BARBARA
TAYLOR
BRADFORD

Three Complete Novels

BARBARA TAYLOR BRADFORD

Three Complete Novels

Love in Another Town
Everything to Gain
A Secret Affair

SMITHMARK

This edition contains the complete and unabridged texts of the original editions.
They have been completely reset for this volume.

This omnibus was originally published in separate volumes under the original titles:

LOVE IN ANOTHER TOWN copyright © 1995 by Barbara Taylor Bradford, published by HarperCollins Publishers, Inc.
EVERYTHING TO GAIN copyright © 1994 by Barbara Taylor Bradford, published by HarperCollins Publishers, Inc.
A SECRET AFFAIR copyright © 1996 by Barbara Taylor Bradford, published by HarperCollins Publishers, Inc.

This edition published in 2000 by
SMITHMARK Publishers
a division of U. S. Media Holdings, Inc.
115 West 18th Street
New York, NY 10011

Smithmark books are available for bulk purchase for sales promotion and premium use. For details, write the manager of special sales, SMITHMARK Publishers, 115 West 18th Street, New York, NY 10011

ISBN 0-7651-1772-X

Printed in the United States of America

10 9 8 7 6 5 4 3 2 1

Library of Congress Cataloging-In-Publication Data
Bradford, Barbara Taylor, (date)
    [Novels. Selections]
    Three complete novels / Barbara Taylor Bradford.
        p. cm.
    Contents: Everything to gain—A secret affair—Love in another town.
    ISBN 0-7651-1772-X
    1. Love stories, American.   I. Title.

PS3552.R2147 A6 2000
813'.54—dc21   99-052867

CONTENTS

Love in
Another Town

For my dearest husband, Bob,
to whom I owe so much

1

Jake Cantrell slowed his pickup truck as he approached Lake Waramaug near the Boulders Inn, braked to a standstill, and gazed out the window.

The lake was still, calm with a glassy sheen that looked almost silver in the late afternoon light of this cool April day. He lifted his eyes to the etiolated sky, so bleached out it, too, seemed as pale and as unmoving as the water. In stark contrast were the rolling hills rising up around the lake, darkly green and lush with trees.

Jake could not help thinking yet again how beautiful the view was from this angle of vision, a dreamy landscape of water and sky. To Jake, it was somehow evocative, reminded him of another place, yet he was not sure of where . . . someplace somewhere he had never been, except in his imagination perhaps . . . England, France, Italy, or Germany, maybe even Africa. Someplace he would like to go one day. If he ever got the chance. He had always wanted to travel, dreamed about going to exotic lands, but thus far in his twenty-eight years of life on this planet he had only been to New York City a few times, and twice to Atlanta where his sister Patty was now living.

Shading his eyes with one hand, Jake scanned the vistas of land, water, and sky once more, then nodded to himself. How incredible the light is today, almost otherworldly, he thought, as he continued to stare ahead.

He had always been fascinated by light, both natural and artificial. The latter he worked with on a daily basis, the former he frequently endeavored to capture on canvas, when he had time to pick up a paintbrush and indulge himself. He loved to paint whenever he could, even though he wasn't very good at it. It gave him a great sense of satisfaction, just as did creating special lighting effects. He was working on a big lighting job now, one that was tough, tested his talent and imagination, and fired his creativity. He loved the challenge.

The car behind him honked him forward, and, rousing himself from his thoughts, he pushed his boot down on the accelerator and drove on.

Jake headed along Route 45 North, which would take him up to Route 341 and all the way to Kent. And as he drove he kept noticing the unusual clarity of the light today; it echoed the light over the lake and seemed to get even brighter the farther north he drove.

Lately he had come to realize that this clear bright light was endemic to this part of the state, called the northwestern highlands by some, the Litchfield Hills by others. He did not care what people called the area. All he knew was that it was beautiful, so breathtaking he thought of it as God's own country. And the extraordinary, incandescent skies, which were almost uncanny at times, very frequently inspired awe in him.

This particular area was relatively new to him, even though he had been born in Hartford, had grown up there, and had lived in Connecticut all his life. For the past four and a half years he had been a resident of New Milford, but he had rarely, if ever, ventured beyond the town's boundaries. That is until a year ago, just after he had finally separated from his wife, Amy.

He had stayed on in New Milford, living alone in a small studio on Bank Street for almost a year. It was around then that he had started driving into the countryside, going farther afield, looking for a new place to live, something a bit better than the studio, an apartment or, preferably, a small house.

It was on Route 341, near Kent, that he found the little white clapboard three months ago. It had taken him a few weeks to get it cleaned up, painted, and made reasonably habitable, then he had scoured the local junk shops and tag sales looking for furniture. He was surprised at the things he managed to find, and at the prices, which he considered reasonable. In no time at all he had managed to make the little clapboard fresh looking and comfortable. His final purchases were a brand new bed, a good rug, and a television set, all bought in one of the big stores in Danbury. He had finally moved in three weeks ago and had felt like a king in his castle ever since.

Jake drove on at a steady speed, not thinking about anything in particular except getting home. *Home.* He found himself contemplating that word all of a sudden.

It hovered there in this mind. "Home," he said out loud. And yes, he *was* going home. Home to his house. He savored this thought, liking it. A smile lingered on his sensitive mouth. *Home. Home. Home.* The word suddenly had a very special meaning to him. It signified so much.

It struck him then that never in nine years of marriage to Amy had he ever called their various apartments home; usually, whenever he referred to them, he would say *our place,* or *back at the ranch,* or some such thing.

Now he realized that until today the word *home* had always meant the house in Hartford where he had been raised by his parents, John and Annie Cantrell, both dead for several years.

But the little white clapboard on Route 341, with its picket fence and neat garden, was indeed home, and it had become his haven, his place of refuge. There were several adjoining fields with a large barn standing in one of them, and this he had turned into a workshop and studio. Currently, he was renting the property, but he liked it so much he was seriously thinking of buying it. *If* he could get a mortgage from the bank in New Milford. *If* the owner would sell. Jake wasn't sure about either possibility at this moment. He could only hope.

Apart from being the right size, the house was close enough to Northville, where he had moved his electrical business a few weeks ago. He had wanted to be out of New Milford altogether because Amy still lived and worked there. Not that there was any animosity between them; in fact, they were quite good friends in spite of their breakup.

Their separation had been reasonably amicable, although initially she had not wanted to let him go. Eventually she had agreed. What option did she have? He had been long gone from her emotionally and physically, even when they still shared the same apartment in New Milford. The day he had finally packed his bags and made his intentions clear for the last time, she had exclaimed, "Okay, Jake, I agree to a separation. But let's stay friends. *Please.*"

Long absent in spirit, and with one foot already out the door, he had willingly agreed. What harm could it do? And anyway if it mollified her to a certain extent so much the better. Anything to make his escape easier, to get away from her at long last, in a peaceful way and without another row.

Jake's thoughts centered entirely on Amy for a moment or two. In many ways he felt sorry for her. She wasn't a bad person. Just dull, unimaginative, and something of a killjoy. Over the years she had become an albatross around his neck, dragging him down, and inducing in him an unfamiliar state of depression.

He knew that he was smart and quick and clever. He always had been, even as a child. And he was good at his job. His former boss at Bolton Electric had constantly told him he was a genius with lighting and special effects. And because of his drive, hard work, and talent he had moved up in life; he had wanted to move even farther, but she had held him back.

Amy was always afraid, afraid things would go wrong if they did anything out of the ordinary, or if he made a move to better himself and them and their existence. She had fought him two years ago when he had left Bolton Electric and started his own business.

"It's not going to work, it'll fail and then where will we be?" she had wailed. "Anyway, what do you know about being a contractor?" she had gone on nervously, her face pinched and white and tight around the mouth. When he hadn't answered her, she had added, "You're a good electrician, Jake, I know that. But you're not good at business."

He had been infuriated by her remark. Glaring at her, he had shot back, "How do you know what I'm good at? You haven't been interested in me or anything I do for years."

She had gaped at him, obviously shocked by his words, but he was speaking the truth. It seemed to him now, as he remembered those words, that Amy had lost interest in him during the second year of their marriage.

Jake sighed under his breath. It had all become so sad and discouraging, and he wondered, for the umpteenth time, how it could have gone so wrong. They had grown up together in Hartford, had been childhood sweethearts, and had married right out of school. Well, almost. In those days the future had glittered brightly for him, had been full of promise.

He had his dreams and ambitions. Unfortunately Amy had neither. Within a few years he had come to realize that she not only fought change with great tenacity but actually feared it.

Whatever plans he had to grow, to make things better for them, she threw cold water on. Five years into the marriage he had begun to feel that he was drowning in all that cold water of hers.

The future with Amy had begun to look so bleak, so without promise or happiness he had eventually begun to drift away from her.

Content to plod along, following her usual routine, she had never even noticed when he was gone from her in body and spirit. He might have lived in the same apartment, but he was no longer really there.

Inevitably, he strayed and had a couple of affairs with other women and discovered he didn't even feel guilty. He had also realized at the time—over two years ago now—that the game was up between them. Jake was not a promiscuous man, and the very act of infidelity told him that there was nothing left of their relationship, nothing left to salvage. At least for him.

Through her apathy and fear, her lack of trust in him and in his ability, Amy had killed their marriage. Also, she had taken hope away from him.

Everyone needed hope . . . everyone needed dreams. What did a man have, for God's sake, if not his dreams? Amy had trampled on his.

And yet he did not blame her; he felt sorry for her, perhaps because he had known her for so long, nearly all of his life. Then again, he was aware that she had never meant to hurt him in any way.

He sighed under his breath. Amy gave so little of herself she therefore had so little. She was missing out on life.

Amy was still pretty in a pale blonde way, but she did nothing to help her delicate coloring, so she appeared faded and drab.

She'll never get married again, Jake thought with a sudden flash of insight, and groaned inwardly. He would probably end up paying her alimony forever, until the day she died. Or he did. But what the hell, he didn't care. He knew he could always make money. He had an unfailing self-confidence.

Jake slowed the pickup when he came to his white clapboard house, pulled into the yard, and parked in front of the garage. Walking around to the back, he let himself into the kitchen.

Home, he thought, and glanced around the kitchen. Then he grinned. He *was* home. He *was* free. He had his own business now, and it was doing well. He had a bright future again. His dreams were intact after all. Nobody could take them away. He was at peace with himself. And with the world at large. He was even at peace with Amy, in his own way. Eventually they would divorce and truly go their separate ways.

And if he was lucky he would meet another woman one day and fall in love. He would get married again. And hopefully there would be a child. Maybe even children. A wife, a home, a family, and his own business. Those were the things he wanted and it seemed to him that they were simple, fundamental things. Certainly there was nothing complicated about them. Yet Amy had made them seem unattainable because she had not wanted them. She hadn't even wanted to have a child. She'd been afraid of that too.

"What if there's something wrong with the baby?" she had said to him once, just after he had told her he wanted to have a child. "What if the baby's born defective in some way? What would we do, Jake? I wouldn't want a defective baby."

Startled, he had stared at her in complete bafflement, frowning, not understanding how she could mouth such things. It was then that he had felt a spurt of anger inside, and that anger had stayed with him for a very long time.

Just over a year ago he had suddenly realized that Amy had cheated him of life for the entire time they had been married. To him that was a crime. But then he had allowed her to do it, hadn't he? You were only a victim if you permitted yourself to be one, his mother had told him once. He reminded himself not to forget that.

He had tried to help Amy change, but she had looked at him blankly, obviously not understanding what he was getting at.

Suddenly impatient with himself, he pushed away thoughts of Amy. After all, she was on her own now. As was he.

Opening the fridge door, Jake took out a beer, pried off the cap with the opener on the counter, then stood leaning against the sink, drinking the cold beer from the bottle, enjoying it; beer always tasted better from the bottle.

The phone began to ring. He reached for it. "Hello?"

"Jake, is that you?"

He straightened slightly on hearing the voice. "Yes, it is. How're you, Samantha?"

"I'm fine, Jake, thanks. You haven't forgotten the meeting tonight, have you?"

"No, I haven't. But I'm running late. Just got in from work. I'll be there soon. Real soon."

"Don't kill yourself. I'm late myself today. I'll see you at the theater."

"Okay." He glanced at the kitchen clock. It was just turning five-thirty. "In about an hour?"

"That's good for me. 'Bye."

"See you later," Jake said, and hung up.

He finished the beer and went through into the bedroom. After pulling off his boots and jeans he stripped off his heavy sweater and underwear, then strode into the bathroom to take a shower.

Five minutes later he was toweling himself dry, and after putting on a terrycloth robe he padded through into the small living room.

Standing in front of his CD player, his eyes scanned the shelf of discs next to it. He had inherited his love of music from his mother, especially classical music and opera. She had had a beautiful voice, and he had been reared on Verdi and Puccini, as well as Mozart, Rachmaninoff, Tchaikovsky, and other great composers. He'd always thought it a pity his mother had not been able to have the proper musical education and training, since in his opinion she'd had a voice worthy of the Metropolitan Opera in New York City.

Automatically, his hand reached for one of her favorites, Puccini's *Tosca*, but after looking at the Maria Callas disc for a moment he put it back, pulled out another one, a selection of Puccini and Verdi arias sung by Kiri Te Kanawa, whose voice he loved and who was his preferred opera star. After turning the volume up, he went back to the bathroom, leaving all of the doors open so that he could enjoy the music.

Staring at himself in the bathroom mirror, Jake ran a hand over his chin. No two ways about it, he needed a shave. He lathered himself with soap and scraped the razor over his chin, rinsed his face, combed back his damp black hair, and then went back into the bedroom, all the while listening to Te Kanawa singing arias from Verdi's *Don Carlos*, *Il trovatore*, and *La traviata*.

By the time he was dressed in clean blue jeans, a fresh blue-and-white checked shirt, and a dark blue sports jacket she was still singing Verdi.

One of the arias he liked the most was "Vissi d'Arte" from *Tosca*, and now he walked through into the living room, touched the track number for *Tosca* on the CD player and sat down. He didn't want to be late for the meeting with Samantha Matthews, but he did want to hear his favorite piece from *Tosca*.

As Te Kanawa's voice filled the room, soared up to the rafters, Jake was engulfed. He felt himself falling down into her wonderful voice, falling into the music, which never failed to touch him with its beauty and sadness.

Te Kanawa was Tosca, and she was singing of her sorrow, her tribulation, her hour of need, and Jake leaned his head back against the chair, closed his eyes, gave himself up to the music.

Unexpectedly, he felt choked. Tears welled. His emotions were suddenly laid bare . . . he was filled with yearning for something . . . although he was not exactly sure what he yearned for. Then he knew . . . he wanted to *feel* again. I know there's more, he thought, there's got to be more in life.

He let the music wash over him, relaxing his body, and he remained very still even after the aria finished. In repose his lean, sharply sculpted face looked much less troubled.

After a short while Jake roused himself, pushed his lean frame out of the chair, and went to turn off the CD player. He had to be in Kent in five minutes, and it would take him longer than that to get there.

He left the house through the kitchen and ran to his pickup truck.

On the way to Kent he thought about the meeting he was about to have with Samantha Matthews. He had met her a few weeks ago on the big lighting job he was doing at a mansion in nearby Washington. She was a resident of the town who designed and produced unusual handmade fabrics, which the owner of the mansion, his current client, was using throughout the house.

He and Samantha had started talking over a cup of coffee one day, when they were at the house together, and she had been interested in hearing more about the special lighting effects he was creating inside the house and on the grounds.

Several days later she had phoned him with an invitation. It was an invitation to work with her on the stage sets for an amateur dramatic group she was involved with in Kent.

He had agreed to come to one meeting at least. And it was tonight. He had no idea what to expect, and he wasn't sure whether it would be the first and the last, or the first of many.

Although he had not told Samantha, he was excited about working in the theater, if only with an amateur group such as hers. It was a wonderful challenge and a way to learn more, he felt.

As he drove toward Kent, his mind preoccupied with lighting techniques, Jake Cantrell had no idea that he was being propelled toward his destiny. Nor did he have any way of knowing that his life was about to change, and so profoundly it would never be the same again.

And later, when he looked back to this night, he would do so wonderingly, reminding himself how ordinary it had seemed. He would ask himself why he had not sensed that something momentous was going to happen, why he had not realized that he was about to set out on the journey of his life.

2

Samantha Matthews looked up from the script she was making notations on and stared across the table at her friend Maggie Sorrell, frowning. "Now you tell me you think I've chosen the wrong play! Just when I've got it cast and everyone's madly learning their lines!" she exclaimed, her voice rising slightly.

"I didn't say that!" Maggie protested. "I asked you *why* you'd chosen it. I was merely thinking out loud. Honestly."

"Thinking out loud or not, you sounded *critical.*"

"I didn't, Sam!"

"Doubtful, then."

"Not doubtful either. You know very well I never doubt you, or anything you do. I really was only wondering why this particular play, that's all."

Samantha nodded. "Okay, I believe you. I know you're my true-blue friend who's stuck to me through thick and thick and thin and thin over the years. My very best friend in the world."

"Just as you're mine," Maggie murmured. "So come on, tell me. Why did you pick *The Crucible*?"

"Because last year, before you'd come to live here, we did *Annie Get Your Gun,* and I didn't want to direct a musical again. I wanted to stage a drama. Preferably one by a great American playwright who was still alive, that's why I chose an Arthur Miller play. But I must admit, there's also another reason—"

"Because we did it at Bennington all those years ago," Maggie cut in knowingly, smiling. "That's it, isn't it?"

Samantha sat back in her chair and regarded her friend intently for a moment, then she shook her head slowly. "No, not at all."

"And I thought you'd chosen it for sentimental reasons." Maggie made a face and shrugged. "Oh silly me."

"Sentimental reasons?" Samantha echoed.

"Of course. We were nineteen and rapidly becoming fast friends. Best friends, actually. We'd both fallen in love for the first time; also, we were treading the boards for the first time. In *The Crucible*. It was a very special year for us, but you'd forgotten, hadn't you?"

"No, I do remember that year at college. It was 1971. In fact, I thought about it only the other day. And in a way you're correct. When I selected *The Crucible* I *was* playing it a bit safe, because I do know it so well. But when I said I chose it for another reason it was because Arthur Miller lives in Connecticut and we're a Connecticut theatrical group. So, call me sentimental if you like, Mag."

"You are a sentimentalist at heart, even though you like to pretend you're not," Maggie answered.

"Maybe I am," Samantha agreed and laughed. "Although there are those who call me bossy."

"Oh you're that all right!" Maggie shot back, laughing.

"Thanks a lot, friend. Anyway, getting back to the play, you know it pretty well too, and that's going to be a decided advantage when you start designing the sets."

"You do realize I'm very worried about this whole project, don't you, Sam? I can't imagine how I ever let you talk me into it. I've never designed a stage set in my life."

"But you have designed some beautiful rooms, especially lately, and anyway there's a first time for everything. You'll be okay, you'll do fine."

"I wish I felt as confident as you sound. To tell you the truth, I'm not sure where to begin. I read the play through again last night and my mind went totally blank. In fact, I balked at the project. Are you certain there's no one else to do the sets for you?"

"There isn't, Maggie. Besides, you're only suffering from a touch of stage fright, and that's quite normal. Look, you'll be fine as soon as you pick up your pencil and start sketching. *Trust me.*"

"I'm not so sure I should do that, Sam. When I've trusted you in the past it's only got me into a heap of trouble."

"No, it hasn't," Samantha countered and pushed her chair away from the card table. She stood up, walked across the stage, gesturing as she did.

"You'll have to create some sort of major scenic backdrop here, Mag, and the furniture must be representative of the period. Early American, obviously. But you're an expert on furniture, so I don't really know why I'm even mentioning it."

Samantha swung to face her old friend. "I see something dramatic in my mind's eye, something really unusual for the backdrop. Black and white, maybe even a few grays, something like a painting in grisaille. What do you think?"

Maggie rose and went to join her, nodding as she did. "Yes!" she exclaimed, suddenly sounding excited by the project for the first time. "I know exactly what you mean. It needs to be stark. Bleak almost. Certainly somber, very eye-catching, as well. I think the set has to be a little offbeat, not the usual thing. Let's take the audience by surprise." Maggie raised a brow. "Don't you agree?"

Samantha grinned at her. "I sure do, and I knew you'd catch the bug, once I got that clever little brain of yours working.

You're so talented, Maggie, and very imaginative, and I'm certain you'll come up with exactly the right thing."

"I hope so, I'd hate to let you down—" She broke off, looking thoughtful, then added, "You know, I think I'll drive into New York later this week, pick up some books on theatrical design and stage sets."

"Yes, do that. No, wait a minute, there's no need to go into Manhattan. Try the bookstore in Washington and the one in Kent. I know they're both well stocked. They have everything from soup to nuts."

Maggie laughed, as always amused by her friend's colorful expressions, as she had been since their college days.

The two women stood center stage, discussing ideas for the backdrop and the sets for a few minutes longer. At one moment Maggie went and got her notebook, began to sketch rapidly, all the time listening to Samantha and nodding.

Both women were forty-three and good-looking, but they were strikingly different in appearance and personality.

Samantha Matthews was of medium height and slim, with prematurely silver hair cut short with bangs. The silver color did not seem at all aging since she had a youthfully pretty face and a fresh complexion. Her large eyes, set widely apart, were dark brown and full of soul.

Energetic, enthusiastic, and gregarious, she had an outgoing personality and a friendly nature. Somewhat given to taking control, she liked to be in charge. Nonetheless, she was kind, good-hearted, and easy to get along with.

In contrast, Maggie Sorrell was tall, willowy, with the brightest of light blue eyes that were, at times, highly appraising. Her thick mane of chestnut hair was shot through with auburn lights and she wore it brushed back and falling to her shoulders. Although her face was angular and arresting rather than pretty, she was attractive and appealing in her looks.

Maggie had a fluidity and a gracefulness when she moved. Though she appeared to take things at a more leisurely pace, she had as much energy and vitality as Samantha. Very simply, her style was different. It was calm, controlled. She was the quieter and more reserved of the two. And yet she was a vibrant woman, full of life and optimism.

Even in their style of dressing they were uniquely true to themselves. Tonight Samantha wore what she termed her uniform: well-tailored blue jeans, a white cotton shirt, a black gabardine blazer with brass buttons, and highly polished black Oxfords with white socks.

Maggie, who tended to be less tailored, was dressed in a full, three-quarter-length skirt made of brown suede, matching suede boots, a cream silk shirt, with a brown cashmere stole flung over her shoulders.

Both women had a casual style about them that reflected an understanding of clothes and what suited them; it also bespoke their privileged backgrounds.

Best friends since college days, they had remained close even though they had been separated by thousands of miles for many years. They had managed to meet quite frequently, at least twice a year, and they had spoken to each other on the phone every week for as long as they could remember. Maggie had moved to Connecticut eight months ago, after a dreadful upheaval in her life, and they had become inseparable again.

The banging of a door at the back of the theater startled both women, made them jump. Automatically they swung around, peering into the dimly lit auditorium.

"Oh it's only Tom Cruise," Samantha said immediately, a look of pleasure settling on her face. She waved with a certain eagerness to the man walking down the aisle toward the proscenium.

"*Tom Cruise*," Maggie hissed, grasping Samantha's arm, following the direction of her gaze. "Why didn't you tell me, for God's sake! Has he moved here? Is he taking an interest in the theater group? Oh my God, I hope he's not slumming, doing a part in the play just for kicks. I'll never be able to design the sets! Not with a real pro around."

Samantha burst out laughing. She said, in a low voice, "As far as I know, Mr. Cruise is still living in California. The guy walking toward us could be him though, and that's why I call him Tom Cruise."

Maggie let go of Samantha's arm as the young man walked across the stage to join them.

"Sorry I'm late," he said to Samantha, stretching out his hand, shaking hers.

"No problem," Samantha answered. "Come and meet my friend. Maggie, this is Jake Cantrell. Jake, this is Margaret Anne Sorrell, usually known as Maggie. She's an interior designer and will be designing our sets. Maggie, Jake's a genius with lighting and special effects. I hope he's going to become part of our little group and work with us. We certainly need a lighting expert of his caliber."

Jake gave Samantha a small smile that hinted of shyness and then turned to Maggie. "I'm very pleased to meet you," he said politely and offered her his hand.

Maggie took it. His hand was cool, his grasp firm. "I'm happy to meet you too," she murmured.

They stood staring at each other briefly.

Maggie thought how extremely good-looking he was, realizing at once that he was completely unaware that he was. He's a troubled man, she thought, recognizing the sadness in his eyes.

Jake was thinking that he'd never met a woman like this in his life, so beautifully groomed and well put together. He was suddenly awed by this woman who was looking at him so thoughtfully through her cool, intelligent eyes.

3

The three of them sat down at the table on the stage and Samantha handed Jake a copy of the play.

"Thanks," he said, glancing at it, then looking up at her as she continued, "As you can see we're doing *The Crucible*, and I think you should read it as soon as possible." She flashed him a vivid smile, and added, "Basically, the meeting tonight is for us to become acquainted. I was hoping the three of us could get together again later this week, maybe on Friday or Saturday, to have our first detailed discussion about the scenery and the lighting. By then you'll have a better understanding of what's required."

"I know the play," Jake replied giving her a pointed look. "And very well. From high school. I also saw a revival of it a few years ago. I've always liked Arthur Miller."

If Samantha was surprised to hear this she certainly disguised it. Merely nodding, she murmured, "That's great, and obviously I'm delighted you know the play, it'll save us a lot of time in the long run."

"I've never done any stage work before, as I told you when you phoned," Jake said. "But what's required for this play in particular is real mood, that I *do* know. All stage lighting should underscore the meaning of the drama, the scenes being acted, and create an atmosphere. In *The Crucible* it should be one of . . . mystery. Deep mystery, I think. And revelation . . . impending revelation. And I believe it's important to introduce a sense of time as well as place. In this instance, Salem, Massachusetts, in the seventeenth century. Candles are going to be important, as are special effects. It's necessary to simulate dawn and nighttime. I remember a nighttime scene in the wood. You'll need interesting combinations of light and shadow—" He stopped, wondering if he'd said too much, even worse, made a fool of himself.

Jake sat back in his chair and looked at the women. They were both staring at him intently. He felt himself flush and experienced a surge of acute embarrassment.

Maggie, who had been observing him closely and giving him her entire attention, sensed that he was suddenly feeling uncomfortable, although she wasn't sure why. Wishing to put him at ease, she said swiftly, "You've hit it right on the mark, Jake. I'm fairly familiar with the play myself, but I know the scenery is going to be tough for me to do. This is *my* first stab at theatrical design. Like you I'm a bit of a novice. Maybe we'll be able to help each other as we go along."

Smiling, Maggie finished, "Samantha has a good point about meeting again later in the week, once we've both had a chance to refresh our memories about the play. I'm available either Friday or Saturday." She glanced at Samantha and then back at him. "Which day do you both prefer?"

"Saturday," Samantha answered.

Jake was silent. An unfamiliar discomfort had settled over him. They were taking it for granted he was going to get involved with their drama group, but he still wasn't sure that he would. Or whether he even wanted to. He wondered if he'd said too much a moment ago, if he had led them to believe he intended to participate.

"Would Friday be better for you, Jake?" Maggie asked.

He shook his head. "No, I don't think so. I—" He cut himself off abruptly, suddenly wary of making any kind of commitment to them. It might take up too much of his time; after all, he did have a business to run these days. Also, he was beginning to feel a bit out of his depth with these two women. They were so sure of themselves, were from another world, one he didn't know at all. And there was another thing, it seemed to him that they took their amateur theatrical group very seriously. Certainly they were determined to put on a good production, he could tell that. He knew Samantha Matthews was a perfectionist, his client in Washington had indicated that only the other day. It was apparent to him that she would be a hard taskmaster, very demanding. Better to skip it, he thought.

Clearing his throat several times, he looked across at Samantha and said, "I agreed to come tonight because I'm always interested in extending my knowledge, so the idea of designing stage lighting appealed to me. But I have the feeling you want a real commitment from me, Samantha, and I can't give you that. What I mean is, I'm very busy with my electrical business. I work late most nights—"

"Oh, Jake, don't be so hasty," Samantha interrupted. "Maggie and I are also up to our necks with work. We've all got to earn a living, you know."

Once again she offered him that vivid smile of hers, and added, "Whatever you might think, you wouldn't be making such a huge commitment. Not really. Once you'd created the lighting effects you wouldn't have anything else to do. I'd take it from there. I've got several good stagehands to help me and an electrician as well."

"Lighting isn't easy," he answered. "In fact, it's very complicated and especially so for *this* play."

"You're absolutely correct," Maggie interjected. "But I do wish you'd reconsider. From what Sam's told me about your work at the Bruce house, you really do know what you're doing.

Look, I know how you feel, I just started a new business myself a few months ago, and I'm totally committed to it. Nonetheless, I think I'll learn a lot from this little theatrical venture." She smiled at him winningly.

He looked at her, looked right into her eyes, and he felt the hairs on the back of his neck bristling. Maggie Sorrell was not pretty in the given sense. But there was something about her that went beyond mere prettiness. She was arresting, intriguing, the kind of woman a man would look at twice. She had an elegance that had nothing to do with her clothes, but with her herself. He felt oddly drawn to her. Instantly, he pulled back. He had never known a woman like this; he was not sure he wanted to.

Since he had remained mute, Maggie continued talking, "You did say yourself that initially you thought you'd learn something. Actually, Jake, we'll both benefit, and in innumerable ways. For instance, there's the publicity. We'll get quite a lot, and that can't be bad for your business or mine. Anyway, I've come to realize that whatever I'm doing I'm usually meeting a potential client somewhere along the line."

"Bravo! Said like a true professional!" Samantha exclaimed. "And Maggie's correct, Jake, you can profit from this and in a variety of different ways."

When he still said nothing, she pressed, "What do you have to lose?"

Hesitating for a moment longer, he finally said in a quiet voice, "It's the time that's involved, I can't let my business suffer."

"None of us can," Maggie pointed out. "Come on, Jake, give it a try. I am. The whole project is challenging and I love a challenge, don't you?" Not waiting for his answer, she said, "In any case, I think we'll have a lot of fun together."

Before he could stop himself he agreed. He wondered what he was doing, making such a commitment. To cover himself, he added swiftly, "If it gets to be too much, gets in the way of my work, I'll have to quit. You do understand that, don't you?"

"Of course," Samantha replied.

"What about the next meeting, Jake? Do you prefer Friday or Saturday?" Maggie asked.

"Saturday's definitely better," Jake told her. "I'm working late on Friday, and on Saturday morning. Can we make it Saturday afternoon? Late afternoon?"

"Fine by me," Maggie murmured.

"You've got a deal!" Samantha cried, her voice suddenly full of excitement. "We're going to make a great team! And you'll enjoy it, Jake, you'll see. It's going to be a gratifying experience. Incidentally, I was impressed with what you said earlier, about the lighting for the play. Your ideas are brilliant. Personally, I think you've already got the lighting licked."

"I hope so," he replied, trying not to look pleased at her compliment. "I've always found that play very powerful."

"Yes, it is, and frightening in a sense, when you think it all hinges on lies—the terrible lies people tell," Maggie remarked.

It was a few minutes before nine when Jake walked back into his kitchen. He realized how hungry he was as he opened the fridge door and took out a cold beer.

After swallowing a few gulps, he went into the living room, draped his sports jacket over a chair back, and returned to the kitchen. Within a few minutes he had opened a can of corned beef and a jar of pickles and made himself a sandwich.

Carrying the plate and the beer back into the living room, he put them on the small glass coffee table, sat down, picked up the remote control, and flicked on the television. He ate his sandwich and drank his beer, staring at the set. He wasn't paying much attention to the sitcom on one of the networks.

Jake was preoccupied with the drama group, *The Crucible*, and the two women he had left a short while before. They were opposites, but they were both very nice and he liked them. And so he had let himself be persuaded to do the lighting for the play. Now he wished he hadn't agreed. He had done so against his better judgment and instinctively he knew it was going to be more trouble than it was worth. Why did I let myself get swept up into this? he asked himself yet again.

Suddenly impatient with the television and with himself, he flicked off the set and leaned back in the chair, taking an occasional swallow of beer.

After a moment Jake got up, walked over to the window, and stood looking out at the night sky. He wondered what she was really like, Maggie Sorrell, but he figured he would never get to know her well enough to find out.

4

Maggie Sorrell awakened with a start. Reaching out, she turned on the bedside lamp and looked at the alarm clock. It was three-thirty.

Groaning to herself, she doused the light, slid down under the covers and attempted to go back to sleep. But her mind raced when she began to think about the living room and library of the house in Roxbury she was redecorating for a client. Fabric patterns, carpet swatches, paint colors, and wood finishes swirled around in her head.

She finally gave up trying to envision a scheme. Jake Cantrell kept intruding into her thoughts. There was something about him that was appealing, very engaging, and of course he was stunning looking. But he doesn't know it, not really, she thought again, as she had a few hours ago. And then remembering the sadness she had detected in his light green eyes, she wondered what had gone awry in *his* life.

Obviously someone had hurt Jake Cantrell and very badly. She recognized that look only too well. The shell-shocked look she called it.

A woman did him in, Maggie thought, still focusing on Jake. She sighed to herself. Women. Men. What they did to each other in the name of love was diabolical. It bordered on the criminal. She ought to know, it had been done to her.

Mike Sorrell had destroyed her just as surely as if he had stuck a knife in her. But then he'd been killing her soul for years, hadn't he?

The big upheaval had happened two years ago, but the memory of it was still there. Although most of the pain had receded, there were moments when it came rushing back, took her by surprise with its intensity. She tried to squash the bad memories but they seemed determined to linger.

I'll be forty-four next month, she thought. *Forty-four*. It didn't seem possible. Time had rushed by with the speed of light. Where had all the years gone? Well, she knew the answer to that. Mike Sorrell had devoured them. She had devoted most of her life to Michael William Sorrell, attorney-at-law by profession, and to their twins, Hannah and Peter, college students both, soon to be twenty-one years old.

The three of them were gone from her life and she had learned to live without them, but it still pained her when she thought of the twins. They had sided with their father, even though she had done nothing wrong. He was the guilty party. But then he was Mr. Money Bags and that apparently carried weight with them.

How terrible it was to know your children were greedy, avaricious, and selfish, when you'd tried so hard to bring them up right, to instill proper values in them. But there it was. They had proved to her that she had failed with them.

In taking his side they had destroyed something fundamental deep within her. She had borne them, brought them up, looked after them when they were sick. She had always been there for them and guided them all of their lives. What they had done to her was rotten, in her opinion. They had flung all that caring back in her face. Flung her love for them back at her, as if it were meaningless.

In a sense, their cold-hearted defection had stunned her more than Mike's ugly betrayal of her. He'd dumped her when she was forty-two for a younger woman, a woman of twenty-seven who was a lawyer in another Chicago law firm.

But I survived, Maggie reminded herself, thanks mainly to Samantha. And myself, of course.

It was Samantha who had reached out to her two years ago, that awful day in May, the day of her birthday when she had finally admitted to herself that she would be spending it alone.

Hannah and Peter were both attending Northwestern, but were far too busy with their own lives to make time for their mother's birthday celebration. And their father had left that morning on a business trip without wishing her a happy birthday. Apparently he hadn't even remembered it.

That May morning, sitting alone in the kitchen of their apartment on Lake Shore Drive, she had felt totally, completely alone. And without her husband and children she was. Her parents were dead and she had been an only child. That special morning she had felt something else—abandoned, cast aside, of no use to anyone anymore. Even now, so long after, she was unable clearly to pinpoint her exact feelings, but she had been disturbed, she knew that.

When the phone had rung and she had answered, had heard Samantha singing, "Happy birthday to you, happy birthday best friend, happy birthday dear Maggie, happy birthday to youuuu!" she had burst into tears. Between sobs she had explained that she was spending her birthday alone because the kids didn't have time for her and Mike had gone away on a business trip.

"Pack a bag, get out to O'Hare and take a plane to New York! *Immediately!*" Samantha had exclaimed. "I'll book us into the Carlyle. I have some pull there, I can usually get rooms. I'm taking you out on the town tonight. Somewhere posh and smart. So pack your fanciest gear."

When she had tried to protest, Samantha had said, "I'm not listening to your excuses. And I won't take no for an answer. There's a plane leaving every hour on the hour. Just get on one and get yourself to New York. *Pronto, pronto, pronto,* honey. I'll meet you at the hotel."

True to her word, Samantha had been there when she arrived, full of warmth and love, sympathy and support. They had enjoyed their two days together in Manhattan, doing a little shopping and eating at nice restaurants. A Broadway play and a trip to the Metropolitan Museum had been mandatory; they had also found time to talk endlessly, reminiscing about their days at Bennington College, where they first met, and their lives thereafter.

Samantha had married several years after Maggie. Her husband had been a British journalist based in New York. She and Angus McAllister had tied the knot when she was twenty-five and he was thirty-one. It had been a very happy marriage, but Angus had been tragically killed in a plane crash five years later, en route to the Far East on an assignment.

Only a few months later, Samantha, who was childless, moved back to Washington, Connecticut, where her parents had long owned a country house they used at weekends. Heartbroken though she had been, she had managed eventually to get her grief under control. She had never remarried, although there had been several men in her life in the intervening years.

At one moment, during the birthday visit, Maggie had asked Samantha why this was so. Samantha had shaken her head and said, in her colorful way, "Ain't found the right man, honey chile. I'm looking to fall head over heels in love, the way I did with Angus. I want my stomach to lurch and my knees to wobble." She had laughed, and finished, "I want to be swept off my feet, into his arms, into his bed and his life forever. It *must* be like that for me or it won't work. And I'm still waiting to meet him."

Later, on the plane going back to Chicago, Maggie had admitted to herself that her marriage to Mike was growing more and more unsatisfactory with the passing of every day. She did not know what to do about it. He did. A day later he returned from his trip. He walked into the apartment, announced he was leaving her for another woman, and walked right out again.

Once the shock had subsided and she had recovered her equilibrium to a degree, she had set about cleaning up the mess his unexpected departure had created.

Divorce proceedings were started, the apartment went on the market, and, once it was sold, she moved back east, back to her hometown, New York.

She had lived there for six months in a small, rented studio. Her parents were already dead, she had no family, and she'd lost touch with all of her old friends from her youth. It was a lonely life for her.

It didn't take much persuasion on Samantha's part to get her to start looking at houses in the northwestern part of Connecticut.

Samantha also talked her into working as an interior designer again. Some years ago, she had been the junior member of a successful Chicago decorating firm and had loved every moment working there. She had finally given up her job because of pressure from Mike.

But she did what her best friend suggested and hung out her shingle once she was installed in her small Connecticut colonial in Kent. The house, a little gem in her opinion, was only a few miles from Washington, where Samantha lived.

Thanks to Samantha's many contacts, design work had started to come Maggie's way quickly. They were small jobs. However, they had helped to pull her back into the swing of decorating, and the money she earned paid part of the mortgage.

Samantha, the eternal optimist, kept telling her a really big job would come her way one day soon. Maggie believed her because she was also an optimist.

Soon Maggie began to accept that sleep would elude her for the rest of the night. Putting on the light, she peered at the alarm clock again and decided to get up. It was just turning four o'clock and she often rose at this hour, accomplishing a lot before eight whenever she did.

An hour later Maggie sat at her desk, sipping a mug of coffee. She was dressed and made up and ready for the day ahead. Later in the morning she would be driv-ing over to Samantha's studio in Washington to look at her latest handpainted fabrics for a bedroom she was doing in New Preston. Then she would be presenting the scheme for the library to the owner of the house in Roxbury. Pulling the swatches and samples together for this room was the order of the day and of vital importance.

Maggie began to assemble the small samples from various canvas bags at her feet. There were a variety of different greens and reds, colors the owner wanted, but not one of them was pleasing to her. Most of the reds were too bright, the greens too pale. Something somber, she muttered under her breath. And then for a reason she couldn't explain she thought of *The Crucible,* and of the meeting last night.

And again Jake Cantrell insinuated himself into her thoughts. If she were honest with herself, she'd have to admit she felt rather foolish, believing as she had, if only for a few moments, that he was Tom Cruise. But Samantha had sounded so convincing when she'd spotted him coming down the aisle of the auditorium. He'd taken them both by surprise when he started to talk about his ideas for the lighting. It was obvious to her from that moment on that he was knowledgeable about his work, and most likely as brilliant as Samantha said. Of course, you never knew with Sam. She had always liked a pretty face, Maggie thought, as she shuffled the samples on the desk, and then she stopped and sat back in her chair, staring into space. "But he's too young for her," she muttered aloud. And for you too, she added to herself silently.

5

Jake heard the phone ringing as he stepped out of the shower. He reached for a towel, partially dried himself, and pulled on his terrycloth robe.

Walking into the bedroom he heard Maggie Sorrell's voice saying good-bye. The answering machine clicked off; he depressed the button and played the message back.

Her voice filled the room. "Jake, this is Maggie Sorrell. I've just been hired to do a big job in Kent. A farm. It's a beautiful old place but it needs a lot of work. The grounds are superb. I was wondering if you would be interested in doing the electrical? Interiors and exteriors. Please call me. I'm here at home." She then repeated the number she'd given him last Saturday at the drama group meeting.

Jake sat down on the bed and played the message again. He loved her voice. It was light, musical, cultured. It suited her. He had met her three times now at meetings about *The Crucible*, and he realized that his attraction to her was powerful. He thought about her a lot, but he had no intention of doing anything about it. She'd never be interested in him.

He would like to do the electrical work, though. The major job he had been doing in Washington was just about completed, and he and his crew would finish up in the next couple of days.

With four men on the payroll he had to pull in as many jobs as possible to keep them busy. Two were married and had families to support, and he felt a great sense of responsibility.

He picked up the phone to call Maggie back, and then he dropped the receiver in the cradle. He did not want to seem too anxious. Then again, he always felt a bit nervous around her.

Returning to the bathroom, he combed his wet hair and finished his toilet, then went to get dressed, pulled on blue jeans and a sweater.

Fifteen minutes later he sat down at the desk in the small room at the back of the house, which he used as an office. Pulling the phone toward him, he dialed Maggie's number.

She answered immediately. "Hello?"

"It's Jake, Maggie."

"Hello, Jake, you got my message?"

"Yes, I did. I was in the shower when you called." He wondered why he'd told her that. Rushing on, he continued quickly, "The farm job sounds interesting. Where is it exactly?"

"It's not too far from Kent, near Bull's Bridge Corner, actually. It's a pretty property and the house has great charm."

"Is it really a big job?"

"I think so. To be honest with you, Jake, the entire farmhouse needs rewiring, and it needs remodeling and restoring. It hasn't been touched in thirty years, in my opinion anyway. The woman who's bought it, my client, wants air conditioning and central heating systems put in, all new appliances in the kitchen, and she wants to build a laundry. Then there're the grounds. The exterior lighting will be extensive. She wants to build a pool and patio, oh, and there's an old cottage to be remodeled for guests, as well as a caretaker's apartment over the cottage." She laughed. "So I guess it is a huge job."

"It sounds like it to me, Maggie. What are we looking at? About six or seven months work?"

"Probably. Maybe a bit longer. Can you handle it?"

"Yes, I'm pretty sure I can. And thanks for thinking of me."

"Samantha's always said you're the best, and yesterday I saw the work you've done in the Washington house, and on the grounds there. I was very impressed."

"Thanks. When can I see the farm? I'd like to, before I commit to it."

"We could go over there later this week."

"Okay."

"How does Friday sound? That's the fourteenth of April."

"Great. What time?"

"Could you do it around eight?"

"Sure thing. Whereabouts is it?"

"It's hard for me to give you the right directions . . . it's up a lot of twisting roads. I think we should meet at my house, since you know where it is, and we can go from here. It's easier and it'll save time."

"I'll be there at eight sharp. And Maggie?"

"Yes, Jake?"

"Thanks for thinking of me."

After hanging up from her, Jake wrote the appointment in the small pocket diary he carried around with him, and also put it in the agenda on the desk. Then he got up and left the house.

As he walked out to the pickup truck it struck him that perhaps he hadn't been so foolish after all, getting involved with the drama group. It looked as if he was getting a job because of it. But he knew the real reason he had become involved with the theater group. It was because of her, of course. He had done it because of Maggie Sorrell.

He sat at the steering wheel without moving for a few seconds, bracing himself. He was on his way to an appointment, and he wasn't looking forward to it.

*   *   *

Amy Cantrell stood in the center of the living room of her apartment, looking around slowly, all of a sudden noticing the untidiness of the place. Dismay swamped her.

She had managed to talk Jake into coming over tonight, for the first time in months, and she knew he would be furious. He loathed mess and disorder. He was as neat as a pin himself, and had been as long as she had known him, which was forever. Her lack of organization and her untidiness had been a bone of contention between them. She never understood how she could create chaos in a room within seconds. She never meant to, it just happened.

Shaking her head and frowning, she began quickly to pick up the newspapers and magazines scattered all over the coffee table and on the floor underneath. She put them on a chair, plumped up the pillows on the sofa, and took the newspapers out to the kitchen.

When she saw the dirty dishes in the sink, she groaned. She had forgotten about them. Flinging down the papers angrily, she opened the dishwasher; it was stacked to the brim and had not been turned on. Everything was dirty. Endeavoring to stack more items into it and moving quickly, she dropped a mug. It shattered.

The phone rang shrilly. She grabbed it. "Hello?"

"Amy, it's me. Has he arrived yet?"

"No, Mom, he's not coming until after eight."

"Why so late, Amy?"

"I don't know. He works, Mom."

"Tell him about the alimony. That you want alimony."

"Mom, I gotta go. Honestly I do. I'm trying to tidy up here. Jake hates mess."

"So what do you care? He left you."

"I gotta go, Mom. 'Bye." She hung up before her mother could say another word.

Moving across the kitchen floor in the direction of the dishwasher, she crushed the shards of pottery from the broken mug under her feet. Amy looked down, bit her lip. She went to find the brush and dust pan; she was on the verge of tears.

For the next few minutes she attempted to bring order to the kitchen before going through into the bedroom. The bed was unmade, as it usually was these days. The mere thought of making it up overwhelmed her, and, defeated by the domestic chores that needed doing, she scurried into the bathroom.

After washing her face and cleaning her teeth, she combed her pale blonde hair. It hung listlessly around her face.

Amy Cantrell sighed as she regarded herself in the mirror. She wondered how she could make herself look better, and reached for the Cover Girl foundation, patted some of it on her face, and added powder. Once she had highlighted her cheek bones with the blush-on, she outlined her mouth with pale pink lipstick.

The image of herself in the mirror infuriated her. She didn't look any better than she had a few seconds ago. Tears flooded her eyes. She was a mess. The apartment was a mess. She had never known what to do about either.

Her friend Mandy had once offered to show her how to use cosmetics, but she had never taken her up on it. She wondered why. As for the state of the house, there was never any time, and the more she did to clean it up, the more chaotic it became. Reaching for a tissue, she blew her nose and wiped her eyes. It just wasn't fair. Other people seemed to get through life so easily, so flawlessly. All she could do was stumble along, dragging mess in her wake.

The doorbell rang, making her jump.

My God, was he here already! She hurried out into the little entrance foyer, realizing, as she went to open the door, that she was still wearing the cotton housedress she had donned earlier when she had started the housework.

"Who is it?" she asked through the door.

"It's Jake."

Glancing down at her grubby housedress, she made a face and then opened the door.

"Hi, Amy," he said, coming in.

"Hi, Jake," she echoed, closing the door, trailing after him lethargically.

"How've you been? All right, I guess."

"I guess. And you?"

"Busy. With the business."

"Oh."

Jake glanced around and then sat down on one of the chairs.

Amy could not help noticing the distaste on his face. She winced inside. He had always been particular about the apartment, and his appearance. She glanced at him obliquely. He looked impeccable tonight. As he always had. Always did. He was wearing a beige turtleneck sweater and dark blue jeans with a navy blazer. His boots shone, his hair shone, so did his teeth and his face. He looked brand spanking new, like a freshly minted coin.

More conscious than ever that she looked awful, if not worse than awful, Amy simply sat down on the chair opposite and smiled at him.

Jake cleared his throat. "You said you had to see me. You were very insistent. What do you want to talk about, Amy?"

"The divorce."

"We've discussed it so much we've worn the subject out," he answered in an even tone.

"I just want to be sure you're sure, Jake."

"I am, Amy. I'm sorry, but there's no going back."

Her pale blue eyes filled. She blinked the tears away, pushed her hair out of her face. Trying to get a grip on her emotions, she took several deep breaths. "Well, I have been to see the lawyer. Finally. I'm sure you're pleased about that."

"When did you go?" he asked.

"Yesterday."

"I see. I'm glad you did, we should get this over, Amy, so that we can settle everything."

"He asked me if we'd tried to solve our problems. I told him yes, but that it wasn't any good, that it wouldn't work. Are you really sure, Jake? Maybe we should try again."

"I can't, Amy, honestly honey, I can't. It's finished."

The tears rolled down her cheeks.

"Oh, Amy, please don't cry."

"I still love you, Jake."

He said nothing.

"All those years," she said, staring hard at him. "We've known each other since we were twelve. It's a long, long time."

"I know. And maybe that's the problem. Perhaps we know each other too well. We've become like brother and sister. Listen to me, Amy, you've got to face up to the fact that our marriage is over, and it's been over for years and years." He cleared his throat and finished gently, "You just never noticed."

"I don't know what I'm going to do without you," she wept.

"You're going to be fine. I know you are."

"I don't think I am, Jake. Would you get me a glass of water, please. Do you want a beer?"

"No, thanks. I'll get the water for you." Jake maneuvered himself through the living room into the kitchen, and he could not help noticing how dirty the apartment was. He bent down, picked up the broken mug and put it on the countertop. His eyes fell on the dishwasher jammed with dirty dishes and the sink piled even higher, and he grimaced. Once he had found a relatively clean glass in the cupboard, he rinsed it, filled it with cold water, and took it to her.

Amy thanked him, sat sipping it for a few moments, staring at him over the rim of the glass. She was trying to think of something to say to him, but no words would come, and her head was empty of thoughts. All she really wanted was for him to come back to her. Then she wouldn't feel so lonely.

Jake said, "I'll have to be going, Amy, I've work to do tonight."

"You're not dressed like you're going to work!" she exclaimed, giving him a furious look, suddenly filled with jealousy.

"Paperwork, Amy, I've loads of it."

"Do you want me to come and help you?"

"No, no," he said hurriedly, standing up. "But thanks for the offer." He began to edge his way to the hall.

Amy put the glass down and stood up. She followed him to the front door. "The lawyer says I'm entitled to alimony," she announced.

"That's no problem, Amy, and it never was. I always told you I would look after you."

"Then stay with me."

"I can't. And what I meant was I'd look after you financially. Tell the lawyer to go ahead and talk to my lawyer. Serve me with papers, Amy. Let's get this over with."

She did not answer him.

"So long," he said. "I'll talk to you soon." When she chose not to answer him he simply closed the door behind him quietly and left. Poor Amy.

6

On Friday morning Jake set out for Maggie Sorrell's house in Kent.

He knew where it was. He had gone there with Samantha Matthews the previous week to have another meeting about the lighting for *The Crucible*. It was not too far from where he lived, on the other side of town, halfway down Route 7.

As he pulled out of his yard and headed up Route 341 in the direction of the town center in Kent, Jake thought what a glorious morning it was, the way you always hoped an April day would be. It was crisp and dry, with bright sunlight and a vivid blue sky filled with puffed white clouds, the kind of day that made him feel good to be alive. Opening the window of the pickup, he took a few deep breaths of the pure clean air.

Jake was finally feeling better in spirits. After his meeting with Amy on Tuesday night, he had been depressed for almost two days. She always managed to drag him down, to drain the energy out of him with her negative personality and her total lack of direction and purpose.

Sometimes Jake wondered how Amy managed to keep her job in the store, where she had worked for a number of years; it baffled him. It was a bath specialty store, selling everything for the bathroom from towels to accessories. Seemingly the owner liked her enough to keep her on, despite the constant mistakes she made.

Jake glanced out of the pickup's window, noted that the light was crystalline today. Perfect. He wished he had time to get out his paints this weekend, but he knew it was not possible. He had paperwork to finish; also, if he was lucky, and Maggie hired him, he would have to start analyzing the electrical work required at the farm.

He had allowed himself half an hour to get to Maggie's house, but since there was no traffic he arrived there fifteen minutes early. He parked in the backyard and walked toward the kitchen door, noting how pristine and well-cared-for the traditional Connecticut colonial looked. The clapboard walls were painted white and all of the shutters were dark green.

Before he reached the kitchen door, Maggie opened it. She stood there on the step, smiling at him.

The minute he saw her his chest tightened and he felt himself grow hot around the neck. To cover his nervousness, his sudden confusion, he coughed several times, then murmured, "Good morning, I'm afraid I'm early."

She stretched out her hand. He took it in his. She said, "Good morning, Jake, and that's no problem, I've been up since dawn. Come on in and have a cup of coffee before we leave." She smiled at him once more and extracted her hand.

He didn't want to let go of it, but he did. "Thanks, coffee would be good." He followed her into the immaculate kitchen, stood there glancing around, feeling slightly awkward.

Maggie said, "Sit down, Jake, over there at the kitchen table. You take your coffee black, if I remember correctly, black with a spoonful of sugar." One of her dark brows lifted questioningly.

"That's right, thanks," he answered, and took a seat at the old pine table at one end of the kitchen, noticing it had been set for breakfast for two.

She moved past him, and he caught a faint whiff of shampoo in her thick, luxuriant hair, the scent of her perfume on her skin, something light and floral; he heard the gentle swish of her suede skirt against her suede boots, the tinkle of the gold bracelets she always seemed to wear on one of her slender wrists.

Maggie moved around the kitchen quickly, but with the gracefulness he had noticed before. She was tall and slender, full of life and energy; he could not take his eyes off her. Eventually he did so, realizing he was staring.

Jake looked away quickly, let his eyes roam around the kitchen. Again he was struck by its singular charm, as he had been last week. It was decorated to make a statement, but it was certainly not overdone. Everything was in the best of taste, from the white walls and cabinets and the terra-cotta tile floor, to the blue accents and the sparkle of copper.

Delicious smells were suddenly wafting on the air . . . freshly baked bread, cooked apples and the hint of cinnamon mingled with the smell of coffee. He inhaled, then sniffed.

Maggie, who had turned around at this moment, said, "I baked the bread earlier this morning and it's still warm. Would you like a slice? It's delicious, even though I say so myself."

"I would, thanks very much. Can I do anything to help?" He started to rise.

"No, no, I can manage. The coffee's coming up, and then I'll bring the bread and honey." As she spoke she glided across the kitchen floor, carrying the mugs of coffee, and a second later she was back again with the homemade bread, a honeycomb, and a bowl of baked apples on a tray. She placed this in the center of the table and sat down opposite him.

"I love baked apples," she confided. "Try one, they're great with a slice of warm bread and honey.

"I will," he said, as tongue-tied as ever, then thought to say thank you.

Maggie sipped her coffee and regarded him surreptitiously. He had helped himself to a baked apple and was eating it with relish, then he took a slice of the warm bread, spread it with butter and honey, took a bite.

He said, a second later, "I haven't had homemade bread since I was a kid. It's nectar."

"I know what you mean," she answered, laughing, glad he was enjoying the breakfast. She had prepared it especially for him. It had struck her the other day that he probably didn't have very many proper meals. She knew from Samantha that he was single and lived alone in a charming white clapboard house on Route 341.

Maggie wondered if he had a girlfriend. Obviously he did. Looking the way *he* looked, and being as nice as he was, it was more than likely that women chased after him. She felt a little twinge of something, of what she was not sure. Envy? Jealousy? Or a bit of both? Of course he'd never be interested in her, so why daydream about him? Which is exactly what she had been doing since their first meeting. Actually, she couldn't get him out of her mind. The other night she had even had fantasies about making love with him, and now, as she remembered those images, she felt herself flushing.

Maggie stood up swiftly and hurried over to the counter, convinced that her face had turned scarlet. She was extremely conscious of Jake's presence in her kitchen. He seemed to fill it with his masculinity and strength. And his sexuality. She had not felt like this for years and years.

Pouring herself another cup of coffee, Maggie Sorrell cautioned herself to put Jake Cantrell out of her mind. And at once. He was, after all, much younger than she. Beyond her reach in so many ways.

From the other side of the kitchen, Jake's eyes were riveted on her. She was half turned away from him, so he was seeing her partly in profile, and he was struck yet again by her unusual beauty. There was a great deal of strength there, and yet she was the most feminine woman he had ever met, and vulnerable. He wanted to protect and cherish her. And love her. He already did. He had fallen for her the first night they met.

And he wanted to make love to her. He had done this so many times in his mind he was beginning to think it had really happened. But of course it hadn't; he fervently wished it had. Jake wanted to make love to her right now, had a terrible urge to get up and walk across the floor, take her in his arms and kiss her passionately. And he wanted to tell her exactly how he felt about her, but he didn't dare. It took all of his self-restraint to remain seated.

Jake picked up his coffee cup and discovered, to his dismay, that his hand shook slightly. Whenever he was near her she had the most extraordinary effect on him. I want her in every possible way, he thought, yet I know I can't have her. Oh God, I don't know what to do. Or what to do about her.

Maggie turned around.

Taken by surprise, he gaped at her.

She exclaimed, "Are you all right, Jake?"

"Yes. Why?"

"You're looking a bit pale. And a bit odd."

"I'm fine, thanks."

"Would you like another cup of coffee?"

He shook his head. "No, thanks. I'll finish this and then perhaps we'd better be on our way," he answered, and was surprised his voice sounded so normal.

"I'll just go and get my things," she said. "I won't be a minute. Excuse me."

Left alone he leaned back against the chair and exhaled. He wondered how he would be able to work with her on a continuing basis and experienced a sudden surge of panic. For a split second he considered turning the job down if she offered it to him. Instantly he dismissed this idea. He needed another big job if his business was to grow and flourish. Not only that, he needed to be with her on a daily basis, needed to be near her, however torturous that might prove to be.

Jake Cantrell knew deep within himself that his wild imaginings about Maggie Sorrell would never come to pass. They were from wholly different worlds. She had never shown the remotest interest in him since the day they first met, other than to offer him this chance to bid on the electrical job at the farm she was decorating. It was obvious to him that his work and his knowledge about lighting impressed her. That would have to suffice.

Jake drove them to the farm in his pickup truck, following Maggie's directions once they had left the center of Kent.

Since he was so drawn to her, so smitten, and therefore needed her to think well of him, he was reluctant to say a word. Very simply, he was afraid he might say the wrong thing. And so he sped to their destination in total silence.

For her part, Maggie believed he was naturally shy, a little withdrawn. Days ago she had decided he was a troubled man, one who had been badly hurt; he needed to be handled with gentleness, in her opinion.

Because of her own painful experiences, Maggie empathized with him and felt that she understood him without really knowing him. After two years struggling with her own pain, she had finally managed to regain her self-confidence, but she was only too well aware that emotional damage could take a long time to heal. After Mike's rejection of her, and the breakup of their marriage, she had felt nothing for so long.

And so she began to talk to Jake quietly, discussing the play they were involved with and their designs for the scenery and lighting. She was able to draw him out a little; he became enthusiastic and articulate as he began to speak about the lighting techniques he was planning to use.

She listened attentively, making an occasional comment.

Mostly she let him do the talking, recognizing that as he opened up to her he became more sure of himself. He was gaining confidence as he spoke fluently about his work.

In no time at all they were turning through white gates and heading up the driveway of Havers Hill, the farm Maggie had been hired to remodel, restore, and decorate.

Jake parked near a big red barn and then walked around to help her get out of the pickup. He offered her his hands and she took them. As she jumped down she lost her balance and stumbled against him. He caught her, held her in his arms for a brief moment, and she clung to him. They drew apart quickly, staring at each other self-consciously.

Maggie turned away, straightened her jacket to cover her sudden confusion, and then reached into the truck for her briefcase and handbag.

After she had moved away, Jake, swallowing hard, closed the door of the pickup and swung around, glancing about him as he did.

The property was magnificent.

Well-kept green lawns sloped away from the drive, rolled as far as the eye could see. Beyond were pastures, and even farther beyond mountains partially encircled the property. Nearby, an old stone wall bordered a smaller lawn where a gazebo sat in the shade of an ancient gnarled maple, and the wall itself made a fitting backdrop for an English-style border of perennials.

He shaded his eyes with his hand. In the distance he could see an apple orchard. "What a place!" he exclaimed. "It's beautiful. I'd like to own something like this one day."

"Then I'm sure you will," she replied, smiling at him. "If you want something badly enough you can usually get it, if you work hard at it, of course."

Gesturing to a series of buildings just ahead of them, she went on, "That's the caretaker's house over there, Jake, and the farmhouse is the bigger building to the right. Come on, I want to show you around."

She began to walk rapidly toward the house, continuing, "I told the caretaker, Mrs. Briggs, that we'd be coming over, so the front door's open." She glanced over her shoulder at him as she spoke.

Jake caught up with her and they went into the house together, their shoulders brushing in the narrow entrance.

Even though the lights were on, the hallway was dark and Jake blinked, adjusting his eyes to the murkiness of the interior.

"It's very old," he said to Maggie, peering about, moving forward, looking inside several rooms that opened off the entrance hall.

"Yes, it is. About 1740 or 1750, somewhere thereabouts," she told him. "And it was furnished in Early American style; most authentically, in fact. Most of the furniture's been sold though. My client only wanted to keep a few choice pieces."

"Think about it, Maggie, this house was built before the American Revolution. My God, what these walls could tell us if they could talk!"

Maggie laughed. "I know exactly what you mean. I've often thought that myself. About other places I mean, and especially in England and France."

"Who owned the farm?" he asked, turning to her.

"A Mrs. Stead. It had been in the Stead family for several hundred years. The last Mrs. Stead died about a year and a half ago. No, two years ago, to be exact. She was very old, ninety-five, when she died. Her English granddaughter inherited the property, but since she's a married woman with children and lives in London, obviously her life is on the other side of the Atlantic. So she put the property, the farmhouse and its contents, on the market two years ago. She thought she'd sell Havers Hill immediately, because it is such an idyllic place. But the asking price was in the millions and it's no longer the 1980s.

So naturally she didn't have any takers. She finally had to drop the price."

Jake said, "A lot of people who want to sell their weekend homes up here are beginning to realize the prices of the eighties are finished. Anyway, who finally bought it? Who's your client?"

"A married couple. Anne and Philip Lowden. They own an advertising agency on Madison Avenue. They live in Manhattan during the week and wanted a retreat in the country. Anne fell in love with this place, especially the grounds. She came to me through a client in New Preston. Anne told me she liked my understated style. 'No nouveau riche folderol for me,' she said when we met. She didn't even bother to interview any other designers, just hired me to do it all. Anne wants me to modernize the farmhouse and the guest cottage."

"The farmhouse certainly needs it," Jake remarked, and turned to look at Maggie. "Okay, where shall we start?"

"Let's go into the kitchen first. We can put our things there, it's the only place with any furniture in it anyway."

Maggie led the way down a short corridor and into the kitchen. This was a medium-sized room with two adjoining pantries, a couple of small windows, and a beamed ceiling. It overlooked a vegetable garden, an old stone well, and, to the right, a cutting garden.

"A decent-sized room," Jake commented as they surveyed the kitchen together. "But it's too dark, not much natural light coming in, you'll have to supplement it with really good artificial lighting."

"I know," Maggie murmured. "And that's the problem with the whole house, Jake. It's so . . . so gloomy. Personally, I find it quite depressing. I like airiness, pale colors, a sense of space. My aim is to get rid of the somber feeling without having to put in too many additional windows. I don't want to kill the period look of the place. After all, it's one of the reasons my clients bought it. For its rustic charm and antiquity."

"I understand." Jake's eyes scanned the kitchen once more. He looked up at the ceiling and then walked around the room a few times, a thoughtful expression settling on his face.

Maggie placed her briefcase and handbag on the kitchen table, took out a notebook and made a few notations.

Jake said, after a moment, "I don't think this room presents too many problems. We could use several large-sized ceiling fixtures, such as old lanterns, something like that, plus wall sconces, in order to introduce proper artificial light. And you might want to think about putting in a new kitchen door, one that has panes of glass in the upper portion."

"Yes, I had thought of that . . . it would let in additional natural daylight."

"What about high hats? Would you or the clients object to a few in the ceiling?"

"No, since they're fairly unobtrusive. But can you do it?"

"I think so. I'll have to cut into the ceiling first, to investigate what's going on up there. But it shouldn't present any real problems. If I get the job that is."

Maggie stared at him, frowning slightly. "Jake, surely you know you're going to get the job."

"You might not like my estimate, it might not fit into your budget."

"We'll make it fit into my budget, won't we, Jake?"

He gave her a long look and was silent for a few seconds. Then he said, "I guess so. Have you found a contractor yet?"

"I'm thinking of hiring Ralph Sloane. He's done a bit of other work for me, and I've seen some of his really huge jobs in the last few days. I like the way he operates, I like his style. Do you know him?"

"Yes, I've worked with him before. He's a good guy. Are you going to hire an architect? Or don't you plan on making structural changes?"

"The answer is yes to both of those questions, Jake. I met with Mark Payne the other day—"

"He's the best!" Jake cut in, sounding enthusiastic.

"That's what I thought. I've seen a lot of his work now, and he seems to be an expert when it comes to Colonial architecture. He'd like the job, I know that, and I was impressed with his ideas." There was a small pause and then she finished, "I think I'm putting together a good team, don't you?"

He glanced at her and nodded, gave her half a smile and then headed out of the kitchen. "Shall we go through the rest of the house?"

"Yes, let's look at the rooms on this floor first."

Three hours later they came out of the farmhouse together, blinking in the sunlight. Slowly they walked back to the pickup truck.

Jake leaned against the hood, and said, "It's a huge job, Maggie, bigger than I initially thought. The whole place needs rewiring. It obviously hasn't been touched in years. And there's so much else to do. We haven't even thought about the exterior lighting for the grounds."

"I know." She threw him a worried glance. "You're not saying you don't want to tackle it, are you?"

"No. I want the job. I need it. As you know, I'm building a new business. Anyway, I like a challenge. And I want to work with you, Maggie." He paused and stared into her face. Suddenly making a decision, taking control of the situation, he said in a firm voice, "Let's go. I'll take you to lunch. I know a good place for a hamburger or a salad, whichever you prefer."

"Good idea," she responded. "I'm starving."

7

When Jake knocked on Maggie's kitchen door and there was no answer, he opened it and went inside.

She was nowhere in sight, so he wandered through the kitchen and into the small back hall, heading for her office. He stopped at once, stood perfectly still, listening.

In the few weeks he had known Maggie Sorrell he had never seen her ruffled. Nor had he ever heard her raise her voice. But she was doing so now, obviously speaking on the phone in her office.

"He did it on purpose!" she exclaimed. "Nothing you say will convince me otherwise. And he did it to hurt me. He simply doesn't want me there to celebrate with you."

There was a sudden silence.

Jake guessed she was now listening to whomever it was on the other end of the line. Wanting to be polite, to make sure she was aware of his presence, he walked across the hall, knocked on the open door, poked his head around it, and raised his hand in greeting.

Maggie stared at him so blankly he realized at once how preoccupied she was. Then she nodded quickly, acknowledging him.

He half smiled in return and ducked out. Swinging around, he headed toward the small sitting room opposite. After placing the envelope he was carrying on the coffee table, he walked over to the window and stood looking out at her garden, lost for a moment in his thoughts of her.

It was apparent to him that Maggie was not only angry but upset as well, and this disturbed him. He had become very protective of her.

Jake glanced at his watch. They had agreed to meet at six o'clock tonight, and as usual he was far too early. It seemed to him that he was continually ahead of himself whenever they had an appointment. He just couldn't help it. He wanted to be with her all the time; he hated it when they finished their work and he had to leave her.

They had only known each other five weeks, yet it seemed so much longer to him. He had discovered that they were compatible, liked the same things. She loved music as much as he did and she was impressed with his knowledge of it. He enjoyed talking to her because she was so well informed; she was a news buff and, as he was, a great fan of CNN.

There were other things that he liked about her. She had a good sense of humor, laughed a lot, and she was a truly feminine woman. For all her ability and talent, strength and independence, she was not hard. Just the opposite. He forever felt the urge to look after her.

Since his first visit to the farmhouse, two weeks ago now, Jake had begun to relax with her and, at the same time, he had acquired more self-confidence. In fact, ever since that Friday morning, when he had taken her for a hamburger in Kent, he had considered himself to be in command of the situation.

Lately she had seemed to defer to him, and frequently she used him as a sounding board about the work to be done at the farmhouse. It had struck him only the other day, and quite forcibly, that she depended on him, and he was pleased about this. They had become good friends; he wished it could be more.

Tonight he had come over to discuss the detailed estimate for the electrical work at the farmhouse. He had given her a ballpark figure a week ago; then he had had to spend endless hours over at the farm, studying every aspect of the property inside and out. Now he was anxious to talk to her, get her approval of the figures.

From the doorway, Maggie said, "Hello, Jake."

He spun around, looked across at her. She was very pale. When she remained standing in the doorway, looking hesitant, he hurried across the room.

"Are you all right?" he asked quietly, drawing to a standstill in front of her, his black eyebrows puckering together in a frown.

"I'll be fine in a minute," Maggie answered. "I'm afraid I became angry—" She broke off, biting her lip.

"Anything I can do to help?"

"No, thanks anyway." Her voice was trembling and she paused again. Suddenly tears welled in her blue eyes and she looked at him helplessly.

"Maggie, what's wrong?" He could not bear to see the pain settling on her face. Concerned, he took a step toward her.

And as he did she moved toward him.

He reached for her, drew her to him, enfolded her in his arms.

"Maggie, Maggie, what is it? Please tell me what's bothering you?"

"I don't want to talk about it . . . I'll be all right in a minute . . . really I will . . . "

But she wept on his shoulder, clinging to him fiercely.

He stroked her hair and kissed the top of her head, murmured gently, "I'm here, I'll look after you. Please don't cry. I'm here for you."

Turning suddenly, she twisted her face to stare up into his.

Their eyes locked. He felt her trembling in his arms, and he tightened his grip on her.

Maggie's lips parted slightly, almost expectantly, and before he could stop himself he bent down and kissed her fully on the mouth.

She kissed him back, pressing her body against his. Because she was tall, almost as tall as he was, their bodies fit together.

We're a perfect fit, Jake thought, his heart racing.

After a few moments of intense kissing, they stopped, drew apart, and stared at each other breathlessly, wonderingly.

Jake said softly, "I've been wanting to do that for a long time."

"I've been wanting you to do it," Maggie whispered.

Emboldened, still staring hard at her, he went on, "I've wanted to make love to you since that first night we met."

"And I . . . "

"Oh Maggie, Maggie."

"Jake."

He drew her toward the sofa; they sank down onto it. Pushing her gently against the cushions, he leaned over her, looking deeply into her eyes. Bending closer, he kissed her eyelids, her nose, her face and lips, moved his mouth down into the hollow of her neck, then he began to unbutton her blouse. His hand slipped inside, cupped her breast; somehow he managed to release it from her bra.

When his mouth found her nipple, Maggie sighed deeply and moaned. And then she gave herself up to her feelings entirely, her hurt and pain of a short while ago forgotten for now.

She had thought of Jake constantly, had envisioned making love to him so often, she could scarcely believe it was happening now.

His mouth was soft, if insistent, his touch gentle, but firm, and when he stopped with suddenness she held herself perfectly still, wondering why he had stopped. She wanted him to continue.

A moment later his face was resting against her hair, and he said softly, "Please, Maggie, let's go upstairs."

"Yes," she answered and he straightened, pulled her off the sofa; together they went up the wide staircase, their arms wrapped around each other.

Maggie pushed open her bedroom door, led him inside, and walked to the center of the room.

Jake closed the door behind them and followed her.

The light outside was changing. The sky had turned a warm golden color and it was flooding the room with a soft radiance.

He took hold of her shoulders and stared into her face. "Be sure of this, Maggie."

"I am, Jake."

"Once this happens there's no going back. Not for me."

"Nor me."

He brought her into his arms.

They stood there for a long time, kissing, touching, familiarizing themselves with each other. They pulled apart, gazed at each other, started kissing again, their ardor growing.

Eventually, Jake began to undress her, taking off her blouse, unfastening her bra, then her skirt. Everything fell on the floor around her feet.

She stepped over the heap of clothes and stood gazing up at him intently, her emotions written all over her face: She wanted him.

Jake returned her gaze, recognized the need in her eyes, and nodded slightly. He pulled his sweater over his head; Maggie stepped closer to him, began to unbutton his shirt, then took it off. He struggled out of his boots and jeans, and she took off her stockings and they came together totally naked.

They held each other tightly. Jake ran his strong hands over her shoulders, across her back and down onto her buttocks; she smoothed her hands over his shoulders, pushed them up into his thick hair.

Finally he led her over to the bed. After he had pressed her down onto it, he bent forward, kissed her, then said, "I'll only be a minute."

Maggie lay waiting for him, her heart beating rapidly. It was years and years since she had felt like this, had wanted a man so much. She wished he would hurry, come back. She could hardly wait.

Jake walked across the room toward the bed.

She thought he looked magnificent.

He stood next to the bed, staring down at her. He noticed that her eyes had turned the darkest of blues, so dark they were almost purple, the dark bluish-purple of pansies. They were full of urgent desire for him, he recognized that once more and he felt heat rising in him, his excitement growing as he stood looking at her.

How beautiful she was in her nakedness, in the soft golden radiance of the fading light, he thought. He had not realized what a lovely body she had, covered as it always was with her bulky sweaters and heavy jackets and long, flowing skirts.

She was very slim, he noted, with curving hips, and long, long legs. She had perfect breasts, softly rounded, and her skin was smooth and pale.

As Maggie returned his long, contemplative gaze she thought that a man's body could be beautiful. His was. Jake was tall and slim; he had a broad chest and wide shoulders above slender hips and long legs. He was splendid to look at. She could hardly tear her eyes away.

Jake joined her on the bed at last.

He took her in his arms and held her close to him, kissing her hair and her neck, smoothing his hands over her marvelous breasts. He began to kiss her mouth.

Maggie kissed him back ardently. Their kisses grew hot, harder and hotter still, more passionate than before.

Jake propped himself up on one elbow, looked into her face and traced his finger along the line of her mouth. "I want you so much," he murmured. "But I don't want us to hurry. I want to prolong this, savor it." He bent into her. "You really excite me, Maggie; if we're not careful it'll be over all too quickly."

She half smiled, said nothing.

He went on quietly, "I've wanted this for so long, ached to be with you."

"I felt the same." She paused, eyed him carefully. "But I thought you weren't interested in me."

"I thought the same . . . of you."

Reaching up, she touched his face lightly with her fingertips. "We're a couple of fools." She ran a finger around his mouth, thinking how sensual it was.

He took hold of her hand, put her finger in his mouth and began sucking it, curling his tongue around it. Maggie felt the heat surging through her, settling in her loins. He was exciting her . . . there was something so erotic about the way he was sucking. She felt herself growing moist.

After a moment he stopped and said, in a voice thickened by emotion, "I love you, Maggie. I want you to hear this now. Not in the heat of it all, when I might well say it. I want you to know it's true, not just the sex talking."

Startled, she simply nodded.

Putting her arms around his neck, she drew his face down to hers. She kissed him deeply, as he did her. Their mouths locked together, their tongues entwining. Maggie felt as though he were sucking the breath out of her, and she grew more excited than ever. Desire flooded her, blinded her to everything except him.

Abruptly Jake moved his head, began to kiss her breasts, cupping them together in both of his hands, moving his mouth from one nipple to the other, brushing his lips over them until they stood erect in the center of their dark, plum-colored areoles.

Moving on, thrilling to her, tremendously aroused now, Jake trailed his mouth down over her stomach, and his hands followed, smoothing and stroking until they came to rest in the tangle of hair at the top of her thighs.

Jake lifted his head, looked at her face. Her eyes were closed. "Maggie," he said softly.

"Yes?"

"Am I pleasing you? Can I love you this way?"

"Oh yes."

He began to make love to her tenderly, wanting to give her pleasure. He touched the core of her lightly at first, but as his supple fingers began to know her they became more insistent. He explored and massaged the flower of her womanhood, did so expertly, tantalizingly, enjoying touching her in this most intimate way, feeling her coming alive under his hands.

Maggie lay very still, hardly breathing. Her longing for him was rampant; her body ached to be joined to his. She felt herself opening up to him more and more as his mouth followed where his fingers had been. He lavished her with kisses and his tongue was a darting arrow hitting its mark. She began to pulse under his kisses.

And then suddenly she was spiraling up into ecstasy as wave after wave of pleasure rolled over her. She convulsed, her body arching slightly as he brought her to a climax; and she cried out his name harshly.

Jake moved his body onto hers, parting her legs wider with his own. He had an enormous erection but she was ready for him, and he slid right into her, thrusting deeply.

Maggie was panting, moving against him, matching his rhythm, floating with him somewhere she had never been before.

Higher and higher she rose as he moved deeper and deeper into her, and once again the waves of ecstasy started, began to engulf her.

Jake knew he was touching the core of her with the core of himself. He was strong and hard inside her, riding the crest of her second climax with her. This was the way it was meant to be. The way it should always be and never had been for him. Until her.

She was cresting higher and higher, flying into the unknown, saying his name over and over.

He let himself go, crested with her, gave himself up to her, flowed with her and into her. And he shouted out, "Oh Maggie! Oh my love!"

The colors of the sky had changed again, the bright golden radiance laced through with crimson, magenta, and violet. It was that magic hour, twilight, just before darkness falls, when everything looks soft and rosy and at peace.

Jake lay on top of Maggie, his head between her breasts. Her hands rested lightly on his shoulders. After a while she began to stroke his back and then his hair.

His voice was muffled when he said, "I don't ever want to move. I want to stay right here forever."

Maggie said nothing. She bent over him and kissed the top of his head, thinking of his words earlier, before their passionate lovemaking. He had told her he loved her, startling her with this declaration. But she believed him. Jake always meant what he said and he was very sincere. She felt the same way about him, but for days now she had been suppressing her feelings, convinced he had no interest in her. How wrong she had been. But nothing could ever come of this, there was too big a difference in their ages.

Before she could stop herself, Maggie said, "I'm a lot older than you, Jake."

"I like older women," he laughed. "They're more interesting." He chuckled again. "Anyway, you don't look it."

"But I am. I'm almost forty-four."

"Numbers don't mean anything. And I told you, you don't look much older than thirty-two, thirty-three. But who cares?"

"I do. How old are you?"

"How old do you think I am?" he asked in a teasing voice.

"Thirty, thirty-one."

"Wrong. Guess again."

"I can't. Please tell me."

"I'll be sixteen in June."

"Be serious, Jake!"

He laughed. "Okay, okay. I'm twenty-eight until June the twelfth. Then I'll be twenty-nine."

"That makes me fifteen years—"

"Who's counting!" he exclaimed peremptorily, cutting her off. He lifted himself up, lay next to her, taking her in his arms.

Jake started kissing her, quietly at first and then more passionately, and soon he was moving on top of her. He was fully aroused and he entered her quickly, without preamble, possessing her more forcibly than before.

"Oh God, how I want you," he groaned against her hair. "I've never wanted a woman the way I want you, Maggie. I want all of you, every bit of you. Come to me, please come to me."

"Oh Jake," she cried, "I want you too, you must know that."

He pushed his hands under her buttocks, brought her even closer to him. They moved together with rhythmic grace, rising and falling as one. They soared, crested on the heat of their passion for each other.

Finally they lay still, their breathing rapid and harsh.

When Jake regained his breath he said against her neck, "And you think age matters. . . this is what counts. This . . . this chemistry between us, Maggie. It doesn't often happen, at least not like this, with such intensity. It's very rare . . . "

When she was silent, he said, "You do know that, don't you?"

"Yes."

"What we have together is something very powerful, and believe me, age has nothing to do with it."

They ate supper together in the kitchen. It was a simple meal that Maggie had prepared quickly: scrambled eggs, English muffins, and coffee.

"More like breakfast, I'm afraid," Maggie said, smiling across the table at him. "I haven't had a chance to do much marketing this week."

"I don't mind. I was starving." Jake smiled back at her and added, "Can I have it again for breakfast, please? You are going to let me spend the night, aren't you?"

"If you want to," she replied and felt suddenly shy with him.

"I want." He reached out and took hold of her hand and squeezed it. Then he lifted it to his lips and kissed her fingers. "You have beautiful hands, Maggie, such long, supple fingers. And *you're* beautiful." He shook his head. "Oh God, you do have a terrible effect on me . . . I could take you back to bed right now and do it all over again."

As he finished speaking he began to kiss the tips of her fingers, her knuckles and the spaces in between. Then he turned her hand over and kissed the palm. After a second he lifted his eyes and looked at her. "Don't ever doubt this, Maggie. It's real and it's the best."

She stared back. His face was serious, his deep green eyes intense, and there was so much yearning for her in them she was touched. She felt herself choking up for a reason she couldn't fathom. "Oh Jake," was all she could say, and for a split second she thought she was going to weep.

As if sensing this, and wishing to avert it, Jake rose and said, "How about some more coffee?"

She shook her head. "No, thanks."

He went and filled his own cup, returned to the table, and sat down opposite her once more.

There was a small silence between them. It was broken by Jake, who said in a low voice, "You were very upset earlier, Maggie."

"Yes, I was," she agreed. Giving him a candid look, she continued, "I think I should explain something."

"If you like, but it's up to you. I don't want to pry."

"A few weeks ago Samantha made a reference to my divorce. So I know you know I was married once. You do, don't you?"

"Yes, I'd gathered that."

"What you don't know is that I have two children. Twins. A boy and a girl. They'll be twenty-one in a couple of weeks. They live in Chicago. They're attending Northwestern. Anyway, I had hoped we could all be together for their birthday, but their father is taking them away for a long weekend in California. Without me. When you arrived earlier this evening I was talking to my daughter, Hannah, who was explaining this to me. Naturally, I was very upset to be excluded."

"I don't blame you. That's kind of a lousy thing to do, isn't it?" He raised a brow quizzically, then rushed to add, "In my opinion it is."

"I agree." Maggie shook her head. "But it's par for the course."

"What do you mean?"

She sighed. "You've never been married, never had children, Jake, so it would be hard for you to understand all the ramifications. In any case, I prefer not to talk about it anymore. I just wanted you to know I was upset about something personal and not business."

He nodded and changed the subject.

8

The jangling telephone brought Maggie out of the shower swiftly. Grabbing a large bath towel, she wrapped it around herself and raced through into her bedroom.

Reaching for the phone, she said, "Hello?"

"It's me."

"Hello, Jake!" she exclaimed, as always delighted to hear his voice. "We're still on for ten o'clock, aren't we?"

"You bet," he answered quickly. "The only thing is, I'd like to meet you a bit earlier. Is that possible?"

"Of course, Jake, but is there something wrong?"

There was the merest hesitation before he said in a rather tentative voice, "No, not really, Maggie. I just want to talk to you about something, that's all."

"What? You sound odd. Tell me now, Jake, tell me on the phone."

"I prefer to talk to you in person, Maggie, face-to-face. Really I do."

There was something in his voice that alarmed her, but knowing him the way she did she knew he would not succumb to pressure from her. She said, "All right then. What time do you want to meet?"

"Nine-thirty. If that's okay with you?"

"It's fine. Do you want to come here?"

"No. I'll meet you at the site," he answered swiftly.

"All right."

"See you then."

"'Bye Jake."

Maggie stood with her hand resting on the phone, a puzzled look on her face. His voice had been peculiar and so had his words and his delivery. He had been almost, but not quite, abrupt with her. This was unlike him. Also, she had detected a nervousness in him, and she could not help thinking he was about to break off with her. What else could it be?

She sat down heavily on the bed, shivering suddenly, even though it was a lovely May morning, warm and sunny outside. Her heart sank. Yes, that was it. He was going to end their relationship. Sighing, she lay back on the pillows and closed her eyes, thinking of Jake Cantrell. It was exactly a week ago today that they had first made love here in this bed.

Crazy, exciting, passionate love. He had been insatiable, unable to get enough of her, bringing her back to bed after they had eaten her potluck supper of scrambled eggs. And she had felt the same way; desire had overwhelmed her.

It seemed to Maggie that they hadn't stopped making love since then, although this was not strictly true. They had managed to do an enormous amount of work together at the farmhouse, or the site, as he called it.

But, now that she looked back, he had been odd for the last couple of days, withdrawn and shy with her. It suddenly struck her that his demeanor had been the same as it had on the first night they had met with Samantha to discuss *The Crucible.*

Opening her eyes, Maggie resolutely pushed herself up and left the bed. She went back to the bathroom, finished her toilet, and then returned to the bedroom to dress for the working day ahead.

Since it was warm and sunny, she chose a pair of light-weight navy blue gabardine pants with a matching jacket and took out a white cotton T-shirt. Once she was dressed, she hurried downstairs to her office and put her papers in her briefcase.

A few minutes later, just before nine, she left the house, knowing it would take her a good half hour to drive to the farm near Bull's Bridge Corner in South Kent.

Jake's pickup truck was already parked outside the old red barn when she arrived. Bringing her Jeep to a standstill, Maggie alighted, picked up her briefcase, and slammed the door.

As she went into the farmhouse, heading for the kitchen, she braced herself, not knowing what he was going to say to her, not knowing what to expect.

He stood up when he saw her and smiled faintly, almost apologetically, but he made no move in her direction, as he would normally have done.

Maggie thought he looked drawn, on edge, and his light green eyes, usually so full of vitality and life, were dull and anxious.

"Hi," Maggie said from the doorway.

He nodded. "Thanks for coming early. I wanted a chance to talk to you before the other guys arrived. Come and sit here at the table, Maggie. I brought a thermos of iced tea. Would you like some?"

She shrugged, then walked into the room briskly. "Why not." Sitting down at the table she waited for him to pour the tea, thanked him, and said, "Why didn't you want to talk to me on the phone, Jake? What's this all about?" Maggie heard the strain and anxiety in her voice and she was annoyed with herself.

Jake cleared his throat several times and explained, "I've been feeling terrible this past week, Maggie, really awful. Ever since we made love last Wednesday." He cleared his throat again. "I . . . I . . . look, I just haven't been fair to you."

Staring hard at him, she asked, "What do you mean, Jake?"

He shook his head, and looked embarrassed when he said in a sudden rush of words, "I haven't been exactly honest with you. It's not that I've lied to you, because I haven't, but there's something I should have told you. And I guess I've had a very guilty conscience. I just couldn't stand it any longer. That's why I wanted to see you this morning, why I wanted to explain . . . "

"What is it, Jake?" Maggie asked, sounding slightly perplexed. "What are you trying to say to me?"

"Last Wednesday night you made a remark about me not understanding why you were upset because I'd never been married, never had children. But I have been married, Maggie, and I should have told you so then. I didn't though, and I lied by omission. It's been troubling me."

Maggie sat back in the chair, her large blue eyes riveted on him. "Are you a married man cheating on his wife? Is that what you're trying to tell me?"

Color suffused his face and he exclaimed vehemently, "No! I'm not! I've been separated for over a year. I'm in the middle of a divorce. I live alone and I rarely ever see Amy. And I hope to be single again soon. But look, I should have told you before. I'm sorry," he finished quietly.

She heard the misery in his voice, saw the contrite expression on his handsome face, and reached out and took hold of his hand. "It's all right, Jake, really it is."

"You're not mad at me?"

Maggie shook her head and smiled at him. "Of course not. Anyway, I don't get mad that easily. It has to be something really important to get me going . . . like my children's defection, for example."

Jake said, "You didn't explain that to me . . . I'm not sure I understand what's going on."

Taking a deep breath, Maggie said, "We've never had a proper talk, you and I, Jake. We were friends involved in a drama group, and then we started to work together profession-ally, when suddenly, unexpectedly, we became lovers. We don't know very much about each other. Let me tell you about me. Okay?"

"Yes, I want to know all about you, Maggie."

She chuckled. "I'm not so sure I'm going to tell you *every-thing*. I think I should remain a little mysterious, don't you?"

He laughed with her and nodded.

"Two years ago my husband left me for a younger woman. Mike Sorrell's a very successful lawyer in Chicago, and he dumped me for a twenty-seven-year-old lawyer he'd met and was working with on a case. I ought to have known something like that was going to happen, things hadn't been right between us for a very long time. But what threw me, truly hurt me, was my children's defection. I've never really been able to under-stand why they took Mike's side when he was the guilty party." Maggie gave Jake a long, thoughtful look, and added softly, "Except that he's the one with all the money, of course."

"Little shits," Jake said, and then flushing slightly, he mur-mured, "Sorry, I shouldn't be making remarks like that."

"It's okay, Jake, I understand, and I've often thought the same thing. Anyway, I wanted them to celebrate their twenty-first birthday with me, and I had written to Hannah, some weeks ago actually. When I didn't hear from her, I phoned her. You came in on the tail end of my conversation. The upshot is that she and her twin brother, Peter, are going to spend their birthday with their father. He's taking them to some beautiful inn in Sonoma for the weekend."

"And you're not invited."

"No."

"I'm sorry, Maggie, really sorry they're hurting you in this way. I wish I could make it up to you."

"Thanks, Jake," she said, squeezing his hand. "But I'm better now, I'm over it. Well, more or less." Maggie sighed and said in a low voice, "In a way, I think I'd written them off . . . they haven't shown much interest in me ever since all this happened." Forcing a laugh, she added, "I guess I wasn't a very good mother."

"Knowing what I know about you, I bet you were a hell of a mother!" Jake exclaimed. "And kids in this kind of situation can be very . . . treacherous. I think that's the best word. I know my sister Patty is going through something similar. She got married a couple of years ago. Her husband was a divorced man, and his children have been behaving very badly lately. Not only toward him but Patty as well. And she had nothing to do with their parents' divorce. Bill had been single for four years when she met him. Things were apparently relatively okay between him and his kids until he married Patty. Then they turned nasty and adopted a very hostile stance." Jake shook his head. "God knows why."

"You said you were separated, Jake. Do you have children?"

"No, I don't. Sadly. Well, perhaps I shouldn't say that now that we're getting divorced. I wanted children, though. Amy didn't."

"I see," Maggie murmured, looking at him through thoughtful eyes, then she said, "You must have been married very young."

"Nineteen. We were both nineteen. We'd been friends since we were twelve, sort of childhood sweethearts in high school."

"I married young, too, just after I left Bennington College, when I was twenty-two. I had the twins a year later."

"And you were living in Chicago all those years?"

"Yes, that's Mike's hometown. I come from New York, I grew up in Manhattan. Where are you from, Jake? Kent?"

"No, Hartford. I was born there. After Amy and I were married we lived there for a while, then we moved to New Milford. Once we separated last year I lived in a studio apartment on Bank Street. Until I found the house on Route 341, that is."

"Where does Amy live now?"

"She's still in New Milford." Jake took a long swallow of his iced tea and went on, "Do you know Samantha from New York? From when you were growing up, I mean?"

"No, we met at Bennington. And we became instant friends. Best friends." Maggie smiled as she thought of Samantha with affection. "I don't know what I would have done without her. Especially in the last couple of years. I don't think I would have managed to survive without her."

"Oh yes you would," Jake remarked in a knowing voice. "You're a born survivor. That's one of the things I admire about you, Maggie. Your strength of character, your resilience. You're a very special woman. I've never met anyone like you."

"Thank you. I've never met anyone quite like you, Jake."

He stared at her.

She stared back.

Jake said softly, "You do care about me then?"

"Oh yes, I do," she answered.

"Is everything all right between us?"

She nodded, smiled.

He also smiled, relief flooding his eyes. "I couldn't stand it if you were angry with me."

Suddenly Maggie laughed, feeling relieved herself. "I feel the same way."

"Can I see you tonight?"

"I'd love it."

"Would you like to come to my house? I could make pasta and a salad. I'd like to go over the final lighting designs for *The Crucible* with you."

"That's a good idea! I'd like to show you my drawings for the sets and finalize everything with you. There's not much time left, especially since Samantha and I are going away."

"Oh. When is that?" he asked swiftly, sounding surprised.

"In about six weeks. In July."

"Where are you going?"

"To Scotland. And then we're stopping off in London for a few days, on our way home. The trip's been planned for a long time. It's partly business."

"I'll miss you," Jake said. But he didn't really know how much until she had gone.

9

In his whole life Jake had never missed anyone the way he missed Maggie Sorrell. She had only been gone five days, but to him it seemed like five months.

It would be another ten days before she returned to Kent, and he knew he was going to be miserable until then. He was glad they were involved professionally as well as personally, working on the remodeling of Havers Hill. It made him feel closer to her, especially when he went to the old farmhouse. Her presence was everywhere.

For the same reason, he'd been up to the Little Theater in Kent twice, to tinker around with the lighting for the play, and he planned to go there again before she returned.

The woman designing the costumes, Alice Ferrier, was a friend of Samantha's and Maggie's, and he enjoyed chatting with her and with the stagehands working on Maggie's sets. It gave him a sense of belonging to Maggie's group; it was like being part of a large family, and he enjoyed the camaraderie. Also, it helped to deflect the loneliness he was feeling in Maggie's absence.

Until he met Maggie, Jake had been self-sufficient, going about his business, doing his own thing, seeing the odd male friend occasionally, and he'd had a couple of short-lived affairs. But he had never relied on anyone for anything.

Now he felt that Maggie was necessary to his well-being, his very existence, and this bothered him. He disliked being dependent on another human being; it made him feel vulnerable.

At the outset of their relationship, the night they had slept together for the first time, Jake had come right out and said it— told Maggie that he loved her. It was true, he did. But Maggie had not declared herself. He was not really worried, although he would like to hear her say it, because he knew she cared about him. Cared a lot. She gave herself away constantly.

Thoughts of Maggie continued to swirl in his head as he went out of the kitchen and crossed the yard, heading for the old red barn in the field at the back of the house. He had turned it into a studio and workshop, and he wanted to complete the plans he was drawing up for the exterior lighting at Havers Hill Farm. He wished Maggie had been with him at the farm today; finally he had come up with solutions for some of the more intricate lighting problems and he would have enjoyed explaining them to her.

Jake paused as he walked down the path, staring at an unusual brown-colored bird with an orange breast that had just flown out of the giant oak that shaded the lawn. As the bird hopped along at the edge of the grass he wondered what species it was. He had never seen this kind of bird before. The garden and fields surrounding his house were full of wildlife, as were the wetlands that stretched beyond. Canada geese and ducks made the wetlands their habitat.

Wandering on toward the barn, he stopped again as a chipmunk skittered across his path and disappeared into the innards of an old stone wall; the entire place was a haven for these funny little creatures and squirrels and rabbits. A fleeting thought crossed his mind—that this place would be a natural wonderland for a child.

As Jake struggled with the lock on the barn, which was stuck, he could hear the phone ringing inside, but by the time he managed to get the door opened it had stopped.

Could it have been Maggie phoning from Scotland? he wondered. He hoped so; she had said she would give him a call this week. He depressed the button on the answering machine.

"It's me, Jake," he heard Amy's voice saying. "I've got to talk to you. It's urgent. Please call me."

Immediately he dialed her apartment. The phone rang and rang. There was no answer. Just as there had been no answer yesterday, even though he had received the same kind of message on his machine last night. Obviously she wanted to talk to him about something, but when he returned her calls she was not there.

Walking over to the long table that served as a desk for him, he resolved to buy her an answering machine. Since she hadn't bothered to get one, as he had suggested months ago, he was going to have to do it for her.

Jake sighed under his breath. That was the story of his life with Amy. For as long as he could remember, ever since they were twelve, he had always been the one to take care of everything, and he had always had to look after her. She was like a baby. She couldn't manage to do the simplest task. Eventually it had begun to irritate him.

The odd thing was he *wanted* to take care of Maggie, to look after *her*, even though there was no need. She was such a competent woman and well able to take care of herself. Over the last few months he had come to know her well. He was aware that she was clever and practical, but he still felt the need to protect her. Certainly he saw a vulnerability in her, a softness he found most appealing.

Pushing aside thoughts of Maggie and Amy, Jake turned on the architect's lamp he used on the old oak table, pulled a drawing pad toward him, and began making sketches for the exterior lighting systems at Havers Hill Farm.

The red barn where he was working had become a refuge for him since he had moved into the house. He found the big open space conducive to work, whether it was designing lighting effects, tinkering with lamps and other electrical equipment at the bench, or painting at the easel under the big window situated at the far end of the barn. These three areas were quite separate and self-contained. He had furnished the barn sparsely. It was austere, painted white, and only the things required for his work had been used. His one luxury was a CD player, so that he could listen to music whenever he felt like it.

Jake concentrated on the plans for lighting the trees at Havers Hill for an hour, and then he tried Amy's number again. There was still no answer, and immediately he turned his attention back to the plans in front of him. He had always had tunnel vision, and this had served him well.

At nine he stopped working, shut off the lights, left the barn, and went back to the house. He found a cold beer in the refrigerator, made himself a cheese-and-tomato sandwich, and took his evening snack into the living room. After turning on the television, he sat down in the chair, ate his sandwich, drank his beer, and channel surfed absentmindedly. He was preoccupied with thoughts of Maggie, missing her, wanting her, longing to see her.

When the phone rang again Jake jumped up, grabbed it and exclaimed, "Hello?" hoping it was she.

"It's me," Amy said. "I've been trying to get you for two days. Why haven't you called me back, Jake?"

"I have, Amy," he answered, striving not to sound impatient. "I got your message when I came home from work last night. I phoned you. No answer. I tried you at the store this morning and was told it was your day off. I just missed your call by a few seconds tonight. You must have gone out immediately, because there was no answer and I dialed you within minutes."

"I went to the movies with Mavis."

"I see." He cleared his throat. "You said you wanted to talk to me urgently. What about?"

"Something important."

"Then tell me, Amy, I'm listening," he said, sitting down on the arm of the sofa. When there was no response from her, he said in an even tone, "Come on, Amy, tell me what this is about."

"Not on the phone. I need to talk to you in person. Can't you come over?"

"*Now?*"

"Yes, Jake."

"Amy, I can't! It's too late! It's turned ten, and I have to be up very early. Let's talk now if it's so important to you."

"*No!* I have to *see* you."

"Well, I'm not driving over to New Milford at this hour, so you can forget that!"

"Can I see you tomorrow? It's really urgent that we meet."

"All right," he agreed, although he did so reluctantly.

"Tomorrow night, Jake? I could make you supper."

"No, no, that's not necessary," he replied and thinking swiftly, he improvised, "I have to go to New Milford tomorrow morning to pick up some equipment. I need it for the job I'm doing in South Kent. How about if I come to the store around noon? I'll take you to lunch."

"I guess so . . . I wish you could come over now . . . "

"I'll see you tomorrow," he said firmly. "Good night, Amy."

"'Bye, Jake," she muttered and hung up.

Later, as he undressed, Jake asked himself if he had made a mistake, agreeing to see Amy. There was no question in his mind that she was going to grumble about the divorce, try to talk him out of it. She was already procrastinating; there had been no word from her lawyer. He wasn't even sure she had been to see him again. He was going to have to do something about it himself, take matters into his own hands, he decided, if he ever wanted to be free. As usual, Amy was incapable of handling it.

When they met the following day, the first thing Jake noticed about Amy was that she had made an effort with her appearance. Her wispy blonde hair was pulled back in a ponytail and tied with a blue ribbon, and she had applied a little makeup.

Nevertheless, as he sat looking at her across the table in the Wayfarers Cafe in New Milford, where he had brought her for lunch, he thought she looked tired. She was only twenty-eight, but it struck him now that she appeared older, a little worn down. But this was nothing new, really; there had been something lackluster about her for the past few years. Amy had faded quickly. It saddened him really, and he couldn't help feeling a little bit sorry for her. She wasn't a bad person, just unfocused, disorganized, and isolated.

They chatted about inconsequential things, looked at the menus, discussed what they would like to eat. In the end they both settled on the Cobb salad and iced tea.

Once the waitress had taken their order and they were alone, Amy said, "So what's the job you're doing in Kent?"

"A farmhouse," he explained. "A very old place, actually. It's picturesque and has beautiful grounds. It's a challenge, especially the interiors. I'm also doing the outside, creating lighting for the landscaped areas and the pool. It's a big job for me and I'm pretty excited about it."

She nodded. "I know you like doing intricate work, the fancy stuff, and you're good at it, Jake."

"Thanks." He gave her an appraising glance and said, "What is it you want to talk to me about, Amy?"

"Let's wait until after lunch."

"Why? You've been calling me for two days, asking me to meet you, saying it's urgent, and now you want to wait."

She nodded. Her mouth settled in a stubborn line.

Jake let out a small sigh. "Whatever you say, Amy, but I do have to go back to work you know. In a couple of hours."

"My mother doesn't think we should get a divorce," she blurted out, and then took a quick sip of water, eyeing him over the rim of the glass.

"I know that," he replied, his eyes narrowing slightly. "Is that why you wanted to see me? To discuss the divorce? Has your mother been going on at you?"

She shook her head. "Not really."

Jake leaned forward over the table and pinned her with his eyes. "Look, Amy, I'm sorry it didn't work out, really sorry. But there it is . . . these things happen, you know that."

Before she could answer the waitress was back, placing the salads in front of them, returning a second later with the glasses of iced tea.

They ate in silence for a while. Or rather Jake ate; Amy picked at her food.

Finally she put down her fork and leaned back in her chair.

Jake glanced at her, frowning slightly. Suddenly she looked pale, paler than usual, he thought, and she seemed to be on the verge of tears.

"What is it, Amy? What's wrong?" he asked, putting his fork on the plate. When she didn't answer, but gaped at him oddly, looking scared, he pressed, "What's the matter, honey?"

"I'm sick," she began and stopped abruptly.

His frown intensified. "I'm not following you. Do you mean you feel nauseous at this moment? Or are you saying you have an illness?"

"Yes. I went to the doctor, Jake. I haven't been feeling well." Her eyes brimmed. "It's cancer. He told me I've got ovarian cancer."

"Oh my God! Amy! No! Is he sure?" Jake leaned forward and took her hand, holding it tightly in his. "Is the doctor certain?"

"Oh yes," she whispered.

For a moment Jake was at a loss for words. A compassionate man and kind by nature, he filled with sympathy for her. He wondered how he could comfort her, and then realized there was no way. His words, if he could find the right ones, would be cold comfort. Far better to leave them unsaid. And so he sat there, holding her hand, patting it from time to time, hoping he was making her feel less alone.

10

It had rained earlier and as Maggie walked down the path that led through the garden of Sunlaws House Hotel she paused for a moment and lifted her eyes to the sky. The sun was coming out again, penetrating the light clouds, and quite suddenly a rainbow trembled up there above the trees, a perfect arc of pink and blue, violet, and yellow.

Maggie smiled inwardly, thinking it was a good omen. Her mother had been the most positive person she had ever known, one who had always believed in the pot of gold at the end of the rainbow, silver linings, and bluebirds bringing happiness.

Mom was an eternal optimist, she thought, still smiling to herself, filled with the fondest of memories. I'm glad I inherited that trait from her. If I hadn't I don't think I would have survived the debacle with Mike Sorrell. They would have taken me away in a straitjacket. But she had indeed survived and life had never been better for her, she decided. And then she thought: How many people get a second chance at life?

When she reached the end of the path, Maggie turned around and headed back to the hotel. She and Samantha were staying there overnight, en route to London by rented car. They had driven down from Edinburgh and Glasgow and had arrived at Sunlaws in time for lunch today.

The manor was in Kelso, in the area known as the Borders, so called because it was close to the borders between Scotland and England in the heart of Roxburghshire. The gracious old house, which belonged to the Duke and Duchess of Roxburghe, had been turned into the most charming of country hotels.

Sunlaws was handsomely furnished, full of mellow antiques and fine paintings, and it was imbued with the comfort and welcoming warmth that Maggie loved. It was a look and an environment that she strove hard to create in her own decorating schemes for her clients.

The landscape around the hotel was equally captivating, and it reminded her of the northwestern highlands of Connecticut. The moment she had set eyes on it she had begun to feel homesick.

Maggie now realized that she couldn't wait to get back to her house in Kent. And to Jake. He was constantly on her mind; she rarely stopped thinking about him, wishing he were here, wishing he could be sharing this trip with her. And she wished he had been with her when she bought the antiques in Edinburgh and Glasgow. They were for the farmhouse and were good pieces made of dark, ripe woods, some of them handcarved, and all were very old and beautifully made. They would sit perfectly in the rooms at Havers Hill Farm, would underscore the mood of the house and its overall feeling of antiquity.

Maggie was glad she had come to Scotland with Samantha. The trip had been highly successful for both of them. Aside from the antique furniture she had purchased, she had also found other interesting things: antique lamps, porcelains, and all sorts of unique accessories.

Samantha had invested in a variety of fabrics that she planned to sell in the studio shop she was opening in three months. Maggie's favorites were the Scottish wools, mohairs, and tartans, which had taken her fancy as well as Samantha's.

All in all they had done well, and Maggie made up her mind to come back next year. With Jake. He had never traveled abroad and recently confided that he would enjoy making a trip to England one day.

Once more her thoughts settled on Jake. She had missed him, missed his warmth and affection, his sense of fun, his dry humor, his passion, and his constant cosseting of her. He made her feel so wanted, so loved, and in a way that Mike Sorrell never had.

She heard her name and glanced up, peering ahead, shading her eyes against the bright light with her hand. She waved when she saw Samantha coming down the path toward her.

"I've been looking all over for you!" Samantha exclaimed, tucking her arm through Maggie's, falling into step. The two of them continued on to the hotel together.

Maggie said, "I love this time of day, just before dark. It's magic."

Samantha nodded. "So do I. And that's what they call it in the movie business. . . *the magic hour.* Apparently cinematographers think it's the most wonderful light for filming." Samantha shivered. "Let's go inside, Maggie, it's turned coolish. There's a breeze blowing up for one thing, and it smells of rain."

"I'm a bit cold myself," Maggie admitted.

They increased their pace, and once they were inside the hotel Samantha looked at her watch. She said, "It's nearly seven. Let's go and have a drink in the lounge. There's a huge fire blazing in there. It might be July, but they know something about these cool Scottish nights, the locals do."

A short while later the two friends sat in the comfortable lounge. It was furnished with deep leather chairs and sofas, and there were wonderful old paintings on the walls. Vases of flowers were everywhere and their mingled scents filled the air. The only sounds were the ticking of a clock somewhere at the other end of the room and the hiss and crackle of the logs burning in the huge marble fireplace. Silk-shaded lamps had been turned on and the lounge had a soft glow to it.

Samantha looked around and said, "It's so intimate and cozy in here, and the room has a real country-house feeling to it, don't you think?"

"It's a look that's hard to reproduce properly," Maggie said. "The British do it so well, maybe because it's endemic to their way of life."

Samantha merely smiled and took a sip of her white wine. Then she glanced across at Maggie. "I've really enjoyed the trip, haven't you?"

"Yes, I have."

Now Samantha eyed her carefully and murmured, "But you've missed Jake, haven't you?"

Maggie smiled. "A bit . . ." She laughed, added, "A lot actually. How did you guess?"

"You've seemed distracted sometimes, and sort of . . . well, *faraway* is the best way of describing it."

Maggie was silent. She averted her face for a brief moment, sat gazing into the fire, a quiet, reflective expression settling in her eyes. After a moment she glanced at her best friend and said, "There's something I want to tell you."

Samantha nodded. "And oddly enough, I've got something to tell you. But you go first."

There was a fractional silence. Maggie then said, "I'm pregnant, Sam."

"Good God! You can't be! Surely not! Not in this day and age! Don't tell me you didn't use anything, for God's sake!"

"Yes, I'm very pregnant. I missed my period for the second time last week, when we first got here. And no, we didn't use anything."

Samantha sat back, gaping at her, askance. "There's something out there called AIDS, Maggie."

"I know. But . . . well . . . I trust Jake, I know he's not promiscuous."

"When you slept with Jake you slept with everybody else he's ever been with . . . you don't know anything about *them*."

Maggie did not respond. She leaned back against the tapestry cushions in the leather chair and stared into space. Then finally rousing herself, she muttered, "You said you had something to tell me. What is it?"

Samantha hesitated, cleared her throat, and leaning closer to Maggie, she said quietly, "You'd better know this, even though it might hurt more than ever. Jake's a married man, Mag. I found out just before we left, but I didn't want to tell you then and upset you. However, I thought you should know, now that we're heading back home. I purposely waited so as not to spoil your trip."

Maggie said quickly, "But I already know that! He told me himself, weeks ago. Actually, it was a few days after we became lovers. He was very honest with me, Sam. He said he had been separated for a year, living alone for that time, and was in the middle of a divorce. Are you suggesting he's still living with his wife?"

Samantha shook her head and said swiftly, "No, no, I'm not."

"Who told you he was married?"

"A client. She bought me a present at the bath and body shop in New Milford. When she gave the basket of goodies to me, all kinds of aromatherapy products, she said they'd been recommended by Amy Cantrell. I suppose I must have reacted to the name, and my client said something about Amy being the wife of Jake Cantrell, the lighting expert. But if you say he's separated, then I'm sure he is."

"And he does live alone." Maggie asserted. "I've been to his house several times."

"Why didn't you tell me he was in the middle of a divorce?"

Maggie shrugged. "I didn't think it was particularly important, Sam."

"What are you going to do about the baby, Maggie?"

"I'm going to have it, of course."

Samantha gave her a questioning stare. "What about Jake? I mean, what do you think he'll say? Do?"

"I'm sure he'll be pleased. I hope so. But in any case it's my choice, and only mine. I'm certainly not going to have an abortion."

Maggie leaned forward, and her face was suddenly bright with happiness and hope when she added, "While I was walking in the garden earlier, I couldn't help thinking that not many people get a second chance in life. I did. The baby's my second chance, and Jake of course. I think I'm very lucky."

"Do you think he'll want to marry you?"

"I don't know . . . I don't really care . . . about making it legal. I can bring up a baby myself and support a child. I'm very competent, Sam."

"You don't have to tell me! I know that only too well," Samantha remarked pithily.

"Maybe you think I'm crazy," Maggie ventured. "Here I am, forty-four years old, pregnant by my much younger lover of twenty-nine, who's not even divorced yet, whom I'm not sure even wants to marry me." She began to laugh and lifted her hands in a helpless gesture. "And do I want to marry him?" Maggie shrugged and lifted a dark brow.

Samantha shook her head wonderingly. "There's nobody like you, Maggie, when it comes to coping. Let's not forget that you came through a pretty rotten situation when your husband of twenty-odd years decided to take a walk. A situation that might have felled many another woman."

"Don't spoil my day! Don't mention Mike Sorrell. Anyway, getting back to Jake, he does love me."

"He told you?"

"Yes, he did."

"Do you love him, Mag?"

"Yes. Very much."

"You're very brave, Maggie."

"Oh, Sam, I'm very lucky . . . "

Samantha Matthews was glad she had insisted that they stay at Brown's Hotel. It was handy to Piccadilly, Bond Street, and just about everywhere else, being the center of the West End. It was easy to walk to all the shops, and cabs were readily available.

Now as she hurried down Albermarle Street, making her way back to the hotel, she could not help wondering what Maggie had been doing this afternoon. Her friend had insisted on going off alone, and had behaved in the most secretive way. But she would soon know; Maggie would eventually tell her.

It was hot and muggy this afternoon and a storm threatened. Samantha decided to ask the head porter to order a car and driver for the evening ahead. They were going to the theater and then to dinner at the Ivy and the last thing they needed was to be caught in the rain.

When she entered the lobby Samantha made straight for the porter's desk. After ordering a car, she took the elevator up to the suite she and Maggie were sharing. It was her treat, her birthday present to Maggie. "But you've already given me that gorgeous bag!" Maggie had protested when she had made the announcement in Scotland. Samantha had merely smiled at the time and refused to listen.

Maggie was still out.

Samantha dropped her bag and packages on the sofa in the sitting room and went through into the bedroom. Taking off her dress and stepping out of her high-heeled shoes, she put on a silk robe and lay down on her bed. She was tired from rushing around all day and wanted to relax before dressing for the evening.

After a moment her thoughts settled on Maggie. She loved her like a sister she had never had, and there was no one she felt closer to or cared more about. Not unnaturally, given the circumstances, she was worried about Maggie. It was she who had introduced Maggie to Jake Cantrell, and she felt responsible for the current situation. On the other hand, Maggie was a forty-four-year-old woman who was highly intelligent and extremely smart. If she didn't know what she was doing, then Samantha didn't know who did.

Samantha sighed under her breath. There were no doubts in her mind about Maggie's capabilities, and in many ways she admired the attitude she was taking about the baby. But what about Jake? Would he come through for Maggie? And what if he didn't? Could Maggie really manage to bring the baby up on her own? That took guts, which Maggie had, of course. She'll be all right, no matter what, Samantha decided. And I'm there to help her. Samantha smiled to herself. Their motto had always been: Through thick and thick and thin and thin.

The telephone on the nightstand between the two beds began to ring. Reaching for it, Samantha said, "Hello?"

"Is that you, Samantha?"

"Yes, it is. Who's this?" she asked, failing to recognize the somewhat gruff male voice at the other end of the line.

"It's Mike Sorrell, Sam."

Samantha was so surprised she almost dropped the receiver. "Oh!" she exclaimed and then added in an icy tone, "What can I do for you, Mike?"

"I'm looking for Maggie."

"She's not here."

"When do you expect her, Sam?"

"I don't know," Samantha replied, as cold as ever, ignoring his attempt at friendliness.

"Have her call me, please."

"Where?"

"I'm staying at the Connaught."

"You're in London!"

"I'm here on business."

"How did you know where we're staying?"

"I tracked you down, via your assistant in Connecticut. When all I could get was Maggie's machine, I phoned your studio."

"I see. I'll give her the message."

"Thanks," he said.

"Good-bye," Samantha muttered and slammed the phone down. She glared at it. *Son of a bitch*, she thought and angrily zapped on the television set. She got the BBC and the evening news, but watched it somewhat absentmindedly, wondering what Maggie's ex-husband wanted with her.

Half an hour later Maggie walked into the suite laden with shopping bags. "Hi, Sam," she said, walking through into the bedroom, putting the packages on a chair and kicking off her shoes. "It's just started to rain. Perhaps we'd better get a car for tonight."

"I already did," Samantha replied and pushed herself into a sitting position on the bed. "Sit down, Maggie darling. And brace yourself."

Maggie stared at her. "Why? What's wrong?" She frowned, went on, "There is something wrong. I can tell from the dour expression on your face."

"Guess who's in London? No, you'll never guess. Don't even try. It's Mike Sorrell. He just called you, about half an hour ago. He wants you to phone him. He's staying at the Connaught."

"Good God!" Maggie flopped into the nearest chair and stared at Samantha, shaking her head in disbelief. "How did he find us? Not that it's a secret where we are."

"Through Angela. When he couldn't raise you he called my studio."

Maggie bit her lip, suddenly thoughtful. "Out of the blue he wants to talk to me. I wonder why."

"As do I, Mag. Are you going to call him?"

"I don't know. What for? It can't be anything to do with Peter or Hannah, he would have told you if there was some sort of problem or emergency."

"I think he would. He sounded calm enough and controlled."

Maggie thought for a moment and then made a decision. Pushing herself to her feet, she looked at Samantha and said, "I'm going to talk to him now, get this out of the way." She walked into the sitting room looking brisk and businesslike.

Samantha slid off the bed and followed her.

Maggie lifted the phone on the desk and asked the operator to connect her to the Connaught Hotel. A few seconds later she was talking to Mike Sorrell.

"It's Maggie. I hear you want to talk to me."

"Hi, Maggie! Yes, I do. I was hoping we could get together."

"Oh. Why?"

"I need to go over something with you. How about tonight? I thought we could meet for a drink. Or dinner."

"Certainly not."

"Not even the drink?"

"No. I'm busy this evening."

"Tomorrow?" he suggested.

"Why can't we talk now, on the phone? That's what we've been doing, off and on, for the last two and a half years."

"I need to see you in person, Maggie."

"Are the twins okay?"

"Oh yes, they're fine. Look, I think we have some unfinished business to discuss."

Startled to hear this, Maggie was silent for a moment. Then she made another decision. "Nine o'clock tomorrow morning. Here at Brown's Hotel. I'll meet you in the lounge."

"Okay! Great. 'Bye, honey."

Maggie put the receiver in its cradle and turned around,

stood leaning against the desk, staring at Samantha. "You're not going to believe it, but that snake in the grass just had the temerity to call me honey."

"Something's not kosher in the House of Denmark, to paraphrase Hamlet!" Samantha exclaimed indignantly. "Since you've seen fit to meet with him, I'm glad you made your venue here. I'll be ready and waiting in case you need me . . . to kill that son of a bitch."

Maggie couldn't help laughing. "Oh Sam darling, I do love you. No matter what, you can always bring a smile to my face."

Grinning, Samantha leapt to her feet and went over to the small bar. "Let's have a vodka on the rocks before we get ready for the theater."

"Well . . . you fix one for yourself. I want to get something from the bedroom."

Maggie returned a moment later, carrying a small package. "This is for you, Sam. It's just to say thank you for all this—" She glanced around the sitting room. "But mostly it's because you're always there for me, and always have been."

Samantha took the package, tore off the wrapping paper, and opened the red velvet box. It contained a pair of delicate chandelier earrings made of gold and malachite.

"Oh Maggie how sweet of you! The earrings I admired in that shop in the Burlington Arcade. Thank you so much, they're gorgeous. But you shouldn't have." She went over and hugged Maggie, and added, "Your friendship is the most important thing in the world to me."

Maggie drew away from her, and smiled lovingly. "Through thick and thick and thin and thin . . . "

The following morning when Maggie got up she wondered, for a moment, why she was feeling so tense. Instantly she remembered. Mike Sorrell was coming over to the hotel to see her, and she was not looking forward to it at all.

Very simply, she had nothing to say to him, and she didn't particularly want to hear what he had to say to her. As far as she was concerned they had no unfinished business, as he termed it. Their business was well and truly finished and had been for a very long time.

"You look fantastic!" Samantha exclaimed, when Maggie walked into the sitting room of the suite a few minutes before nine. "The bloom is on the rose, and then some, Maggie. You look so well and so happy he's going to be gnashing his teeth."

"I doubt it," Maggie said, and grinned. "I'm sure he's very happy with his lady love, his new wife. He's probably in the midst of starting a brand-new family, that's what these second, trophy wives want, isn't it? Kids galore and an insurance policy for the future?"

Samantha laughed. "Who knows? And who cares. Listen, Mag, I've been thinking about your situation with Jake, and I'm really glad. I know it's going to work out."

Maggie patted her stomach. "And the baby?"

"I think you're doing the right thing, having it, I mean. Just make sure I'm godmother."

"Who else but you?" Maggie looked at herself in the mirror, straightened the lapel of her navy blue gabardine pantsuit, adjusting the collar of her white silk shirt as she did. "Give me twenty minutes with him and then come downstairs and get me."

"I will. Our appointment at Keith Skeel's antique place is set for ten o'clock anyway."

"See you in a few minutes," Maggie murmured and left the suite.

Mike Sorrell was already waiting for her in the lounge when she arrived a few seconds later. He rose to greet her, seemed at a sudden loss, as if he didn't know whether to kiss her or shake her hand. He opted for the latter, and thrust his hand at her.

Maggie shook it quickly and sat down opposite him. She could not help thinking that he looked weary, worn, and sad. His face was lined and jowled, his hair very gray, and in general there was a tired air about him. He wasn't wearing well, she decided, looked much older than forty-nine. An image of Jake, twenty years his junior, flashed before her eyes. She blinked and averted her face, not wanting him to see the sudden smile of pleasure that had settled there. He might misunderstand that smile.

She said, "Let's order coffee, shall we?"

"Thanks. I could use another cup." As he spoke he signaled to a waiter. Turning to Maggie he asked, "Do you want anything to eat?"

She shook her head.

Once he had given the order for coffee, Mike turned back to her, again looking uncertain.

Maggie seized the moment and said, "Why did you want to see me?"

Mike cleared his throat nervously. "I was in New York at the end of last week, en route to London for a client. I thought we could get together there. I'm sure Samantha told you I called her studio when I couldn't reach you."

"Yes, she did. But *why* do you want to see me at all? You dumped me unceremoniously almost three years ago now and have hardly been in touch since then. Why the unexpected change of heart?"

When he remained totally silent, Maggie added, "*I* don't think we have any unfinished business. Quite the contrary, our business is well and truly finished." She laughed a little acidly. "You made that quite clear to me when you left me for your legal colleague."

"Don't be bitter, Maggie," he murmured. "I realize now that—"

"Bitter!" she exclaimed, cutting him off. "I'm not bitter. I've better things to do with my time than waste it feeling bitter about you, or mourning your loss, Mike. I have a life to live, and believe me I'm living it. To the hilt."

"You look very well . . . glowing," he said, eyeing her thoughtfully.

Maggie decided he sounded slightly regretful and briefly wondered what was happening in his new life. She really didn't care, and she didn't want to know. She said, "Look, Mike, I have an appointment with an antique dealer this morning, so my time is limited. What's this unfinished business you mentioned on the phone? Let's get to the point."

He took a deep breath and said, "*Us*, Maggie. We're the unfinished business. We were together for so long, we had a good life, and we have the kids . . . " His voice trailed off as he became aware of her icy demeanor, the disdainful expression on her face.

Maggie's voice was frosty when she said, "Are you trying to tell me you made a mistake? Is that it, Mike?"

"Yes, for my sins, I did. I should never have left you, honey. We were the best, so good together. As I said, we had a great life—"

"*You* did," Maggie interrupted. "I didn't, now that I look back. You were pretty selfish and self-involved, you never really thought about my needs, and the one time I was happy, doing so well at the design firm, you made me leave my job. You just couldn't stand the fact that I had an interest other than you."

"Don't be like this, Maggie. *Please.*"

She laughed in his face. "You bastard! You dump me in the most cold-hearted way, barely talk to me for nearly three years, and now come around making nice talk. What's all this about? Don't tell me your new wife's left you?"

When he sat back in his chair and glared at her, Maggie knew she had hit the mark. "Well, well, well," she said, biting back an amused smile. "And more than likely for a younger man. Right?"

Mike Sorrell flushed deeply, but still he said nothing.

Maggie said, "Ironic reversal."

"I suppose it is," Mike agreed at last. "And yes, Jennifer has left me. She took up with a guy about six months ago, unknown to me, of course. Anyway, she's gone off with him. Permanently. To Los Angeles. She wants a divorce."

"Never mind, Mike, you'll manage to cope somehow. I did."

"Can't we try again, Maggie?" he pleaded. "Let's give it a shot. The kids are all for it, too. And I need you."

"Oh really. Well, it might surprise you to know that I don't give a damn that you need me. Also, what Peter and Hannah think doesn't concern me very much. They have behaved in the most unconscionable way to me. So, my attitude is exactly the same as theirs has been toward me since you dumped me for a younger woman. Let's not forget what you did."

"Don't be so resentful and bitter!" Mike exclaimed, glaring at her. "I'm offering you this chance to start all over again, to put the family back together again, and you're behaving as if I'm asking you to commit suicide or murder."

"Apt words, very apt words indeed!" Maggie exclaimed. "To come back to you *would* be suicide. And you murdered my soul for years, all the years I knew you, Mike. You never let me be me, be myself."

"You don't want to end up a lonely old woman, all by yourself do you?" he asked and then paused as the waiter arrived with the coffee.

Once he had left, Maggie said in an icy tone, "You egotistical idiot. What on earth makes you think I'm alone? As a matter of fact, I'm very involved with someone."

"Is it serious?" he asked, and he was unable to keep the angry look off his face.

"Yes, very serious. I expect to be married soon."

"Who is he?"

"I don't think that's any of your business. We're divorced, remember." Maggie pushed back her chair, stood up and stepped away from the table. Then she paused and murmured, "Good-bye."

As she walked through the lounge she saw Samantha hovering in the doorway. She raised her hand in greeting and smiled. She felt freer and happier than she had in years. In a few days she would be back with Jake. Her future.

11

Jake had to keep reminding himself that the speed limit was forty-five miles an hour to resist the temptation to press his boot down hard on the gas pedal. He was on his way to Maggie's, and he couldn't wait to get there.

She had called him on his beeper the minute she had arrived at her house in Kent from Kennedy Airport, and when he had asked her if he could come over she had agreed at once. He thought she had sounded glad to hear his voice, excited even, and this pleased him. He had missed her; he wondered if she had missed him.

Ten minutes later he was driving into her yard.

Before he had even turned off the ignition she was coming through the kitchen door and running down the back steps. Her face was wreathed in smiles.

"Hi, sweetheart!" he cried, slamming the truck's door behind him and almost running toward her.

They met in the middle of the backyard and he swept her into his arms and swung her around. They were both laughing when he finally set her down on the ground.

Jake held her away from him, looked into her face, smiling widely.

Maggie smiled back at him and exclaimed, "I've missed you so much, Jake! I can't begin to tell you how much!"

"I know. I've missed you too," he said and brought her into his arms, kissing her deeply on the mouth. Once he started kissing her he couldn't stop. He showered her with kisses. Her forehead, her eyes, her face, and her neck. "I'm happy you're home, Maggie."

"Yes, so am I. Let's go inside, Jake." She cocked her head on one side and gave him a flirtatious look. "I have something for you."

"You do?" He looked at her questioningly.

She nodded, took hold of his hand, and led him into the house. Her suitcases were still in the kitchen, along with her raincoat and a shopping bag; she reached into the latter and pulled out a package.

Turning, she offered this to him, feeling suddenly rather shy and girlish. "This is for you, Jake. It's from Scotland."

Grinning, and just a bit flustered, he took the gift from her and stared at it for a moment. "What is it?" he asked finally.

"Open it and see," she answered, gazing up at him.

He did so, pulled out a heavy fisherman's sweater made of thick cream wool and then looked at her. "Maggie, this is great. But you're spoiling me."

"I just hope it fits. I had to guess your size. Large, right?"

He nodded and then held it against himself. "I'm sure it's perfect. Thanks, Maggie." Putting the sweater down on a chair he moved forward, pulled her into his arms and kissed her on the cheek. "Thanks . . . for thinking of me when you were away . . ."

"I never stopped, Jake."

The adoration reflected in her eyes told him what he wanted and needed to know. He bent into her, placed his mouth on hers, and kissed her passionately.

Maggie held on to him tightly, returning his kissing, matching his ardor, pressing herself against him, needing to feel his warmth and his love.

Finally, he slackened his hold on her and stared down into her face. "Can we go upstairs?"

Maggie nodded.

Together they climbed the stairs holding hands.

It occurred to Jake that their lovemaking was more frantic and passionate than ever. They shed their clothes and came into each other's arms with a rush of excitement and urgency; they seemed to grasp at each other, their faces full of intensity and longing.

Jake found himself taking her to him at once, on her urging, and she was hot and yielding and ready for him, as he was for her. They soared together, clutching each other tightly, calling each other's name as they soared higher and higher, lost in the wonder of each other.

When he finally fell against her he felt drained, almost exhausted from their passion. "Oh God, Maggie," he gasped. "It's never been like that. Not ever. Not any time. Not anywhere. Not even with you. Until now." He lifted himself on one elbow and looked down at her. "That was a first."

She smiled and touched his face. "Jake . . . "

"Yes, sweetheart?"

"I love you . . . I love you so much . . . more than I've ever loved anyone."

"Oh Maggie, Maggie." He wrapped his arms around her, held her close to him. "I've wanted to hear you say that for ages. I love you too. But then you know that . . . I told you the first night."

"I felt the same way, but I just wanted to be sure. About my own feelings, I mean."

"And are you sure now?"

"*Absolutely.*"

"I'm glad."

Maggie lay next to him, her arms wrapped around him, drifting with her thoughts. Finally rousing herself, she said, "Jake, I have a surprise for you."

"Mmmmmm," he murmured lazily without moving.

Maggie endeavored to sit up. He held her tightly in his arms, would not release her. Struggling slightly, she said softly, "Let me get up, Jake. I have something to tell you."

"Tell me then."

"I'd like to be looking at you when I do."

"Oh." Intrigued, he let go of her and sat up himself.

Maggie crawled in front of him, then sat up, hugging her knees, staring into his face.

"So go on, tell me, sweetheart," he said, eyeing her curiously.

Maggie smiled. "I'm pregnant, Jake. I'm expecting a baby. Our baby."

A beatific smile spread across his face and his eyes lit up. "That's wonderful! *A baby.* That's great, Maggie! It really is."

"You *are* pleased then?" she asked.

"Sure I am. I always wanted a child. I told you that. When did you realize? When is it due? I wonder if it's a boy or a girl?" For a few moments he was full of questions.

Maggie answered each one, enjoying his excitement and happiness, relieved that he had reacted in this way.

Later they made love again. "To celebrate the baby," Jake whispered in her ear and then they fell asleep in each other's arms.

It was Jake who awakened first, about half an hour later. He slid out of bed and went into the bathroom to take a shower.

When he returned to the bedroom, wrapped in a towel, Maggie was putting on a loose silk caftan. She turned around as he came in; as always she felt the impact of him . . . his dark good looks, the soulful green eyes, the black hair slicked back after his shower never failed to surprise her. There were moments when he took her breath away.

"You're staring," he said.

"I know. Sorry. It's just good to see you that's all." For a moment she was tempted to tell him about the night they first met at the Little Theater in Kent, when Samantha had called him Tom Cruise. But she refrained, knowing that the story would not sit well with him. He disliked references to his good looks and his physique.

Maggie moved across the room swiftly, the caftan flaring out behind her. "I picked up some groceries on the way in from the airport. Steaks and salad for dinner. How does that sound?"

"Great. I'll be down in a minute. If you open a bottle of Perrier we can have a drink outside, while I grill the steaks on the barbecue."

"It's a deal," she said and went out.

After he had buttoned his white shirt, pulled on his blue jeans and boots, Jake went downstairs. He found Maggie outside on the back terrace, sitting at the table, the bottle of Perrier in a bucket of ice. She poured two glasses as he sat down next to her.

"Cheers," they said together, clinking glasses.

After taking a long swallow, Jake remarked, "Things are going great at Havers Hill, Maggie, as I told you when you phoned the other day. And I know Mark and Ralph have been giving you progress reports. But I can't wait for you to come out to the site tomorrow. You'll be very surprised, pleasantly surprised."

She grinned. "I know I will. I guess I'll have to make two trips tomorrow. One in the morning and one at night. I do want to see the outside lighting after dark. You said some of it was in place already."

"But only temporarily. For you to see. I've rigged it up in such a way that if you don't approve we can change it. My guys haven't done the channeling in the ground for the wires. We'll do that once you've made your final decision."

"I wish you'd been with me in Scotland, Jake. I found some wonderful antiques."

They sat talking about the work at Havers Hill for a while, and then they went into the kitchen. Maggie took the green salad she had made earlier out of the refrigerator and put it on a tray, along with plates, knives, forks, and napkins. Jake insisted on carrying this outside for her; Maggie followed him with the plate of steaks.

"I've rarely seen fireflies," Maggie said, clutching Jake's arm. "Look! Over there! The little lights dancing among the bushes."

"You're right!" he exclaimed. "I haven't seen them since I was a kid myself. When I was about fourteen. Amy and I would go to her aunt's—" Jake broke off, sat back in his chair, sipped a little coffee, suddenly silent and tense.

Maggie said, "Why did you stop?"

"It's not a very interesting story," he mumbled and got up. He walked along the terrace and stepped down onto the lawn that stretched in front of it.

Aware of the sudden change in his mood, sensing that something was troubling him, Maggie rose and went after him. She caught up with him on the lawn, took hold of his arm, and pulled him around to face her.

"What is it, darling?" she asked, filling with apprehension.

He stood staring down at her and shook his head. A deep sigh escaped him. "I really didn't want to tell you this tonight. Not on your first evening back. I just wanted us to enjoy being together. But I guess I have to tell you . . ." He sighed again, then put his hand on her shoulder, peered into her face. "I've got some really bad news, Maggie."

She stared at him. "What kind of bad news?"

"It's about Amy . . ."

"The divorce has stalled, is that it?"

He shook his head. "No, not in the way you mean. But it is stalled."

"You always said she was very reluctant to divorce you, and I can't say I blame her," Maggie murmured, feeling deflated after the excitement of earlier and their intimate dinner.

"It's not really her," Jake began, and stopped. He coughed, and said in a low voice, "While you were away I found out that Amy has cancer. Ovarian cancer."

"Oh no, Jake, how terrible! I'm so sorry. Is she getting treatment?"

"Chemotherapy. She started at the beginning of this week. Maybe the treatment will arrest the cancer."

"Let's hope so," Maggie said, and moving away, she trailed across the lawn, knowing what he was going to say before he said it. She knew because she knew him. He was a decent man, and he was sensitive, compassionate.

Jake caught up with her and put his arm around her shoulders. "I have to help her as much as I can, do what I can for her, Maggie. You do understand that, don't you?"

"Yes. Of course."

"I just can't pressure her about the divorce right now."

"I understand . . ." Maggie paused, took a deep breath and went on quietly, "Are you moving back to New Milford? Are you going to live with Amy again?"

"No, I'm not! How could you think that?" he cried and turned her to face him. "I love you, Maggie. I don't want to lose you. I just want you to understand that I'll have to do what I can for her, especially financially. She's on my medical insurance, I can't pull that away from her. If we got divorced she'd lose her benefits. She needs me to be there for her right now. She's like a child, she's always been dependent on me. As soon as the cancer's arrested I'll talk to her again about seeing her lawyer."

Maggie compressed her lips and nodded. She was afraid to speak. She didn't want to say the wrong thing. She didn't want to lose him either. Her eyes filled with tears.

In the dim evening light he saw them glittering on her dark lashes, and he brought her into his arms, pressed her head against his shoulder. "Don't cry. I know what you're thinking. You're thinking about the baby."

"Yes," she whispered against his shirt, which was soaked with her tears.

"Will you marry me, Maggie? When we can?"

"I will, Jake. I love you."

"I love you. I want you and I want our baby. But I have to stand by Amy. Until she's better. You do understand that?"

Maggie nodded. "If you weren't the kind of man you are, I don't believe I would love you as much as I do. I'll wait for you, Jake. I'll wait."

12

"It's me, Amy," Jake called out as he opened the door of her apartment. Bending, he picked up the bags of groceries he had deposited on the floor and went into the hall. Walking across to the living room, he stood in the doorway. "Hello, honey," he said, smiling at her.

Amy was sitting on the sofa in the dimly lit living room, watching television. "Hi, Jake," she said in a low voice and gave him a wan smile.

"I'll be with you in a minute, Amy. After I put all of this stuff in the kitchen."

Amy nodded and leaned back against the sofa. She was so happy to see Jake, but she didn't seem to have the strength to show it.

Jake thought she looked excessively pale today and weaker than usual, but he made no reference to her health. Turning, he hurried into the kitchen; after placing the groceries on the table he glanced around. For the past few weeks Mary Ellis, the wife of one of his electricians, had been keeping the apartment clean. She was doing it more as a favor to him and out of the goodness of her heart rather than for the money, and he was pleased with the results. The kitchen was not only neat and clean, it sparkled.

Once he had put everything away, Jake went back to the living room and sat down opposite Amy. "How're you feeling today?" he asked, inspecting her face closely, thinking she was thinner than ever.

"Tired, Jake, a bit done in," she answered.

"Do you want me to make you something to eat before I go back to work?"

She shook her head. "I'm not hungry . . . I'm never hungry these days. But you eat something."

"No, thanks anyway. I can't stay too long. I have to get back to the site as quickly as possible, we're doing some special wiring. When do you have to go to the hospital again?"

"Tomorrow. My mother's going to take me."

"What does the doctor say? Are you in remission yet?"

"I think so. But that doesn't mean I'm not going to die, Jake. Not many people survive cancer. We all know that," she murmured in a low voice.

"You mustn't be negative, Amy," he replied gently but firmly. "And you must keep your strength up. Not eating is the worst thing you can do. You need nourishment, some good food in you. Why don't you let me make you something? I did a lot of shopping at the supermarket. I bought all sorts of things, special things you've always liked."

"I'm not hungry, Jake," she began and stopped, her voice quavering. Amy took a deep breath, opened her mouth to say something and stopped again. The tears came then, welling in her eyes. Slowly they trickled down her pale cheeks.

Jake got up immediately and went and sat next to her on the sofa. He put his arms around her and held her close. "Don't cry, Amy. I said I'd look after you, and I will. It's going to be all right, you're going to get better. This is the hard part, you know, undergoing the treatment, suffering through it. I know it's making you weak, but you'll get your strength back eventually. And when you do I'm going to send you and your mother to Florida for that vacation I promised you."

"You'll come won't you, Jake?" Amy asked, looking at him with wistfulness.

"You know I can't. I've got to work, I must make sure things keep running smoothly. I can't let anything slip, not now."

"I wish you *could* come though."

"I know you do. Listen to me, Amy, you and your mother are going to enjoy getting away. It'll do you both good."

"Jake—"

"Yes, honey?"

"I don't want to die." She began to cry again, sobbing against his shoulder. "I'm frightened. I think I'm going to die. I don't want to, I'm afraid, Jake."

"Hush. Hush. Don't upset yourself like this. Remember what I've said to you before, it's the worst thing you can do, getting yourself so overwrought in this way. You've got to stay calm, be positive. Everything's going to be all right, Amy. Hush now."

Eventually she stopped weeping, and once she was composed Jake got up and went to the kitchen where he boiled a kettle and made a cup of tea. He brought it to her on a tray and sat talking to her for a while, wanting to allay her worries and fears, hoping to help her reach a better frame of mind.

Jake was preoccupied with thoughts of Amy as he drove to South Kent. He was doing everything he could to help her, but she had to help herself. Her doctor had told him that a positive attitude could work wonders, and that many people had licked cancer because of this. Jake knew only too well how negative Amy was; he wished he could make her understand how important it was for her to look on the bright side, to vow to get better and to do everything she could to achieve this goal. But she was more negative than ever, apathetic and gloomy. He was doing everything he could, from providing financial support and doing the marketing to coming over whenever he could to sit with her, to cheer her up.

By the time he arrived at Havers Hill Farm Jake had decided to have a talk with Amy's mother. Maybe she could make more of an impression than he had been able to with Amy.

After parking the pickup, he made directly for the kitchen before going to check up on Kenny and Larry, who were working on the exterior wiring.

Maggie's briefcase was on the floor and her papers were spread out on the old kitchen table, as they usually were, but she was nowhere in sight. He ran up the stairs and found her in the master bedroom, measuring one of the walls.

Hearing his footsteps, she swung around and her face lit up at the sight of him. "Good morning!" she cried coming toward him.

His smile was wide, and he was so intent on sweeping her into his arms he did not notice the frown of concern, the worry lurking at the back of her eyes. She knew how much he was juggling—the business, his own work, Amy's illness, and herself. That he was exhausted was apparent.

Hugging her to him, Jake said, "How're you feeling, Maggie? How's the baby feeling?"

She smiled up into his face, pushing her worry to one side. "We're both terrific and all the better for seeing you. Were you at Amy's?"

"Yes. I got her some groceries."

"How is she, Jake?" she asked, her brows puckering in a frown.

He shook his head. "Not too good. Down. Depressed, I think."

"Who can blame her? How awful for her to be so ill. She's so young. It's very sad, troubling."

"I just wish she had your kind of spirit, your positive nature, Maggie, that would help a lot, I think."

Maggie nodded and slid out of his arms. "Come on, I'd like to show you something." She was purposely changing the subject, wanting to distract him, to cheer him up, since he seemed to have been infected by Amy's dourness this morning.

Taking him by the hand she led him downstairs and into the dining room. "Yesterday the table arrived from the antique dealer in New York. Take a look." As she spoke she whipped off the dustcloth, and stood back, admiring the table yet again.

"What beautiful wood!" Jake exclaimed. "And it's an old piece, I can see that."

"Fairly old, nineteenth century. And it's yew wood."

Jake glanced around. "This room's really taking shape," he remarked and walked over to a wall where Maggie had glued on swatches of fabric and carpet, plus a paint chip. "Tomato red?" he said, raising a brow eloquently.

Maggie laughed. "That's right. Heinz tomato ketchup with a dash of cream. Avocado-green carpet . . . that's as far as I've got with possible colors."

He laughed with her, much to her relief. At least she had managed to take his mind off Amy's illness for a moment or two.

Jake said, "I've noticed something lately. Whenever you speak about colors you do so in terms of food."

"I'm pregnant remember. I've got all sorts of cravings."

"You don't have to remind me, I could never forget." He leaned into her, kissed her on the cheek. "I'm going outside to see the guys. How about supper tonight? I'll feed you."

"You're on," she answered, grinning at him.

13

"Are you listening to me, Amy?" her mother said, quickly glancing at her daughter out of the corner of her eye, not wishing to take her eyes off the road ahead.

"Yes, Mom, I am. You said Jake thinks I'm too negative about my cancer."

"That's correct," Jane Lang murmured. "He says it would be better for you if you got out more, *did* things when you're well enough, when you're not in pain. Are you in pain now, Amy?"

"No, Mom, I'm not. I don't know what he means by *do* things. We didn't do much when we were married. He was always working, working, working, a real workaholic that guy is for sure."

"What do you mean *were* married? You're still married to him, Amy, and let's not forget that. If you would only concentrate on Jake I'm sure you and he could get back together. He loves you, honey, and I know you love him, it was ridiculous of you to split up. He's so nice, I've always liked him since you were kids."

"I don't think he wants to come back, Mom."

"But just consider the way he's looking after you right now, Amy, taking care of you financially, doing so many things, like getting you this woman to help you in the apartment, and paying for it. And going to the supermarket for you. He loves you, I'm certain."

"Oh, I don't know, maybe he's just being nice. He's like that."

"Like what, honey?"

"*Nice*, Mom. Jake's always been kind to me, ever since we were kids in high school," Amy responded, sounding slightly impatient.

"You never did tell me exactly *why* you and Jake broke up, *why* you decided to get a divorce. What was the reason?" Mrs. Lang asked.

"I don't really know, to be truthful, Mom. I guess we just sort of drifted apart, you know . . ." Amy's voice trailed off. She wasn't really sure how the whole mess *had* come about.

"You can win him *back*! It will give you a goal . . . you must try very hard, Amy, put all your heart and soul into it. You and Jake were always right for each other, it's such a shame all this came to pass." Mrs. Lang sighed and then applied pressure to the brake as she turned a difficult corner on the slippery road. "And it's such a shame you didn't have children. I don't know why you never planned a family. Amy—"

"It's a good thing I didn't!" Amy exclaimed, cutting her mother off, "now that I'm dying. Where would they have been? Practically orphans with their mother dead of cancer at the age of twenty-nine and their father working night and day, never home."

"Don't talk like that, Amy, it's very upsetting to me. And you're *not* dying. Dr. Stansfield told me you're doing well."

"He did?"

"Certainly he did."

"When, Mom?"

"This afternoon. When you were getting dressed. He thinks you're making wonderful progress."

"I don't feel that I am," Amy mumbled. "I'm not really in pain but I feel crummy, Mom. Really crummy. I told Aunt Violet that when I was in the kitchen tonight, you know, when she was cooking the hamburgers. She offered me a vodka, said it would make me feel better."

"That woman is incorrigible at times!" Mrs. Lang exclaimed.

"She's your sister, Mom."

"And we're as different as chalk and cheese."

"I guess so."

"I know so. Anyway, honey, we're going to take that trip to Florida next month. You'll enjoy it very much. Jake mentioned it to me again this morning when he called. Do you remember when your Daddy took us to Florida? You were six. You loved it so much."

"Perhaps I'll get to see Mickey Mouse before I die," Amy murmured.

"Don't, Amy, *don't*," her mother whispered.

"Sorry, Mom. But I do hope I get to meet Mickey."

"You will, you will, when we go to Disney World," Mrs. Lang said, peering ahead. Although it was a wet night the rain had stopped; knowing Amy was tired, wanting to get her home, Mrs. Lang pulled out, impatient with the slow-moving Toyota in front of her.

She did not see the vehicle coming directly at her down the other lane on the two-lane road. Blinded by glaring headlights, Jane Lang took one hand off the wheel to shade her eyes and in so doing relinquished a degree of control of her car. But she didn't have a chance. The oncoming truck, moving at an even greater speed, smashed into them head on.

Amy heard her mother screaming and the sound of glass shattering. She felt the impact most forcibly, was thrown forward and then back, like a helpless rag doll.

"Mom," she said before she blacked out.

Amy was suddenly and inexplicably outside the car, floating above it in the air, just in front of the windshield. She could see her mother inside the car, pinioned by the steering wheel against the front seat. And she was there, too, sitting next to her mother in the other seat. At least her body was there. Amy realized that she and her mother were both unconscious in the car.

Below her, there were other people milling around now. The driver of the truck that had struck their car, who was himself unscathed; other drivers whose cars were backed up behind because of the crash. Then she heard the sound of sirens and saw two state troopers arriving on their motor bikes.

I'm dying, Amy thought, no, I'm actually dead. I've already died and left my body. She could see that body. She was floating over herself, looking down at the empty shell.

Amy was not afraid. Nor did it matter to her that she was dead. In fact, she felt extremely happy, free of all pain and sadness, and without a care in the world.

Unexpectedly, Amy was being sucked forward as if by a giant vacuum hose. She was in that hose. It was not a hose, she discovered, but a long tunnel. She was being pulled up it by some great force. She was not in the least upset, even though she knew she was dead.

At the very end of the long tunnel she could see a tiny pinpoint of light. As she continued on her way, rushing toward the light, it grew bigger and bigger, and so much brighter. Soon she emerged from the tunnel, blinking, adjusting her eyes to the light. It was the most magnificent light. She was surrounded by it, enveloped in its warmth and brilliance. The light embraced her, made her feel lighthearted, and so happy. She had never experienced feelings like this in her life before. They were feelings of tranquillity and peace and unconditional love, and they came from the all-embracing light. She basked in it.

Amy was floating in the light, totally weightless; she had shed her cumbersome human body. And she realized she had entered another world, a different dimension, and that she was pure spirit.

Soon she became aware of other spirits, floating in the brilliant light. They were sending her love and warmth without speaking, but somehow they were communicating. She reciprocated their loving feelings, and she knew they welcomed it.

The light changed, its white brilliance picking up prisms of color, all of them rainbow hues. Another spirit drew closer to her, accompanied her, and Amy understood that she was being guided now, gently wafted toward a destination by this spirit. She knew without being told that this spirit was an old soul, that her name was Marika. It was Marika who was moving her along, but tenderly so, and with great love.

The light was growing softer and softer, losing its sharpness. Amy was moving out of it and into the most beautiful landscape she had ever seen. It was a place without a blemish, perfection, paradise. And it was a place without pain, one that was filled with purity and goodness.

The landscape where Amy floated was one composed of green pastures, flower-filled glades, wooded hillsides above a shimmering blue lake. Surrounding this pastoral setting were mountains capped with glittering white snow, and everything was bathed in golden sunlight.

Floating over the glades were many spirits like herself. Somehow Amy knew that there were old spirits mingling with younger souls. And then she saw him. Her father. The sight of him took her breath away. She knew it was he. Even though he was in spirit form, pure essence, as she was, Amy felt that special love flowing from him to her, and it was the self-same love she remembered from her childhood.

At this moment she felt her mother's spirit floating toward her father. Her mother's aura was radiant and serene, not the crushed human body that Amy had last seen behind the wheel of the wrecked car. Her parents joined each other and came over to her. They spoke to her. Although no actual words were used, she understood everything. They told her how much they loved her. They said they were waiting for her, but that she must go back for a while. *It is not time,* her mother was saying to her. *It was my time, Amy, but not yours. Not yet.* Their great love for her was enveloping her, and she was not afraid; she was happy.

Marika, the old soul guiding her, explained that she must move on. Soon they were floating through the bright light once more, entering a crystal cave that shimmered and radiated an intense and most powerful light.

Amy was immediately aware that she was in the presence of two women, that they were ancient spirits of great wisdom, and that some of their wisdom was going to be imparted to her. She was told by Marika that she would understand it all, understand the universe, the meaning of everything.

The cave was beyond imagining, made entirely of crystal rock formations and giant stalactites that glittered in the white light, sent out hundreds of thousands of prisms of colored light, ranging from pale yellow to pink and blue.

Amy was momentarily blinded by the clarity of light in the crystal cave, and she blinked several times.

A moment later she saw more clearly than she had ever seen before. She saw her past life, saw herself, and she understood at once why she had failed in her earthly life. It was because of her negative approach, her apathy; and she was made to understand that she had wasted much, had thrown away special gifts she had been given. The two women spirits explained this, and Amy felt contrite and sorry.

Then she saw Jake. She saw him at this very moment in time, as if he were right here with her. But he was not. He was in a room somewhere, and he was with a woman, a woman he cared about. A woman he loved. Deeply loved. She recognized the fulfillment and warmth between them. Instantly Amy understood his life. She saw him in the past, in the present, in the future. His whole life was there for her to view, as if she were seeing it on film.

Now Marika was conveying something, saying that she must leave, must move on, but Amy did not want to go. She fought going. She wanted to stay here. Suddenly she was spinning out of the cave, pushed along by Marika.

Marika was urging her in a gentle way to go back to the tunnel. She did not want to and she fought it. She yearned to stay here in this paradise where there was only peace and happiness and unconditional love. But Marika would not permit it. She said Amy must return.

Amy was hurtling down the tunnel, moving through the darkness, leaving that shimmering dimension behind, leaving the light.

She felt a sudden push and there she was back on an earthly plane, floating again above her mother's wrecked car with their bodies trapped within.

Amy saw the truck driver and the other drivers and state troopers hovering near the car. And then an ambulance slowed to a stop. She continued to watch as her mother was removed from the car, and then her own body was lifted out and put on a stretcher.

With a sudden, awful jolt and a whoosh Amy went back into her body.

Eventually she opened her eyes. And then she closed them again. She felt so tired, so exhausted. There was a pain in her head, a terrible pain as if someone had been hammering on her forehead. She fell into unconsciousness immediately.

Amy's aunt, Violet Parkinson, and her daughter, Mavis, rarely, if ever, left Amy's side at the New Milford Hospital. Jake had to come and go because he had to attend to his business, had to work, but he was genuinely concerned about her, apprehensive about her reaction on learning, when she finally regained consciousness, that her mother had been killed in the terrible car crash.

Jake was also worried about Amy's own injuries. She was badly cut and bruised, and whilst the doctors believed she had no internal injuries, she was in a coma.

Now, on the third evening after the accident, Jake sat by the bed in the hospital, holding Amy's hand. They were alone for the time being. He had sent Mavis and Aunt Violet downstairs to have coffee and sandwiches, since they had apparently been sitting with Amy throughout the day.

His thoughts drifted for a while. He worked out some complicated wiring systems for the farm in his head, and thought for a moment or two about Maggie, and then he looked up, startled, when Amy said: "I'm thirsty."

Immediately bringing his attention to her, he exclaimed, "Amy, honey! Thank God! You're awake!"

"I've been in another place, Jake," she began in a whispery voice. "I want to tell you about it."

He nodded. "I'll say you have, Amy. Unconscious for three days. Did you say you were thirsty? Let me get you some water."

"Jake!"

"Yes, Amy?"

"My mother's dead."

He was so startled he gaped at her, and he was unable to say a word for a moment.

"Don't tell me she isn't, trying to protect me, because I know she's dead."

Jake, who had stood up, now bent closer to her, gave her a puzzled look. "Let me go and fetch the water, and tell the doctor you've regained consciousness, honey."

"I died too, Jake, but I came back. That's how I know my mother's dead. I saw her spirit with my father's spirit."

Sitting down on the chair again, he asked gently, "Where, Amy?"

"In Paradise, Jake. It's such a beautiful place. Full of light. A place you'd like, you've always been fascinated by light."

Jake was speechless. He simply sat there holding her hand, not knowing what to say, truly startled by her words.

Amy sighed lightly. "My mother's safe there. And she's happy now. She's with my father. She always missed him, you know."

"Yes," he answered, still at a loss. He wondered whether it was the drugs talking. Certainly the doctors had given her a number of injections, although he was not sure what these were. She was so calm, so in control, and this was slightly mind-boggling to him. He had known Amy most of his life, and he would never have expected her to act like this after her mother's death. They had always been close, and why Amy wasn't hysterical he would never know. Yes, perhaps it was the drugs talking when she had said, a moment ago, that she had died herself but had come back.

As if reading his mind, Amy remarked quietly, "I did die, Jake. Believe me."

He stared at her, a small frown knotting his brow.

Amy sighed. "I'm tired. I want to go to sleep."

"I'll get the doctor, Amy." He extracted his hand from hers, and rose, moved to the door. "I'll bring the nurse so that she can give you a drink of water."

"Thanks, Jake."

He nodded and left the room.

"It was the weirdest thing, Maggie," Jake said quietly, looking across at her intently. "When Amy finally came out of her coma tonight she told me her mother was dead. She wasn't hysterical like I thought she would be, but calm. In control."

Jake shook his head, took a swallow of his beer. "She also said something else that was strange." He hesitated.

"What was that?" Maggie asked.

"She said her mother was with her father. In another place. A place she'd been to . . . she called it Paradise. I thought about her words all the way here from the hospital. How did Amy *know* her mother had died in the crash, Maggie? She's been unconscious since it happened." He exhaled. "That's what mystifies me."

Maggie sat back in her chair and regarded him for a long moment, then she said, "Maybe Amy knew her mother had died because she did see her in another place, just as she claims."

"I'm not following you," he answered, giving her an odd look.

"It's possible that Amy had an NDE."

"What's an NDE?" Jake asked, lifting a brow.

"Near-death experience. There's been a lot written about them in the last few years. Doctor Elisabeth Kubler-Ross, the social scientist, who used to practice in Chicago, wrote an article on the terminally ill during her tenure at Billings Hospital at the University of Chicago. This eventually became the basis for her book, *On Death and Dying*, which I found fascinating. She wrote a number of other books, and appears to believe in near-death experiences. As do many people actually, Jake. And doctors as well. Doctor Raymond Moody did the first anecdotal study of the phenomenon. Another expert is Doctor Melvin Morse, who has also written several books about near-death experiences."

"So you're saying that Amy told me the truth?"

"Very possibly . . . most probably, actually."

"How do you explain an NDE, Maggie?"

"I don't know, I don't think I can . . . because I don't really know enough, Jake," Maggie murmured. "There are a few good books available, as I just mentioned. Perhaps you should read one." Leaning forward slightly, pinning him with her eyes, Maggie went on, "Did Amy describe this place she went to?"

"No. She just said it was very beautiful."

"Did she mention anything about light?"

"Well, yes, she did. How did you know that?"

"Because light, very bright light, always figures in near-death experiences. People feel as if they are embraced by the light. Some even think they are transformed by it."

"Amy did say it was a place I'd like because it was full of light."

"Anything else?"

"No, I don't think so."

"And when exactly did she tell you this?"

"The moment she woke up—when she first came out of the coma."

"Then perhaps she did have a near-death experience. She certainly didn't have enough time to invent such a thing, invent that kind of story. Anyway, deep unconsciousness, or coma, is supposed to wipe the slate clean, wipe the mind clean," Maggie pointed out.

"Okay, so let's say Amy did have an NDE, what exactly does that mean? To her?"

"It's an experience that she's not likely to forget, for one thing. Apparently people who have them never do, the experience stays with them always, for the rest of their lives. Of course they are as baffled by them as everyone else, and they generally look for meanings, special meanings behind them. An NDE does make people change . . . that brush with death and a glimpse of the afterlife does have an effect."

"You seem to know a lot about near-death experiences, Maggie," Jake murmured, eyeing her speculatively.

"Well, I haven't had one myself, but I have talked with several people who have. I did quite a lot of charity work when I lived in Chicago, and I worked at a hospice for terminally ill people several afternoons a week for over four years. That's when I first heard about NDEs. People recounted their experiences to me, and the thing is, they drew such enormous comfort from them."

"So you do believe there is such a thing then?"

"I guess so, Jake. I don't *disbelieve*. I'm not that arrogant. One would be a fool to dismiss these things out of hand. How can anyone debunk near-death experiences? Or life after death? Or even the idea of reincarnation, for instance? None of us knows anything. Not really. There are far too many unexplained things in this world. I'd be the last person to say that the paranormal doesn't exist. Or couldn't happen. I've got an open mind."

"Amy doesn't read a lot," Jake volunteered. "So I'm sure she doesn't know anything at all about near-death experiences from books, Maggie."

She nodded. "There has been quite a lot on television about them, over the past few years, but I'm quite positive Amy did have some sort of experience. I don't think she's inventing this, not for one moment."

"Why do you say that?"

"From what you've told me about her, Jake, Amy doesn't have the imagination to invent such a thing."

"You're correct there," he agreed. Jake leaned back in the chair, stifling a yawn.

Maggie exclaimed, "Oh Jake, you're so tired after your vigil at the hospital. I think you'd better go to bed. You need your rest, you've got to be up so early tomorrow. We've got the meeting at the farm."

He nodded. "I am pretty bushed. But thank God we've finally finished the last design plans for the farm. Lately they seem to have been endless."

She laughed. "Only too true. But isn't Havers Hill now looking perfectly wonderful?"

"It sure is, thanks to you, Maggie of mine."

14

It was a golden October day, a shimmering day. The foliage had already changed, and the trees were a mass of copper and gold, russet and pink, brilliant in the bright sunshine.

Amy feasted her eyes on the landscape in the back of Jake's little house on Route 341, thinking how magnificent everything looked today. Such breathtaking colors, such fire in the trees. And the sky was a perfect blue, without a single cloud. It was a mild day, mild enough for her to sit here without a jacket, which she had shed earlier when she and Jake were having lunch.

She rested her head against the chair and closed her eyes, enjoying the warmth of the sun on her face. She felt relaxed, at peace.

Earlier in the week Jake had asked her what he could do to make her feel better, and she had said she wanted to have a picnic out in the country. It had been his idea to bring her here to his white clapboard house, and she was glad he had. It was nice to see where he lived, now that they were no longer together. Also, she liked his yard with its beautiful trees, pretty garden, and the pastures beyond. He had even shown her around his studio-workshop in the red barn, which had pleased her.

Hearing his footsteps on the path, Amy opened her eyes and sat up.

Jake said, "Here we are, honey, ice cream and apple pie, just as you requested."

Amy smiled at him. "You're spoiling me. And I'm enjoying every minute."

He placed the tray on her lap. "Tea or coffee later?"

"Tea please, and thanks for this." She glanced down at the ice cream. "Oh Jake, you remembered how much I love pistachio and raspberry mixed together."

Jake nodded and grinned, pleased that she was happy. She never complained, but he knew she was frequently in pain these days. If bringing her here and having a picnic with her helped to alleviate her suffering then he was all for it.

"Be back in a minute, honey," he said, and strode down the path to the kitchen. "And don't wait for me. I'm only having coffee."

Amy ate some of the ice cream, enjoying it, but she couldn't finish it all. Her appetite was poor, and she was only able to take a few bites of the apple pie. She leaned back in the chair again, waiting for Jake to return to the garden.

Strains of music suddenly filled the air and she smiled to herself, knowing that he had somehow managed to wire the garden and put speakers outside. Kiri Te Kanawa singing "Vissi d'Arte" filled the air, her magnificent voice soaring into the sky.

"Where's the music coming from, Jake?" Amy asked when he was back, standing over her, offering her the cup of tea.

"The singing rocks, just over there in the flower beds," he explained.

She laughed in delight and he laughed also. Then he said, "Don't you want any more dessert, Amy?"

"No, thanks, Jake, but what I ate was delicious."

He took the plate away, and then sat down next to her with his mug of coffee. "I hope you've enjoyed the picnic, being out in the country," he murmured, glancing at her.

"I have, and it was nice of you to give up your one free day. I know how precious Sundays are to you."

"I've enjoyed it too, Amy, you know I'll do anything to help, to make you feel better."

Turning slightly in the chair, Amy focused her eyes on him. She loved him very much. He was the only man she had ever loved . . . since she was twelve years old. He had always been so special to her; he had made *her* feel special. And he had been so kind. Always. Amy had considered herself the luckiest of women to have him, to be his wife. Her friends had envied her, but she knew they were focusing on his good looks. Only she really knew what a truly nice person he was.

Jake said, "You're staring at me, Amy. What's wrong? Do I have dirt on my face?"

She shook her head. "I was just thinking how long we've known each other." She paused, cleared her throat, and then went on carefully, "Mavis took me to see the lawyer on Friday, Jake, and I—"

"But Amy you don't have to worry about the divorce right now. Just get yourself better first."

"I didn't go to see him about the divorce. A divorce is not necessary."

He sat looking at her, his expression unchanging. He was not sure how to answer her.

She said, "I'm dying, Jake. I'm not going to see the end of the year . . . I know that—"

"But Amy, the doctor said you were making good progress!" he cut in swiftly.

Amy shook her head. "He might think so, but *I* know I'm not. Anyway, I went to see the lawyer because I wanted to make a will. It's necessary now that my mother's dead. She left me her house in New Milford, you know, and her furniture and everything else she owned. And a little money. So, I made a will and I've left everything to you."

Jake stared at her speechlessly. Then he said, "But what about Aunt Violet and Mavis? They're your next of kin."

"No, they're not. You are, Jake Cantrell. You're my husband. We're still married, even though we might not be living together. And as your wife I am leaving you all my worldly possessions. Except for a few items for Aunt Violet and Mavis, you know, some bits of my mother's jewelry, china, that kind of thing. I want you to have everything else."

"I don't know what to say," he began and stopped abruptly, staring at her.

Amy gave him a small smile. "You don't have to say anything, Jake."

"If that's the way you want it, then thank you, Amy," he murmured, not knowing what else he could say.

"There's something I want to say . . . I want to apologize to you, Jake, tell you how sorry I am that I was a bad wife."

"Amy, for God's sake, you weren't a bad wife!" he cried. "You did the best you could always. I know that."

"My best wasn't good enough. Not for you, Jake. I was always so negative and apathetic, and I never helped you when you were trying to make a better life for us. I did everything wrong, and I'm truly sorry."

He stared at her silently, again at a loss for words.

Amy said, "I really did die the night of the crash. I did leave my body. My soul did, I mean. Or my spirit, if you prefer to call it that. I went to another plane, to another dimension. And I saw my father. Then my mother joined him. That's how I knew she was dead. There was an old soul there looking after me, and she took me into a crystal cave of wisdom. There were two wise women spirits, and they told me things. And they showed me how wrong I'd been. I saw my whole life, Jake; I saw my past and I saw your past."

Jake was silent.

Amy said, "I can't change anything in my life now because I have no time to do so. I have become the person I should have always been, and I must try to make amends." Amy leaned back in the chair and focused her eyes on Jake. "You're skeptical aren't you? I mean about my dying and coming back."

"No, as a matter of fact, I'm not," he replied. "I do know there are other people who have had similar experiences, and a number of books have been written about them."

"I didn't know that, although I didn't think it could have only happened to me."

"What happened to you is called a near-death experience, Amy."

Amy nodded then closed her eyes. After a moment she opened them. Leaning forward, she focused them on Jake.

He blinked. They seemed brighter, more full of life than he'd ever seen them, and the smile spreading itself across her face was one of pure radiance.

Amy said, "I not only saw my past, and your past, Jake. I also saw your future. I didn't see mine because I don't have one. Not on this plane at least."

"You saw my future," he repeated.

"Yes, I did. There's a woman in your life, Jake, and you love her very much. She is older than you, but that is of no consequence. You and she are meant to be together. You were always meant to be together, and your whole life has been a journey toward her. As hers has been a journey toward you. Once you were souls who were joined together as one, and then you were split asunder. Your whole lives have been spent trying to get back to each other. When you found each other you became whole. Never doubt her in any way."

Jake opened his mouth but no words came out.

She said, "This woman, your soulmate, is carrying your child. She's five months pregnant. The baby is due in February. It's a boy, Jake, you're going to have the son you always wanted. The future is good for you. You will be prosperous; you were always right to start your own business. It will go well, and this woman, who is devoted to you and will be your wife, will also be your partner in your business. You are going to have all the things you always wanted, Jake, and somehow never managed to get with me. But you must not let your success change you, or turn your head. You're such a good person. You must cling to your values always."

"Amy, I don't know what to say. It's true, I did meet someone. In April. I never mentioned her to you because I didn't want to hurt your feelings—"

"Don't say anymore; it's not necessary. I am the one who hurt you. This was shown to me, and I was sent back in order to put things right with you and to help you with your future."

"Help me how?"

"To show you the way, to set you on the right path. You have already started out on it with your soulmate. She is strong, wise, and you must always listen to her." Amy nodded. "You must take her advice. And you must also follow all of your instincts. You are usually right. Trust yourself more."

"I don't know what to say," Jake began and stopped. Amy was looking at him intently and he realized how lovely she was. It seemed to him that at this moment she had undergone a startling transformation. Her face was radiant, her pale blue eyes bright and sparkling, and even the curly blonde wig she was wearing looked suddenly right on her.

"Now it's my turn to say you're staring at me," Amy exclaimed.

"I was thinking how radiant you looked."

"I am. *Inside.* I want you to promise me something, Jake."

"Yes, Amy, I will. Tell me what it is."

"I want you to promise me you'll get married immediately after I die. I don't want you to have any mourning period. That would be false anyway, since we've been separated for almost two years." She paused and gave him a very direct look. "Longer, if you think of the years we lived together without communicating. Do you promise?"

Jake nodded.

Amy went on, "I think I'll die soon, Jake."

"Oh Amy . . . "

"There's something else I need to say to you and it's this: Love is the most important thing in the whole world."

"I know you're right," Jake responded.

Amy smiled her radiant smile and said softly, "I'm not afraid to die. Not anymore, Jake. You see I know there is life after death. Not life as we know it here, but life on another plane. I will be glad to shed my body then my spirit will be free at last . . . "

15

Maggie stood staring out of the kitchen window, wondering what happened to Jake. It was snowing hard, the tiny crystalline flakes sticking to the panes. She always worried about him in bad weather. The roads could be so treacherous.

Christmas traffic, she decided, that's what was holding him up. He had promised to be here by two, but perhaps he had been delayed at the Little Theater in Kent. At Samantha's request he had gone up there to look at one of the lighting systems that had blown the night before. None of the stagehands knew how to fix it permanently. Since Jake had designed it, Samantha and Maggie knew he would be able to solve the problem.

Maggie's thoughts drifted to the play for a moment. *The Crucible* had opened in September and, much to everyone's surprise and delight, it was still running. It was a sell-out at weekends; Samantha was in her element as the producer, director, and owner of the theater.

Turning away from the window, Maggie walked across the room, her steps slower these days. She was seven months into her pregnancy. The baby, a boy, was due in two months and she couldn't wait to deliver. The baby was big and she was heavy; and every day she seemed to grow slower and slower.

Sitting down at the kitchen table, she looked at her list of gifts. She had finished almost all of her Christmas shopping, having started it earlier in the year. Today was Saturday, the sixteenth of December, and anything else she still needed Jake would have to buy. Maggie knew she did not have enough energy to struggle through the stores, the big stores at any rate.

At least she wouldn't have to do much cooking. She and Jake were going to spend Christmas Day with Samantha. That was the big day, of course; on Christmas Eve Samantha was coming to them along with some of the cast and other members of the theatrical group. Weeks ago Maggie had decided to make the supper a cold buffet, so much simpler for her to handle.

Rising, Maggie lumbered into the small sitting room and walked over to the tree. Jake and she had trimmed it slowly, gradually, over the past two weeks, mostly because he was so busy with business. And she was unwieldy, not very much help to him.

Maggie smiled inwardly and put her hands on her stomach. The baby was her treasure. Hers and Jake's. He couldn't wait for the child to be born, and was forever pampering her, treating her like a piece of crystal.

Stepping up to the tree, she eyed it critically, knowing that certain branches were still rather bare. Perhaps today they would have time to stop at The Silo to buy some more gold and silver icicles, gold angels, and fruits. She and Jake had created a gold and silver tree, with touches of red and blue here and there; and it was eye-catching, she thought.

Maggie walked slowly back to the kitchen and stood at the window again, waiting for him, wishing he would get home. After a while, she moved away, went to the radio and turned it on.

"*Hark the herald angels sing, glory to the newborn king. Peace on earth and mercy mild . . .* " a female voice was singing.

Maggie was immediately distracted. She heard the pickup coming into the yard and stood looking at the door expectantly, waiting for him.

As always, she felt the impact of him in the pit of her stomach whenever she saw him, even after a very short absence. What it was to be so in love. Sometimes she worried that she loved him far too much.

"Hi, sweetheart," Jake said, striding over to her, tracking snow across her clean floor. But Maggie did not care. "Hello, darling," she answered, beaming at him. "I was beginning to worry, wonder what was taking so long."

"That stupid system I invented!" he exclaimed, brought her into his arms and kissed her cheek.

"Oh Jake, your face is cold, and your hands. Why didn't you put on your gloves and a scarf?"

He grinned at her boyishly. "Oh stop worrying about me. I'm fine. Anyway, the system's okay for tonight and tomorrow. But I think I'll have to rig up something else next week. Samantha's going to kill me if I don't get it perfect, and this one's not."

"Do you want a cup of coffee?"

Jake shook his head. "I think we'd better get going. It's snowing hard, and the snow's settling. It's going to take us a good half hour to New Milford. Do you have the plant for Amy?"

"It's over there on the countertop."

Jake walked over and looked at it. "You've made it look pretty with the blue and silver bow, Maggie."

She nodded. "Shall we go, Jake?"

"Yes. Let me get your coat."

The snow had stopped falling by the time they arrived in New Milford, and the sun was shining in the brilliantly blue sky.

Maggie held onto Jake's arm tightly as they walked down the path. There was a light covering of snow on the paving stones, and she was afraid she might slip.

"Here we are," Jake said a few seconds later. "Now, just let me undo this." As he spoke he pulled the wrapping paper off the plant and shoved it in his pocket. Bending down, he placed the miniature evergreen on the new grave.

Straightening, he turned to Maggie and put his arm around her. "I'm glad we came," he murmured. "I gave her my word we would. 'Come and visit my grave as soon as you can after you're married,' she said and then she made me promise."

"She's at peace now," Maggie said. "Out of her pain and suffering."

Jake nodded. "Her soul is free. She wasn't a bit afraid to die in the end."

Maggie pulled off her gloves. Leaning over the grave, she straightened the blue and silver bow. Her broad gold wedding ring gleamed brightly in the afternoon sunlight. "That's because Amy knew where she was going," Maggie murmured.

Jake merely nodded and put his arm around his wife protectively. Together they stood in silence at the grave for a few moments, lost in their own thoughts. Jake was thinking of Amy, who had died two weeks ago. He had known her most of his life, and she had been his high-school sweetheart. Somehow everything had gone awry with them. Still, in the end, they had remained friends. He was glad of that, and happy that he had been able to give her comfort in the end, had helped her through her illness. He had been with her when she died, and her last words had been for him. "Bless you, Jake," she had said. "And your soulmate and the baby."

A week after her death he and Maggie had married, fulfilling Amy's wish that they do so immediately. He had wanted it that way himself, and he knew that Maggie had too. The wedding had been at Samantha's house in Washington; Sam had insisted. She also arranged for a local judge, who was a friend of her family, to perform the short ceremony. She and Alice Ferrier, the costume designer from the drama group, had been the witnesses.

Jake knew he would never forget last Saturday morning. Their wedding day. Maggie had looked so beautiful and full of life. She had worn a blue wool maternity dress that reflected the color of her eyes but did little to conceal the fact that she was seven months pregnant. Neither of them cared. Maggie's eyes had been full of tears when the judge pronounced them husband and wife, as his had been. They had both been very emotional that morning, and for days afterward.

Sam had given a small lunch and members of the cast of *The Crucible* had come in to toast them and wish them well before going off to the Little Theater in Kent. It had been the most special day of his life.

Jake said, "I think we'd better go, Maggie. It's starting to snow again."

Together the two of them walked along the path that led to the gate of the cemetery. At one moment Maggie glanced up at the sky, and high above them she saw the arc of a rainbow. It was indistinct, but it was there. She blinked in the bright sunlight and looked away. When she turned her eyes to the sky again the rainbow had disappeared.

She held Jake's arm as they continued on down the path, and at one moment she said quietly, "The cycle of life is endless, and it never changes."

"What do you mean?" he asked, glancing down at her, frowning.

"There has been a death . . . and soon there will be a birth. That's the way it is. *Always.* One soul has gone to her rest, a new soul is about to be born."

Jake nodded and was silent as they made their way out of the cemetery and back to the Jeep. Once he had helped Maggie in and settled himself in the driver's seat, he leaned in to her and kissed her cheek. "I love you, Maggie of mine," he said. Looking at her huge stomach he placed his hand on it and added, "And I love our baby. He's going to be born well blessed."

"Oh I know that," Maggie said, smiling into his eyes. "Come on, darling, it's time to go home."

Home, Jake thought, as he put the key in the ignition and turned it. *Home.*

Everything
to Gain

For Bob, ever true-blue, with my love

CONTENTS

PROLOGUE

Connecticut, August 1993

I have been alone for so long now, it is almost impossible for me to think in terms of living with another person again. But that is what Richard wants me to do. To live with him.

When he asked me last night to marry him, I told him I could not. Undaunted by my answer, and bravely, as is his way, he suggested we move in together. A sort of trial marriage, he said, with no strings, no commitment necessary on my part. "I'll take my chances, Mal," he said with a small, wry smile, his dark eyes anxiously holding mine.

Yet even this idea seems as out of the question to me now, this morning, as it did last night. I suppose, if I am scrupulously honest with myself, I fear the intimacy living with another human being entails. It is not so much the sexual intimacy that appalls me but the physical closeness on a day-to-day basis, the emotional bonding that weaves two people together and makes them part of each other. I am convinced I cannot handle this, and the more I think about it the more I am coming to understand truly my reaction to Richard's suggestion.

I am afraid. Afraid to make a commitment . . . afraid of caring for him too deeply . . . afraid of becoming too attached to him . . . perhaps even of falling in love with him, if, indeed, I am capable of such a strong emotion.

Fear has paralyzed me emotionally for a number of years. I am well aware of that, and so I have created a life for myself, a life alone; this has always seemed so much safer. Brick by brick by brick I have erected a wall around myself, a wall built on the foundations of my business, my work, and my career. I have done this in order to protect myself, to insulate myself from life; work has been my strong citadel for such a long time now, and it has given me exactly what I have needed these few years.

Once I had so much. I had everything a woman could possibly want. And I lost it all.

For the past five years, since that fateful winter of 1988, I have lived with pain and heartache and grief on a continuing basis. I have lived with a sorrow that has been, and still is, unendurable. And yet I have endured. I have gone on; I have fought my way up out of a terrible darkness and despair when I had hardly any strength left and when I had lost even the will to live. I have managed, somehow, to survive.

And I taught myself to live alone, have grown used to doing so, and I'm not sure that I can ever share myself again, as I once did, certainly not in the way I did in the past, in that other life which I once had.

But this is exactly what Richard is asking of me. He wants me to share my life with him and therefore to share myself. He is a good man. I don't think there is one better anywhere on this earth, and any woman would be lucky to have him. But I am not any woman. I have gone through far too much, have been scarred forever, my soul damaged irretrievably, beyond repair, so I believe. And I'm fully aware that I can never be the kind of woman he deserves, a woman who can give him her all, a woman without a past, with no heavy baggage, no burdens or sorrows weighing her down, such as I have.

The easiest thing for me, emotional cripple that I have become, would be to send Richard Markson away, to tell him *no* much more firmly than I did last night, and never see him again. Yet I cannot . . . something holds me back, prevents me from saying those words. It is Richard himself, of course, I realize that. In my own way, I do have certain feelings for him, and have come to rely on him lately, perhaps more than I care to admit.

Richard came into my life quite by accident about a year ago, not long after he rented a house near mine in this pastoral corner of northwestern Connecticut, just above Sharon near Wononpakook Lake and Mudge Pond, close to the Massachusetts border. I have always called these western highlands of Connecticut God's own country, and so I was somewhat startled when he used exactly those words to describe his appreciation of this magnificently beautiful part of the world.

I liked Richard the moment he walked into my house. On that winter's evening, over supper in my kitchen, I was convinced it was my friend Sarah Thomas with whom Richard was taken. It was not until a few weeks later that he made it perfectly clear to me *I* was the object of his interest, the one he wished to know better.

Wary, I held him at bay for a long time; then, slowly, cautiously, I allowed him to enter a small corner of my life. Yet in many ways I've withheld much of myself. So it's not without reason that I was stunned last night when he proposed to me. I promised to give him an answer today.

My eye caught the top of *The New York Times* which lay on my desk, and I read the date: Monday, August 9, 1993. I wondered if he would remember this date later, recall it as the day I rejected him, just as I remembered so many dates myself . . . markers along the path of my life that brought back so many memories when they rolled around every year.

On the spur of the moment, I reached for the phone, wanting to get it over with, and then almost instantly my hand fell away. There was no point dialing his apartment in Manhattan, since I was not sure how to couch the words I knew must be said. I didn't want to hurt him unduly; I must be diplomatic.

Suddenly irritated with myself, I sighed under my breath, impatiently pushed back my chair, and went to turn on the air conditioner. It was unusually humid this morning, the air heavy and oppressive in my office here at the back of the house. My skin was clammy, and I felt stifled, claustrophobic all of a sudden.

Returning to my desk, I sat down and stared into space, my thoughts continuing to focus on Richard. Last night he'd said I was too young to lead such a solitary existence. There's truth in this, I suppose. After all, I *am* only thirty-eight years old. Still, there are days when I feel like an old woman of eighty, older than that, even. I realize this is because of the things which have happened to me, as well as my newfound knowledge about life and people. Certainly I've learned a lot about their insensitivity and selfishness, their callousness and indifference. I've learned about evil too, firsthand; yes, and even about good. There *are* some good people in this world, those who are kind and concerned and compassionate, but not many, not really. I have come to understand only too well that for the most part we are entirely alone with our troubles and pain. I suspect I've become something of a cynic these days, as well as much wiser, more self-protective, and self-reliant than I ever was before.

A few weeks ago I railed on about the doers of evil who inhabit this planet, and Richard listened attentively, as he always does. When I finished and discovered I was on the verge of unexpected tears, he joined me on the sofa, simply took my hand in his and held it tightly. We sat together like that for a long time, surrounded by the silence, until he said finally, ever so quietly, "Don't try to understand the nature of evil, or analyze it, Mal. It's a mystery, one nobody has ever been able to fathom. Evil has touched your life, more so than it's touched most people's. You've been through hell, and I certainly have no proper words with which to console you. Anyway, words are empty, cold comfort at best. I just want you to know that I'm always there for you whenever you need me. I'm your friend, Mal."

I know I will always be grateful to him, not only for expressing those lovely sentiments that particular day, but because he did not attempt to placate me with platitudes, those meaningless words the well-meaning tend to offer when confronted with another person's pain or anger or despair. Also, I must admit, I admire Richard Markson. He is a decent human being, a man of integrity and compassion, qualities that mean a great deal to me. Although he has never been married, he has not passed through this life totally unscathed—that I know. He is thirty-nine, a year older than I, and now it strikes me, and quite forcibly, how ready he is to make a commitment, to embark on a long-term relationship. He is willing to accept everything this means. But am I? Ambivalent, uncertain, wary, scared, caught on an eddying tide of fears and deep-rooted problems, I feel completely helpless this morning, unable to think with clarity.

I snapped my eyes shut, leaned forward, and dropped my head onto the desk, realizing, as I did, that I was spiraling down into a cold funk. There was no way I could make that call to Richard, as I had promised I would. Very simply, I had nothing to say to him, no answer to give him.

The shrill ring of the telephone a few moments later brought me upright in my chair with a start, and I reached for the receiver and said, "Hello?"

"Mallory?"

"Yes."

"It's me. Richard."

"I know."

"Mal, I have to go out of town. On an assignment."

"Oh," I said, surprised by his announcement. "This is very sudden, isn't it?"

"Yes. It just came up a short while ago. The magazine's sending me to Bosnia. I'm leaving immediately. This United Nations-NATO situation is turning out to be something of a fiasco. So off I'm going to—"

"But you don't usually cover things like this, do you?" I cut in. "I mean, you don't cover *wars*."

"Nor am I doing so now. Not really. I'm going to be writing one of my special think pieces, based on the kind of things we've all been saying about the wholesale carnage going on over there, the dithering of the Western leaders and the terrible indifference the world is showing to such human suffering." He paused, then murmured, "It's a replay of everything that happened in Nazi Germany sixty years ago . . . " His quiet, concerned voice trailed off into silence.

"It's the most hideous situation!" I exclaimed, my voice rising. "We're no more civilized now than we were in the tenth century! Nothing's changed, we've learned nothing. Man *is* rotten. *Evil*."

"I know that, Mal," he answered, sighing imperceptibly.

Striving to adopt a more normal tone, I said, "And so you're leaving today?"

"I'll be heading for Kennedy in a couple of hours." There was a little pause, and then he said, "Mal."

"Yes, Richard?"

"Do you have an answer for me?"

I was silent for a moment or two. Eventually, clearing my throat, I said, "No, I'm afraid I don't. I'm sorry, Richard, I need time. I told you that . . . " Now it was my turn to let my voice fade away.

Richard did not say a word.

I held the phone tightly, waiting, wondering how he was going to take my negative attitude.

Suddenly, he spoke. "Perhaps when I get back from Bosnia," he said in a firm, strong voice, "you'll have good news for me, tell me what I want to hear. You will, won't you?"

"When will you be back?" I asked, not rising to the bait.

"In a week to ten days."

"Be careful, Richard. It's dangerous where you're going."

That light, careless laugh I had grown to know echoed down the wire. "I don't aim to catch a stray bullet, if that's what you're getting at. That's not part of my destiny."

"Nevertheless, just be careful."

"I will. And take care of yourself, Mal. So long."

He hung up before I could say good-bye.

After a moment or two I walked out of my office, across the back hall, and out into the garden.

I took the stone-paved path that led across the vast lawns at the back of the house, walking rapidly until I came to the ridge overlooking part of my property and the valley far beyond. Hills darkly green with lush and splendorous trees soared high above this valley, giving it some shelter from the elements in the harsh winter months. The two small houses nestled in the bed of the valley, always so forlorn in bad weather, now looked cool and inviting with their white-painted shingles and dark rooftops, their gardens bright with vivid color.

Presently I shifted my gaze, let it rest just below me. Here, at the bottom of verdant lawns sloping away from the ridge where I stood, the horses grazed contentedly in the long meadow. To the left of them, and adding to this bucolic scene, were the old barns, freshly painted dark red with white trim. To the right of the long meadow, the pond, calm and glassy as a mirror, shimmered in the sun; a family of Canada geese swam, one after the other, in a straight line across its dark surface, where water lilies, waxy and pale pink, floated in profusion.

After a short while, my eyes wandered, my glance sweeping over the resplendent rosebushes, luxuriant in full flower, then moved on to survey my vegetable garden behind its white picket fence, the cutting garden bursting with perennials in a galaxy of the gayest hues. Everything blooms so well here; how beautiful the land is, so rich, so ripe with life.

I lifted my head and looked up at the sky. It was the brightest, most piercing of blues, banked high with pure-white flossy clouds, and dazzling. I blinked several times against the coruscating light, and then I realized, suddenly, that I was crying.

As the tears ran down my cheeks unchecked, I thought of Richard's words a short while before: "I don't aim to catch a stray bullet," he had said, almost dismissively.

I shivered in the sunlight, unexpectedly cold in the sultry air. No one ever knows what life holds, I thought, what destiny has in store. I understand that better than anyone.

Five years fell away.

I stepped back into the past, into the summer of 1988, a summer which would be etched on my heart forever.

PART ONE

INDIAN MEADOWS

1

Connecticut, July 1988

I awakened with a sudden start, as though someone had touched my shoulder, and I half expected to see Andrew standing over me as I blinked in the dim room. But he was not there. How could he be? He was in Chicago on business, and I was here in Connecticut.

Pulling the covers over me more securely, I slid farther down into the bed, hoping to fall asleep again. I soon realized there was no chance of that, since my mind had already started to race. Andrew and I had quarreled earlier in the week, and that silly little row, over something so petty I could scarcely bear to think about it now, still hovered between us.

I should have swallowed my pride and called him last night, I admonished myself. I *had* thought about it, but I had not done so. He hadn't phoned me either, as was his custom normally when he was away, and I was worried things would get blown out of all proportion; then our weekend together, which I had been so looking forward to, would be spoiled.

I'll make it right when he gets here tomorrow, I resolved. I'll apologize, even though it really wasn't my fault. I hated to have rifts with anyone I loved; it has always been that way with me.

Restlessly, I slipped out of bed and went to the window. Raising the shade, I peered out, wondering what kind of day it was going to be.

A band of clear, crystalline light was edging its way along the rim of the distant horizon. The sky above it was still ashy, cold and remote, tinged slightly with green at this early hour just before dawn broke. I shivered and reached for my cotton robe. It was cool in the bedroom, almost frosty, with the air conditioner set at sixty degrees, where I'd positioned it last night in an effort to counteract the intense July heat. I flicked it off as I left the bedroom and headed along the upstairs hallway toward the staircase.

It was dim and shadowy downstairs and smelled faintly of apples and cinnamon and beeswax and full-blown summer roses, smells which I loved and invariably associated with the country. I turned on several lamps as I moved through the silent, slumbering house and went into the kitchen; once I had put on the coffee, I swung around and made my way to the sunroom.

Unlocking the French doors, I stepped outside onto the wide, paved terrace which surrounded the house and saw that the sky had already undergone a vast change. I caught my breath, marveling as I always did at the extraordinary morning light, a light peculiar to these northern Connecticut climes. It was luminous, eerily beautiful, and it appeared to emanate from some secret source far, far below the horizon.

There were no skies like this anywhere in the world, as far as I knew, except, of course, for Yorkshire; I have come across some truly spectacular skies there, most especially on the moors.

Light has always fascinated me, perhaps because I am a painter by avocation and have a tendency to look at nature through an artist's eyes. I remember the first time I ever saw a painting by Turner, one of his masterpieces hanging in the Tate Gallery in London. I stood in front of it for a full hour, totally riveted, marveling at the incandescent light that gave the picture its breathtaking beauty. But then, capturing light on canvas so brilliantly and with such uncanny precision was part of Turner's great genius.

I don't have that kind of gift, I'm afraid; I'm merely a talented amateur who paints for pleasure. Nonetheless, there are times when I wish I could re-create a Connecticut sky in one of my paintings, get it just *right,* just *once,* and this morning was one of those times. But I knew, deep down, that I would never be capable of doing it.

After lingering for a few minutes longer on the terrace outside the sunroom, I turned and walked around the house, heading for the back. Heavy dew clung to the grass, and I lifted my nightgown and robe as I walked across the lawns, not wishing to get them drenched.

The light was changing yet again. By the time I reached the ridge overlooking the valley, the sky above me was suffused with a pale, silvery radiance; the bleak, gray remnants of the night were finally obliterated.

Sitting down on the wrought-iron seat under the apple tree, I leaned back and relaxed. I love this time of day, just before the world awakens, when everything is so quiet, so still I might be the only person alive on this planet.

I closed my eyes momentarily, listening.

There was no sound of any kind; nothing stirred, not a leaf nor a blade of grass moved. The birds were silent, sleeping soundly in the trees, and the stillness around me was like a balm. As I sat there, drifting, thinking of nothing in particular, my anxiety about Andrew began slowly to slip away.

I knew with absolute certainty that everything would be all right once he arrived and we made up; it always was whenever there had been a bit of friction between us. There was no reason why this time should be different. One of the marvelous things about Andrew is his ability to put events of today and yesterday behind him, to look forward to tomorrow. It was not in his nature to harbor a grudge. He was far too big a man for that. Consequently, he quickly forgot our small, frequently silly quarrels and differences of opinion. We are much alike in that, he and I. Fortunately, we both have the ability to move forward optimistically.

I have been married to Andrew Keswick for ten years now. In fact, next week, on the twelfth of July, we will be celebrating our wedding anniversary.

We met in 1978, when I was twenty-three years old and he was thirty-one. It was one of those proverbial whirlwind romances, except that ours, fortunately, did not fizzle out as so many do. Our relationship just grew better and better as time went on. That he swept me off my feet is a gross understatement. I fell blindly, madly, irrevocably in love with him. And he with me, as I was eventually to discover.

Andrew, who is English, had been living in New York for seven years when we met. He was considered to be one of the boy wonders of Madison Avenue, one of those naturals in the advertising business who can make an agency not only fabulously successful but incredibly famous as well, attracting a flock of prestigious multinational clients. I worked in the copy department of the same agency, Blau, Ames, Braddock and Suskind, and at the time, despite my lowly position, I rather fancied myself a writer of slick but convincing advertising copy.

Andrew Keswick seemed to agree.

If his compliments about my work went to my head, then he himself went straight to my heart. Of course, I was very young then, and even though I was a graduate of Radcliffe, I think I was most probably rather naïve for my educational background, age, and upbringing. I was a slow starter, I suppose.

In any event, Andrew captivated me entirely. Despite his brilliance and his standing on Madison Avenue, I soon came to realize that he was not in the least bit egotistical. Quite the opposite, in fact. He was unassuming, even modest for a man of his considerable talents; also, he had a great sense of fun and a dry humor which was often rather self-deprecating.

To me he was a dashing and sophisticated figure, and his very Englishness, as well as his mellifluous, cultivated voice set him apart. Medium of height and build, he had pleasant, clean-cut looks, dark brown hair, and candid eyes set wide apart. In fact, his eyes were his most arresting feature, of the brightest blue and thickly lashed. I don't think I've ever before seen eyes so vividly blue, nor would I ever again, except years later, in Clarissa and Jamie, our six-year-old twins.

Every young woman in the advertising agency found Andrew immensely attractive, but it was I whom he eventually singled out for special attention. We began to go out together, and at once I discovered that I was completely at ease with him; I felt comfortable, very natural in his presence. It was as though I had known him forever, yet there was so much that intrigued me about him and his life before we met, so much to learn about him.

Andrew and I had been seeing each other for only two months when he whisked me off to London for a long weekend to meet his mother. Diana Keswick and I became friends instantly, actually within the first hour of knowing each other. You could say we fell in love, and that is the way it has been between us ever since.

To some people, the term "mother-in-law" inevitably conjures up the image of an enemy, a woman who is overly possessive of her son and in competition with his wife for his attention and affection. But not Diana. She was lovely to me from the moment we met—a female Andrew. Or rather, I should say, Andrew is a male version of his mother. In a variety of different ways, she has proved to be loyal and devoted to me; I truly love, respect, and admire her. Many qualities make her unique in my eyes, not the least of which is her warm and understanding heart.

That weekend in London, which was actually my first trip to England, remains vivid in my mind to this very day. We had only been there for twenty-four hours when Andrew asked me to marry him. "I love you very much," he'd said, and taking hold of me, he had pulled me close and continued in that beautiful voice of his, "I can't imagine my life without you, Mal. Say you'll marry me, that you'll spend the rest of your life with me."

Naturally I said I would. I told him that I loved him as much as he loved me, and we celebrated our engagement by taking his mother to dinner at Claridge's on Sunday night before flying back to New York on Monday morning.

On the return journey, I kept glancing surreptitiously at the third finger of my left hand, admiring the antique sapphire ring gleaming on it. Andrew had given me the ring just before we had gone out to our celebration dinner, explaining that it had belonged first to his grandmother and then to Diana. "My mother wants you to have it now," he said, "and so do I. You'll be the third Keswick wife to wear it, Mal." He smiled in that special, very loving way of his as he slipped it on my finger. And in the next few days, every time I looked at it, an old-fashioned phrase sprang into my mind: "With this ring we pledge our troth." And indeed we had.

Twelve weeks after our first dinner date, Andrew Keswick and I were married at Saint Bartholomew's Church on Park Avenue. The only person who was not entirely overjoyed by this sudden union was my mother. Liking Andrew very much though she did and approving of him, she was nonetheless filled with disappointment about the extreme hastiness of the nuptials. "Everyone is going to think it's a shotgun wedding," she kept muttering, throwing me piercing glances as she rushed to have the invitations engraved and hurriedly planned a reception to be held at the Pierre Hotel on Fifth Avenue.

My glaring eyes and stern, obstinate mouth must have warned her off, warned her not to ask if I *was* pregnant, which I wasn't, by the way. But my mother deems me impractical, has for years characterized me as an artistic dreamer, a lover of poetry, books, music, and painting, with my head forever in the clouds.

Some of what she says was true. Yet I am also much more pragmatic than she could ever imagine; my feet have always been firmly planted on the ground, despite what she thinks. We married quickly simply because we wanted to be together, and we saw no reason to wait, to drag out a long engagement.

Not all brides enjoy their weddings. I loved mine. I was euphoric throughout the church ceremony and the reception. After all, it *was* the most important day of my life; but furthermore, I had also managed to outwit my mother and get my own way in everything. This was no mean feat, I might add, when it came to social situations.

By my own choice, and with Andrew's acquiescence, the whole affair was tiny. Both our mothers were present, of course, as well as a few relatives and friends. Andrew's father was dead. Mine wasn't, although my mother behaved as though he was, inasmuch as he had left her some years before and gone to live in the Middle East. In consequence, she thought of him as nonexistent.

But exist for me he did, and very much so. We corresponded on a regular basis and spent as much time together as we could, whenever he came to the States. And he flew to New York to give away his only daughter. Much to my astonishment, my mother was pleased he had made this paternal gesture. And so was I, although I had expected nothing less. The thought of getting married without him by my side as I walked down the aisle had appalled me. Once Andrew and I became engaged, I had called him in Saudi Arabia, where he was at the time, to tell him my good news. He had been overjoyed for me.

Even though my mother barely spoke to my father the entire time he was in Manhattan, she at least behaved in a civilized manner when they were together in public. But, not unnaturally, he departed as soon as it was decent to do so, once the reception at the Pierre was drawing to a close. My father, an archaeologist, seems to prefer the past to the present, so he had rushed back to his current dig.

He had fled my mother permanently when I was eighteen. I had gone off to Cambridge, Massachusetts, and my new life at Radcliffe College, and it was as though there was no longer a good reason for him to stay in the relationship, which had become extremely difficult for him to sustain. That they have never divorced I've always found odd; it is something of a mystery to me, given the circumstances.

We left the wedding reception together, my father and I and my bridegroom, and rode out to Kennedy Airport in one of the grand stretch limousines my mother had hired. Just before we headed in different directions to catch our planes to different parts of the world, he had hugged me tightly, and as we said our good-byes, he had whispered against my hair, "I'm glad you did it your way, Mal, had the kind of wedding *you* wanted, not the big, splashy bash your mother would have preferred. You're a maverick like me. But then, that's not half bad, is it? Always be yourself, Mal, always be true to yourself."

It had pleased me that he'd said that, about being a maverick like he was. We had been very close since my childhood, an emotional fact that I suspect has been a constant irritant to my mother. I don't believe she understood my father, not ever in their entire life together. Sometimes I've wondered why they married in the first place; they are such opposites, have come from worlds that are completely different. My father is from an intellectual family of academics and writers, my mother from a family of affluent real estate developers of some social standing, and they have never shared the same interests.

Yet something must have attracted Edward Jordan to Jessica Sloane and vice versa, and they must have been in love, or thought they were, for marry they did in 1953. They brought me into the world in May of 1955, and they stayed together until 1973, struggling through twenty years of bickering and quarreling, punctuated by stony silences that lasted for months on end. And there were long absences on the part of my father, who was always off to the Middle East or South America, seeking the remains of ancient civilizations lost in the mists of antiquity.

My father aside, my mother has never understood me, either. She is not remotely conscious of what I'm about, what makes me tick. But then, my mother, charming and sweet though she can be, has not been blessed with very much insight into people.

I love my mother, and I know she loves me. But for years now, ever since I was a teenager, I've found her rather trying to be with. Unquestionably, there is a certain shallowness to her, and this is something which dismays me. She is forever concerned with her social standing, her social life, and her appearance. Not much else interests her, really. Her days revolve around her dressmaker, hair and manicure appointments, and the luncheons, dinners, and cocktail parties to which she has been invited.

To me it seems such an empty, meaningless life for any woman to lead, especially in this day and age. I am more like my father, inasmuch as I am somewhat introspective and serious-minded; I'm concerned, just as he is, about this planet we inhabit and all that is happening on it and to it.

In many ways, the man I married greatly resembles my father in character. Like Daddy, Andrew *cares,* and he is honorable, strong, straightforward, and dependable. *True-blue* is the way I categorize them both.

Andrew is my first love, my only love. There will never be anyone else for me. We will be with each other for the rest of our lives, he and I. This is the one great constant in my life, one which sustains me. Our children will grow up, leave us to strike out on their own as adults, have families of their own one day. But Andrew and I will go on into our twilight years together, and this knowledge comforts me.

Suddenly, I felt the warmth of the sun on my face as its rays came filtering through the branches of the big apple tree, and I pushed myself up from the wrought-iron seat where I sat. Realizing that it was time for the day to begin, I walked back to the house.

It was Friday, the first of July, and I had no time to waste today. I had planned a special weekend for Andrew, Jamie, and Lissa, and my mother-in-law, who was visiting us from England, as she did every year. Monday, the Fourth of July, was to be our big summer celebration.

2

As I approached the house, I could not help thinking how beautiful it looked this morning, gleaming white in the bright sunlight, set against a backdrop of mixed green foliage under a sky of periwinkle blue.

Andrew and I had fallen in love with Indian Meadows the minute we set eyes on it, although it wasn't called Indian Meadows then. It didn't have a name at all.

Once we had bought it, the first thing I did was to christen it with a bottle of good French champagne, much to Andrew's amusement. Jamie and Lissa, on the other hand, were baffled by my actions, not understanding at all until I explained about ships and how *they* were christened in exactly the same way. "And so why not a house," I had said, and they had laughed gleefully, tickled by the whole idea of it. So much so that they had wanted their own bottle of Veuve Clicquot to break against the drainpipe as I had done, but Andrew put a stop to that immediately. "One bottle of good champagne going down the drain is enough for one day," he quipped, laughing hilariously at his own joke. I'd rolled my eyes to the ceiling but couldn't resist flashing a smile at him as I appeased the twins, promising them some cooking wine with which to do their own house christening the following day.

As for the name, I culled it from local lore, which had it that centuries ago Indians had lived in the meadows below the hill upon which our house was built. And frequently, when I am standing on the ridge looking down at the meadows, I half close my eyes and, squinting against the light, I can picture Pequot squaws, their braves, and their children sitting outside their wigwams, with horses tethered nearby and pots cooking over open fires. I can almost smell the pungent wood smoke, hear their voices and laughter, the neighing of the horses, the beat of their drums.

Highly imaginative of me, perhaps, but it *is* a potent image and one which continues to persist. Also, it pleases me greatly to think that I and my family live on land favored centuries ago by Native Americans, who no doubt appreciated its astonishing beauty then as we do today.

We found the house quite by accident. No, that's not exactly true, when I look back. The house found us. That is what *I* believe, anyway, and I don't suppose I will ever change my mind. It reached out to us like a living thing, and when for the first time we stepped over the threshold into that lovely, low-ceilinged entrance hall, I knew at once that it would be ours. It was as though it had been waiting for us to make it whole, waiting for us to make it happy again. And this we have done. Everyone who visits us is struck by the feeling of tranquility and happiness here, the warm and welcoming atmosphere that pervades throughout, and which envelopes everyone the moment they come through the front door.

But in June of 1986 I had no idea that we would finally find the house of our dreams, or any house, for that matter. We had looked for such a long time for a weekend retreat in the country, and without success. And so we had almost given up hope of ever finding a suitable place to escape to from New York. The houses we had viewed in various parts of Connecticut had been either too small and pokey, or too large, too grand, and far too expensive. Or so threadbare it would have cost a fortune to make them habitable.

That particular weekend, Andrew and I were staying with friends in Sharon, an area we did not know very well. We had taken Jamie and Lissa to Mudge Pond, the town beach, for a picnic lunch on the grassy bank that ran in front of the narrow strip of sand and vast body of calm, silver-streaked water beyond.

Later, as we set out to return to Sharon, we inadvertently took a wrong turn and, completely lost, drove endlessly around the hills above the pond. As we circled the countryside, trying to get back to the main highway, we unexpectedly found ourselves at a dead end in front of a house.

By mistake, we had gone up a wide, winding driveway, believing it to be a side road which would lead us back, we hoped, to Route 41. Startled, Andrew brought the car to a standstill. Intrigued by the house, we stared at it and then at each other, exchanging knowing looks. And in unison we exclaimed about its charm, which was evident despite the sorry signs of neglect and disuse which surrounded it.

Made of white clapboard, it had graceful, fluid lines and was rather picturesque, rambling along the way it did on top of the hill, set in front of a copse of dark green pines and very old, gnarled maples with great spreading branches. It was one of those classic colonial houses for which Connecticut is renowned, and it had a feeling of such mellowness about it that it truly captured our attention.

"What a shame nobody cares enough about this lovely old place to look after it properly, to give it a fresh coat of paint," Andrew murmured, and opening the door, he got out of the car. Instructing Jenny, our English au pair, to stay inside with the children, I quickly followed my husband.

In a way I cannot explain, certainly not in any rational sense, the house seemed to beckon us, pull us toward it, and we found ourselves hurrying over to the front door, noticing the peeling paint and tarnished brass knocker as we did. Andrew banged the latter, whilst I peeked in through one of the grimy windows.

Murky though the light was inside, I managed to make out pieces of furniture draped in dust cloths and walls covered with faded, rose-patterned wallpaper. There were no signs of life, and naturally no one answered Andrew's insistent knocking. "It looks totally deserted, Mal, as if it hasn't been lived in for years," he said, and after a moment, he wondered out loud, "Could it be for sale, do you think?"

As he put his arm around my shoulders and walked me back to the car, I found myself saying, "I hope it is," and I still remember the way my heart had missed a beat at the thought that it may very well be on the market.

A few seconds later, driving away down the winding road, I suddenly spotted the broken wooden sign, old and weather-worn and fallen over in the long grass. When I pointed it out to Andrew, he brought the car to a standstill instantly. I opened the door, leaped out, and sprinted across to the grass verge to look at it.

Even before I reached the dilapidated sign, I knew, deep within myself, that it would say that the house *was* for sale. And I was right.

During the next few hours we managed to find our way back to Sharon, hunted out the real estate broker's office, talked to her at length, then followed her out of town to return to the old white house on the hill, almost too excited to speak to each other, hardly daring to hope that the house would be right for us.

"It doesn't have a name," Kathy Sands, the real estate broker, remarked as she fitted the key into the lock and opened the front door. "It's always been known as the Vane place. Well, for about seventy years, anyway."

We all trooped inside.

Jamie and Lissa were carefully shepherded by Jenny; I carried Trixy, our little Bichon Frise, listening to Kathy's commentary as we followed her along the gallerylike entrance, which, Andrew pointed out, was somewhat Elizabethan in style. "Reminds me of Tudor interior architecture," he explained, glancing around admiringly. "In fact, it's rather like the gallery at Parham," he added, shooting a look at me. "You remember Parham, don't you, Mal? That lovely old Tudor house in Sussex?"

I nodded in response, smiling at the remembrance of the wonderful two-week holiday we had had in England the year before. It had been like a second honeymoon for us. After a week with Diana in Yorkshire we had left the twins with her and gone off alone together for a few days.

Kathy Sands was a local woman born and bred and a font of information about everything, including the previous owners—over the last couple of centuries at that. According to her, only three families had owned the house from the time it had been built in 1790 to the present. These were the Dodds, the Hobsons, and the Vanes. Old Mrs. Vane, who was formerly a Hobson, had been born in the house and had continued to live there after her marriage to Samuel Vane. Eighty-eight, widowed, and growing rather frail, she had finally had to give up her independence and go to live with her daughter in Sharon. And so she had put the house, which had been her home for an entire lifetime, on the market two years earlier.

"Why hasn't it been sold? Is there something wrong with it?" I asked worriedly, giving the broker one of those sharp, penetrating looks I had learned so perfectly from my mother years before.

"No, there's nothing wrong with it," Kathy Sands replied. "Nothing at all. It's just a bit off the beaten track, too far from Manhattan for most people who are looking for a weekend place. And it *is* rather big."

It did not take Andrew and me long to understand why the real estate broker had said the house was big. In actuality it was huge. And yet it had a compactness about it, was not as sprawling and spread out as it appeared to be from the outside. Although it did have more rooms than we really needed, it was a tidy house, to my way of thinking, and there was a natural flow to the layout. Downstairs the rooms opened off the long gallery, upstairs from a central landing. Because its core was very old, it had a genuine quaintness to it, with floors that dipped, ceilings that sloped, beams that were lopsided. Some of the windows had panes made of antique blown glass dating back to the previous century, and there were ten fireplaces, eight of which were in working order, Kathy told us that afternoon.

All in all, the house was something of a find, and Andrew and I knew it. Never mind that it was farther from New York than we had ever planned to have a weekend home. Somehow we would manage the drive, we reassured each other that afternoon. Andrew and I had fallen in love with the place, and by the end of the summer it was ours, as was a rather large mortgage.

We spent the rest of 1986 sprucing up our new possession, camping out in it as we did, and loving every moment. For the remainder of that summer and fall our children became true country sprites, practically living outdoors, and Trixy reveled in chasing squirrels, rabbits, and birds. As for Andrew and myself, we felt a great release escaping the tensions of the city and the many pressures of his high-powered job.

Finally, in the spring of 1987, we were able to move in properly, and then we set out taming the grounds and planting the various gardens around the house. This was some task in itself, as challenging as getting the house in order. Andrew and I enjoyed working with Anna, the gardener we had found, and Andrew discovered he had green fingers, something he had never known. Everything seemed to sprout under his hands, and in no time at all he had a rose garden, vegetable patch, and herb garden under way.

It did not take either of us long to understand how much we looked forward to leaving the city, and as the weeks and months passed we became more and more enamored of this breathtaking corner of Connecticut.

Now, as I walked through the sunroom and into the long gallery, I paused for a moment, admiring the gentle serenity of our home.

Sunlight was spilling into the hall from the various rooms, and in the liquid rafts of brilliant light thousands of dust motes rose up, trembled in the warm July air. Suddenly, a butterfly, delicately wrought, jewel-tinted, floated past me to hover over a bowl of cut flowers on the table in the middle of the gallery.

I caught my breath, wishing I had a paintbrush and canvas at hand so that I could capture the innocent beauty of this scene. But they were in my studio, and by the time I went to get them and returned, the butterfly surely would have flown away, I was quite certain of that. So I just continued to stand there, looking.

As I basked in the peacefulness of the early morning, thinking what a lucky woman I was to have all that I had, there was no possible way for me to know that my life was going to change so profoundly, irrevocably.

Nor did I know then that it was this house which would rescue me from the destructiveness within myself. It would become my haven, my refuge from the world. And in the end it would save my life.

But because I knew none of this at that moment, I walked blithely on down the gallery and into the kitchen, happy at the prospect of the holiday weekend ahead, lighthearted and full of optimism about my life and the future.

Automatically, I turned on the radio and listened to the morning news while I stood toasting a slice of bread and drinking a cup of coffee I had made earlier. I studied a long list of chores I had made the night before and mentally planned my day. Then, once I had eaten the toast, I ran upstairs to take a shower and get dressed.

3

I have red hair, green eyes, and approximately two thousand freckles. I don't think I'm all that pretty, but Andrew does not agree with me. He is forever telling me that I'm beautiful. But, of course, beauty lies in the eye of the beholder, so I've been told, and anyway, Andrew is prejudiced, I have to admit that.

All I know is that I wish I didn't have these irritating freckles. If only my skin were lily-white and clear, I could live with my vivid coloring. My unruly mop of auburn curls has earned me various nicknames over the years, the most popular being Ginger, Carrot Top, and Red, none of which I have ever cherished. Quite the opposite, in fact.

Since I have always been somewhat disdainful of my mother's preoccupation with self, I have schooled myself not to be vain. But I suspect that secretly I am, and just as much as she is, if the truth be known. But then I think that most people *are* vain, care a lot about the way they look and dress and the impression they make on others.

Now, having showered and dressed in a cotton T-shirt and white shorts, I stood in front of the mirror, peering at myself and grimacing at my image. I realized that I had spent far too long in the garden unprotected yesterday afternoon; my freckles seemed to have multiplied by the dozen.

A few fronds of hair frizzled around my temples and ears, and I sighed to myself as I slicked them back with water, wishing, as I so frequently did, that I were a pale, ethereal blonde. As far as I'm concerned, my coloring is much too vibrant, my eyes almost unnaturally green. I have inherited my coloring from my father; certainly there is no mistaking whose daughter I am. My eyes mirror his, as does my hair. Mind you, his is a sandy tone now, although it was once as fiery as mine, and his eyes are not quite as brightly green as they once were.

That's one of the better things about getting older, I think—everything starts to fade. I keep telling myself that I'm going to look like the inestimable Katharine Hepburn when I'm in my seventies. "Let's only hope so," Andrew usually remarks when I mention this little conceit of mine. And it *is* wishful thinking on my part; what woman, redheaded or not, doesn't want those lean, thoroughbred looks of hers?

Brushing back my hair, I secured it with a rubber band, then tied a piece of white ribbon around my ponytail and ran down the stairs.

My little office, where I did paperwork and household accounts, was situated at the back of the house, looking out toward the vegetable garden. Seating myself at the large, old-fashioned desk, which we had found at Cricket Hill, a local antique shop, I picked up the phone and dialed our apartment in New York.

On the third ring my mother-in-law answered with a cheery, very British "Hello?"

"It's me, Diana," I said, "and the top of the morning to you."

"Good morning, darling, and how is it out there?" she asked. Not waiting for my response, she went on, "It's frightfully hot here in the city, I'm afraid."

"I thought it would be," I answered. "And we're having the same heat wave in Connecticut. All I can say is, thank God for air-conditioning. Anyway, how are my holy terrors today?"

She laughed. "*Divine.* And I can't tell you how much I relish having them to myself for a couple of days. Thanks for that, Mal, it's so very sweet and considerate of you, letting me get to know my grandchildren in this way."

"They love you, Diana, and they enjoy being with you," I said, meaning every word. "And what are you planning to do with them?"

"I'm taking them to the Museum of Natural History, after breakfast. You know how they are about animals, and especially dinosaurs. Then I thought I'd bring them home for a light lunch, since it's so nice and cool in the flat. I promised to take them to F.A.O. Schwarz after their nap. We're going shopping for toys."

"Don't spoil them," I warned. "Doting grandmothers have been known to spend far too much money at certain times. Like when they're on holiday visits."

Diana laughed, and over her laughter I heard my daughter wailing in the background. Then Lissa said in a shrill voice, "Nanna! Nanna! Jamie's broken my bowl, and the goldfish is on the carpet. *Dying!*" The wailing grew louder, more dramatic.

"I didn't do it on purpose!" Jamie shouted.

My mother-in-law had not spoken for a moment, no doubt distracted by this sudden racket exploding around her. Now she exclaimed, "Oh, God, hang on a minute, Mallory, the fish *is* gasping. I think I'd better grab a glass of water and pop the fish in it. Won't be a tick." So saying she put the phone down, I strained to hear my children.

Jamie cried plaintively, "I'm sorry, Lissa."

"Pick up the phone and speak to your mother," I heard Diana instruct from a distance, sounding very brisk and businesslike. "She's waiting to say hello to you, darling. Go on, Lissa, speak to your mummy," my mother-in-law commanded in a tone that forbade argument.

After a moment, a small, tearful voice trickled down the wire. "Mommy, Jamie's killed my goldfish. *Poor* little fish."

"No, I haven't!" Jamie shrieked at the top of his lungs.

"Don't cry, honey," I said to Lissa, then added in a reassuring voice, "And I'm sure your goldfish isn't dead. I bet Nanna has it safely in water already. How did the bowl break?"

"It was Jamie that broke it! He banged on it with a spoon, and all the water fell out and my little fish."

"He must have been banging awfully hard to break the glass," I said. "Perhaps it was already cracked. I'm sure it was an accident, and that he didn't do it on purpose."

In the background, Jamie cried again, "I'm sorry."

Lissa said, "He *was* banging hard, Mommy. He's mean, he was trying to frighten Swellen."

"Swellen?" I repeated, my voice rising slightly. "What kind of name is that?"

"She means Sue Ellen," Diana said to me, having relieved my daughter of the phone. "And I suspect the fishbowl was defective, Mal. In any case, the goldfish is alive and kicking, or should I say *swimming,* in one of your Pyrex dishes. I'll get a goldfish bowl later, at the pet shop where I bought the goldfish yesterday. That'll make her happy."

"You don't have to bother buying a new one," I said. "There's a bowl from the florist's in the cupboard where I keep the vases. It's perfectly adequate."

"Thanks for the tip, Mal. Jamie wants to speak to you."

My son took the phone. "Mom, I didn't do it on purpose, honestly I didn't. *I didn't!*" he protested.

"Yes, you *did!*" Lissa yelled.

She must have been standing directly behind Jamie, I heard her so clearly. "I'm sure you didn't mean to break it, honey," I murmured. "But tell Lissa you're sorry again and give her a kiss. Then everything will be fine."

"Yes, Mom," he mumbled.

Because he still sounded tearful, I tried to reassure him. "I love you, Jamie,"

"I love you, too, Mom," he answered a bit more cheerfully, and then he dropped the receiver down with a clatter.

"Jamie, ask Nanna to come to the phone!" I exclaimed, then repeated this several times to no avail. I was about to hang up when Diana finally came back on the line.

"I think peace reigns once more," she said, chuckling. "Oh, dear, I do believe I speak too soon, Mal."

A door banged; there was the sound of Trixy barking. "I guess Jenny just came back from walking the pooch," I said.

"Exactly. And I'd better prepare breakfast for my little troop here, then get the twins ready for their outing. And seriously, Mal, everything seems to be all right between them. They've kissed and made up, and Sue Ellen is happily contained in the bowl, swimming her heart out." She chuckled again. "I'd forgotten what a handful six-year-olds can be. Either that or I'm getting too old to cope."

"You, old! *Never*. And if you remember, their little spats never last long. Basically, they're very close, like most twins are."

"Yes, I do know that."

"I've loads of chores, Diana, so I must get on. I'll talk to you tonight. Have a lovely day."

"We will, and don't work too hard, Mallory dear. Bye-bye now."

"Bye," I said and hung up.

My hand rested on the receiver for a few moments, my thoughts lingering with my mother-in-law.

Diana was a sweet and caring woman, truly loving, and I've always thought it was such a shame she never remarried after Andrew's father died in 1968, when he was very young, only forty-seven. Michael Keswick, who had never been sick a day in his life, had suffered a sudden heart attack that proved fatal.

Michael and Diana, who originally hailed from Yorkshire and went to live in London after university, had been childhood sweethearts. They had married young, and Andrew had been born two years after their wedding; it had been an idyllic marriage until the day of Michael's untimely death.

Diana once told me that she had met quite a few men over the years since then, but that none of them had ever really measured up to Michael. "Why settle for second best?" she had said to me during one of our treasured moments of genuine intimacy. On another occasion, she had confided that she much preferred to be on her own, rather than having to cope with a man who didn't meet her standards, did not compare favorably with Michael.

"I'd always be making mental notes about him, passing private judgments, and it wouldn't be fair to the poor man," she had said. "Being on my own means I'm independent, my own boss, and I can therefore do what I want, when I want. I can come to New York to see all of you when the mood strikes me. I can work late every night of the week, if I so wish, and I can go up to Yorkshire whenever I feel like it. Or dash over to France on a buying trip, on the spur of the moment. I don't have to answer to anyone, I'm a free agent, and believe me, Mal, it's better this way, it really is."

I had asked her that day whether Michael had been her only love, or if she had ever fallen in love again. And she had muttered something and glanced away. Intrigued by the way she had flushed, albeit ever so slightly, and averted her head with sudden swiftness, I had been unable to resist repeating my question. After a moment's hesitation and an unexpected stiffening of her shoulders, she had finally turned her face back to mine. Her gaze had been direct, her eyes filled with the honesty I'd come to appreciate and rely on. I always knew where I stood with her, and that was important to me.

Slowly, she had said in the softest of voices, "The only man I've ever been remotely interested in on a serious level, and very strongly attracted to is . . . not free. Separated for the longest time, but not actually divorced, God knows why. And that's not good. I mean, it would be impossible for me to have a relationship with a man who was *legally* tied to another woman, even if not actually living with her. Untenable, really, and certainly no future in it."

Her shoulders had relaxed again, and she had shaken her head. "I came to the conclusion a very long time ago that I'm much better off living on my own, Mal. And I *am* happy, whatever you think. I'm at peace with myself."

Yet it has often struck me since that Diana must have moments of great sadness, of acute loneliness. But Andrew doesn't agree with me.

"Not Ma!" he had exclaimed when I first voiced this opinion. "She's busier than a one-legged toe dancer doing *Swan Lake* alone and in its entirety. She's up at the crack, behind her desk at the antique shop by six, cataloguing her stock of antiques, bossing her staff around, and floating over to Paris to buy furniture and paintings and *objets* at the drop of a hat. Not to mention wining and dining her posh clients, and fussing over us, her dearest darlings. Then there's her life in Yorkshire. She's forever racing up there to make sure the old homestead hasn't tumbled down."

Shaking his head emphatically, he had finished, "Ma, *lonely?* Never. She's the least lonely person I know."

At that time I had thought that perhaps she keeps herself so frantically busy in order not to notice her loneliness, perhaps even to assuage it. But I hadn't mentioned this to Andrew. After all, he was her son, her only child, and he ought to know her well, if anybody did. And yet there have been times over the years when I have noticed a wistful expression on Diana's face, a sadness in her eyes, a look of longing, almost. A yearning, maybe, for Michael? Or for that love who was not entirely available? I wasn't sure, and I have never had the nerve to broach the subject.

Nora startled me, and I jumped in my chair as she came crashing into my office. I sat bolt upright, gaping at her.

"Sorry I'm late, Mal," she exclaimed, striding forward and flopping down in the chair opposite my desk.

For a dainty, petite person she could certainly make a lot of noise.

"Phew! It's hot today! A real scorcher!" She fanned herself energetically with her hand and gave me a smile. Then her face dropped as she took in my expression.

"Oh, sorry, did I give you a start when I came in?"

I nodded. "You did. But then, I was miles away, I must admit. Daydreaming."

A look of incredulity swept across Nora's face. Narrowing her eyes, she uttered a dry little laugh. "Daydreaming! Not you, Mallory Keswick! That's the last thing you'd be doing. You're a human dynamo. I've never seen *you* waste a minute."

Her words amused me, but I made no comment.

Rising, I said to her, "How about a glass of iced tea, before we get down to the task of putting this house in order for the weekend?"

"Sounds good," she answered, immediately jumping up and leading the way out of the office. "I didn't stop at the market stand on the way here. It's better I buy your vegetables and fruit tomorrow, Mal. They'll be fresher for Monday's barbecue."

"That's true. Listen, are you and Eric coming? You haven't really given me a proper answer."

She swung her head, looked over her shoulder at me, gave a quick nod. "We'd love to, and thanks, Mal, for including us. It's good of you."

"Don't be so silly, you and Eric are like part of the family."

She didn't say anything, just moved on into the kitchen, but there was a small, pleased smile on her face, and I knew she was happy that I'd asked her again, that I had not taken no for an answer.

Nora, who was about forty, was a slender pixie of a woman, with unusual, prematurely silver hair, an intelligent but merry face, and silvery-gray eyes. She had been my helper for the past year and a half, almost since we had moved in, and her husband, Eric, who worked at the local lumberyard, did carpentry and outdoor chores for us on weekends. Married for nearly twenty years, they were childless, and both of them doted on the terrible twins, as I jokingly called Jamie and Lissa at times.

Nora was a practical, down-to-earth, no-nonsense woman, a real Connecticut Yankee with her feet on the ground, which made us totally compatible, since I tend to be pragmatic and plain-speaking myself.

Utterly without pretension, she refused to be called a housekeeper. "Too fancy for me," she had said the day I had hired her. "Let's just say I'm your helper, Mal. All right if I call you Mal, isn't it?"

I had nodded, and she had continued, "It's friendlier. Anyway, that's the way it is in the country. First-name basis." She had laughed then. "*Housekeeper* sounds a bit formidable to me. Makes me think of a woman in a black dress with a grim expression and a bunch of keys tied to her belt." The silvery-colored eyes had twinkled. "Maybe I've read too many gothic novels."

As far as I'm concerned, Nora Matthews can call herself anything she wants. She is invaluable to me; I couldn't manage without her.

Pouring two glasses of iced tea, Nora remarked in her clipped way, "Fourth's going to be a lot hotter than today. Weather forecast says we're in for it. Better think about dressing cool on Monday. Lightweight all the way." She eyed my T-shirt and shorts. "You've got the right idea. Stick to that outfit for the barbecue."

"Aw, shucks, Nora, there goes my plan to wear my new cocktail dress!" I exclaimed, arranging a suitably disappointed expression on my face.

Swiftly, she glanced at me. Her brow furrowed. Nora was never absolutely certain about my humor, never knew whether I was teasing her or not.

I burst out laughing. "This is *exactly* what I intended to wear. Shorts and a T-shirt. You know very well they constitute my summer uniform."

"I guess so," she muttered.

For a split second I thought that I had offended her, teasing her in this way, but then I saw a glint of hidden laughter in her eyes, and I relaxed.

"Come on, let's get this show on the road," I said, adopting a bustling manner.

"Beds first?"

"You bet," I answered, and gulping down the last of my iced tea, I followed her out of the kitchen.

4

Four hours later I carried a turkey sandwich and a Diet Coke out to the low wall which surrounds the terrace in front of the sunroom.

Selecting a corner which was well-shaded by one of the large old maples, I sat down and took a bite of the sandwich, enjoying it. I was starving, having been up since before dawn. Also, besides changing all the bed linens, Nora and I had done a marathon job of cleaning the bathrooms and the bedrooms. The hard work had helped to give me an appetite. Not only that, I wanted to fortify myself for the rest of the day; there was still the entire downstairs to clean.

I take great pride in Indian Meadows.

I love it most of all when everything sparkles and gleams and looks perfect. Diana has always said I should have been an interior decorator. She thinks I have great talent for putting furniture and things together to create unique and attractive settings. The idea doesn't appeal to me; I don't think I would enjoy doing this kind of work for clients in the way that Diana buys antiques, paintings, and beautiful objects for the customers who patronize her prestigious antique shop in London. I am sure it would be far too frustrating, trying to please other people, not to mention convincing them that my taste is superior to theirs.

I prefer to be an amateur decorator creating a home which pleases Andrew and me, just as I paint for my own pleasure, for the satisfaction and gratification it gives me.

Nora never joins me on this wall for a picnic. Invariably, she eats her lunch inside, preferring the cool, air-conditioned interior. Certainly it is much more comfortable inside the house today; it is positively grueling out here. A great yellow orb of a sun seems to be burning a hole in the fabric of the sky, which is of such a sharp and brilliant blue it almost hurt my eyes to look at it.

The wall where I'm sitting is wide, with big flat stones along the top, and it is very old, built by hand by a local stonemason many years ago.

In Yorkshire, drystone walling, as it is called, is an ancient craft. All of the stones have to be perfectly balanced, one on top of the other, so that they can remain tightly wedged together without the benefit of cement. It is done by the crofters on the Yorkshire moors and in the lush green dales, but it is a dying craft, Diana says, almost a lost art. I'm sure it is here, too, and more's the pity, since these ancient walls are beautiful, have such great character.

I am extremely partial to this particular wall on our property, mostly because it is home to a number of small creatures. I know for a fact that two chipmunks live inside its precincts, as well as a baby rabbit and a black snake. Although I know the chipmunks well and have spotted the bunny from time to time, I have never actually seen the snake. But our gardener, Anna, has, and so have the twins. At least, that is what they claim, most vociferously.

Ever since my childhood, I have loved nature and the wild creatures who inhabit the countryside, and I have encouraged Jamie and Lissa to respect all living things, to treasure the animals, birds, and insects that frequent Indian Meadows.

Unconsciously, and very often without understanding what they are doing, some children can be terribly cruel, and it always makes me furious when I see them hurting small, defenseless animals, pulling wings off butterflies, grinding their heels into earthworms and snails, throwing stones at birds. I made my mind up long before the twins were born that no child of mine would ever inflict pain on any living thing.

To make nature more personal, to bring it closer to them, I invented stories about our little friends who inhabit the garden wall. I tell Jamie and Lissa tales about Algernon, the friendly black snake, who has a weakness for chocolate-covered cherries and wishes he owned a candy store; about Tabitha and Henry, the two chipmunks, married with no children, who want to adopt; and about Angelica, the baby bunny rabbit, who harbors an ambition to be in the Fifth Avenue Easter Parade.

Jamie and Lissa had come to love these stories of mine; they can't get enough of them, in fact, and I have to repeat them constantly. In order to satisfy my children, I'm forever inventing new adventures, which entails quite a stretch of the imagination on my part.

It's struck me several times lately that perhaps I should write down the stories and draw pictures to illustrate them. Perhaps I will, but only for Jamie and Lissa. This idea suddenly took hold of me. What a wonderful surprise it would be for the twins if I created a picture book for each of them, and put the books in their Christmas stockings.

I groaned inside; how ridiculous to be thinking of Christmas on this suffocatingly hot summer's day. But the summer will soon be drawing to an end; it always does disappear very quickly after July Fourth weekend. Then Thanksgiving will be upon us before I can blink, with Christmas not far behind.

This year we are planning to spend Christmas in England. We will be staying with Diana at her house in West Tanfield in the Yorkshire dales. Andrew and I are really looking forward to it, and the children are excited. They are hoping it will snow so that they can go sledding with their father. He's promised to take them on the runs he favored when he was a child; and he is planning to teach them to skate, providing Diana's pond has frozen solid.

I was ruminating on our winter vacation ten minutes later when Nora poked her head around the sunroom door. "It's Sarah on the phone," she called.

"Thanks," I called back, but she had already disappeared.

I slid off the wall and went inside. Flopping down on a chair, I picked up the phone, which sat on a nearby end table. "Hi, Sarah. When are you coming out here?"

"I don't think I will be coming," she replied.

I thought she sounded woeful, a little glum for her; she was normally so cheerful.

"What's wrong?" I asked, gripping the phone a bit tighter, instinctively aware that all was not right.

We had been best friends all of our lives, ever since we were babies in prams being walked on Park Avenue by our mothers, who were also friends. We had attended the same kindergarten and then Miss Hewitt's. Later on we had gone off to Radcliffe together, and we have always been extremely close, inseparable. I know Sarah Elizabeth Thomas as well as I know myself, and so I understood that she was upset about something.

Since she had remained totally silent, I asked again, more insistently, "What's the matter?"

"It's Tommy. We had a foul row last night, the worst we've ever had, and he's just informed me, by phone no less, that it's over between us. Finished, terminated, kaput. He doesn't want to see me . . . ever again. And he says he's going to L.A. this afternoon. To be succinct, Mal, I've been dumped. *Dumped! Me!* Can you imagine that! It's never happened to me before."

"I know. You've always done the dumping. And I'm sorry you're upset. I realize you cared about Tommy. On the other hand, I've always felt—"

"You don't have to say it," she cut in softly. "I know you never liked him. You were always a bit wary of him. I guess you were right. As usual. How come you know men better than I do? Don't bother to answer that. Listen, recognizing that Tommy's a bit of a louse doesn't make it any easier for me. I sort of—liked him."

Her voice had grown tiny, and I knew she was on the verge of tears.

"Don't cry, it'll be all right, Sash," I soothed, using the nickname I had given her when we were children. "Admittedly it's cold comfort, but it *is* better this way. Honestly. Tommy Preston the third isn't worth weeping over. The break was bound to happen sooner or later. And preferably now than later. Think how awful it would be if you married him and then this kind of thing happened—"

"He did ask me," Sarah interrupted. "Half a dozen times, to be exact."

There was a sniffling sound, and then I heard her blowing her nose.

"I know he proposed. You've told me about it—numerous times, actually," I muttered. "And I'm glad you were cautious and didn't plunge. But why aren't you coming for the weekend? I don't understand."

"I can't come by myself, Mal. I'll feel like a spare wheel."

"That's ridiculous! You'll be with me, your very, *very* best friend, and Andrew, who loves you like a sister. And your god-children, who adore you. And Diana, who thinks you're the greatest thing since Typhoo tea."

"Flattery will get you everywhere, but then, you know that," she said, and I heard the laughter surfacing in her voice. "However, I think I'll stay in Manhattan and lick my wounds."

"You can't do that!" I protested, my voice rising. "You'll only pig out on ice cream and all those fattening things you love to eat when you're upset. And just think of the hard work you've put in, losing ten pounds. Besides, it's going to be hotter than hell in Manhattan. Nora told me they predict a hundred and twenty degrees in the shade."

"I'm afraid *I* take Miss Nora's weather forecasts with a grain of salt, Mal."

"Honestly, it *is* going to be hot in the city. I heard it on television myself. Last night. Just think how much cooler it will be out here in Sharon. And then there's the swimming pool, some shady corners in the garden. You know how much you love it here. This is your second home, for heaven's sake."

"Nevertheless, at the moment I think I prefer the blistering sidewalks of Manhattan, the lonely confines of my stifling apartment. At least I can wallow unashamedly in my memories of Tommy," she intoned dramatically. "My lost love, my greatest love."

Her theatricality, such an integral part of her personality, was coming through all of a sudden, and I was relieved. It told me she wasn't quite so heartsick as she had first made herself out to be at the outset of our conversation. I began to chuckle.

"Don't you dare laugh at me, Mallory Christina Jordan Keswick. Stop laughing, I tell you!" she cried indignantly. "I'm heartbroken. *Heartbroken.*"

Still laughing, I whooped, "That's a load of cod's wallop!" This was one of Andrew's favorite expressions, and I had made it my own over the years. "You're no more heartbroken about him than I am. Your pride's injured, that's all it is. I'll tell you something else, I bet if the truth be known, that . . . that . . . that little creep was always intending to go off to the West Coast for the July Fourth weekend. To see his family. You've always said he dotes on his mother and adores his sisters and constantly complains about their recent move to California."

"Oh." She said nothing more for a moment, then she murmured thoughtfully, "I must admit, I hadn't thought of that." There was another brief pause. I could visualize her digesting my point. "But we *did* have a terrible row, Mal."

"No doubt one he manufactured," I replied sharply. I had never liked Thomas Preston III. An Eastern seaboard uptight WASP, he was tight with a buck as well as his emotions, high on snobbery and low on brains. He was employed by a famous private merchant bank as a vice president only because the bank bore his family name and was run by his uncle. My beautiful, generous, talented, loving Sarah deserved much better; she deserved the best. Personally, I thought Tommy Preston was the worst, a poor excuse for a man. He wasn't even all that good-looking; at least I could've understood it if she'd fallen for a pretty face.

I took a deep breath. "So, when are you coming out to Connecticut? Tonight or tomorrow?"

"I've just arranged to take one of my buyers to dinner tonight. I'll come sometime tomorrow, is that okay?"

"It sure is, Sashy darling. July Fourth wouldn't be quite the same without you."

5

After Nora had left for the day, I toured the house as I generally do on Fridays, checking that everything was in order in all of the rooms.

I was happy with the way things looked, and even though I say so myself, the house *is* beautiful; I stood in the doorway of each room, admiring what I saw, taking the most intense pleasure and gratification from our home.

In the sitting room, the antiques I had so lovingly waxed and polished that morning gleamed in the soft, early-evening light, the smooth wood surfaces darkly ripe and mellow with age. The pieces of old silver on display in the small dining room glittered brightly on the sideboard, and everywhere there was the sparkle of mirrors, the shine of newly cleaned windows. The many flowering plants and vases of cut flowers, which I had placed in various strategic spots throughout the house, added splashes of intense color against the cool, pale backgrounds, and their mingled fragrances filled the air with sweetness.

There was a lovely feeling of well-being about the house tonight. It was completely ready for the holiday weekend, comfortable, warm, and welcoming, truly a home. All that was missing was my family. But they would be with me tomorrow morning, to enjoy the house and everything in it and to fill it with their happy voices and laughter. I could hardly wait for Andrew, the twins, Diana, and Jenny to arrive. Andrew was going to drive them out very early, at least so he had said before leaving for Chicago at the beginning of the week.

After a few more moments of wandering around scrutinizing everything, I ran upstairs to our bedroom. Stripping off my clothes, I took a quick shower, toweled myself dry, put on a pair of white cotton trousers and a clean white T-shirt, then tied my hair in a ponytail with a red ribbon.

Later I would make myself a bowl of spaghetti and a green salad, but right now I wanted to relax after my hard day's work. I would call Diana to check on her and the twins and then settle down with a book.

There is a long, low room opening off one end of our bedroom, and I went into it now. I had made it mine right from the beginning when we first bought the house. It is such a peculiar shape and size, I can't imagine what it was ever used for before, but I have turned it into a comfortable sitting room, my private inner sanctum, where I sit and think, listen to music, watch television, or read.

Because of its odd shape and size, I painted it white with just the merest hint of green in the paint mix. The pale, apple-green carpeting I chose matches the green-and-white plaid I found for floor-length draperies, the sofa, and armchairs. There are floor-to-ceiling bookshelves along one wall; pretty porcelain lamps grace two tables, skirted in pale-green silk, which stand on either side of the sofa. Some of my watercolors line the walls, and above the sofa hangs the portrait in oils of the twins I painted two years ago. Another oil, this one of Andrew, takes pride of place above the mantelpiece, and so my husband and children keep me company here the entire time, smiling out at me from their gilded frames.

All in all, it's a charming room, pleasant and inviting, with its wash of white and pale greens, a room which benefits from a great deal of sunshine in the afternoons because of its southern exposure. Yet it has a restful feeling to it, especially at this hour of the day when the sun has set and twilight begins to descend. It is one of my favorite corners of Indian Meadows, and as with the rest of the house, decorating it was a labor of love on my part.

Sitting down at the country French *bureau plat,* I pulled the phone toward me and dialed our apartment in New York. After speaking briefly to Diana, I wished my children a loving good night, told them I would see them tomorrow morning, and hung up.

Rising, I crossed to the sofa, stretched out on it, and picked up the book I was reading. This was two novels in one volume, *Cheri* and *The Last of Cheri* by Colette; I had always had a love of her books, and lately I had begun to read her again. And so quickly I found my place, looking forward to becoming a captive of this author's imagination once more.

I had read only a couple of pages when I heard the sound of a car in the driveway. Putting the book down, I got up and hurried to the window, glancing at the carriage clock on the mantelpiece as I did, asking myself who it could be. Very few people came calling on me unannounced, especially at night.

Although the bright summer sky had dimmed considerably, it was still light, and much to my surprise, I saw Andrew alighting from the back of the car, his briefcase in his hand. I dropped the lace curtain, flew out of the room, and tore down the staircase at breakneck speed.

We met, he and I, in the long entrance gallery and stood staring at each other.

He had his luggage with him, and I exclaimed, "You came straight from the airport!" My surprise at his sudden unexpected arrival was quite evident.

"That's right, I did," he answered, eyeing me carefully.

I gazed back at him, searching his face, trying to determine his frame of mind; I wondered if he was still angry with me. I saw nothing but love and warmth reflected there, and I knew instantly that everything was all right between us.

My eyes remained fixed on his face as I asked, "But what about Jamie and Lissa, and your mother and Jenny? How are they going to get out here?"

"I've arranged for a car and driver to pick them up tomorrow morning, very early," he explained, and moving toward me, he took hold of me, drew me into his arms, and embraced me tightly. "You see, I fancied an evening alone with my wife."

"Oh, I'm so glad you did," I exclaimed, clinging to him harder.

We stood holding each other like this without speaking for a second or two. Eventually I said quietly, "I'm sorry for being petty about Jack Underwood, or rather, about his girlfriend. I don't mind if they come for the Fourth, really I don't, Andrew."

"I was petty too, Mal. Anyway, as it turns out, Jack can't come after all. He has to fly to Paris on business, and Gina wouldn't dream of coming alone. Listen, I'm sorry we quarreled. It was my fault entirely."

"No, it was mine," I protested, genuinely meaning this.

"Mine," he insisted.

We pulled apart, looked at each other knowingly, and burst out laughing.

Bending toward me, Andrew kissed me lightly on the mouth, then taking hold of my arm, he said, "Let's have a drink, shall we?" And so saying he propelled me in the direction of the kitchen.

"What a good idea," I agreed and looked up at him, smiling broadly, happy that all was as it should be between my husband and me and that he and I were about to spend an evening alone together for once.

When we got to the kitchen, Andrew slipped off his jacket, undid his tie, and threw both on a chair. I took ice out of the refrigerator and made two tall glasses of vodka and tonic with wedges of lime, and handed one to him.

"Cheers, darling," he said, clinking his drink against mine.

"Cheers," I answered, and I couldn't resist ogling him over the rim of my glass. Then I winked.

He laughed, gave me a quick peck on the cheek, and said, "Shall we sit on the terrace?"

"It's a bit hot out there," I answered, then seeing his face drop in disappointment, I added, "Oh, but why not, the garden's so pretty at this time of day."

"My grandmother used to call this hour the gloaming," he remarked as we walked through the sunroom heading for the terrace beyond the French doors. "It's an old north-country word, I think. Or perhaps it's a Scottish term. You know my mother's mother was originally from Glasgow, before she went to live in Yorkshire, after her marriage to Grandfather Howard. That's why she dressed my mother in so much tartan when she was little, and then me." He chuckled. "She loved me to wear a kilt and a sporan and a little black velvet jacket. She always chose the Seaforth Highlander's dress tartan. Her father, my great-grandfather, had been in the Seaforths, you see."

"Yes, you've told me all about your Scottish ancestry before," I said, glancing at him over my shoulder.

He grinned at me. "Oh, sorry. I do seem to have a bad habit of repeating family history."

"It's not a *bad* habit," I said, "just a habit, and I don't mind."

Once outside we settled down at the circular table with the big white canvas market umbrella, where we usually ate meals in the summer months. We sipped our drinks and were silent for a while, comfortable in this silence, as happily married people frequently are, content simply to be together. Words were not necessary. We communicated without them, as we always had.

Andrew and I usually seemed to be on the same wavelength, and often he would say something I had been thinking only a few seconds before, or vice versa. I found that uncanny.

It was not as stiflingly hot outside as I'd expected it to be, now that the sun had gone down. Although the air was balmy, there was a soft breeze moving through the trees, rustling the leaves. Otherwise everything was absolutely quiet, as tranquil as it always was up here atop our lovely Connecticut hill.

The lawn which flowed away from the terrace wall on this side of the house sloped down to a copse of trees; beyond were protected wetlands and a beaver dam. Soaring above the copse and the stretch of water were the foothills of the Berkshires covered with trees densely massed and of a green so dark they were almost black tonight under that midsummer sky now completely faded. Its periwinkle blue had turned to smoky gray edging into anthracite, with wisps of pink and lilac, saffron and scarlet bleeding into one another along the rim of those distant hills.

Andrew lolled back in the chair and breathed deeply, letting out a long, contented sigh. "God, it's so great here, Mallory. I couldn't get back fast enough . . . to you and this place."

"I know." I looked at him through the corner of my eye and said in the quietest of voices, "I thought you'd call me from Chicago . . . " I let my voice trail off, feeling suddenly rather silly for even mentioning it.

A half smile flitted across Andrew's mouth. He looked somewhat amused as he said, "And *I* thought you'd call *me.*"

"Aren't we a couple of stubborn idiots," I laughed, and lifting my glass, I took a sip of my drink.

He said, "I don't know how my stubborn idiot feels about me, but I adore her."

"And I adore mine," I responded swiftly, smiling warmly at him.

He smiled back.

There was another small silence. After a short interval, I said suddenly, "Sarah's broken up with the Eastern seaboard's greatest snob."

Andrew chuckled. "Yes, he is that. And I know about it, be—"

"How?" I cut in peremptorily.

"Sarah told me."

"She did! *When?*"

"Today. I called her this afternoon, just before I left Chicago. I asked her not to come out here tonight, if that was what she was planning to do. I explained that I wanted to get you alone, to have you all to myself for a change, that I was a bit sick of sharing you with the world at large."

Leering at me wickedly, he continued, "That's when she said she wasn't coming at all, because she had just finished with Tommy Preston that very morning. I'm afraid I couldn't persuade her otherwise. She was quite adamant about staying in New York for the weekend."

"I got her to change her mind. She's going to drive out tomorrow sometime."

"That's good to hear, and I'm glad you had more success than I did. To tell you the honest truth, I'm not surprised in the least that she's finished with Tommy. He never measured up, in my opinion."

"I wish . . . "

"Wish what, darling?" Andrew leaned closer to me, searching my face, no doubt picking up on my wistfulness as he observed my sad expression.

"I wish that Sarah could find a really nice guy to fall in love with, so that she could get married and have babies, just as she wants to. I really do wish *we* knew somebody for her."

"So do I, Mal, but we don't. In the meantime, I think she's quite happy in her own way. She does love her job, you know, and that's quite a career she's carved out for herself as fashion director of Bergman's."

"That's true. Still, I do think she'd like to be married."

"I suppose she would." Andrew fell quiet. A thoughtful expression settled on his face; he finished his drink in a fast little gulp, put his glass on the table, and turned to me. "Talking of careers and jobs, I've just had another offer."

"From the Gordon Agency again?" I asked eagerly, knowing how much he admired this advertising group.

He shook his head. "No, from Marcus and Williamson."

I sat up a bit straighter, staring at him. "That's a fantastic agency. What's the offer?"

"A great one, as far as the money's concerned. But they didn't offer me a partnership. Unfortunately."

"Well, they should have, you're the best in the business," I shot back. "And I guess you didn't take it, did you?"

"No. I didn't want to move just for the money. In all honesty, it would have been worth considering only if Marcus and Williamson had offered me a slice of the pie. Also, to tell you the truth, I did have rather a pang at the thought of leaving Babs."

This was the name everyone on Madison Avenue used for Blau, Ames, Braddock and Suskind, and I did understand how Andrew felt. He had been with them for a number of years, and he was sentimentally attached. He also earned a big salary and had many privileges and benefits aside from being a partner in the firm. But I knew only too well that he thought the agency had begun to stagnate of late, and he had grown increasingly restless this past year.

I voiced this now.

He listened quietly to everything I had to say. He respected my opinion. I was ambitious for him; I always have been. Now I enumerated some of the reasons why I thought he ought to consider leaving, not the least of which was his frustration with Joe Braddock, the senior partner.

When I finished, he nodded. "You're right, you make a lot of sense. I agree that Joe is hardly the most visionary of men, and especially when it comes to the future of the agency. He's in a time warp these days, living in the past and on past glories."

After taking a sip of his drink, he went on, "Joe didn't used to be like that, and certainly not when I started there twelve years ago. I guess he's just getting too old." He gave me a long, rather thoughtful look. "Tell you what, I'm going to talk to him, mention the various offers I've had this past year. It can't do any harm."

"No, it can't," I agreed.

He hurried on, "Actually it might shake him up a bit. Perhaps he'll come around to my way of thinking about certain aspects of the agency. I know Jack Underwood and Harvey Colton would like me to have a go at Joe. Actually, Mal, they deem it high time he retired, and I'm afraid I have to agree with them. On the other hand, he *is* the last of the original founding quartet, the only one still alive, and something of an industry giant. It's going to be a tough situation to deal with."

I reached over and squeezed his hand. "I'm glad you've decided to talk to Joe. I've wanted you to do that for the longest time, and it'll work out, you'll see. Now, do you want another drink, or shall we go inside and I'll make supper?"

He nodded. "I'm starving! What's on the menu?"

"I was going to prepare spaghetti and a green salad for myself, but if you prefer something else, I can defrost—"

"No, no," he interrupted, "that sounds great. Come on, let's go inside and I'll help you."

Much later, when we had finished dinner and were drinking the last of the wine, Andrew said, "You remember that time my mother talked to you about the only man she'd been seriously attracted to since my father's death?"

"Of course I do. She said he was separated but not divorced—"

"And therefore verboten as far as she was concerned," Andrew interjected.

"That's right. But why are you bringing this up now?"

"I think that man might be your father."

I gaped at him. I was so taken aback I was momentarily speechless. Quickly I found my voice. "That's the most preposterous thing I've ever heard, Andrew. What on earth makes you think such a thing all of a sudden?" I knew he had to have a good reason for this comment, since my husband was not given to flights of fancy, and least of all where his mother was concerned.

Clearing his throat, he explained, "Last Tuesday morning, after you'd gone out and just before I left for Chicago, I asked my mother if she could change a hundred-dollar bill for me. She told me to get her wallet out of her handbag in her bedroom. So I did, but there was an envelope caught in the flap and it fell to the floor. When I picked it up I couldn't help noticing your father's name on the back and his return address in Jerusalem. I thought it a bit odd that he was writing to my mother. Anyway, I put the envelope back in her bag and took the wallet to her. Obviously I didn't say anything. How could I?"

I sat back in my chair, frowning. "It does seem strange," I murmured. "But it might be quite innocent."

"That's true. I sort of dismissed it myself as being a trifle far-fetched, but the other night in Chicago I got to thinking about them, and all sorts of little things kept cropping up in my mind."

"Such as what?" I asked, leaning over the table, pinning my eyes on his.

"Edward's behavior, for one thing. He's very solicitous, gallant with her, and a bit flirtatious, I'd say."

"Oh, come on, he *isn't*! He's actually quite distant with Diana. No, *remote* is a better word. And cool, almost cold even."

"He's really only like that when your mother is present, on those family occasions when we're all together for a short while.

Then he is rather . . . " Andrew paused, and I could see him
mentally groping for the right word. "Strained," he finished.

I pondered what he had said, staring down into my glass of
red wine.

Andrew pressed on: "Listen, Mal, consider the times when
he's been in London with us and the twins and Diana. Really
think about them. There's a change in him. A subtle change, I
have to admit, and it's not noticeable unless one is looking for it,
but there *is* a change, nonetheless."

I cast my mind back to those occasions in the past to which
Andrew was referring when seemingly quite coincidentally my
father had had archaeological business in London at the same
time we were there. Now I wondered how coincidental those
visits of his had been. Perhaps they had been carefully planned
so that we could all be together like one big happy family. Also,
looking back, I realized how eager he always was to come to
Yorkshire with us. I tried my best to recall my father's demeanor,
and as I did I began to see that there was some truth in what
Andrew was saying. My father did treat Diana the way an
admirer would, and she too, showed another side of herself
when he was around.

As I visualized them together, I had a flash of comprehen-
sion, and I knew, suddenly, exactly *how* she was different. She
didn't flirt with him, nor did she display any signs of affection.
It was nothing like that. Diana acted younger when she was in
my father's presence. It was as simple as that. And it was barely
discernible, so I had not been conscious of it, had not recognized it until now.

"That's it," I said.

"What is?" Andrew asked, looking across at me in bafflement.

"There is definitely a change in your mother when Daddy's
around. It's ever so slight, but it's there. She acts younger, she even
looks younger. In fact, she's almost girlish. Don't you think so?"

"Yes, you're right, Mal! My mother does seem more . . . *carefree* when Edward is with us, and he appears much younger, too. Actually, that's the difference in him, what I was striving to pinpoint before."

I nodded. Then I asked slowly, "Do you think they're having an affair?"

Andrew began to laugh. "Perhaps they are." His face changed instantly, became sober once more, and he gave a little, noncommittal shrug. "I honestly don't know."

"My mother wouldn't like it if they were."

"For God's sake, Mal, your parents have been separated for donkey's years. They can't stand each other."

"Nevertheless, she wouldn't like it. She's always been terribly jealous of him, and I think she still is."

"Mmmmm. Perhaps that's the reason Mother *isn't* having an affair with your father. It would be too close for comfort for her. She'd feel awkward, embarrassed."

"Yes, she would," I agreed. "And Diana did tell me that she didn't see the special man because he was legally tied to his wife, and so the situation was untenable to her, she said. Well, I guess there's nothing between my father and your mother after all. He was probably just dropping her a friendly note, the way parents-in-law do."

"*Do* they do that, darling?"

I laughed at the skeptical expression on his face. "How do I know?" I lifted my hands in a small, helpless gesture. "Look, getting back to your original statement, Andrew, I'm certain there couldn't be anything between them. You see, I'd *know*. I really would. I'm very close to Diana, and to my father, and I think I'd feel it in my bones." But as I said these words, truly meaning them, I couldn't help thinking that Andrew might well be correct in his initial assumption, and I quite wrong.

Apparently my husband decided the conversation was finished, for he rose suddenly and began to clear the kitchen table.

I also got up and helped him to carry the dishes over to the sink. But all the while I kept thinking about Diana and my father, and at one moment I had to turn my head away so Andrew would not see the sudden, pleased smile on my mouth. It gladdened my heart to think that these two people, whom I cared so much about, might be involved with each other. They both deserved a little happiness, considering the bereftness of their years alone.

6

The arc of the sky was the darkest of blues, and it was clear, without a single cloud. The stars were very bright, crystalline, sparkling, and there was a thin sliver of a crescent moon.

It was the most perfect night, and there was even a cool breeze blowing up now as Andrew and I walked over the ridge and down toward the long meadow and the big pond. After helping me tidy the kitchen, he had said he wanted to see the horses, and so a few minutes ago we had set out from the house, walking in silence, holding hands, enjoying the beautiful evening.

Our two horses and the children's ponies were stabled in one of the big red barns near Anna's little cottage. She was an extraordinary gardener whose talent and skill had turned the wilderness surrounding Indian Meadows into a true beauty spot, and she was worth every penny we paid her. We gave her the cottage rent-free in return for caretaking chores and for looking after the horses, feeding and grooming them and mucking out the stalls. Her nephew Billy came to help her every day after school, and we paid him for his work in the stables. Although Anna's true vocation was gardening, she was an enthusiastic and expert equestrian and enjoyed exercising our horses as well as her own.

The cottage was misnamed, since in reality it was a barn, one of the smaller ones which we had remodeled last year, turning it into a comfortable studio with a sleeping loft, bathroom, and kitchen.

Anna loved it, and she had been thrilled to move in with Blackie, her Labrador, and her coffee-colored Persian cat, Miss Petigrew. She had come along at exactly the right time for us, and seemingly so, had we for her. She had just separated from her boyfriend, moved out of his house in Sharon, and was staying with friends at their farm near Lake Wononpakook until she found a place of her own. Our remodeled barn and the offer we made had solved her immediate problems as well as ours.

As we drew closer, I saw there were lights on in the cottage, but she did not come out to speak to us, and since we never intruded on her in the evenings unless there was a specific reason to do so, we wandered on in the direction of the biggest of our barns.

Once we were inside, Andrew turned on the powerful overhead lights and walked forward, moving down between the stalls. He petted and nuzzled Blue Boy and Highland Lassie, and spent a few minutes with them, before going to see the ponies, Pippa and Punchinella. But we did not stay with the horses very long and were soon heading back to the house.

Andrew had not said much on the way down, and he was equally as quiet as we went up the hill. He seemed to be lost in thought, preoccupied, and I decided not to pry. If there was something on his mind, something he wanted to tell me, he would do so in his own good time. From the beginning of our marriage he had always shared everything with me, and continued to do so, as had I with him.

Diana once said that we were each other's best friend as well as husband and wife and lovers, and this was true. We loved each other on many different levels, and even though Sarah was my dearest girlfriend and Andrew was close to Jack Underwood, he and I were inseparable and spent almost all of our free time together. He was not the kind of man who went off on his own, drinking and carousing with his male companions or following his own pursuits; in many ways he was something of a home-body, and certainly he was a wonderful father, very close to his children.

At one moment Andrew put his arm around my shoulders and drew me closer. Glancing up at the incredible night sky, he sighed deeply several times. I recognized that these were sighs of contentment, and I was pleased he felt so relaxed and at peace, as I was now that he was back with me and close by my side.

We lay together, my husband and I, on top of our bed. The room was cool from the air conditioning and dimly lit by two small lamps on each of the bedside tables. But because I had left the draperies open to the night sky, moonlight cast a silvery sheen over everything, bathing the room in a soft radiance.

Andrew moved closer to me, pushed himself up on one elbow, and looked down into my face, moving a strand of hair away as he did. "I missed you this week," he murmured.

"I missed you too, and I hate it when we quarrel."

"So do I. But it was merely a small storm in an even smaller teacup. Let's forget it, shall we, and move on. To more impor-tant things."

He paused for a moment or two, and as I looked up at him, I saw a reflective expression settle on his face. He seemed to be thinking deeply. Finally, he said, "There's something I want to say . . . to tell you . . . how I feel about something."

"What? What is it?" I asked quickly, sensing that this was important.

Leaning closer to me, he said softly, "I'd like another child. Wouldn't you, Mal?"

"Yes. Yes, I would," I answered without a moment's hesita-tion, thinking how like him it was to suddenly voice an idea I had been turning over in my mind of late.

I felt him smile against my cheek, and I knew he was happy at my unequivocal positive response.

"Let me love you," he said against my hair, stroking my cheek as he spoke. Then he touched the strap of my nightgown a little impatiently. "Take this off, darling. Please."

As I pulled the short silk shift up and over my head and dropped it onto the floor, he got off the bed, slipped out of his pajamas, and a split second later he was next to me again, taking me in his arms, bending over me intently, seeking my mouth with his.

He kissed me over and over again, his lips moving from my mouth to each of my eyelids, onto my nose and forehead, and down to nestle in my neck. He stroked my shoulder and my breasts, tenderness in his every movement; then he began to kiss my nipple while his hand slid down onto my inner thigh. An instant later his questing fingers had found the innermost core of me, and he caressed me expertly, delicately, and I felt a sudden surge of warmth spreading through me.

Sighing, I stirred in his arms, arching my body, pressing closer to him, my longing for him paramount in my mind. I put my arms around his neck, and as I did so he began to kiss my mouth again, his passion rising. And I knew that he wanted me as much as I wanted him. It had always been like this between us; our desire for each other had never waned in all the years of our marriage.

He was ready for me now, just as I was ready for him, and I met his passion with intense ardor, arching up, cleaving to him as he entered me. Instantly we found our own rhythm, moving against each other with mounting excitement.

Suddenly, abruptly, Andrew stopped.

I snapped my eyes open and looked up into his face hovering so close. His hands were braced on either side of me, and he was holding his body very still above mine. He stared down at me for the longest time, searching my face.

His eyes were vividly blue, so blue they almost blinded me, and as we gazed at each other, drowning in each other's eyes, neither one of us was able to look away. It was as though we were plunging deeply into each other's souls, merging to become one.

The silence between us was a palpable thing. He broke it when he said in a voice that was low and thickened by emotion, "My wife, my darling wife. I love you, I've always loved you and I always will."

"Oh Andrew, I love you too," I breathed. "Forever." And reaching up, I touched his face, my love for him spilling out of me.

A faint smile flickered onto his mouth and was instantly gone. He brought his face down to mine, kissing me lightly, tenderly. His tongue slid into my mouth, mine curled against his, and we shared a moment of the most profound intimacy.

Sudden heat flared in me again, took hold of me. "I want you," I whispered.

"And I want you," he answered, and in the pale light I saw the need and urgency in his eyes, the excitement on his face.

Slowly, gently at first, Andrew began to move once more. His speed increased, as did mine; our movements became almost violent as we spun out of control.

I closed my eyes, swept along by wave after wave of ecstasy, excited by the things Andrew was whispering to me. We clung to each other, and as I felt that first sharp surge of intense pleasure, I gasped, then called his name.

Like an echo coming back to me, I heard him crying mine, and we rushed headlong toward a rapturous climax, reaching fulfillment together.

We had turned out the lights and lay in the darkness, curled up under the quilt, wrapped in each other's arms. I felt languorous, satiated after our explosive sexual release and overwhelmed by the love I felt for Andrew. He was my life, my whole existence. I was so lucky. There was no woman luckier.

I nestled into him, listening to his even breathing, thankful that it was normal again. During our hectic lovemaking he had started to pant, then gasp, and even after he had collapsed against me, his breathing had been extremely labored.

Now I said quietly, "Your breathing was so strange, I was worried."

"Why, darling?"

"For a split second I thought you were having a heart attack."

He laughed. "Don't be silly. I was very turned on, overexcited. I thought I was going to explode. If you want the truth, Mal, I couldn't seem to get enough of you tonight."

"I'm glad of that," I murmured. "The feeling's mutual."

"I'd rather gathered that." He kissed the top of my head. "Happy?"

"Deliriously, ecstatically." I turned my face, buried it against his chest. "You're the very best."

"I'd better be."

"What do you mean?"

"I don't want you looking elsewhere," he said in a teasing tone, laughing again.

"Fat chance of that, Mr. Keswick!"

He tightened his arms around me. "Oh, Mal, my beautiful wife, you're such a wonder, the best thing that's ever happened to me. I don't know what I'd do without you."

"You won't have to . . . I'll be with you all the days of our lives."

"Thank God for that. Listen, do you think we made a baby tonight?"

"I hope so." I craned my neck to look up at him, but his face was obscured in the murky light. Slipping out of his arms, I pushed myself up until my head was next to his on the pillows. I bent over him, took his face between my hands, and kissed him.

When we finally drew apart, I said with a small smile, "But don't worry if we haven't. Think of all the fun we're going to have trying."

7

I knew immediately that my mother was going to pick a fight with me. I suppose that over the years I have acquired a second sense about her moods, and I recognized she was not in a very pleasant one this morning.

Perhaps it was the set of her shoulders, the tilt of her head, the way she held herself in general, so rigidly, with such tautness. In any case, her body language telegraphed that she was spoiling for a fight.

I was determined not to react, not today, the Fourth of July. I wanted this to be a happy, carefree day; after all, it was our big summer celebration. Nothing was going to spoil it.

She was so uptight when I greeted her on the doorstep that I had to steel myself as I kissed her on the cheek. She was not going to be easy to deal with; all of the signs were there.

"I don't know why you have to have your barbecue so early," she complained as she came inside the house. "I had to get up at the crack of dawn to make it out here."

"One o'clock is not so early, Mother," I said quietly, "and you didn't have to arrive at this hour." I glanced at my watch. "It's barely ten—"

"I wanted to help you," she shot back, cutting me off. "Don't I always try to help you, Mallory?"

"Yes, you do," I answered quickly, wishing to placate her. I eyed the bag she was carrying; she had not said anything about spending the night when we had spoken on the phone yesterday, and I hoped she wasn't planning to do so. "What's in the bag?" I asked. "Are you sleeping over?"

"No, no, of course not!" she exclaimed.

She had such a peculiar look on her face, I wondered if the mere idea of this was distasteful to her. However, I did not say a word, deeming it wiser to remain silent.

She added, "But thanks, anyway, for asking me. I have a dinner date tonight. In the city. So I must get back. As for the bag, I have a change of clothes in it. For the barbecue. I do get so creased driving out here." She glanced down at her black gabardine trousers. "Oh, dear!" she cried. "I hope this dog isn't going to cover me with hairs."

Trixy, ever friendly, was jumping up against her legs. Stifling a sudden flash of annoyance with my mother, I automatically reached for the dog and picked her up.

"The Bichon Frise doesn't shed, Mother." I said this as evenly as I possibly could, exercising great control over myself.

"That's good to know."

"You've always known it," I retorted, unable to keep the acerbity out of my voice.

She ignored this. "Why don't I go into the kitchen and start on the potato salad."

"Oh, but Diana's going to make that."

"Good heavens, Mallory, what does an Englishwoman know about making an all-American potato salad for an all-American celebration like Independence Day? Independence from the British, I might add."

"You don't have to give me a history lesson."

"*I'll* make the salad," she sniffed. "It's one of my specialties, in case you've forgotten."

"Fine," I answered, eager to promote a peaceful atmosphere.

My mother began to move in the direction of the kitchen, obviously anxious to start preparing the famous potato salad.

I said, "I'll take your bag up to the blue guest room; you can use it for the day."

"Thank you," she replied, walking on, not looking back.

I stared after her slim, elegant figure, wondering how my father had resisted the temptation to strangle her. Then I hoisted the bag and, still holding Trixy, ran upstairs to the blue room. I came back down immediately, still carrying the puppy, and in the hall outside my little office I kissed the top of her fluffy white head and put her down.

"Come on, Trixola," I muttered, "let's go and attack her, shall we?"

Trixy looked up at me and wagged her tail, and as I so often am, I was quite convinced she understood exactly what I'd just said. I laughed out loud. Trixy was such a gay little animal; she always brought a smile to my face and made me laugh.

As I hurried toward the kitchen with the dog trotting behind me, I was more determined than ever not to let my mother ruin my day. I wondered whether she purposely wanted to upset me or was merely in a bad mood and taking it out on me. I wasn't sure. But then, that was an old story when it came to my mother and me. I never *really* knew where I stood with her.

I found her positioned at one of the counters, slicing the chilled boiled potatoes I had made earlier. She had a cup of coffee next to her, and a cigarette dangled from her mouth. It took a lot of self-restraint on my part not to admonish her; I hated her to smoke around us, and most especially when she was working in the kitchen.

"Where are the children and Andrew?" she asked without looking at me.

"They've gone to the local vegetable stand, to buy fresh produce for the barbecue. Corn, tomatoes, the usual. Mother, do you mind not smoking when you're preparing food?"

"I'm not dropping cigarette ash in the salad, if that's what you're getting at," she answered, still sounding peevish.

Once again, I endeavored to placate her. "I know you're not. I just hate the smoke, Mom. Please put it out. If not for your own health or mine, at least for your grandchildren's sake. You know what they're saying about secondhand smoke."

"Lissa and Jamie live in Manhattan. Think of all the polluted air they're breathing in there."

"Only too true, Mother," I snapped. "But let's not add to the problem of air pollution out here, shall we?" I knew my voice had hardened, but I couldn't help myself. I was furious with her, angered that she was taking such a cavalier attitude, and in my house.

My mother swung her beautifully coiffed blonde head around and stared at me over her shoulder.

There was no doubt in my mind that she recognized the unyielding expression which had swept over my face. Certainly she had seen it enough times over the years, and now it had the desired effect. She stubbed out the cigarette in the sink and threw the butt into the garbage pail. After gulping down the last of her coffee, she carried the bowls of potatoes over to the kitchen table and sat down. All of this was done in a blistering silence.

After a moment or two, she said slowly, startling me with her dulcet tones, "Now, Mallory darling, don't be difficult this morning. You know how I hate to quarrel with you. So upsetting." She proffered me the sweetest of smiles.

I was flabbergasted. I opened my mouth, then snapped it shut instantly. She was the most exasperating woman I had ever met, and once again I felt that old, familiar rush of sympathy for my father.

In her own insidious and very clever way, she had somehow managed to twist everything, had made it sound as if I had been the one itching for a fight. But experience had taught me there was nothing to be gained by taking issue with her or trying to present my point of view. Silence or acquiescence were the only viable weapons that could defeat her.

I walked over to the refrigerator and brought out the other ingredients for the potato salad, all of which I had prepared at six o'clock this morning, long before her arrival. There were glass bowls of hard-boiled eggs, chopped celery, chopped cornichons, and chopped onions; these I placed on a large wooden tray, along with the salt and pepper mills and a jar of mayonnaise.

Carrying the laden tray over to the old-fashioned kitchen table, I placed it in the middle and got another chopping board and knife before taking the chair opposite her. I began to methodically chop an egg, avoiding her eyes. I was seething inside.

We worked in silence for a while, and then my mother stopped slicing a large potato, put the knife down, and leaned back in her chair. She sat gazing at me, studying me carefully.

So intense was her stare, so acute her scrutiny, I found myself reacting almost angrily. She had always had that effect on me; I felt like she was putting me under a microscope and dissecting me like a bug.

I frowned. "What is it, Mother?" I demanded coldly. "Do I have dirt on my face or something?"

She shook her head, exclaimed, "No, no, you don't." There was a little pause, then she went on, "I'm sorry, Mal, I *was* staring at you far too hard. I was examining your skin, actually, gauging the elasticity of it." She nodded quite vigorously, as if confirming something important to herself. "Dr. Malvern is right. Young skin does have a special kind of elasticity to it, a different kind of texture than older skin. Mmmm. Well, never mind. I can't get the elasticity back, I'm afraid, but I can get rid of the sag." As she spoke she began to pat herself under her chin with the back of her hand. "Dr. Malvern says a nip and a tuck will do it."

"Mother! For God's sake! You don't need another face job. Honestly you don't. You look wonderful." I truly meant this. She was still a lovely-looking woman who defied her age. The face-lift she had had three years ago had helped, of course. But she was naturally well preserved. No one would have guessed that this slender, long-legged beauty with the pellucid hazel eyes, high cheekbones, and the most perfect complexion, wrinkleless, in fact, was actually a woman approaching her sixty-second birthday. She appeared to be much younger, easily fifteen or sixteen years younger, in my opinion. One of the few things I admired about my mother was her youthfulness and the discipline she exercised in order to achieve it.

"Thank you, Mal, for those kind words, but I do think I could use just a *little* tuck . . . " Her voice trailed off, and continuing to stare at me, she let out several small sighs. There was an unfamiliar wistfulness about her at this moment, and it took me by surprise.

"No, you *don't* need it," I murmured in a gentler voice, a rush of love for her filling me. She suddenly seemed so open and vulnerable that I felt a rare touch of sympathy for her.

Another silence fell between us as we continued to observe each other; but we were really caught up in our own thoughts and drifted with them for a while.

I was thinking of her, thinking that vain and foolish though she might be, she was not a bad person. Quite to the contrary, in fact. Intrinsically, my mother was a good woman, and she had done her level best to be a good mother. There were times when she had been hopeless at this, others when she was more successful. Admittedly, she had instilled in me some excellent values, which were important to me. On the other hand, we rarely agreed about anything, and frequently she misread me, misjudged me, and treated me as if I were a witless dreamer.

It was my mother who finally broke the silence. She said in

an unusually low voice for her, "There's something else I want to tell you, Mal."

I nodded, gave her my full attention.

She hesitated fractionally.

"Go on then," I muttered.

"I'm going to get married," she told me, finally.

"*Married*. But you *are* married. To my father. It might be in name only, but you're still legally tied to him."

"I know that. I mean, after I get a divorce."

"Who are you going to marry?" I asked, leaning forward and staring at her questioningly, unexpectedly riddled with curiosity.

"David Nelson."

"Oh."

"You don't sound very thrilled."

"Don't be silly . . . I'm just taken aback, that's all."

"Don't you like David?"

"Mother, I hardly know him."

"He's very nice, Mal."

"I'm sure he is . . . he's seemed pleasant enough, very cordial on those few occasions I've met him."

"I love him, Mal, and he loves me. We're very good together, extremely compatible. I've been lonely. Very lonely, really, and for a *very* long time. And so has David, ever since his wife died seven years ago. We've been seeing each other fairly steadily for the past year, and when David asked me to marry him, last week, I suddenly realized how much he meant to me. There doesn't seem to be any good reason why we *shouldn't* get married."

Something akin to a quizzical look had slipped onto my mother's face, and her eyes now searched mine; it occurred to me that she was seeking my approval.

I said, "There's no reason at all why you shouldn't get married, Mom. I'm glad you are." I smiled at her. "Does David have any children?"

"A son, Mark, who's married and has one child. A boy, David, named for his grandfather. Mark and his wife, Angela, live in Westchester. He's a lawyer, like David."

A son, that's a blessed relief, I thought. No possessive, overly protective daughter floating around Papa David, one likely to upset the apple cart. Now that I knew about it I was all in favor of this union. I wanted it to go ahead without a hitch. I probed, "And when do you plan to get married, Mother?"

"As soon as I can, as soon as I'm free."

"Have you started divorce proceedings?"

"No, but I'm going to see Alan Fuller later this week. There won't be a problem, considering that your father and I have been separated such a long time." She paused, then added. "Fifteen years," as though I didn't know this.

"Have you told Daddy?"

"No, not yet."

"I see."

"Don't look so pained, Mal. I think he might—"

"I'm not looking pained," I protested, wondering how she could ever think such a thing. I didn't have any pained feelings about anything. Actually, I was pleased she wasn't living in a kind of decisionless limbo any longer.

"I was going to say, before you interrupted me, that I believe your father will be relieved I've finally taken this step."

I nodded. "You're right, Mother. I'm *positive* he will be."

The sound of heels clicking against the polished wood floor of the gallery immediately outside the kitchen made my mother sit up straighter. She brought her forefinger to her lips and, staring hard at me, mouthed silently, "It's a secret."

I gave her another swift, acquiescent nod.

Diana pushed open the door and glided into the kitchen just as my mind was focusing on secrets. There were so many in our family; instantly I pushed this thought far, far away from me, as I invariably did. I never wanted to face those secrets from my childhood. Better to forget them; better still to pretend they did not exist. But they did. My childhood was constructed on secrets layered one on top of the other.

Faking insouciance, I smiled at Diana. It was a beatific smile, belying what I had been thinking. I asked myself if she *was* my father's lover. And if so, would this sudden change in his circumstances affect his life with her? Would the seemingly imminent divorce make him think of marriage—to her? Was my mother-in-law about to become—my stepmother? I swallowed the incipient laughter rising in my throat; nevertheless, I still had to glance away as my mouth twitched involuntarily.

Diana was cheerfully saying, "Good morning, Jessica dear. It's lovely to see you."

My mother immediately sprang to her feet and embraced her. "I'm glad you're here, Diana. You look wonderful."

"Thanks, I feel good," Diana responded, smiled her sunny smile, and added, "I must say, you look pretty nifty yourself, the picture of good health."

I studied them as they talked.

How different they were in appearance, these two women of middle age, our mothers.

Mine was all blonde curls and fair skin, with delicate, perfectly sculpted features. She was a very pretty woman, a cool Nordic type, slim and lissome with a special kind of inbred elegance that was enviable.

Diana was much darker in coloring, with a lovely golden complexion and straight silky brown hair, pulled back in a ponytail this morning. Her face was broader, her features more boldly defined, and her large, luminous eyes were of a blue so pale and transparent they were almost gray. She was not quite as tall as my mother. "I'm a Celt," she had once said to me. "There's more of my Scottish ancestry in my genes than the English part." Diana's appeal was in her warm, tawny looks; she was a handsome woman by any standard, who, like my mother, carried her sixty-one years well, seeming years younger.

Their characters and personalities were totally different. Diana was a much more serious woman than my mother was, more studious and intellectually inclined. And the worlds they occupied, the lives they lived, were not remotely similar. Diana was something of a workaholic, running her antique business and loving every minute of it. My mother was a social butterfly who did not care to work, and who fortunately did not have to. She lived on a comfortable income derived from investments, family trusts, and a small allowance from my father. Why she accepted this from him I'll never know.

My mother was actually somewhat quiet and shy. At times I even thought of her as being repressed. Yet she was a social animal, and when she wanted to she could exude great charm.

My mother-in-law was much more spontaneous and outgoing, filled with a *joie de vivre* that was infectious. I always felt happy when Diana was around; she had that effect on everyone.

Two very disparate women, my mother and my mother-in-law. And yet they had always been amiable with each other, appeared on the surface to get on reasonably well. Perhaps *we* were the bond between them, Andrew and me and the twins. Certainly they were thrilled and relieved that we had such a happy marriage, that our union had been so successful, so blessed. Maybe the four of us validated their troubled lives and diminished their failures.

The two of them sat down, continuing to chat, to catch up, and I rose and walked to the far end of the kitchen. Here I busied myself at the sink, pulling apart several heads of lettuce, washing the leaves scrupulously.

My mind was preoccupied with marriage, my mother's impending one, to be precise. But then my thoughts took an unexpected curve, zeroed in on my father. His life had not been a happy one, far from it—except for his work, of course. That had given him a great deal of satisfaction and still did. He was proud of his standing as an archaeologist. His marriage had been such a disappointment, a terrible failure, and he had expected so much from it, he had once confided in me. It had gone hopelessly awry when I was a child.

What a pity my father had never been lucky enough to have what Andrew and I have. Sadness for him filtered through me; I was saddened even more that he had never found love with someone else when he was a younger man. He was sixty-five now; that was not old, and perhaps it wasn't too late for him. I sighed under my breath. I blamed my mother for his pain, I always had; he had never been at fault. In my eyes he had always been the hero in a bitter, thankless marriage.

As this random thought surfaced, floated to the front of my head, I examined it as carefully as I was washing the lettuce leaves under the running water. Wasn't I being just a little bit unfair? No one in this world is perfect, least of all my father. He *was* a human being, after all, not a god, even if he had seemed like one to me when I was growing up. He had been all golden and shining and beautiful, the most handsome, the most dashing, the most brilliant man in the world. And the most perfect. Of course. Yes, he had been all those things to me as a child. But he must have had his flaws and his frailties, like we all do, hangups and weaknesses as well as strengths. Should I not perhaps give my mother the benefit of the doubt?

This was so startling a thought I took a moment to adjust to it.

Finally, I glanced over my shoulder at her. She was calmly sitting there at my kitchen table, talking to Diana, methodically making her famous potato salad, one she had prepared so religiously every Fourth of July throughout my entire childhood and teenage years.

Unbidden and unexpected, it came rushing back to me, a *fragment* of a memory, a memory prodigiously beaten into submission, carefully boxed and buried and thankfully forgotten. Suddenly resurrected, it was flailing at me now, free-falling into my consciousness. And as it did I found myself looking down the corridor of time. I saw a day long, long ago, twenty-eight years ago, to be exact. I was five years old and an unwilling witness to marital savagery so shocking, so painful to bear I had done the only thing possible. I had obliterated it.

Echoing back to me along that shadowy, perilous tunnel of the past came a mingling of familiar voices which dredged up that day, dragged it back into the present. Exhumed, exposed, it lived again.

My mother is here, young and beautiful, an ethereal, dream-like creature in her white muslin summer frock, her golden hair burnished in the sunlight. She is standing in the middle of the huge kitchen of my grandmother's summer house in Southampton. But her voice contrasts markedly with her loveliness. It is harsh, angry, and accusatory.

I am afraid.

She is telling my father he cannot leave. Not today, not the Fourth, not with all the family coming, all the festivities planned. He cannot leave her and her parents and me. "Think of your child, Edward. She adores you," she cries. "Mallory needs you to be here for her today." She is repeating this, over and over and over again like a shrill litany.

And my father is explaining that he *must* go, that he has to catch his plane to Egypt, explaining that the new dig is about to start, telling her that as head of the archaeological team he must be there at the outset.

My mother starts to scream at him. Her face is ugly with rage. She is accusing him of going to *her*, to his mistress, not to the expedition at all.

My father is defending himself, protesting his innocence, telling my mother she is a fool, and a jealous fool, at that. Then he tells her more softly that she has no reason to be jealous. He vows that he loves only her; he explains, very patiently, that he must go because he must do his work, must work to support us.

My mother is shaking her head vehemently from side to side, denying, denying.

The bowl of potato salad is suddenly in her hands, then it is leaving her hands as it is violently flung. It is sailing through the air, hitting the wall behind my father, bouncing off the wall, splattering his dark blue blazer with bits of potato and mayonnaise before it crashes to the floor with a thud, like a bomb exploding.

My father is turning away angrily, leaving the kitchen; his handsome face is miserable, contorted with pain. There is a helplessness about him.

My mother is weeping hysterically.

I am cringing in the butler's pantry, clinging to Elvira, my grandma's cook, who is my best friend, my only friend, except for my father, in this house of anger and secrets and lies.

My mother is storming out of the kitchen, running after my father, in her anguish not noticing Elvira and me as she races past the open door of the pantry.

Again she is shouting loudly. "I hate you! I hate you! I'll never give you a divorce. *Never.* Not as long as I live. Mercedes will never have the pleasure of being your wife, Edward Jordan. I swear to you she won't. And if you leave me, you'll never see Mallory again. Not ever again. I'll make sure of that. I have my father's money behind *me.* It will build a barrier, Edward. A barrier to keep you away from Mallory."

I hear her running upstairs after my father, railing on at him remorselessly, her voice shrill and bitter and condemning.

Elvira is stroking my hair, soothing me. "Pay no mind, honeychile mine," she is whispering, her plump black arms encircling me, keeping me safe. "Pay no mind, chile. The big folks is always mouthing the stupidest things . . . things they doan never mean . . . things no chile needs hear. Pay no mind, honeychile mine. Your momma doan mean not a word she ses."

My father is here.

He does not leave. An armed truce is struck between them; it lasts only through the Fourth of July. The following morning he kisses me good-bye. He drives back to Manhattan and flies off to Egypt.

He does not come back for five months.

I closed my eyes, squeezing back the tears, pressing down the pain this unexpected memory, so long concealed, has evoked in me.

Slowly, I lifted my lids and stared at the kitchen wall. With infinite care, I placed the lettuce leaves in the colander to drain, covering them with a large piece of paper towel. My hands felt heavy, like dead weights, and nausea fluttered in my stomach. Holding on to the edge of the sink, I calmed myself and endeavored to regain my equilibrium before I walked across the kitchen.

Eventually, I was able to move.

I paused at the kitchen table and looked down at my mother.

It struck me, with a rush of clarity and something akin to shock, that she had probably suffered greatly as a young wife. I should stop my silent condemnation of her. All of my father's long absences must have been difficult to endure, unimaginably lonely and painful for her. *Had* there been a mistress? *Had* a woman called Mercedes really existed? Had there been many other women over the years? Most probably, I thought, with a sinking feeling. My father was a good-looking, normal, healthy man, and when he was younger he must have sought out female company. For as long as I could recall, he and my mother had

had separate bedrooms, and this situation had existed long before he had left for good, when I was eighteen. He had stayed in that terrible marriage for me. I had long believed this, had long accepted it. Somehow, today, I knew it to be true.

Perhaps my mother had experienced humiliation and despair and more heartache than I ever realized. But I would never get the real truth from her. She never talked about the past, never confided in me. It was as if she wanted to bury those years, forget them, perhaps even pretend they never happened. Maybe that was why she was so remote with me at times. Maybe I reminded her of things *she* wanted to expunge from *her* memory.

My mother was looking up at me.

She caught my eye and smiled uncertainly, and for the first time in my adult life I asked myself if I *had* been unfair, if I had done her a terrible injustice all these years.

"What is it, Mal?" she asked, her blonde brows puckering, a spark of concern flickering in her hazel eyes.

I cleared my throat and took a moment to answer. At last I said in a carefully modulated voice, "Nothing, Mom. I'm fine. Listen, I've just washed all the lettuce. It's draining. Could you put it in the fridge in a few minutes, please?" It seemed important to me at this moment to speak of mundane things.

"Of course," she answered.

"What can *I* do to help, Mal? Should I fix the salad dressing?" Diana asked.

"Yes, please, and then perhaps the two of you could take out the hamburger meat and start making the patties."

"Done," Diana said, immediately jumping up and going into the pantry.

Looking at my mother again, I said, "I'm going to go and set the tables."

She nodded, smiling at me, and this time her smile was more sure. She turned back to her potato salad, mixing in the mayonnaise.

Pushing open the kitchen door, I went outside into the garden with Trixy at my heels, leaving the two women alone.

I paused near the door and took several deep breaths. I felt shaken inside, not only by the memory but by the sudden knowledge that all the years I was growing up I had been terrified my father would leave us forever, my mother and I, terrified that one day he would never come back.

It was very hot and airless in the garden, and within seconds my
T-shirt was damp and clinging to me. Even Trixy, trotting along
next to me, looked slightly wilted; wisely, she flopped down
under one of the trestle tables when we reached them.

Late last night Andrew and I had placed the tables under the
trees, and now I was glad that we had.

The maples and oaks which formed a semicircle near my
studio were old, huge, and extravagant, with thick, gnarled
trunks and widely spreading branches abundant with leaves.
The branches arched up to form a wonderful, giant parasol of
leafy green that was cool and inviting and offered plenty of protection from the sun. We were going to need such a shady spot;
by one o'clock it would be a real scorcher of a day, just as Nora
had predicted to me on Friday.

Early this morning I had carried red-and-white checked
cloths and a big basket of flatware out here, and now I began to
set the tables. I had almost finished the largest table, where the
adults would sit, when I heard someone calling, "Coo-ee!"

I recognized Sarah's voice at once and looked up. I waved;
she waved back.

She was wearing a white terrycloth robe and dark glasses.
Her jet-black hair was piled up on top of her head, and there

was a mug in her hand. As she drew closer, I could see that her face was woebegone.

"God, I feel *awful*," she moaned, lowering herself gingerly onto the bench in front of the smaller table.

"I'm not surprised," I said, "and good morning to you, Miss Parfait." This was one of my affectionate nicknames for her.

"Good morning, Little Mother," she answered, using one of her pet names for me.

I grinned and tipped the remainder of the knives and forks out onto the table.

"Oh, please, Mal," she groaned, "have a heart. Hold the noise down. My head's splitting, I feel positively ill."

"It's your own fault, you know, you really did tie one on last night."

"Thanks a lot, friend, for all your sympathy."

Realizing that she wasn't overdramatizing for once, I went and put my hand on her shoulder. "Sorry, I shouldn't tease you. Do you want me to get something for you? Headache pills? Alka Seltzer?"

"No, I've already taken enough aspirin to sink a battleship. I'll be okay. Just move around me very, very carefully, please, tiptoe on the grass, don't clatter the tableware, and talk in a whisper."

I shook my head. "Oh, Sarah darling, you do punish yourself, don't you? Thomas Preston the third isn't worth it."

Sarah paid no attention to my last comment, saying, "I guess it must be the Jewish half of me, the Charles Finkelstein half . . . that's what I inherited from good old Dad, a penchant for punishing myself, a tendency to treat everything like an ethnic drama, lots of Jewish guilt, and dark looks."

"Dark *good* looks," I said. "And have you heard from Charlie Boy lately?"

She smiled and made a moue. "No, I'm afraid I haven't. He's got a new wife, yet another WASPy blonde like my mother, so

I'm the last thing on his mind. I'll call him next week to see how he is, and I'll make a date with him and Miranda. I don't want to lose touch with him again."

"No, you mustn't. Not after he's finally forgiven you for taking your stepfather's name. And a WASPy name, at that."

"Forgiven my mother, you mean!" she cried, her voice rising slightly. "She was the one who changed my name to Thomas, not I, when I was seven and not old enough to understand or protest."

"I know she did," I murmured, walking to the far side of the smaller table, which I now began to set for the children.

Sarah took a long swallow of her coffee, then put the mug down. After taking off her sunglasses, she placed her elbows on the table and rested her head in her hands. Her dark brown velvety eyes followed me as I moved about.

"How many are we going to be for lunch, Mal?" she asked.

"About eighteen. I think. Let's see, there's my mother and Diana, you and the twins and Jenny, plus me and Andrew, which makes eight. I've invited Nora, Eric, and Anna, bringing us up to eleven. Then there're three couples, the Lowdens, the Martins, and the Callens, making seventeen, and two more kids. Vanessa, the Callens' little girl, and Dick and Olivia Martin are bringing their young son, Luke. So I guess that makes nineteen altogether."

"All I can say is, thank God *we* don't have to do the cooking."

I laughed at the expression on her face. "I know what you mean. Luckily, Andrew has everything under control, and he's roped in all the men to do the barbecuing. Nora and my mother and Diana will help me to fetch and carry."

"I'm hoping I'll feel better by lunchtime, that I'll be able to pitch in."

"It's not necessary, Sash. Just relax. And in any case, I'm setting up a buffet table here. It'll hold most of the other food, such as the salads, the breads, the baked beans, baked potatoes, and corn. It's only the hot dogs, hamburgers, and chops that'll have to be brought over from the barbecues on the kitchen patio."

Sarah nodded but didn't say anything for a few minutes. She sat staring into space with a reflective expression on her face. Eventually, she said slowly, "Your mother looks like the cat that's swallowed the canary this morning."

"What do you mean?"

"Her eyes are bright and shiny, and she did nothing but smile at me when I was having my toast. And I couldn't help thinking that it was a very self-satisfied smile. Even a bit smug."

"I guess I can tell you," I began, and then I hesitated.

"Sure you can, you've been telling me everything since the day you could talk."

"It's supposed to be a secret."

"So what, you've always told me your secrets, Mal. Yours and everybody else's, actually."

"Well, so have you too!" I shot back.

"I bet it's to do with a man." Sarah grinned at me and winked.

"I'm impressed. How did you guess?"

She burst out laughing. "She has that look. *The* look, the one that says, 'I have a man and he's all mine.' A guy might not recognize it, but every woman does."

"My mother's getting married."

"Golly gee whiz! You've got to be kidding!"

"No, I'm not."

"Good for Auntie Jess. Who's the man?"

"David Nelson. I think you've met him once or twice when he's been at my mother's."

Sarah let out a low whistle. "He's quite a catch, I'd say. Very good-looking and successful, and younger than her."

"Are you sure he's younger?"

"Yes, I am. My mother said something to me a few months ago about Aunt Jess and David, and she mentioned he was about fifty-eight."

"Oh, only four years, that's not much. Anyway, my mother looks a lot younger than he, don't you think?"

"Yes, she does."

"I can't imagine why she wants to get another face job, though. She doesn't need it, in my opinion."

If Sarah was startled by my comment, she did not show it. She said, "No, she doesn't, but she may feel insecure, worried about her age. That's the way my mother is now that she's turned sixty, always attempting to look younger. A lot of women think that's a milestone, I guess."

I shrugged. "Maybe. On the other hand, sixty's not old. In fact, it's considered young these days. This morning, when my mother mentioned she wanted to have a little nip and tuck, I tried to convince her she didn't need it. But she'll do what she wants. She always has."

"I wonder if she's told my mother? About getting married."

"I don't know. But don't say anything, Sash, just in case she hasn't. As I said, it's a secret. Mom hasn't even informed my father yet, nor has she talked to her lawyer about a divorce. She just made her mind up in the last couple of days . . . at least, that's the impression she gave me."

"I won't tell a soul, I promise, Mal. And I'm really glad for Auntie Jess, glad she's happy."

"I am too." I paused, staring at Sarah without saying anything for a moment, then I flopped down opposite her.

"Is something wrong?" she asked, frowning slightly, pinning her beautiful dark eyes on mine.

I shook my head. "No. I had a sort of . . . well, a sort of revelation earlier. My mother was fussing with the potato salad, and I suddenly found myself remembering an incident with a potato salad that happened on another Fourth of July morning. When I was five. I'd buried it deep and forgotten all about it. Anyway, the memory came back, at least a fragment of it, and I started thinking about my parents and their relationship when I was little, and I suddenly felt rather sorry for my mother. It struck me she must have suffered greatly when she was a younger woman."

Sarah nodded in agreement. "Looking back, she probably did. She was always alone. You *two* were always alone. At least that's the way *I* remember it."

I was silent for a moment, before murmuring, "I had the most awful feeling inside this morning, Sashy . . . "

"What kind of feeling?"

"I felt sick at heart. I suddenly understood that I'd been unfair, that I'd probably done my mother a terrible injustice—and for years."

"What do you mean?"

"I blamed her for their marital problems, but now I'm not so sure it was always her fault."

"I'm certain it wasn't. Anyway, it takes two to tango, Mal." Sarah sighed under her breath. "Your father was hardly ever in this country, the way I recall it. The normal thing was for him to be sitting on a pile of rubble in the Middle East, examining bits of old stone and trying to ascertain how ancient they were, which millennium they came from."

"He had to be away a lot for his work, you know that, Sarah," I said, then realized I sounded defensive.

"But he *never* took you and your mother with him. He always went off alone."

"I had to go to school."

"Not when you were little, you didn't, and when you were older you could have gone to a local school wherever your father's dig was, or you could have had a tutor."

"Going to a local school wouldn't have been very practical," I pointed out. "I wouldn't have been able to speak the local language, for one thing. After all, I was a little kid, I wasn't fluent in Arabic or Urdu or Portuguese or Greek. Or *whatever.*"

"You don't have to be sarcastic, Mal, and look, there are ways to make unusual situations work. Many ways."

"Perhaps my parents couldn't afford a tutor," I muttered.

Sarah was silent.

I studied her for a moment, then asked, "Are you blaming my father?"

"Hey, I'm not placing the blame anywhere, on anyone!" she exclaimed. "How do I know what went on between your parents. Not even you really know that. Jesus, I didn't understand what was happening between mine, either. Kids never do. But it's always the kids who suffer. Ultimately."

When I said nothing, Sarah continued, "Maybe your mother felt it was better, wiser for you to be brought up in New York, rather than in some broken-down, flea-bitten hotel somewhere in the middle of the Arabian desert."

"Or maybe my father simply preferred to leave us behind, to go off alone. For his own personal reasons." I stared hard at her again.

"Come on, Mal, I never said that, nor did I even remotely imply it!"

"I'm not being accusatory or trying to put words in your mouth. Still, it might well have been so. But I suppose I'll never know about their marriage, what went wrong with it."

"You could ask your mother."

"Oh, Sarah, I *couldn't.*"

"Sure you could. There'll be a moment in time when you'll be able to ask her. You'll see. And I bet she won't bite your head off, either. In fact, she'll probably be glad you asked, relieved to talk about your father and her. People do like to unburden themselves, especially mothers to their daughters."

I doubted my mother would feel this way, but I said, "I hope so, Sash. You know only too well that she and I have our differences. But my mother does love me, and I love her, even though she can be exasperating. And today I felt something else for her, something different—a rush of genuine sympathy, and a certain kind of . . . aching sorrow. I realized that she probably hadn't had it easy with Daddy. It was at that moment it occurred to me that I was being unfair, unjust. I think I've always been somewhat blinded to reality because of my adoration of my father."

"You might have been unjust, yes, but you can't change that now, honey. What's done is done. I'm glad you had this . . . this revelation, as you call it." Sarah cleared her throat, and looking me straight in the eye, she said, "Your father was never there for you, Mal. Your mother *always* was."

I gaped at her, about to protest, but clamped my mouth firmly shut. I realized that Sarah had spoken only the truth. Whenever there had been a crisis during the years I was growing up, my father had inevitably been abroad. It was my mother who had coped with my problems during my adolescence and teenage years and even when I was older.

I nodded. "You're right," I said at last, acknowledging the veracity of her words. Then with a twinge of dismay I realized this was the first time I had ever been disloyal to my father in my thoughts, let alone in my words. But he had most likely been as much at fault as my mother, when it came to the disintegration of their marriage.

She got up and walked around the table to my side, hugged me against her body. "I love you," she whispered.

"And I love you, Best Friend," I said, squeezing her hand, which rested on my shoulder.

Straightening, she said with a light laugh, "I'd better go inside and get dressed. I don't want to be caught in my robe when your guests arrive."

I also stood. "And I must finish setting these tables." As I spoke I picked up a handful of red-and-white checked napkins and began to fold them in half.

Sarah was a few yards away from me when she swung around and said, "It's going to be a good day, Mal. *This* Fourth of July is going to be the best you've ever had. I promise."

I believed her.

9

I could see them through the French doors of the sunroom, playing together on the terrace. My beautiful children.

And how glorious they looked this morning. They were like little Botticelli angels, with their sun-streaked blonde hair, the most vivid of blue eyes which echoed their father's, and rounded baby cheeks as smooth and pink as ripe peaches.

I drew closer to the glass, listening to them chattering away together. They were close to each other, quite inseparable, in fact. They were so alike, yet in many ways they were very different.

Lissa was saying, "Yes, Jamie, that's *good*. Give them a flag *each*. We've got a big flag on our house, so they should, too."

"I don't know when they'll *see* their flags," Jamie muttered, casting his sister a quick glance before turning back to the work at hand.

My six-year-old son was sticking a small Stars and Stripes into the top of the wall, trying to secure it between the cracks. "This one's for Tabitha and Henry. But they won't come out to look at it when there are lots of people here, and Mom's having a *big* lot of people for lunch. Vanessa and Luke are coming, too."

"Ugh!" Lissa made an ugly face. "How do you know?"

"Grandma Jess told me."

"Ugh," Lissa said again. Stepping over to her twin, she put her arm around his shoulders in a companionable way and gazed at the flag stuck on top of the wall. "Don't worry, Jamie, the little chipmunks'll see their flag tonight."

"Are you sure?"

"Oh, *yes*. They come out to play at night. They all do, the black snake and the bunny, as well," Lissa reassured her twin, sounding as self-confident as she usually did. My daughter was one of the most positive people I've ever met. "Now," she continued, "let's put the flag in the side of the wall over there, for Algernon. And another one for Angelica."

Jamie nodded and ran to do what she suggested. But almost at once the flag fell down onto the terrace. "It won't stay," he cried, turning to Lissa, as always seeking her guidance. She had been born first and was the more aggressive of the two; Jamie was often diffident, more sensitive about certain things, and he had inherited my artistic nature.

"Does Dad have any of that funny glue he sometimes uses?" Lissa asked. "Mom says it'll stick anything."

"Yes, it will," I said, pushing open the door and stepping out onto the terrace. "But I don't want you messing around with Krazy Glue this morning. It's tricky to use and dries very quickly, and it can stick to your skin."

"But Mommy—" Lissa began.

I cut her off. "Not today, honey. Anyway, I think I have a much better solution to your problem, Jamie. Why not use some of your Silly Putty? You can press a small mound of it onto the wall where you want to place the flag, and then stick the flag into the Silly Putty. I bet the flag'll hold very securely."

"Oh, that's a good idea, Mom!" Jamie exclaimed, grinning from ear to ear. "I'll go and get it."

"Slow down, you'll fall!" I shouted after him, watching him race away as fast as his little legs would carry him. Trixy was hard on his heels, bouncing along by his side.

I looked down at Lissa and smiled, thinking how adorable she was in her pink T-shirt and matching shorts. "So, you decided to give flags to all of our little friends who live in the wall," I said. "That's nice."

She nodded, gazing up at me solemn-faced and serious. "Yes, Mommy. We can't leave them out on the Fourth of July. Every American house should have a flag, *you* said so."

"That I did, and where did you get your flags?"

"Daddy bought them in that shop near the vegetable stand. And he bought you some flowers." She stopped abruptly, her eyes opened wider, and she clapped a hand over her mouth. "Oh, Mom, I shouldn't have told you that. It's a surprise. Pretend you don't know when Dad gives you flowers."

I nodded. "I've just forgotten what you said."

Jamie came back with Trixy in tow, and he began to work with the Silly Putty, breaking off small pieces and making mounds.

Lissa stood watching him for a moment, then she swung her head to me and said, "It's hot, Mommy. Can I take my T-shirt off?"

"I don't think you should, darling. I don't want you to expose yourself to the sun. You know how easily you get a sunburn."

"But it's soooo hot," she complained.

"How about a dip in the pool?" I suggested.

"Oh, yes! Goody! Goody!" She clapped her hands together and beamed at me, then cried to Jamie, "Let's go and get our swimsuits, Fishy."

"*Fishy?*" I repeated. "Why do you call your brother that?"

"Daddy says he's like a fish in the water, the best swimmer, too."

"That's true, but you're not so bad yourself, Pumpkin."

"Mom, can we take Swellen into the pool for a swim with us?"

"Don't be ridiculous, Lissa, of course you can't. Sue Ellen's only a goldfish. She'd drown in the pool. And she'd be scared to death."

"She wouldn't, Mom, honest. And she's a *brave* little fish." Lissa threw Jamie a pointed look, and added, "A very, very, very brave little fish."

"I didn't hurt your fish," Jamie mumbled without looking at his sister.

"Of course you didn't, honey," I exclaimed. Turning to Lissa, I went on, "You really can't take her into the pool with you, even though she is an *extremely* brave little fish. You see, the chlorine might poison her, and you wouldn't want that to happen, would you?"

My daughter shook her head; her blue eyes had grown larger and rounder.

I explained carefully, "Sue Ellen's better off in the goldfish bowl in your bedroom. Truly she is."

"How do you like the flags, Mom?" Jamie stepped back, his head to one side, looking proudly at his handiwork.

"They're great! You've done a terrific job," I enthused.

"Hi, Mrs. Keswick," Jenny said, coming around the corner of the house.

"There you are, Jen dear," I replied, returning her smile. I was going to miss our pretty, young au pair when she went back to England in November. I must talk to Diana about finding a replacement; it wouldn't be easy. Jennifer Grange was unusual, special, and we had all become very attached to her.

"Can I do anything to help with lunch?" Jenny asked, joining Jamie near the wall. An approving expression settled on her face as she glanced at the flags, and she squeezed his shoulder affectionately.

"You can't do a thing, Jen," I said. "Just keep an eye on your charges, make sure they don't get into any mischief. And you—"

"Mommy says we can go swimming," Lissa interrupted.

"But I want you *in* that pool with them, Jenny," I said.

"Of course, Mrs. Keswick. I'd never let them go into the water alone, you know that. I'll just go inside and get their swimsuits."

Lissa said, "We don't have to sit at the kids table, do we?"

"Well, yes, of course you do." I looked down at her, frowning slightly, wondering what this was all about.

"We don't want to, Mom," Jamie informed me.

"Why ever not?"

"We want to sit with you and Dad," he explained.

"Oh, Jamie, there just isn't room, honey. Anyway, you should be with your little guests. You have to look after them."

"Vanessa and Luke. Ugh! Ugh!" He grimaced, squeezed his eyes tightly shut, and grimaced again.

"Don't you like them?" I was baffled by this sudden antipathy toward our neighbors' children, with whom they had frequently played, and quite happily so, in the past.

Opening his eyes, Jamie muttered, "Vanessa smells funny, Mom, like Great-grandma's fur coat."

"*Mothballs*," I said. "Like mothballs?" I stared at him, raising a brow. "How peculiar. Are you sure, Jamie?"

He nodded vigorously. "Yep." He grinned at me. "Maybe they keep *her* in mothballs, Mom, like Great-grandma Adelia keeps her fur coat in mothballs. In that funny wood closet of hers. Ha ha ha ha." He laughed hilariously in the way that only a little boy can.

I had to laugh myself.

Lissa giggled and began to sing, "Smelly old mothballs, smelly old mothballs, Vanessa stinks of smelly old mothballs."

"Ssssh! Don't be naughty," I reprimanded. But I found myself still laughing indulgently. Glancing at Jamie, I now asked, "And why don't you like Luke all of a sudden?"

"He wants to be the boss, and we're the boss."

I threw my son a questioning look.

Jamie said, "Me and Lissa, *we're* the boss."

"I see. However, I think you will have to sit with them for lunch today. There's not much alternative, kids. Come on, do it as a favor to me, please."

"Can the grandmas sit with us?" Lissa asked. "Please, Mommy."

"I don't know . . . Well, maybe. Oh, why not. Okay, yes."

"Oh, goody, we like *them*," Jamie said.

"I'm glad to hear it," I murmured, wondering how I would have coped if they had hated their grandmothers.

"We *love* them," Jamie corrected himself.

"They give us lots of presents," Lissa confided.

"And money," Jamie added. *"Lots of it."*

"They're not supposed to do that!" I exclaimed, shaking my head and averting my face to conceal a smile. There was nothing quite so startling as the honesty of children; it could be brutal, and invariably it took my breath away.

Jamie tugged at my hand.

"Yes, darling, what is it?"

"Who did you belong to before Dad got you?"

"Your grandmother, I guess. Grandma Jess. Why?"

"So we belong to you and Dad, don't we?" Lissa asserted.

"You bet!" I exclaimed.

Hunkering down on my haunches, I swept them both into my arms and hugged them to me. They smelled so sweet and young and fresh. I loved that small child's smell . . . of shampoo, soap, and talcum powder, and milk, cookies, and sweet breath. And I loved *them* so much, my little Botticelli angels.

It was Jamie who pulled slightly away, looked into my face intently, and touched my cheek with his grubby, warm little hand. "Mom, will the new baby belong to all of us, or just you and Dad?"

"*Baby!* What baby?"

"The one you and Dad are trying to make." His fine blond brows drew together in a frown. "And what do you *make* it out of, Mom?"

I was so taken aback I was speechless for a moment. Then before I could think of an answer, Lissa announced with some assurance, "They make it out of love." She smiled up at me, obviously extremely pleased with herself, and nodded her head, looking like a little old woman imbued with wisdom.

"What do you mean, Lissa?" her brother asked before I had a chance to say anything.

I jumped in swiftly. "Well, we are trying to make a baby, that's true. When did your father tell you this?"

"When he was giving us breakfast this morning," Jamie said. "He was cross with us, we were making too much noise. He said we'd soon have to fend for ourselves, that we'd better start growing up real quick. He said we'd have to look after the new baby when it came, be responsible children and take care of it. Who *will* it belong to, Mom?"

"All of us. If we succeed, of course."

"You mean you might not be able to make it?" Lissa asked.

"Afraid so," I admitted.

"Good. Don't make it. I like it this way, just us and Trixy!" she exclaimed.

"If you do make it and we don't like it, can we give it away?" Jamie asked.

"Certainly not," I spluttered.

"But when Miss Petigrew had kittens, Anna gave them away," he reminded me.

"This is not quite the same thing, Jamie darling. A baby's a baby, a kitten's a kitten."

"Can we call the baby Rover, Mom?"

"I don't think so, Jamie."

"That's a dog's name, silly," Lissa cried.

"But it's my favorite name," Jamie shot back.

"It's the name for a boy dog. You can't call a baby girl that," Lissa told him, sounding very superior.

"If it's a girl, we could call it Roveress or Roverette."

"You're stupid, Jamie Keswick!" his sister shrieked, throwing him the most scornful look. "You're a stupid boy."

"No, I'm not. You're stupid!"

"Stop it, both of you," I admonished.

"Mom." Jamie fixed his vivid blue eyes on me. "Please tell me, how do you make a baby out of love?"

I thought for a moment, wondering how to effectively explain this to them without resorting to a pack of lies, when Lissa leaned toward Jamie and said, "*Sex.* That's what makes a baby."

Startled, I exclaimed, "Who told you that?"

"Mary Jane Atkinson, the girl who sits next to me at school. Her mother just made a baby with sex."

"I see. And what else did Mary Jane tell you?"

"Nothing, Mom."

"Mmmm."

Thankfully, Jenny came back just then, and the conversation about babies was curtailed. Jenny was already wearing a bathing suit and carrying swim wear for the children.

"Come on, put these on," she said, handing Jamie a pair of trunks and Lissa her minuscule pink-and-yellow bikini, which Diana had bought for her in Paris.

"I want them to wear their water wings, Jen, they mustn't go in the pool without them. Or without you," I cautioned.

"Don't worry, Mrs. Keswick, I'll look after them properly." So saying she turned to Lissa and helped her to put her bikini top on, and then she led the twins to the shallow end of the swimming pool. Picking up a set of water wings she slipped these onto Lissa's arms before doing the same for Jamie.

Within seconds the three of them were in the pool, laughing and splashing around in the water, having the best of times.

I watched them for a few minutes, enjoying their antics, pleased they were having such fun. I was about to go into the kitchen to see what was happening when Andrew appeared at my side. After kissing me on the cheek, he handed me a huge bunch of red and white carnations.

"Sorry they didn't have any blue ones to make exactly the right color scheme for today," he murmured against my cheek and kissed me again.

"They only have those odd colors occasionally. Usually on Saint Patrick's Day, when they dye them green," I said. "And thank you, darling." I peered at him closely. "The twins think we're trying to make a baby, Andrew."

"Well, we are."

"They're riddled with curiosity about it. Why on earth did you tell them?"

He laughed. "I didn't mean to, it wasn't planned. Honestly, Puss. It just popped out. They were being impossible this morning, and Lissa's become something of a Miss Know-It-All. I wanted to bring them up short, so I gave them a lecture about being more adult in their behavior. And that's when I mentioned a new baby. The kids were rendered speechless, so it had the desired effect. Momentarily." He chuckled again. "I can tell you this, the grannies were delighted. Absolutely thrilled."

"What did you just call me?" Diana exclaimed, stepping out of the sunroom onto the terrace.

"Oh, hi, Ma," Andrew greeted her. Then another laugh broke free, and he hugged her to him. "*Granny.* I called you and Jessica grannies, Ma. But I have to admit, you're the greatest-looking grannies I've ever seen in my entire life. The most beautiful. And you both have fabulous legs."

"Your husband's quite the flatterer," his mother said to me and winked.

"He's only telling the truth, Diana," I answered and edged toward the sunroom door. "I've got to go in and change for lunch now, if you don't mind."

"Go right ahead, Mal, I'll just sit here and watch my grand-children frolicking in the water." She sat on a white terrace chair, her eyes immediately focusing on the pool.

"I'll come with you." Andrew said to me. He took hold of my arm, and together we went through the French doors. Trixy followed us automatically, scampering along behind.

As we crossed the sunroom, Andrew whispered in my ear, "Want to try for the baby now? Or don't you have time?"

"Oh, you! You're impossible! Incorrigible!" But despite my words, I smiled up at him.

Bending over me, Andrew kissed the tip of my nose. "I do love you, Puss," he murmured, his expression suddenly serious. Then his face changed yet again, and a mischievous glint flickered in his blue eyes as he said, "Listen, I'm willing to try any time, anywhere. All you have to do is say the word."

I laughed. "Tonight?"

"You've got a date," he said.

10

Connecticut, October 1988

The birds had come back.

A great flock of them had landed on the lawn not far from the swimming pool, just as they had done yesterday. They perched there now, immobile, silent, creating a swath of black against the grass, which was strewn with fallen autumn leaves of burnished red and gold.

I could see them quite clearly through the windows of my studio. They looked for all the world like birds of prey to me. An involuntary shiver ran through me at this thought, bringing gooseflesh to my neck and face.

Putting down my paintbrush, I stepped around the easel and opened the door.

Observing the birds from the threshold, I could not help wondering why they still sat out there. Several hours ago, when I was in the bedroom, I had seen them land, and the amazing thing was that they continued to linger, not moving a single feather nor making the faintest twitter of a sound.

Out of the corner of my eye I caught a flash of color, and I swung around to look over at the house.

Sarah was coming down the steps of the terrace, carrying a tray. She was bundled up against the autumnal chill, dressed in an oversized gray sweater, gray wool pants, and black suede boots. A long, scarlet wool scarf was flung around her neck, and it was this which had caught my attention a second before.

"What were you staring at so intently?" she asked as she drew closer.

"Those black birds over there," I answered, gesturing toward them. "They keep coming back."

Pausing in her tracks, Sarah glanced over her shoulder and grimaced. "They look so strange," she murmured. "So . . . ominous."

"I know what you mean," I said and opened the door wider to let her come into the studio.

"I thought you might like a cup of coffee," she said. "Mind if I join you? Or am I interrupting your work?"

"No, you're not, and I'd love a cup." Turning away from the peculiar gathering of birds, I closed the door and followed her inside. Moving a box of watercolors and a jar of water, I made room for the tray on a small table in front of the old sofa.

Sarah sat down and poured the coffee. As she glanced up and looked through the window, she exclaimed, "Jesus, what *are* those birds doing on the lawn? There're so many of them, Mal."

"I know, and it *is* weird, isn't it? The way they sit like that, I mean. But we do get a lot of wildlife out here these days. The wetlands down there near the beaver dam are a sanctuary, and Canada geese and mallard ducks come and occupy the pond, and sometimes a blue heron pays us a visit. Andrew's even seen a hawk from time to time. At least, he thinks it's a hawk."

"Are those blackbirds?"

"Crows," I replied. "Or maybe rooks. What do you think?"

"Search me, I'm not a bird-watcher, I'm afraid."

I laughed, took a sip of coffee, and bit into a macaroon.

Sarah did the same, then looked over the rim of her coffee cup and asked, "Have you made your mind up yet? About going to London to meet Andrew next weekend?"

"I think so. I'd like to go, Sarah, since he's going to be stuck there for another two weeks. That's if you don't mind coming up here with Jennifer and the twins. Actually, if you prefer it, you could move into the apartment in the city for the few days I'll be gone."

"You know I love to play Mommy, how much I adore Jamie and Lissa, and I'm delighted to come up here. Frankly, these quiet weekends far from the maddening crowd are a blessing. I seem to be able to really recharge my batteries out here. And, God knows, I need to do that these days. There's such a lot of pressure at work. So make your plans. I'll hold down the fort, and very happily. In any case, I—" She broke off and stared out the window facing onto the lawn.

I followed her glance, then sprang up and ran to the door. I pulled it open and stepped outside. The birds had taken off in a great flurry all of a sudden, rising up off the lawn with a flapping and whirring of wings. I craned my neck backward to watch them soar upward into the gray and bitter fall sky. I saw at once that the span of their wings was very wide; they were big birds. They climbed up higher, wheeling and turning against the leaden sky, then circled over the studio, casting a dark shadow across its roof.

"They're not blackbirds or crows," I said. "They're far too large. Those birds are ravens."

"Shades of Edgar Allan Poe," Sarah intoned in a low voice directly behind me.

She startled me. I hadn't realized she had followed me to the door. I swung around to face her. "You made me jump! Gave me quite a start!" I exclaimed. "I didn't know you were standing there. And what do you mean, shades of Edgar Allan Poe?"

"Ravens are very Poe-ish," she said, "always in his writings. They're considered to be birds of ill omen, harbingers of death, you know."

A coldness trickled through me. I felt myself shivering. "Don't say things like that, Sash; you frighten me."

"Don't be so silly," she laughed. "I'm only kidding."

"You know very well I've never liked anything that's macabre or ghoulish or has to do with the occult—" I didn't finish my sentence. Sarah was staring at me, concern reflected in her eyes.

"What is it?" I asked. "Why are you looking at me like that? So *oddly*."

"You've gone quite pale, Mal. I'm sorry, honestly I am. I'd forgotten that you're a bit squeamish about those sort of things."

"And you're not," I retorted, trying to recoup, forcing a laugh. But I was still cold all over, and irrational as it was, I felt a peculiar sense of apprehension.

"Only too true," Sarah agreed. "The more ghoulish and scary something is, the better I like it, whether in a film or a book." She laughed again. "Poe was my favorite until Stephen King and Anne Rice came along."

"I'm afraid I have different tastes," I remarked. Closing the door behind me, I walked back to the sofa.

Sarah strolled over to the long table under the window at the back of my studio and stood looking down at the watercolors spread out on it. "These are terrific, Mally!" she cried, sounding surprised. Her voice was suddenly full of merriment. "Oh, I love these drawings of the creatures in the wall! Here's Algernon, the black snake, with his head in the cookie jar, or I should say the chocolate-covered cherry jar. And how adorable—Angelica in her Easter bonnet off to the Fifth Avenue parade, and the chipmunks making a cradle for the baby they're going to adopt." She turned around; her face was wreathed in smiles. "Mal, you're brilliant, a genius. These are delightful paintings, full of charm and humor. You've missed your way. You should be illustrating children's books."

"That's sweet of you to say, but I have my hands full with so many other things, quite aside from Andrew and the twins," I said. "But I'm pleased you like them. I had fun creating the books, and Andrew helped me with the editing of the stories."

"The kids are going to love the books when they find them in their Christmas stockings," Sarah said.

"I hope so, considering all the time I've put into them."

"You ought to try to get them published, Mal."

I shook my head. "I'm not sure they're good enough."

"Take my word for it, they're good enough."

"I wrote and painted them for Jamie and Lissa—just for them, and that's the way I prefer it."

After Sarah left the studio, I picked up my brush and went back to the portrait on the easel. It was of Diana, and I was painting it as a Christmas gift for Andrew.

I had done the initial drawings in July, when she was visiting us, and taken a number of photographs of her in this pose at that time. Working in oils for the past two months, I was now almost finished. I spent a good hour concentrating on Diana's hair color, trying to capture the reddish lights in it, and once I felt I had it exactly right and couldn't improve upon it, I put the brush down. I needed to step away from the portrait for a couple of hours, to get a new perspective on it; also, it was almost lunchtime, and I wanted to eat with the twins, Jenny, and Sarah.

Taking up a rag, I dipped it in turpentine and cleaned the brushes I had used this morning. When I finished, I turned off the lights, pulled on my heavy cardigan, and headed for the door. But before I reached it the phone began to ring, and I picked up the receiver. "Hello?"

"It's me, darling," Andrew said from London.

"Hi, honey, how are you?" I asked, smiling into the phone, glad to hear his voice.

"I'm okay, Mal, but missing you and the twins like hell."

"We miss you, too."

"You are coming over here next weekend, aren't you?" he asked, sounding anxious.

"Nothing could keep me away! Sarah's agreed to bring the twins and Jenny up here, and they'll have fun together."

"And so will we, Puss, I can promise you that," my husband said.

PART TWO

KILGRAM CHASE

11

London, November 1988

On Thursday morning at nine-thirty I flew to London on the *Concorde*.

Andrew had insisted that I take the supersonic flight because it was so fast, only three and a half hours long, reasoning that since I was going for just a few days, it would give us more time together. He had overcome my objections with the assurance that his office was paying for my very expensive ticket.

I quickly discovered it was a terrific way to fly. I had hardly had a chance to eat a snack, relax, and read my Colette when we were landing at Heathrow. Another good thing about flying Concorde was the way the luggage came off the plane and onto the carousel so quickly. The porter I found was soon stacking my cases on his trolley and whizzing me through customs. As we came out into the terminal I was still blinking at the efficiency and speed with which everything had moved.

I looked around for Andrew and saw him before he saw me. He was standing just beyond the barrier, looking handsome and dashing with a trenchcoat thrown nonchalantly over his shoulders. He wore a gray pinstripe suit, a pale blue shirt, and a plain gray silk tie, and as always he was immaculate, not only in his clothes, but from the top of his well-groomed head to the tip of his highly polished brown shoes.

A rush of excitement hit me at the sight of him. It always did when we had been apart. He was the only man I had ever loved, the only man I would ever want.

Suddenly he saw me, and his face broke into smiles. I raised my hand in greeting, smiled back, and hurried forward as he moved toward me. A split second later he was holding me in his arms, hugging me to him and kissing me. As I clung to him I thought how extraordinary it was that less than four hours after leaving Kennedy I was standing here on English soil, embracing my husband.

We drew apart finally, and I said, "My bags are on the trolley," looking over my shoulder as I spoke.

Andrew glanced at the porter and nodded.

"'Evening, guv'nor," the porter said. "Got a car waiting, have you?"

"Yes, in the parking area just outside this building," Andrew told him.

"Right ho!" The porter went trundling ahead of us, pushing the trolley. We walked after him.

Andrew turned to me and lifted a brow. "You've come for the duration, have you?"

"Duration?"

"Of my stay. You've certainly brought enough luggage."

I laughed. "Only two cases and a makeup bag."

"Rather large cases, though," Andrew murmured, half smiling.

I threw my husband a flirtatious look and said, "But I'll stay if you want me to."

"Will you really, darling?" His face lit up, and there was a sudden eagerness in his eyes, excitement in his manner.

Instantly I regretted teasing him and explained in a more serious tone, "I'd love to stay longer than we'd planned, Andrew, but you know I can't. I've got to go back on Monday."

"Why?"

"I can't leave the children for longer than a weekend."

"'Course you can, darling. The twins'll be fine. They've got Jenny and your mother, *and* Sarah to watch over them."

"Sarah's working during the week," I pointed out.

"Your mother isn't, and Jenny is very reliable. They're as safe as houses with her."

"But we agreed I'd only come here for the weekend," I reminded him. I stopped. Staring hard at him, I said, "I shouldn't have risen to the bait just now, and I shouldn't have teased you, said I'd stay longer. Honestly, it's just not possible. I'd feel uneasy, Andrew."

Suddenly he looked awfully glum, but he made no further comment. We walked on in silence.

Making a snap decision, I stopped again, turned to him, and said, "Look, I'll stay on until Tuesday, honey. I think that'll be all right. Okay? Is that okay with you?"

Smiling, he nodded and exclaimed, "Mal, that's great, just great!" Then taking hold of my elbow firmly, he hurried me forward.

We went through the glass doors of the terminal, crossed the road, and entered the parking area where the porter was already waiting with my suitcases on the trolley.

I shivered. It was a damp November night and quite cold, typical English winter weather.

A dark green Rolls-Royce moved slowly toward us and braked. A uniformed chauffeur jumped out, nodded to me, and said, "Good evening, madam," and went to help the porter load the bags into the trunk before I even had a chance to acknowledge him.

Turning to the porter, I said, "Thanks for helping me," and walked over to the Rolls. Andrew tipped him and followed me. Bundling me into the car, Andrew then stepped in behind me and closed the door. Immediately he took me in his arms and gave me a long kiss, then pulling away, he said, "It's so good to have you here, Mal."

"I know. It's the same for me," I answered. "Wonderful to be here with you."

The chauffeur got in and turned on the ignition. A few seconds later we were leaving the airport buildings behind and heading out onto the main road in the direction of London.

As the car sped along, I glanced at my husband. My eyes lingered on his face, and I saw, on closer examination, that he looked much more tired than I had realized. There were dark smudges under his eyes, and in repose, his face appeared unexpectedly weary. A general air of fatigue enveloped him.

Frowning, I said, "You've had a much rougher time than you've told me, haven't you?"

Andrew gave a quick nod, squeezed my hand, and inclined his head in the direction of the driver, obviously not wanting to speak in front of him. He murmured, sotto voce, "I'll tell you later."

"All right." Opening my bag, I took out two envelopes with *Dad* printed across their fronts in uneven, wobbly, childlike letters. Handing them to Andrew, I said, "Lissa and Jamie have each written you a card."

Looking pleased, he put on his horn-rimmed glasses, opened the envelopes, and began to read.

I leaned back against the soft cream leather of my seat and stared out the window. It was just six-thirty, and dark, so there was not much to see. The road was slick with rain, and the traffic at this hour was heavy. But the Rolls-Royce rolled steadily along at a good speed, and I knew that in spite of the rain, which was now falling in torrents, we would arrive at Claridge's in an hour, or thereabouts.

Later that evening, after I had called Jenny in New York, unpacked, showered, redone my makeup, and changed my clothes, Andrew took me to dinner at the Connaught Hotel.

"For sentimental reasons, Mal darling," he said as we walked from Claridge's to the other hotel, which was situated on Carlos Place.

It was still cold and damp, but the heavy downpour had long since ceased, and I was glad to get a little air after being cooped up on the plane. Anyway, I always liked to walk in London, especially in Mayfair around the dinner hour.

The traffic was far lighter and the streets were much less crowded; in fact, they were almost empty at this time of day. There was something charming and beautiful about this lovely old part of London. Certain streets in Mayfair were still residential, although some of the elegant Georgian mansions had been turned into offices; nonetheless, the section was very special to me, and it held many fond memories of my courtship.

Once we were settled at our table in the restaurant of the Connaught, Andrew ordered a glass of white wine for me and a very dry martini for himself. As we waited for the drinks to materialize, he started to talk about the London office of Blau, Ames, Braddock and Suskind, and without any prompting from me.

"I think I got over here just in the nick of time," he explained, leaning across the table, pinning me with his eyes. "The place is in a mess, as I sort of indicated to you on the phone the other night. It's been badly managed for the last few years. Joe Braddock's son-in-law doesn't know his ass from his elbow, and Jack Underwood and I will have to do a lot of fancy footwork in order to keep it afloat."

I was incredulous. It had always been a financially successful operation. Until recently, apparently. Startled, I exclaimed, "Do you mean you might have to close the London office?"

He nodded emphatically. "Yep, I sure do. Malcolm Stainley's one of the biggest dummies I've ever met. I don't know what got into Joe. Giving him the European end to run was more than foolhardy. It was criminal. And it *is* the European end, not merely the London office, since most of our French,

German, and Continental business is handled and billed out of here."

"Nepotism, of course," I said. "That's why Malcolm is where he is." Then I asked, "But what exactly did he do, Andrew?"

"He made one hell of a mess, that's for sure," Andrew muttered, falling silent as the waiter arrived with our drinks.

After we had clinked glasses, Andrew went on, "The trouble with Malcolm Stainley is that he hasn't got a clue about people. He can't keep staff, for one thing, and in my opinion that's because he pits people against one another. Anyway, morale is at rock bottom here, and everyone hates his guts. Then again, he's a bit of a cheapskate, so he's always trying to save money—in the wrong ways. For instance, he hires second-rate talent instead of going for the best and the brightest. In consequence, we lose out on a lot of bids we make to potential clients, because the presentations are lousy." Andrew shook his head. "He's shown very flawed judgment on many different levels."

"But what's the solution? After all, Malcolm is married to Joe's daughter, and Ellen likes living in London. So you can bet Joe isn't going to remove her husband, or fire him. At least, that's the way I read it."

Andrew looked thoughtful as he sat and sipped his martini without responding.

Finally, he said, "No, I don't suppose Joe is going to do anything about Malcolm, so Jack and I will have to render the bugger helpless and take his power away to boot."

"And how do you plan to do that?" I asked, raising a brow.

"Appoint someone else to run the London office, get it on the straight and narrow."

"But Joe may not agree to that. And Malcolm *surely* won't," I ventured.

Andrew gave me a small, very knowing smile. "Joe *will* agree to certain things, Mal. Jack, Harvey Colton, and I have been talking retirement to him, and in no uncertain terms, these last few months, and he will agree to do what we propose. In order to stay on with the agency himself. He loathes the idea of retiring, as I thought you'd realized."

I nodded but made no comment. Joe Braddock was close to senile, in my opinion, and should have been put out to pasture eons ago.

Andrew continued, "You're right, of course, in that Joe won't like seeing his son-in-law demoted or displaced. And neither will Malcolm the Great himself. He'd put up one hell of a bloody fight, no two ways about it, if we said we wanted him to go. So we're not going to do that. Instead we're going to kick him upstairs, give him a fancy title." Andrew paused dramatically, then finished, "And we'll tie his hands. Manacle them, if necessary." He grinned at me conspiratorially. "That leaves the way open for a new, hands-on guy who'll pull the company out of the mire, get it back on course. And lead it to financial security. *We hope.*"

"Do you have someone in mind?" I wondered out loud.

"Jack and Harvey wanted me to take it on. However, I said thanks but no thanks. Frankly, Mal, I didn't want to uproot us all, take the kids out of Trinity, move to London for a couple of years. Because that's what it would mean. It's going to take two, maybe even three years to pull this operation around."

"Oh," I said, staring at him. "But I wouldn't have minded living in London for two or three years, Andrew, really I wouldn't. If you haven't already hired someone else yet, why don't you take the position after all?"

He shook his head. "No way, Mal, it's not my cup of tea, cleaning up somebody else's mess. Besides which, Harvey, Jack, and I have been streamlining the New York operation. I want to keep on doing that, it's very important to me." Narrowing those brilliantly blue eyes at me, he said softly, "Oh, hell, darling, you're disappointed, aren't you?"

"No, I'm not," I protested, although he had read my thoughts very accurately.

"I *know* you, Mallory Keswick," my husband said in the quietest of voices. "And I think you *are* disappointed . . . just a little bit."

"Well, yes," I admitted. Then I gave him a reassuring smile. "But I'm not important in this instance. It's your decision. After all, it is *your* career, and you're the one it affects the most. Whatever you decide about where you work, be it agency or city or country, it'll be okay with me, I promise you."

"Thanks for that. I just don't want to live in England," he answered, "but then you've always known this. I love Manhattan and working on Madison Avenue. The rhythm of the city excites and invigorates me, and I love my job. Not only that, I'd miss Indian Meadows, and so would you."

"That's true, I would. So who have you hired? Or haven't you found anyone yet?"

"Jack Underwood. He's going to move over here and tackle the job. In fact, he's flying in next Wednesday so that we can go over things together before I leave. He'll stay on, as of this coming week, and assume the running of the British company immediately. It's going to be a permanent move for him. At least, he'll be here for a few years. I'm going to miss him."

"So you and Harvey will have to cope on your own in New York?"

"That we will. And we do have our jobs cut out for us. But we both believe we can bring the agency back to its former standing. Although it has been losing ground a bit, we're still big in certain areas of advertising, and we have a roster of good and very loyal old clients."

Reaching out, I took hold of his hand, which rested on the table. "I haven't seen you looking so tired for a long time, darling. I guess it has been pretty rough whilst you've been here in London. Much rougher than you've let on to me."

"Mal, that's true to a certain extent." He sighed under his breath. "And I have to admit that very long hours and a disgruntled staff have had their debilitating effect, no two ways about it." Then he winked, taking me by surprise, and in a lighter, gayer tone, he added, "But now you're here, my darling. We're going to have a lovely weekend together, and we're not going to discuss business. Not at all. Agreed?"

"I agree to anything you say or want."

A dark brow lifted, and he laughed a deep-throated laugh. He said, "Let's order another drink, and then we'll look at the menu."

12

It was gray and overcast on Friday morning, and as I left Claridge's Hotel, heading toward Berkeley Square, I glanced up at the sky. It was leaden and presaged rain, which Andrew had predicted before he had left for the office earlier.

Instead of walking to Diana's, which I liked to do, I hailed a cab and got in. Just in time, too. It began to drizzle as I slammed the door and gave the cabbie the address. English weather, I thought glumly, staring out the taxi window. It's always raining. But one didn't come to England for the weather; there were other, more important reasons to be here. I had always loved England and the English, and London was my most favorite city in the entire world. I loved it even more than my hometown, New York.

I settled back against the cab seat, glad to be here. On second thought, it could hail and snow and storm for all I cared. The weather was quite irrelevant to me.

My mother-in-law's antique shop was located at the far end of the King's Road, and as the cab flew along Knightsbridge, heading in that direction, I made a mental note to go to Harrods and Harvey Nichols later in the day, to do some of my Christmas shopping. Since we would be spending the holidays with Diana, I could have gifts for her, the children, and Andrew shipped directly to her house in Yorkshire. Certainly it would save me the trouble of bringing everything with me from New York in December. The stores would probably gift wrap them, too.

Andrew had kept it a secret from his mother that I was joining him in London for a long weekend; when I had announced my presence to her on the phone last night, she had reacted in her usual way. She was full of excitement, so very pleased to hear my voice, and she had immediately asked me to have lunch with her today.

Once we arrived at the shop, I paid off the cabbie and stood outside in the street, gazing at the beautiful things which graced the window of Diana Howard Keswick Antiques.

I feasted my eyes on a pair of elegant bronze *doré* candlesticks, French, probably from the eighteenth century, which stood on a handsome console table with a marble top and an intricately carved wood base, also eighteenth-century French, I was quite sure of that.

After a few moments, I looked beyond these rare and priceless objects, peering inside as best I could. I could just make out Diana standing at the back of the shop near her desk, talking to a man who was obviously a customer. She was gesturing with her hands in that most expressive way she had, and then she turned to point out a Flemish tapestry, which was hanging on the wall behind her. They stood looking at it together.

Opening the door, I went inside.

I couldn't help thinking how marvelous she looked this morning. She was wearing a bright red wool suit, simple, tailored, elegant, and her double-stranded pearl choker. Both the vivid color and the milky sheen of the pearls were perfect foils for her glossy brown hair and tawny-gold complexion.

It particularly pleased me that she was wearing red today, since I had painted her in a scarlet silk shirt and the same choker, which she usually wore and which was her trademark, in a sense. Observing her, I was instantly reassured that I had captured the essence of her on my canvas—her warmth and beauty and an inner grace that seemed to radiate from her. I hoped Andrew was going to like my portrait of his mother, which Sarah says is one of the best things I've ever done.

The moment Diana saw me she excused herself and hurried forward, a wide smile lighting up her face, her pale gray-blue eyes reflecting the same kind of eagerness and joy which I usually associate with Andrew. He always has that same happy, anticipatory look when he is seeing me for the first time after we've been apart; it is spontaneous and so very loving.

"Darling, you're here!" Diana cried, grasping my arm. "I can't believe it, and it's such a lovely surprise. I'm so happy to see you!"

My smile was as affectionate as hers, and my happiness as keenly felt. "Hello, Diana. You're the best thing London has to offer, aside from your son, of course."

She laughed gaily, in that special warm and welcoming way of hers, and we quickly embraced. Then she led me forward.

"Mal, I'd like to introduce Robin McAllister," she said. "Robin, this is my daughter-in-law, Mallory Keswick."

The man, who was tall, handsome, distinguished, and elegantly dressed, inclined his head politely. He shook my hand. "I'm pleased to meet you, Mrs. Keswick," he said.

"And I'm happy to meet you, Mr. McAllister," I responded.

Diana said, "Mal, dear, would you please excuse me for a moment or two? I wish to show Mr. McAllister a painting downstairs. I won't be very long, then we can get off to lunch."

"Don't worry about me," I said, "I'll just wander around the shop. I can see at a glance that you have some wonderful things. As you usually do."

Before my mother-in-law had a chance to say anything else, I strolled to the other side of her establishment, my eyes roving around, taking everything in.

I loved antiques, and Diana invariably had some of the best and most beautiful available in London, many of them garnered from the great houses of Europe. She traveled extensively on the Continent, looking for all kinds of treasures, but mostly she specialized in eighteenth- and nineteenth-century French furniture, decorative objects, porcelain, and paintings, although she did carry a few English Georgian and Regency pieces as well. However, her impeccable credentials and reputation as a dealer came from her immense knowledge of fine French furniture, which was where her great expertise lay. But like every antiquarian of some importance and distinction, Diana was extremely learned in other areas, well versed in a variety of different design periods from many countries.

I noticed that she was currently showing a collection of Biedermeier furniture in the special-display area of the shop, and even from this distance I could see that it was superb. I was instantly drawn down to the far end of the store, near the staircase leading to the upper floors. Here a small raised platform held the furniture, which was roped off.

I stood looking at the German pieces in awe, admiring the rich, gleaming woods and the incredible craftsmanship. I was especially taken by a circular dining table made of various light-colored woods, most likely fruitwoods, and inlaid with ebony. This was a combination often used in Biedermeier designs at the turn of the century, when the furniture was at the height of its popularity.

What I wouldn't give for a table like that, I thought. But quite aside from the fact that it probably cost the earth—I was positive it did—I had nowhere to put it. Not only that, Indian Meadows was furnished with a mixture of antique English and French country furniture, and although Biedermeier was versatile and plain enough to blend with almost any period or style, it wasn't quite right for us, either for our country home or our Manhattan apartment. Pity, though, I muttered under my breath as I walked on.

Pausing in front of an eighteenth-century French *trumeau*,

which was hanging on a side wall, I admired its beautifully carved wood frame and painted decorative scene set in the top of the frame, wondering what mantelpiece it had hung over, and in which great house? A château in the Loire, I had no doubt. Then I took a peek at myself in its cloudy antique mirror.

My reflection dismayed me. I decided I looked a bit too pale and tired, almost wan under the mass of red hair, but nonetheless quite smart in my dark delphinium-blue wool coat and dress. No wonder I'm looking tired, I suddenly thought, recalling last night. Andrew and I had been very carried away with each other. A small smile slid onto my face, and I glanced down at the floor, remembering. My husband and I hadn't been able to get enough of each other, and despite his tiredness in general, his fatigue over dinner, he had been imbued with an amazing vitality, a rush of energy the moment we had climbed into bed. If we hadn't made another baby last night, I couldn't imagine when we ever would.

"Hello, Mallory, how are you?" a voice said, and I gave a little start and swung around swiftly. I found myself staring into the smiling face of Jane Patterson, Diana's personal assistant.

Taking a step forward, I gave her a quick hug. "How are you, Jane?"

"I couldn't be better," she said, "and you're obviously in the best of health and thriving."

I nodded and told her I was.

She inquired about the twins. I asked about her daughter, Serena. We stood chatting amiably for several seconds.

Out of the corner of my eye, I became aware of sudden movement. I saw Mr. McAllister striding toward the door. He nodded to us curtly as he went out into the street. Right behind him came Diana, hurrying forward on her high heels, throwing a red wool cape around her shoulders with a flourish as she headed in our direction.

"Shall we go, Mal?" she said to me briskly.

Turning to her assistant, my mother-in-law added, "Percy says he'll be happy to hold down the fort whilst you go to lunch, Janey. I should be back around three."

"No problem, Diana," Jane murmured.

She and I said our good-byes.

Diana rushed out into the street, put up her umbrella, and stood on the edge of the sidewalk enthusiastically flagging a cab, ignoring the rain.

Diana took me to the Savoy Hotel in the Strand for lunch.

Even though it was a bit far from her shop, she knew it was one of my favorite places, and she wanted to please me, as she usually did. I protested. Knowing how busy she was, I tried to persuade her to go somewhere closer, but she wouldn't hear of it. She could be as stubborn as her son at times.

We sat at a window table overlooking the Thames in the main restaurant, which I have always preferred to the famous Grill Room where Fleet Street editors, politicians, and theatrical celebrities frequently lunch and dine. It was quieter in here, more leisurely, and anyway, I could never resist this particular view of London. It was superb.

I gazed out the window. There was a mistiness in the air, and the sky was still a strange metallic color, but the heavy, slashing rain had stopped finally. Even the light had begun to change, now casting a pearly haze over the river and the ancient buildings, bathing them in a gauzy softness that seemed suddenly to make them shimmer; the winter sun was finally breaking through the somber clouds. Light on moving water, Turner light, I said to myself, thinking, as I so often did, of my favorite painter.

I lolled back in my chair. I was relaxed and happy, filled with the most extraordinary contentment. How lucky I was—to be in London with my husband, to be here with Diana at the Savoy having lunch, to have my beautiful children. I might even be pregnant again. My life was charmed. I was blessed.

I sipped my wine and smiled at Diana. And she smiled back, reached out, squeezed my hand.

"Andrew's so lucky to have found you, and I'm so lucky to have you, Mal. The daughter I always wanted. You're the best, you know, the very best."

"And so are you, Diana. I was just thinking how lucky *I* am."

She nodded. "I believe we're both rather fortunate." She sipped her wine, continued, "I was so sorry not to be able to come to your mother's wedding. It was simply the worst time for me. I had made my plans such a long time before she invited me. I had to go to a sale in Aix-en-Provence, and then on to Venice. I just couldn't get out of my commitments."

"It was all right, Diana, Mom understood, honestly she did. To tell you the truth, I think she was relieved to keep it small. That's unusual for her, I must admit, since she's such a social animal, but she seemed glad to have just a few people. Us, and David's son and daughter-in-law and grandson. Oh, and Sarah and her mother, of course. Mom's been close to Aunt Pansy ever since Sarah and I were little kids, babies. She didn't even invite her mother, Grandmother Adelia, but then I don't believe *she* was up to it anyway. She's getting a bit senile, poor thing. Such a pity. She used to be so vital."

"She's very old now, isn't she?"

"Ninety-one."

"Oh, my goodness, that *is* old."

"I wouldn't mind living to that age," I said, "as long as I had all my marbles."

Diana laughed, and so did I.

I said, "David Nelson's a nice man, by the way. I've gotten to know him a bit better over the past few months, and he's very genuine. He really does care for Mom."

"I'm glad Jessica finally got married. She's been so lonely for so very long. Marrying David is the wisest thing she could've done."

I looked across the table at Diana, studying her for a second. And then before I could stop myself, I blurted out, "And *you* must be very lonely too, Diana. After all, you're *alone*."

"I think most women, no, let me correct myself, most *people* who are on their own get extremely lonely at different times in their daily lives," she said, smiling faintly.

There was a slight pause, and I saw a look of sadness creep into her eyes before she said slowly, "In a way, loneliness is another kind of death . . . " She did not finish her sentence, merely sat gazing at me.

I was lost for words myself, feeling her wistfulness, her sense of loss and regret more profoundly than I ever had before. She touched me deeply.

A silence fell between us. We sipped our wine, looked out the window, and quietly ignored each other for a moment or two, lost in our own thoughts.

Quite unexpectedly, I had a terrible urge to ask her about my father, to tell her what Andrew and I had concocted about the two of them this past summer. Yes, I will ask her, I made up my mind. But when I turned my face to focus on her, I lost my nerve. I didn't dare say a word to her. Not because she intimidated me, which she didn't, but because she was essentially such a private person. I could not intrude on her privacy, nor could I probe into her personal life.

She caught my eye and flashed me the most brilliant of smiles. She said cheerfully, "But my loneliness doesn't last very long, Mal, only an hour or two, and it only hits me every now and then. Let's face it, I'm very fortunate to have the business. It keeps me fully occupied night and day—traveling abroad, going to auctions and sales on the Continent, taking clients and would-be clients to lunch and dinner, seeing and entertaining foreign dealers, not to mention running the shop. I never seem to have a moment to spare these days. I'm always flying off to France or Italy or Spain. Or somewhere or other."

"And haven't you ever met someone *delicious* on your travels?" I asked. "A suave, sophisticated Frenchman? Or a lyrical, romantic Italian? Or perhaps a dashing, passionate Spaniard?" I couldn't resist teasing her.

Giggling like a schoolgirl, her eyes as merry as I've ever seen them, she shook her head. "'Fraid not, Mal," she said, then lifted her glass to her mouth and took a sip of the wine, a very good Montrachet. She knew her French wines.

At this moment the waiter appeared with our first course.

Diana had ordered leek-and-potato soup, "to fight the chill in the air," she had said to me a short while before as we studied the menus.

I had selected oysters, and a dozen of the Savoy's best Colchesters were staring up at me temptingly. They looked delectable. My mouth watered. I said to Diana, "Whenever I'm here in London, I manage to make a pig of myself with all of the wonderful fish, I love it so much. And I'm afraid I'm about to become Miss Piggy again."

"It's the best fish in the world, at least I think so; and don't forget, it's not fattening."

"As if *you* had to worry," I murmured. I had always admired Diana's sleek figure. Not that I was fat, but she was very slender and shapely for her age.

Pushing my small, sharp fork onto the shell and underneath a plump, succulent oyster, I lifted it up and plopped it into my mouth. Instantly, I could taste the salt of the sea and seaweed and the sea itself in that little morsel, all of those tastes rolling around in my mouth at the same time. It was refreshing and delicious. As the oyster slid down my throat, I reached for another without pause, and then another, unable to resist. I was going to have to restrain myself, or I would bolt them all down in the space of a few minutes.

Out of the blue, Diana said, "I wonder if your father will get married, now that he's free to do so?"

My eyes came up from my plate of oysters, and I gaped at her. Putting my fork down, I sat back in the chair, my eyes leveled at her. I felt a tight little frown knotting the bridge of my nose.

Finding my voice eventually, I said slowly, "He'd have to have . . . someone . . . someone in his life . . . *someone* to marry, wouldn't he?" I discovered I could not continue. I leaned against my chair, too nervous to say another word. I wanted Diana to tell me, to break the news about her and Daddy. I felt awkward, tongue-tied, and therefore I couldn't probe.

"Oh, but he does have somebody," she said, and that brilliant smile of hers played on her pretty mouth again.

"He *does*?"

"Why, of course. Whatever makes you think that a man like your father could be alone? He's far too dependent a creature for that." She stopped short, staring hard at me. She must have noticed the expression on my face.

I sat there still somewhat dumbfounded, staring back at her stupidly. I had been rendered mute.

Diana frowned. "I thought you knew . . . I thought your mother had told you years ago . . . " Once again, her voice trailed off.

"Told me what?" I asked in a tight voice.

"Oh, dear," Diana muttered, almost to herself. "What have I done now? Gone and put my foot in it, I suspect."

"No, you haven't, Diana, truly you haven't!" I protested, eager to hear more. "What did you mean? What did you think my mother had told me?"

She took a deep breath. "That there have been other women in his life. I mean after your mother and he agreed to separate, all those years ago when you were eighteen, when you went off to Radcliffe. Jess once told me about his—affairs, relationships, whatever you wish to call them. I simply assumed that she had confided in you when you grew older. Especially after your marriage."

"No, she didn't. I must admit, though, that I've thought about his life, lately, anyway. Thought about him . . . having other women, I mean."

Diana nodded.

"And there's someone now, isn't there? Someone *special* in my father's life."

Again she nodded, as though she did not trust herself to speak, the way I had felt a few minutes before. I could certainly understand why.

Taking a deep breath, I said in a rush, "It's you, isn't it, Diana? Just as Andrew and I have suspected for months now."

My mother-in-law looked as if she'd been struck in the face, stared at me in absolute amazement, and then she burst out laughing. She continued to laugh so much tears came into her eyes. Only by exercising enormous control did she manage to finally stop. Reaching for her bag, she took out a lacy handker-chief and dabbed her eyes.

"Oh, do excuse me, Mal darling," she said after a moment, still gasping slightly. "I'm sorry to behave this way, but that's the funniest thing I've heard in a long time. Your father and I? Good Lord, no. I'm much too practical and down-to-earth, far too sane for Edward. He needs someone a lot more helpless and sweeter than I. He needs a woman who is romantic, idealistic, and fey. Yes, *fey* is a very good word with which to describe Gwenny."

"Gwenny! Who's *Gwenny*?"

"Gwendolyn Reece-Jones. She's a great friend of mine, a the-atrical designer, and when she's not up here in London design-ing sets and scenery and all that sort of thing for plays and shows in the West End, she lives in a sixteenth-century manor house in the Welsh Marshes. She's imaginative and charming and funny and dear, and yes, very, very *fey*."

"And she's Daddy's girlfriend?"

"Correct. She's been good for him, too." Diana cleared her throat and after a pause added, "And I'm afraid I introduced them, for my sins."

"Is it serious?"

"Gwenny is serious, I know that for a fact. She's positively dotty over him. Very much in love." Diana sat back, her head held on one side; a thoughtful look spread itself across her face. "I *think* Edward's serious about her, but I couldn't say definitely. That's why I wondered aloud if he would marry. Perhaps. Hard to say, really."

"Has he known her long?"

"Oh, about four years, thereabouts."

"I see."

After a moment, Diana asked, "Tell me something. What on earth made you and Andrew think *I* was involved with your father? That's a most preposterous idea, and in many ways, I might add."

I told her then about Andrew finding the letter in the summer. I explained how the two of us had speculated about them, had analyzed the way they behaved when they were together, concluded how different they were when in each other's company. And in consequence of all this had assumed they were having an affair.

Diana had the good grace to chuckle. "If you think I act differently when I'm around Edward, you're perfectly correct. I do. I suppose I'm more of a woman, my *own* woman, less of a *mother*, less of a *grandmother*. I'm more myself in certain ways. What I mean by this is that I'm like I am when I'm alone, when I'm not with you and Andrew and the twins. I behave in a very natural way with him. You see, there's something in your father's personality that makes every woman feel . . . good, and—"

"Except for Mom," I cut in.

"Touché, darling," she said. "And as I was saying, he has that knack, that ability, to make a woman feel her best—attractive, feminine, and desirable. Edward can make a woman believe she's special, *wanted*, when he's around her, even if he's not particularly interested in her for himself. And he's very flirtatious, says flattering things. It's hard to explain, really. I will say this: Your father's very much a woman's man, not a man's man at all. He adores women, admires them, respects them, and I guess that is part of it." She leaned across the table and finished, "It's all about *attitude*, Mal. His attitude."

"Will he marry . . . Gwenny? What's your opinion, Diana?"

"I told you, I don't know." She pursed her lips, looking thoughtful again, but only for a fraction of a second. "If he's smart, he will. She's made him happy, that I do know."

"I wonder if he'll bring her out in the open, now that Mom's divorced him and married someone else?"

Diana threw me an odd look. "He's not made much of a secret about Gwenny in the past. In fact, no secret at all. At least, not here in London. He probably didn't mention Gwenny to you because he didn't want to hurt your feelings."

"Maybe."

"I'm sure that's the case," Diana said in her firmest tone.

It occurred to me that she was suddenly out to defend my father. He didn't need any defense, as far as I was concerned. I had always loved him, and I still did. After all, his marital battles with my mother were old hat. I had grown up with them. Besides which, I was the one who had always thought they should have divorced years ago. I had never understood their behavior.

Clearing my throat, I asked, "Did he ever bring Gwenny to the States? To New York?"

"Not to New York, as far as I know. However, I believe she was with him when he gave those archaeological lectures at U.C.L.A. last year."

"How old is she?"

"About fifty-three or fifty-four, not much more than that."

"Has she ever been married? Tell me something about her, Diana."

Diana nodded. "Of course. It's not at all unnatural for you to be curious. But there's not much to tell. She *was* married. To Laurence Wilton, the actor. As you probably know, he died about twelve years ago. No children. She's a rather nice woman, and she's very interested in archaeology, anthropology, art, and architecture. She shares many common bonds with your father. I think you'd approve of Gwenny."

"I wish he'd trusted me enough to tell me about her," I muttered, dropping my eyes. I ate the rest of my oysters in silence.

Diana dipped her spoon into the soup and took a few mouthfuls. "I'm afraid I've let this grow cold," she murmured.

"Let's get you some more," I suggested, and swiveling in my chair, I endeavored to catch the waiter's eye.

"No, no," Diana demurred. "This is fine, really. It hasn't lost its taste. It's like . . . vichyssoise now, and it's still very good."

I nodded and took a long swallow of the white wine.

My mother-in-law's eyes rested on me, and she studied me for a while. Eventually, she said in a low, concerned voice, "You know, your father has always been a very discreet man, from all that I've heard, and from everything I know about him personally. He's never flaunted his . . . lady friends. And you must always remember that old habits die hard. With everyone. Edward is a gentleman, and so he's discreet. He doesn't know any other way to be. I am quite certain that he thought he was doing the right thing in not telling you about Gwenny. Or introducing you to her. And there's something else. I'm sure he didn't want to upset you."

"I guess so," I agreed, but I was a bit miffed with my father all of a sudden.

I turned my head and looked out the window, staring at the hazy gray sky but not really seeing it. I was disappointed he had not understood that *I* could handle it, had not understood that *I* would have understood everything, understood about Gwendolyn Reece-Jones and his need at this time in his life to have a bit of happiness. I was thirty-three years old, married and a mother, for God's sake. I was a mature, adult young woman, not a little girl anymore.

13

The suite at Claridge's was not all that large, but it was very comfortable, and the sitting room was one of the most charming I've ever seen, redolent of the Victorian period.

What made it so unusual and special was the fireplace that really worked and the baby grand that stood regally in a corner near the tall, soaring windows. These were dressed with plum-colored velvet draperies, handsomely swagged and tasseled, and they punctuated the soft, dove-gray brocade walls, while an oriental carpet spread rich, jewel-toned colors underfoot.

A big, squashy sofa covered in plum silk and matching armchairs, along with an antique coffee table, were arranged in front of the white marble fireplace; here, an eye-catching chinoiserie mirror hung over the mantel and made a glittering backdrop for a gilt-and-marble French chiming clock with cupids reclining on each side of its face.

Adding to the turn-of-the-century mood created by the elegant background were such things as a Victorian desk, a china cabinet filled with antique porcelain plates, and various small occasional tables made of mahogany. In fact, so authentic was the decorative scheme I felt as if I had been whisked back into another era.

Vases of flowers, a bowl of fruit, a tray of drinks, newspapers and magazines all helped to make the room seem even more homey and inviting. It was especially cozy this November night, with the fire burning merrily in the grate and the pink silk-shaded lamps turned on.

A television set stood in a corner on one side of the fireplace; I turned it on and sat down on the sofa to watch the evening news. But it was the tail end of it, with sports coming up, and within a few minutes I became bored and restless.

Turning it off, I wandered through into the bedroom, asking myself when Andrew would manage to get away from the office. We had spoken earlier, in the late afternoon just after I had returned from a visit to the Tate, and he had told me that he had booked a table at Harry's Bar for dinner. But he had not indicated what time the reservation was for, nor had he said when he would return to the hotel.

To while away a little time, I read several chapters of my Colette, and then, realizing it was almost eight, I undressed, put on a robe, and went into the bathroom. After cleaning off my makeup, I redid my face and brushed my hair. I had just finished coiling it up into a French twist on the back of my head when I heard a key in the door. I rushed into the sitting room, a happy and expectant look on my face.

Andrew was hanging up his trenchcoat in the small vestibule of the suite. Turning around, he saw me. "Hi," he said. He lifted his briefcase off the floor and took a step forward.

I found myself staring at him intently. I saw at once that he was totally exhausted. I was appalled. The dark smudges under his eyes seemed more pronounced than ever tonight, and his face was drawn, much paler than usual.

Hurrying to him, I hugged him tightly, then taking hold of his arm, I led him into the room. But he paused by the fireplace, stepped away from me, and put the briefcase on a nearby chair. After leaning toward the fire and warming his hands, he straightened and propped himself against the mantelpiece.

Looking at him closely, I asked, "Don't you feel well?"

"Tired. Bone bloody tired."

"We don't have to go out to dinner," I volunteered. "We could have room service."

He gave me a peculiar, rather cold look. "I don't care whether we go out to dinner or not. What I do care about, though, is dragging myself up to Yorkshire. What I should say is that I'm certainly *not* going to trail up there to my mother's." He said this in a snappish tone that was most unlike him. "I've just had her on the phone, railing on about my working too hard, and insisting we go up there tomorrow. So that I can have a rest, she said. Is that what the two of you were concocting at lunch today?"

"We hardly spoke about it!" I exclaimed a bit heatedly. "In fact, Diana only mentioned it to me in passing."

"Well, she didn't to me!" he snorted, glaring. "She gave me a bloody lecture. She also said *you* wanted to go, that I was not being fair, making you stay in town for the weekend—"

"Andrew," I interjected sharply, "I don't care whether we go or not!" I could tell he was not only tired but angry, and I had an awful sinking feeling it was with me, as well as with his mother.

"I'm glad to hear you feel that way, because we can't go. It's out of the question altogether. I have to work tomorrow, and Sunday as well, most probably."

"Oh," I said, at a loss.

"And what does *that* mean?"

"Nothing, just *oh*. However, if you have to work this weekend, why did you ask me to fly over here? Just to sit in this suite waiting for you? I might as well have stayed in New York with the twins, or taken them out to Indian Meadows."

Instead of answering me, he ran his hand through his hair somewhat distractedly, then rubbed his eyes. "It's been one hellish day," he grumbled in the same belligerent voice. "Malcolm Stainley's been behaving like an idiot. Which he *is*, of course . . .

goes without saying. He's also a bastard, the worst. And full of himself, has an ego the size of a house. *Ego.*" Andrew compressed his lips. "Ego always gets in the way, and it gets more people into trouble than I care to think about," he muttered in a voice so quiet now it was barely audible.

I said nothing.

Suddenly straightening his shoulders, he glanced across at me. "I stumbled on yet another of Stainley's messes this afternoon, and it may take a bit of time to clear up. There's a possibility I'll have to stay in London for an extra week."

"I thought Jack Underwood was coming over on Wednesday," I said. "To take over from you."

"He may need help. *My* help."

I opened my mouth to protest and promptly closed it. I sat down heavily on the sofa, and after a moment I said, "Why don't I call Harry's Bar and cancel our reservation? Obviously you're in no mood to go out to dinner."

"And *you* are. So we'll *go.*"

"Andrew, *please.* You're being so argumentative, and I don't know why." I bit my lip, feeling unexpected tears pricking the back of my eyes. Impatiently, I pushed them away, swallowed hard, and said, as steadily as possible, "I just want to do what *you* want. I only want to please you."

"I need a drink," he mumbled and marched over to the console table that stood between two of the high, graceful windows.

I watched him as he poured himself a neat scotch, noticing the taut set of his shoulders, the way he held himself. He gulped it down in two swallows and poured another one for himself, this time adding ice and a drop of water from the glass jug. Then without a word to me of any kind, he walked across the room and went into the bedroom, carrying his drink.

I stared after him speechless.

It had been a long time since I'd seen him in such a contrary and difficult mood. Because my feelings were hurt, because I felt he had been terribly unjust, I jumped up and ran after him. I was furious.

He was standing near the bed, where he had thrown his jacket, and was loosening his tie. Hearing me come into the room, he pivoted swiftly, stood glaring at me.

I said, "I realize you've had a bad day, and I'm sorry for that. God knows, you of all people don't deserve it. But you're not going to take it out on me! I won't let you! *I* haven't done anything wrong!"

"It's a bad couple of *weeks* I've had, not merely a bad *day*," he shot back, adding with ill grace, "I'm going to take a bath," and so saying began to unbutton his shirt.

"And stick your head under the water and keep it there! For several hours!" I shouted, my temper flying to the surface. I turned on my heels abruptly and flounced out, banging the door after me with a resounding crash. The crystal chandelier in the sitting room rattled and swayed slightly, but I didn't care. I had had such a wonderful day, and he had just ruined it, in the space of only a few seconds. I was trembling inside and angrier than I had been in a very long time.

A split second later the bedroom door was wrenched open, almost violently, and Andrew strode over to me, where I was standing by the piano.

Grabbing hold of me by the shoulders, he held me tightly and looked into my eyes. "*I'm sorry*, so very sorry, Mal. I *did* take it out on you, and that was wrong of me, very unfair. There's no excuse for it, really there isn't. The problem is, my mother got my goat tonight. Railing on about going up to spend the weekend with her, complaining she's seen nothing of me whilst I've been in London. That's true, of course, and she means well, but—" He shook his head. "I guess my nerves are pretty raw tonight."

He searched my face.

When I said not one kindly word nor showed a glimmer of friendliness, he murmured in a low, weary voice, "Forgive me, Puss?"

His tiredness was a most palpable thing; all of my anger dissipated as rapidly as it had erupted. "There's nothing to forgive, silly."

Smiling now, his eyes as soft and loving as they usually were, he kissed the tip of my nose. "Oh, Puss, whatever would I do without you?"

"And me you?" I asked.

Lifting my hand, I touched his cheek gently. "Listen, tough guy, let me cancel the dinner reservation, order a good bottle of wine and your favorite soul food, and we can stay here, have supper in front of the fire. Just the two of us. All cozy and warm and loving. So, what do you say?"

"I say okay, you've got a date."

"Good. Now, come on," I bustled. "Let's get you into a nice hot tub. You can soak for a while in some of my bubbly stuff. It's got pine oil in it, and it'll relax your muscles."

"Join me?" he asked, lifting a brow, giving me a suggestive look.

"*No!*"

He laughed for the first time since he had come in, and so did I.

"No hanky-panky tonight, Andrew Keswick. You're far too tired."

"Afraid so, even for you, Puss."

The dinner was perfect. And so was the evening, as it turned out.

Whilst Andrew soaked his weary bones in a tub filled to the brim with the hottest water and a generous portion of my pine bubble bath, I ordered supper from room service.

Wanting to pamper and spoil him, make him feel better, I chose all of his favorite things: Morecombe Bay potted shrimps, baby chops from a rack of lamb with mint sauce, mashed potatoes, *haricot vert,* and carrots. I selected a wonderful red wine, Château Lafite-Rothschild, and to hell with the price. For dessert I picked bread pudding. I wasn't particularly fond of this, but Andrew loved it; it was a favorite of his from boarding school days, and I knew he would enjoy it tonight.

Refreshed, relaxed, and replete with food and wine, my husband was in a much mellower mood by eleven o'clock. Nevertheless, he still took me by surprise when he said suddenly, "Okay! We're going to Yorkshire tomorrow after all, Puss-Puss."

I was lolling against him on the sofa, vaguely watching the television news, and I sat up with a jerk and stared at him.

"But I thought you had to go to the office tomorrow!" I exclaimed. "I thought you had another mess to sort out."

"That's true, yes. But I don't think I can really sort it out by myself. I need Jack as a sounding board. It's financial, which is where his expertise lies. And look, I can take some paperwork with me, clear some of it up on the way to Ma's."

"Are you sure, darling?"

"I'm positive."

"You're not doing it for me, are you? Because you don't want me sitting around the hotel waiting for you? That's not it, is it?"

"I'm doing it for both of us, Mal. And for my mother. Anyway, I think it'll do me good to get away for forty-eight hours. It'll give me a better perspective about everything. And quite frankly, I need to get out of that office, stand away from the situation and take stock of everything."

"If you're really sure . . . " I knew I sounded hesitant, but I couldn't help myself.

"I *want* to do this," Andrew reassured me. "Scout's honor."

"Shall we go on the train?"

He shook his head. "No, I don't think so. I'd like to leave early, about six-thirty, so that we miss the worst of the traffic on the motorway. If we set off then, we'll get to Ma's in the middle of the morning, in time for lunch. I can even work on my papers on Saturday afternoon. We can relax all day Sunday and drive back with my mother early on Monday morning."

"But how are we going to get there tomorrow? We don't have a car, and your mother left earlier this evening. She told me she wanted to be on the road by eight at the latest."

"Yes, I know that. But there's no problem, we're in a hotel, remember, and one of the best in the world." He pushed himself to his feet and walked over to the desk. "I'm going to call the hall porter right now and ask him to have a car and driver outside for us tomorrow morning at six-thirty. How does that sound?"

"Wonderful," I answered and smiled at him. "And your mother's going to be delighted to have us for the weekend."

"Whether your father marries Gwenny Reece-Jones or not doesn't affect you much, does it, Mal?" Andrew asked as he switched off the bedside light and pulled the bedcovers over him.

I was silent for a moment, and then I said, "No, not really. I just want him to be happy, that's all."

"She's very nice."

"I thought you couldn't remember her."

"I couldn't at first. But she's started to come into focus in the past few hours, and I've got a really good picture of her now. Ma's known her for donkey's years. Gwenny's older sister Gladys was at Oxford with my mother, and that's the connection. When I was little we used to go and stay with the family. I vaguely remember an old house that was quite beautiful, in the Welsh Marshes."

"Your mother mentioned it to me earlier. But go on, you said you had a good picture of her. What's she look like?"

"Tall, slender. Dark, like a lot of the Welsh are, with a rather lovely face, a gentle face, and I can visualize pretty eyes, hazel, I think, big and soulful. But she wore odd clothes."

"What do you mean?"

"Long floaty skirts and boots and peasant blouses, trailing scarves, dangling earrings, and flowing capes." I heard him laugh in the darkness, and then he went on in an amused voice, "Looking back, I think she was a cross between a gypsy, a Russian peasant, and a hippie. I mean in her appearance. And she was most eccentric, as only the British can be. But don't get me wrong, she was awfully sweet. I'm sure she still is."

"Yes, and talented, at least, so your mother said."

"Mal?"

"Yes, honey?"

"Don't sound so grudging about Gwenny. I know you're irritated because your father didn't confide in you, but I'm sure it was only because he didn't want to embarrass you or upset you. Ma's right about that."

"I guess so. And I didn't mean to sound grudging. I'm glad Dad has Gwenny. I hope I get to meet her soon. After all, Dad might be in Mexico next year for six months. So no doubt he'll come to New York more often if he's based there."

"Is he going to accept the invitation from U.C.L.A. to be part of the dig in Yaxuna?"

"Possibly. After all, he's had an interest in the Mayan civilization for a long time, as you well know, and I think he'll be glad to get away from the Middle East. He wrote in his last letter that he'd had it out there."

"I can't say I blame him."

"I hope he goes to Mexico. I hope he marries Gwenny, and that they spend a lot of time with us. It'll be nice for the twins to get to know their grandfather better, and I'm sure Gwenny will be a good sport. I got that impression from your mother, anyway—that she's fun, I mean. Listen, Andrew, Dad might come to Yorkshire for the Christmas vacation. Anyway, Diana said she was going to phone Gwenny and invite them. That would be nice, don't you think?"

Andrew did not respond, and I realized that he had fallen asleep. He was breathing evenly but deeply, and this did not surprise me at all, since he was so exhausted. It was a miracle he hadn't fallen asleep over supper.

I lay next to him in the darkness, thinking about my father and Gwenny, hoping they were happy. One thing I was certain of, in this uncertain world, was that my mother was happy with David Nelson. In the beginning I'd had a few misgivings about him, inasmuch as he was a criminal lawyer of some standing and celebrity; he had always sounded too street-smart, too tough and slick in the past. But what a lovely man he had turned out to be, and not in the least like my original impression. Charming without being smarmy, intellectual without being pompous, and brilliant without being a show-off. He had a good sense of humor, but most important, I had discovered he was a kind and compassionate man, blessed with a great deal of understanding and insight into people. He adored my mother, and she adored him; that was good enough for me.

I fell asleep with a smile on my face, thinking how nice it was that my mother had started a whole new life at the age of sixty-one.

14

Yorkshire, November 1988

Andrew worked on his papers all the way to Yorkshire.

Lulled by the warmth and the motion of the car, I dozed on and off as we headed north on the motorway. I roused myself fully at one point, sat up straighter against the seat, and glanced at my watch. I saw that it was almost nine-thirty. This surprised me, and I said to Andrew, "We've been on the road well over three and a half hours. We must be in Yorkshire already, aren't we?"

"That we are, Puss," he answered, looking up from the folder on his lap, giving me a half smile. "And you've slept most of the way. In any case, we left Harrogate behind a while ago."

I swung my head and stared out the car window. I saw that it was a pristine morning, clear and sunny, the sky a high-flung canopy of palest blue and white above the undulating pastoral dales. And as I continued to look out of the window, thinking what a great day it was, I experienced a sudden rush of anticipation and excitement knowing that we would soon be with Diana at her lovely old house just outside West Tanfield.

Ever since our marriage, Andrew and I had come to England at least once a year for a holiday, and we had never left without making a trip to Yorkshire. So, not unnaturally, I was happy we were coming for the weekend. During the last ten years I had grown to love this beautiful, sprawling county, the largest in England, with its bucolic green dales, vast, empty moors, soaring fells, ancient cathedrals, and dramatic ruins of medieval abbeys. It was a rich corner of the north, blessed with immense tracts of fertile, arable land and great industrial wealth, and it boasted more castles and stately homes than any other county in the whole of Britain. Also, I had developed a deep affection and respect for the canny, down-to-earth folk who lived here, and whose pragmatism, dry wit, and hospitality were legendary.

Wensleydale and the valley of the Ure, which we were presently driving through, was the area I knew best, since this was where the Keswick ancestral home was located. The house had been in the family for over four hundred years; even though Michael and Diana had settled in London after their youthful marriage straight out of university, they had spent almost every weekend there with Michael's parents, and all of the main annual holidays as well.

Andrew had been born in the house, as had most of the other Keswicks who had gone before him. "My mother made sure my actual birth took place in Yorkshire, not only because of the Keswick tradition, but because of cricket," Andrew had told me somewhat cryptically, on my first trip to West Tanfield when we had come to England on our honeymoon.

I had asked him what he meant about cricket, and he had chuckled, then explained, "Cricket is Yorkshire's game, Mal. My father and grandfather wanted me to be birthed in the county, because only men actually born within the boundaries of Yorkshire can play cricket for it. They had high expectations of me, hoped and prayed I might turn out to be another Len Hutton or a Freddy Trueman. You see, Dad and Grandpa were cricket addicts."

Since I knew nothing about cricket, that most British of British games, Andrew had gone on to explain that Hutton and

Trueman were world-famous Yorkshire cricketeers who had played for England and had been national champions, if not, indeed, national heroes.

As it happened, Andrew loved cricket and had played it at boarding school. "But I was never inspired, only an average batsman. I just didn't have the talent," he had confided to me on another occasion, a warm summer day the following year when he had taken me to Lords to watch my first test match.

Continuing to gaze out the window, I spotted the shining tower of Ripon Cathedral outlined dramatically against the distant blue horizon. The cathedral was one of the most extraordinary edifices I have ever seen. Founded in the year 650, it was imposingly beautiful, awe-inspiring. Andrew was christened there, and it was in the cathedral that his parents were married. Now the sight of its great tower told me that we were about thirty minutes away from Andrew's family home.

"I'm hungry," Andrew said, interrupting my thoughts. "I hope old Parky has a good breakfast waiting for us. I could eat a horse."

"I'm not surprised," I laughed. "I'm pretty hungry myself, we left London so early. And I hope the hall porter phoned your mother, as you asked him to do. I'd hate to arrive unexpected."

"Good Lord, Mal, you ought to know better than that by now. I'd stake my life on the hall porters at Claridge's; they're the salt of the earth, and very reliable."

"True. Still, perhaps we ought to have stopped on the way up, called her ourselves,"

"Not necessary, my sweet," he murmured. "And it wouldn't matter if we did arrive unannounced. We're going to my mother's, for God's sake."

I said nothing, simply nodded, then I reached for my handbag. Taking out my compact, I powdered my nose and put on a little lipstick. Settling back, I glanced out the window once more to see that we were passing through the marketplace in Ripon.

Here, every night at nine o'clock, the horn blower blew his horn at each corner of the neat little square, sounding the ancient curfew, wearing a period costume that came from an era of long ago. It was a centuries-old tradition, which the English, and most especially the locals, took in their stride, but one that an American like me found quite amazing—and extremely quaint.

Within seconds we had left the center of town behind. The driver pointed the car in the direction of Middleham, following Andrew's explicit instructions, and soon we were out in the open countryside again, making for West Tanfield. This was situated between Ripon and Middleham, but closer to the latter, a place renowned for its stables and the breeding and training of great racehorses; it was also a treasure trove of history, had been known as "the Windsor of the North" at the time of the Plantagenet kings, Edward IV and Richard III.

We continued to barrel along, following the winding country lanes and roads, narrow and a bit precarious under the shadow of those lonely, windswept moors. This morning they looked somber and implacable. In August and September they took on a wholly different aspect, resembling a sea of purple as wave upon wave of heather rippled under the perpetual wind; they were a breathtaking sight.

"We're almost there," I murmured half to myself as the car rolled over the old stone bridge which spanned the River Ure and led into the main street of West Tanfield. It was a typical dales village—charming, picturesque, and very, very old.

I glanced to my left to see the familiar view, a line of pretty stone cottages with red-tiled roofs standing on the banks of the Ure, their green sloping lawns running down to the edge of the river. And behind them, poised against the pale wintry sky, were the old Norman church and the Marmion Tower next to it, both surrounded by ancient oaks and ash and a scattering of evergreens.

I reached over and squeezed Andrew's hand. I knew how much he loved this place.

He smiled at me and began to straighten his papers, quickly putting them back into his briefcase and closing it.

"Did you get a lot done?" I asked him.

"Yes, I did, and probably more than I would have in that damned office. I'm glad Ma put the screws on me yesterday, that I finally made up my mind we should spend the weekend with her. It'll do us both good."

"Yes, it will, and maybe we can go riding tomorrow."

"That's a good thought, Mal. We'll zip up to Middleham and join the stable boys and grooms on the gallops when they're exercising the racehorses. If you don't mind getting up very early again."

"I'm always up early, aren't I?" I laughed. "But Andrew, how stupid I am. I'd forgotten—we don't have our riding gear with us."

"Don't worry about that. I know I've got some historic old stuff at Ma's from years ago. I'm sure it's gungy, but it'll do, and my mother will lend you a pair of her boots and old jeans or riding breeches. And she's got masses of warm jackets, barbours, green Wellies, stuff like that. So we'll manage."

"Yes, it'll be fine." I studied him carefully and asked, "Does it feel good to be home?"

A small frown creased his smooth, wide brow as he returned my steady gaze. "These days, home for me is wherever *you* are, Mal. You and the twins." He leaned into me, kissed my cheek, and added, "But yes, it does feel good to be back in Yorkshire, to come back to my birthplace. I suppose everybody must feel that way—that atavistic pull. It's only natural, isn't it?"

"Yes," I agreed, and turning away from him, I looked straight ahead, peering over the driver's shoulder and out the front window of the car. We had left the village behind a good ten minutes ago and had taken the road which led up to the moors of Coverdale and the high fells. Following a bend in the road, we turned a corner. Now I could see them straight ahead, the high stone wall and the wrought-iron gates which opened onto the long winding driveway leading up to Diana's house.

15

We drove through the gates and progressed up the driveway rather slowly, since there were sheep and fallow deer wandering around the grounds, and the latter were skittish.

Far in the distance, I got just the merest glimpse of the house, of its tall chimneys poking up into the sky.

Its name was Kilgram Chase. It had always been called that, ever since its beginnings. Built in 1563, five years after Elizabeth I ascended to the throne, it was typically Tudor in style. A solid, stone house, it was square in shape yet graceful and with many windows, high chimneys, pitched gables, and a square tower built onto each of its four corners. In every crenellated tower there were only two mullioned windows, but these were huge and soaring, set one above the other, creating a highly dramatic effect and filling the tower rooms with extraordinary light.

Kilgram Chase stood in a large expanse of parkland, its green sweep of lawns and grazing pastures encircling the house, stretching up from the iron gates we had just left behind. Surrounding the edge of the park on three sides, to form a semicircular shape behind it, were dense woods, and rising up above these woods were the moors and, higher still, the great fells. Thus the house, the park, and the woods were cupped in a valley that protected them from the wind and weather in the winter months and, in times past, from political enemies and marauders, since the only access to the house and its park was through the front gates.

The first time I came here I had naturally been intrigued by Andrew's childhood home. Diana had given me the grand tour, told me everything I wanted to know about the house and the family. She was proud of Kilgram Chase and an expert on its history.

Its unusual name came, in part, from the man who had built it 425 years ago, a Yorkshire warrior knight called Sir John Kilgram. A close friend of Robert Dudley, the Earl of Leicester, he was a member of Queen Elizabeth's loyal faction, and one of the *new men,* as they were called, in palace politics. Kilgram had been given the great park and woods by Queen Elizabeth's royal decree for special services to the Crown. But long before Elizabeth Tudor's reign, when the Plantagenets had ruled, it had been a chase, that is, a stretch of open land where wild animals roamed and could be hunted by the local gentry. Later it was owned by the monks of nearby Fountains Abbey; they lost it when Elizabeth's father, King Henry VIII, confiscated all lands owned by the church. After the dissolution of the monasteries it became the property of the Crown.

The house and its park had come to the Keswicks quite legally, through a marriage which took place in the summer of 1589. Sir John had an only child, a daughter named Jane, and when she married Daniel Keswick, the son of a local squire, he gave them Kilgram Chase as part of her dowry. It had been in the family's possession ever since, passed down from generation to generation. One day it would belong to Andrew, and then to Jamie, and Jamie's son, if he had one.

Diana called it a typical country manor and constantly protested that for all of its prestige and historical significance, it was by no means a grand house anymore, and this was true. Architecturally, it was extremely well designed, skillfully planned, even somewhat compact for this type of Tudor manor, and in comparison to some of the great homes of Yorkshire, it was small. Despite its size, for a long time now Diana had found it difficult to run, in many respects. Not the least of it was the cost in time and money for its overall upkeep. For these reasons she lived in only two wings and kept two closed most of the year.

The house was maintained with the help of Joe and Edith Parkinson, who had lived and worked at Kilgram Chase for over thirty years. With their daughter, Hilary Broadbent, they took care of all the interiors, in both the open and closed wings, and did the laundry and cooking. Joe was also the handyman; he did a certain amount of outdoor work as well, looking after Diana's two horses and the sheep and mucking out the stables.

Hilary's husband, Ben, and his brother Wilf were the two gardeners responsible for the grounds; they mowed the many lawns, tended the flower beds, pruned the trees in the orchard, cleaned the pond once a year, and made sure the walled rose garden remained the great beauty spot it had been for hundreds of years.

Roses were my favorite flowers, and I had always gravitated to this particular garden at Kilgram Chase. But I did not plan to visit it this trip; I knew it could only be bereft, without color or life, just as everything at Indian Meadows was brown and faded. It was a bleak period for a gardener like me, these cold, cheerless months when the earth was hard as iron, the air sharp with frost, and all growing things lay dormant and still.

Glancing out the car window, I noticed that many of the giant oaks, which stood sentinel at intervals along the driveway, were already shedding their leaves, now that it was November and the first chill of winter had settled in. Everything was dying. Winter was a time of death in gardens and in the countryside; quite unexpectedly I felt melancholy, and I filled up with sadness. Shivering, I hunched further into my coat, pulling it tightly around me. But the death of the land in winter only meant its rebirth in the spring, I reminded myself, attempting to shake off this curious sense of sadness which had enveloped me. I shivered again. Some poor ghost just walked over my grave, I thought.

And in less than a moment it *was* gone, the sadness, for suddenly there was the house, rising up in front of us in all its glory. Kilgram Chase. It stood there under the shadow of the moors, proud and everlasting as it had been for four centuries, seemingly untouched by time. My heart lifted at the sight of the lovely old manor. Its pale stones gleamed golden in the clear morning air, and the many mullioned windows shone brightly in the sunlight. I lifted my eyes, saw smoke puffing out of the chimneys, curling up like strands of gray-blue ribbon thrown carelessly into that silky, shining sky.

How welcoming it looked in all its mellowness and charm— my husband's ancestral home, the place where he had grown up.

The car had hardly come to a standstill in front of the house when the great oak door flew open and Diana appeared. She ran down the steps; her smile was wide, her face glowing with happiness at the sight of us alighting.

"Hi, Ma," Andrew cried, waving to her.

I rushed toward her and hugged her close. "Diana!"

"Aren't you the best girl in the whole wide world," she greeted me, "getting this obstinate son of mine to come up here after all."

Laughing, I pulled away from her and shook my head. "Not me, I didn't persuade him, Diana. *He* had a change of heart on his own accord. Late last night, far too late to call you. And we left so early this morning, at six, we didn't want to disturb you. That's why we asked the hall porter to phone. He did, didn't he?"

"Yes, darling." Turning to her son, she embraced him and went on, "As long as you're both here, that's all that matters. We'll have a nice cozy weekend together, and I know Parky plans to spoil you both."

Andrew grinned at her. "We expected nothing less." Leaning closer, he said, "Before I let the car go, should I ask the driver to come back for us tomorrow night? Or can we cadge a lift to town with you on Monday morning?"

"Of course you can. Anyway, it's hardly worth coming up here, if you don't stay through Sunday night. And I'll be glad to have your company and Mal's on the way back to London. In fact, you can drive part of the way, Andrew dear."

"You bet," he said, "and thanks, Ma. There's just one thing: We'll have to leave here fairly early on Monday morning. About six-thirty. Is that all right?"

"I usually set out about that time," Diana answered.

Andrew nodded and hurried off to speak to the driver.

Diana took hold of my arm and drew me toward the stone steps leading up to the front door. Joe Parkinson was hovering at the top of them. He came striding down.

"Morning, Mrs. Andrew," he said, giving me a big smile. "It's lovely to have you back, by gum it is."

"Thank you, Joe, I'm really glad we could come up for the weekend."

"I'll just get along, help Mr. Andrew with the luggage." And so saying Joe moved down the steps, calling out, "Nay, Mr. Andrew, I'll do that. Let me handle them there suitcases."

I glanced back over my shoulder and saw Andrew and Joe shaking hands, greeting each other affectionately. Andrew had been eight years old when the Parkinsons had come to work at Kilgram Chase. Joe had taught him so much about the countryside and nature, and they had always been firm friends. As Andrew said, Joe was the salt of the earth, a real Yorkshireman through and through, hardworking, canny, wise, and loyal.

"It's a raw morning," Diana said, shivering and pulling her cardigan around her. "Come on, let's go in and have a cup of tea."

Waiting for us in the small entrance hall were Edith Parkinson, Joe's wife, whom Andrew had called Parky since childhood, and her daughter, Hilary. Both women welcomed me warmly, and I returned their greetings.

Parky said, "If only the little ones were with you, Mrs. Andrew, they'd be a sight for sore eyes."

Smiling at her, I said, "Don't forget, they'll be here next month for Christmas, Parky. In fact, we're planning on staying through the New Year. Mr. Andrew promised."

"That's just wonderful," Parky exclaimed, beaming at me. "I can't wait to see the wee bairns." Glancing at Diana, she added, "We'll have to have a *big* Christmas tree this year, Mrs. Keswick, and maybe Joe'll play Santa Claus, get dressed up in his red Santa suit and whiskers, like he does for the Sunday school class at the church."

"Yes, that's a marvelous idea," Diana agreed. Taking my coat, she hung it up in the hall closet. "Now, let's go into the kitchen, Mal. Parky's been busy for the last hour whipping up all sorts of things. Andrew's favorites, of course."

The kitchen at Kilgram Chase was as old as the house itself, and it had altered little over the years. Painted cool white, it was long in shape. The ceiling was low and intersected with dark wood beams. The floor was still covered with the original flagstones, so ancient they were worn in places by the steps of centuries, steps which had gone from the fireplace to the window and across to the door, and back and forth, time and time again, so that deep grooves now scored the stones.

The fireplace at the far end of the kitchen was high to the ceiling and wide, made of local brick and stone and braced with old wood beams to match the ceiling. It had a great, raised hearth, an overhanging mantel shelf, and old-fashioned baking ovens set in the wall next to the actual fireplace. The ovens had not been used for years and years; long ago Diana had installed a wonderful Aga, that marvelous English cooking stove I would give my eyeteeth for. I agreed with her that this was the best stove in the world, and it also helped to keep the rather large kitchen warm the year round. It was welcome, since the kitchen with its thick old walls and stone floor was always cool even in the summer months.

A butler's pantry, which opened off the kitchen, had been updated and remodeled by Diana, so that it better served her and Parky. She had put in a double-sized refrigerator, two dish-washers, and countertops for food preparation; above the counters were lots of cabinets for storing china as well as all of those practical items that made the wheels of a kitchen turn.

A series of mullioned casement windows opened onto a view of the back lawns, the pond, and the ever-present moors reaching up to touch the edge of the sky. Opposite the window wall an antique Welsh dresser took pride of place, and this lovely old piece was filled to overflowing with willow-patterned china of blue and white. Nearby, in the center of the room, there was an old-fashioned country table with a deal top and stumpy legs, where Andrew and I now sat. A green Majolica jug filled to the brim with branches of bittersweet stood on the table, and I couldn't help thinking how perfect it looked.

Marching along the mantel shelf was a diverse collection of wood and brass candlesticks in the barley-twist style bearing white beeswax candles, and underneath the mantel were all kinds of horse brass that glittered and winked in the bright fire-light. And everywhere there was the sparkle of copper in such things as jelly and fish molds and pots and pans all hanging from a rack on the ceiling, and in ladles, spoons, and measuring scoops on a side table.

I had always loved this kitchen, thought it one of the most welcoming I had ever seen; it was not only cheerful in its ambience but comfortable as well. As Diana said, it was the hub of the house, a room you could easily live in.

Diana was over by the Aga stove making a pot of tea; she carried this over to the table but suggested we let it stand for a few moments.

"Aye, that's right, Mrs. Andrew, don't pour it yet, it has to mash," Parky instructed.

"Yes, Parky," I said dutifully and smiled at Andrew. She had been telling me this for ten years.

Pervading the air in the kitchen was the tantalizing smell of bacon sizzling on top of the Aga and the mouth-watering aroma of freshly baked bread just out of the oven. Parky had left the loaves and tea cakes to cool for a few minutes on one of the countertops, and the mere smell made me salivate.

Swinging around to face us, Parky said, "In case you haven't guessed, I'm going to make bacon butties. Your favorites, Mr. Andrew." She smiled at him fondly before turning back to her task of lifting the bacon out of the frying pan and onto a large platter. Parky had mothered him as a little boy, and he had been like a second child to her in some respects.

"What a treat, Parky," Andrew exclaimed, and added to me, "*You've* got to make them for me, Mal, when we're home at Indian Meadows."

Diana joined us at the table and poured the steaming hot tea into big blue-and-white cups, and a moment later Parky was beside her, serving the bacon butties. These were thick slices of the warm new bread, spread with butter and with rashers of the fried bacon between the slices—hot bacon sandwiches, really.

"Here goes my cholesterol!" Andrew groaned cheerfully, "But oh, God, how wonderful!" he added after taking the first bite.

"I know, they're *sinful*," Diana said, laughing, then cautioned, "But don't eat too many, Parky's making fish cakes and parsley sauce for lunch."

"With chips," Parky cut in. "To be followed by another of your favorites. Treacle pudding."

"Oh, God, Parky, I think I've just died and gone to heaven," he exclaimed, laughing, enjoying Parky and the fuss she was making over him. He had always had a soft spot for her.

"But, darling, it *is* heaven here," Diana said, smiling at him lovingly. "Or had you forgotten?"

Andrew shook his head, kissed her warmly on the cheek. "No, Ma, I hadn't forgotten. Not only that, I'm here with three of my four favorite women."

"And who's the fourth?" I asked swiftly, staring.

"Why, my daughter, of course," he answered, winking at me.

16

I found the books on Saturday afternoon. And quite a find they were.

After lunch Diana drove off to West Tanfield to do some errands; she asked me to go with her, but I declined, preferring instead to stay at Kilgram Chase with Andrew, only to discover that he wanted to work.

"I must go over the rest of this stuff," he explained apologetically, holding up his briefcase. "I'm sorry, Mal."

"It's okay," I said, although I was disappointed he was going to be poring over the papers in Diana's office for the rest of the afternoon, rather than going out for a walk with me.

"I won't be long, about an hour and a half, two hours at the most." He shook his head as he paused on the threshold of the office. "Some of it's rather complicated, that lousy financial stuff I mentioned to you in London. I could use Jack's nimble brain. He's much better than I am when it comes to figures."

"Maybe I could help you," I suggested.

He smiled at me ruefully. "I'm afraid you can't, darling. Look, you don't mind if I work, do you? At least for a while. We'll go for a walk later, just before tea."

"That's great, don't worry," I said, giving him a quick peck on the cheek. I walked off in the direction of the library, which had always fascinated me. I loved to poke around in there, looking for literary treasures or family memorabilia. Unfortunately, I'd never come across anything remotely interesting or out of the ordinary.

Like the kitchen, the library had not changed much in four hundred years, except, perhaps, for the acquisition of more and more books by the Keswicks over the centuries. And it seemed to me that they never threw anything away. It was larger than most of the other rooms at Kilgram Chase, since it was situated in one of the square towers, the one on the northeast corner of the house, overlooking the moors.

The coffered ceiling was over thirty feet high, balanced by the huge window set in the middle of the center wall, a beautiful window of unusual dimensions and shape which filled the room with the most extraordinary light at all times of the day. Paneled in light oak, the library had floor-to-ceiling bookshelves throughout, and these held many thousands of volumes, most of them very old. A handsomely built fireplace of local limestone was set in the wall facing the window, and around this had been arranged several comfortable chairs, an oak coffee table, and a Knole sofa. Directly behind the sofa stood a library table, also of carved oak, and on this was stacked the latest magazines, many of them to do with antiques, as well as today's *Times*, an assortment of other national and local newspapers, and a few current novels.

I did a cursory check of everything on the table, but there was nothing of particular interest to me, and so I began to wander around the room, my eyes scanning the lower shelves where everything was in easy reach. But, of course, because these shelves were readily accessible to me, I had looked at almost every book countless times before. There was nothing new.

Suddenly realizing it was cool in the library, and shivering slightly, I went over to the fireplace, pulled out the damper, and put a light to the paper and chips of wood under the logs in the grate. Within minutes I had a good blaze going, and soon the logs had caught and the fire was roaring up the chimney.

Glancing around, I saw the set of polished mahogany library steps at the other side of the room, and I pulled these over to the fireplace wall. On either side of the fire there were shelves rising to the ceiling, and since I wanted to stay warm, I decided to investigate these first.

Climbing up, I examined a series of books covered with dark green leather that I'd never noticed before, undoubtedly because they were placed so high. Much to my disappointment most of them were old atlases and maps of Yorkshire and other counties.

Leaning my head back, I looked up, scanned a higher shelf immediately above me, and spotted a large-sized volume bound in purple leather. The royal color of the binding intrigued me, and I climbed a bit farther, until I stood on the top step. I stretched my arm, endeavoring to reach the book; I had no idea what it was, but naturally, because it was beyond my reach, I wanted to look at it.

I tried once more but lost my balance and almost fell. I clutched frantically at the nearest shelf and managed to steady myself. I took a deep breath; my heart was suddenly pounding hard. That had been a close call. After a few seconds, when I recovered, I made a slow descent, moving carefully, having no wish to fall off the library steps. And once I was on the floor, I let out a sigh of relief. Hurrying out, I went in search of Joe.

I found him in the kitchen talking to Parky, and after explaining what I wanted, I returned to the library.

Within a few minutes he came in carrying one of the very tall stepladders he kept in his workshop.

"That *is* a big one, Joe," I said, eyeing it.

He nodded. "Aye, it is that, Mrs. Andrew. I need it for cleaning the chandeliers. And doing some of the windows. I've got a brush with an expanding handle, o'course, but t'brush isn't always long enough, you knows. Windows in the tower rooms, like the library here, are right high, for example, and difficult to get to, by gum they are. Now, then, where exactly do you want this ladder, Mrs. Andrew?"

"Here, Joe, please. I would like to look at that book on the shelf up there." I pointed to the shelf in question.

Joe followed my gaze. "What's it called?"

"I don't know, but it's the purple leather one. Next to the one with the torn, moldy-looking binding."

Almost immediately I realized he wasn't quite focused on the shelf I meant, and so I said, "Don't worry, Joe, I'll go up and get it. Just hold the ladder steady for me." As I spoke, I moved closer to him.

"Nay, Mrs. Andrew, I can't let you climb up there! Goodness me, no! What if you had a fall? Mr. Andrew would be right vexed with me, that he would, and so would Mrs. Keswick. The whole house would be in an uproar, you can bet your last shilling on that." He shook his head vehemently. "Oh, no, no, no, you can't go up there. I'll bring the book down for you. Now, just let me get on the ladder, and then you can direct me to the volume you mean."

"All right," I said, knowing it was no use arguing with Joe. I had tried to do so in the past without success. He was very stubborn, and once he had made up his mind, it was hard to persuade him or to coerce him into doing anything against his wishes. Obviously he thought I was incapable of climbing that ladder, and I wasn't going to make a fuss about it. After all, I'd almost had a mishap on the library steps.

After showing him where to place the ladder immediately behind the shelf, I pointed to the book once more.

"I see it!" he exclaimed, and went up the steps with amazing speed and sureness of foot. Of course he was able to reach it without any problem, since he was taller than I and had much longer arms.

"What is it, Joe?" I asked as he opened it.

"It looks like a ledger. An accounts book, for carpentry items. It says, *nails one halfpenny,* and there are a few other things mentioned, but there's nowt much else in it," he said, leafing through the ledger. "It's got a date in it. 1892. By gum, almost a hundred years ago!"

"Interesting. What's next to it?"

"Looks like another ledger. This one's got a cloth cover." He turned the pages, then glanced down at me. "Definitely a ledger, only one entry. It says *fresh fish two pennies.* No nothing else in it, and no date."

"And that torn book, which is still on the shelf? The moldy-looking one. What's that, Joe?"

He took it down. After a second or two spent scanning it, he said, "Well, this one looks like a diary, aye, summat like that."

"*Diary?* Do you mean it's handwritten?"

"Aye, it is, Mrs. Andrew."

"Could you bring it, Joe, along with the other two, please? The two ledgers. I'd like to take a look at them."

"Right-oh, Mrs. Andrew."

There was a long refectory table in front of the big mullioned window, with a porcelain bowl of flowers in the center and, at either end, a high-backed chair covered in green cut velvet.

I went over to this table, pulled one of the chairs closer to it, and sat down.

Joe brought me the books and put them in front of me.

"Thanks, Joe," I said.

"I'll leave the ladder, shall I, Mrs. Andrew?"

"Yes, do. You can put the books back for me later. After I've studied them. I'll come and find you when I'm ready."

He nodded and went to the door, where he stopped abruptly and swung around to face me.

"Don't start climbing up that there ladder! If you want summat else, another book brought down, come and get me, Mrs. Andrew."

"I will, Joe. I promise."

I looked inside the two ledgers first and quickly laid these on one side. There was nothing much of interest in either of them. But the diary intrigued me, and now I opened this book with its tan leather binding, torn and a bit frayed on the spine. The end-papers were of a feather design, a kind of paisley pattern in shades of brown and ochre, rust and beige, with just the merest hint of blue.

Turning the first few pages, which were blank, I came to a handwritten frontispiece.

Slowly I began to read, filled with growing anticipation and excitement.

> *I, Clarissa Keswick, wife of Robin Keswick and Mistress of Kilgram Chase, discovered this day the diary and private household book penned by my dear Husband's ancestor, one Lettice, born 1640 died 1683. Fortuitously I stumbled upon her private book in the library here at Kilgram Chase, when my dear Husband asked me to fetch for him a copy of that great tragedy* Hamlet *by William Shakespeare. The words of Lettice Keswick were interesting to me and so I bethought myself to copy them in order to preserve them. This is done for the future generations of this family who will follow me and mine.*
>
> *I started my work on this tenth day of August in the year 1893 in the glorious and prosperous reign of our great Queen and Empress of India Victoria Regina. God Bless Her Gracious Majesty and Long May She Reign.*

Clarissa was a Keswick family name, one we had chosen for our own daughter, and there had been several Clarissas before ours was born six years ago. The Victorian Clarissa whose elegant copperplate handwriting I was now reading had been one of the earlier ones.

Elated by my discovery and eager to read more, I turned the first page, and once again I was staring at a frontispiece, the words set out in the center.

Lettice Keswick
Her Book
Kilgram Chase
Yorkshire

Flipping this page, I read the first words of Lettice's diary, so carefully copied by the Victorian Clarissa nearly a hundred years ago.

I, Lettice Keswick, begin this diary on the twenty-fifth day of May in the Year of Our Lord 1660 A.D. On this very day' all England rejoices and is glad and light of heart. Our Sovereign, Charles Stuart, returned from Exile and at Dover his feet have trod again on English soil this day.

The Monarchy will be restored forthwith. He will be crowned King Charles II and the foul and bloody execution of his father is avenged in part.

Death to the traitors who led his father to the block.

On this day in Yorkshire and o'er all the land did cathedral and church bells ring forth in praise of our gracious Sovereign, restored to us as if by a great Miracle. And bonfires burned tonight and messengers rode the length and breadth of England to spread the good and glorious news.

My dear Husband, Lord and Master Francis, did lead us all in prayer this day, servants and family together, in the blue tower and we gave our grateful thanks to the dear Lord Our God for His Goodness and Mercy. Our true Monarch is safe. We are all reborn.

I write my words late this night, well nigh past midnight, by the light of my tallow candle. It was this night that my beloved Husband Francis came to me and took me to him in bodily love and we loved each other well. Perhaps this joyful night I have conceived, God willing, and from our great happiness and love will be born another child. So does my Lord and Husband pray, as do I, and God willing it will be a son and a male heir at last, to carry on the pride of the Keswicks. I pray that it is. I pray.

It is growing late. My candle splutters. My Husband sleeps. Outside the May moon rides high across a dark sky. It is very late. I hear my Husband stir. I must put down my pen and snuff my candle, step over to the bed to sleep, to share his dreams. This I will do. I will pick up my pen tomorrow and I will continue.

I went on reading avidly, my eyes moving swiftly across page after page. I was eager to know more, fascinated by Lettice Keswick's jottings about her life in Yorkshire in the seventeenth century.

There were several more short sections, dated the end of June; then she moved on to cover a few days in July and August. Once more she was writing about her everyday life and her doings. She wrote of her two little daughters, Rachel and Viola, her life as a country squire's wife and the lady of the manor. The last entry for August was a joyful notation that she was at last pregnant and hopeful it was with a son.

I paused for a moment and gazed out the window reflectively. Nothing has changed since time immemorial. We all harbor the same dreams and hopes and desires as those who have gone before us. Here I was, reading about Lettice's desire for another child in 1660, and this was mine and Andrew's dream at the moment, now in 1988. I smiled to myself thinking how very little really changed in life, and, dropping my eyes, I continued to read.

The diary as such stopped quite abruptly. I experienced a genuine sense of disappointment, even irritation, so taken was I by Lettice Keswick's words.

But she had digressed, writing pages of household hints, which I merely glanced at, then listing all sorts of recipes— recipes for making potpourri and pomanders from dried flowers, herbs, and certain fruits and spices. There were instructions on how to make beeswax candles and soap; copious notes about herbs—sweet-smelling herbs for freshening rooms and closets, others for making ointments to treat various ailments, still others to add flavor to the cooking pot.

Her next section was devoted to preserves. Now came Lettice's recipes for rhubarb-and-gooseberry jam, quince jelly, bilberry jelly, lemon curd, mincemeat and sweet apple chutney. Once again I simply scanned these and moved on.

Finally the diary of her daily life began anew, the dates of entry running through October to December. I was completely engrossed as I read about winter life at Kilgram Chase, the various family activities, her needlework and embroidery, her husband's hunting and shooting skills, his expertise with horses. She wrote about the winter solstice, the weather, and her difficult pregnancy.

But before she continued with her daily doings into the new year of 1661, she had indulged in another domestic diversion, writing endless pages about the making of pies, puddings, and pastries, elderberry and nettle wine, even ale.

The diary was a veritable treasure trove, in a variety of ways. Unfortunately, I did not have time to read it scrupulously and in its entirety. At least not now. So I scanned, speed-read the rest of it, still admiring Clarissa's wonderful copperplate handwriting. Not once did it falter; her script was impeccable, a work of art.

As I swiftly turned the pages, I saw that Lettice Keswick's diary covered the early months of 1661 and finished in the spring. She spoke of the birth of her son, Miles, in the April of that year, after a long and difficult labor, and she wrote about her husband's birthday in May.

The very last page was dated May 29. There were no more entries, because there were no more pages left in the book. She had filled it.

Again, I found myself feeling disappointed. Until it struck me that the diary had only ended because the book she was writing in was full. Surely Lettice had continued her diary, for she was a natural writer with an easy, flowing style, almost conversational, and a great eye for detail. There *must* be another volume somewhere here in this library, and Clarissa must have found it and copied it. Just as I wanted to know more, so must she have been riddled with curiosity.

Jumping up, I headed for the ladder, in my anxiety totally ignoring Joe's warnings about climbing it. I did just that, in fact, until I came to the second-to-last step from the top. I did not dare climb higher, for fear of having an accident.

But I was quite high enough, it seemed. I stood immediately below the shelf from which Joe had taken the ledgers and the diary, and it was easy for me to read the titles of the books which remained. There were two novels by Thomas Hardy, three by the Brontës, and six by Charles Dickens, as well as a volume of sonnets by Shakespeare. But nothing else, just a gap on the shelf where the ledgers and Clarissa's copy of the diary had been.

Liking the look of the book of sonnets, which had a gorgeous red binding with gold lettering, I took this off the shelf. It was then that I saw it. A small, thick book with a black leather cover, which lay just behind the Brontë novels against the back of the shelf. For a moment I thought it was a Bible, but when I looked at it I saw that it had a totally plain front. Certainly no gold lettering proclaimed its title.

Balancing myself carefully at the top of the stepladder, I opened the black book. With a little thrill and a rush of excitement, I recognized it at once. It was the *original* Lettice diary, written in her own hand, the one Clarissa had so carefully copied in 1893. I poked around behind the Brontë, Hardy, and Dickens volumes, but there was nothing else there.

Holding the diary tightly in one hand, I edged my way down the stepladder and hurried over to the table in front of the window. Sitting down, I opened Lettice Keswick's original diary.

I stared at it in awe, turning the pages slowly, carefully, afraid that I might damage it if I handled it roughly.

The diary was over three hundred years old, but to my amazement it was undamaged. Some pages felt slightly brittle, but not very many, and there were tiny wormholes here and there. But for the most part, it was wonderfully intact.

What a miracle it was that it had lasted all this time. But then, no one had known of its existence, and so no one had handled it. Except for Clarissa, of course, who had found it, copied it, and presumably put it back for safety's sake. Then again, the temperature in the library remained the same, year in, year out, exactly as it had for centuries, I was certain. It was always cool and dry; there was no dampness, and certainly the heat from the fire would not cause any damage to any of the old books. It barely warmed the room. No wonder, then, that the seventeenth-century diary had been so well preserved.

The original, written by Lettice herself, was penned in a spidery, rather elaborate script, typical of the century in which she had lived, but her writing was clear and legible. And I discovered, to my delight, that the original diary contained something unique: exquisite little pen-and-ink drawings and watercolors of flowers, fruit, and herbs, and vignettes of Lettice's gardens here at Kilgram Chase, which illustrated the diary throughout.

It was obvious to me that I had stumbled upon a small treasure. Of course, it was of no real value and probably of little interest to anyone except the Keswicks, and I couldn't wait to show it to Diana and Andrew.

Glancing at my watch, I realized that the last hour and a half had sped by. It was almost four o'clock.

Rising, I left the library and went down the corridor to Diana's office. I peeked in. Andrew's grim expression as he spoke on the phone registered most forcibly. He was no doubt talking to Jack Underwood in New York. He sounded angry in that quiet, controlled way of his, and he wasn't even aware that I had cracked open the door. I closed it softly, deeming it wiser to leave him in peace to attend to his business.

I really did need a breath of fresh air now, having been in the house since our arrival that morning, and after the long drive north in the car. In the nearby mudroom I sat down on the bench, took off my shoes, pulled on a pair of Diana's green Wellington boots, and lifted a barbour off the peg. I loved these fleece-lined waterproof jackets that are so snug and can be worn in all kinds of weather. In each pocket I found a woolen glove. After putting these on, I took a red wool scarf off the coat stand, threw it around my neck, and went out through the side door.

It was chilly. The morning sun had long ago disappeared, leaving a sky that was a faded, pale blue, almost without color.

The smell of autumn assailed me: dampness, rotting leaves, and wood smoke, acrid on the air. Somewhere, not far away, one of the gardeners had a bonfire going. It was that time of year, when dead plants and roots, dried leaves, and garden debris in general went into the flames; I had just had my own winter bonfire last weekend at Indian Meadows.

As I turned the corner of the house, I practically stumbled over Wilf, the gardener, who was shoveling dead leaves and roots into a pile, obviously fodder for the fire.

He glanced up when he heard my sharp exclamation.

"Aw, it's you, Mrs. Andrew." He touched his cloth cap and grinned at me. "How you be doing then?" He rested his filthy hands on top of the shovel and stood gaping at me, staring right through me.

"Fine, thank you. And how are you feeling these days, Wilf?"

"Can't complain. Me rheumatism's a bit of a bother, but there's nowt much else wrong with me. I don't expect to be kicking up t'daisies in yon cemetry for a long time." He laughed. It sounded like a cackle.

"I'm glad to hear it." I nodded and hurried away, heading for the pond. There was something odd about Wilf Broadbent. He always seemed to have a baleful glint in his eye when he talked to me. I thought he might be a bit touched. Andrew said he was just gormless, using the Yorkshire word for dumb, stupid. Diana laughed at us when we discussed Wilf. She believed him to be the salt of the earth.

Four brown ducks swam away as I approached the water.

I stood watching them paddling as fast as they could to the far bank, absently wondering if it would freeze by Christmas. The twins so longed to skate on this pond, just as their father had done when he was a little boy. But I didn't think it would be cold enough to freeze; it was a decent-sized body of water.

I set off to walk around the pond, my mind focusing on Lettice and Clarissa, those two other Keswick women who had been the brides of Keswick men, and who had lived out their entire lives here. If only walls could talk to me, what marvelous secrets they would reveal, what tales they could tell.

On the other hand, the *diary* had talked, hadn't it? Only for a short while, but still, it had spoken to me of a time past, given me a bit of the family history.

Even Clarissa's frontispiece, short as it was, and her act of copying it so meticulously had told me quite a lot about her. She must have been a good woman, conscientious, God–fearing, a typical Victorian, but obviously an intelligent and caring person. Certainly she had cared about the diary, had understood what it meant to the family. Also, she had had the foresight to realize that the original might not survive the passage of time; and she had considered it important enough to preserve it for posterity. Of course she lacked artistic talent because she had not copied the drawings or watercolors, but that wasn't so important.

And what did the diary tell me about the diarist herself?

First and foremost that Lettice was a born writer, articulate and with a thorough knowledge of the language and an understanding of its beauty. It was at her fingertips, and she had made excellent use of it. The illustrations indicated that she had been artistically inclined, the household hints and recipes proclaimed her to have been a good housekeeper and cook, not to mention an excellent herbalist and wine-maker. Her many references to her husband and children revealed that she had been a loving wife and mother, and lastly, I decided that she had had a political turn of mind. There were innumerable references to Parliament in her diary, and acerbic comments, and certainly she had been a dyed-in-the-wool royalist, elated, no, *overjoyed* when Charles II returned to England to accept the throne.

It struck me again that there must be another volume of her diary *somewhere* in that vast library. A truly natural writer such as Lettice Keswick would not stop just like that, with such terrible abruptness. But how to find it amongst those thousands of books lining the hundreds of shelves?

There was no time for me to look for it now, not today or tomorrow. Perhaps when we came back for Christmas I could have a stab at it. The effort would be worth it. After all, in my opinion the diary was a little jewel. I knew Diana would be intrigued by it and so would Andrew, if I could ever tear him away from that briefcase and those wretched papers. I couldn't imagine what that awful Malcolm Stainley had done, unless he had been cooking the books, God forbid. If he had, Andrew would go for the jugular, and Jack wouldn't be far behind, wielding a very sharp knife, figuratively speaking.

As I walked up the wide path carved out between the expanse of green lawns, I saw a car approaching the house. It was moving at a snail's pace up the driveway between the giant oaks, and it was not Diana returning, I knew that. This was not her car.

Within a few seconds the car and I had drawn closer. I saw that it was a pale blue Jaguar.

Was Diana expecting a visitor? It was odd that she hadn't mentioned it, if she were. She usually told us if someone was coming to tea, warned us, really, in case we felt we had to escape. Usually Andrew did, since her guests for this truly English ritual were people like the woman who ran the church institute, the vicar and his wife, the head of the garden club, or some such local character.

The car slowed, then came to a standstill at the bottom of the stone steps. I strode across the terrace to the top of the steps and stood looking down expectantly.

The door of the Jaguar finally opened. A woman alighted.

She was tall and slender, with a mass of dark, wavy hair that tumbled around a rather narrow but attractive face. Her eyes were dark, intense, and her generous mouth was a slash of bright red lipstick.

At first glance, her clothes looked like a gypsy's odd assortment, but as my eyes swept over her swiftly, I realized there was a degree of coordination about them. At least as far as the colors were concerned. She wore a long, full, green wool skirt, topped by a short bomber jacket made of red, green, purple, and yellow patches. Joseph's coat of many colors. Or so it seemed to me. Long scarves of yellow, purple, and red were wrapped around her neck and trailed down her back. Her boots were red, her handbag yellow.

I did not have to be introduced to this colorful woman.

I knew exactly who she was.

Gwendolyn Reece-Jones in person.

My father's mistress.

17

We stared hard at each other, she and I. And for a split second neither of us spoke.

I was aware from the expression in her eyes that she knew who I was, had recognized me as Edward Jordan's daughter, but I doubted that she would acknowledge this. Certainly she would not confide her relationship with my father or even say that they were friends. I knew this instinctively.

She spoke first.

Moving closer to the bottom step, she said, "I'm looking for Mrs. Keswick. Rude. To come without calling first. Tried. Your phone's been engaged for a long time. Is Mrs. Keswick in?"

I shook my head. "No, I'm afraid she isn't, she went off to do a few errands. But she should be back any moment. Would you like to come in and wait for her?"

Gwenny bit her lip, and an anxious expression crossed her angular face. "Don't want to impose."

"I'm sure Diana won't be long. I know she'd be very upset if she missed you."

"Frightfully kind. Yes, well, er, thank you. Perhaps I will hang around for a few minutes." She began to mount the steps. Drawing level to me, she held out her hand. "Gwendolyn Reece-Jones."

"Mallory Keswick," I answered, shaking her hand. Immediately I swung around, stepped up to the front door, opened it, and ushered her into the small entrance foyer. "Can I take your jacket?" I asked politely.

"Just the scarves, thank you," she replied, unraveling the three of them from around her neck.

After hanging these in the coat closet, I took her into the parlor next door to the dining room. This was a small, comfortable room, rather cozy, with a Victorian feeling to it, a sort of den, which we used all the time. It was there we watched television and usually had afternoon tea and drinks in the evening.

Parky had turned on the lamps and started the fire. This burned merrily in the grate, and the room looked inviting.

"Please make yourself comfortable," I said. "If you'll excuse me, I'll go and take off my boots and tell Andrew you're here. He'll come and join us. If he's off the phone."

"No rush. Take your time." She reached for the current issue of *Country Life* which lay on the tufted ottoman and sat down in an armchair next to the fire.

Once I had shed Diana's barbour and Wellingtons and put on my shoes in the mudroom, I went in search of my husband. Andrew was still on the phone in Diana's office, but this time when I opened the door he saw me, smiled, and raised an eyebrow questioningly.

"We have a visitor," I said rolling my eyes to the ceiling.

"Just a minute, Jack," he murmured into the receiver and looked across at me, frowning slightly.

"Who is it?" he asked.

"You'd never guess in a million years, so I'm going to tell you. *Gwendolyn Reece-Jones.* She's here looking for your mother. She tried to phone first, but she couldn't get through." I laughed. "For obvious reasons."

"Gwenny!" he exclaimed. "I'll be damned! Since Ma isn't

back yet, offer her tea, and I'll join you in a few minutes. I'm just finishing up with Jack."

I nodded. "Give him my best."

"I will."

As I turned away I heard him say, "That was Mal, she sends her love. Well, that's about it, old buddy. Just wanted to run all this by you."

Parky was in the kitchen putting cups and saucers on a large tray; she glanced up as I walked across the floor and hovered next to the table where she was working.

"Hi, Parky," I murmured. "You'll have to add another cup and saucer. A friend of Mrs. Keswick's has just arrived. Miss Gwendolyn Reece-Jones. I'm sure you know her. Anyway, she'll be having tea with us."

"*Oh.*" Parky pursed her lips. "Miss Reece-Jones can't have been expected, or Mrs. Keswick would have told me before she went out. She's very precise about things like that, Mrs. Keswick is."

"She wasn't expected, Parky."

"A bit rude, if you ask me," Parky sniffed, "dropping in like that." She marched into the pantry and came back with an extra cup and saucer. "Most people telephone first."

"She did try to get through," I explained, hiding a smile, amused at Parky's irritation. But then, she was a stickler for good manners; I always remembered that about her. For a reason I didn't quite understand, I felt I had to defend Gwenny, so I now added, "Mr. Andrew's been on the phone to New York for well over an hour, Parky, that's why Miss Reece-Jones was unable to get us."

"Hurrumph," was all Parky said as she went on fussing with the teapot and the other things she needed for afternoon tea. But after a few seconds she threw me a warm smile, and leaning closer, she said, "I've made a luvely caraway-seed cake for tea, Mr. Andrew's favorite. And nursery sandwiches. He did enjoy them when he was little. Four sorts today. Tomato, cucumber, watercress, and egg salad. Homemade scones, too, with home-made strawberry jam and Cornish cream."

"Goodness, we're not going to want any dinner!" I exclaimed, before I could stop myself. "So much food, Parky."

"But it's what I always serve, Mrs. Andrew, and I've been doing so for thirty years," she announced, taking a step back and staring at me. She looked slightly put out.

Realizing that I might have hurt her feelings unintentionally, I said quickly, "The tea sounds wonderful. I just know Mr. Andrew is going to enjoy it, and so will I. Why, my mouth's watering already."

Mollified, she beamed. "In any case, dinner's a simple meal tonight, Mrs. Andrew. Just Morecombe Bay potted shrimps, cottage pie, and a green salad."

"No dessert?" I teased.

Taking me quite seriously, she cried, "Oh, yes! I always make a dessert for Mr. Andrew. You know how he loves them. But I haven't decided which one to make yet—English trifle or cus-tard flan."

"It'll be delicious, whatever it is," I muttered and hurried to the door. "I'll go and keep Miss Reece-Jones company. By the way, Parky, did Mrs. Keswick say what time she'd be back?"

"She's never later than a quarter to five for tea. *Never.*"

"As soon as she arrives perhaps you can serve it," I suggested.

"I will that. And I expect Mr. Andrew'll be needing a bit of sustenance by then, working all afternoon the way he has, poor thing. On a Saturday too."

"Yes," I agreed and slipped out.

Gwenny Reece-Jones was leafing through the magazine when I returned to the parlor. "Andrew will join us in a minute," I told her, closing the door behind me. "And Diana's expected back imminently, so I hope you'll join us for tea, Miss Reece-Jones."

"How nice. Love to."

"Good."

As if she felt she needed to explain her sudden and unexpected arrival, she cleared her throat and said, "Working in Leeds. Doing *A Midsummer Night's Dream.* At the Theatre Royal. Sets. I design sets."

"Diana told me you were a theatrical designer."

"Oh." She looked momentarily taken aback. "Came over to Kilburn today. Know it, do you?"

"I think so. Isn't that the place where there's a giant-sized horse carved into the side of the hill?"

"Correct. On the face of Roulston Scar. Wanted to order a hall table from the Robert Thompson workshop. The great Yorkshire furniture maker and carver. Dead now. His grandsons run the workshop. Continue his work. Thought it a good idea to stop on my way back to Leeds. Say hello to Diana."

"I'm glad you did. As a matter of fact, Diana mentioned you to me only the other day."

"She did?"

I took a deep breath and plunged in. "She told me that you know my father, Edward Jordan, that you're a friend of his. A very good friend."

Startled, Gwenny gaped at me. A bright pink flush spread up from her neck to flood her face. "Good friends, yes," she admitted. She glanced away swiftly and stared into the fire.

I had a terrible feeling that I had embarrassed her, which I hadn't meant to do at all. I simply wanted to have everything out in the open. I said quickly, "I'm glad you and Daddy are friends. I worry about him, worry that he's lonely. It's comforting to know he has some companionship when he's in London, Miss Reece-Jones."

"Call me Gwenny," she said and bestowed a huge smile on me.

I thought I detected a look of relief on her face as I smiled back at her.

At this moment the door flew open and Andrew came in. "Hello, Miss Reece-Jones, remember me?" he said, grinning from ear to ear. "You used to bounce me on your knee when I was a little boy." He strode over to her and shook her hand.

"Never forgot you," she laughed, staring up at him, affection softening her face. "Mischievous." She glanced across at me. "Mischievous boy."

Before I could make any kind of comment, the door opened again, and Diana walked in, obviously not at all surprised to see Gwendolyn Reece-Jones sitting in her parlor. Undoubtedly she had seen the car in the drive.

"Hello, Gwenny dear," Diana said, crossing the room to the fireplace.

Gwenny jumped up and the two women embraced, then Gwenny said, "Rather rude. Dropping in like this. Wanted to say hello."

"Please don't apologize, it's lovely to see you," Diana said in a warm voice. "You must stay for tea. I'll just pop into the kitchen and tell Parky to bring it in. Excuse me for a moment."

"I'll come with you," I exclaimed, moving toward the door. "To help."

Diana looked at me curiously but made no comment, and we left the parlor together.

Of course later in the evening, after Gwendolyn Reece-Jones left and went on her way to Leeds, we held a little postmortem on her. It was only natural, I suppose, given the circumstances.

"She has such an odd way of speaking," I said to Diana, shaking my head. "It's sort of staccato."

"I know, she talks in little sharp bursts, and she has a predilection for using one-word sentences. But she's a good sort, awfully kind and considerate, and she doesn't have a bad word for anybody, or a bad bone in her body, for that matter," Diana answered.

"I liked her very much," I murmured.

"And she liked you," Diana replied. "Furthermore, she was rather relieved that you know about her relationship with your father."

"I hope I didn't embarrass her, I just wanted to level with her, let *her* know *I* knew." I gave Diana one of my piercing looks. "Did she say anything when you went out to the car with her, Diana?"

"Only that you'd taken her by surprise when you'd mentioned Edward, and what a lovely young woman you were, so pretty. She was very admiring of your beautiful red hair."

"I thought *she* was rather attractive, too, and I can just see her and Daddy together. I approve; she *is* very nice."

"But as eccentric as hell!" Andrew exclaimed. "A genuine character. And whenever I hear the name Gwendolyn, I think of scarves. She's always worn masses of them, rain or shine, all kinds of weather, and as far as I remember they've been made of every type of fabric. Gwenny's a regular Isadora Duncan, if you ask me." He laughed and stood up. "Would you like another glass of wine, Ma?"

"Not at the moment, darling," Diana said, "I've still got half of this one left."

"I think I will," he said and walked across the parlor to the skirted table in the corner, where Parky had put a tray holding a bottle of white wine in an ice bucket and a syphon of soda water. "How about you, Mal?"

"I'm fine, Andrew, and listen, you two, before we have supper I want to show you my finds."

"Finds? What do you mean?" Andrew asked, turning around and smiling at me fondly.

"I was poking around in the library this afternoon, and I found a diary by one of your ancestors, Lettice Keswick, which she wrote in the seventeenth century. Actually, what I found was a *copy* of the original, and it was in the most beautiful copperplate handwriting. It was done by Clarissa Keswick, who copied it in 1893 in order to preserve it."

"Good Lord! So that's what you were doing all afternoon, digging around amongst those moldy old books. Better you than me, my love." Andrew squeezed my shoulder as he came back to the fireplace, bent over me, and kissed the top of my head. "And trust *you* to come across something unusual."

Diana cut in, "But you said *finds*, Mal, in the plural. What else did you unearth?" She had a puzzled expression in her eyes as she looked at me across the room.

"I actually found the *real* diary, as well as Clarissa's copy of it," I said, and I went on to explain what I had done earlier in the day. Then, standing up, walking toward the door, I finished, "Let me go and get them; they're in the library. Once you see both books, you'll understand what I'm talking about."

Firelight danced on the walls and across the ceiling, filling our bedroom with a rosy glow. There was no other light in the room, and I felt relaxed, drowsy, encased in a cocoon of warmth and love as I lay within the circle of Andrew's arms.

Earlier, a high wind had blown up, and now I could hear it howling over the moors. In the distance was the sound of thunder, and lightning flashed spasmodically, illuminating the bedroom with a bright white brilliance for a moment or two.

I shivered slightly, despite the warmth of the bed, and put my arm around my husband, drew closer to him. "I'm glad we're not out in that. Quite a storm's blown up since we came upstairs."

He chuckled. "Yes, it has, and we're in the best place, you and I. Snug as two bugs in a rug. But you know what? When I was little I always wanted to be out in it, in the rain and the wind and the hail, don't ask me why. I just loved storms. Maybe the inherent drama of such dreadful weather appealed to something in me. And once, when I was about seven, my father told me that it was our ancestors in their armor crashing about up there in the heavens, that their ghosts were riding out to conquer their enemies, as they had done centuries ago. I'm certain that must've sparked my imagination when I was a kid."

"And *did* you go out in the storm when you were a boy?"

"Sometimes I managed to sneak out of the house, but not if Ma could help it. She was always a bit overprotective."

"What mother isn't? Anyway, I don't blame her; storms can be dangerous. People have been struck by lightning—"

"Like I was, when I first met you!" he interrupted, putting his hand under my chin and turning my face to his. He kissed me softly, tenderly on the mouth, then broke away. "The French call it a *coup de foudre*, that instantaneous falling in love just like that." He snapped his thumb and a finger together. "In other words, struck by lightning."

I smiled against his chest. "I know what it means."

There was a small silence. We were content to lie together like this, so at peace with each other.

After a few minutes I said, "It's been such a lovely weekend, Andrew, I'm glad we came to Yorkshire, aren't you?"

"I am, and anyway, it's not over yet. We still have Sunday here. We can go riding tomorrow morning if you like, up on the gallops as I promised. And then we can take it easy for the rest of the day, be lazy. We'll have a good Sunday lunch, read the newspapers, watch television."

"You're not going to do any work?" I asked, my voice rising a fraction in my surprise.

"Certainly not. Anyway, I've done as much as I can. Now I've got to wait for Jack to come in from New York next week."

"I have a feeling you've discovered something about Malcolm Stainley, something awful."

When he was silent, I went on, "Something . . . unpleasant, unsavory, perhaps?"

His answer was simply a long, drawn-out sigh.

"What is it? What's he done?" I pressed, riddled with curiosity. I turned my face to look at his in the firelight, but it betrayed nothing.

"I don't want to go into it now, darling, honestly I don't." He sighed again. "But always remember: Beware of guys selling snake oil."

"He's crooked, Andrew! That's what you mean, isn't it?"

Pushing himself up on one elbow, he bent over me, smoothed the hair away from my face, and kissed me full on the mouth. Then he stopped and stared deeply into my eyes. "I don't want to discuss it. I've got other, more important things on my mind right now."

"Such as what?" I teased.

"You know *what*, Mrs. Keswick," he murmured, a half smile playing around his mouth.

I looked up into his face, that beloved face which was so dear to me. His expression was intense, and his extraordinary blue eyes had turned darker, almost navy in the firelight; they overpowered me.

"*You*," he said at last. "I've got you on my mind. I love you so much, Mal. You're my whole reason for being."

"I love you, too." I stroked his face. "Make love to me."

Bending over me, he brought his mouth down to mine and kissed me for a long time, gently at first. But his desire overtook him, and his kisses became wilder, more passionate.

"Oh, Mal, oh, my darling," he said between his hot kisses. Then pulling the bedcovers away, he slipped off the straps of my nightgown and released my breasts, stroking them. "Oh, look at you, darling, you're so beautiful, my beautiful wife." Lowering his head, he kissed my nipples, and his hand slid down my thigh, along the silky length of my nightgown until he caught the hem of it in his fingers. He raised it to my waist, began to kiss my stomach, then my inner thighs. And all the while his hand stroked my body in long caresses, and I trembled under his touch.

Eventually, his mouth came to rest at the center of me, and I felt myself stiffen with pleasure. I was swept along, lost in my love for him. He came and knelt between my legs and brought me cresting to a climax, then he stopped suddenly and slid inside me, filling me. We clung together, and as always we became one.

The fire had burned low, and the shadows had lengthened across the bedroom walls. Outside, the wind howled and rain slashed violently against the panes of glass. It was a wild November night here at the edge of the moors, and growing wilder, by the sound of it.

Andrew stirred against me and murmured, "Shall I put another log on the fire?"

"Not unless you're cold."

"I'm fine. And we should let the fire die out anyway."

Sitting up, I climbed out of bed, padded over to the window, and pulled the cord to close the draperies, shutting out the storm. As I walked back, I said, "That was nice of your mother, wasn't it?"

"Inviting Gwenny for Christmas, you mean?"

"Yes." I got into bed, pulled the covers over me, and snuggled up to Andrew. "I hope she'll come, and that she'll bring Daddy with her. That way it'll be a real family occasion."

"I don't think your father could stay away. And the twins are going to love it here. It's going to be a wonderful Christmas, Mal. The best."

PART THREE

NEW YORK CITY

18

New York, December 1988

"Have a wonderful baby shower, and we'll see you tomorrow," Andrew said, moving across the hall to the front door of the apartment.

"It won't be the same without you, but I do understand your reasons for fleeing," I said, laughing.

He laughed with me. "Sixteen women in this apartment is a bit too much even for me to cope with." He picked up Trixy's lead and his canvas bag and opened the front door. "Come on, kids, let's get this show on the road. It'll be teatime before we get to Indian Meadows, if we don't leave soon."

"Coming, Dad," Jamie said, buttoning his quilted, down-filled jacket but getting the buttons in the wrong holes.

I bent down to help him do it correctly, then kissed him on the cheek. He looked at me through solemn eyes and asked, "Is it *our* baby shower, Mom?"

I shook my head. "No, Alicia Munroe's. She's the one having the baby, honey."

"Oh," he said, and his little face fell. "Any news of our baby, Mom? Have you made it yet?" he asked, fixing me with his bright blue eyes, a hopeful look flashing across his face.

"Not yet," I answered, standing up. I glanced at Andrew and we exchanged amused looks, and he winked at me.

Lissa said, "Don't forget to feed Swellen, Mom, will you?"

"No, I won't, darling, I promise." I hunkered down on my haunches and kissed her. She put her little arms around my neck and showered me with fluttery kisses on my cheek. "Butterfly kisses for you, Mommy, like Daddy gives me," she said, then holding her head on one side in that old-fashioned way she had, she continued, "Did you tell Santa to bring me the big baby doll?"

"Yes. Well, at least Daddy told him."

"Will Santa know where to come?" she asked, suddenly sounding anxious. Her expression grew worried when she added, "Will he find Nanna's house in Yorkshire?"

"Of course. Daddy gave Santa her address."

She beamed at me, and I buttoned her coat and pulled on her blue woolen cap that exactly matched her eyes. "There! You look beautiful! You're my beautiful little girl, the most beautiful girl in the whole wide world. Now, put your gloves on. Both of you," I said, glancing at Jamie. "And I don't want either of you running outside to play without your coats when you're in the country. It's far too cold. And don't give Trixy any tidbits from the table."

"No, Mom," they said in unison.

"Hear that, Trixy?" I said, glancing down at the puppy. Our little Bichon Frise looked up at me through her soulful black eyes and wagged her tail. I picked her up and cuddled her, kissed the top of her head, then put her back down on the floor.

I walked with them to the front door and stood in the outside foyer waiting for the elevator to come. Andrew hugged me and kissed me on the cheek, then asked, "Did you put the list in the canvas bag? The list of the things you want me to bring back tomorrow?"

"Yes, I did. And there's not much, really, just a few items for the twins and our shearling coats, yours and mine, to take with us to Yorkshire."

"Okay, no problem, Puss." He kissed me again and ushered the kids and the puppy into the elevator. "See you."

"Drive carefully," I said just as the elevator doors started to close.

"I will," he called back. "And I'll ring you when we get there, Mal."

It was quiet in the apartment now that they had left. I went to my desk in the bedroom, sat down, and carefully wrote the card to go with Alicia's gift.

Alicia Munroe was a good friend of Sarah's and mine and had been at Radcliffe with us. A fellow New Yorker, she had married Jonathan Munroe two years ago and moved to Boston with him. She had come to Manhattan for the weekend to see her parents and to attend the baby shower Sarah and I were giving in her honor at the apartment.

When he heard, three weeks ago, what we were planning, Andrew had exclaimed. "It's the country for me, Mal! In any case, I want to give Indian Meadows the once-over before we take off for Yorkshire for Christmas. I'll take the twins and Trixy with me, get them all out of your hair, and you can have a real girls' weekend with Sarah."

When I had worried out loud how he would manage without Jenny, our former au pair, who had finally returned to live in London, he had grinned at me and said one word: *"Nora."* And, of course, hearing her name had set my mind at ease at once. Nora loved the twins and enjoyed cooking for them, fussing over them. She would be in her element without me hovering around, as would Eric, who was devoted to Jamie and Lissa.

I glanced at the small calendar on my desk. Today was Saturday the tenth. In exactly eleven days we were flying to London and then taking the train to Yorkshire the following morning.

Diana had invited Sarah to join us for Christmas, and she had been thrilled to accept, and we were all going to stay at Kilgram Chase until early January. Gwenny Reece-Jones and my father were going to be with us too; in fact my father had called me yesterday from London. He had wanted to tell me how much he was looking forward to spending the holidays with me, Andrew, and his grandchildren. He had also told me how glad he was I liked Gwendolyn.

There were still quite a lot of preparations to make for the trip, and tomorrow Sarah and I were going shopping for last-minute gifts. Now I began to make a list on a yellow pad and was stumped when I came to Gwenny's name. Last night, tongue in cheek, Andrew had suggested we buy her a scarf. And although he had been joking, it wasn't a bad idea after all, since she did seem to like them. Perhaps I would find something special and unusual at Bloomingdale's.

Once I had finished the list, I put the card in the shopping bag with the gift for Alicia, an antique silver christening cup. Then, carrying the bag, I went into the living room.

Josie, our housekeeper, a lovely, motherly woman from Chile, was already plumping up cushions on the two big traditional sofas and armchairs.

She glanced up as I came in and said, "I've dusted the dining room, and I'll get to the kitchen next, Mrs. Keswick."

"Thanks, Josie, but perhaps you'd better make the beds and tidy the bedrooms first. Miss Thomas should be here any minute, and then we'll start preparing some of the food. I guess you ought to leave the kitchen until last."

"You're right, and I can help with the sandwiches as soon as I've finished cleaning."

"Thanks," I said, and went into the adjoining dining room, where I put the shopping bag in a corner. I added, "I'm going to start setting the table for the tea."

By the time Sarah arrived half an hour later, I had already

put out cups, saucers, and plates, as well as crystal flutes, since we had called the shower a champagne tea, and we were going to serve Veuve Clicquot.

"You haven't left me very much to do," Sarah said, as she surveyed my handiwork in the dining room.

"Don't kid yourself," I shot back. "There's a lot to do yet. Roll your sleeves up, and let's go to the kitchen."

But the first thing we did was to have a cup of coffee together. This we drank at the table in front of the window, chatting about the shower and Sarah's hectic week and gossiping in general.

Finally, fifteen minutes later we started to work on the food, cutting the slices of smoked salmon into small pieces, boiling eggs for the egg salad, slicing cucumbers and tomatoes, and mashing sardines. All of these things we would use for the tea sandwiches later in the afternoon, just before the guests were due. They had been invited for three o'clock and it was still far too soon to make the sandwiches.

At one moment Sarah said, "I'm glad we made it early, Mal. Everyone'll be gone by six, no later than six-thirty, and maybe we can go to a movie, have supper out somewhere."

"Great idea. And how about a snack now? I don't know about you, but I'm starving." I looked at the clock on the wall. "It's nearly one thirty-five."

"I'm on a diet. In readiness for Christmas."

I laughed. "But Sarah, you look fantastic. You are *svelte*."

"I could still lose a few pounds. But okay, why not? I'll have a taste of the smoked salmon."

"Coming up," I said, reaching for a slice of bread. The phone rang, and I picked it up.

"Hello, Puss, it's me, and we're here," Andrew said. "And guess what, it's snowing! Mal, it's gorgeous, just like a fairyland. All white. And the snow is glistening in the sun. I promised the kids a snowball fight later."

"That's great, but make sure they wear their Wellies and are wrapped up well, honey, won't you?"

"I will, don't worry so, Puss."

"Is Nora there, Andrew?"

"She certainly is, and so is Eric. He's got the fires going throughout the house, and Nora made a wonderful vegetable soup and baked a loaf. We're going to have lunch in a few minutes. And this soup! It smells delicious! So don't worry your little head about us, everything is fine at Indian Meadows."

"Just goes to show how well you can manage without me," I muttered.

"Oh, no I can't," he asserted, his voice dropping. "There's *no way* I can manage without *you*, Mal."

"Nor me you," I responded. "I love you."

"And I love you. Big kiss, darling. And a big kiss to Sarah. I'll see you both for supper tomorrow night. Tell her I'm looking forward to her spaghetti primavera."

"I will, and have a nice time with the kids."

19

It was snowing again, as it had yesterday. But tonight the snowflakes were light, and as I glanced out the window, I noticed that they were melting the moment they hit the pavement. So it couldn't be the weather which was making Andrew late getting home.

Putting my glass of white wine down on the coffee table, I left the den, crossed the entrance hall, and went into the kitchen.

Sarah swung around when she heard me come in. "I've turned off the water for the spaghetti. No point boiling it yet. I'll make everything at the last minute, once Andrew and the twins arrive."

I nodded, and automatically my eyes went to the kitchen clock. It was ten past eight. "I can't imagine where he is, why he's not home yet, Sash," I said.

"Anything could be holding him up," Sarah answered, putting the lid on the pot of hot water. "Traffic. Snow."

"It can't be the snow. I just looked out the den window, and it's not even settling on the ground."

"Not on East Seventy-second Street, maybe, but if it's snowing in Connecticut, it could be slowing Andrew down, and everyone else who's coming back to the city on Sunday night. There's probably a backup of cars."

"That's true, yes," I said, seizing on this possibility, wanting to ease my worry. But the fact was, Andrew was rarely, if ever, late, and that was what troubled me now. Sarah knew it as well as I did, but neither of us was voicing this thought at the moment.

I said, "I'm going to try Anna again, maybe she's home by now."

"Okay, call her," Sarah agreed.

Lifting the receiver off the wall phone in front of me, I dialed the gardener's number at Indian Meadows. It rang and rang as it had earlier this evening. I was about to hang up when the phone was finally answered.

"Hello," Anna said.

"It's me. Mal," I said. "You must have been out, Anna, I've been trying your number for ages."

"I was in Sharon. I went to visit my sister, and I—"

"Did you see Andrew before he left today?" I interrupted, wanting to get to the point.

"Yes, I did. Why?"

"What time was that?"

"About two, somewhere around there."

"*Two.* But that's over six hours ago!" I cried, and looking across at Sarah, I couldn't help transmitting my anxiety to her. She came and stood next to me, her face suddenly as full of concern as mine was.

"You mean he's not arrived home yet?" Anna asked.

"No, he hasn't, and I'm starting to worry. It never takes more than three hours at the most, and Andrew does it in less time than that."

"There's snow up here, Mal, and he may have hit more of it on the way down to the city. Oh, and there's another thing, he did say something about needing to do some Christmas shopping. That could've delayed him."

"That's true, yes, and maybe he did stop off at a couple of shops on the way in. Everything's open at this time of year, and stays open late. I guess that's what happened, and thanks, Anna, you've made me feel less anxious."

"Try not to worry, Mal, I'm sure he'll be there any second. And you'll call me before you leave for England, won't you?"

"Yes, during the week. Bye, Anna."

"Bye, Mal."

We hung up, and turning to Sarah, I said, "Andrew told Anna he needed to do some Christmas shopping. I'm sure that's the explanation. Don't you think?"

Sarah nodded, giving me a reassuring smile. "He loves all those little antique shops in the area. Also, the twins might have wanted to go to the bathroom, or wanted something to eat, and so he could've stopped several times. We often stop, if you think about it, for those very reasons."

"But why hasn't he called me? It's not like him not to be in touch, you know that," I muttered, biting my lip.

The doorbell rang several times.

Sarah and I looked at each other knowingly, and we both broke into happy smiles.

"There he is! And wouldn't you know he doesn't have his key!" I exclaimed, laughing with relief as I hurried into the entrance hall.

As I unlocked the front door and pulled it open, I cried, "And where have all of you be—" The rest of my sentence remained unsaid. It was not my husband and children who stood there, but two men in damp overcoats.

"Yes?" I stood staring at them blankly, and even before they told me who they were, I knew they were cops. As a New Yorker, I recognized them immediately, recognized that unmistakable look. They were plainclothes police officers from N.Y.P.D. My chest tightened.

"Are you Mrs. Andrew Keswick?" the older of the two cops asked.

"Yes, I am. Is there—"

"I'm Detective Johnson, and this is Detective DeMarco," he said. "We're from the Twenty-fifth Precinct. We need to talk to you, Mrs. Keswick."

They both showed me their shields.

I swallowed several times. "Is there something wrong?" I managed to say, my eyes flying nervously from him to his partner. I dreaded the answer; my heart began to clatter.

"Can we come in?" Detective Johnson said. "I think it would be better if we spoke inside."

I nodded, opened the door wider, and stepped back to let them enter the apartment.

DeMarco closed the door.

Sarah, who had been hovering in the background, said, "I'm Sarah Thomas, an old friend of Mrs. Keswick's, a friend of the family, actually."

Detective Johnson nodded, and Detective DeMarco murmured, "Ms. Thomas," and inclined his head, scrupulously polite.

I led them into the living room and said, "Is there some sort of problem? My husband's late getting home. I, we, that is, Sarah and I, have been a bit worried. He's not been in an accident, has he?"

"Let's sit down, Mrs. Keswick," DeMarco said.

I shook my head. "Just tell me what's wrong, please."

DeMarco cleared his throat and began, "Something tragic has happened. I think we should sit down."

"*Tell me.*" My voice quavered as I spoke, and a dreadful trembling took hold of me. Sudden fear surged through my body, and reaching out, I gripped the top of the wing chair to steady myself.

"We found your husband's Mercedes on Park Avenue at One Hundred Nineteenth Street. Your husband was hurt—"

"Oh, my God! Is he badly injured? Where is he? Oh, God, my children! Are they all right? Where are they? Where's my husband?"

My heart was racing. Filled with a mixture of panic and dread, I moved forward and grasped DeMarco's arm. Urgently, I said, "Why didn't you bring my children home? Which hospital is my husband in? The twins must be frightened. Take me to them, please."

Gasping, fighting my tears, I swung to Sarah and cried, "Come on, Sash, let's go! We must go to the twins and Andrew. *Come on!* They need me."

"Mrs. Keswick, Ms. Thomas, just a minute," DeMarco said.

I stopped, looked at him. There was something odd in his voice. My stomach lurched. He was going to say something awful, something I didn't want to hear. I knew it instinctively.

He said, "I'm sorry to have to tell you this, Mrs. Keswick, but your husband has been shot. He's—"

My eyes opened wide. "*Shot!* Who shot him? *Why?*" The blood was draining out of me; my legs had gone weak.

My eyes flew to Sarah. Her face had turned the color of bleached bone. In an unusually high voice, she exclaimed, "I thought the car was in some sort of accident."

I stood staring at her; somehow I had thought the same thing.

"No, Ms. Thomas," DeMarco said.

"He's not badly hurt, is he?" Sarah asked, endeavoring to speak in a more controlled voice.

"Where are my children?" I demanded before either of the detectives could answer her. "I want to go to my children and my husband."

"They're all at Bellevue," Detective DeMarco said. "And so is your dog. I'm very sorry to have to tell you this, but your—"

"My children . . . are . . . all right . . . aren't they?" I interrupted, speaking very slowly, fearfully.

Detective Johnson shook his head. He looked dour.

DeMarco said, "No, Mrs. Keswick. Your husband, your children, and your dog were all fatally shot this afternoon. We're very sorry."

"No! No! Not Andrew! Not the twins! Not Jamie and Lissa! It's not possible! It can't be true," I cried, gaping at DeMarco, uncomprehending. I began to shake.

I heard Sarah saying over and over again, "Oh, my God, my God!"

I stepped away from DeMarco, stepped away from the chair, and went lurching across the room to the entrance hall, shaking my head from side to side, denying, denying. Blindly I reached out, grabbing at air, at emptiness.

I had to get out of here.

Get to Bellevue.

Bellevue.

That's where they were.

My husband.

Get to Andrew.

To Lissa and Jamie.

Get to my children.

My children needed me.

My husband needed me.

My little Trixy needed me.

He'd said they were dead.

All dead.

The four of them.

NO!

The room became very bright, and it began to sway and move.

I heard it then. The noise.

It was a terrible, piercing scream that went ripping right through me. A bone-chilling scream rising higher and higher. It sounded like the scream of an animal being tortured, of an animal in torment.

It grew louder and louder until it filled my mind absolutely. And it deafened me.

As the floor came up to hit me in the face, I knew that it was I who was screaming.

20

When I regained consciousness, I was lying on one of the sofas in the living room.

As I opened my eyes, it was Sarah's face I saw. She sat in a chair next to me.

"Mal," she whispered, reaching out, taking hold of my hand. "Oh, Mal, darling." Her voice broke, and tears welled in her dark, compassionate eyes. I saw the pain on her face.

I grasped her hand tightly, pinning her with an intense gaze. "Tell me it's not true, Sash," I pleaded tearfully. "Tell me it's not. They're all right, aren't they? It's been a horrible mistake, hasn't it?"

"Oh, Mal," was all she could say, in a muffled voice. She was unable to continue speaking, and tears trickled down her strained white face.

I saw him then.

Detective DeMarco.

He was standing near the living room window, looking across at me. Fleetingly, a look of pity washed over his face and was instantly gone; but I knew without a doubt that it was true.

It *had* happened.

It was not a bad dream from which I had just awakened.

It was *real*, this nightmare.

My eyes shifted. Through my tears I could see his partner, Johnson. The older detective was standing by the small antique desk in front of the window overlooking Seventy-second Street. He was speaking on the phone. I heard him say, "Yes, that's correct."

I shouted in a shrill, angry voice, "I want to go to my husband and my children. I want my family. I want my dog. I want to be with them." I tried to struggle off the sofa, but Sarah put her arms around me, held me still, endeavored to soothe me.

"I want my babies," I shouted through my wracking sobs. "I want my family. I'm going to them now." I continued to struggle against Sarah, but she held me tightly.

"Yes, we *are* going, Mal, in a few minutes." Sarah's voice was low, drained. She went on. "The detectives are going to take us to the mor—to Bellevue. I just gave Detective Johnson your mother's number. He's been talking to her and David. They're coming now; they'll be here in a couple of minutes."

I clung to Sarah, sobbing against her shoulder. I wanted Andrew, I wanted the twins. What had happened this afternoon? I didn't understand. Who had shot my family? And why? Why had this happened to us? Why would anybody shoot a decent man like Andrew? Shoot innocent little children and a dog? *Why?*

Suddenly I heard the front door and my mother's voice exclaiming, "Where's my daughter? Where's Mrs. Keswick? I'm Mrs. Nelson, her mother."

I pulled away from Sarah. My mother was rushing toward me across the living room. Her face was stricken, ashen, her eyes full of horror and disbelief.

"Oh, Mom!" I cried out. "Oh, Momma! Andrew and the twins have been shot. And Trixy. Why, Mom? I don't understand."

My mother sank down heavily on the sofa, wrapped her arms around me, and held me close to her. "It doesn't make sense," she whispered, and she kept repeating this like a litany. She began to weep, and we held on to each other desperately, struggling with our pain and heartbreak.

Between sobs, my mother said, "I don't know how to help you, Mal, but I'm here for you, darling. Oh, God, how can anybody help you? This is too much for anyone to bear." She rocked me in her arms, weeping, and whispered in a cracking voice, "I can't believe it. Lissa and Jamie gone, Andrew gone. It doesn't make any sense. What has this world come to? It's godless. *Godless.*"

After a few minutes, David left the detectives and came over to the sofa, knelt down on the floor in front of us, and put his arms around my mother and me.

His voice was gentle, caring. "I'm so very, very sorry, Mal. I'm here for you and your mother. I'll do anything to help you both. All you have to do is ask me. Anything at all, Mal."

Eventually I managed to sit up. Gently, I extricated myself from my mother's arms. She lay back against the sofa; her face was haggard.

David rose, came and sat in a chair near me. "Take your time, Mal, we're in no hurry."

I looked at him, tried to speak, but I couldn't say anything. I began to weep once more. Wrapping my arms around my body, hugging myself, I moved backward and forward on the sofa, making low, keening noises. I was distraught, I was in an agony of mind, soul, and body. Every part of me felt as if it had been bludgeoned.

Finally I stopped moving and leaned back, closing my eyes. But the tears kept coming, seeping out from underneath my lids.

Opening my eyes at last, I gazed at David helplessly. He gave me his handkerchief.

After I wiped my eyes, I said in a shaky voice, "I want to see my family."

"Of course, and you shall," David said. "The detectives are ready to take you to Bellevue, Mal. We'll all come. Your mother and Sarah and I. We'll be with you."

I could only nod my understanding.

David said, "Can I get you anything? Anything to drink? Brandy, maybe?"

I shook my head. "Just water, please."

My mother stood up shakily. "I'll get it, I need a glass myself."

Sarah said, "I'll come with you, Auntie Jess."

David took hold of my hand, held it tightly in his, wanting to comfort me. His light gray eyes were full of sympathy, and his tactfulness and concern were palpable. I was thankful he was here. I had grown to know him quite well since he'd married my mother, and he was kind and considerate. He was also quick, efficient, and smart, and as a criminal lawyer he knew how to properly and effectively deal with the police.

After a second, he said, "I need to talk to the detectives, Mal. I didn't learn much from them on the phone. My fault, I didn't give them a chance to fill me in. Your mother and I just raced around here within minutes of receiving their call."

He started to get up, but I wouldn't let go of his hand.

Puzzled, he looked at me closely. "What is it, Mal?" he asked.

"Can you bring them over here? I want to hear what they have to say."

Nodding, he rose and strode across the floor. He stood talking to Johnson and DeMarco for a few minutes, and then the three of them came back and sat down near me.

Detective Johnson said, "We don't know what happened, Mrs. Keswick." He threw David a quick glance, and went on in a low voice. "It could have been a crime of opportunity, such as robbery, we're just not sure. And we won't be able to give you any real answers until we've done a proper investigation."

David said, "You told me you found the car on Park Avenue at One Hundred Nineteenth Street. At the traffic light there."

"Yes," Johnson said.

"Was the family in the car?"

Johnson said, "Yes. Mr. Keswick was in the front seat, the driver's seat, and he'd fallen across the passenger seat. His door was open, and his legs were out of the car, as if he'd been trying to get out. One back door was also open, and the children were on the backseat together, with the dog."

I pushed myself to my feet. On shaking legs I half walked, half staggered out of the living room. I managed to get to my bathroom. Closing and locking the door, I knelt on the floor and vomited into the toilet, retching until there was nothing left inside me. Then I fell over on my side and curled into a ball, sobbing my heart out. I was in shock, disbelieving. This couldn't be happening, it couldn't. This morning I had been talking and laughing with Andrew on the phone, and now . . .

"Mal, Mal, are you all right?" Sarah called, knocking on the bathroom door. "We're concerned about you."

"Give me a minute." I dragged myself to my feet, splashed cold water on my face, and looked at myself in the mirror. The face staring back did not look like mine. It was stark, the cheekbones sticking out like blades, and it was as white as chalk under all the freckles. I felt stunned, dazed, and my glazed eyes reflected this.

Not me, that's not me. But then, I would never be me again.

There were two medical examiners waiting for us at Bellevue Hospital, where the New York City Morgue was located. I followed them into the morgue, accompanied by Detectives Johnson and DeMarco as well as David Nelson.

I had protested to Detective DeMarco, begging him to let me go in alone except for the two doctors. It was Johnson who had explained the law; the police officers who were the first to arrive on the scene of a crime must be present at the identification of the body or bodies. It was mandatory.

David had insisted on coming in with me, and I hadn't had the strength to argue. In any case, the medical examiners seemed to think his presence was essential.

When they pulled out Andrew's body and showed it to me, I gasped and cried out in anguish, then pressed my hands to my mouth. I felt my legs buckle, but David was there, standing right behind me, and he put his arm around my waist, held me upright.

Oh, Andrew, my darling, my heart cried out.

My eyes were streaming as they led me to the next two compartments, pulled out the slabs, and showed me Lissa and then Jamie. My children, my darling babies. I could barely see their faces for my blinding tears. They were so still, so quiet, so cold. All I wanted was to keep them warm, to keep them safe. Oh, my poor babies.

Looking at one of the medical examiners, I gasped through my tears, "They didn't suffer, did they?"

He shook his head. "No, Mrs. Keswick. None of them suffered. Death was instantaneous."

Detective Johnson was edging me away, edging David and me away from my children.

"I want to stay with them," I whispered. "Please let me stay."

"We can't, Mrs. Keswick," Johnson said. "You can be with them tomorrow at the funeral parlor, after we've released them." Then he added, very quietly, "Your dog's here. Normally it would have gone to an animal hospital, but it was required for evidence."

"She," I said. "She's a she, not an it."

"You must have a vet, don't you?" Johnson said. "We'll need the name and address. The dog can go there tomorrow."

All I could do was nod. I was sobbing uncontrollably.

One of the doctors took me to Trixy, showed her to me. I bent over her and touched the top of her furry head, and my tears fell down on my hands.

Trixy. My little Trixola.

I was still weeping when David guided me out into the corridor. He led me down to the waiting room, but I could barely walk; waves of shock and heartbreak were washing over me.

As we went into the waiting room, my mother stood up and so did Sarah. They both hurried over.

"Oh, Mom, oh, Momma," I wept. "It is them. They're dead. Whatever am I going to do without them?"

21

"Park and One Hundred Nineteenth Street is a very bad area, Mrs. Keswick; there's drug dealing on the street, prostitution. So, what do you think your husband was doing up there on Sunday afternoon?" Detective Johnson asked.

I stared at him, clenching my hands in my lap, endeavoring to control their constant trembling. "I know what he was doing up there," I said quietly. "He was on his way home with our children. He was coming from Connecticut."

"Where in Connecticut?" DeMarco inquired, shifting slightly in his chair, leaning back in it. There was a sympathetic look in his eyes.

"Sharon," I said. "We have a house there."

Detective Johnson frowned. "And did he usually drive through the heart of Harlem?"

I nodded. "Yes. Andrew always takes—" I stopped, steadied myself, and went on, "Andrew always took Route 684, which leads into the Saw Mill River Parkway and then the Henry Hudson Parkway. That's an absolutely straight line from Sharon to Manhattan. And by going through Harlem he came out at the top of Park Avenue."

"Where did he get off the Henry Hudson?" Johnson asked.

"At the One Hundred Twenty-fifth Street exit, in order to zip right over to the East Side. He never varied this route, and we would go all the way across One Hundred Twenty-fifth, past Twelfth Avenue and Amsterdam, until we came to Park."

DeMarco said, "Did he go under the elevated section of the Metro North railway tracks at One Hundred Twenty-fourth, passing North General Hospital and the Edward M. Horan School around One Hundred Twentieth?"

"That's right. Then my husband would drive all the way down Park Avenue, turning right on Seventy-second Street. He believed it was the quickest way to get home. And it is."

"It's a well-traveled route. A lot of New Yorkers use it to hit the East Side quickly, but that area around One Hundred Nineteenth Street has become very dangerous lately," DeMarco said. "Huge quantities of crack cocaine are sold up there, underneath those stone arches of Metro North, just near the traffic light where your husband's . . . car was found."

"He wasn't on drugs," I exclaimed angrily. "Furthermore, he had our children with him. He wasn't doing anything wrong. He was simply driving home." My mouth began to tremble, and I covered it with my hand. I felt the tears sting the back of my eyes.

"We know he wasn't doing anything wrong, Mrs. Keswick," Detective Johnson said in a kindly voice, and I glanced at him in surprise. His partner had seemed to be the nicer of the two.

"Why were my husband and children shot?" I asked again, repeating the question I had been asking nonstop for two days.

DeMarco cleared his throat. "Your husband either stopped for the red light there, or he was forcibly stopped by one or more perpetrators. He was either getting out of the car, to see what was going on, or the door of the car was wrenched open. Then the shootings occurred, around four-thirty, five o'clock, according to the medical examiners. And we're not sure why he and the children *were* shot, Mrs. Keswick."

I stared at him. I could not speak.

Johnson said, "We think it might have been a carjacking gone wrong, in other words, an *attempted* carjacking."

"Carjacking?" I repeated. "What's that?"

"It's a crime that's occurring more and more frequently these days," Johnson explained. "It usually happens when a car is waiting at a red light or is parked in a rest area. The car is attacked, usually by several perpetrators. The occupants are made to get out, and the car is driven away. What might have happened, in your husband's case, is that the perpetrators were startled by something or someone, or taken by surprise, and so they fled without the car. It's possible they left the scene of the crime in panic or fear, or both, because one of them or more got trigger-happy. There might have been witnesses, and we're hoping someone will come forward."

DeMarco said, "We know from Mr. Nelson that your husband always wore a gold Rolex and carried a wallet. These items were missing, as we informed Mr. Nelson yesterday. But was there anything else in the car? Luggage?"

"Our shearling coats, Andrew's and mine. A few small items, clothing and a pair of riding boots, things like that, which he packed in a suitcase. Nothing very valuable, as far as I know," I said.

"Those things were not found in the car. It was empty," DeMarco reminded me, and continued, "The car will be released tomorrow, so you should have it back in another day. It was dusted for fingerprints on Sunday, and these have been sent to the FBI to be checked."

I did not respond. I did not want the car. I never wanted to see it again.

Johnson rose. "I'll be back in a minute," he said to DeMarco and went to the door. As he opened it and walked out, the din of the Twenty-fifth Precinct penetrated the quiet office.

Detective DeMarco said, "I've got to ask you a few other questions, Mrs. Keswick."

"Yes."

"Ruling out a possible carjacking, an attempted carjacking, that is, can you think of any reason why someone might want to shoot your husband? Why someone might wish to do him harm?"

I shook my head.

"Did he have any enemies?"

"No, of course he didn't," I said.

"Did he have any bad business dealings with anyone?"

"No."

DeMarco cleared his throat. "Any girlfriends, Mrs. Keswick?"

"What?"

"Could your husband have had a relationship with another woman? I realize that you might not have known about it, but was it a possibility?"

"No, it wasn't, Detective DeMarco. No, he didn't have any girlfriends. We were very happily married," I said in a cold little voice, and once again it was all I could do not to burst into tears. I resented the fact that I'd had to come to the precinct to be questioned rather than making a statement to them at home. But last night David had told me that I must go, that it was simply police procedure.

A moment or two later Detective DeMarco escorted me out into the corridor, where Sarah was sitting on a bench waiting for me. After I'd said good-bye to DeMarco, who told me he'd be in touch if there were any developments, Sarah took my arm and hurried me out of the precinct.

Once inside the car waiting for us outside, she told the driver to take us back to Park Avenue and Seventy-fourth Street, where my mother lived. I had been staying with her and David since Sunday night; my mother had not wanted me to be alone. In any case, her apartment, which David had moved into after their marriage, had been my home until I married Andrew. I had grown up there.

I leaned back against the car seat, feeling weak and drained. Since the shooting I had been trying to hold myself together as best I could, but most of the time I felt as though I was flying apart. I could not let that happen—not until after the funeral, anyway.

Sarah held my hand and glanced at me worriedly from time to time, but we were silent as the car sped down Park.

Finally, I looked at her and said, "The police think it might have been an attempted carjacking."

"What?" She stared at me in puzzlement. "What's that?"

"Apparently a carjacking is a relatively new crime that's been recurring constantly lately. The thieves attack a car that's either parked or at a red light, usually at gunpoint, and after they've made the occupants get out, they steal the car."

"Good God!" Sarah looked at me aghast.

"Johnson and DeMarco think Andrew's car was attacked in this manner, but that the thieves got scared off." I went on to repeat everything the two detectives had told me.

"Nobody's safe anymore," she said quietly, when I had finished, and I felt a shiver run through her.

22

My father was the first person I saw when I entered my mother's apartment with Sarah.

He must have heard my key in the door, for he came out of the small library. Anxiousness and concern ringed his mouth, and his thin, patrician face was taut with strain.

Sarah said, "Hello, Uncle Edward," and disappeared in the direction of the kitchen before he could answer, discreetly leaving us alone.

"Mal!" my father exclaimed, hurrying across the entrance hall. But there was no joy in his voice at the sight of me, only anguish.

"Oh, Dad," I cried and ran to him. I threw myself into his arms and held on to him tightly. "Oh, Daddy, I can't bear it. I can't. I can't live without Andrew and Lissa and Jamie. I should have been with them. Then I would have been killed too, and we would be together." I broke down, sobbed against his chest.

He stroked my hair, trying to console me. But I was inconsolable. He held me for a few moments. At last he said, "When Diana reached me I couldn't believe it. It's *not* believable . . . that such a thing could happen to Andrew and the twins—" He stopped, unable to continue, his voice broken; tears shook him, and we stood there in the middle of the entrance hall, weeping and clinging to each other.

After a short while we both managed to gain control of ourselves, and we drew apart.

My father took out his handkerchief and wiped away my tears, tenderly, as he had when I was a child. Then he wiped his own eyes and blew his nose.

After helping me off with my black wool coat, which he hung in the closet, he put his arm around my shoulders and walked with me into the library.

Looking up at him, I said, "Where's Diana? I thought you traveled together from London."

"We did. She's in your mother's bedroom, freshening up. The minute she walked in and saw your mother, she began to cry. So did your mother, of course. It's difficult to comprehend that we don't have Andrew and our grandchildren anymore—" My father's strong, resonant voice faltered, and I saw the tears glistening at the back of his eyes.

Silently, we sat down next to each other on the sofa. My father said, "I wanted to comfort you, to help you, but I'm afraid I'm not doing a very good job of it, am I, darling?"

"How can you?" I replied in a strangled voice. "You're grieving too. We're all grieving, Dad, and we're not going to stop, not ever."

He nodded, took my hand and held it tightly in his. "When David picked us up at Kennedy this morning, he explained that you'd gone to the precinct to make a statement, that this was just normal procedure. But did they tell you anything? Pass on any new information?"

"No, they didn't, except that they thought the shooting was a carjacking."

My father looked as puzzled as Sarah had. I explained and repeated everything the detectives had told me.

He shook his head in wonder, his tanned, freckled face registering a mixture of pain and anger. "It's so horrific one can hardly bear to think of it, never mind comprehend it." A deep sigh escaped him, and he shook his head again.

"And all for a watch, a wallet, and possibly a car, until something, or someone, made them run." My voice wavered, and fresh tears surfaced. "And they may never be caught."

My father's voice was gentle and loving as he said, "I'm here for you, darling. I'll do whatever I can to help you bear this . . . this . . . this unbearable sorrow and pain."

"I don't want to live without them, Dad. I don't have anything to live *for*. Life without Andrew and the twins is no life for me. I want to die."

"Ssssh, darling," he said, gentling me. "Don't say that, and don't let your mother and Diana hear you. It will destroy them afresh if they hear you speaking in this way. Promise me you'll put such thoughts out of your head."

I remained silent. How could I make a promise I knew I couldn't keep?

When I did not answer him, my father said, "I know that you—"

"Mal!" Diana said from the doorway, and it sounded like a cry of pain.

I leapt up and went to her as she came toward me.

All of her emotions were on her face; I could see her raw grief, her immense suffering. I tried to be strong for her as I put my arms around her and embraced her.

"You're all I have left now, Mal," she said in a low, shaking voice, and the tears came and she wept in my arms, just as I had wept in my father's a few minutes ago.

He rose and came to us and led us both back to the sofa, where she and I sat down.

Daddy took a chair opposite us and said, after a few moments, "Shall I go and get you a cup of tea, Diana? And one for you, Mal?"

Diana said, "I don't know . . . I don't care, Edward."

I murmured, "Yes, why not. Go and get it, Dad, please."

"All right." He got up and strode across the carpet but paused in the doorway. "Your mother's in the kitchen, helping the maid make sandwiches. Not that I think anyone is going to eat them."

"I can't, and I'm sure Diana feels the same way."

Diana said nothing. She dabbed her eyes with her handkerchief and blew her nose several times. "I simply can't absorb it, Mal," she began, shaking her head. "I can't believe they're . . . gone. Andrew and Lissa and Jamie. My son, my grandchildren, cut down like that—so senselessly, so cruelly."

"They didn't suffer," I managed to say in a tight voice. I was so choked up it took a moment for me to continue. "I asked the medical examiners if they had, and one of them assured me they hadn't, that death had been instantaneous."

Diana bit her lip, and her eyes filled, and at that precise moment I realized how much Andrew had resembled his mother. I covered my mouth with my hand, pressing back the tears.

"I don't know what I'm going to do without him," I whispered. "I loved him so much. He was my life, the twins were my life."

Reaching out, Diana clasped my hand. "I know, I know. I want to see them. I want to see my son and my grandchildren. Can we go and see them, Mal?"

"Yes. They're at the funeral home. It's nearby."

"And the service is tomorrow, your mother said. In the morning. At Saint Bartholomew's."

"Yes."

Diana said nothing more. She simply sat there staring at me, stupefied. I knew she was in shock, as was I. As we all were, for that matter.

Swallowing a few times and trying to get a grip on myself, I said, "I need you to do something for me, Diana."

"Oh, Mal, anything, anything."

"Will you come to our apartment? I have to choose . . . choose . . . their . . . clothes . . . the clothes they'll wear . . . in their coffins," I managed to say brokenly, the horror of it all sweeping over me yet again, as it had constantly in the past forty-eight hours.

"Of course I'll come," Diana said in a choked voice that sounded suddenly exhausted and old.

Without warning and without another word, she jumped up and rushed out, and I knew she was barely managing to hold herself together.

I knew exactly how she felt.

I leaned back on the sofa, and my gaze turned inward as I sat and reflected about my life and how it had been destroyed beyond redemption.

PART FOUR

INDIAN MEADOWS

23

Indian Meadows, January 1989

I was alone.

My husband was dead.

My children were dead.

My little pet, Trixy, was dead.

I should be dead too.

And I would have been if I had come with them to Indian Meadows that weekend in December. But I had stayed in the city to give the shower for Alicia Munroe, and because of that I was alive.

I didn't want to be alive. I had nothing to live for now, no reason for being.

A life without Andrew had no value.

A life without my children had no meaning.

I did not know what to do without them; I did not know how to cope with the business of everyday living, or how to function properly.

It seemed to me that I walked around like a zombie, doing everything automatically, by rote. I got up in the morning, showered, dressed, and drank a cup of coffee or tea. I made my bed and attended to chores in the house, helping Nora as I always had.

Sometimes I visited Anna and the horses in the stables; I spoke on the phone to my mother and Sarah. Several times a week I called Diana, or she called me, and my father was more in touch with me than he had ever been, phoning me constantly.

But for the most part I did nothing. I had no strength, no initiative; I was filled with apathy.

Occasionally I did come to my small office at the back of the house, where I sat now, trying to answer some of the condolence letters I had received. There were hundreds of them, but I could face only a few at a time, they were so harrowing to deal with.

Frequently I sat upstairs in my sitting room, thinking about Andrew, Lissa, and Jamie, grieving for them and for Trixy. My little Bichon Frise had been my constant companion before the children were born, forever at my heels, following me everywhere. She had been a genuine little presence.

I could not understand why this terrible thing had happened to us. What had we done to deserve it? Why had God allowed them to be murdered? Had I done something to offend Him? Had we all done something wrong? Something which displeased Him?

Or was there no God?

Was there only evil in this world?

Evil was man's invention, not God's. It had existed since the beginning of time and would continue to exist until this planet blew itself up, which it would, because man was evil and destructive, intent on killing and destroying.

My life, *our lives,* had been touched by evil when that animal had pulled the trigger, wiping out two innocent children, a little puppy, and a decent man who had never done any harm to anyone in his forty-one years.

Andrew had been cut down in the prime of his life, my children at the beginning of their lives, and it made no sense to me. Some of my friends had told me that it was God's will, and that we should never question Him. Or ask why He did certain things, that we must *accept* them, however painful.

How could I accept the deaths of my husband and my children? And so I kept on asking *why*. I wanted to understand why it had happened. I needed to know why God permitted the human race to commit the crimes it did. *Did God want us to suffer?* Was that it? I did not know. I had no answers for myself. Or for anyone else.

Perhaps there were no answers; perhaps there was no God, which was something I'd been pondering for five weeks. My mother said we lived in a godless world, and she might just be right.

We knew now from the ballistics report that the gun used to shoot my family had been a nine-millimeter semiautomatic handgun, which carried seventeen or eighteen bullets in the clip and did not have to be reloaded. DeMarco had told David this, explaining that it could be bought on the streets quite easily, adding that it was the gun of choice.

Gun of choice.

What had we come to? Had we learned nothing over the centuries?

According to DeMarco, the same type of bullet had killed all of my family, so he and Johnson were fairly certain there had been only one gunman. But that did not rule out an attack by a gang, DeMarco had told David. Unfortunately, there were still no suspects. And no witnesses had come forward.

Nothing was happening, as far as I knew, despite the intense media coverage, which still continued. The shooting of my family, the funeral service, and the police investigation had attracted the media in droves; it had become a circus in the end, with newspaper and television reporters hounding us on a daily basis. Even the British press had descended on us, much to our distress.

I no longer read the newspapers or watched the television news. I did not want to get caught by surprise by something about me or mine. Certainly I no longer cared what was happening in the world. The world was irrelevant.

I had fled to Indian Meadows.

I had also wanted to escape the apartment and New York, which I now loathed. The city filled me with disgust and fear.

David had told me not to be too disdainful of the media and their constant coverage of this tragedy.

"They're keeping the pressure on the police," he had pointed out again just the other day. "Be glad about that, Mal. The N.Y.P.D. doesn't want to get roasted alive. They'll only intensify their efforts to find the perp." After a pause, he had thought to add, "Mind you, DeMarco and Johnson are hell-bent on solving this crime, and DeMarco especially has made it a personal crusade."

Everything David said was true. And DeMarco did seem to be very personally committed. Yet I doubted that the monster who had so cold-bloodedly taken the lives of my family would ever be tracked down.

He was long gone with his lethal weapon.

He was free.

Free to live his evil life. And kill again, if the whim took him.

And I was left to grieve.

I grieved for my husband and my children, grieved for the lives they would never lead, grieved for the future which had been stolen from them, grieved for all that might have been and never would be now.

I wanted to die.

And I was going to die.

Soon. Very soon.

I had been unable to kill myself up until now because I had not been left alone for a moment. There was always someone with me.

Did they all suspect my intentions?

I had been surrounded since the day after the funeral, when I had driven up to Sharon with Diana and my father. Sarah had followed with my mother and David, and they had stayed for days.

They had given me love. And they had tried to comfort me, as I had endeavored to console them. But none of us had succeeded. The loss was too great, the pain too excruciating. It lingered deep inside, never beginning to fade.

Eventually they had all left, although some of them only temporarily, such as my mother, David, and Sarah. She had had to go to work at Bergman's, David to his law office. But they were all back within a few days, and Nora and Anna were never far from my side. Even Eric, Nora's husband, seemed to hover constantly when he was not at work.

Diana had decided to return to London toward the end of December. She had wanted to stay with me here, at least to help get me through the holidays, as had my father. I had pointed out that my mother, David, and Sarah would be coming to Indian Meadows for Christmas, and that they should go, should try to get on with their lives as best they could.

"Perhaps you're right, Mal," Diana had said. "You and I will only feed on each other's pain and grief if I remain here." It struck me she was only saying this to help me feel better. Certainly I knew it was heart-wrenching for her to leave me. In fact, at the last minute, just before she and my father had set out for Kennedy, she had begged me to quickly pack a bag and go with her to London, then up to Yorkshire.

My father had also pleaded with me to accompany them. He had asked me to spend Christmas with him, Diana, and

Gwenny at Kilgram Chase, or, if I felt that that was impossible, he would take us all away. We could go somewhere in France, he had said.

But there was nothing for me in London or Yorkshire or France or anywhere else for that matter. I was no longer comfortable on this earth. I craved another, distant place.

And so I had shaken my head, kissed them both good-bye, and sent them on their way. I wanted to be here with my memories. And I wanted to make my plans for my death.

There was another reason why I had not done it yet. I was waiting for something to be delivered. It had not arrived. But once it did, I would kill myself and join my husband and babies. We would be together, and the pain would end.

I glanced at today's date in my engagement book. It was Tuesday, January 17. The package was due to arrive tomorrow, the eighteenth.

There was no doubt in my mind that I would do it on the nineteenth.

So be it.

I got up and walked out of the office, down the corridor to the coatroom, where I kept boots and raincoats. Earlier this morning Anna had asked me to go down to the stables, and now seemed as good a time as any. Before I reached the coatroom I ran into the ever-present Nora carrying a tray.

"Mal! I was just bringing you this bowl of soup."

"I don't really want it, Nora, I'm not hungry. Thanks. Anyway, I'm going out."

"No, you're not," she said, blocking my way. "Not until you've got something inside you." She stared me down. "You've not eaten a thing for days. Tea, coffee, a slice of toast. What good is that going to do you? You're going to have this soup."

"All right," I said. I couldn't be bothered to argue with her. Anyway, she had that obdurate look in her eyes, which lately I had come to know only too well. Also, it occurred to me that she might physically prevent me from going outside unless I ate the soup.

She softened a bit. "Where do you want it?"

"In the kitchen," I said.

Without saying anything, she turned on her heels and went in the direction of the long gallery, which in turn led into the kitchen.

I could tell from the way she held herself that she was annoyed with me, hurt even, and this troubled me. I wouldn't offend Nora for the world. She was a good woman, and she too was grief-stricken and sorrowing. She had adored the twins to the point of distraction and had cared deeply for Andrew. She, Eric, and Anna had come to New York for the funeral service, and they had been devastated ever since.

Wanting to make amends for my curtness, I said as I sat down, "I'm sorry, Nora. I didn't mean to speak so crossly to you."

She placed the tray on the kitchen table in front of me and put her hand on my shoulder. She began to speak, but there was a catch in her throat, and she hurried away before I could say another word.

Even though it was the middle of January, it was not very cold, and so far this year there had been little snow. A light dusting of it covered the flat ground near the house, but it was not particularly deep on the lawns, only on the hill which sloped down to the barns, the pastures, and the pond.

Eric had cleared a path through the snowdrifts which covered the hill and had put down sand and salt. I followed this path, heading for Anna's cottage. I was almost there when she came out of the stables, turned, saw me, and waved.

I waved back and increased my pace.

After greeting me affectionately, as she always did, she said,

"It's about . . . the ponies, Mal. You told me to do what I wanted about them, and . . . well, I have a customer."

I frowned. "A customer? What do you mean, Anna?" I asked, staring hard at her.

"I have someone who wants to buy them," she answered quickly, and there was a baffled expression in her soft brown eyes.

"Oh, I couldn't sell them!" I exclaimed. *"Never."*

My voice must have sounded harsh, for she colored and stammered, "I guess I misunderstood."

I put my hand out, touched her arm reassuringly. "No, no, you didn't misunderstand, Anna. *I* didn't make myself clear. And I'm sorry if I spoke harshly just now. When I told you to do what you wanted about the ponies, I meant that you should give them away. I could never sell Pippa and Punchinella."

Her face broke into a smile. "I have this friend who wants them. She'll take good care of them, Mal, and her children will, too. It's a lovely gift, thank you."

I nodded. "Is there anything else you wanted to talk about?"

"No, that was it," Anna replied.

"I think I'll go in and look at the ponies, say good-bye to them," I muttered half to myself as I walked across to the stables.

Anna had the good grace not to follow me.

I went to the stalls and pulled a carrot out of my pocket for Punchinella, then another one for Pippa. After feeding them, patting their heads, and nuzzling them, I whispered, "Go off to a new home. And be sure you give two other children the same pleasure you gave mine."

Slowly I walked back up the hill to the house.

When I reached the top I sat down on the seat under the apple tree. It looked so bare, so bereft at this time of year, but in the spring and summer it was leafy and filled with delicate white blossoms. A beautiful tree, I have always thought.

This was one of my favorite spots at Indian Meadows. Andrew had called it Mommy's Place, for whenever I had a moment or two to spare I would come here—to relax, to think, to read, occasionally to paint, and very often just to sit and day-dream. Eventually it had become theirs, too, the children's and Andrew's. If ever I was missing for a while, it was here they usually found me, and they always wanted to stay, to share this place.

Underneath this tree I had told the twins fairy tales and read to them, and sometimes we had had picnics on the grass. It was never anything but cool and shady even on the hottest of summer days, and it was one of the prettiest spots I had ever known.

And it was here that Andrew and I had come just to be alone, especially on warm nights when the sky was inky and bright with stars. Enfolded in each other's arms, we had sat together quietly talking about the future, or not talking, if we didn't want to, always at peace here.

How we had all loved it beneath the old apple tree.

I closed my eyes, shutting out the powder-blue sky and the January sunlight, squeezing back my tears.

24

"Mal, there's a truck here, a delivery truck," Nora said, bending over me and touching my shoulder.

I sat up with a start, blinking.

"I'm sorry I had to wake you up. I know you hardly ever sleep these days. But the delivery guy needs these papers signed, and he wants to know where you want the safe."

Pushing myself to my feet, I said, "Up here. I want it up here, Nora, in my clothes closet."

"Oh," she answered, throwing me a puzzled glance. "Why do we need a safe, Mal?"

"I have things I want to put in it," I replied. "Private papers, jewelry, documents." This was a lie, but I had to give her some sort of answer.

"You'd better come down and speak to him," she muttered, handing me the papers she was holding.

I followed her out into the corridor and down the stairs, relieved that the safe company had delivered my order on time. I had placed it several weeks ago, sent a check immediately, and had been waiting for it patiently.

The truck had driven up to the back door, and the driver was standing in the kitchen when Nora and I walked in.

She disappeared into the pantry. I said, "Hi, I'm Mrs. Keswick. I want you to bring the safe upstairs, but it might be a problem. The staircase is narrow."

"I got my helper in the truck," he said gruffly. "Can you show me where it's going?"

"Come with me."

I took him upstairs to my little sitting room, led him into the deep, walk-in closet where I kept my clothes, and said, "I want it against the back wall. There." I indicated the spot.

"Okay," he said and went back downstairs.

I was hard on his heels. In the kitchen I sat down at the table, gave the papers a cursory glance, found a ballpoint pen near the phone, and signed them.

Nora poked her head around the pantry door and asked, "Is Sarah coming tomorrow or Friday?"

"She's not coming this weekend."

"Oh." Nora looked taken aback. After a second she said, "So your mother's coming."

I shook my head. "No, I'll be by myself."

"But it's the first time you'll have been alone." She stood there uncertainly, staring at me, looking worried.

"I'll be fine," I reassured her. "There are things I have to do."

She did not move for a second, and then she turned and went back into the kitchen, a helpless expression settling on her face.

A moment later the delivery man from Acme and his helper were rolling in a dolly with the safe on top. "I'm gonna take the door off," the delivery man announced, and he proceeded to do just that. Once the door had been lifted off its hinges, he placed it on the floor. Then he laid the safe flat on the dolly, and he and his helper pushed the dolly through into the long gallery, heading toward the stairs. They returned for the door, and within fifteen minutes the safe had been reassembled and stood in my walk-in closet exactly where I wanted it.

Once I was alone, I practiced opening and closing it, following the instruction chart the delivery man had given me. When I had the knack of it, I erased the factory code and entered my own into the digital panel, using the date of my marriage.

It seemed to me that it was taking Nora longer than ever to finish up today.

Several times I looked at the clock on the mantelpiece in the office, baffled as to why she was still here. It was now four o'clock.

I had the answer in a flash. Eric was probably coming to see me, as he so often did during the week these days, and she wanted to be here when he arrived from work.

Now that the safe was here, I could clear up all my affairs, and I was writing checks, fulfilling my obligations. When I had finished paying the bills, I added up everything on my yellow pad, entered the balance, closed the checkbook, and put it in my desk drawer.

Without Andrew's monthly salary check, I had nothing coming in, and my funds were getting extremely low. And I had not yet received the money from his insurance policy. There was some money in our savings account, but it wasn't much, certainly not a fortune. Andrew and I had always lived life to the hilt, and frequently beyond our means.

Anyway, what did it matter now? I wasn't going to need money. I was going to be dead.

My mother would sell the apartment in New York and this house, pay off the two mortgages, and use whatever money remained to settle any other debts that were left. Everything would be neat and tidy; that was exactly how I wanted it to be.

I had had my last will and testament drawn up a few days ago, using a local lawyer in New Milford rather than the law firm in Manhattan which handled my mother's affairs. It would only throw her into a panic if she knew I'd made a will.

She and Sarah were the executrixes, and my mother would get the bulk of my estate, such as it was. But I had left my pearls and most of my jewelry to Sarah, except for my engagement ring, which I had willed to Diana. After all, it was a Keswick heirloom and had been hers before it was mine. I had made other small bequests, such as small pieces of jewelry and some of my own paintings to Nora, Eric, and Anna. The rest of the paintings my mother could dispose of as she wished.

I loved Sarah. She was my closest and dearest friend, the sister I had never had. I knew only too well that she was going to be devastated and that she would miss me. But I couldn't bear to go on living, not without my family.

The office door suddenly opened, and Eric stuck his head around it. "Hi, Mal, how're you doing?"

"I'm all right," I answered, attempting a smile without much success. "And you?"

He made a face, shook his head. "Things are a bit tough down at the lumberyard. The boss had to lay a couple of guys off this week. But so far so good, I'm not too concerned."

"I'm glad *you're* okay, Eric. Nora's upstairs; I heard her footsteps a few minutes ago."

He grinned. "I'll see her shortly. I'm going down to the basement to bring up some more logs, then I'll take a look at that third heater in the stables. Anna told Nora it's been on the blink for the past few days. Got to keep the barns warm for the horses."

"We certainly do, and thanks, Eric, I appreciate it."

"No trouble, Mal. Just let me know if there's anything else you need fixed. The furnace isn't acting up again, is it?"

"It seems to be running fine, thanks."

"I'll pop in and see you before I leave." He smiled and was gone.

Eric Matthews was a kind man. Ever since I had been living permanently at Indian Meadows, he had gone out of his way to do all of the jobs Andrew had done and which were too hard for Nora or me. Like his wife and Anna, he was grief-stricken, and although he tried to be cheerful whenever he came to say hello, I could see the pain of loss in his eyes.

Nora and Eric had finally driven off, she in her ramshackle old Chevy, he in his battered pickup truck, and as much as I cared for them, I breathed a sigh of relief.

At last I was alone.

After locking the doors, I ran upstairs and went to the chest of drawers in my bedroom where I kept T-shirts and sweaters. The bottom drawer was deep, and in it, at the back, I had hidden the four cardboard boxes.

Taking them out one by one, I carried them carefully into the sitting room adjoining the bedroom and put them on the sofa.

First I opened the box with the vet's label on it and took out the small cream-colored can. Next I opened the three others, which bore the name of the crematorium. Placing the four canisters on the coffee table side by side, I sat down on the sofa and looked at them. When David had collected them and brought them out here to me, I had immediately labeled each container, writing the name and the dates of birth and death of Andrew, Lissa, Jamie, and Trixy.

There they were—all that I had left of my family. Four cans of ashes.

Tears rushed into my eyes, but I pushed them back, reached for a tissue, and blew my nose.

Immediately getting a grip on myself, I picked up the two

canisters containing Lissa's and Jamie's ashes and carried them into the walk-in closet. I placed them on the shelf in the safe, then I went back to the sitting room, returning a moment later with Andrew's ashes. Finally I brought in Trixy's.

After I had arranged the four of them next to one another, I closed the door, locked it, and put the key in my pocket.

"You're safe now. Absolutely safe. No one, nothing, can hurt you ever again," I said out loud, talking to my family as I did frequently these days. "Soon I'm going to be with you. We'll be together forever."

The following day I passed the morning making phone calls.

I spoke to Diana in London, my mother and Sarah, who were both in New York, and finally to my father, who was in California, attending meetings at U.C.L.A.

I chatted to them all pleasantly, made sure I sounded cheerful, and told each of them that I was feeling much better.

I think they believed me. I could be very convincing when I wanted to be.

In the afternoon I wrote my farewell letters to the four of them. There was a fifth letter to David Nelson, thanking him for all that he had done for me and asking him to look after my mother, to cherish her. I also gave him instructions about our ashes. Sealing the envelopes and writing each name on them, I placed these in the desk drawer next to my checkbook.

Tonight I would kill myself. My body would be discovered tomorrow morning. And not too much later the letters would be found.

I lay on the sofa in my upstairs sitting room, sipping a vodka and listening to Maria Callas sing *Tosca*. It had been one of Andrew's favorite operas.

The winter sun had long since fled the pale wintry sky, and the light was rapidly fading. Soon it would be twilight—*the gloaming,* Andrew had called it. A northern name, he had once said.

A deep sigh escaped me.

Soon my life would be over.

I would shed this mortal coil. I would be free. I would go to that other plane where they waited for me. All my suffering would finally cease. I would be at peace with them.

In the dim light of the room I could see Andrew's face looking down at me from the portrait I had painted of him. I smiled, loving him so much. And then my eyes shifted, and I gazed at the portrait I had done of the twins. Jamie and Lissa. How beautiful they looked, my little Botticelli cherubs. I smiled again. They had been my two small miracles.

Reaching for the glass, I gulped down some more of the vodka, closed my eyes, and let myself drift with the music.

When this side of the disc ended, I would end my life.

"Mal! Mal! Where are you?"

I sat up with a jerk, dropping the glass of vodka I was clutching, startled out of my mind.

Before I could recover myself, Sarah came bursting into the little sitting room, her eyes anxious, her face pale.

"No wonder you couldn't hear me banging on the front door!" she exclaimed. "What with Callas screaming her lungs out like that!" Stepping over to the stereo, she lowered the volume. "I've been outside for ages. Banging and banging on the door."

I was stunned that she was here. "How did you get in?" I asked in a faint voice.

"Through the kitchen door."

"But it was locked!"

"No, it wasn't, Mal."

"But it was!" I cried, my voice rising shrilly. "I locked it myself." As I spoke I cast my mind back to this afternoon. I had walked Nora across the kitchen, we had said good-bye as I saw her out. I had then closed the kitchen door and swung the bolt. Demented I might be, but there was no question in my mind about that door. Who had unlocked it?

Sarah was standing there, looking down at me.

I said, "What are you doing here, anyway?" She had spoiled my plans, and I was furious.

Throwing her coat onto a chair, she came and sat next to me on the sofa, took my hand in hers. "Why am I here, Mal? Because I was worried about you, of course. Very worried."

I stared at her speechlessly.

25

Sarah had obviously come to Indian Meadows for the weekend. As we went into the kitchen, I saw her suitcase, which she had dumped on the floor near the back door.

The first thing I did was to walk over and check that door. I turned the knob, and it opened. "I guess you didn't lock this before you came upstairs looking for me," I said.

"No, I didn't, Mal. It was open, so I left it open. Sorry."

"It's okay. I just don't understand. I did lock it earlier. It's a mystery."

Sarah made no comment. She walked over to the pine cabinet, took out a glass, and poured herself a vodka. Looking at me, she asked, "How about you, Mal? Do you want one?"

"Why not," I replied. If I couldn't kill myself tonight, I might as well get drunk. I could put myself out of my misery for a few hours at least.

Opening the freezer, I took out a tray of ice and gave it to Sarah, then went back and peered into the refrigerator.

"There's some hot pot here," I said. "Nora made it this morning. Or I can fix you an omelette."

Plopping ice cubes in our drinks and adding chunks of lime, Sarah said, "No eggs, thanks. I'll try the hot pot. What're you having?"

"The same," I murmured, although I wasn't even hungry. I never was these days. After I had emptied the hot pot into a pan and put this on the stove over a low light, I said, "It's going to take about half an hour to heat up."

Together we headed for the sunroom. Although it had a lot of windows and French doors, it was warm, centrally heated like the rest of the house. As we went in, I switched on the lights and noticed that it was snowing outside. The lawns had a coating of white; the trees looked as if they had just burst into bloom with white blossoms.

I sat down on a side chair with my back to the window.

Sarah took a big armchair, propped her feet on the coffee table, and lifted her glass in silence.

I did the same.

Sarah didn't say anything, and neither did I; we sat together like that for quite a while.

Finally rousing herself and focusing her eyes on me, she said, "My cousin Vera's coming back to New York, Mal."

"Oh," I said, looking at her swiftly. "Didn't she like the West Coast?"

"Yes, but her husband's left her. Moved in with another woman. Apparently he wants a divorce, so she's decided to pack up and come home."

"I'm sorry," I murmured, wanting to be polite.

Sarah went on, "Vera's flying to New York in about two weeks. To look for an apartment, and driving up here tonight it suddenly occurred to me that yours might be perfect for her. She has a teenage daughter, Linda, if you remember, and a housekeeper who's been with her for years. Your apartment is just the right size."

I took a sip of my vodka and said nothing.

"So, what do you think?" Sarah asked, eyeing me.

I shrugged indifferently.

"Do you want to sell it, Mal?"

"Yes, I guess so."

"You sound uncertain. But weeks ago you told me you never wanted to see New York ever again, that you hated the city. Why keep an apartment in a city you hate?"

"You're right, Sash. If Vera wants to buy the apartment, she can. Show it to her whenever you want. Or my mother can. She has a set of keys."

"Thanks, Mal." She smiled at me. "It'll be nice if I do you both a good turn."

"What do you mean?"

"Vera wants a nice place to live. And I'm sure you can use the money, can't you?"

I nodded. "Andrew's insurance policy is not a big one."

"There's a mortgage on the apartment, isn't there?"

"Yes," I said. "And one on this house."

Sarah gave me a long stare. "How're you going to manage?" she asked quietly, her concern apparent. "What are you going to do for money?"

I won't need it, I'll be dead, I thought. But I said, "There's a little bit coming from the advertising agency, but not much. Jack Underwood told me they're in trouble. They've lost a number of big accounts, and there are all kinds of financial problems at the London office. But you knew that. Andrew told you, when he came back in November."

"When did you talk to Jack?"

"He came out to see me a couple of days ago. He'd just returned from London. He's been heartbroken about Andrew—they were very close—and distressed about the agency. He and Harvey are leaving. They're going into business for themselves. Andrew had instigated the whole thing . . . " My voice trailed off, and I stared at her blankly, then sitting up, I finished in a stronger, firmer voice. "And so they're going ahead with their plans, even though Andrew's no longer here."

Sarah was silent. She sat sipping her drink, gazing out the window at the snow-covered lawns, her face miserable.

I got up and lowered the lights, which were a little too bright for me tonight. Then I sat down again.

"I'm worried about you, Mal," Sarah suddenly said.

"You mean about the money, the fact that I haven't got any?"

She shook her head. "No, not that at all. Auntie Jess and David will help you, and so will I. You know anything I have is yours. And your father and Diana will chip in until you're on your feet."

"I guess so," I said. Of course this would never be necessary; I would not be here.

Sarah said softly, "I'm worried about your well-being, about your health. But, most importantly, about your state of mind. I know you're in the most excruciating pain all the time, that your sorrow and suffering are overwhelming. I just want to help you. I don't know how."

"Nobody can help me, Sash. That's why it's better if I'm alone."

"I don't agree, honestly I don't. You need someone with you, to comfort you whichever way they can. You need someone to talk to, to cling to if necessary. You mustn't be alone."

I did not answer her.

"I know I'm right," she pressed on. "And I know *I'm* the right person. It's *I* who should be with you. We've known each other all our lives, since we were babies. We're best friends . . . I should be with you now when you need someone. It's *me* that you need, Mal."

"Yes," I said softly. "You're the best one. And the only one who knows how to cope with me, I suppose."

"Promise me I can come every weekend, that you won't try to push me away, as you have several times lately."

"I promise."

She smiled. "I love you, Mal."

"And I love you too, Sash."

A small silence fell between us once more.

"It's the nothingness," I said finally.

"Nothingness?"

"That's what I face every day. *Nothingness.* There's just nothing there. Only emptiness, a great void. For ten years my focus has been on Andrew and our marriage and his career, then later it encompassed the twins. But now that they're gone, I have no focus. Only nothingness. There's simply nothing left for me."

Sarah nodded. Her eyes had welled up, and she was obviously unable to speak for a moment. But also she would never offer me meaningless pap, the kind of empty words that I had heard from so many of late.

I stood up. "Let's not talk about this anymore."

We ate supper in the kitchen. Actually, only Sarah ate—I just picked at my food. I had lost my appetite, and it had never come back. But I had opened a bottle of good red wine, and I drank plenty of it as the meal progressed.

At one moment Sarah looked at me over the rim of her glass and said, "Not now, because I don't think you're up to it, but later, in six months or so, maybe you could work. It would keep you busy. I know it would help you."

I merely shrugged. I wasn't going to be around in six months, but I could hardly tell her that. I loved her. I didn't want to upset her.

"You could work out here in the country, Mal, doing what you love."

I stared at her.

She continued, "*Painting.* You're very talented, and I think you could easily get some assignments illustrating books. I have a couple of friends in publishing, and they'd help; I know they would. You could also sell some of your watercolors and oils."

"Don't be silly. My paintings are not good enough to sell, Sash."

"You're wrong, they are."

"You're prejudiced."

"That's true, I am. But I also know when someone's good at what they do, especially in the artistic field, and you're good, Mallory Keswick."

"If you say so," I murmured, pouring myself another glass of Andrew's best French wine.

26

It snowed again on Sunday.

Even though I was low in spirits, I could not help noticing the beauty of the grounds at Indian Meadows. They were breathtaking. They resembled a monochromatic painting in black and white below a crystal-clear sky of the brightest blue washed over with golden sunlight.

As I walked down to the pond with Sarah, my heart tightened. I thought of Lissa and Jamie, and how much they would have enjoyed playing in the snow with Andrew, making snowballs, building a snowman, and sledding down the hill below the apple tree.

I missed them all so much; my yearning for them was constant, ever-present in my heart.

But now I pushed my heartache away, burying it deep inside me, hoping to conceal it. I did not want to burden Sarah. She was so loving and understanding, and she worried about me all the time. I felt I must act as normal as possible around her today. She was going to Paris tomorrow with her fashion team from Bergman's, and I wanted her to leave feeling that I was in a better frame of mind.

"I've never seen so many ducks here before!" she exclaimed when we got to the pond. "There must be at least two dozen!"

"Yes, and they're mallards. They've made Indian Meadows their home this winter," I answered. "Obviously because we're feeding them every day."

As I spoke I put the shopping basket I was carrying down on the snow, took out the plastic container of scratch feed and turkey-grower pellets, and went to the edge of the pond.

The ducks took off immediately. Some rose up into the air and flew to another part of the property, others hopped onto the portion of the pond that was frozen and waddled away.

Our first winter at Indian Meadows, Andrew had installed a recirculating pump at one end of the pond. Electrically operated, it constantly churned the water surrounding it and thus prevented that area from freezing, even when it was below zero.

Sarah came and stood with me as I scattered the grain at the edge of the water, then she took a handful herself and walked to the frozen part, throwing it down for them.

"Silly ducks," she said, looking at me over her shoulder. "They're not coming to eat."

"They will, once we leave."

She joined me again and stood staring at the pump agitating the water.

"This really works," she said, glancing at me quickly. "What a good idea it was, to put it in for the ducks and the other wildlife that come around in winter. How did you know about it?"

"Eric told Andrew. In fact, they installed it together. This kind of pump is mostly used by farmers, who need to keep small parts of their ponds unfrozen, so that their cows can drink in winter," I explained.

"Hi, Mal! Hi, Sarah!"

We both swung around and waved to Anna, who waved back as she walked toward us across the snow.

She was as heavily bundled up against the weather as we

were, dressed in a crazy collection of clothes, and I had a flash of Gwendolyn Reece-Jones in my mind's eye.

Like Gwenny, Anna was sporting lots of bright primary colors this morning, noticeable in the three scarves wrapped around her neck. These were turquoise-blue, red, and yellow, and they matched her long jacket, which looked as if it had been made from an Apache blanket. On her head was a royal-blue woolen ski cap with yellow pom-poms, and she wore a pair of jodhpurs, riding boots, and green wool gloves. Could she be color-blind?

"Anna, I love your jacket," Sarah exclaimed as Anna drew to a standstill next to us. "It's not only beautiful but very unusual. Is it authentic American Indian?"

"Not really," Anna said. "Well, maybe in its design."

"Did you get it out West? Arizona?"

Anna shook her head. "No, I bought it from Pony Traders."

"Pony Traders," Sarah repeated. "What's that? A shop?"

"No. Pony Traders is a small crafts company, up near Lake Wononpakook. I know one of the two women who own it, Sandy Farnsworth. They make jackets, capes, skirts, waistcoats, even boots and moccasins. Everything has an Indian look to it. And I fell in love with this jacket."

"I don't blame you, it's great," Sarah responded. "I'm off to Europe tomorrow, but maybe when I get back you'll take me up to meet them. Perhaps I'll put in an order for the store."

"Hey, that'd be fantastic," Anna said. Turning to me, she went on, "I thought you might like to come in for a cup of hot chocolate, or coffee, whatever you'd like, Mal." She eyed the basket and added, "I see you've got carrots for the horses. Why not come to my barn first?"

I was about to decline her invitation but changed my mind. She was trying to be nice, and I didn't want to offend her. She had always been so sweet with my children and had spent a lot of time with them when they rode, helping them to handle their ponies correctly. And so I said, "I won't say no to a cup of coffee, Anna. What about you, Sarah?"

"I crave the hot chocolate, but it'll have to be black coffee," Sarah said, grimacing at Anna. "I'm always watching my weight."

Anna laughed and shook her head, "You're a beautiful woman, Sarah. *You* don't have to worry."

Together the three of us walked toward the small renovated barn where Anna lived. It had been months since I had been here, and as I followed her inside, I was instantly struck by its rustic charm and comfort.

She had a big fire going in the fieldstone hearth, and her black Labrador, Blackie, lay stretched out on the rug in front of it. He got up when he heard us and came trotting over, nuzzling at Anna's legs and wagging his tail furiously at me.

"Hello, Blackie," I said, stroking his head. The Labrador looked past me to the door, his tail still wagging. I experienced a sudden pang as I realized he was expecting to see Trixy, who had always accompanied me wherever I went on the property.

I think Anna had probably realized the same thing. She looked at me, her eyes worried, and said in a brisk, cheerful voice, "Come on, give me your coats, and I'll get us the coffee. It's already made. Would you like anything to eat?"

Sarah muttered, "I would, but I won't."

"Just coffee, Anna, thanks," I said. I sat down on the sofa in front of the fire.

"Can I look around, Anna?" Sarah asked. "It's ages since I've seen your home."

"Sure, feel free. Go up to the sleeping loft if you like."

I leaned my head against the Early American quilt that covered the back of the big red sofa and closed my eyes, thinking of

Lissa and Jamie. They had loved Anna, had loved to come here for milk and cookies and special treats. She had loved the twins in return, had always spoiled them, and had cared for them like they were her own.

Later, walking back up the hill to the house, Sarah said, "The barn looks great. Anna's done wonders with it. It's packed to the hilt with stuff, but somehow she's made it all work."

"Yes, she has," I murmured, shrugging further into my quilted coat, feeling the nip in the air all of a sudden.

"You know, Mal, she's very pretty, all that blonde hair, those soft brown eyes, doe eyes. Very appealing, really. But she could be absolutely stunning if only she wore a bit of makeup, especially eye makeup. Blondes always look so faded, so washed-out, if they don't do their eyes right."

"I know exactly what you mean, Sash. But I don't think she really gives a damn how she looks most of the time."

"No incentive, you mean?"

I shook my head. "No, I don't mean that." I hesitated thoughtfully, then said finally, "I think Anna's happy with *herself*. And with the way she looks these days. Healthy, full of vitality, no black eyes or bruises. She had a really bad experience with that guy she lived with, before she came here. And I think she gave up on men a long time ago. He used to beat her up constantly. He was *extremely* abusive, actually, and she was smart to get away from him when she did."

"I remember your telling me about it at the time. Well, I guess it's better to be on your own without a man than—" She broke off and stared at me, looking horrified, then grabbed hold of my arm. "I'm sorry, Mal, I'm so thoughtless."

I turned into her, put my arms around her, and hugged her to me. "You can't keep watching yourself, Sash, watching every word and what you say all the time. Life does intrude, I'm very aware of that."

"I'd give anything to make you feel just a little bit better," she murmured. "Anything, Mal, anything at all." She stood gazing at me, her dark eyes moist, brimming with emotion, all of the love and friendship she felt for me spilling out of her.

"I know you would, Sarah darling, and it *is* easier when you're around," I replied. I wanted to reassure her, and so ease her worry about me.

The stillness in the house was so acute it was tangible.

I stood in the middle of the long gallery, listening to that stillness, letting it wash over me, and I began to feel less agitated than usual.

Ineffable sadness dwelt within my heart, and yet I felt oddly comforted all of a sudden.

It was the house, of course.

It had always been a peaceful place, tranquil, benign, enfolding my family and me in its loving embrace. Ever since I had first set eyes on it, I had thought of it as a living thing, an entity rather than an edifice. I had never believed we had found the house all by ourselves, rather, that it had beckoned to us, drawn us to it, because it wanted us to occupy it, to love it and give it life.

And we had for a while.

My children had laughed here and run along its twisting corridors and played in its many rooms; Andrew and I had loved each other here and loved our family and our friends, and for a short time the house had truly lived again, had been happy. Certainly it had given us joy.

I walked from room to room, looking at everything for the last time before locking the outside doors and switching off the lights. Then I slowly climbed the stairs to my upstairs sitting room.

When I pushed open the door and went in, I saw that the room was dim and filled with shadows. It had grown much darker outside in the last hour or so since Sarah had left. But the logs spurted and hissed in the grate and threw off sparks, and there was a lovely warmth up here on this icy night.

I turned on a lamp and undressed, put on a nightgown and robe.

After pouring myself a vodka, I sat down in front of my portrait of the twins and studied it for a long time. I really had captured them on the canvas; this realization pleased me.

Eventually, my gaze settled on Andrew's portrait hanging over the fireplace. It was not quite as good as the one I had done of the twins, but the likeness was there, and I had caught his extraordinary blue eyes perfectly. They were exactly right.

I finished my drink, poured another one, lingered over this, then drained the glass suddenly, in one big gulp.

Rising, I went into the bathroom. I turned on the taps and ran a bath. When it was full, I took off my robe, threw it across the bath stool, and walked across to the sink.

My art knife was there, where I'd put it earlier, its razor blade encased in a sheath of plastic. The blade was sharp, very sharp. I knew. I had used it for cutting thick paper, posterboard, and sometimes canvases. It would do the job nicely.

I had read somewhere that this was a painless way to die, if one can think of dying as painless. Lying in a tub of water, slitting each wrist, bleeding gently until unconscious, until death came. *Painless.*

Picking up the knife, I examined it before stepping over to the bath. I placed it on the edge of the tub near the taps and lifted my nightgown.

As I began to pull it up over my head, I heard the faintest sound. It was laughter. *Someone was laughing.* In the next room. I was so startled I was frozen to the spot. Finally I let the hem of my nightie fall.

I went out into the sitting room.

Lissa stood there in the center of the floor wearing her night-gown.

"Mommy! Mommy!" she cried and laughed again, her light, tinkling laugh. It was the same laughter I had heard a moment ago.

"Lissa!" I took a step forward.

She laughed and ran out into the corridor.

I rushed after her, calling her name, shouting for her to stop, to come back, as I followed her down the stairs, along the entrance gallery and into the kitchen. She wrenched open the back door and flew out into the snow, laughing, saying my name.

It was dark outside.

I couldn't see her.

I stumbled around in the snow, calling and calling her.

Suddenly she was there, standing right next to me, tugging at my nightgown. "Hide and seek, Mommy, let's play hide and seek."

She ran away, ran into the house.

I chased her. My heart was pounding, my breath coming in gasps as I raced up the stairs. I saw her dash through the door of my upstairs sitting room, but when I got there the room was empty. I looked in the bathroom, hurried into the adjoining bedroom, only to discover I was alone.

Shivering, I glanced down at my nightgown.

It was soaking wet at the bottom, and my feet were frozen. I had run outside with nothing on my feet. My teeth began to chatter, and I got my robe and put it on. I dried my feet on a towel and found a pair of slippers in my clothes closet.

Where was Lissa hiding?

I went from room to room on this floor and covered every room downstairs. I even made it to the basement.

The house was empty except for me.

I'm not certain exactly how long I searched for her, but eventually I gave up. Returning to my little sitting room, I threw some logs on the fire and poured a vodka to warm myself.

Puzzled by what had just happened, I sat down on the sofa to think.

Had it been a dream? But I hadn't been asleep.

I had been in the bathroom, and I had been wide wake.

Was it wishful thinking? Possibly. No. Probably.

Had I just seen Lissa's spirit? Her ghost?

But were there such things?

Andrew used to say this house was full of friendly ghosts. He *had* been joking, hadn't he?

I didn't know anything about parapsychology or ectoplasm or psychokinesis. Or the occult or any of those things. All I knew was that I had seen my daughter, or thought I'd seen her, and that the image had been so strong I had believed her to be real.

Baffled, sighing to myself, I finished the glass of vodka, lay back against the sofa's cushions, and closed my eyes. Suddenly I felt exhausted, wiped out.

"Mommy, Mommy."

I paid no attention. Her voice was in my head.

"Butterfly kisses, Mommy," she said, and I felt her child's soft lips against my cheek, felt her warm breath.

Snapping my eyes open, I sat up with a jerk.

Lissa was standing there, looking at me.

"Oliver's cold, Mommy," she said, handing me her teddy bear, and then she climbed onto the sofa and snuggled down into my arms.

Sunlight streaming in through the lace curtains awakened me, and I turned and stretched, almost falling off the sofa. Pushing myself up into a sitting position, I glanced around, feeling completely disoriented.

I had obviously fallen asleep on the sofa. I had a crick in my neck, my back ached, and my mouth was dry. I felt parched. My eye fell on the half-empty bottle of vodka, and I shuddered.

It was then that I remembered.

Everything came rushing back to me. Lissa had been here last night. She had been in her nightgown, holding Oliver, and she had said he was cold; she had given him to me and had crept into my arms.

I *had* held her. I know I had.

No, it was a dream. A hallucination. My imagination playing tricks. The vodka.

I heard Nora's step on the stairs and her voice calling, "Mal, Mal, are you up there?" And when I glanced at the clock, I saw to my shock that it was nine-thirty.

Nine-thirty.

I hadn't slept like this since Andrew had been killed. In fact, I had hardly slept at all until last night.

"Freezing cold out," Nora announced coming into the sitting room. She stood in the doorway, eyeing me. "Not like you not to be up and about," she went on, "lolling around like this. You haven't even made the coffee this morning."

"No, I haven't. I only just woke up, Nora. I must have fallen asleep on the sofa. I've been on it all night."

She glanced at the vodka bottle, said succinctly, "Not surprising. But a good sleep was what you needed."

"I'll be down soon."

"Don't rush. Coffee takes a few minutes," she said as she hurried out.

I went into the bathroom and bent over the tub to flip the plug and saw, to my amazement, that the bath was empty.

But it couldn't be. I'd filled it last night. Filled it to the brim. I had been going to kill myself last night by slitting my wrists with my art knife.

The knife was not there.

This is ridiculous, I thought, looking around for it. I had put the knife on the edge of the tub near the taps. It was gone.

I spent a good twenty minutes searching for my art knife, but without success. It had vanished.

The whole business of the empty tub, the missing knife, and the kitchen door both puzzled and disturbed me. Demented with grief I might be, but I knew I wasn't crazy.

27

"I'll be in my studio if you want me," I said to Nora a little later that morning.

"Oh, that's good to hear," she said, and there was a pleased note in her voice.

"I'm going to clean out some of my stuff, not paint," I said, looking at her as I pulled on my barbour.

Her face fell, but she made no comment, simply went back to preparing the vegetables for yet another one of her interminable soups. She was determined to feed me, and about the only thing she could get me to eat was soup or porridge. I was never hungry these days.

The icy wind stung my face as I walked quickly down the path which led past the terrace and the swimming pool. The studio door was locked, and as I fumbled with the key I shivered. Nora had been correct again. It was freezing cold today, below zero.

Warm air greeted me as I stepped inside my studio.

Last year I had installed gas heating, and I kept it at fifty degrees in the winter months. I went over to the thermostat and pushed the switch up to sixty-five.

Glancing around the studio, I saw that Nora had made an effort to tidy it since I had last been in here in November. But even so, there was a lot of mess and clutter. Brushes were lying around, and there were palettes with dried paint on them, a stack of new canvases piled haphazardly on a table, and several of my oils propped up against the side of the old sofa.

Taking off my barbour, hanging it on the coat stand, I ignored the mess I had supposedly come to clean. Instead I looked for another art knife with a razor blade. I was certain there was a new one in a drawer of the chest I used for storing supplies. But I was wrong. All I could find were new sable brushes, crayons for drawing pastels, small pots of oil paints, a new paintbox of watercolors, and a lot of colored pencils.

I stood staring at the chest, biting my lip. Apparently the only art knife I had was the one which had gone missing.

How was I going to cut my wrists if I didn't have a blade?

I could gas myself instead. My eyes focused on the gas fire set in the wall.

The intercom on the phone buzzed, and I picked up the receiver, "Yes, Nora?"

"Were you expecting your mother, Mal?"

"No."

"Well, she's here. At least her car's coming up the front drive."

"Okay. I'll be right there."

"Good thing I'm making this soup for lunch," she said, then hung up.

After lowering the heat in the studio, I went out, locked the door, and ran back up the path to the house. It was not like my mother to come without calling me first; also, I was surprised she had ventured up to Connecticut in this bitterly cold and snowy weather.

She was coming in the front door as I strode into the long gallery.

"Mom, this is a surprise," I said, embracing her. "What's brought you up here on a day like this?"

"I wanted to see you, Mallory. I thought you might try to put me off if I phoned first. So I just came."

"You know you're always welcome, Mom."

She gave me an odd look but didn't say anything, and I took her heavy wool duffel coat and carried it out to the coatroom in the back of the house near my office.

"Would you like a cup of coffee?" I asked when I returned.

"Tea would be nice," she answered, following me into the kitchen. I went to put the kettle on.

Nora said, "Hello, Mrs. Nelson. Roads bad, are they?"

My mother shook her head. "No, they've been well plowed. And good morning, Nora, how are you?"

"Not bad. And you?"

"As well as can be expected, under the circumstances," my mother responded. She half smiled at Nora, then looked at the stove and sniffed. "Your soup smells delicious."

"It's lunch," Nora said. "And I can make you a sandwich. Or an omelette, if you like."

"Anything will do, thanks, Nora. I'll have whatever Mal's having."

Nora went over to one of the cupboards and took out a cup and saucer for my mother's tea. Looking over her shoulder, she asked, "What about you, Mal? Do you want a cup too?"

"Yes, it'll warm me up," I said, and turning to my mother, I asked, "How's David?"

"He's well. Very busy right now."

"Has he heard anything? From DeMarco?"

"No. Have you?"

"No."

We stared at each other. I saw the tears rising in my mother's eyes. She blinked, pushed them back, and took a deep breath. "Are you feeling a bit better, darling?"

"Yes, I'm doing fine," I lied.

I walked over to the kitchen stove, turned off the kettle, and made the pot of tea. I began to put everything on a wooden tray, and looking up, I said to my mother. "Let's go into the sunroom. It's really very pleasant in there today."

"Wherever you wish, Mal."

We sat opposite each other on either side of the big glass coffee table, sipping our tea.

When she had finished her cup, my mother put it down on the table, looked across at me, and said, "Tell me the truth, Mal, are you really all right?"

"Of course, Mom!"

"I do worry about you, and about your being alone out here all the t—"

"I'm not alone. Nora's here, and Eric's in and out almost every day, and there's Anna down in the barn."

"They're not with you at night."

"True, but I'm okay, honestly. Try not to worry so much, Mother."

"I can't help it. I love you, Mallory."

"I know, Mom."

"And then there are the weekends." She stopped, studied me for a moment, then asked, "Don't you want David and me to come out anymore?"

"Yes. Whenever you like. Why do you say that? And in such a peculiar tone?"

"I've felt that you've been pushing us away recently."

"Not true. I told you before, you're welcome anytime, and so is David."

"It disturbs me that you're alone so much," she said again.

"I'm not. And Sarah's always here. She was here this weekend."

"I know. She called me last night when she got back to the city. She wanted to tell me about her cousin Vera, about Vera looking at your apartment. So you are going to sell it, then?"

"Why not? I don't want to live there."

"Yes," she said quietly. "I understand."

"Vera's coming to New York in a couple of weeks, so Sarah said. Do you mind showing her the apartment? That is, if Sarah's working or away on business."

"I'll be happy to do it, darling."

"I guess Sarah told you she was going to Paris today?"

My mother nodded. "You and Sarah are very lucky, you know."

I stared at her. *I* was *lucky?*

"To have each other, I mean," she said swiftly, no doubt noticing the startled expression on my face. "To be so close—"

"Yes, we are," I agreed, cutting her off.

"To be best friends," she continued. "To be lifelong friends, to have such unconditional love for each other. You're both so fiercely loyal, and in many ways you're very dependent on each other."

"We bonded long ago, Mom."

"Yes, it's rare, that kind of friendship."

"But surely you have it with Auntie Pansy?"

"To a certain extent, but we were never as close as you and Sarah. I don't think Pansy wanted that kind of intimacy. She's not a bit like her daughter. Sarah's much warmer."

"Well, there's nobody like my Sarah, I must admit. They threw the mold away."

"She is unique, Mal, I agree. But I've been wondering lately—do you think she's enough?"

"I don't know what you mean, Mom." I sat up straighter and focused my eyes on her. "What are you getting at?"

"I'm not talking about friendship, darling. I'm talking about your pain and grief, your heartbreak. Maybe you need more help than Sarah or I can give you. Perhaps it would be a good idea to see a professional. A psychiatrist."

"A *psychiatrist.* Do you think I need one, Mother?"

"Perhaps. For grief counseling. There are many who specialize in that, and I understand they help people come to grips—"

"I don't want to see a shrink," I interrupted. "You go if you want."

"Perhaps we can go together."

"No, Mom."

"There are groups, you know, who counsel mothers and fathers who have lost children to violent crimes."

I sat staring at her, saying nothing.

She went on, "I've heard of this young woman who lost her child in a car accident. She was driving, and walked away alive. She's started a group. People in similar circumstances, who have lost children, get together to talk. My friend Audrey Laing wants me to go. Do you want to come with me, Mal? It might help you."

"I don't think so," I said in a low voice. I began to shake my head vehemently. "No, no, it wouldn't help, Mom, I'm sure of that. I know you mean well, but I just couldn't . . . couldn't talk about Lissa and Jamie and Andrew to strangers, to people who had never known them. Honestly, I just couldn't."

"All right, I understand what you're saying. But don't dismiss it out of hand. At least think about it, will you?"

"I much prefer to talk to you and Sarah. And Diana, Daddy when he calls. People who know firsthand what I've lost."

"Yes, darling." My mother cleared her throat. "I do worry about you so. Maybe I should get you another dog."

"Another dog!" I cried, jumping up, gaping at her. "I don't want another fucking dog! I want *my* dog! I want *Trixy.* I want my *babies*! I want my *husband*! I want my *life* back!" I glared at my mother, then swung around and flew to the French doors. Opening them, I ran outside. Something inside me had snapped, and I was crying and shaking with rage.

I stood there in the snow, pressing my hands to my face, sobbing as if my heart would break. I was oblivious to the icy wind and the snow, which was falling again.

A moment later I felt my mother's arms around me. "Come inside, Mal. Come inside, darling."

I let her lead me back into the sunroom, let her press me down onto the sofa. She sat next to me, pulled my hands away from my face, and looked into my eyes. I looked back at her, the tears still trickling down my cheeks.

"Forgive me, Mal. I didn't mean it the way it came out, the way it sounded. I really didn't," she whispered in a choked-up voice.

Her own grief and heartache stabbed at me, and my anger dissipated as swiftly as it had flared inside me. "I know you didn't, Mom, and there's nothing to forgive. I know you'd never hurt me."

"Never," she wept, clinging to my arm. "I love you very much."

"And I love you, Mom."

She lifted her head, looked into my eyes again. "It was always your father with you—" she began and stopped short.

"Perhaps I favored him because he was hardly ever there, and so he seemed very special to me. But I've always loved you, Mother, and I know you've always been there for me."

"And I still am, Mal."

A few days after this visit of my mother's I fell into a deep depression.

I became morose, filled with a strange kind of melancholia, and I felt listless, without energy. I could hardly bear to move, and my limbs ached as if I were an old woman suffering from an ague. It was a kind of physical debilitation I was unaccustomed to, and I was helpless, almost an invalid.

All I wanted to do was curl up in my bed and sleep. And yet sleep always eluded me; I only ever dozed. I would soon be wide awake, my mind turning and turning with endless distressing and painful thoughts.

Wanting to end my life though I did, I discovered I did not have the strength to get out of bed, never mind actually kill myself. Apathy combined with a deep-rooted loneliness to render me useless to myself.

There were moments when despair overwhelmed me, brought me to tears again. I was alone, without purpose. I had no future. The absence of my family appalled me, and the loneliness, the yearning for them was destroying me.

At times different emotions intruded, bringing me to my knees: Guilt that I had not been with them, guilt that I was alive and they were dead; rage that they had been victims of street violence, rage that I could not avenge their deaths. These were the moments I felt murderous, wanted to kill whoever had killed my children and my husband.

On those occasions I would call the Twenty-fifth Precinct to talk to Detective DeMarco, wanting to know if any new evidence had turned up.

He never sounded anything but regretful, even sad, when he told me no. He promised they would break the case. He meant well. But I was unconvinced. I never believed him.

Memories were my only source of comfort. I fell down into them gratefully, recalling Lissa, Jamie, Andrew, and little Trixy with the greatest of ease. I relived our life together and took joy from this.

But then one abysmal day the memories would no longer come at my bidding. And I was afraid. Why could I no longer recall the past, our past? Why were my children's faces suddenly so blurred and indistinct? Why did I have such trouble picturing Andrew's face in my mind's eye?

I did not know. But when this loss of total recall persisted for a week, I knew what I had to do. I must go to Kilgram Chase. I wanted to be in Andrew's childhood home, the place where he had grown up. Perhaps there I would feel close to him once more, perhaps there he would come back to me.

PART FIVE

KILGRAM CHASE

28

Yorkshire, March 1989

Spring had come early, much earlier than anyone here at Kilgram Chase had expected.

I had arrived from Connecticut toward the end of January to find everything covered in snow, and the first part of February had been bitter, with sleet, freezing rain, and intermittent snowstorms. But the weather had changed in the middle of the month. The rain and harsh winds had ceased unexpectedly; there had been a general softening, a warming much welcomed by everyone here, most especially the farmers.

Now, on this first Friday in March, the trees were bursting with tender green shoots and the first fluttering little leaves. Grass was beginning to sprout, and the borders at the edges of the lawns were alive with purple, yellow, and white crocuses and delicate, starlike snowdrops. Daffodils danced down near the pond and under the trees in the woods. Tall and graceful as they nodded in the light breeze, their brilliant yellow bonnets reflected the bright afternoon sun.

I stood at the mullioned window in the library, looking out toward the moors, thinking that perhaps I ought to take a walk later.

I had not been able to go out much since I had arrived almost five weeks ago. Within the first few days I had fallen sick, felled by a bad bout of flu, and I had spent over ten days in bed.

Diana, Parky, and Hilary had nursed me through it, done the best they could to make me better. But I had been a bad patient, not very cooperative at all; I had refused almost all of the medicines they had offered me and done little to speed my recovery, hoping to catch pneumonia and die. I had not. But then neither had I been very well; I was slow to get up on my feet and about. When I first arrived I had been exhausted and undernourished, and the aftermath of the flu virus left me feeling even weaker. This physical debilitation combined with my mental apathy to make me more listless and enervated than I had been at Indian Meadows.

Although I was here in Andrew's childhood home, I continued to face dreary empty days and sleepless nights, and that awful nothingness was ever-present.

Not even Diana could cheer me up very much when she came back to Yorkshire on the weekends, after working at her shop in London all week. How right my mother had been when she had told me that you don't leave your troubles behind you when you go to another place.

"Pain and heartache travel well," she had said to me the day she took me to Kennedy to catch my plane to London. And indeed they did.

Yet I did feel closer to Andrew here at Kilgram Chase, as I had believed I would. My memories of him and my children now came back to me unbidden, and their well-loved faces were clear, distinctive in my mind's eye once again. Very regularly my thoughts turned inward, and I was able to live with them within myself, in my imagination.

The days passed quietly, uneventfully. I did very little. I read occasionally, watched television; sometimes I listened to music, but for the most part I sat in front of the fire in the library, lost in my own world, oblivious to everyone most of the time. Of course Diana made her presence felt when she was here and tried to rouse me from my lethargy. I really made an effort, tried to perk up, but I wasn't very successful. I had no one and nothing to live for. I simply existed. I had even lost the will to kill myself.

Now, moving away from the window, I crossed to the fireplace and piled more logs on top of those already crackling and burning up the chimney. Then lifting the tray with the coffee things on it, I took it back to the kitchen.

Parky looked up as I came in and exclaimed, "Nay, Mrs. Mal, you needn't have bothered with that! I would have sent Hilary or Joe for it later."

"It's no trouble, Parky, and thank you, it was a lovely cup of coffee. Just what I needed."

"You didn't eat much lunch, Mrs. Mal," she said, her eyes filled with worry. "Picking at your food is no way to improve your health and get your strength up."

"I know. I do try, Parky. And what I did eat I really enjoyed. The grilled plaice and chips were delicious."

She went on rolling out the pastry on the big slab of marble, saying, "It's a right bonny afternoon. Too bonny to stay cooped up in that there library, if you don't mind me saying so. You should get out, have a good blow on the moors. It'll do you good, that it will, Mrs. Mal."

"I was just thinking about taking a walk, actually, Parky."

She smiled at me, nodded her approval, and continued. "Mrs. Keswick will be arriving a bit earlier than usual this weekend. About four-thirty, or thereabouts. In time for tea," she said.

"That's nice," I answered. "Parky, can I ask you something?"

"Of course you can, Mrs. Mal."

"I've been wondering why you and Joe and Hilary and the gardeners call me that? For ten years I've been Mrs. Andrew to you all. But since I came back in January, it's been Mrs. Mal. Why?"

She stared at me, flushing slightly and looking discomfited. "It's just that . . . that . . . well, we didn't want to upset you further," she began haltingly. "We thought that to keep mentioning Mr. Andrew's name would be . . . well, painful."

"No, Parky," I interrupted softly. "It wouldn't. I *am* Mrs. Andrew, and I really would prefer you to keep on calling me that."

"I'm sorry if we've upset you," she said, sounding concerned. "We'd never do anything to hurt you. We were only trying to be mindful of your feelings."

"I know you were, and honestly, I do appreciate that, and I am grateful to you for the kindness you've shown me these last few weeks."

"You were in such a bad way when you got here, and we didn't want to distress you anymore than you already were. We felt we had to be careful. It was like . . . like walking on eggs."

"I'm sorry, Parky."

"Oh, there's no need to apologize, Mrs. Mal, I mean Mrs. Andrew. We understand. We loved Mr. Andrew and the wee bairns—" Her mouth began to tremble and her eyes filled, but she took a deep breath and finished. "Such a tragedy, so hard to live with . . ."

"Yes, it is." I coughed behind my hand, trying to control myself. I knew I might easily break down if I didn't keep a tight grip on my emotions. My grief was never very far below the surface.

Parky said quietly, almost to herself, "Like my own child, he was," and then she put down the rolling pin and hurried into the adjoining pantry. "Got to find that big pie dish for the steak-and-kidney pie," she called to me in a muffled voice without looking around.

"I shall go for a walk," I said, and went out of the kitchen swiftly, knowing it was wiser to leave her by herself to recoup. Otherwise we'd both be in a flood of tears.

I headed in the direction of the mudroom. Once there, I took off my penny loafers, pulled a pair of Wellingtons on over my jeans, and struggled into one of Diana's old barbours. Wrapping a scarf around my head, I went outside.

It was a clear day, crisp but not really cold, and there was the lightest of breezes rustling through the trees, making the new leaves flutter and dance. I dug my hands into the pockets of the barbour and struck out toward the pond down near the woods. Behind the pond there was a narrow path, which the gardeners had cut through the dense mass of trees some years ago, and this led up to the lower moors.

The grounds were deserted, I noticed as I walked.

Usually Ben and Wilf were somewhere or other, digging, planting, and pruning, or burning leaves. This afternoon they were nowhere in sight.

But by the time I got closer to the pond, I saw Wilf pushing a wheelbarrow along the path that led from the orchard up to the house. When we drew level with each other, he stopped and touched his cap. "Afternoon, Mrs. Mal."

"Hello, Wilf."

"You're not going up on yon moors?"

"Yes, I was thinking about it," I answered.

"Aye, no, don't be doing that." He turned his head, shaded his eyes with his hand, and peered toward the hills silhouetted against the distant horizon.

"B'ain't wise. Weather's right dicey up on yon moors this time o'year. Sunny for a bit, like now, but then t'clouds roll in and t'rain comes down in torrents. Blows in from yon North Sea, it does that."

"Thanks for telling me, Wilf," I murmured and hurried on down the path, thinking what an old fool he was, gormless, as Andrew had always said. It was as clear as a bell today; the sky was blue and without a single cloud.

But something about his words must have registered at the back of my mind, because in the end I avoided the moors. It was such a long, steep climb, anyway. Instead, I went for a more leisurely walk through the woods, and a half hour later I came back and circled the pond, before taking the wide stone path that cut through the lawns. I had been out long enough today. I already felt tired. Obviously I was out of shape and still quite weak.

As I approached the house, I saw Hilary coming toward me, waving and beckoning.

I increased my pace, and when we met in the middle of the stone path, she said, "There's a phone call for you, Mrs. Andrew. From New York. It's Mr. Nelson."

"Thanks, Hilary."

Together we went around the side of the house to the back door, and as we hurried in, I said to her, "Would you tell him I'll be there in a moment, please. I just want to get my Wellies off."

"Yes, Mrs. Andrew," she answered, disappearing down the back hallway.

A few seconds later I was picking up the phone on the long refectory table in the library. "Hello, David, how are you?"

"Good, Mal, and you?"

"I've finally recovered from the flu. There's nothing wrong, is there? My mother's all right, isn't she?"

"Yes, she is, and everything's fine. She worries about you, of course, and keeps talking about coming over to see you. She wants us to take a trip to England, if you're planning on staying in Yorkshire for a while."

"Why don't you come? Is that the reason you're calling, David?"

"No, it isn't. I have some news for you, Mal."

I caught the change in his voice, the tension. My chest tightened. I gripped the receiver harder as I said, "From DeMarco?"

"Yes. There's been a break in the case. He just called me about fifteen minutes ago. Luckily, I wasn't in court today."

"Have they caught the killer? The gunman?" I asked in a tight voice.

"No, but they will, and very soon, Mal. This is what happened. Twenty-four hours ago, Johnson and DeMarco arrested a small-time narcotics dealer who operates in that neighborhood. Those arches under the elevated train tracks are part of his territory. Anyway, he's trying to strike a deal, to plea-bargain. He says he knows who shot Andrew and the children. Four local youths who hang out together, one of whom has talked about it. He's given their names and addresses to DeMarco, and he and Johnson hope to take them into custody today, bring them into the Twenty-fifth Precinct for questioning immediately. DeMarco's got a strong feeling that those unidentified fingerprints found on Andrew's Mercedes will match up with theirs. He's banking on it."

My legs suddenly felt weak, and I sat down heavily on the cut-velvet chair. I could hardly speak, but finally I managed to say, "If the fingerprints do match, what happens then?"

"The perpetrators will be taken down to Central Booking in Police Plaza and booked on charges of murder in the second degree. And all four of them will be booked, Mal, you see—"

"I thought there was only one gunman?" I cut in.

"That's what DeMarco believes, yes. But a person doesn't have to pull the trigger to be booked or found guilty of murder. Just being there, just standing there when the crime is committed, is enough to convict," David explained. "It's called *acting in concert*. If there's enough evidence, within seventy-two hours they'll go in front of a grand jury in criminal court downtown. And if they're indicted in the grand jury hearing, they'll go on trial."

"When would that be?"

"I'm not sure. It could take several months. Not only to get on the docket, but the assistant district attorney will want to be sure he has every scrap of evidence he can get, that he has a watertight case. DeMarco and Johnson will have to work their butts off on this one, and they will, I've no doubt. The prosecutor wants a guilty verdict, not an acquittal, and so do they."

"And if the youths *are* found guilty?"

"There's no death penalty in New York State, Mal. They'll get twenty-five or thirty years to life. No parole."

"I see. Could they—" I paused, took a deep breath, and asked, "Could they get off?"

"No way. DeMarco and Johnson are convinced they've struck pay dirt with the drug dealer, that they'll turn up all the evidence they need for a conviction."

"I hope so."

"They will. It's a personal crusade with them, especially DeMarco. Also, I know the judicial system inside out, and the judge will go for the maximum, trust me on this. The killers will never see daylight again; they'll never get out."

"Should I call DeMarco, David? What do you think?"

"You don't have to, Mal. He asked me to pass the news on to you. Anyway, I doubt that you'd get him right now. He's on the investigation full blast. Now that he's got this lead, he wants results fast. He wants to put these . . . animals away. He wants them under lock and key. Today."

"I understand. And thank you, David, for everything."

"I'm always here for you, Mal. Give Diana my best."

"I will. Oh, does Mom know about the break in the case?"

"Yes. I told her before I called you. She sends her love."

"Give her mine."

"I'll be in touch as soon as I have more information from DeMarco."

"When you speak to him, thank him for me."

"I will, honey. Bye."

"Bye, David."

After we hung up I sat with my hand resting on the phone, pondering everything David had told me. I felt nothing, only emptiness inside. Knowing the killers of my family were about to be arrested did not relieve my pain and grief. And it would not bring them back.

Gazing out of the mullioned window, I drifted with my thoughts for a while. But at one moment the sky darkened, and I lifted my eyes. The garden was still filled with sunlight, but on the moors the blue sky had turned, was curdled and gray. Ominous dark clouds were blowing in, and up there it had started to rain, just as old Wilf had predicted. Shivering involuntarily, feeling suddenly cold, I walked over to the fire and sat down on the sofa to get warm. And to wait for Diana.

I must have fallen asleep, for I woke up with a start when I heard her voice. She was coming into the library with Hilary in her wake carrying the tea tray.

"Hello, darling," Diana said, hurrying forward. "Are you feeling a bit better today?"

I would never feel better. But I nodded; it was the easiest thing to do.

She bent over me, kissed me on my cheek, and then went and stood with her back to the fire, as she often did, just as Andrew had done. Saying nothing, she surveyed me for a few moments. As soon as Hilary had put the tea tray down and departed, she said, "What is it, Mal? You look as if you have something to tell me."

"I do," I replied. "David called me a short while ago. There's been a break in the case at last."

"Tell me all about it!" she exclaimed. She came and sat down next to me on the sofa.

Her eyes did not leave my face as I recounted my entire conversation with David.

When I finished, her reaction was the same as mine had been. "Thank God," she said quietly. "But it won't bring my son and my grandchildren back to life ... " Her voice wavered slightly, and she took a moment to regain her composure, then she added, "But at least we know that justice will be done, and that those responsible will be punished."

"It's small comfort," I murmured. "But it's better than knowing they are free."

"And that they might kill again," Diana said.

29

"I have to go to Paris on Wednesday," Diana said. "Why don't you come to London with me tomorrow? And then we'll go to Paris together. I think it would do you good, Mal."

Diana and I were sitting in the library on Sunday morning, reading the newspapers. Or rather, she was reading; I was merely glancing through them.

Looking up, I shook my head. "I don't think so. I'm still feeling a bit debilitated after the flu."

Diana stared at me for the longest moment, and then she said, "Nonsense, Mal, you're much better, and you have been for the last week. Your problem is your mental apathy."

Startled by her brisk, matter-of-fact tone as well as her words, I recoiled slightly, then said, "Maybe you're right."

"I know I am," she replied and put down her newspaper. Leaning forward, focusing every ounce of her attention on me, she continued, "Mal, you can't go on like this."

I returned her steady gaze, but I remained silent.

"What are you going to do? Sit on that sofa in this library for the rest of your life? Is that your plan?"

"I have no plans," I said.

"But you do have a *choice*. Actually, you have three choices. You can sit around forever, as you're doing now, letting your life drift away from you. You can kill yourself, which I know you've contemplated more than once, from the things you've said to me. Or you can pull yourself together, pick up the pieces and go on from here."

"Go where?" I muttered. "I just don't . . . don't know . . . what to do . . . what to do with myself," I began hesitantly, at a loss in more ways than one.

Diana sat studying me, her eyes full of love, her expression sympathetic, as it always was. Her voice was caring when she murmured softly, "I know only too well what you've lost—those you loved with all your heart, those most precious and dear to you. But as hard as it may seem, you must begin again. That is your *only* choice, Mal darling. Trust me, it is. God knows, you've nothing to lose, you've already lost it all, but you do have everything to gain."

"I do?"

"Yes. Your *life*, for one thing, a new life. You must try, darling, not only for yourself, but for me."

I sighed and looked away, and then I felt the tears rising to flood my eyes. "I can't," I whispered, fighting the tears, the pain, and the grief. "I'm weighted down. My sorrow is unendurable, Diana."

"I know, I know. I'm suffering too . . . " Diana could not finish her sentence. Her voice choked up, and she came and sat next to me on the sofa. Taking my hand in hers, she held on to it tightly and said finally, "Andrew wouldn't want to see you like this, Mal. He always said you were the strongest woman he'd ever known, other than me."

"I can't live without him. I don't want to live without him and the twins."

"You're going to have to," Diana said in a voice that was low, suddenly quite stern. "You've got to stop feeling sorry for yourself, right now. Do you think you're the only woman who has ever lost loved ones? Lost a family? What about me? I've lost my son, my only child, and my grandchildren, and before that I lost a husband when I was still a young woman. And what about your mother? She is as grief-stricken and heartbroken as we are."

Taking a deep breath, she added, "And what about the millions of other people in the world who have had to survive the loss of their families? You only have to think about the survivors of the Holocaust—those who lost husbands and wives and children and mothers and fathers in the death camps, to realize we are not alone. Loss of loved ones is part of life, I'm sorry to say. It's terrible, so difficult to accept—"

Diana could not continue speaking. Her emotions got the better of her, and she began to weep, but after only a moment or two she said through her tears, "There isn't a day goes by that I don't think about him, think about my Andrew, and about little Lissa and Jamie. And my heart never stops aching. But I know I can't give in, that I mustn't. And so I try to keep myself together, the best way I can. Mal, listen to me. You can't throw your life away. You have to try, just as I try."

The tears trickled down her cheeks, and she looked at me helplessly. I put my arms around her and held her close to me. And I wept with her.

Her words had found their mark, had touched the core of me, and I realized with a small shock how badly I had behaved; I had thought only of myself.

"I've been so selfish, Diana," I said at last. "Very selfish. You're right, I've only thought about my feelings, about *my* loss, *my* pain, not yours or Mom's."

"I didn't mean to sound harsh, darling," she murmured, extricating herself from me, sitting up on the sofa and drying her cheeks. "I was only trying to make you see . . . see things a little more clearly."

I didn't say anything for a few minutes, then glancing at Diana, I asked quietly, "What did you mean when you said I had everything to gain?"

"I told you, your *life*, primarily. But that also means your health, your well-being, your sanity. You're only thirty-three, Mal, still so very young, and I simply won't allow you to become a vegetable, a blob sitting around doing nothing except mourning and feeling sorry for yourself. It's vital that you mourn, yes. We must do that, we must get the grief out. But I can't, I *won't* permit you to throw your future away."

"Do I have a future, Diana?"

"Oh, yes, you do. Of course you do. That's another thing you have to gain. Your future. But you must reach out, grab life with both hands and start all over again. It will be the hardest thing you've ever had to do, the most painful, even, but it *will* be worth it, I promise you that."

"I don't know what to do. How would I begin again?" I asked, my mind starting to work in a more positive way for the first time since Andrew's death.

"First, I think you have to get yourself completely fit physically. You're far too thin, for one thing. You must start eating properly, and walking and exercising, so that you regain your strength, that vigor and energy of yours which I've always admired. And then you must think of the kind of job you'd like to find. You must work, not only because you need to earn money, but because you must keep yourself busy."

"I wouldn't know where to start." I bit my lip and shook my head. "I realize I have to begin to support myself, and very quickly. I can't let my mother and Dad go on helping me. But I don't have any idea what I could do. Or what I'm capable of doing, for that matter."

"You wrote advertising copy once," Diana reminded me.

"That was a long time ago, and I'm not sure how good I was, even if Andrew did say I was brilliant. Besides, I don't think I'd enjoy working in an office, and I know I can't live in New York. So we can forget Madison Avenue."

"You could live in London," she suggested, eyeing me intently. "I'd like that. You're all I have left, Mal, the only family I have."

I nodded. "I know, Diana, and you're very much a part of me, part of my life. It's a possibility, living in London, I mean. I suppose I could always sell Indian Meadows."

"What's happening with the apartment? You haven't said anything lately about Sarah's cousin and her plans."

"Vera wants to buy it, and she's agreed to the price my mother asked. But she hasn't gone before the board yet, the board of the cooperative. I think she's supposed to be interviewed by them this coming week. I'm not worried though, Diana; I know she'll pass."

"Getting back to a job for you, if you stay in London, you might consider working with me at the shop. You do love antiques, and you know a lot about them. I could certainly use your expertise. And your obvious talents as a decorator."

When I said nothing, Diana sat back, stared at me for a few seconds, and then reached out and took my hand in hers. "I'd like you to become my partner, Mal."

"Oh, that's so generous of you! Thank you, Diana. I'm not sure. Can I think about it?"

"Yes. Take your time." She half smiled and then reached out, touched my cheek. "You're like my daughter. No, you *are* my daughter. And I love you."

"I love you, too, Diana. You're very special to me."

"I started to say I could use your talents as an interior designer. You're awfully good at decorating, and I have a lot of clients who don't just want to buy antiques from me. They also want me to put together whole rooms for them. Whole houses, in fact."

"I do enjoy decorating, but I'm not sure I'd want to do it for other people," I said. "But it is a possibility, I guess."

"We could always have a trial run. We've nothing to lose."

"What do you mean?"

"There's no good reason why you shouldn't stay on in London for a few months. You could work at the shop, travel with me to France on buying trips, even make trips on your own. Then you could spend weekends up here with me. It's always lovely at Kilgram Chase in the summer months. At the end of the summer you could go back to Connecticut, if you wanted to, if that's what you decided was best for you."

"There's nobody like you, Diana, you're so kind, so loving." I leaned my head against the cushions and closed my eyes. A small sigh escaped me.

She said softly, "I won't press you anymore, but do think seriously about it, Mal. And remember, it would please me enormously to have you as my partner."

That night when I went to bed, I lay awake for a long time, watching the light from the fire flickering across the ceiling and the walls.

Here in this room that had once been his as a boy, Andrew was always close to me. And tonight I felt his presence more acutely than ever. It was as if he stood at the foot of the bed, keeping watch over me.

I talked to him, asked him what I should do, and it seemed to me that he was telling me to stay here with his mother at Kilgram Chase. If that was what he wanted me to do, then I would do it. Here in Yorkshire I was far away from New York and the terrible violence that had claimed my family. I felt safe here, just as I felt safe in London. Yes, perhaps it would be best to stay in England, best to start my new life here.

I turned this thought over and over in my mind until I finally fell asleep.

30

Diana had gone off to London en route to Paris, and I was alone at Kilgram Chase once more.

The library had become my sanctuary in the last few weeks, and now as I sat here on Monday morning, glancing at the newspapers and drinking a cup of coffee, I thought of the things Diana had said to me over the weekend.

She had been right, had spoken only truths.

I had acknowledged this to her and to myself. Self-delusion was not one of my faults. Nonetheless, I knew already that it was going to be hard for me to come to grips with my grief, that it would take me a long time to get it totally under control. The pain inside me was relentless, never seemed to diminish; my sorrow was overwhelming; my loneliness filled me with desolation.

The memory of the terrible violence that had taken my family from me and changed my life forever would always be there in my heart. That was a given. But I *would* try to make a new start. Somehow. I had promised Diana I would; I owed it to her and to myself. And that, at least, would be some sort of a beginning.

I still did not know what I was going to do with the rest of my life, where I was going to live or how I would earn a living.

The first thing I had to do was pull myself up out of my despair, rise above it if I could. I was not sure how to do this.

Earlier this morning it had occurred to me that I ought to find something to focus on, if only for a short while, something to take my mind off my troubles, take me out of myself. Going back to my painting, as Sarah had suggested before I left Indian Meadows, did not particularly interest me now, and therefore, it was not a solution.

However, there *was* one thing that had fascinated me when I was here at Kilgram Chase last November, and that was the diary I had found in this very room. I realized, as I thought of it again, that the seventeenth-century Lettice Keswick still intrigued me. And I could not help wondering, as I had last year, whether or not there was another volume, perhaps even volumes of her writings somewhere in this house.

The diary had no monetary value as far as I knew, and certainly it had nothing to do with my earning a living. On the other hand, looking for another volume, a continuation of the first book, would give me something to focus on. And that in itself would be a step in the right direction.

I would do it. I would start a search. It would keep me busy until I had worked out some sort of plan for my future, bleak though this seemed at the moment.

The library steps were at the other side of the room, and I dragged them over to the fireplace, deciding to look at all the books in this area first. After all, Clarissa's copy and the original had been found on one of the shelves here.

I had just started to mount the steps when there was a tap on the door; Hilary came in for the coffee tray.

"Do you remember those diaries your father and I found last year, Hilary?" I asked, peering down at her.

"Yes, I do, Mrs. Andrew. Quite a find they were. Mrs. Keswick showed them to the vicar. Very impressed, he was."

I nodded. "I thought at the time that there might be more of them, but I never did get around to doing a search before I left. So I've decided to start one today."

"My father and I have already done that, Mrs. Andrew," Hilary explained quickly. "You see, Mrs. Keswick thought the same as you, that there might be another one knocking around, and anyway, she wanted all the books dusted, so we've been working the entire library section by section for some time."

"Oh," I said, feeling a small stab of disappointment. "And you found nothing?"

"No, I'm afraid we didn't. Not so far, anyway. We haven't done the two walls on either side of the fireplace yet, where you're standing. And not that one down there." She nodded in the direction of the end wall with its door leading out into the corridor.

"All right. I'll continue looking here, Hilary."

"And I'll come back and help you if you like, Mrs. Andrew," she said. "I'll just take the tray to the kitchen, I won't be a minute."

"Thanks, I'd really appreciate the help," I said, going higher on the library steps, peering at the leather-bound volumes in front of me. Once I'd read every title, I pulled a couple of books out and felt behind them, hoping for hidden treasures.

Within minutes Hilary returned with Joe, who was carrying the tall ladder he used for cleaning the chandeliers.

"It'll be right grand if we find another diary, Mrs. Andrew," Joe said as he propped the ladder against the end wall. "Mrs. Keswick'll be ever so chuffed if we do."

"So will I, Joe," I said, adding, "By the way, I'm not dusting any of these. Do you think perhaps I should?"

"Aye, no, don't worry about that!" Joe exclaimed. "Hilary can give the books a bit of a flick with the feather duster later. Hilary," he turned to his daughter and said, "Run back t'kitchen, like a good lass, and bring the small stepladder. That way you can follow on behind Mrs. Andrew and dust them there books once she's looked at them."

I was about to protest, but then I remembered how obstinate he could be and decided I'd better not interfere. I continued reading titles and poking around on the shelves, as did Joe and eventually Hilary in other parts of the library.

When Parky appeared at one point to announce that my lunch was ready, I was completely taken aback. I glanced at my watch and saw to my astonishment that it was exactly one o'clock. How quickly the time had flown this morning.

We had a fruitless afternoon, came up empty-handed, and both Joe and Hilary had long faces. Their disappointment was quite evident. It struck me that for some unknown reason they had expected *me* to find something truly special, even if it wasn't another volume of Lettice's diaries.

"Never mind," I said, as we abandoned the search for the day. "Maybe we'll be luckier tomorrow. I fully intend to keep going, to investigate every shelf you two haven't already tackled."

"And we'll help you, Mrs. Andrew," Hilary said. "It's a challenge."

"Aye, it is that," Joe added over his shoulder, going out with the ladder.

That evening Diana called me from London, as she usually did, and I told her what I'd been doing all day.

"I was so intent on finding another Lettice diary, I forgot about the time," I said. "Not only that, I even met with Parky's favor today."

Diana chuckled softly at the other end of the phone. "Don't tell me. You actually *ate* something, is that why she was pleased?"

"Yes. I managed a small plate of cottage pie. Parky was flabbergasted. To tell you the truth, Diana, so was I."

"I'm glad you've started to eat again, however small the plate. It's a start, and you need to build yourself up. I'm relieved that you took my words to heart. I must admit, I worried driving back to London this morning, worried that I'd been too strong with you, but I needed to get through to you."

"Tough love," I replied.

"Is that what you call it?"

"Yes, and Mom says it's the best kind of love when somebody's in trouble and needs help."

"I'm here for you, Mal, with tough love and whatever else you need."

"I know, and I'm here for you. We have to support each other now, get each other through this—"

"We will, darling."

We chatted for a few minutes longer about other things; Diana told me she would be staying at the Crillon in Paris, then gave me the number. After saying good night, we hung up. But within minutes Diana called me back.

"I've just thought of something, another place for you to look for the diaries, or rather, a copy by the Victorian Clarissa, who was so intent on preserving things for the future."

"You mean a place other than the library?" I asked.

"The attics in the west wing," Diana explained. "There are several steamer trunks up there. They've got torn old labels on them, you know, labels from steamship lines, such as the P & O and Cunard. Anyway, in those trunks are all sorts of items from the Victorian era. My mother-in-law showed them to me years ago, just after Michael and I were married. She said they'd been packed up by one of the Keswick wives years before her time, at the turn of the century, in fact. Perhaps it was Clarissa who put those things in the trunks."

"And you think she might have included the diaries, if they exist, in amongst them?" I said.

"There's that possibility. In any case, it's worth looking, don't you think?"

"I certainly do," I said. "And thanks for calling back."

"Good night, Mal."

"Night, Diana."

"Look at this embroidery, it's exquisite, Mrs. Andrew," Hilary said, glancing up at me.

She was kneeling on the attic floor in front of one of the old trunks, and she handed me a claret-colored velvet cushion covered in beads. It was obviously Victorian.

I examined the work, surprised that the cushion and the beading were in such good condition after these many years. One entire side was covered with claret bugle beads, with gray, black, white, and silver beads used for the design. This was a combination of roses and leaves, bordered by delicate ferns around the edge. In the center of the cushion, white beads had been worked to form three words.

"*Amor vincit omnia,*" I read out loud. "Latin. It's quite a well-known phrase. I think it means 'love conquers all.'" Staring at Hilary, I lifted a brow questioningly.

"Don't look at me like that, Mrs. Andrew," she exclaimed with a laugh. "I never studied Latin. Mrs. Keswick would know what it means, though, she took Latin at Oxford University. At least, I think she did."

"Yes, she did," I concurred.

Bending over the trunk, Hilary pulled out another cushion, this one larger and cut from olive-green velvet. Silver, gold, and bronze beads formed the background; white beads made a pattern of calla lilies, with green beads for the stems. Once again there was a Latin phrase at the bottom, worked in green beads.

I took the cushion from Hilary and read, "*Nunc scio quid sit*

Amor. I'm afraid I don't know this phrase at all, but again, it has something to do with love."

"Yes," Hilary agreed, plunging her hands into the treasure trove. She pulled out two more cushions, both Victorian, heavily embroidered with beads and bearing Latin phrases.

As she showed them to me, I shook my head. "I can't tell you what they say, but let's take them downstairs. Mrs. Keswick will be interested in seeing them when she gets back from Paris."

"I can't believe she's forgotten how beautiful they are," Hilary murmured. "What I mean is, you told me she'd seen them years ago. You'd think she'd want to have them out. On the sofas and chairs, I mean."

"Yes. But then perhaps she *has* forgotten, Hilary, just as you said. After all, it was quite a long time ago when she was shown them. Forty years, as a matter of fact."

"Look at this, Mrs. Andrew!"

Hilary now passed me the most beautiful piece of black lace, cut in a large square, edged with jet beads, and encrusted with black bugle beads.

I held it up to look at it in the lamplight.

"What do you think it is?" Hilary asked me. "A mantilla? Like Spanish women used to wear?"

"I don't know. I don't think so, though, it's not quite long enough for a mantilla. But you're right, it's gorgeous. Is there much else in there?"

"Just old linens at the bottom of the trunk."

Hilary began to lift out this collection of items, which had been carefully folded years ago, and handed them to me one by one. Then she pushed herself up on her feet. "This trunk's empty now, Mrs. Andrew."

Together we examined the folded white linens, discovered several Victorian nightgowns made of cotton, half a dozen hand-embroidered pillowcases, and six matching, hand-embroidered sheets.

"Mrs. Keswick can probably make use of these antique linen sheets and pillowcases," Hilary announced. "In the two guest rooms. But I don't know what she'll do with the nightgowns. They're a bit old-fashioned." As she spoke Hilary held one of them against herself. "It smells of mothballs," she muttered and made a face.

For the remainder of the week, Hilary and I spent most of our afternoons poking about in the attics of Kilgram Chase.

There were quite a lot of them located in the four wings of the house, and we ventured into all of them. I had never been up in the eaves before, and I was fascinated by these vast spaces and all that they contained.

Aside from the Victorian steamer trunks in the west-wing attics, we found a variety of other trunks, huge cardboard boxes, and many wooden tea chests stored at the top of the house.

Inside them we discovered a wealth of lovely old things, from more beaded cushions, needlepoint samplers, and a big selection of old linens to china, glass, and all manner of Victoriana: tortoiseshell stud boxes, mother-of-pearl calling-card cases, papier mâché trays, decorative boxes, and tea caddies.

But no books. No diaries by Lettice Keswick. No copies by Andrew's Victorian ancestor, Clarissa.

On Friday afternoon, Hilary and I were in the northeast attic above the library when I stumbled on an old leather trunk. Not quite as large as the other ones we had come across, it was decorated with brass nailheads, now badly discolored, and looked very ancient.

"This might prove to be interesting," I said to Hilary. "But wouldn't you know, it's locked."

"I've got this kitchen knife with me," Hilary answered. "Let me try to prise it open." She came and knelt with me in front of the trunk. She worked away at the lock but was unable to get it to open.

"What about a hairpin?" I suggested. "That sometimes works."

"I don't have one. Do you, Mrs. Andrew?" she asked, looking at my pile of red hair upswept onto the top of my head.

"No, I'm using combs today," I explained. "But there are some pins in my bedroom, I'll rush down and get them."

"Wait a sec. I'll have a go with one of these old keys we found the other day," Hilary replied, pulling a diverse collection of small, very ancient keys out of her apron pocket.

Selecting one at random, she tried to push it into the lock; it did not fit. After trying a number of others, she finally found one that slid into the lock with ease.

"This just might work," she muttered to herself, twisting the key and jiggling it around. It took a few seconds, and then there was a distinct, if slight, click.

"I think I've done it!" she cried with a triumphant look at me.

"Go on, then, open it," I said.

She lifted the lid, and together we looked inside.

"Books!" I exclaimed, bending over the edge of the leather trunk.

"I'm not going to touch them, Mrs. Andrew; they might be very valuable. I wouldn't want to go and damage one."

"I know what you mean, Hilary." I began to nod to myself as I added, "Maybe we've struck gold."

And we had, as it happened.

The first book I put my hands on turned out to be a treasure indeed, although at first glance it looked like nothing of much importance. Bound in black leather, worn, and torn a bit on the spine, it had a frontispiece written in a hand I instantly recognized. There was no mistaking that elegant, feathery, seventeenth-century script.

Lettice Keswick Her Garden Book, the frontispiece said, and as I turned the pages, I caught my breath in surprise and delight.

Lettice had written a charming little book about the gardens at Kilgram Chase, *her gardens*: She told how she had planned and designed them, what she had planted, and why. But most important, the book was beautifully illustrated with watercolors and drawings by Lettice herself. In this it resembled the original diary we had come across last November, but there were many more illustrations in this particular book.

Hilary also exclaimed about its beauty when I showed it to her, and she went as far as to say it was better than the diary.

I did not agree. But there was no doubt that Lettice's illustrations of flowers, trees, shrubs, and plants were superb, as were her actual plans of the various gardens.

Investigating the trunk further, I pulled out four other old books, hoping against hope that they were all Lettice's work.

One was bound in purple leather, and it looked a little less scratched and used than the others. I discovered, on opening it, that it was a volume of Victorian recipes. All were written out in Clarissa's wonderful copperplate handwriting, which I had so admired before. There was no doubt in my mind that it was of her own compilation and that it reflected her own tastes in the culinary art.

There was also a cookbook by the prolific Lettice, and this contained all kinds of seventeenth-century recipes, along with household tips and advice on the use of herbs for medicines.

But it was the last two books which thrilled me the most. One was Lettice Keswick's diary for the year 1663; the other was Clarissa's careful copy of it, again written out painstakingly in her unmistakable copperplate. I could hardly wait to read it.

"It's been worth all the hard work this week, Hilary," I said, struggling to my feet and bending down to pick up the books. "These are very special."

"What will Mrs. Keswick do with them, do you think?" she asked, a quizzical expression settling on her face.

"I'm not sure. Probably nothing in the end, because I don't

know what she could do, Hilary, to tell you the truth. But they're nice to have, aren't they?"

"Yes. Maybe she'll put them on display, you know, in a glass case, like they do with old books in libraries," Hilary murmured, sounding thoughtful all of a sudden. "Mrs. Keswick has the garden fête for the church every summer. Maybe people could pay something extra to come into the house and see the books. Proceeds to go to the church, of course."

"That's a good idea, Hilary. Clever of you."

Looking pleased at my compliment, she went on more confidently, "There're a lot of people around here would be interested to get a tour of this house, too, but Mrs. Keswick will never open it to the public."

I didn't say anything.

Hilary said, "Well, she wouldn't, would she?"

"I don't know. I'd have to ask her," I said.

After I had had my cup of tea, which Parky usually brought to me at about four-thirty, I went back and sat at the refectory table in front of the soaring, mullioned window. It was a clear, sunny afternoon, and anyway, the light was always good on this side of the library.

I had just begun to read Lettice's diary, which she had started in January of 1663, when the loud shrilling of the telephone made me jump slightly.

Automatically, I reached for it and picked up the receiver.

"Kilgram Chase," I said.

There was the sound of static, and then I heard David's voice saying, "Mal, is that you?"

"Yes, it is," I said and found myself clutching the phone all that much tighter. "Do you have news?"

"DeMarco's done it!" he exclaimed. "He and Johnson arrested the four youths over the weekend. I didn't call you earlier, because I was waiting for further developments, and—"

"Did they do it?" I cut in, my voice rising an octave.

"Yes. DeMarco and Johnson are positive the four of them are the perpetrators. Two sets of fingerprints from the car match those of two of the youths. Another was in possession of the gun, the nine-millimeter semiautomatic. It went to ballistics, and the report is conclusive: It is the gun that was used."

"So they'll go before a grand jury?"

"They have already. DeMarco and Johnson moved with great speed, on Monday. The hearing was yesterday, and the grand jury has voted to indict them on charges of murder in the second degree. They'll be going to trial."

"When will that be?" I asked.

"DeMarco's not sure. The prosecutor has to prepare the case, as I explained to you last week. Bail was denied, naturally. And all four currently are in jail. Which is where they'll spend the rest of their lives. They're not going to get off, I can assure you of that."

"Was it . . . " I stopped and took a deep breath. "Was it like Detective DeMarco said . . . was it an attempted carjacking, David?"

"Yes, it was. Gone wrong, of course."

"Did DeMarco tell you why . . . why Andrew and the twins were shot?" I asked, my voice so low it was barely audible.

"He told me that two of the youths were hopped up. Doped up, Mal, full of drugs. They'd apparently been smoking crack cocaine, and one of them just went wild for no reason at all. Just started to fire the gun wildly . . . "

"Oh, God, oh, God, David," I whispered. I could hardly speak.

"I know, I know, honey," he answered, his voice loving and as sympathetic as it always was. "Are you all right?"

I couldn't respond. I sat there in the library, gripping the phone, my knuckles white and my eyes staring blindly into space.

"Mal, are you there?"

I swallowed hard. "I'm here." I took another deep breath. "Thanks for calling, David. I'll be in touch."

"Take care of yourself, Mal. We'll phone you on Sunday. Bye."

I hung up without saying another word and went out of the library. Crossing the hall, my body hunched over and my arms wrapped around myself, I made it to the staircase without anyone seeing me.

Grabbing hold of the bannister, I dragged myself upstairs, slowly lifting one foot after the other. They felt as heavy as lead.

Once I was inside my bedroom, I fell onto the bed and pulled the comforter over me. I had begun to shake, and I couldn't stop. Reaching for a pillow, I buried my face in it, wanting to stifle the sound of my dry, wracking sobs.

My husband and my babies had died needlessly, for nothing, for no reason at all.

31

Yorkshire, May 1989

Up here on the wild, untenanted moors it was a truly pretty day. The sunlit air was soft, balmy, and the vast expanse of sky was cerulean blue, scattered with wispy white clouds.

The air was pure, and I breathed deeply as I walked along the path that had led me from the woods of Kilgram Chase, across the adjoining field, and up onto the lower reaches of the moors.

At one moment I looked up and caught my breath, as always awed by the high-flung fells that soared above me like giant cliffs. They dwarfed everything below, made the floor of the valley and the pastoral green dales seem so much gentler.

I would not go up to the fells today; distances were deceptive in these hills, and they were much farther away than they appeared. In any case, it was too difficult a trek.

But it did not take me long to reach my destination. This was the spot that Andrew had loved from his childhood, and where he had often brought me in the past. It was a stretch of moorland above Kilgram Chase, under the shadows of the great Ragland Fell, up near Dern Ghyll. It was a deep ravine, with an extraordinary waterfall cascading down over its sheer drops and rough-hewn stones.

I had discovered long ago that I was never very far away from the sound of running water on these moors. They were seamed with tinkling little becks and larger streams, and water-falls that came effortlessly tumbling down over the rocks and crags in the most unexpected places.

Feeling quite warm after my walk, I took off my jacket, spread it on the ground, and sat down on it. I stared at the vast panorama stretching out before me; there was nothing but rolling moors sweeping down to the dales and the fields, for as far as the eye could see. No dwellings here. Except, of course, for Diana's house nestled against the trees directly below me.

After a short while, I lay down with my head on my jacket and closed my eyes. I enjoyed the peace up here; I was trans-ported into another world.

There was no noise at all, except for the gentle sounds of nature. The faint buzzing of a bee, the scurry of rabbits rustling through the bilberry and bracken, the occasional bleat of a stray sheep, the trilling of the birds, and that ever-present rush of water dropping over the edge of Dern Ghyll close by.

Today was Thursday, the fourth of May.

My birthday.

I was thirty-four years old today.

I felt older, much older than my years, and scarred by the deaths of my children and my husband. Without them my life would never be the same, and sorrow was my constant compan-ion.

But I no longer had the overwhelming urge to kill myself, and those terrible, debilitating depressions took hold of me less frequently these days. On the other hand, I had not solved the problem of earning a living or finding a job that I liked. I was at a loss, living in a kind of limbo.

I sighed and brushed a fly away from my cheek.

Lulled by the warmth and the sun on my face and bare arms,

I felt suddenly drowsy. I drifted off, calmed by the peacefulness of this place.

Big drops of rain splashing on my face awakened me, and I sat up with a start, groaning out loud when I saw the darkening sky, the rain clouds gathering just above Ragland Fell.

In the distance there was the crack of thunder sounding off like cannon, and a sudden flash of bright white lightning lit up the sky. It ripped through the blackened clouds which had suddenly begun to burst.

A moment later I was already drenched by the most ferocious, slashing rain. Snatching up my jacket, I struggled into it and began to run down past Dern Ghyll, making for the winding path which would lead me back to Kilgram Chase.

In my haste I stumbled several times, and once I almost slipped, but somehow I managed to keep my balance. I went on running, pushing my wet hair away from my face, trying to keep up a steady pace. And I kept asking myself why I never heeded Wilf's warnings about the unpredictable weather up here.

Later, when Diana asked me what happened, I was unable to tell her because I had absolutely no idea how I came to fall. But fall I did. Without warning, I went sprawling at the top of an incline, and before I could check myself I was sliding and rolling down the side of the steep moorland.

I finally came to rest in a gully, and I lay there for a few minutes, gasping, catching my breath. I was winded and felt slightly battered after tumbling such a long way.

Struggling into a sitting position, I looped my wet hair behind my ears and tried to get up. Instantly, I felt the pain shooting from my ankle up my leg, and I sat down again. I realized I had either wrenched or sprained it; I didn't think it was broken. I slithered along the ground until I reached the rock formation at one side of the gully. Here I gripped a protruding rock, endeavoring to pull myself to my feet. I discovered I had difficulty standing, let alone walking.

Thunder and lightning had started raging again, and it seemed to me that the rain was much heavier than before. Uncertain what I ought to do, I decided it would be wisest to shelter here under the rocks until the storm abated. Only then would I try to make it back to Kilgram Chase.

The rocks offered me some protection because they formed an overhang. By crouching down, I was able to shuffle myself under this, where it was reasonably dry. I attempted to wring out my hair with my hands, and then I squeezed the bottom of my trousers. My loafers were wet through and covered in mud, as were the rest of my clothes.

Much to my dismay, the rain continued to come down in great streams; the thunder and lightning were a constant barrage and seemed never-ending. Shivering with cold, my teeth chattering, I pushed myself against the back wall of the rocks, praying that the weather would calm down as quickly as it had erupted.

But it did not, and it grew darker by the minute. Hardly any blue sky was visible now as the thunderheads came scudding in, whipped along by the wind, which had started to blow quite fiercely. From this spot I could just make out the trees bending and swaying in the fields below me.

I sat under the rocks for over two hours, shaking with cold, trying to keep myself calm. The light had grown much dimmer, and I was afraid I was going to be stranded up here in the dark. Even when the rain stopped, I knew I would not get very far hopping or limping my way back to the house.

Growing more stiff and cramped and numb, I twisted my body, stretched out my legs, and lay lengthwise. This was a bit more comfortable, but not much.

From time to time the rumbling clouds parted and I saw a sliver of gray sky. Then it changed unexpectedly, and a peculiar white light began to shimmer on the edge of the horizon, suf-fusing the dark clouds with an aureole of radiance.

The sky was looking strange, almost eerie, but it was never-theless quite beautiful. The light grew brighter, sharper, and I held my breath. Eerie or not, it was magnificent.

As I lay staring at that brilliant sky, trying to still my worry, I heard his voice. Andrew's voice. *Mal.*

It was clear, very close, so close I pushed myself up swiftly and changed my position under the rocks. Again I heard my name.

Mal.

"I'm here," I answered, almost to myself.

Don't be afraid. You'll be all right. Listen to me now. You must be strong and brave. As long as you are alive you will carry the memory of me in your heart. I will live on in you. As Jamie and Lissa will live on in you. We are watching over you, Mal. But it's time for you to move on. Gather your strength. You must go on with your life. Go forward into the future.

"Andrew," I said, looking about me anxiously. "Are you there? Don't leave me, don't go away."

I am always with you, darling. Always. Remember that.

The thunder and lightning stopped.

I peered around again.

I was alone.

The rain ceased abruptly, without any warning. The bright light streaming out from behind the clouds was beginning to diminish and fade, and the stormy clouds were speeding away across the heavens. A fragment of blue appeared above me.

I closed my eyes, thinking.

Had Andrew spoken to me? Or was it all in my own head?

Was my imagination playing tricks again?

"She never paid me any mind, Mrs. Andrew didn't," Wilf grumbled. "I allus told her not to come up on these 'ere moors, Joe. I did that. Dangerous they are."

"Let's just try and find her," Joe said. "Stop yakking."

When I heard their voices nearby, I managed to push myself to my knees. "Help!" I shouted weakly. "Help! I'm down here! Joe! Wilf! Down in the hollow!"

"That's Mrs. Andrew calling us, Joe," Wilf cried excitedly. "She's tummeled in yon gully, I bet she has. Come on, Joe."

A fraction of a second later Wilf and Joe were peering down at me, relief spreading across their weather-beaten faces.

"Whatever's happened to you, Mrs. Andrew?" Joe cried, clambering down into the hollow.

"I fell, rolled down the moor, and ended up in here. I hurt my ankle," I explained, "I'm not sure how well I can walk, Joe. I think I can only hop or limp."

"Don't you worry, we'll have you back home in two shakes of a lamb's tail," Joe said. "Now, come along. Put this barbour on, it'll keep you warm. By gum, you're as white as a sheet, and you must be frozen. You're shaking like a leaf."

"I be warning you afore, Mrs. Andrew," Wilf said. "But you never paid me no mind."

"I'm sorry, Wilf, I should have listened. And you're right, the weather *is* unpredictable up here."

"It is, by gum. Many a poor soul's been lost on these moors, not found till it was too late. Dead as a doornail, they was," Wilf intoned in a dolorous voice.

"That's enough, Wilf," Joe said. "Now, Mrs. Andrew, just put one arm around my neck, and let's see if I can help you up out of this gully."

32

Joe and Wilf half walked me, half carried me back to the house.

We made slow progress because of my ankle; I felt ill, frozen through to my bones, and I had a raging headache. But at least it was no longer raining, and the wind had dropped considerably.

When we finally arrived at Kilgram Chase, Parky, Hilary, and her husband Ben were all waiting for us in the kitchen, their faces anxious.

"Oh, dear, Mrs. Andrew, what happened to you?" Parky cried. "Have you hurt yourself, then?"

"Sprained her ankle, she has," Joe answered.

"I'm all right, Parky," I reassured her, although I didn't feel it at this moment.

"Found her up near yon ghyll, we did, she'd tummeled in a gully," Wilf said. "And I—"

"It could have been worse," Hilary exclaimed, cutting him off sharply. Taking charge with sudden briskness, she went on, "There's no point standing around here nattering. Now, Mrs. Andrew, let's get you upstairs, get those wet clothes off you. A hot bath is what you need, and something hot inside you."

Hilary came to me, put her arm around my waist, and helped me across the kitchen.

"I'll ring up Dr. Gordon, ask him to come, shall I?" Ben said, looking at Hilary.

"Yes, you'd better," she replied.

"I'm okay, honestly I am," I interjected. "I'm just cold. Very cold. A bath will do the trick."

"I think the doctor had better look at your ankle. Best to be on the safe side," Joe said as we went out into the corridor.

I heard Parky say, "I'll put the kettle on."

And then Joe replying, "Nay, Mother, what yon lass needs is a shot of good scotch whiskey, not tea."

Hilary tightened her grip on me as we started up the stairs. "Can you make it all right?" she asked worriedly.

I nodded.

Once we were in my bedroom, she went to run me a bath.

I stripped off my muddy clothes, threw them on the floor, and put on a dressing gown. I limped into the bathroom.

Hilary looked around as I came in and said, "Shall I put some of these Epsom salts in the bath? They're good for aches and pains."

"Yes, that's a good idea," I answered, sitting down on the bathroom stool.

"I'll be back in a few minutes with the tea and the whiskey," Hilary said, walking over to the door. "I'll leave it in the bedroom for you. Oh, and I'll put a bottle of aspirin on the tray."

"Thanks, Hilary. Thanks for everything."

"You're welcome," she murmured and closed the door behind her.

I sat soaking in the hot tub for a long time, enjoying the heat of the water, feeling myself thawing out. The Epsom salts did help my bruised body and my ankle; and even though this was badly sprained, I was now certain it was not broken.

But it was quite obvious that I had had a lucky escape.

When I had gone for a walk earlier this afternoon, I hadn't told anyone where I was going, and it was only by chance that I had seen Wilf in the orchard as I had walked past. He had waved. I had waved back, and then I had gone on down the path into the woods. When the storm had started and I had not returned, he must have been the one to sound the alarm. I experienced a stab of guilt as I thought of the way Andrew and I had always characterized him as stupid—*gormless,* as Andrew said.

Andrew.

I closed my eyes, concentrating, picturing my husband in my mind's eye.

Had he really spoken to me this afternoon? Freezing cold, in pain from my ankle, frightened that I might not be found before nightfall, that I might easily be lost on the moors, might I not have simply imagined it? Might I not have conjured him up for comfort?

I did not know. Just as I did not know whether I had dreamed that Lissa had slept in my arms all those months ago at Indian Meadows.

Was there such a thing as an afterlife? Certainly religions have preached for thousands of years that there is. And if there is an afterlife, then there must be ghosts, spirits of the dead who come back to this physical plane for a reason. To comfort and calm those loved ones left behind grieving? To show themselves as guardian angels?

Suddenly I remembered a book I had seen the other day in the library. It was about angels and ghosts; I had leafed through it quickly. Later I would look at it again.

"You've been very lucky, Mrs. Keswick," Dr. Gordon said, putting his stethoscope away in his bag. "Very lucky indeed."

"I realize that," I responded. "I could have broken something, not just sprained my ankle."

"Very true. But what I meant is, you're fortunate you're not suffering from hypothermia. You were out in that wretched storm for over two hours, and one's body temperature drops very quickly with that kind of exposure to the elements. And when hypothermia does occur, a person can be in serious trouble."

"But Mrs. Andrew *is* all right, isn't she?" Hilary asked, her concern apparent.

"Yes, she's fine." He glanced from Hilary back to me. "Your temperature is normal, and you don't seem to have suffered too much damage. Even the sprain is not that serious. A couple of days, you'll be all right. But do be sure to keep that ankle of yours bandaged."

"I will, Doctor, and thank you for coming over."

"I was glad to pop in, and if you have any problems at all, please don't hesitate to ring me."

"I will. Thanks, Dr. Gordon."

"Good-bye, Mrs. Keswick."

"Bye."

Hilary jumped up.

"I'll see you out, Doctor," she said and hurried after him. Turning back to look at me from the doorway, she asked, "Do you need me for anything else, Mrs. Andrew? Shall I come back and help you get dressed?"

"Thanks, Hilary, that's sweet of you, but I can manage."

Left alone, I took off my robe, put on a pair of gray flannels, a russet-colored silk shirt, and a matching wool jacket. Sitting down on the bench at the bottom of the bed, I pulled on a pair of white wool socks and slipped my feet into a pair of suede moccasins.

Picking up the walking stick Parky had brought upstairs for me, I hobbled out of my bedroom, went along the hall and down the staircase, taking steps very carefully, walking sideways.

The library had become my favorite room at Kilgram Chase these past four months, and knowing this, Joe had turned on the lamps and started the fire earlier, whilst I had been with the doctor.

Even though it was May, the great stone house could be chilly at night, especially this room, with its high-flung ceiling and overscaled proportions. The fire blazing up the chimney and the warm glow of the lamps gave it a cheerful ambience on this rainy evening.

Once I had found the book about angels and ghosts, I went over to the fireplace and sat down in the wing chair. I would look at it whilst I waited for Diana. She was driving up from London tonight instead of tomorrow, so that she could spend the evening with me; she did not want me to be alone for my birthday. She was due in about an hour, and I was glad she was coming.

A memory of my last birthday insinuated itself into my mind, and I couldn't help recalling how happy it had been. My mother had given an early dinner at her apartment, and Lissa and Jamie had come with me and Andrew and Sarah. There had been champagne first and a cake after dinner, and the twins had sung "Happy Birthday" to me. Andrew had given me mabe pearl earrings; the twins had painted their own special cards for me and saved up all year to buy me a pretty silk scarf.

My throat tightened, and I felt the tears sting my eyes as the memories came rushing back. I pushed them aside, took hold of myself, leaned back in the chair, and closed my eyes. Eventually the pain of yearning for them passed.

I began to leaf through the book about angels and ghosts, and I soon found the section I was looking for, the references I wanted.

I read that angels were considered to be messengers of the divine, that they only ever brought good news and aid to those in need of it. People who had seen them said they were filled with goodness and warmth and were surrounded by light, that frequently they were vividly and brilliantly colored, and that a special kind of radiance emanated from them.

Other people interviewed for the book said that when they had seen an angel, or several angels together, they had felt themselves filling with joy, bursting with happiness; some said they had filled with sudden laughter.

The section on ghosts came next, and I read that they were the spirits of the dead, and always took their own form when they materialized. The idea that ghosts did exist was apparently found in every country and culture, and that in general most people agreed on how they actually looked. They were misty, cloudy, transparent, and floating.

Usually, ghosts came to help their loved ones, according to the book. They brought messages of hope and love and frequently materialized in order to tell us that everything was all right. Seemingly, ghosts were attached to the physical world, our world, by their longing for those they had left behind.

The book said there were also bad ghosts, evil spirits who could do harm and who sometimes took demonic possession of a person. I began to read about the Roman Catholic church's attitude toward evil spirits, and the exorcisms which were performed by priests. I found this a bit frightening and closed the book. I did not want to know about evil spirits. I had experienced enough evil to last me a lifetime.

After returning the book to its place on the shelf, I went and sat in front of the mullioned window, staring out at the moors. They were a peculiar blue-black color at this twilight hour, rainswept and formidable, and a shiver ran through me as I thought of being out on them in this weather tonight.

And yet, curiously, I had been close to Andrew up there this afternoon in the storm, closer than ever, and at one moment I had felt his presence most acutely.

Was this because he had always loved storms? Because he had wanted to go out in them when he was a boy, had wanted to become at one with his ancestors riding out to fight their enemies?

I smiled inwardly, thinking of him with such love. My heart was full of him. Unexpectedly, I experienced a feeling of great calmness. It was flowing through me, suffusing my entire being; it was the kind of calmness I had forgotten existed.

I sat there for a long time, looking out the window, thinking about Andrew's words to me today. My birthday. Had he spoken to me *because* it was my birthday?

I sighed to myself. I was still not sure what had happened out there this afternoon, whether his voice had been real or simply inside me, conjured up because of my yearning for him.

"Here's to you, darling," Diana said, touching her glass of white wine to mine. "I'm glad you're here. I'm glad we can spend your birthday together."

"So am I, Diana."

Placing her goblet on the coffee table, she picked up the small gift-wrapped package she had brought into the library with her a few minutes ago. Handing it to me with a smile, she said, "This is for you, and it comes with all of my love."

"Thank you," I answered, taking it from her and unwrapping it. The small black leather box I held in my hands was worn, a bit rubbed on one side, and when I opened it, I let out a little gasp. Lying on the black velvet was an antique cameo, one of the most exquisite I had ever seen. "It's beautiful, Diana, thank you so much."

Rising, I went over to the sofa and kissed her on the cheek, and then I pinned the cameo onto the lapel of my jacket.

"My mother-in-law gave it to me years ago, for one of *my* birthdays," Diana explained. "I thought it was a nice idea to pass it on to you, since it's a Keswick heirloom."

"You're always so thoughtful, so loving," I murmured, going back to the chair and sitting down. "You spoil me."

"There's something else I want to talk to you about," Diana went on. "And now is as good a time as any."

She sounded suddenly rather serious, and I looked at her questioningly. "Yes, of course."

"It's about this house, Mal."

"What do you mean?"

"You're my heir now . . . " She paused for a moment, and I saw the emotion crossing her face. But she recovered herself immediately. "My only heir, and I just wanted you to know that I have had my will redrawn. I've left Kilgram Chase to you, and everything else I own, actually."

"Oh, Diana, I don't know what to say . . . thank you, of course . . . " I was at a sudden loss and couldn't find the right words to express myself.

Diana said, "You're young, Mal, only thirty-four today, and much of your life is still ahead of you. And one day I'm sure you'll remarry, perhaps even have children again, and I like to think of you being here with them."

I gaped at her. I was aghast. "No!" I exclaimed. "I won't remarry—"

"You don't know what's going to happen," she said, interrupting me. "I know how you feel at this moment, and perhaps I was wrong to bring the subject up tonight. So I'm not going to continue this conversation. Certainly not now. However, I do want to say one thing, and it is this, Mal darling. You must go on. We must all go on. Life is for the living, you know."

I had a strange affinity with Lettice Keswick.

I felt curiously drawn to her, and yet she had been an ancestor not of mine, but of Andrew's. Nonetheless, I did feel oddly close to this seventeenth-century Yorkshirewoman, dead now for several hundred years though she had been.

I had grown to know Lettice through her writing—those two diaries covering two years of her life in Stuart England, her cookbook full of recipes for food and wine, and her enchanting, illustrated garden book.

As I sat in the library at Kilgram Chase this morning, leafing through those various books again, I could not help thinking that Lettice had been a lot like me, in many ways. A homemaker, a cook, a gardener, a painter, a woman interested in furnishings and all those things which made a home beautiful. And she had been a devoted mother and an adoring wife, just as I had.

Basically that was my problem. I had not known anything else after college; certainly a few months in an ad agency didn't count. And without my husband and my children, I had no focus, no purpose. Certainly I had nothing to do, and that was not good, not good at all, as Diana kept pointing out. A job was essential.

But what kind of job?

That old question came back to nag me, as it had for some months.

Sighing under my breath, feeling suddenly impatient with myself, even irritated, I pushed back my chair and went outside. I also felt the need for some air before lunch.

I found my steps were leading me toward the walled rose garden, always a favorite spot of mine. But perhaps more so of late, since I knew it had been designed almost three hundred years ago by Lettice. It was exactly the same today as it had been then.

Opening the oak door which led into the garden, I walked down the three steps and stood looking around for a moment or two. It was not a large garden, but it had a special kind of charm, due in no small measure to its ancient stone walls and paths covered with moss and chamomile, two sundials, and various wooden garden seats placed here and there.

Lettice's design was simplicity itself, but that was the reason it worked. There were hedges of shrub roses, ramblers climbing the ancient walls, rectangular beds of floribundas, and circular beds of hybrid tea roses. My favorites were the Old-Fashioned roses, a variety raised before the twentieth century; I liked to think these resembled the roses planted by Lettice so long ago.

It was late May, and since most of the roses currently planted bloomed in June, the garden was not as beautiful or as colorful as it would be then and through the rest of the summer. But because the walls gave the garden shelter and the sun shone on it in the afternoons, a few of the June roses were already starting to flower.

I sat down on one of the garden seats, my mind still focused on a job. I had no idea what I could do or what I wanted to do. I had decided weeks ago that I did not want to work in an office, and of course that limited my choices.

Last weekend, when my father and Gwenny had come to stay with us, he had been in favor of my going to work with Diana at her antique shop in London. And she herself was all for it, was waiting for an answer, in fact.

"You should be with people, Mallory," my father had said. "That's why a shop's ideal. And in this instance, it's the perfect shop for you, loving antiques and art the way you do." Gwenny and Diana had agreed, and all three of them had tried to talk me into the partnership she had so generously offered.

I thought about this idea one more time, assessing the pros and cons. Perhaps they were right. I did care about antique furniture, objects of art and paintings, and I had quite a wide knowledge of them. Though I didn't want to decorate for people, I wouldn't mind selling things to them. Actually, the thought of being in a shop appealed to me.

Except . . .

Except what?

I wasn't sure exactly what it was that was making me balk.

Then it hit me. I had a moment of truth, of such extraordinary clarity of vision I was momentarily stunned.

I didn't want to work in Diana's shop or become her partner because I didn't want to stay in England.

I wanted to go home.

Home to Indian Meadows. My home. The place Andrew and I had so lovingly made ours. I missed it. I was homesick. I needed to be there in order to get on with my life.

Everybody had been telling me I must do that, but I hadn't been able to make a move. I had been stationary, marking time here, because England was the wrong place for me at this juncture of my life. I loved it; I would always come back to Yorkshire. But now I must move on. Immediately.

I must go home. Whatever my life was going to be, I suddenly knew that I wanted to, no, *must* live it in Connecticut, in that old house. I needed to be in its lovely cool rooms, to be close to my old apple tree and my barns. I longed to see the horses in the long meadow, the mallards on the pond. I wanted to be with Nora and Eric and Anna.

Indian Meadows was mine. Andrew and I had created it together, made it what it was. I felt *right* there, at ease. I had fled Indian Meadows in January in search of Andrew. But I no longer had to look for him here in his childhood home. He was with me always, inside my heart, part of me, just as Jamie and Lissa were part of me. And would be for as long as I lived, for all the days of my life.

But if I were to keep my Connecticut homestead, I had to earn a living.

I could open my own shop. Right there at Indian Meadows.

This thought took me by surprise.

I pondered it, realized at once that it was not a bad idea at all. Except that there were innumerable antique shops in the area, stretching from New Milford and New Preston all the way up to Sharon.

But it didn't have to be an antique shop, did it?

No. What kind of shop, then?

A shop for women like me. Or rather, women who were married with children, the way I had been once. Homemakers. Mommies. Besotted wives. I could sell them all of the things I knew about, from the days when I was a wife and mother: kitchenware, cooking utensils, and baking tins; beautiful pottery for beautiful tables; herbs and spices, jams and jellies; potpourri, fancy soaps, and beeswax candles. All of these things women had loved since Lettice Keswick's time.

Lettice Keswick. Now there was a name to conjure with. I could call it Lettice Keswick's Kitchen. That had a nice ring to it. No, I preferred Indian Meadows. Why not keep *that* name? It had always meant a lot to us. It was the name of the house, but there was no reason why it shouldn't also be the name of the shop.

My shop.

My very own shop. Indian Meadows. A Country Experience.

That also had a nice ring to it. But why was it a country experience? It would only be a shop, after all. But it could be an experience if something special happened there. It could be a café as well. A small café in the center of the shop, serving coffee, tea, cold drinks, soups, small snacks, and quiche.

A country shop and café in an old red barn in the foothills of the Berkshires, the northwestern highlands of Connecticut. God's own country, Andrew and I had always called it.

Nora and Anna could help me run it. They'd enjoy it; certainly they'd enjoy making the extra money. And perhaps Eric could be a part of it; after all, things were not very good at the lumberyard, Nora had written to tell me. She had also said she missed cooking for me. Well, she could make jams and jellies, chutneys and spreads to her heart's content. There were enough recipes in Lettice's cookbook to keep her busy. That was it. Our own label. *Lettice Keswick's Kitchen.*

I experienced such a rush of excitement I could hardly contain myself. All kinds of ideas were rushing into my head, ideas for other labels, other lines of products. There might even be a catalogue one day.

A catalogue. My God, what a great idea that was.

I jumped to my feet and glanced around the rose garden.

Thank you, Lettice Keswick, I thought. Thank you. For there was no question in my mind that Lettice had had a hand in this.

PART SIX

INDIAN MEADOWS

33

Connecticut, June 1989

It was a warm Friday afternoon at the end of the month, and Sarah had driven up to stay with me for the weekend.

Even before she had changed from her chic city clothes into her country-bumpkin togs, as she called them, she had wanted to see the barns, to review the progress I had made in her absence.

And so here we stood in the middle of the biggest of my four barns, surveying the work which had been done by my building contractor, Tom Williams, whilst she had been away on business.

"I can't believe it, Mal!" she exclaimed excitedly, her dark eyes roaming around, taking everything in. "Tom *has* moved with great speed, you're right."

"And Eric's been just as fast," I pointed out. "He's already painted the second floor, and tomorrow he'll start down here."

"It was such a good idea of yours, extending the old hayloft. Now you've got a second floor, but without losing the feeling of spaciousness."

As she spoke Sarah looked up toward the new loft at the far end of the barn.

"The café will be under the loft," I said, "if you remember the architect's plans. And I think it's kind of cozy to have it there. Tom's suggested putting in a big potbellied stove for the winter months, and I think it's a terrific idea, don't you?"

"Yes, and you might want to consider one of those gorgeous porcelain stoves from Austria. They're awfully attractive, Mal."

"And expensive, I've no doubt. I've got to keep an eye on the budget, Sash. But come on, let's walk down there, and I'll tell you a bit more about the café."

Taking hold of her arm, I drew her to the other end of the barn. "Now, here, Sarah, in the very center of this space, I'm going to have little tables for four. Green metal tables and chairs, the kind you find in sidewalk cafés in Paris. I've already ordered ten from one of the showrooms you sent me to last week, and that means I'll be able to seat forty."

"So many!" she exclaimed. "Can you handle that number of customers? Serve them, I mean?"

"Yes, I could if I had to. But I honestly don't think there will ever be forty people crowding into the café all at the same time. They'll drift in and out, since they'll mainly have come to shop. At least I hope that's why they'll be here."

Drawing her farther into the café area, I continued, "The counter and cash register will be down near the back wall, just in front of those doors Tom has already put in. They lead outside to the kitchen addition."

"When's he going to start that?" Sarah asked, walking over, opening a door, and peering out.

"Next week."

"I thought Philip Miller's plans for the kitchen were really on target, Mal, didn't you?"

"At first the kitchen seemed a bit too big to me. But when I really thought it through, I realized he had taken growth into consideration. Not that we can grow that much."

Sarah said, "Better to err on the side of largeness, rather than building a kitchen you discover too late is too small."

"I took Philip's advice. And when I saw him last Friday, I also listened to him when it came to the appliances. I've ordered two restaurant-size freezers and two restaurant-size refrigerators, as well as two heavy-duty cooking stoves. Oh, and two microwave ovens for reheating and warming food."

"Are you planning to serve a lot of hot dishes now? Has the menu changed, Mal?"

I shook my head. "It's still the same one we discussed. Various soups, quiche lorraine, maybe cottage pie, but that's it. The rest will be sandwiches and cakes, plus beverages. However, don't forget that Nora will be making our own line of jams, jellies, lemon curd, mincemeat, and chutneys."

"Lettice Keswick's Kitchen," Sarah said, a smile crossing her face. "I love it, and it's a great name for a label."

Turning slowly in the center of the floor, Sarah waved an arm around and continued, "And the walls here in the café will be lined with floor-to-ceiling shelves displaying cooking utensils, pots, pans, cookware, and pottery."

"And the Lettice products as well," I reminded her.

"It's going to be great, Mal! A fabulous success. I can just smell it," Sarah enthused.

"From your mouth to God's ear, as my mother would say."

"My money's on you, Mal, it really is. Oh, Tom's already put in your new staircase. Can we go upstairs to the loft?"

"Yes, but just be careful," I warned. "As you can see, there's no bannister yet."

I led the way up into the old hayloft, now totally remodeled and revamped. Tom had, in effect, created a gallery which floated out into the middle of the barn. It had a high railing at the edge, instead of a wall, and because of this it was airy and light-filled.

Sarah prowled around, nodding to herself as she did. "Up here you're going to sell china, pottery, ceramics, glass, cutlery, linen, tabletop items for dining, that's right, isn't it?"

"It's what you and I decided before you went away. You said it was better to keep the food items downstairs."

She nodded. "The whole idea of the shop-café was inspired. Having the café makes it just that little bit different, and yes, the food should be downstairs. Have you decided what you're going to do with the other barns, if anything?"

"One of them will have to be an office. Mine in the house simply won't be big enough. But it can also double as a place for storing products and—"

"I thought you were going to use the basement of the house for that?" Sarah cut in. "That's what you said the last time I was here."

"I *am* going to use the basement, yes. But to store the bottled food stuff, the nonperishable things, mainly the Lettice Keswick line. It's cool and roomy, and Eric's cleaned it out and given it a fresh coat of white paint. Tom's got two of his crew putting up shelves down there, but what I need is a storage place for inventory, for my stock."

"You're right, you *will* need plenty of space," Sarah agreed, and then she began to laugh. "I can see that my lessons in retailing over the past few weeks have served you well. But then you always were a fast learner, Mal."

"And you're a good teacher. Anyway, to continue, I thought I'd make the third barn into a little boutique called Indian Meadows, and the fourth into a gallery, which I'm naming Kilgram Chase."

"Catchy," Sarah said, and then grinning at me, she teased, "expanding before you've even opened, eh?"

"That's thanks to you again. You did tell me two weeks ago that I ought to have more than one private label, in order to give

the shop a certain kind of cachet. So I did a bit of creative thinking and came up with the idea of the Kilgram Chase label and a
gallery, and an Indian Meadows label for the boutique."

"What are the products?" she probed.

"Let's go over there, and I'll tell you on the way," I answered.

Within seconds we were outside, heading in the direction of
the other barns on my property. These were clustered together
on one side of Anna's cottage and the stables.

"That big barn at the back, the one closest to Anna's place,
will be the administration office and the storage barn," I
explained. "The two smaller ones I'll turn into the gallery and
the boutique."

"Tell me what you're going to sell, Mally. You know I'm a
born retailer, and I'm riddled with curiosity."

Pushing open the door of the barn I had chosen to become
the gallery, I went in first, saying over my shoulder, "Everything
in here will be English in feeling or made in England, Sash. I've
found a crafts and embroidery company up here, and they're
going to make small needlepoint pillows for me. What will make
my pillows different is their design. They'll be copies of those
Victorian beaded cushions I found in the attics of Kilgram
Chase. The designs will be exactly the same, and so will the Latin
mottoes. What do you think?"

"Clever idea, but what about quantity? Can this company
make plenty for you? As many as you want?"

"I don't plan to have more than about a dozen at a time, and
I'll take special orders," I told her. "I'm going to sell English
watercolors, botanicals, and vegetable prints, already framed.
And Diana's going to seek out bits and pieces in London, you
know, small antique items such as stud boxes, snuffboxes, tea
caddies, and candlesticks. She says it's easy for her, a snip, and
she'll just ship them over or bring them when she comes. I'm also
going to feature English soaps and scents, beeswax candles, and

potpourri. Oh, and Ken Turner perfumed candles, as well as some of his smaller dried-flower arrangements. Again, I'm getting those through Diana."

"I think such items will move very well. People do like things that are different, even if they are slightly more expensive. And you've got a good market for them up here. But tell me about the Indian Meadows boutique."

"Come on, let's go over to the barn where I plan to house it," I said.

Once we were inside, Sarah strolled around and asked, "Are you going to sell clothes? You *are* calling it a boutique."

"Yes, I am, but I'm also going to have other things as well. Everything will be American, from my own watercolors, which you tell me are good enough to sell, to Early American and Colonial-style quilts and cushions, soft toys, all handmade, and some really beautiful American Indian blankets from the Southwest."

"And the clothes?"

"They'll be made by Pony Traders, the company Anna knows up near Lake Wononpakook. But I need your help with them."

"I'll do anything to get this project off the ground, you know that, Mally, what do you need me to do to help you with Pony Traders?" A dark brow lifted quizzically.

"You know every aspect of fashion and retailing, you're the fashion director of Bergman's, for heaven's sake. I'd like you to talk to the two women who own the company. Maybe you could persuade them to give me some items on an exclusive basis, and then there's the pricing. If I'm buying a large quantity of their stuff, shouldn't I get some sort of special deal? A discount?"

"It depends," Sarah replied thoughtfully. "But of course I'll come with you, and I'll do what I can. Anyway, now that you're going to sell clothes, I'll come up with some other vendors for you. I guess it's a sort of ethnic look you're after? American Indian?"

"Not necessarily, but certainly casual, comfortable, country-style clothing. Thanks, Sashy. Your help's going to be invaluable."

"I'm just so thrilled about this project of yours, and as I just said a few minutes ago, I feel really good about it in my bones. I just know it's going to take off. And it's going to give you a whole new lease on life. It already has, actually."

Linking her arm through mine, Sarah guided me out of the barn, and we walked back up to the house together.

"Andrew would be so proud of you—" Sarah stopped with that awful suddenness she had adopted lately whenever she mentioned him. She glanced at me swiftly, looking chagrined.

"I know he would be *very* proud of me," I said calmly. "And you don't have to avoid mentioning him, Sashy darling, or stop midsentence when you do. As I told Mom yesterday, Andrew Keswick lived, he existed, he was my husband for ten years, the father of my children. He was on this planet for forty-one years, Sarah, and he made a big difference to a lot of people, not only his mother and me and the children. He loved me. I loved him. He was my lover, my best friend, my true soul mate, and my dearest companion. He meant everything to me, he was my whole life, you know that. So I don't want you to stop yourself every time his name crops up in conversation."

"I won't, I promise, Mal. And I understand, I really do. You're right, we risk negating him by never speaking about him."

"It's the same with Jamie and Lissa. I want you to talk about them to me, remember them, discuss them whenever you feel like it. You will, won't you?"

"Of course."

"It's comforting, you know," I went on softly. "And it helps to keep them alive."

"I'm so glad you've told me. I *was* being scrupulously careful."

"I know . . . " I let my sentence trail off. We walked on up to the house in silence for a few seconds. Then I said, "They were so special, weren't they, Sash? Your godchildren."

"Yes, they were. Your Botticelli angels, your small miracles, and mine, too. How I loved them. And Andrew."

"They loved you, Sarah, and he loved you, just as I do. I'm so glad you're my friend."

"I am, too. We're very lucky to have each other."

"I was thinking the other day . . . about Andrew," I said, looking at her. "Do you remember when you first met him, Sash?"

"I certainly do. I was bowled over, and jealous to death of you!"

"You called him Dreamboat. Do you remember that?"

"Yes, I remember," she murmured, returning my long look. Her lovely dark eyes grew suddenly moist, and I saw her swallow hard. "I remember everything," she said in a whisper.

"Don't cry," I said softly. "Don't cry, Sashy."

She could only nod.

34

As we entered the house, Sarah said, "I'll go and change out of these clothes. I'll be down in a few minutes."

"There's no hurry, Sash," I answered. "I'm going to be in my office. When you're ready, join me there. I want to show you the sign for the main gate, the labels for the different products, all the things I've designed this past week."

"Give me ten minutes, Mal," she murmured with a faint smile as we walked down the back hall together.

"No problem, Sashy."

I stood outside my office, my eyes following her as she ran upstairs. She had been quite upset a few moments ago; I realized she wanted to be alone for a while, to compose herself.

Turning, I stepped into my little office and sat down at the desk, where I spread out the various labels. Leaning forward, I studied them for a few moments. "Keep it simple," Sarah had said to me before she left for California. "Remember what Mies van der Rohe said—'Less is more,' and he was right."

I was glad to have Sarah's advice. There was always the temptation to add some sort of decorative element to a label, along with the name. But I resisted, used only the words *Indian Meadows* and *Kilgram Chase*, concentrating on a distinctive type of lettering.

I had also kept simple the drawing for the sign for the main gate into Indian Meadows, using the name and the slogan I had dreamed up in Lettice's rose garden at Kilgram Chase a few weeks ago: *A Country Experience.* I hadn't even added anything about a café or shops. I wanted to keep the sign uncluttered, and people would soon know what we were about.

The phone rang, and I reached for it. "Hello?"

"Mal, it's me. How are you?"

"Hi, Mom, I'm okay. Sarah's here. She arrived a short while ago, and I've been showing her around. She's impressed, excited about everything."

"So am I, darling, and I can't wait to see how it's progressed in the last couple of weeks. You're still expecting us on Sunday for lunch, aren't you?"

"Yes, of course I am."

"What time?"

"I thought about eleven-thirty, twelve. You can take a stroll around, and then we can have lunch at about one. How does that sound?"

"Wonderful, darling. We'll be there. Here's David, he wants a word with you."

"Bye, Mom." I frowned to myself, wondering what David had to tell me. Had he heard from DeMarco? Most probably. I felt myself automatically stiffen and gripped the phone that much tighter.

"Hello, Mal," David said. "I'm looking forward to seeing you on Sunday."

"Hi, David. You've heard from DeMarco, haven't you?"

"Yes, this afternoon. He wanted me to know that the date for the trial has been set, and—"

"When is it going to be?"

"Next month. The end of the month."

"Will it be in criminal court downtown? Like you said?"

"Yes, it will."

"I want to go. I can, can't I?"

"Yes, you can, but I don't think you should."

"David, I have to be there!" I cried, my voice rising.

"Mal, listen to me. I don't think you should expose yourself to something like this. You've never been to a criminal trial, you don't know what it's like. But I do. I'm in criminal court almost every day of my life. You're going to be very upset again—"

"I'll be all right," I interrupted quickly, "Honestly, I will."

"No, you won't. Please take my word for it. Mal, I understand *why* you think you want to be there, but you mustn't go, not under any circumstances. I don't want you exposed to that . . . filth, and neither does your mother."

"My family was exposed to it; they're dead because of those animals."

"I know, honey. Listen to me, I want you to think very carefully about the trial and going to it, and we'll discuss it when I come out on Sunday."

"We don't have to, David. I've made up my mind."

"Don't do that. Keep an *open* mind. I'll explain things to you, tell you what the trial's going to be like, and then you can make a decision."

Knowing it was useless to argue with him, I said, "All right, David. We'll talk about it on Sunday."

"Good. See you then."

We said our good-byes and hung up.

I sat staring into the middle of the room, thinking about the impending trial and those who had been responsible for killing my family, and I began to tremble. The calmness I had acquired of late instantly disappeared; I was suddenly filled with agitation and anxiety.

I heard Sarah's footsteps on the staircase, and I glanced toward the door as she came into the room.

"What's wrong?" she asked, staring at me.

"I just spoke to David. DeMarco called him today. The trial's set for late July."

"Oh," she said, walking across the little office and sitting down in the chair near the fireplace. "I've been wondering when it was going to be."

"I want to go to it, Sash, but David doesn't think I should."

"I tend to agree with him."

"I have to go!" I exclaimed.

"If you really feel you must, then I'll go with you, Mal. I'd never let you face that alone. I don't suppose your mother would either."

"How can you come with me? There's your job."

"I'll take some of my vacation time."

"But you were going to spend your vacation out here with me, getting Indian Meadows ready," I reminded her.

"I know, and I'd much prefer to do that. On the other hand, I couldn't stand it, knowing you were in court without me, even if your mother were with you. Anyway, what did David say?"

I told her quickly, then continued, "I feel funny about not being there, Sarah. Those youths are going to be on trial for the cold-blooded murder of Andrew and Lissa and Jamie, and I ought to be in that courtroom."

Sarah did not speak for a moment or two. She sat thinking; eventually she said slowly, "I know you, Mal, and I know how your mind works, so I know you feel you should be present to see justice done. I'm right, aren't I?"

"Yes," I admitted. "I want justice."

"But whether you're there or not won't affect the verdict. The evidence against those guys is conclusive and overwhelming, Mal. According to everything DeMarco has said, forensics has a make on the fingerprints found on the car, and ballistics on the gun. And then there's the confession of one of the youths. You know they're going to be found guilty and sentenced to life.

There's no way out for them. So, if I'm truthful with you, I agree with David. I don't think you should go. You can't contribute anything, and it would be painful for you to bear."

I said nothing, simply sat there looking at her, biting my lip worriedly.

Sarah went on, after a moment's reflection, "Why put yourself through it all over again?"

"I feel uneasy about *not* going . . . "

"You've been so much calmer since you came back from Yorkshire, and made such progress. I think it's important to forge ahead, to think about the project here, to get on with it. And listen, there's another thing . . . the press. Can you honestly cope with another media circus?"

I shook my head. "No, I couldn't."

Sarah got up and walked to a window, then stood looking out. She was silent. I stared at her for a moment, noticing that she held herself rigidly; her shoulder blades protruded slightly under her thin cotton shirt. She was tense, worried; I knew her so well, as she knew me.

Leaning back in my chair, I closed my eyes, turning the whole thing over in my mind. Eventually I sat up and said quietly, "I just feel Andrew would want me to be in court."

Swinging around to face me, Sarah exclaimed vehemently, "No, he wouldn't! That'd be the last thing he'd want! He would want you to take care of yourself, look to the future, do exactly what you *are* doing now. He'd hate you to cause yourself unnecessary heartache, Mal, he really would. Please believe me, there is nothing to be gained by going to that trial."

"But you'd go with me, wouldn't you?"

"How could I let you go alone? But honestly, David knows what he's talking about. He's been a criminal lawyer all his life, he knows how horrendous these kinds of trials are; and then again, he cares about you, wants the best for you. I'd listen to him, if I were you."

I nodded slowly and reached for the phone. I dialed my mother's apartment.

David answered. "Hello?"

"It's me," I said in a subdued voice. "Sarah's here, David, and she agrees with you about the trial. I've made a decision, but I just wanted to ask you again . . . do you really think I shouldn't be there?"

"I do, Mal."

"I've decided not to go."

I caught a note of relief in his voice as he said, "Thank God. But there's something I should point out to you, something you may not know. You can be present for the sentencing, to make a statement to the judge, if you so wish, stating your feelings about the kind of sentence you think should be imposed on the criminals."

"I didn't know that."

"How could you? In any case, Mal, you may very well want to go to court at that time. And naturally I would come with you, and so would your mother. Think about it."

"I will, David."

"You made the right decision. I'll tell your mother, I know she's going to be pleased. Good night, honey."

"Good night, David."

I told Sarah what he had just said; she listened carefully as she always did, and then she went and sat down in the chair. Finally, she said, "Maybe you *should* go to the sentencing, Mal. Somehow that makes sense. Sitting through a trial, no. It would make you ill. But saying your piece to the judge, expressing your loss, your pain, well, that's a whole different thing, isn't it?"

"It is. Maybe I'll do it," I said. Then I got up and walked to the door. "Come on, Sash, I'll buy you a drink. I don't know about you, but I could really use one."

35

Connecticut, July 1989

Once I had made up my mind not to be present at the trial, I managed to push it to the back of my mind.

There was no point dwelling on it, since that served no good purpose and only tended to deflect me from my goal. This was forging ahead with the shops and the café at Indian Meadows.

Every day there was something new to keep me busy, yet another decision to be made, plans to be approved, additional merchandise to be ordered, labels to be manufactured, and countless other jobs.

There were times when I would stop in the middle of doing something and wonder at myself and all that had happened in two months.

I had come back from Yorkshire with the idea of opening a shop and a café, and everything had taken shape immediately. I had formed a company, applied to the town of Sharon for commercial zoning permits, borrowed money from my mother, my father, David, and Diana, and opened a business bank account.

They had all wanted to give me the money, to become my partners, but I had refused. I did not wish to have any partners, not even Sarah, who had also volunteered to be an investor.

I told them I would repay their money with interest, as soon as I could, and I had every intention of doing so.

Armed with my newly printed business cards and my checkbook, I had gone to the product showrooms in New York. Two were housed in a building on Fifth Avenue and another in one on Madison Avenue, and it was there that I found everything I needed for the kitchen shop. It was Sarah who had told me about these showrooms, pointing me in the right direction, explaining that I didn't have to travel to foreign countries to buy the merchandise for my different lines.

"You'll find the best of everything right there in Manhattan," she had explained. "I talked to various buyers on the home floors at Bergman's, and they recommend these particular showrooms." She had handed me the list and gone on, "You'll see from the notations next to each showroom that you can get French, Italian, Portuguese, and Spanish pottery, porcelains, and cookware, all that kind of stuff, and table linens as well. Everything you want for the tabletop, in fact."

She had also told me that the International Gift Show was held twice a year in New York at the Jacob Javits Convention Center. "And there are other gift shows, held on the piers at the passenger-ship terminal on the Hudson. There's a wealth of American products as well as merchandise from all over the world."

I felt as if I had walked across the world, the first day I went on a buying trip to Manhattan.

I covered every one of the showrooms on Sarah's long list, and I thought I had lost my feet by the end of the day.

In fact, I was so exhausted by four o'clock that I took a cab up to my mother's apartment, where I promptly collapsed. Even after a rest and dinner with her and David, I hadn't had the strength to drive to Sharon. Since I no longer had an apartment in New York, I spent the night in my old room.

I drove back to Indian Meadows the following morning, feeling that I had accomplished miracles on my first buying trip.

Eric stood poised in the doorway of my studio. "Am I interrupting you, Mal?" he asked.

"No, it's okay, come on in," I replied, putting down the watercolor I was holding. "I'm just trying to sort through these paintings. Sarah's going to take them to that good frame shop in New Preston this afternoon, and I was just trying to select twenty of the best ones to begin with."

He came and stood looking over my shoulder at the watercolors, which I had spread out on the table. After a moment studying them, he said, "They're all beautiful, Mal, it's hard to choose."

"They're not bad, are they?" I said, glancing at him. "But you look as if you're bursting to tell me something, so come on, what is it?"

"They all want to come and work for us, Mal!" Eric exclaimed, grinning broadly. "Billy Judd, Agnes Fairfield, and Joanna Smith. So I thought I'd hire 'em, if that's all right with you."

"Of course it is, Eric. We're going to need three people at the very least. We may even have to take on another two helpers later."

"Billy wants to work with me, serving in the café and the food shop. Joanna Smith is in love with the idea of selling beautiful things for beautiful dining, so she could run the shop upstairs in the new loft. Agnes had wanted to be in the boutique, but I told her that was Anna's territory, and so she's agreed to handle the Kilgram Chase Gallery. It's worked out well, hasn't it?"

"It has indeed, thanks to you. I assume they agreed to the money we're paying."

Eric nodded. "Oh, yes, no problem, and they're all prepared to stay in their current jobs, starting with us in October."

"Good. That gives us six months to get everything ready for the opening in Spring of 1990. There's a lot to do, though. What do you think, Eric? Can we manage to unpack all of the products, get price tags on everything, and put the merchandise on display in that amount of time?"

"I think so."

"I'll discuss it with Sarah later, just to be sure. But originally she did tell me to set aside three months just to deal with the merchandise."

"It's not putting the price tags on that's the problem," Eric volunteered. "It's making attractive displays of everything. Sarah says that's very important."

"Crucial," I agreed. "But she has promised to come out here and supervise us, you know."

He grinned at me.

I handed him a collection of watercolors. "Do you mind helping me with these, Eric?"

"My pleasure, Mal."

I picked up a second pile of my paintings, and together we left the studio.

It was a boiling-hot July morning, and as we left the air-conditioned studio, a blast of warm air almost knocked me over. "It's terribly hot today," I muttered, glancing up at the hazy sky and the brilliant sun already breaking through the clouds.

"It's going to be a real scorcher by noon," Eric commented.

"The sign for the gate is going to be ready tomorrow," I told him as we walked toward the house. "One of Tom's carpenters has made it, and he's bringing it over. Then I can paint the background and our name on it: *Indian Meadows: A Country Experience.* In the meantime, let's go and find Sarah."

"She's in the kitchen, sticking her nose into all of Nora's bubbling pots. She doesn't know which jam to try first. And every time Nora gives her a new one to taste, she declares it's her favorite."

Eric had spoken the truth.

I found Sarah with Nora in front of the stove, taking small samplings of her jams and putting them on a plate.

"What do you aim to do with all of that?" I asked as I walked through the kitchen, heading for my little office at the back of the house.

"Eat it, of course," Sarah said. "On these two slices of home-made bread, also courtesy of dear Nora here. And I know, before you say it, Mal, I'll regret it later. And yes, my diet's gone to hell."

36

New York, August 1989

What I was about to do today would be difficult. But I knew it must be done, no matter what.

In a few hours I was going to stand up in a court of law and speak to the judge in the case brought by the district attorney against those who had killed my family.

I was going to tell the judge, the Honorable Elizabeth P. Donan, about Andrew and Jamie and Lissa and the pain their deaths had caused me. I was going to bare my soul to her and to everyone else who would be seated in that courtroom this morning.

And I was going to ask the judge to mete out the maximum penalty under the law. As David had said: This was my *right* as the victims' next of kin.

The four defendants had been found guilty of murder in the second degree after a trial which had lasted less than a week. There was obviously no doubt in the jurors' minds about their culpability. They had returned the guilty verdict within a couple of hours of going into deliberation.

Soon it would be my turn to say my piece, as David called it. He was going to be with me in criminal court in downtown Manhattan. So were my mother, my father, Diana, and Sarah.

Diana had flown in from London two days ago, after Detective DeMarco had given David the date the sentencing would be held; my father had arrived early yesterday evening from Mexico, where he was currently conducting a special archaeological project for the University of California.

Everyone wished to give me moral support; they also wanted to see justice done, as I did.

"Of course I'm going to be with you," Diana had said when she had spoken to me on the phone from London over a week ago now. "It would be unthinkable for me not to be there. I lost my son and my grandchildren; I must be present. And your father feels the same way. I discussed it at length with him some time ago. This is about family, Mal, about a family standing together in a time of crisis, pain, and grief."

I had driven in from Sharon yesterday afternoon so that I could spend the evening with my family, which included Sarah, of course. Now I finished dressing in my old room at my mother's apartment. Then I went over to the mirror and stood looking at myself for a moment, seeing myself objectively for the first time in a long while. How thin my body was; I looked like a scarecrow. My face was so pale my freckles stood out markedly.

I was gaunt, almost stern in my appearance.

I was wearing a black linen suit totally unrelieved by any other color, except for my red hair, of course, which was as fiery as it always was. I wore it pulled back into a ponytail, held in place by a black silk bow. The only jewelry I had on were small pearl earrings, my gold wedding ring, and my watch.

Stepping into a pair of plain black leather pumps, I picked up my handbag and left the room.

My mother and Sarah were waiting for me in the small den with Diana, who was staying with us. The three of them were dressed in black, and like me, they looked severe, almost grim.

A moment later David walked into the room and said, "Edward should be here any minute."

My mother nodded, glanced at me, and murmured, "Your father is always very punctual."

Before I could comment, the intercom from downstairs rang. I knew it was my father.

The press was present in full force, not only outside the criminal court building on Centre Street but in the courtroom as well.

This was already packed with people when we arrived, and David hurried me down to the front row of seats. I sat between him and Sarah; in the row behind us were my mother, my father, and Diana.

I recognized the chief prosecutor from newspaper photographs and television. He was talking intently to Detective DeMarco, who inclined his head in our direction when he saw David and me. I nodded in return.

Looking around the courtroom, I suddenly stiffened; my hackles rose, prickling the back of my neck.

My eyes had come to rest on the four defendants. I stared at them.

They were seated with their attorneys, and this was the first time I had seen them in the flesh. They were neatly dressed, spruced up for this procedure, I had no doubt. I held myself very still.

Three youths and a man.

Roland Jellicoe. White. Twenty-four years old.

Pablo Rodriguez. Hispanic. Sixteen years old.

Alvin Charles. Black. Eighteen years old.

Benji Callis. Black. Fourteen years old. The gunman.

I would never forget their names.

Their names and their faces were engraved on my memory for all time.

They were the fiends who had killed my babies and my husband, and my little Trixy.

My eyes were riveted on them.

They stared back at me impassively, indifferently, as if they had done nothing wrong.

I felt as though I couldn't breathe. My heart was beating very fast. Then something erupted inside me. All of the anger I had been suppressing for months, ever since last December, spiraled up into the most overpowering rage.

My hatred took hold of me, almost brought me to my feet. I wanted to jump up, rush at them, hurt them. I wanted to destroy them as they had destroyed mine, destroyed those I loved. If I'd had a gun, I would have used it on them, I know that I would have.

This thought brought the blood rushing to my head, and I began to shake all over. Gripping my hands together, I gazed down at them, endeavoring to steady myself.

I knew I dare not look at the defendants again, not until I had done what I had come here to do today.

The court clerk was saying something about rising, and I felt David's hand under my elbow, helping me to my feet.

The judge entered and took her seat on the bench.

We all sat down.

I looked at her with curiosity. She was about fifty-five, I guessed, and she had a strong, kind face. She was quite young-looking but had prematurely silver hair.

She banged her gavel.

I fumbled around in my handbag looking for the statement I had written, peering at my words, blinded by my rage and pain, oblivious to what was going on around me.

The words I had written on the sheet of paper started to run together, and I suddenly realized my eyes were wet. I blinked and pushed back the tears. Now was not the time for tears.

A terrible pain filled my chest, and that feeling of suffocation swept over me again. I tried to breathe deeply in order to steady myself, to keep myself as calm as possible.

Then I became aware of David touching my arm, and I glanced at him. "The judge is waiting, Mal, you must go over to the podium and read your statement," he said.

All I could do was nod.

Sarah whispered, "You'll be all right," and squeezed my hand.

I rose a bit unsteadily and walked slowly to the podium which had been set up in front of the bench. I spread the paper out on the podium and stood silently before the judge. And I discovered I was quite unable to speak.

Raising my face, I looked up into hers.

She returned my gaze with one that was extremely steady; I saw the sympathy reflected in her eyes. It gave me courage.

Taking a deep breath, I began.

"Your Honor," I said, "I am here today because my husband, Andrew, my two children, Lissa and Jamie, and my little dog were all brutally killed by the defendants in this courtroom. My husband was a good man, a devoted and loving husband, father, and son. He never did harm to anyone, and he gave a great deal of himself to all those who knew him and worked with him. I know that everyone benefited from their relationships with Andrew. He made a difference in this world. But now he's dead. He was only forty-one. And my children are dead. Two harmless little innocents, six years old. Their lives have been snuffed out before they had begun. I won't see Jamie and Lissa grow up, go to college, and have careers, fulfilled lives. I will never attend their graduations or their marriages, and I will never have grandchildren. And why? Because a senseless act of violence has torn my life apart. It will never be the same again. I am facing the prolonged anguish of living without Andrew, Lissa, and Jamie. My future has been taken away from me, just as their futures were so cruelly taken away from them."

I paused and took a deep breath. "The murderers of my family have been found guilty by the jury. I ask this court to punish them for their crimes to the fullest extent of the law, Your Honor. I want justice. My mother-in-law wants justice. My parents want justice. That is all I am asking for, Your Honor. Just justice. Thank you."

I stood staring at Judge Donan.

She stared back at me. "Thank you, Mrs. Keswick," she said.

I nodded. Then I picked up the piece of paper, which I had ignored. I folded it in half and walked back to my seat.

The courtroom was totally silent. No one seemed to breathe. The only sound was the faint hum of the air-conditioning.

After a few moments staring at the papers on her desk, Judge Elizabeth P. Donan started to speak.

I closed my eyes, barely listening to her. I felt exhausted by my effort and emotionally drained. Also, the fury still raged inside me; it had taken over my whole being.

Vaguely, I heard the judge speaking of the heinous crime that had been committed, the defendants' lack of remorse for the murders of an innocent man and two children, the great loss I had suffered and my family had suffered, the senselessness of it all. I kept my eyes closed, blocking everything out for the next few minutes, trying to still that rage fulminating inside of me.

David touched my arm.

I opened my eyes and looked at him.

"The judge is about to pass sentence," he whispered.

I felt Sarah reaching for my hand, taking it in hers.

Sitting up straighter, I stared at Judge Donan, all of my senses suddenly alert.

The defendants were told to rise.

Focusing on the youngest, the gunman, the judge said: "Benji Callis, you have been tried as an adult and found guilty on three counts of murder in the second degree. I hereby sentence you to twenty-five years to life on each count of murder, each sentence to run consecutively."

She gave the other three defendants the same sentence: seventy-five years.

Judge Donan had seen to it that they received the maximum punishment under New York State law. It was exactly as Detective DeMarco and David had predicted it would be.

But for me it was somehow not enough.

In a way, I felt my family had not been properly avenged. Certainly I felt no satisfaction, only emptiness inside, and my smoldering rage.

Once the proceedings were over and the courtroom began to clear, David took me over to Detectives DeMarco and Johnson, and I thanked them for everything they had done.

Outside the criminal court building there was a barrage of newspaper photographers, television cameras, and reporters. Somehow David and my father managed to get me through the mêlée and into the waiting car.

From criminal court we sped uptown to my mother's apartment on Park Avenue for lunch. Everybody seemed as exhausted as I was, and slightly dazed. Conversation was desultory at best.

My father was coming to stay with me at Indian Meadows for a few days, before returning to Mexico City. As soon as coffee was finished, he took charge.

"I think we'd better get going, Mal," he said, rising and heading for the door of the library.

I pushed myself to my feet and followed him.

Diana also got up and put her arm around me. "You were wonderful in court, darling. You spoke so eloquently. I know it was hard for you, but I think the judge was touched by your words."

I merely nodded, hugged her, and said, "Thanks for coming, Diana, you gave me courage. Have a safe flight back to London tomorrow."

David came out into the hall. I turned and watched him walking across to me, thinking how well he looked today. Fresh-complexioned, with silver hair and light gray eyes, he was a handsome man, always well dressed. In his circles they called him the Silver Fox, because of not only his appearance but his ability, and it was deserved.

Embracing him affectionately, grateful for everything he had done for me, I said, "Thank you, David. I couldn't have gotten through this without you."

"I didn't do anything," he said with a faint smile.

"You dealt with DeMarco and Johnson, and that was a big help," I answered.

My mother came to me, kissed me, and held me longer than usual. "I'm proud of you, Mal, and Diana's right, you *were* wonderful today."

37

Connecticut, August 1989

"I thought I'd feel better after the sentencing, but I don't, I really don't, Daddy."

My father was silent for a moment, and then he said, "I know what you mean. It's a bit of a letdown in a way, anticlimactic."

"I wanted the death of my family avenged, but even consecutive twenty-five year sentences don't seem to be enough, not to me!" I exclaimed. "They might be incarcerated, but they still can see the sunlight. Andrew, Lissa, and Jamie are dead, and those bastards ought to be dead too. The Bible got it right."

"An eye for an eye, a tooth for a tooth," my father murmured quietly.

"Yes," I said.

"There's no death penalty under New York State law, Mal," my father pointed out.

"Oh, I know that, Dad, I've always known it. It's just that . . . well . . . " Leaving my sentence unfinished, I jumped up, walked to the edge of the terrace, and stood staring out across the lawns. Agitation was suddenly gripping me again, and I tried to clamp down on the feeling, to demolish it completely.

I stood very still, breathing in the beauty of the landscape. It was a lovely August evening, not too hot, with a soft breeze rustling through the trees. In the distance the foothills of the Berkshires loomed up, lush and green against the fading sky. It was dusk. Twilight was descending, and behind the dark hills the sun had sunk low. Now burnt orange bleeding into lilac and mauve, it slowly disappeared below the horizon.

"I'd like a drink, Dad, would you?" I asked, turning around to face him.

"Yes, I would. I'll go and fix them. What would you like, Mal?"

"A vodka and tonic, please. Thanks."

Pushing himself to his feet, he nodded, then went into the sunroom heading for the kitchen.

I sat down on one of the chairs under the big white market umbrella, waiting for him to come back. I was glad that he was with me, that we had this opportunity to spend the weekend together before he went back to his project in Mexico.

My father returned within minutes, carrying a tray with the drinks on it. He sat down opposite me at the table, lifted his glass, and touched it to mine. "Chin-chin," he murmured.

"Cheers," I answered, then took a long swallow.

We sat quietly together for a few minutes, and finally I said, "I have this terrible rage bubbling inside me, Dad. It erupted yesterday in the courtroom. When I saw the defendants, I thought I would go out of my mind. I wanted to do physical damage to them, even kill them. The hatred just overwhelmed me."

"I experienced something very similar myself," my father confided. "I think we all did. After all, we were just a few feet away from the men who attacked and murdered Andrew, Lissa, and Jamie in cold blood. Wanting to strike back is a natural impulse. But, of course, we can't go around killing people. That would bring us down to their level, make animals of us all."

"I know . . . " I stopped and shook my head, frowning worriedly. "But the rage won't go away, Dad."

My father reached out, covered my hand with his. It was comforting. He said quietly, "The only way it will dissipate is if you let go of it, darling."

I stared at him, saying nothing.

After a moment, my father went on slowly, "But that's not easy. I know exactly what you're going through. You're very like me when it comes to your emotions. Sometimes you have a tendency to mask your feelings, as do I. Certainly you've been suppressing your anger for months, but it had to come out eventually."

"Yes," I agreed. "It did."

My father looked at me for a long moment, his eyes thoughtful. "And it *is* all right for you to be angry, Mal, it really is. You'd be abnormal if you weren't. However, if you allow it to, it will eat you up, destroy you. So . . . just let it go, darling, just let it go."

"How, Dad? Tell me how."

He paused, then he leaned forward and stared into my eyes. "Well, there is one thing you could do."

"There is?"

He nodded. "When we were at Kilgram Chase in May, I asked you where you had scattered the ashes, and you told me you hadn't done so. You confided that you had bought a safe and locked the ashes inside it. 'To keep them safe,' you said to me, and you added, 'Nothing can ever hurt them again.' I'm sure you remember that conversation, don't you?"

"Of course I do," I said. "You're the only person I ever told about the safe, Dad. Why I wanted it."

"And are their ashes still in the safe here? Still upstairs?"

I nodded.

"I think it's time to put your family to rest, Mal, I really do. Maybe if they're at peace, you might be able to find a little yourself. Anyway, it would be a beginning . . . "

*   *   *

The following morning I got up at dawn.

I had taken my father's words of the night before to heart, and in the early hours, unable to sleep, I had come to a decision.

I would do as he had suggested.

I would put my family's ashes in their final resting place. It was fitting to do so now.

I dressed quickly in a pair of cotton pants and a T-shirt, and then I went downstairs, heading for the basement. Only last week I had purchased a large metal cash box for the shops, and it was ideal for what I had in mind.

Carrying the box, I returned to my little sitting room upstairs. Putting it down on the sofa, I went into my walk-in closet. The key to the safe was in a hatbox on the top shelf; climbing up on the small stepladder, I retrieved the key, got down, and opened the safe.

First I took out Andrew's ashes and Trixy's; then I went back for the small containers that held Jamie's and Lissa's. I placed the four cans in the metal box, closed it, and took it downstairs with me.

I had always known in my heart of hearts that if I ever buried their ashes, I would put them under the ancient maple tree near my studio.

The tree was huge, with a wide, gnarled trunk and great spreading branches, and it must have been three or four hundred years old. It grew on the far side of my studio and sheltered the building from the fierce heat of the sun in the summer months, yet without blocking the light.

The tree had always been a favorite of Andrew's, as had this shady corner of the property, where we had often had picnics. The twins had loved to play near the tree; it was cool there under its leafy green canopy on those scorching hot, airless days.

I dug a deep hole under the tree.

When I had finished, I straightened, stuck the spade in the earth, and went to get the box.

Kneeling down at the edge of the grave, I placed the box in it, then paused for a moment, letting my hand rest on top of the box. I closed my eyes and pictured them all in my mind's eye.

You'll be at peace here, I said to them silently. *You're forever in my heart, my darlings, always with me. Always.*

Standing up, reaching for the spade, I began to shovel the earth on top of the box, and I did not stop until the grave was filled.

I stood there for a few moments, then I picked up the spade and went back to the house.

Later that morning I told my father what I had done.

Then I took him down to the maple tree to show him where I had buried their ashes.

"If you remember, we used to have picnics under the tree sometimes, and the twins often played here, especially when I was in the studio painting."

My father put his arm around my shoulder and held me close to him. He was visibly moved and could not speak for a few moments.

At last he said, "And there shall be in that rich earth a richer dust concealed."

I looked up at him, my eyes filling. "That's lovely . . . "

He held me tighter against his body. "Rupert Brooke."

"What's the rest of it? Do you know the whole poem, Dad?"

My father nodded. "But it doesn't really apply."

"Why not?"

"Because it's to do with a soldier's death. An English soldier's death. Rupert Brooke wrote it before he died en route to the Dardanelles in the First World War."

"But Andrew was English, and the twins were half English, Daddy. So it is appropriate. Please, I'd love to hear you recite it, the way you used to read to me."

"Well, if you really want me to."

"Please."

My father began to speak slowly, softly, and I leaned into him and closed my eyes, listening.

> *If I should die, think only this of me:*
> *That there's some corner of a foreign field*
> *That is for ever England. There shall be*
> *In that rich earth a richer dust concealed;*
> *A dust whom England bore, shaped, made aware,*
> *Gave, once, her flowers to love, her ways to roam,*
> *A body of England's, breathing English air,*
> *Washed by the rivers, blest by the suns of home.*
> *And think, this heart, all evil shed away,*
> *A pulse in the eternal mind, no less*
> *Gives somewhere back the thoughts by England given;*
> *Her sights and sounds; dreams happy as her day;*
> *And laughter, learnt of friends; and gentleness,*
> *In hearts at peace, under an English heaven.*

38

Connecticut, August 1990

"What a stunning success you've got on your hands!" Diana exclaimed, turning to me and smiling broadly. "It's just wonderful, Mal, what you've accomplished in the first four months of being in business."

"I know, even I've been a bit surprised," I admitted. "And I couldn't have done it without your support and Mom's. And Sarah's help and advice. You've all been terrific."

"That's nice of you to say, but it's actually all due to your own hard work and inspired ideas, and let's face it, your extraordinary business acumen," Diana replied with a laugh, looking pleased. "Who'd have thought you'd turn out to be another Emma Harte?"

"Not quite, not yet," I said. "I've a long way to go."

Diana laughed again. "I like to think of you as a woman of substance for the nineties."

"Let's hope so. I'll tell you this, Diana, I do love retailing. Every aspect of it, in fact. Getting the shops here running properly has been tough, but doing it *and* getting it right has given me a lot of satisfaction."

"Meeting a challenge usually does," Diana answered. "And in my opinion there's nothing quite like hard work. It helps to take our minds off things, and certainly it gives us a great outlet for our energies. I know at the end of the day I'm ready for bed, and I fall asleep immediately, I'm so exhausted."

"I'm the same way," I said.

Diana fell silent, studied me for a moment, and then asked in a careful voice, "How are you really, darling?"

I sighed, "Well, there's not a day goes by that I don't think of them, of course, and the sadness and the grief are there, deep inside me. But I've forced myself to keep going, to function. And as we both know, being so incredibly busy works wonders."

"I learned that myself a long time ago," Diana murmured. "It was the antique shop and my business that saved my life, after Michael died. Work is a great cure-all for anyone with problems."

"Talking of work, I'd like to show you something," I said, getting up and walking across the administration office I'd created in a corner of the big red barn.

Opening one of the filing cabinets, I took out a couple of manila folders; then I returned to the seating arrangement in front of the window, where Diana and I had been having coffee.

Sitting down opposite her, I went on, "Last May at Kilgram Chase, when I had the idea of opening the shop-café, it also occurred to me that I could start a catalogue, that this would be a natural outgrowth of the shops."

"You didn't mention it," Diana said, settling back against the quilted throw pillows and crossing her legs.

"No, I didn't, because I thought you'd think I'd gone totally mad, that I was being too ambitious."

"Nobody can be too ambitious, as far as I'm concerned."

"That's true," I agreed. "Anyway, the shops have been so successful, such good money earners in such a short period of time, I've decided to go ahead with the catalogue. I've already designed it, created the mock-up. Sarah and I have done it together, and she's putting up some of her own money. We're going to be partners in this venture."

"I'm delighted to hear it, Mal. You're so close, and who better to have as a partner than your best friend? Besides which, I'm sure her input will be invaluable."

"It has been already, and she's helped tremendously with the shops as well. I thought it only fair to ask if she wanted to participate. I suggested it months ago, when I'd already started to create the catalogue, and she jumped at the opportunity."

"Is she going to leave Bergman's?"

"No. The catalogue will be a sideline for her." I joined Diana on the sofa and showed her the catalogue.

She took out her glasses, drew closer to me, then looked at the cover. This featured the red barn where the kitchen shop and the café were housed, and underneath the picture, a painting I had done especially for the catalogue. It said: *Indian Meadows,* and on the next line: *A Country Experience.* The third line read: *Spring 1991.*

"So you're not going to bring it out until next year?" Diana asked, raising a brow.

"No, it wouldn't work before then. I've got to stockpile a lot of merchandise to begin with, and then I've got to do a mailing. We've already purchased several mailing lists for key areas across the country, and Eric and Anna have compiled a local list. We'll mail out the catalogue early in January for the spring. There's a lot of planning involved when it comes to a catalogue, you know."

"I can well imagine."

I flipped open the catalogue to reveal the inside cover. "Here's a more detailed painting of the little compound of barns, the pastures, and the stables, and on the page facing is my letter telling them about Indian Meadows," I explained, and handed Diana the dummy of the catalogue, continuing, "It's divided into three comprehensive sections, as you'll see. The first is Lettice Keswick's Kitchen, featuring the jams and jellies and bottled items, as well as a good selection of products from the kitchen shop. All of the things we sell there, such as cookware, pottery, porcelain. The middle section is called Indian Meadows Boutique and offers clothing, accessories, and American quilts, that kind of thing. The last part is Kilgram Chase Gallery, presenting decorative items with an English flavor."

Diana opened the catalogue and began to look through it, exclaiming about the clever way we had presented everything. When she had perused it carefully for a few minutes, she gave it back to me and said, "I'm very impressed, Mal, very impressed indeed."

"Thank you. Mom and David thought it was pretty good, too. Very inviting, with appealing merchandise. My mother said she could buy half of the things without batting an eyelid. But come on, I want to show you two places you haven't seen yet."

"More surprises! How wonderful," Diana exclaimed, as always enthusiastic about everything I was doing.

I led her across the barn. "As you know, I divided this floor of the barn into separate areas. There's the office, where we just were, and this is the packing room," I explained, opening the door and taking her inside.

"The helpers pack everything which has to be mailed out in here, on these trestle tables. Then the packages are stacked up over there, ready for UPS, who already pick up every day."

"Do you still get a lot of orders that people want sent?"

"Yes. As you know, we've always had a good number of mail orders, ever since we opened in the spring. They have steadily increased, and that's what made me believe a catalogue would work very well."

I guided Diana next door, into one of our storage rooms. "This is where the kitchen merchandise is stored."

"And all of the Lettice jams and jellies are in the basement of the house, that I do remember," Diana added.

I nodded. "On the floor above this, which I had built last summer, we store clothing, soft toys, table linen, that kind of thing."

We strolled back to the administration office and sat down. Diana said, "You seem to have covered everything. And let me say it again, Mal. You've worked miracles here."

"Thanks, but I will need some extra storage space soon. That's my only real problem left to solve. In fact, when she arrives tomorrow, Sarah is going to talk to my neighbor, Peter Anderson."

"The stage director?"

"Yes. He owns the big pasture opposite the entrance to Indian Meadows, on the other side of the road, where there are two big barns. He doesn't use them. Sarah's hoping we can buy the land and the barns from him, but I don't think he'll sell."

"Perhaps he'll rent to you."

"We're hoping so, and if anybody can persuade a person to do something they don't want to do, it's Sarah."

An affectionate expression slid onto Diana's face. "She can charm the birds out of the trees, that's true, and I *am* fond of her; she's such a special woman."

"The best, and I don't know what I would have done without her. She's been a rock for me."

"Has she met anyone nice lately?" Diana asked.

I shook my head. "I'm afraid she hasn't. Travel the world though she does, an attractive man has remained elusive."

"I know what you mean," Diana responded, giving me a rueful little smile.

I stared at her, and before I could stop myself, I said, "Whatever happened to the man you told me about years ago, the one you thought was special? You said he was separated but not divorced, and was therefore verboten to you."

"He's still in the same situation."

"So you don't see him?"

"I do occasionally, yes. But only for business."

"Why doesn't he get a divorce, Diana?" I asked, riddled with curiosity, as I had always been about the situation.

"Religion."

"Oh, you mean he's a Roman Catholic?"

"Good God, no, not my Calvinistic Scotsman! It's his wife who's a Catholic and won't divorce him."

"Oh," I said, and fell silent, not wanting to probe any further.

Diana was also silent. She stared out the window for a second or two, her face pensive, her eyes sad. Then, rousing herself, she swung her face around to me and said quickly, "You've met him, you know."

"I have!"

"Yes, of course."

"Where?"

"In the shop, when you were in London with Andrew. In November of 1988. Robin McAllister."

"That tall, very good-looking man?" I asked, staring at her.

Diana nodded. "I was showing him some tapestries, if you recall."

"I remember him very well. He's the sort of man who leaves an impression."

"True." Diana glanced at her watch and stood up. "It's one o'clock. Shall we go and have lunch in the café? I'm feeling a bit hungry."

"Let's go!" I exclaimed, also jumping up, realizing she wanted to change the subject.

"Won't you need a lot of extra help to fulfill your catalogue orders?" Diana asked, taking a sip of her iced tea.

"Not at first, since we're doing our initial mailing in January, for the spring," I replied. "When I started the shops this year, my busy days were Friday, Saturday, and Sunday, so that leaves Monday, Tuesday, Wednesday, and Thursday for the staff to pack and wrap orders. That is, in the early spring. Everybody'll pitch in at first, and then I'll just take it from there. The summer months are obviously more difficult, and we'll have to adjust things. I'm going to play it by ear."

Glancing around, I added, "It's only Wednesday, and look, the café is already very busy."

"And you had quite a lot of people in the Kilgram Chase Gallery earlier, I noticed," Diana said. "But take it one step at a time, one day at a time, Mal, that's always been my motto."

"The thing that's surprised me is the success of the café," I said. "It's been a hit ever since it opened. We're doing a lot of business, and people actually call up to make reservations."

"It's a charming place, with these little green tables, the fresh flowers, and all the plants scattered around. And the products on display make a statement. It reminds me of a big country kitchen," Diana remarked. "And it does smell delicious."

"The food's delicious too. You'll see in a minute."

"And Nora's doing all the cooking?" Diana asked.

"Her niece comes to help her on weekends, when it's really busy, otherwise she's alone except for Billy and Eric. Guess what is her most popular hot dish?"

"Cottage pie, recipe courtesy of Parky," Diana said, winking at me.

"Yes. And the rest of the things on the menu are quiche, soups, and sandwiches. However, she now wants to do a few salads, and I think she's right, in view of the popularity of this place. And speaking of Nora, here she comes."

Nora glided over, drew to a standstill at our table, and thrust out her hand. "Nice to see you, Mrs. Keswick."

Diana shook her hand and said, "And it's wonderful to see you, too, Nora. Quite a success you've got here. Well done, Nora, well done."

"It's all Mal," she answered quickly. "She's the brains." But nonetheless, she looked pleased. She gave Diana one of her rare smiles. "I hope you'll stop by and see my kitchen later. Now, what can I get you?" she asked, handing Diana a menu.

I said, "I'm going to have one of your pita-bread concoctions, Nora, please."

"Don't tell me. You want sliced avocado and tomato."

"However did you guess?"

Nora shook her head. "Oh, Mal, there's not a lot of nourishment in that. Let me put chicken in it as well."

"Okay," I agreed, knowing it would please her. "And I'll have another iced tea, please."

"And I'd like to have the avocado and shrimp on pita bread," Diana said. "And another iced tea, too, please, Nora."

"Back in a minute," Nora said and hurried away.

Diana asked, "Is she waiting on the tables as well, Mal?"

"No, she just wants to serve *you*. She's sort of proprietary at times, possessive, especially with the family."

Diana smiled. "She's always been very devoted. And who's Iris, the young woman who looks after the house now? She seems awfully pleasant. She couldn't do enough for me this morning."

"That's Nora's other niece. Iris's sister, Rose, is the one who helps out in the kitchen on weekends. I had—" I broke off as Eric came hurrying toward the table, carrying the tray of iced teas.

"Here we are, Mal, Mrs. Keswick," he said, giving us each a glass.

We both thanked him.

He half turned to go back to the cash register, which he had made his station, but hesitated.

"What is it, Eric?" I asked, looking up at him.

"Sorry to trouble you now, Mal, when you're at lunch. But I've just had a call from one of our customers, a Mrs. Henley. She wants to know whether or not we do private parties."

I frowned. "Do you mean catering?"

"No. She wants to have a private party here. In the café. A sweet-sixteen party for her daughter and the daughter's young friends."

"When?"

"In September. On a Friday night."

"Oh, I don't know, I don't think so, Eric, that's bound to be a busy time, people will want to come in for cold drinks—"

"Don't say no quite so quickly," Diana interrupted, putting her hand on my arm. "It could be quite profitable to have private parties, and it helps to get the place better known than it is already."

Eric bestowed a huge smile on Diana. "I agree with you, Mrs. Keswick."

"All right, Eric, tell the lady yes, but that you'll have to get back to her about the cost."

"I will, Mal," he said, giving me a little salute, which was a new habit of his, before he disappeared.

"I do like him," Diana said to me. "He's the salt of the earth."

"Just like Joe, Wilf, and Ben," I said.

After we had eaten our pita-bread sandwiches, I sat back in the chair, regarding Diana for a moment. Finally, I said, "I have a proposition for you."

"You do! How wonderful!" she exclaimed, then paused and viewed me intently. "I thought you didn't want any partners."

"I don't, in the shops. But this is something else."

"Well, it can't be the catalogue. Sarah's your partner in that."

"It's an idea I had months ago, but I've only just managed to think it through properly," I explained. "I want to start a small publishing company, and I'd like you to become my partner in it."

Leaning back in her chair, her head on one side, my mother-in-law studied me for a moment or two, then asked, "Isn't publishing rather dicey?"

"I think it can be, yes. But I'm talking about a small country press, publishing only a few specialty books, for sale only through my catalogue and here in the shops."

"It sounds interesting, Mal, but don't you think you have enough on your plate at the moment?"

"I am doing a lot, that's true, Diana. But I'm not thinking of starting the publishing company until next year, and I'm not asking you to put up any money."

"Oh, I see. But you *did* say you had a proposition for me."

"I do. I'd like you to become my partner, as I said, publishing only four books to begin with, in fact, we might never publish anymore, after that."

"Which books?" she asked, giving me a speculative look.

"Your books, Diana. The two Lettice Keswick diaries, her cookbook, and her garden book. Later we might do Clarissa's Victorian cookbook, but I'm not sure. If we went ahead, I would publish the Lettice diaries first, then her cookbook, and finally her garden book. It would be a special series, and therein lies its appeal, in my opinion. Eventually, once they'd all been published, the series could become a boxed set, a gift item. I really think it'll work."

"Where *will* you get the money? You say you don't want it from me."

"Only because I don't think I'll need very much," I pointed out. "Look, you own the books, and you're going to give me the rights. I can type up her text and do copies of her drawings. My only cost will be the printer and the bindery."

"I'm willing to give it to you."

"Thanks, Diana, but by the time I do it next year, I may well be able to finance the publishing project myself."

"Whatever you want. But in any case, I think the idea is brilliant, Mal! Just brilliant! I'd love to be involved. In any way you want."

I reached out and squeezed her hand. "Thanks. By the way, I'm going to call it Kilgram Chase Press. Is that all right with you?"

"I love it! How clever you are, darling." She stared at me for a moment, and then she began to shake her head wonderingly. "What I said earlier is perfectly true, Mal. You *are* going to be a woman of substance for the nineties."

39

Connecticut, May 1992

I lay in bed, staring at the clock in the dim light of the room. I could see that it was only four-thirty.

I had awakened sooner than I usually did. Although I was an early riser, and always had been, I generally slept until six. Lingering in bed for a while, I let myself drift with my thoughts. Then I remembered what day it was: Monday, the fourth of May. My thirty-seventh birthday. *Thirty-seven.* That didn't seem possible, but it was true.

Sliding out of bed, I went to a window, opened a blind, and stood peering out. It was still dark. But far off, beyond the trees and the wetlands, the horizon was tinged with a green luminescence, and wisps of pale light were trickling up into the sky. Soon it would be dawn.

Walking into my little sitting room next door, I sat down and stared at my painting of Lissa and Jamie, then my eyes automatically swung to Andrew's portrait above the fireplace.

Though my grief was held in check, my sorrow contained, my longing for them had not lessened. There was an aching void inside and, at times, moments of genuine despair. And busy though I was with Indian Meadows, loneliness was a familiar companion.

Last year I had finally found the courage to sort through Jamie's and Lissa's clothes and toys. I had given everything away—to Nora's family, Anna's friend, and the church. But I had been unable to part with my children's two favorite possessions, Oliver, Lissa's teddy bear, and Derry, Jamie's dinosaur.

Going to the bookshelves, I took down these well-cuddled toys and buried my face in their softness. Memories of my children momentarily overwhelmed me. My throat suddenly ached, and I felt the rush of tears. Blinking them away, I took firm hold of myself, placed the toys in their places, and went into the adjoining bathroom.

After pinning up my hair under a cap, I took a quick shower. A few minutes later, as I toweled myself dry, I found myself glancing at the corner of the bathtub near the taps, as I frequently did. I had never found my art knife, after it had vanished the night I planned to kill myself. What had happened to it? It was a mystery, just as the empty tub and the open kitchen door were also mysteries.

Recently I had confided in Sarah, who had listened to me attentively.

When I had finished my tale, she had been silent for a moment or two, and then she had said, "I'm sure there's a logical explanation for these things, but I like to think it was something inexplicable, like a special kind of intervention, or perhaps the house itself looking after you."

Sarah and I had long agreed that there was an especially wonderful atmosphere in the house these days. It seemed to us that it was more benign and loving than it had ever been, and there was an extraordinary sense of peacefulness within its old walls.

"It's a house full of loving, friendly ghosts, just as Andrew once said," Sarah had murmured to me only last weekend. We had stared at each other knowingly then, as we realized we were thinking the same thing: Andrew, Jamie, and Lissa were present in the house, for it was alive with our memories of them.

Once I had dressed in my usual working clothes of jeans, a T-shirt, jacket, and penny loafers, I went downstairs.

After putting on the coffee, I drank a glass of water, picked up the bunch of keys for the shops, and went outside. I stood looking around, breathing the air. It was fresh, redolent of dew-laden grass and green growing things; the scent of lilac planted around the house wafted to me on the light breeze.

It was going to be a pretty day, I could tell that. The sky was clear, unblemished by clouds, and it was already pleasantly mild.

As I struck out toward the ridge, a bevy of small brown birds flew up into the sky, wheeling and turning into the haze of blueness soaring above me. I heard their twittering and chirping as I walked, and in the distance there was the *honk-honk* of Canada geese.

Since I had plenty of time this morning before opening up the shops, I sat down on the wrought-iron seat under the apple tree. Like the lilacs, this too was beginning to bloom, bursting with green leaves and delicate little white buds. Soon it would be in full flower.

Mommy's Place. That was what Andrew had always called this spot. I settled back against the seat and closed my eyes, and I heard their voices clear and resonant, saw their images so vividly in my head. They were here with me, as always. Safe in my heart.

This was the fourth birthday I had spent without Andrew and the twins. I knew from past experience that it would be a sad day for me, just as their birthdays and special holidays were always tinged with sorrow, hard for me to bear without them.

And yet despite my pain and loneliness, I had managed to go on living. One day I had finally come to understand that no one could really help me or do it for me. I had to find my courage myself.

To do this I had reached deep inside myself, gone to the very core of my being, the center of my psyche, and there I had found hidden resources, a strength I had never known existed in me. And it was this strength of character, and a determination to start anew, to make some sort of life for myself, that had propelled me forward, brought me to where I stood today.

Perhaps it was not the best place, but given the circumstances of my life, it was a good place to be. I was healthy mentally and physically; I had managed to open a business, become self-supporting, pay off my debts, and keep the house I loved. I had even been able to reduce the loans from my parents, Diana, and David. By the end of the summer I would retire the loans in full, I was certain of that.

You're making it, Mal, I said under my breath. You're not doing badly at all.

I got to my feet and went down the hill toward the compound of barns. As I drew closer, I noticed that the pond was alive with wildlife this morning, mostly the mallard ducks and a few geese. Later in the summer the blue heron would come and pay us a visit, as it usually did. We had all grown attached to it, awaited its arrival eagerly. And brief though its stay was, we loved having it with us. It had become a sort of mascot, and I was thinking of using the name Blue Heron for another label, a line of locally crafted baby clothes.

Unlocking the door of Lettice Keswick's Kitchen, the café-shop, I went inside and was instantly greeted by the delicious smells of apples and cinnamon.

Switching on the light, I stood in the doorway for a second, admiring the café. Painted white, with dark beams floating above, it had a new floor of terra-cotta tile, so much easier to keep clean, we had discovered, and bright red-and-white checked curtains at the few small windows. It was fresh, cheerful, and inviting, with many green plants everywhere and metal shelving filled with our specialties.

Walking forward, I let my eyes roam over some of the shelves stocked to the hilt with jars and bottles of the Lettice items. Marvelous jams and jellies—apple and ginger, rhubarb and orange, plum and apple, apricot, blackberry and apple, pear and raspberry. There were jars of mincemeat, lemon curd, chutneys, pickled onions, red cabbage, beets, and walnuts, and Piccalilli, a mustard pickle which was a favorite of mine and which originally hailed from Yorkshire.

Also, we carried a small selection of pastas, wild rice, and couscous, imported English biscuits, and French chocolates. And Nora's pasta sauces, recent additions.

She had turned out to be something of a miracle in the kitchen, and had found her true vocation. Aside from the pasta sauces, mostly with a tomato base, she made all of the other Lettice products in our own café kitchen. I was very proud of her and of her cooking.

The Lettice Keswick line had caught on quickly, become a huge success here in the shop and in the catalogue. The latter, which Sarah and I had started seventeen months ago, had been another big hit, so much so we were both still reeling.

Only last week I had had to hire three new employees to work in the packing and dispatching department; Eric had taken on two new waiters for the café, since I had just promoted him. He had become the manager of the shops and the café and was now in charge of the twelve other people who worked at Indian Meadows.

Pushing open the kitchen door, I glanced inside. Everything shone brightly in the early-morning sunlight; I nodded to myself, went on upstairs, gave the cookware and tabletop shop a cursory glance, and headed back to the main floor.

Once outside again, I paid a visit to the Indian Meadows Boutique, unlocked the door, looked inside quickly, and then progressed to the Kilgram Chase Gallery.

Although I loved all of my shops and all of my products, in a funny sort of way this little gallery was my favorite. Perhaps this was because it was reminiscent of Yorkshire and Andrew's childhood home. In any case, it had been well patronized so far, and it was hard for me to keep the merchandise in stock. Everything was sold before I could turn around to order more.

The gallery's biggest hit, though, had been and still was *Lettice Keswick's Journal*, published under my Kilgram Chase Press imprint last summer. In the year it had been out, it had sold almost thirty-five thousand copies in the gallery and through the catalogue. Sarah told me that her friends in publishing in New York were quite astounded, although they were admiring of the book and found it fascinating. Apparently so did everyone else.

Once more, I gave the gallery only a cursory glance and, closing the door behind me, made my way back to the house. Things down here were in good order; at seven Anna would be floating around, at nine Eric and Nora would arrive, and by nine-thirty the rest of the workers would be here.

As I walked up the hill, I told myself yet again how lucky I had been with the business. Every different project had worked well here. Each of the shops was a success; all of our products were popular; the catalogue just grew and grew; and the café was a runaway success with locals and strangers alike. Whenever I mentioned the word *lucky* to Sarah, she would guffaw loudly. "If you call working twelve to fourteen hours a day, seven days a week for over two years *lucky*, then yes, you have been," she would exclaim. "Mal, you've made Indian Meadows the success it is because you've worked nonstop around the clock, and because you have tremendous business sense. You're one of the smartest retailers I've ever met."

Of course she was right in certain ways. I had poured all of my energy and drive into Indian Meadows, and I had been highly focused. Tunnel vision had turned out to be a handy asset to have.

But despite all of the hard work, not only on my part, but on the part of the entire staff, I still believed in the element of luck. Everyone needed a bit of it, whatever the business or artistic venture.

When I got back to the house, I stopped at one of the white lilac trees and broke off a small branch. I carried it into the kitchen. I filled an old jam jar with water, tore off stems of the lilac, and arranged them in the jar, then I carried the jar outside.

I made for the huge maple tree near my studio, where I had buried my family's ashes on August 19, 1989. Kneeling down, I removed the jar of drooping flowers from within the small circle of stones I had arranged three years ago and replaced it with the jar of lilacs.

I knelt there for a moment, staring down at the flat paving stone made of granite, which I had placed there in October of that same year.

Engraved upon its dark surface were their names.

Andrew, Lissa, and Jamie Keswick. And Trixy Keswick, their beloved pet. And underneath was the date of their murders, *December 11, 1988,* and below the date were those beautiful words of Rupert Brooke's, which my father had recited to me the morning I had laid them to rest:

"*There shall be in that rich earth a richer dust concealed.*"

"Happy birthday, Mal," Nora said, coming into the kitchen.

"Thanks, Nora," I answered, swinging around.

She came forward, gave me a quick hug, and then stepped away.

Eric, who was behind her, said, "Happy birthday, Mal," and thrust a big bunch of flowers at me. "We thought you'd like these, your favorites."

"Thank you so much, it's so sweet of you both." I took them from him, hugged him, and lowered my face to smell the white lilac, tulips, narcissi, and daffodils wrapped in cellophane paper and tied with a big yellow bow. "They're beautiful. I'll put them in water."

"No, I'll do that!" Nora exclaimed, taking them from me before I could protest and marching over to the sink.

Turning to Eric, I said, "Would you like a cup of coffee?"

He shook his head. "No, thanks, though. I should get down to the café, I'm running a bit late this morning."

"Yes, you'd better do that," I shot back. "Otherwise the boss might be mad at you."

He grinned, saluted, and hurried out.

Nora stood at the sink, arranging the flowers.

I sat down at the kitchen table and took a sip of my second cup of coffee.

Nora said, "I see you mother's car is out front. Did she stay over last night?"

"Yes, she did. She wanted to be here for my birthday today. Sarah took Mr. Nelson back to the city."

"I'm glad they were all here yesterday for lunch . . . it was nice, wasn't it?"

"Yes, thanks to you and all the lovely things you made."

"Oh, I didn't do much, Mal," she murmured. "Anyway, it was my pleasure."

"I thought I'd bring my mother down to the café at about twelve-thirty today, Nora. After lunch she's got to drive back to New York."

"Can I make you something special?"

I shook my head. "My mother loves your Cobb salad, and so do I. Why don't we have that?"

"No problem." She pushed the last spray of lilac into the vase she had found on the draining board, swung her head, and asked, "Where do you want me to put these?"

"In the sunroom, I think, since I spend so much time there."

She carried the vase of the flowers away, came back to the kitchen, poured herself a cup of coffee, and stood drinking it near the sink. After a moment she said, "I liked that woman your father brought by yesterday. Miss Reece-Jones. Is he going to marry her?"

I shrugged. "Don't ask me, Nora, I've no idea."

"Pity, if he doesn't. They seem well suited."

"I think they are." I studied her over the rim of my mug. Nora had always had a way of zeroing in on people, making quick and accurate assessments of them. She was rarely wrong.

After rinsing out the mug, she said, "Got to get down to the café kitchen. See you later, Mal."

"Thanks again for the flowers, Nora. It was so thoughtful of you and Eric."

She nodded. "Try and have a nice day," she said quietly, then hurried out.

Over lunch at the café, I said to my mother, "Do you think Dad will marry Gwenny?"

My mother stared at me for the longest moment before answering. Finally, she said, "No, I don't think he will. But I wish he would. She's very nice."

"Yes, she is, everyone seems to like her. But why do you think he won't get married?"

My mother bit her lip, looked reflective for a moment, then she said slowly, choosing her words with care, "Because your father's a bachelor at heart."

"Oh, so it's nothing to do with Gwenny, you just think he prefers to be single?"

"Put succinctly, yes."

"But he was married to you."

"True, but he was never there—" She cut off her sentence and gave me an odd look.

"Dad wants his cake, and he wants to eat it too, is that what you're trying to say, Mom?"

"No, I'm not, actually. I don't mean to imply that your father is a womanizer, or that he's promiscuous, because he's neither. He's just . . . a bachelor at heart, as I told you a minute ago. He prefers to be on his own, free to roam the world, digging about in ancient ruins, doing as he pleases. He's a bit of a loner, you know. If some woman comes along, and he likes her, well, then, I suppose he gets involved. But basically, he doesn't want to be tied down. I think that sums it up."

"I see. Well, I guess *you* should know," I murmured, pushing my fork into the Cobb salad.

My mother watched me for a moment or two and then said, "Yes, I really *do* know all about your father, Mallory, and perhaps now is the time to discuss my marriage to him. I know it's bothered you for years, I mean, the fact that we separated when we did."

"No, not that, Mom, not that at all! I don't understand why Dad was always away when I was a child growing up. Or why we didn't go with him."

A small sigh escaped her. "Because he didn't really want us to go along on his digs, and anyway, as you got older you had to go to school. Here in the States. He insisted you were educated here, and so did I, to be truthful."

"So he went away on these extended trips for his work, and came back when he felt like it. How could you put up with that, Mom?"

"I loved him. And actually, Edward loved me, and he loved you, Mal, he really did. You were the apple of his eye. Look, I strove very hard to hold our marriage together, and for a very long time."

"You say he went off on his digs, and I understand. After all, that's his work. But there were other women when I was little, weren't there?"

"Eventually," she admitted.

I confided in her then. I told her about my memories of that Fourth of July weekend so long ago, when I had been a little girl of five; told her how that awful scene in the kitchen and their terrible quarrel had stayed with me all these years. Buried for so long because it was so painful and only recently resurrected, jolted into my consciousness four years ago.

She listened and made no comment when I finished.

My mother simply sat there silently, looking numb and far away, gazing past me into space.

At last she said, in a low, saddened voice, "A friend, I should say a so-called friend, told me Edward was having an affair with Mercedes Sorrell, the actress. I'm ashamed to admit that I believed her. I was young, vulnerable. Poor excuses. But anyway, I became accusatory, vile, really, and verbally abusive to your father. You remember that only too well, it seems. It was jealousy, of course. Later I discovered that it wasn't true. It had been a lie."

"But there *were* other women, Mom," I persisted. "You said that yourself."

"I suppose there were sometimes, when he was away on a dig for six months or longer. But it was me he loved."

"And that's why you stayed with him all those years?"

She nodded. "Anyway, your father fought hard against the separation, resisted it for a long time, Mal."

"He did?" I said, my eyes opening wider. I stared at her.

My mother stared back.

"Don't sound so surprised," she said after a second's pause. "And yes, he did resist the separation; what's more, he never wanted a divorce. Not only that, we continued to have a relationship for a long time after we separated."

"Do you mean *sexual?*" I asked, pinning her with my eyes.

She nodded, looked suddenly slightly embarrassed.

"Mother, you didn't!"

"I'm afraid so. In fact, your father and I remained involved with each other, off and on, until I met David."

"Good God!"

"Mal, I *still* love your father, in a certain way. But I knew years ago that he and I could never be happily married."

"Why not? Obviously you continued to sleep with him for years after you split up. You could have fooled me; you always behaved as if he didn't exist."

"I know. A defense mechanism, I'm sure. Why couldn't I be happily married to him? Possibly because I don't want to be with a man who has to wander the earth. Endlessly."

"You could have wandered with him, after I'd grown up."

"It wouldn't have worked, not in the long run."

"But you did have a strong sexual bond—"

"We did. But sex doesn't necessarily make a successful marriage, Mallory. There are so many other factors involved. Your father and I couldn't have made it work, take my word for it."

"Oh, I do, Mom," I said, and I reached out and squeezed her hand. "I've wanted to say this for a long time. Mother, thanks for always being there for me. I know Dad never was."

"In his own way, he was, Mallory. Believe that."

"If you say so, I do, and I love him, Mom, and I love you too, and lately I've come to understand, that I'm quite separate from your marriage. What I mean is, I'm outside your personal relationship with him. What went on between you and Dad never had anything to do with me."

"That's right. It was just between us."

"When I look back on my childhood, I realize that we were a dysfunctional family . . . " My voice trailed away; I looked down at my plate, then at her.

My mother sat there waiting, as if she expected me to say more.

I shifted slightly in my chair, cleared my throat, then took a sip of iced tea. I felt slightly uncomfortable.

Eventually, I said, "I hope you don't mind me saying this, Mom."

"No, I guess not. Actually, if I'm honest, I have to admit it's the truth."

"We *were* a dysfunctional family, and let's face it, I *did* have an odd childhood. I think that's why I wanted to have the perfect family when I got married. I wanted to be the perfect wife to Andrew, the perfect mother to Jamie and Lissa. I wanted it all to be ... to be ... *right* ... "

"It was, Mal, it really was. You were the best wife, the best mother."

I looked at her intently. "I did make them happy, didn't I, Mom?"

Her fingers tightened on mine, "Oh, yes, Mal, you did."

40

Connecticut, November 1992

It was a cold Saturday morning at the beginning of the month. The first snap of frost was in the air, after a mild October of Indian-summer weather. But nonetheless, it was a sparkling day, sunny, with a bright blue sky.

We were always busy at Indian Meadows on the weekends, but this glorious day had brought out more people than usual.

All of the shops were busy, and I was glad we had plenty of merchandise in stock. In the summer I had done a lot of heavy buying, anticipating brisk business over the holiday season. Thankfully, I had been right. If today was any kind of yardstick, then at Thanksgiving and Christmas we would be setting records.

I walked across from the Kilgram Chase Gallery to the café, and when I pushed open the door, I was startled. The place was already full, and it was only midmorning. I hovered in the doorway, looking for Eric. When I caught his eye, he hurried over.

"What a morning," he said. "We're busier than ever in here. Am I relieved we made that second parking lot down by the front gate. It's come in handy today." He grinned at me. "You were right, as usual."

"It didn't cost much, and I do believe we're here to stay, Eric."

"Have you ever had any doubts, Mal?"

I shook my head. "Have you heard from Sarah?"

"No. Why, is there a problem?"

"Probably not, but she hasn't arrived. When she phoned me from the city last night, she said she'd be leaving at six-thirty this morning, that way she'd miss the traffic and be here by nine." I checked my watch. "It's almost eleven."

"She may have been late leaving New York," he responded.

"Perhaps."

"Try not to worry, Mal."

I nodded. "I will. I'll be in the office if you need me," I said. I went out and walked over to the other red barn.

Ever since my family had been killed, I worried excessively if someone close to me was overdue. I just couldn't help it. And in any case, we lived in a dangerous world these days, one more dangerous than it had ever been, in my opinion. Carjacking was a common occurrence, guns had proliferated on the streets to such an extent it was mind-boggling, and the murder of innocent people had become the norm. Every time I picked up a newspaper or turned on the television there was some new horror that chilled me to the bone.

"Mal! Mal!"

I pivoted, saw Anna hurrying toward me.

"Can you spare me a few minutes?" she asked as she drew to a standstill.

"Sure, let's go into the office," I answered, pushing open the door to lead the way.

After we had shed our coats, we headed for the seating arrangement near the window. "Do you have some sort of problem, Anna?" I asked, sitting down on the sofa.

"No, I don't, Mal, but Sandy Farnsworth called me last night," she explained, seating herself opposite me. "She wants to sell Pony Traders. She asked me to ask you if you'd be interested in buying the company."

"No, I wouldn't," I said without hesitation. "I've expected this coming for a while now, Anna. Sandy's sort of hinted at it before. But I don't want to become a manufacturer, which is basically what they are, even if some of their items are hand-made." I shook my head. "No way, Anna, too many headaches. I'm afraid I have to pass."

"I more or less indicated to Sandy that you wouldn't be interested," Anna replied. "I happen to agree with you, and I'm sure Sarah will too. But I promised to pass it by you."

"I understand. Has Sandy indicated what she's going to do? I mean, if she can't sell it? Will she continue the business?"

"I suppose she'll have to, or find herself a new partner. Lois Geery is moving back to Chicago, and that's what this is all about. I guess she wants to pull her money out of the company."

"If Pony Traders goes out of business, we're going to have to find a replacement, another manufacturer who makes their kind of casual country clothes," I pointed out. "I know we have Billie Girl and Lassoo, but we'll need a third."

Anna smiled at me. "I've already thought about that, Mal, and I've started to research it. I'll have a couple of new vendors for us by next week."

The door flew open, and Sarah came bounding in, much to my relief. She was looking harried and windswept.

"What a morning!" she exclaimed. "I'm sorry I'm so late, Mal. I hope you haven't been too worried."

"A little," I admitted. "And what happened to you, Sash? You look a bit disheveled, and you have a smudge on your face."

"I do? I wonder if it was there before? Oh, well, never mind. And what happened is that I had a flat."

"Oh, God, how awful for you, Sarah," Anna said as she got up. "I'd better get back to the boutique, Mal. See you both later."

"I'll be over soon," I answered.

Sarah smiled at her and said to me, "I could really use a cup of coffee, Mal. Shall we go to the café?"

"It's very busy, but Eric will find us a spot. Come on."

We hurried out after Anna.

"How did you manage to change your tire?" I asked as we sipped our coffee a few minutes later, tucked away in a corner of the café near the kitchen.

"I had help, thank God."

"Oh." I looked at her curiously. "Where were you when your tire blew?"

"On Route 41. Just down the road," Sarah explained, grinning at me.

"What's so amusing?" I asked.

"The encounter I had."

"When you blew the tire?"

"Yes, you see it occurred outside a house. Fortuitously for me, as it turned out, otherwise I'd still be sitting there with a flat. It was a small Cape Cod behind a white picket fence, and I went and knocked on the door. I asked the man who opened it if he would mind helping me, and he said he would be glad to. We changed the tire together. Mind you, Mal, he did most of the work. Anyway, while we were working, I managed to find out quite a lot about him. Including his telephone number."

"So he was attractive, Sash?"

"Not bad, not bad at all." Sarah paused, gave me an odd look, and added, "I asked him to dinner."

"You didn't!"

"Yes, I did."

"When?"

"Tonight."

"Sash!"

"Don't say *Sash* in that tone of voice, Mal. And I think it was a great idea."

"But Sash, *tonight.*"

"What's wrong with tonight? You can't say we don't have any food, because this place is stuffed with it."

"That's true."

"Listen, why not have him over? He lives close by, and we don't have many attractive men for neighbors, in fact, none at all, at least none who are available."

"There's Peter Anderson," I reminded her.

"Mr. Lousy Big Shot!" she exclaimed. "He's a pain in the ass. He's strung me along for over two years about those damned barns of his, and now he's finally said no. He doesn't want to sell after all, he says. Not nice, Mal."

"He's a funny bird, I must admit. Eric told me he's had all kinds of tragedies in the last few years. In any case, we're managing all right, and we can always put up another ready-made barn down near the new parking lot, should we need it."

"I suppose so. But Peter's really disappointed me. He seemed so pleasant at first."

"What's his name? The man who's coming to dinner."

"Richard Markson."

I sat back, frowning, and took a sip of my coffee. "It's strange, Sash, but his name sounds familiar. I wonder if I've met him?"

She shook her head vehemently. "No, you haven't. I asked him. He's quite a well-known journalist, and he does a lot of television, so that's probably why you know his name."

"What kind of journalism?" I asked, always wary.

"Political stuff, mainly."

"What time is he coming?"

"I said eight, but I can make it later if you prefer, Mal. I said I'd call to confirm the time."

"Eight is fine. Now, about dinner. We can take one of Nora's cottage pies up to the house, and a container of her chicken bouillon with vegetables. We can make a green salad, there's a Brie cheese and fruit. How does that sound?"

"Great, Mal. The only thing you've forgotten is a loaf of Nora's homemade bread."

I must admit, I liked Richard Markson the moment he walked into the house.

He was a tall man, well built but by no means heavy, with dark brown eyes, dark wavy hair, and a pleasant face.

Almost immediately his presence seemed to fill the house. He was obviously self-possessed and at ease anywhere. Yet he had a quiet demeanor, and his reserved manner appealed to me.

"This is Richard Markson, Mal," Sarah said, bringing him into the kitchen where I was filling a bucket with ice. "Richard, meet my very best friend, Mallory Keswick."

"Thanks for having me on such short notice," he said as we shook hands. "And it's very nice to meet you, Mrs. Keswick."

"Please call me Mal, and I'm happy to meet you, and to welcome you to my home."

He smiled, glancing around. "It looks like a lovely place, and I must say, I'm very partial to these old colonials, they have such charm, as do the old farmhouses in Connecticut."

"Yes, they do. What would you like to drink, Mr. Markson?"

"A glass of white wine, thank you, and I hope you're going to call me Richard."

I nodded and carried the bucket of ice to the hutch, which generally served as a bar. "What about you, Sash? What are you going to have?"

"Me? Oh, I don't know. White wine, I guess. Is there a bottle in the fridge?"

"Yes," I said over my shoulder and took out three wine glasses.

"Let me do that," Richard said to Sarah when he saw her

struggling with the corkscrew, and a split second later he brought the bottle of wine to me. "Here you are, Mal."

"Thanks," I said, then filled the glasses. "Let's go to the small den. It's cozy there. Sarah lit a fire a while ago, since it's turned so chilly tonight."

Once we were settled in front of the blazing fire, Richard lifted his glass and toasted the two of us.

"Cheers," Sarah and I said in unison, and then we all settled back in our chairs and fell silent.

It was Richard who spoke first. Later I came to realize that he was very good at breaking the ice, making people feel comfortable. Perhaps that was part of his great success as a journalist.

Looking at me, he said, "What a fantastic success you've made of Indian Meadows. It's great for us all, none of us knows how we could manage without it now."

"Oh, so you do use the shops, do you?" Sarah said, a brow lifting.

"Certainly do. I bought all of my Christmas gifts here last year, and I fully intend to do the same again. I'm frequently over here browsing around."

"Funny, we've never seen you," Sarah murmured.

I said, "It's nice to meet a satisfied customer. You are, aren't you?"

"Very much so," Richard assured me, smiling. He took a swallow of wine and went on, "And I love Nora and her cooking. To tell you the truth, I don't know what I'd do without her. I buy most of my meals from the café take-out—her soups, her salads, and that delicious cottage pie."

Sarah and I exchanged dismayed glances, and before I could say a word, she exclaimed, "It's a good thing you *do* like it, because that's what you're getting for dinner tonight. Nora's chicken soup and cottage pie."

"Oh," he said. "Oh, that's great. *Great.* As I said, I am her biggest fan."

"I could make something else, spaghetti primavera, if you like!" I suggested swiftly, feeling embarrassed.

"No, don't be silly. The cottage pie's wonderful."

"Bet you had that last night?" Sarah said, making it sound like a question."

"No, I didn't!" Richard protested, and then he broke off. His mouth twitched and he started to laugh. Glancing at me he shrugged. "But honestly, I don't mind eating it again."

The expression on his face was so comical I found myself laughing with him. Between chuckles, I said to Sarah, "We're going to have to start cooking again. We don't have much choice."

"You're right, Mally," she replied, gazing at me for the longest moment.

Richard asked me more questions about Indian Meadows, how I had come to start the shops, and I told him.

He mentioned the Lettice diary and confided how fascinating he had found it.

Sarah listened to us talking, occasionally joined in, went and got the bottle of wine from the kitchen, and kept filling our glasses.

At one moment she came back from the kitchen and said, "I've put the cottage pie in the oven," and pulled a funny face. We all laughed.

Later, when I went into the kitchen myself to check on things, Sarah followed me. "I can do it, really I can," I said. "Go and keep Richard company."

"He's all right, he's looking at the books on the bookshelves. Listen, I want to tell you something."

She sounded so peculiar, I turned around to face her. "What is it?"

"It's lovely to hear you laugh again, Mal. I haven't heard you laugh in years. That's all I wanted to say."

I stood there returning her loving gaze, and I realized that she had spoken the truth.

*   *   *

As it turned out, laughter was the keynote of the evening.

Richard Markson had a quick wit and a good sense of humor, as did Sarah, and their repartee was fast and furious. At one moment they were so amusing I found myself chortling yet again, and so much so I had to stop serving the cottage pie for fear of spilling it.

I sat down at the table for a second, letting my laughter subside, and I looked from one to the other, thinking how well matched they seemed. It struck me that he was the nicest man Sarah had brought around in a long time, and it was quite apparent that he liked her a lot. And why wouldn't he? My Sashy was beautiful and smart, kind and loving, and quite irresistible at times, like tonight. She was inimitable.

Rising, I went back to the oven and brought out the cottage pie again.

Sarah said, "Why don't you put the dish in the middle of table, Mal? We'll help ourselves."

"Good idea," Richard agreed.

I did as Sarah suggested and sat down.

After taking a sip of wine, I watched as Richard served himself, then stuck his fork into the pie on his plate. How awful that Sash and I hadn't been more inventive with the dinner. But how could we have known that he was a regular customer of the take-out kitchen? I began to eat, and a bit later, when I glanced at him out of the corner of my eye, I noticed that he was relishing the pie.

It was over the Brie cheese and green salad that Sarah zeroed in on him. Leaning back in her chair, she asked in an offhand way, "How long have you had a weekend place up here, Richard?"

"Just over a year."

"Your Cape Cod looks very charming from the outside. Do you own it?"

He shook his head. "No, it's a rental. Kathy Sands found it for me, and she's—"

"Kathy was our real estate broker for Indian Meadows," I cut in. "She's a terrific woman, don't you think?"

He smiled. "Yes, she is, and I started to say that she's been looking for a house for me to buy, but the houses are all far too big for me."

"Oh, so you live alone then, do you?" Sarah asked, throwing him a quizzical look.

"I'm single," he said. "And I certainly don't want a large house to roam around in alone."

"That's understandable," Sarah murmured. "I'd feel the same. But of course I come here every weekend to be with Mal." There was a little pause before she said, "I've never been married, have you?"

"No, I haven't," he said. "I've roamed the world as a journalist, been a foreign correspondent until recently, and I guess I was always too involved with my job to think of settling down. I came back to the States three years ago and took a job with *Newsweek*." He pursed his lips, gave a half shrug. "I decided I'd had enough of foreign places. I wanted to come back home to little old New York."

"Are you a New Yorker?" I asked.

"Born and bred. You are too, aren't you, Mal? And you, Sarah?"

"Yes," I answered. "We are."

"We've been friends since we were babies," Sarah informed him, laughing. "Actually, you could say we've been inseparable since our prams. Anyway, what brought you up to this neck of the woods for weekends?"

"I was a boarder at the Kent School before I went to Yale, and I've always loved it up here. To my way of thinking, the northwestern highlands of Connecticut are God's own country."

41

Connecticut, January 1993

The night I met Richard I was quite certain it was Sarah he was interested in, not me. But within a few weeks of knowing him, he had made it absolutely clear he was drawn to me. He liked Sarah as a person, he said, found her delightful, in fact, but that was as far as it went.

I was so taken aback, I found myself stuttering that she was going to be hurt and upset. Richard assured me otherwise; he pointed out that she had no interest in him either.

This, too, had amazed me; after all, she was my oldest and dearest friend. I knew her intimately, as well as I knew myself. I was quite convinced he was wrong in his reading of her.

But he was right.

When I asked Sarah about Richard, she admitted he was not her type. "A nice man, too nice, Mal," were her words. "I've got a horrible feeling I always fall for the rats like Tommy Preston."

Once I recovered from my surprise, I found myself agreeing to go on seeing him. But I did so cautiously. I realized it would take a long time for me to allow him into my life. I had been alone for four years now, and I saw no reason to change the situation.

But as Sarah said, Richard was a nice man, warm, kind, and thoughtful, and he did make me laugh. That dry humor of his constantly brought a smile to my face, and I discovered I looked forward to seeing him on Friday or Saturday, or sometimes Sunday, when he came up for weekends. And yet, for all that, I did withhold part of myself.

I think he knew it, of course. He was too astute not to understand that I was afraid of a relationship, in many ways.

He knew all about me and what had happened to my family. He had never come out and said so, had merely alluded to it. But he was a newspaperman, and a very good one, and he had been living in London in December of 1988. The murders of my husband and children had made headlines there, as well as here.

One of the things I liked about Richard was his sensitivity. On a Saturday evening in January, when I had known him for about three months, I came across him in the sunroom, looking at a framed photograph of Jamie and Lissa.

He held it in both of his hands and was gazing at it intently; there was such a tender look on his face I was touched.

I came in on him unawares, and he looked startled and embarrassed when he saw me. Swiftly he put the photograph back on the table, and still looking uncomfortable, he gave me a small, almost shy smile. He seemed about to say something, then he stopped.

"Say it," I said, walking over to him. "It's all right, really. Say what you're thinking, Richard."

"How beautiful they were . . . "

"Yes, they were. I used to call them my little Botticelli angels, and they were just that. They were adorable, mischievous, naturally, at times, but very bright and funny and . . . just great. They were *great*, Richard."

He reached out, put a hand on my arm gently. "It must have been . . . hard for you, heartbreaking . . . I'm sure it still is."

"Excruciating at times, and I suppose it always will be. But I've learned to go on living somehow."

A troubled expression flickered in his eyes as he said, "Look, I'm sorry, Mal, sorry you caught me staring at their picture. The last thing I want to do is cause you pain by making you talk about them."

"Oh, but it doesn't cause me pain," I said quickly. "I love to talk about them. Actually, most people think like you do, and they avoid mentioning Jamie and Lissa. But I want to reminisce about them, because by doing so it helps to keep them both alive. My children were born, they existed on this planet for six years. And they were such joyous little beings, gave me so much love and pleasure, I want to keep on remembering them, sharing my memories with my family and friends. I know I always will."

"I understand, and I'm glad you've confided in me, Mal," he said, "that you've shared this. It's important to me. I want to get to know you better."

"I've been very damaged," I murmured and went and sat on the sofa.

He took the chair facing me and said, "You're very brave."

"I'm very fragile. There are parts of me that are breakable, Richard."

"I know that, Mal. I'll be careful . . . I'll handle with care, I promise."

It seemed to me that after this discussion we drew a bit closer, but not that much, because *I* would not permit it. Deep down I was afraid of getting involved with him on an emotional level, if indeed I was capable of such a thing. I wasn't sure that I was.

But as the weeks passed and we continued to see each other when he came up on the weekends, the relationship did develop, and we kept discovering new things we had in common.

He had seen the grave under the old maple tree down by my studio, although I had never shown it to him. Perhaps Sarah had. In any case, one lovely April day he brought me a bunch of violets and asked me to put them on the grave. "For Andrew and the children," he said.

This was yet another thoughtful gesture on his part, and it moved me enormously.

After this I began to relax a little, to trust him even more, at least on a certain level. But the barriers I had erected were hard to scale, even harder to break down. As I found myself more and more drawn to him physically, I discovered I was still unable to open up my heart to him.

It was Sarah who pointed out to me how involved with me Richard was, but I pooh-poohed the idea.

"We like each other, we find each other attractive, we enjoy being together. In lots of ways. "But that's all there is to it, Sash. We're just good friends."

She gave me a skeptical look and changed the subject, drew me into a discussion about the catalogue and some of the new items we were including.

Much later on that particular April Saturday, as I got ready for bed, I thought about her words again. And I was convinced she was wrong about him, that she was exaggerating. Loving me as she did, Sarah wanted me to be happy, and in her opinion Richard Markson was part of the answer to that. But she was off track. He *was* a lovely man, I was the first to say so, but I know I could never care for him in the way he deserved. It just wasn't possible.

In May Richard came to see me on the morning of my thirty-eighth birthday, and I was very surprised to see him. It fell on a Tuesday this year, and he was the last person I expected to see strolling over to join me on the wrought-iron seat under the apple tree at eight o'clock in the morning.

"Why aren't you in New York? At work?" I exclaimed as he came and sat down next to me.

"Because I've taken the week off to prepare an outline for a book."

"You're going to write the Great American Novel?"

"No, a nonfiction book." He smiled at me. "Anyway, Mal, this is for you. Happy birthday." He leaned closer and kissed me. "I hope you like it."

"I'm sure I will." I looked at him and smiled, and opened my gift. "Oh, Richard how lovely of you to think of this!" I exclaimed. "Thank you so much." I sat staring at the dark red leather binding of *Collected Poems* by Rupert Brooke. Opening it, I looked inside, slowly turning the pages. "What a beautiful volume. Where on earth did you find it?"

"At an antiquarian bookshop in New York. It's quite old, as you can see. May I have it for a moment, please, Mal?"

"Of course." I handed it to him.

He leafed through the book, found the page he wanted, and said, "This is one of my favorites, Mal. Can I read a few lines to you?"

"Yes, please do."

> *In your arms was still delight,*
> *Quiet as a street at night;*
> *And thoughts of you, I do remember,*
> *Were green leaves in a darkened chamber,*
> *Were dark clouds in a moonless sky. . . .*

Richard stopped, and no words came for a moment.

I said quietly, "How lovely . . . "

"And here are just a few more lines from the same poem, Mal, and again I think they are very fitting." He touched my cheek and smiled that shy smile of his, then read from the book again.

> *Wisdom slept within your hair,*
> *And long suffering was there,*

And, in the flowing of your dress,
Undiscerning tenderness.

I didn't speak for a moment; I just sat there quietly, and then I said, "Thank you, Richard, not only for my birthday present, but for sharing with me."

"Can I take you out to supper tonight?" he asked, leaning back against the seat. "We could go to the West Street Grill in Litchfield."

"Thank you, I'd love that."

"See you later, then," he answered, looking pleased. "I'll pick you up about seven," he added, pushed himself to his feet and walked off briskly.

I watched him go, and then I looked down at the book in my hands and began to turn the pages, reading fragments of poems.

Later that week, on Friday morning, the boxes of books arrived from my printer, and I immediately called Richard. "The second volume of Lettice Keswick's diary has just arrived. Hundreds of them," I told him. "And since you're a fan of her writing, I'd like you to have one of the first copies."

"Thanks, Mal, that's great," he said. "When shall I come over for it?"

"Right now, if you like. I'll give you a cup of coffee."

"See you in half an hour," he replied and hung up.

When he arrived I led him into the sunroom. "I have coffee waiting, and the book for you. I hope you like it. I think they've done a good job, but I'm curious to have your opinion."

It took Richard only a few minutes to peruse the diary and tell me I had another success on my hands. "The layout is beautifully designed, for one thing, and the couple of pages I've read hold up. I suppose the entire diary is of the same high standard?"

"Very much so. It's such a marvelous record of everyday life in England in the seventeenth century. They were very like us, had the same hopes and dreams, troubles and worries."

"People haven't changed much over the centuries," he remarked, putting the book down on the table. "And you certainly stumbled on something very special when you found these."

"There are two more books," I confided.

"Diaries?" he said, looking slightly startled. "Don't tell me you have more of these treasures?"

I shook my head. "No, I don't, unfortunately, because the diaries are the best things she wrote. But I have her garden book and her cookbook, and I plan to publish those next."

"I think Kilgram Chase Press is going to be in business for quite a while," Richard said, smiling at me.

I shrugged. "I hope."

After drinking his coffee, Richard asked, "What's the garden book like?"

"Interesting, because her plans for the gardens at Kilgram Chase are very detailed, as are her lists of the plants, flowers, and trees. But I don't think it will have the same appeal."

"It might. People are very much into gardens these days, Mal. Look at the success of the Russell Page book on his gardens, and Gertrude Jekyll and her writings."

"Maybe you're right."

"Are there many illustrations?"

"Yes, I'll have to start copying them soon."

He laughed. "*Lettice Keswick's Garden Book* might turn out to be just as big a hit as the first diary. And this—" He tapped it and continued, "I'd like to give this to our book editor at the magazine, if you don't mind."

"No, that's fine. I'll get you another copy before you leave," I said.

We sat drinking our coffee and chatting for a few minutes,

mostly about Kilgram Chase Press and books in general. I surprised myself when I said, "I once did a book, Richard."

A look of interest flashed across his face. "Was it published?" he asked.

I shook my head. "It's a special kind of book."

"Do you have it here, Mal?"

"Yes. Would you like to see it?"

"I'd love to. I must admit, I'm very intrigued."

I nodded and hurried out of the sunroom.

I was back within a few minutes. "Actually there are two books," I said. "I wrote and illustrated them for Jamie and Lissa. I was going to put them in their Christmas stockings, but of course they were dead by then."

"Oh, Mal," he said, and his dark eyes looked stricken.

"One is called *The Friends Who Live in the Wall,* and the other is *The Friends Who Live in the Wall Have a Tea Party.* Well, here have a look," I said, handing them both to him.

Richard sat for a long time poring over the books. Finally, when he put the second book down, he had the strangest expression on his face.

"What is it? What's wrong? I asked, staring hard at him.

He shook his head. "Nothing. But Mal, these books are extraordinary, just beautiful. They're enchanting, so imaginative, and your paintings are superb. You *are* going to publish them, surely?"

"Oh, no, I couldn't! I could never do that! I wrote them for my children. They're . . . they're sort of *sacred.* The books were for Jamie and Lissa, and that's the way I want to keep it."

"Oh, Mal, you can't. Not something like these little . . . masterpieces. Small children will love them, and think of the joy and pleasure they'll give."

"No!" I exclaimed. "I can't, I won't publish them, Richard. Don't you understand?" I repeated shrilly, staring at him. "They're sacred."

"What a pity you feel that way," he said quietly.

"Maybe one day," I murmured, suddenly wanting to mollify him.

"I hope so," he said.

I lifted the books from the coffee table and wrapped my arms around them possessively. "I'll just put them away, I'll be back in a moment." I hurried upstairs.

As I laid the books away in the cupboard and locked the door, I suddenly wondered why I had shown them to Richard Markson. Only Andrew and Sarah had ever seen them. I had kept them hidden away for over four years. I hadn't even taken them out for Diana or my mother.

Why did I show him something so personal, so intimate, so meaningful? I asked myself as I went back downstairs to the sunroom. I had no answers for myself. In fact, I was quite baffled.

42

When he left for Bosnia, Richard had said he would be gone for ten days.

But in fact he had been away for almost the entire month. He had been scrupulous about calling me, and in a way I had been grateful to hear from him, to know that he was all right. But at the same time I felt I was being put on the spot.

Whenever he phoned me from Sarajevo, I became self-conscious, almost tongue-tied, certain that he was expecting an answer to the proposal he had made before he left.

I cannot give him one.

I was still ambivalent about my feelings for him. I liked him, cared for him, in fact. After all, he was a good man, and in the ten months I had known him he had proved to me that he was a good friend. Then again, we were compatible, had common interests and enjoyed being together. Yet to me that was not enough for marriage, or even a trial marriage, as he suggested.

I am afraid—afraid of commitment, attachment, bonding, intimacy on a daily basis. And ultimately I'm afraid of love. What if I fell in love with Richard, and then he left me? Or died? Or was killed doing his job? Where would I be then? I couldn't bear to suffer the loss of a man again.

And if I did marry him, as he wanted me to, and did so with-out loving him, there was still the possibility, no, the probability, of children. How could I ever have other children? Lissa and Jamie had been so . . . perfect.

This was how my mind was turning this morning, as I walked toward the ridge carrying a mug of black coffee. I lifted my eyes and looked up at the sky as I usually did.

It was a murky morning, overcast, and rain threatened up in the hills. Yet the sky was a curious color, etiolated, so bleached-out it looked almost white. No thunderheads rumbled above; nonetheless, the air was heavy and thick, and I sensed that the weather was going to break after a blistering August. Anyway, we needed the rain.

Sitting down under the old apple tree, I sipped my coffee and let my eyes roam around. They rested briefly on the cluster of red barns, now my compound of little shops, and I felt a small swell of pride as I thought of their great success. Then my gaze moved on to scrutinize the long meadow, finally settling on the pond. Mallard ducks and Canada geese clustered around the edge; and on the far bank the blue heron stood there proudly on its tall legs, a most elegant bird. My heart missed a beat. It was a welcome sight.

I smiled to myself. We had waited all summer long for the blue heron to pay us a visit. It had been sadly absent, but here it was this morning, looking as if it had never been away.

After finishing my coffee, I sat back, closed my eyes, and let myself sink down into my thoughts. Hardly a few minutes had passed when I knew what I must do, knew what my answer to Richard must be.

No.

I would tell him no and send him away.

Besides, what use to him was a woman who could not love again? A woman in love with her dead husband?

"Life is for the living," I heard Diana's voice saying, somewhere in the back of my mind.

I pushed that voice to one side, trampled on the thought. I would send Richard Markson away, as I had always known I would.

But perhaps he had already gone away of his own accord. I had not heard a word from him for well over a week now. In fact, he had stopped calling me on a regular basis once he'd quit Bosnia.

He had stayed in that war-torn country for ten days, as he had always intended to do. And then he had moved on, had flown to Paris. It was his favorite city, he had told me when he had phoned. He had worked there once, as Paris correspondent for *The New York Times*, and he had loved every minute of his four-year stay in France. Four years was a long time. He undoubtedly had many friends there.

Maybe Bosnia and Paris had cured him of me.

Maybe I wouldn't have to reject him after all.

That would certainly be a relief, if I didn't have to tell him no to his face, if he just stayed away and never came back, or if he let our relationship peter out.

Maybe he had picked up with an old flame. That would be a relief, too. Wouldn't it?

"Hello, Mal."

I sat up with a jerk, so startled I dropped the coffee mug I was holding. It rolled across the grass and disappeared over the edge of the hill.

Speechlessly I gaped at him.

"I'm sorry if I took you by surprise," Richard said, towering over me.

"You made me jump, scared me!" I exclaimed. Taking a deep breath, I asked, "And where did you spring from?"

"My car. I parked over by the house."

"No, I meant when did you get back from Paris?"

"Last night. I drove straight up here from Kennedy. I was going to call you, but it was late. So I decided to come and see you in person this morning." He paused, looked at me closely. "How are you, Mal?"

"I'm fine," I replied. "And you?"

"Great," he said. "But I could use a cup of coffee. Shall we go to the café?"

I dangled the bunch of keys in front of his nose. "Not open yet. It's only eight-thirty. I was just on my way to unlock the doors."

"Oh, God, I'm on Paris time . . . for me it's already the afternoon."

"Come on," I said, "Walk me to the shops. I'll open up, and then we can come back to the house for that cup of coffee."

"It's a deal," he said, and stretched out his hand.

I took it, and he pulled me to my feet.

We walked down the hill in silence. Once we were at the bottom, I opened up the café, the Indian Meadows Boutique, and the Kilgram Chase Gallery, and pocketed the keys.

"That's it," I said. "Let's head for the kitchen. I'll make you some breakfast, if you like. How do scrambled eggs and English muffins sound?"

"Terrific!"

I smiled at him and then moved away from the cluster of barns, heading for the house.

"Mal."

I stopped and turned around.

Richard was still standing near the gallery door.

"What's the matter?" I asked.

Shaking his head, he hurried over to me. "Nothing's the matter. I just wondered . . . " He stopped. "Do you have an answer for me, Mal?"

I didn't say anything at first, having no wish to hurt him. Then I murmured slowly, quietly, "No, Richard, I don't."

He stood staring at me.

"That's not true. I do," I corrected myself. "I can't marry you, Richard. I can't. I'm sorry."

"And you won't live with me? Try that?"

I shook my head, biting my lip. He looked so crestfallen I could hardly bear it.

Richard said, "You know, Mal, I fell in love with you the first moment I saw you. And I don't mean the night ten months ago when I came to dinner, that day I helped Sarah change her tire. I mean when I *first* saw you, the *first* time I came to Indian Meadows. You were unaware of me; we never met. You just bowled me over. I wanted to be introduced to you, but one of my friends in Sharon said you were . . . off limits."

"Oh," I said, surprised.

"Finally meeting you, getting to know you, being with you all these months has been the best thing that's ever happened to me. I love you, Mal."

I stood there looking at him. I was silent.

"Don't you care for me at all?" he asked in a low voice.

"Of course I care about you, Richard, and I worried about you when you were in Bosnia. I worried about stray bullets and air raids and bombs and you getting killed."

"Then why won't you take a chance with me?"

"I . . . just . . . can't. I'm sorry." I turned away. "Let's go up to the house and have coffee," I mumbled.

He made no response. He just walked along by the side of me, saying not one word.

We went up the hill slowly.

I looked at him out of the corner of my eye, saw the tight set of his clenched jaw, the muscle beating on his temple, and something inside me crumbled. My resistance to him fell away.

My heart went out to him in his misery. I felt his pain as acutely as if it were my own. And I knew then that I did truly care for him. I had missed him. I had worried about him. I was relieved he was here, unhurt and in one piece. Yes, I cared.

"Andrew wouldn't want me to be alone," I muttered, thinking out loud.

Richard made no comment.

We walked on.

Again I spoke. I said, "Andrew wouldn't want me to be alone, would he?"

"No, I don't think he would," Richard said.

I took a deep breath. "I'm not sure about marriage, not yet. It scares me. But, well . . . maybe we could try living together." I slipped my hand into his. "Here at Indian Meadows."

He stopped dead in his tracks. And so did I.

Taking hold of my shoulders, he turned me to face him. "Mal, do you really mean it?"

"Yes," I said in a voice so low it was almost inaudible. Then more firmly, "Yes, I do. But you'll have to be patient with me, give me time."

"I've got all the time in the world for you, Mal, all the time you want."

He leaned into me, kissed me lightly on the lips. Then he said, "I know you're very fragile, that pieces of you are breakable. I promise to be careful."

I nodded.

"And there's something else," he began and stopped.

"Yes?"

"I understand that you've had a terrible loss. But you have everything to gain with me—"

"I know that," I said, and remembering Diana's words, I added, "My life. The future—if I have the courage to take it."

"You're the bravest person I know, Mal."

We went on walking up the hill, passed the old apple tree

and the wrought-iron bench, heading for the front door. Richard put his arm around my shoulders as we crossed the wide green lawn.

I looked up at him.

He returned my gaze with one equally as steady and smiled at me.

As we went into the house together he drew me closer to him, his hand firm on my shoulder.

For the first time since Andrew's death I felt safe. And I knew that everything was going to be all right.

A SECRET
AFFAIR

As always, for Bob,
with all my love

1

Sarajevo, August 1995

He was closing the small padlock on his duffle bag when a deafening explosion brought his head up swiftly. He listened acutely, with accustomed practice, fully expecting to hear another bomb exploding. But there was nothing. Only silence.

Bill Fitzgerald, chief foreign correspondent for CNS, the American cable news network, put on his flak jacket and rushed out of the room.

Tearing down the stairs and into the large atrium, he crossed it and left the Holiday Inn through a back door. The front entrance, which faced Sniper Alley, as it was called, had not been used since the beginning of the war. It was too dangerous.

Glancing up, Bill's eyes scanned the sky. It was a soft, cerulean blue, filled with recumbent white clouds but otherwise empty. There were no warplanes in sight.

An armored Land Rover came barreling down the street where he was standing and skidded to a stop next to him.

The driver was a British journalist, Geoffrey Jackson, an old friend, who worked for the *Daily Mail.* "The explosion came from over there," Geoffrey said. "That direction." He gestured ahead, and asked, "Want a lift?"

"Sure do, thanks, Geoff," Bill replied and hopped into the Land Rover.

As they raced along the street, Bill wondered what had caused the explosion, then said aloud to Geoffrey, "It was more than likely a bomb lobbed into Sarajevo by the Serbs in the hills, don't you think?"

"Absolutely," Geoffrey agreed. "They're well entrenched up there, and let's face it, they never stop attacking the city. The way they are sniping at civilians is getting to me. *I* don't want to die from a stray rifle shot covering this bloody war."

"Me neither."

"Where's your crew?" Geoffrey asked as he drove on, peering through the windscreen intently, looking for signs of trouble, praying to avoid it.

"They went out earlier, to reconnoiter, while I was packing my bags. We're supposed to leave Sarajevo today. For a week's relaxation and rest in Italy."

"Lucky sods!" Geoffrey laughed. "Can I carry your bags?"

Bill laughed with him. "Sure, come with us, why don't you?"

"If only, mate, if only."

A few minutes later Geoffrey was pulling up near an open marketplace. "This is where the damn thing fell," the British journalist said, his jolly face suddenly turning grim. "Bleeding Serbs, won't they ever stop killing Bosnian civilians? They're fucking gangsters, that's all they are."

"You know. I know. Every journalist in the Balkans knows. But does the Western alliance know?"

"Bunch of idiots, if you ask me," Geoffrey answered and parked the Land Rover. He and Bill jumped out.

"Thanks for the ride," Bill said. "See you later. I've got to find my crew."

"Yeah. See you, Bill." Geoffrey disappeared into the mêlée.

Bill followed him.

Chaos reigned.

Women and children were running amok; fires burned everywhere. He was assaulted by a cacophony of sounds . . . loud rumblings as several buildings disintegrated into piles of rubble; the screams of terrified women and children; the moans of the wounded and the dying; the keening of mothers hunched over their children, who lay dead in the marketplace.

Bill clambered over the half-demolished wall of a house and jumped down into another area of the marketplace. Glancing around, his heart tightened at the human carnage. It was horrific.

He had covered the war in the Balkans for a long time, on and off for almost three years now; it was brutal, a savage war, and still he did not understand why America turned the other cheek, behaved as if it were not happening. That was something quite incomprehensible to him.

A cold chill swept through him, and his step faltered for a moment as he walked past a young woman sobbing and cradling her lifeless child in her arms, the child's blood spilling onto the dark earth.

He closed his eyes for a split second, steadied himself before walking on. He was a foreign correspondent *and* a war correspondent, and it was his job to bring the news to the people. He could not permit emotion to get in the way of his reporting or his judgment; he could never become involved with the events he was covering. He had to be impartial. But sometimes, goddamnit, he couldn't help getting involved. It got to him occasionally . . . the pain, the human suffering. And it was always the innocent who were the most hurt.

As he moved around the perimeter of the marketplace, his eyes took in everything . . . the burning buildings, the destruction, the weary, defeated people, the wounded. He shuddered, then coughed. The air was foul, filled with thick black smoke, the smell of burning rubber, the stench of death. He drew to a halt, and his eyes swept the area yet again, looking for his crew.

He was certain they had heard the explosion and were now here. They had to be somewhere in the crowd.

Finally, he spotted them.

His cameraman, Mike Williams, and Joe Alonzo, his soundman, were right in the thick of it, feverishly filming, along with other television crews and photographers who must have arrived on the scene immediately.

Running over to join the CNS crew, Bill shouted above the din, "What the hell happened here? Another bomb?"

"A mortar shell," Joe answered, swinging his eyes to meet Bill's. "There must be twenty or thirty dead."

"Probably more," Mike added without turning, zooming his lens toward two dazed-looking young children covered in blood and clinging to each other in terror. "The marketplace was real busy . . ." Mike stopped the camera, grimaced as he looked over at Bill. "A lot of women and children were here. They got caught. This is a real pisser."

"Oh, Jesus," Bill said.

Joe said, "The mortar shell made one helluva crater."

Bill looked over at it, and said softly, in a hard voice, "The Serbs had to know the marketplace would be busy. This is an atrocity."

"Yes. Another one," Mike remarked dryly. "But we've come to expect that, haven't we?"

Bill nodded, and he and Mike exchanged knowing looks.

"Wholesale slaughter of civilians—" Bill began and stopped abruptly, biting his lip. Mike and Joe had heard it all before, so why bother to repeat himself? Still, he knew he would do so later, when he did his telecast to the States. He wouldn't be able to stop himself.

There was a sudden flurry of additional activity at the far side of the marketplace. Ambulances were driving into the area, followed by armored personnel carriers manned by UN troops, and several official UN cars, all trying to find places to park.

"Here they come, better late than never," Joe muttered in an acerbic tone. "There's not much they can do. Except cart off the wounded. Bury the dead."

Bill made no response. His brain was whirling, words and phrases racing through his head as he prepared his story in his mind. He wanted his telecast to be graphic, moving, vivid and hard-hitting.

"I guess we're not going to get our R & R after all," Mike said, a brow lifting. "We won't be leaving today, will we, Bill?"

Bill roused himself from his concentration. "No, we can't leave, Mike. We have to cover the aftermath of this, and there's bound to be one ... of some kind. If Clinton and the other Western leaders don't do something drastic, something especially meaningful, there's bound to be a public outcry."

"So be it," Mike said. "We stay."

"They'll do nothing," Joe grumbled. "They've all been derelict in their duty. They've let the Serbs get away with murder, and right from the beginning."

Bill nodded in agreement. Joe was only voicing what every journalist and television newsman in Bosnia knew only too well. Turning to Mike, he asked, "How much footage do we have so far?"

"A lot. Joe and I were practically the first in the marketplace, seconds after the mortar shell went off. We were in the jeep, just around the corner when it happened. I started filming at once. It's pretty bloody, gory stuff, Bill."

"*Gruesome,*" Joe added emphatically.

Bill said, "It must be shown." Then, looking at Mike, he went on quickly, "I'd like you to find a place where we can film my spot, if possible one that's highly dramatic."

"You got it, Bill. When do you want to start rolling the tape?"

"In about ten minutes. I'm going to go over there first, talk to some of those UN people clustered near the ambulances, see what else I can find out."

"Okay, and I'll do a rekky, look for a good spot," Mike assured him.

William Patrick Fitzgerald was a renowned newsman, the undoubted star at Cable News Systems, noted for his measured, accurate, but hard-hitting reports from the world's battlefields and troublespots.

His fair coloring and clean-cut, boyish good looks belied his thirty-three years, and his tough demeanor stood him in great stead in front of the television camera.

He had earnest blue eyes and a warm smile that bespoke his sincerity, and integrity was implicit in his nature. These qualities underscored his genuine believability, were part of his huge success on television. Because he had this enormous credibility, people trusted him, had confidence in him. They paid attention to his words, listened to everything he had to say, and took him very seriously.

It was not for nothing that CNS treasured him and other networks coveted him. Offers for his services were always being made to his agent; Bill turned them all down. He was not interested in other networks. Loyalty was another one of his strong suits, and he had no desire to leave CNS, where he had worked for eight years.

Some time later he stood in front of the grim backdrop of burning houses in the marketplace, and his sincerity seemed more pronounced than ever. He spoke somber words in a well-modulated voice, as always following the old journalistic rule of thumb: *Who, when, where, what,* and *how,* which had been taught to him by his father, a respected newspaperman until his death five years ago.

"Thirty-seven civilians were killed and many others wounded today when a mortar shell exploded in a busy marketplace in Sarajevo," Bill began. "The mortar was fired by the Serbian army entrenched in the hills surrounding this battle-torn city. It was an obscene act of aggression against innocent, unarmed people, many of them women and children. UN forces, who quickly arrived on the scene immediately after the bombing, are calling it an atrocity, one that cannot be overlooked by President Clinton and the leaders of the Western alliance. UN officials are already saying that the Serbs must be forced to understand that these acts of extreme violence are unwarranted, unconscionable, and unacceptable. One UN official pointed out that the Serbs are endangering the peace talks."

After giving further details of the bombing, and doing a short commentary to run with the footage of the carnage, Bill brought his daily news report to a close.

Stepping away from the camera after his ten minutes were up, he waited until the equipment was turned off. Then he glanced from Mike to Joe and said quietly, "What I couldn't say was that that UN major I was talking to earlier says there *has* to be some sort of retaliation, intervention by the West. He says it's inevitable now. Public anger is growing."

Joe and Mike stared at Bill doubtfully.

It was Joe who spoke, sounding entirely unconvinced.

"I've heard that before," he said and shook his head sadly. "I guess this disgusting war has turned me into a cynic, Billy boy. Nothing's going to happen, you'll see . . . it'll be status quo . . ."

But as it turned out, Joe Alonzo was wrong. The leaders of the Western alliance in Washington, London, and Paris had no choice but to take serious steps to stop the Serbs in their systematic slaughter of Bosnian civilians, or risk being the focus of public outrage and anger in their own countries.

Just two days after the mortar shell exploded in the marketplace, the alliance sent in NATO warplanes to attack the Serbian army in the hills of Sarajevo.

It was August 30, 1995. The bombing began in earnest that day, and it was the biggest attack of the war. There were more than 3,500 sorties in the short space of two weeks, and even Tomahawk Cruise missiles were launched in the assault.

At the end of three weeks, the Serbians had begun to back down, withdrawing their heavy weaponry from the Sarajevo hills at the edge of the city, and making sounds about peace negotiations.

Because of the NATO attack and later developments, Bill Fitzgerald and the CNS crew remained in Bosnia, their week of rest and relaxation in Italy postponed indefinitely.

"But we don't really care, do we?" Bill said one evening when the three of them sat at a large table in the communal dining room of the Holiday Inn.

"No, of course we don't," Mike answered. "I mean, who cares about missing a week in Amalfi, relaxing with a couple of beautiful girls. Nobody would *mind* missing that, certainly not I. Or Joe." He shrugged. "After all, who gives a damn about sun, sea, and sex. And wonderful pasta."

Bill chuckled.

So did Joe, who said, "Me, for one. I give a damn." He grinned at the cameraman, who was his best buddy, then addressed Bill quietly. "I was certainly looking forward to our trip. And you were fixated about Venice, Bill, come on, admit it."

"Yes, it's true, I was. And I plan to make it to Venice soon. Maybe in the next month or two."

It was late September and relatively quiet out on the streets of Sarajevo; the fighting was less intense, with only sporadic sniping and fewer forays into the city on the part of the blood-thirsty Serbs. The entire foreign press corps were fully aware that the intense NATO retaliation had worked far better in curbing the Serbs than the words of appeasement the West had been uttering thus far.

Bill said, "I think things *are* going to ease up here, and very soon."

From their expressions, Mike and Joe were obviously disbelieving, and they did not respond.

Looking at his colleagues intently, Bill added, "With a little luck, this war should end soon."

Joe, ever the cynic, ever the pessimist, shot back, "Want to bet?"

"No, I don't," Bill replied swiftly. "You can never really tell what's going to happen with the Serbs. They talk out of both sides of their mouths."

"And shoot from the hip with both hands. Always fast on the draw, the fucking maniacs," Joe exclaimed. "They started this war and they're only going to end it when it suits them. When they get what they want."

"Which is most of Bosnia, if not, indeed, all of it," Bill said. "This war's always been about territorial greed, as well as power, racial bigotry and ethnic cleansing."

"Greed, power, and hatred, a pretty potent combination," Mike murmured.

The cameraman glanced at his plate of food, his expression glum. He grimaced and put down his fork; his nose curled in distaste. "The soup was watery and tasteless, now this meat is greasy and tasteless. Jeez, this damn curfew has been getting to me more than ever lately. I hate having to eat here every night. I wish we could find somewhere else."

"There's nowhere else to eat in Sarajevo, nowhere that's any better, and you know we can't go out at night anyway," Bill reminded him. "Besides, it's difficult driv-ing without any streetlights." Bill stopped, sat back in his chair, suddenly feeling worried about Mike and Joe. They rarely complained about anything; lately they had done nothing but complain to him. He couldn't say he blamed them. Living conditions in Bosnia never improved, only got worse. He thought of the line he had heard when he first came to the Balkans at the outset of the conflict. It had been told to him by a reporter from a French news maga-zine and he had never forgotten it: *A day in Bosnia is like a week anywhere else; a week is like a month, a month is like a year.* And it was true. The country was wearing and wearying. It killed the soul, drained the spirit, and damaged the psyche. He was itching to get out himself, just as Mike and Joe were.

"It's not much of a menu, I'll grant you that," Joe suddenly said, and laughed hollowly. "It's always the same crummy food every night, that's the problem."

"Most people are starving in Bosnia," Bill began and decided not to continue along these lines.

All of a sudden Mike sat up straighter and announced, "Personally, I aim to be in the good old U.S. of A. in November, come hell or high water. I plan to be out on Long Island for Thanksgiving if it's the last thing I ever do. I want to be with my mom and dad, my kid brother and sister. It's been too long since I've seen them. I'm certainly not going to be in this godforsaken place, that's for sure."

"I know what you mean, old buddy," Joe said. "Me . . . I'd like to be in New Jersey for *my* turkey dinner. With my folks. I don't want to spend Thanksgiving in Bosnia either. Screw that!" Joe threw Bill a pointed look, and finished with, "Let's tell Jack Clayton we want out, Billy boy."

"Sure, I'll do it tomorrow. No problem. I'm positive our grateful and adoring news editor will understand your feelings, and Mike's, and mine. He'll tell us to hop a plane to Paris, any plane we can get, and to hell with the expense, and then board the first Concorde out of Paris to New York. Pronto, pronto. Sure, he'll tell us to do that."

"Sarcasm has never been your forte, Bill," Mike remarked with an engaging grin, then went on: "But very seriously, talk to Jack tomorrow. Our rest period is long overdue. Originally, we were supposed to have it in July, then it got shifted to August, and finally it was canceled altogether. We haven't been out of Bosnia, except for a few long weekends in Hungary, for *three months*. I happen to think that we've all reached the end of our individual bits of rope."

"Could be we have. And you're right, Mike, so is Joe. Our R & R has been postponed for too long now. We're all edgy. Look, the peace talks are about to start in Dayton in October. That's only a few days away. Things ought to be relatively quiet here during that period, so I can't see that there would be any problems. Jack'll just have to send in another news team, should anything serious erupt when we're gone."

"There could easily be trouble," Mike remarked in a thoughtful tone. "Just because the peace talks are on doesn't mean that the guns will be silent. Not here. Anything goes."

"Only too true," Joe agreed. "Let's not hold our collective breath on that one."

"I know Jack's a tough news editor, but he is fair. He'll agree to this. Don't forget, *we* elected to stay when the NATO bombs started falling at the end of August. Jack was very appreciative that we did." Bill paused, thought quickly, and made a sudden decision. "Let's plan on getting out of here in a week. How does that sound, guys? Okay with you?"

Mike and Joe stared at him, dumbfounded. Then they grinned and exclaimed in unison, "*Okay!*"

2

Venice, November 1995

The light in the piazza was silvery, the sky leaden, frosty. A faint mist rising from the lagoon and the many canals swathed everything in a veil of gray on this cold winter's afternoon.

Bill Fitzgerald walked slowly across St. Mark's Square, not caring about the weather in the least. There had been too many abortive attempts on his part to get to Venice, and he was glad he had finally made it.

It was a relief to be here after life in the battlefields of Bosnia; also a relief that the tides and the winds were cooperating and Venice was not flooded, as it frequently was at this time of year. Even if it had been, he wouldn't have cared about that either. The Venetians always managed very well when the city lay under water, so why shouldn't he?

He had been coming here whenever possible for the past few years. It was relatively easy to get to Venice from most cities in Europe, which was where he invariably was, on foreign assignment for his network. And even after only a couple of days here he always felt considerably refreshed, lighter in spirit and uplifted.

La Serenissima, the Venetians called it, this city of churches and palaces floating on water, blazing with color and liquid light, brimming with treasures of art and architecture. Bill thought it was one of the most intriguing and evocative places in the world, its aspects bound to delight even the most jaundiced eye.

On his first visit twelve years ago, he had spent a great deal of time in many of those churches and palaces, gazing at the breathtaking paintings by Titian, Tintoretto, Veronese, Tiepolo, and Canaletto. These masterpieces touched his soul with their incomparable beauty and, thereafter, the Venetian school of painting was one of his favorites.

He had always wished he could paint, but he was not in the least gifted in that respect. His only talent was with words.

"He's kissed the Blarney Stone, that one," his maternal grandmother, Bronagh Kelly, used to say when he was growing up. "True," his mother would agree. "That's his gift, a way with words. And he writes like an angel. We must remember that the pen is mightier than the sword."

Bill was an only child. He had spent a lot of time with adults when he was young, and his lovely Irish grandmother, in particular, was a favorite of his. He had been especially attached to her.

When he was little she had held him spellbound with her stories of leprechauns, lucky shamrocks, and pots of gold at the end of the rainbow. Bronagh had left Ireland with her parents and a younger brother when she was eight, and had grown up in Boston. It was here that she had met and married his grandfather, a lawyer named Kevin Kelly.

"I was born in 1905, and what a birth it was, Billy!" she would exclaim. "I came into this world at the stroke of midnight on the twelfth of June in the middle of the most violent thunderstorm," she'd tell him. "And me darlin' mama said it was a bad omen, that storm." She always embellished the details of her birth with every retelling, obviously enjoying his rapt expression and widening eyes. "And indeed it's been a stormy life I've lived ever since, Billy," she would add, with a huge laugh, which led him to believe she had relished her stormy life.

His wife, Sylvie, had loved Grandma Bronagh as much as he had, and the two had become very close over the years. His grandmother had been a true Celt, spiritual, mystical, and a little fey. Sylvie had shared these traits, been very much like her in many ways.

His only regret, whenever he came back to Venice, was that he had not brought Sylvie here before she died. They had put it off and put it off, and suddenly, unexpectedly, it was too late. Sylvie was gone. Who could have known that she would die like that? In childbirth, of all things in this day and age. "Eclampsia" it was called; it began with seizures and ended in coma and death.

Losing Sylvie was the worst thing that ever happened to him. She had been too young to die, only twenty-six. His grief had overwhelmed him; he had been inconsolable for a long time. In the end, he had managed to come to grips with it, throwing himself into work in an effort to keep that grief in check and at bay.

As he went toward the Basilica, his thoughts were still centered on Sylvie. She had died in 1989; the baby, a little girl, had lived. She was called Helena, the name he and Sylvie had chosen. Now six years old, she was the spitting image of her mother, an adorable creature who entranced everyone she met.

Certainly she was a great joy to him. Whenever he felt depressed and disturbed by the rottenness of the world, he had only to conjure up her face and instantly he felt better. She made life worth living, his beautiful child.

A fleeting smile crossed Bill's face, touched his eyes when he thought of her. Because his job as a foreign correspondent took him all over the world, she lived with his mother in New York. Fortunately, he saw her frequently and the time they spent together was genuinely meaningful. She was a good little girl, spirited, intelligent and not too spoiled, although his mother did dote on her only grandchild.

He had just spent two weeks in Manhattan with them, after covering the start of the Bosnia peace talks in Ohio. He would go back again in December, to celebrate Christmas at his mother's apartment in the East Sixties. When he wasn't in the middle of a battlefield or covering a major story in some far-flung corner of the globe, Bill made a point of being with "my best girls," as he called them. There was nowhere else he wanted to be, especially on important occasions and holidays.

But this week in Venice was his time for himself. He needed it badly, needed to put himself back together after his three-month stint in Bosnia-Herzegovina. Bill felt diminished by the conflict he had witnessed in the Balkans, and he was depleted, weary of war, of the destruction and the killing.

He wanted to forget. Not that he ever really would forget any of it. Who could? But he might at least be able to diffuse some of those horrifying images, still so vivid, that had left such a terrible scar on his mind.

His best friend, Francis Peterson, a war correspondent for *Time* magazine, believed that none of the newsmen would ever be able to expunge the violent images of Bosnia. "They're trapped in our minds like flies trapped in amber, there for all time," Frankie kept saying, and Bill agreed with him. All of them had seen too much savagery; its imprint *was* indelible.

Francis and Bill had met at Columbia University's School of Journalism in 1980, and they had been fast friends ever since. They were often covering the same wars, the same stories, but even when they were not, and were in different parts of the world, they stayed in constant touch.

Francis was currently assigned to Beirut, but he would be arriving in Venice in an hour or two, and they would spend a few days together. Later in the week, Frankie would fly to New York to celebrate his father's seventieth birthday.

Bill was glad his old friend was able to join him. They were exceptionally close, shared the same interests and understood each other well, were usually on the same wavelength.

Suddenly Bill realized he was the only person in St. Mark's

Square, alone except for flocks of pigeons. The birds flew around him, soaring up above the Basilica. Usually the square was the center of animation in Venice, teeming with people, mostly tourists from all over the world. Now he was its solitary occupant, and as he glanced about it seemed odd to him, strangely surreal.

As he continued to walk, he became aware for the first time of the unique paving in the piazza. In the past when he had strolled here, there had been hundreds and hundreds of pairs of feet covering it, obviously the reason he had never noticed it before now.

His eyes followed the flow of the pattern: flat gray stones covering most of the square, balanced on either side by narrow white marble bands set in classical motifs. At once he was struck by the way the motifs directed the eye and the feet toward the basilica. No accident, he thought, walking on. When he came to the church, he did not go inside. Instead, he turned right and went down the Piazzetta San Marco, which led to the water's edge.

For a long time Bill stood looking out across the lagoon. Sky and sea merged to become a vast expanse of muted gray, which soon began to take on the look of dull chrome in the lowering afternoon light.

It was so peaceful here it was hard to believe that just across the Adriatic Sea a bloody war still raged. Nothing ever changes really, Bill thought as he turned away from the water at last. The world is the same as it's always been, full of monsters, full of evil. We've learned nothing over the centuries. We're no more civilized now than we were in the Dark Ages. Man's monstrosities boggled his mind.

Hunching deeper into his trench coat, Bill Fitzgerald retraced his steps across the empty square. He began to hurry now as dusk descended, making for the Gritti Palace, where he always stayed. He loved its old-fashioned charm, comfort, and elegance.

The rain started as a drizzle but quickly turned into a steady downpour. Bill, increasing his pace, was almost running as he approached the side street where the front entrance to the Hotel Gritti Palace was located.

He sprinted around the corner of the street at a breakneck pace and collided with another person also moving swiftly. It was a woman. As her large-brimmed cream felt hat and her umbrella went sailing into the air, he reached out and grabbed hold of her shoulders to prevent her from falling.

Steadying himself, and her, he exclaimed, "Excuse me! I'm so sorry," and found himself staring into a pair of startled silvery-gray eyes. In Italian, he added, "*Scusa! Scusa!*"

She responded in English. "It's all right, honestly," and disentangling herself from his tight grip she ran after her hat, which was blowing down the street.

He followed her, outran her, caught the hat, picked up the umbrella wedged against the gutter, and brought them both back to her. "I apologize again," he said.

Nodding, she took the hat and the umbrella from him. "I'm fine, really." She glanced at the hat. "And this isn't any the worse for wear either." She shook it and grimaced. "Just a *bit* splattered with mud. Oh well, never mind. Who cares? It was never my favorite hat anyway."

"I'm a clumsy fool, barreling around the corner like that. It wasn't very smart of me. Are you sure you're all right?" he asked in concern, unexpectedly loathe to let her go.

She proffered him a faint smile, slapped the hat on top of her dark curls, and sidled away from him, saying, "Thanks again."

He stood rooted to the spot as if paralyzed, watching her walk off when he wanted desperately to detain her, to talk to her, even invite her for a drink. He opened his mouth. No words came out. Seemingly, he had lost his voice, not to mention his nerve.

Suddenly he galvanized himself. Almost running up the street after her, he shouted, "Can I buy you a new hat?"

Without pausing, she called over her shoulder, "It's not necessary, thanks for offering, though."

"It's the least I can do," he cried. "I've ruined that one."

She stopped for a moment and shook her head. "No, really, the hat doesn't matter. 'Bye."

"Please slow down. I'd like to talk to you."

"Sorry, I can't. I'm late." She glided on, swung around the corner.

Bill hurried after her.

It was then that he saw the man coming toward her, waving and smiling broadly.

The woman increased her pace, waving back and exclaiming in Italian, "Giovanni, *come sta?*"

A moment later she was holding her umbrella high over her head so that the man she had called Giovanni could properly embrace her.

Disappointment surged through him. Immediately, Bill turned away, rounded the corner, and went down the street toward the Gritti Palace. He could not help wondering who she was. Certainly she was the most stunning woman he'd seen in a long time. Those luminous silver eyes set in a pale, piquant face, the head of tumbling dark curls, the elegant way she carried herself. She was beautiful, really, in a gamine sort of way. It was just his luck that she was apparently already spoken for. He would have liked to get to know her better.

3

They met in the bar of the legendary Gritti Palace, which faced the Grand Canal.

"It's great to see you, Francis Xavier!" Bill exclaimed, "Just great that you could make it." He enveloped his best friend in a bear hug.

As they drew apart after their rough, masculine embrace, Frank said, "And likewise, William Patrick. It's been too long this time around. I've missed you."

"So have I—missed you."

Still grinning at each other, they both ordered single malt scotch from the hovering waiter and sat down at a small table near the window.

"A lot of wars have been getting in the way," Frank went on, "and we seem to have been covering different ones of late."

"More's the pity we haven't seen the same action."

They exchanged knowing looks for a long moment, remembering the tough situations they had encountered together and had shared. Genuinely close since journalism school, the two men, who were not only friends but colleagues, understood each other on a very fundamental level. And each worried about the other's well-being. They had a great deal in common, always had had—a love of truth and the need to find it, traits which made them superlative newsmen; diligence, honesty, and a zest for adventure. Yet, despite the latter, both were cautious, fully aware of the dangers involved in their work. Whether together or alone on assignments, they always endeavored to minimize the risks they took in order to get the story.

Their drinks arrived, and after they'd clinked glasses, Frank said, "There's no way I'll go back to Bosnia, Bill."

"I know. And I don't blame you. I've sort of had it myself. How is it in Beirut?"

"Fairly quiet. At the moment, anyway. Things are improving, getting more normal, relatively speaking, of course. I don't think it will ever be the Paris of the Middle East again, but the city's perking up. Good shops are opening, and the big hotels are functioning on a more efficient basis."

"Hezbollah's still lurking, though."

"You bet! We have to live with the threat of terrorism around the clock. But *you* know that." Frank lifted his broad shoulders in a light shrug, his dark eyes narrowing. "Terrorism is more prevalent than ever. Everywhere in the world. The bastards are all over the place."

Bill nodded, took a sip of his drink, and leaned back in the chair, enjoying being with Francis Peterson.

Frank said, with a wide smile, "Let's change the subject, get to something more worthwhile. How's my little Helena?"

"Not so little, she's grown a tad. Which reminds me . . ." As he spoke Bill pulled out his wallet, removed a photograph, and handed it to Frank. "Your goddaughter wanted you to have this. She sends you hugs and kisses."

Frank stared at the picture Bill had just handed him. He smiled. "She's the most adorable kid, Billy, you're so lucky. I see she's still got that Botticelli look about her . . . positively angelic."

"To look at, yes, but she's mischievous, a bit of a scamp, my mother says." Bill grinned. "But then who wants a perfect kid?"

"A perfect kid, if there is such a thing, would be insufferable. How's Dru?" he asked, putting the photograph in his own wallet.

"Pretty good, thanks. You know my mother, Frankie, full of piss and vinegar and energy, and as loving of heart as she ever was. She sends you her love, by the way."

"When you speak to her, give her mine. Better still, I'll call her myself when I get to Manhattan, to say hello. Incidentally, I'm sorry I couldn't get home when you were there. I had a really tough deadline for my piece on Lebanon. There was just no way I could take off at that time."

"I understood."

Frank went on, "I gather you weren't particularly impressed with the peace talks in Dayton."

Bill shook his head. "I wasn't. The Serbs are a diabolical bunch. Gangsters. They're never going to agree to a proper and *fair* peace treaty with the Bosnians, you'll see. As for all this UN talk about prosecuting some of the Serbs as war criminals, you can forget it. I assure you it will never happen. They're never going to get those butchers to the Hague to stand trial, for one thing. Just take my word for it. The Serbs are going to get away with their crimes."

"Tragic though it is, you're probably right, Bill."

"It's just wishful thinking on the part of the UN."

"I agree."

A small silence fell between them.

The two men sipped their drinks quietly, lost for a moment in their own thoughts.

They were a good-looking pair, both of them clean-cut and collegiate in their appearance. Any casual observer would have known immediately that they were Americans.

Frank was as dark as Bill was fair. He prided himself on being third-generation Irish-American, and Black Irish at that. He had a shock of dark hair, black eyes, and a fresh complexion.

Like Bill, he was thirty-three, and currently single. His marriage to a television foreign correspondent, Pat Rackwell, one of the rising stars of her network, had foundered on the rocks of her career four years ago.

Fortunately they had had no children, and the divorce had been amicable enough. Whenever they ran into each other on a story, they pooled their information, their resources, and tried to be helpful whenever they could. Very frequently they had dinner together when they were in the same foreign city.

Breaking the silence, Bill said, "I heard a nasty comment about us the other day."

"Back in New York?"

"Yes."

"What was it?"

"That we're war junkies, you and I. That we love danger, love being in the thick of it, and that that's what gives us our jollies. We're characterized as being extremely reckless. A bad example."

Frank threw back his head and roared. "Who cares what people think! I bet it was one of your competitors at another network who made *those* lousy comments."

"As a matter of fact, it wasn't. It was one of the guys at CNS."

"Aha! He wants your job, William!"

"Yeah, he probably does." Bill hesitated for a second, then gave Frank a piercing look. "Do you think the odds *are* against us? That we will get killed one day, when we're covering a war in some godforsaken place?"

Frank was reflective. After a second he murmured, "So many journalists have lost their lives . . ." He let his voice trail off; his expression remained thoughtful.

"But we won't lose ours. I just feel it in my bones!" Bill asserted, his voice positive all of a sudden.

"You're absolutely right, it's just not in the cards. Anyway, you're bulletproof."

Bill chuckled.

"Furthermore, you're my lucky charm."

Bill cut in swiftly, saying, "Except that I'm not always with you these days, Frankie."

"True enough, just wish you were. We've had some experiences in the past, shared some highs and lows, haven't we? Remember the Panama Invasion?"

"How could I forget it? December of 1989. Sylvie had only been dead a few months, and I was so grief-stricken I didn't care what happened to me, didn't give a damn whether I lived or died."

"But you did care about me," Frank said in a low voice, staring at his friend with sudden intensity. "I wouldn't be sitting here tonight if it hadn't been for you, Bill, you saved my life."

"You'd have done the same for me."

"Of course I would! But don't ever forget that I've always been very grateful."

"And so has the female population of . . . whatever city you're living in at the moment."

Frank grinned at his friend, said facetiously, "Aw shucks, Billy, don't start that again. I'm not the only newsman who likes a bit of female company occasionally. And what about you? You're not so shy with the girls either."

"There haven't been many women around lately, I'm afraid, not where I've been."

Frank nodded. "Sarajevo's hardly the place for a romantic interlude."

Bill confided, "Heard another thing in New York, Francis Xavier."

"Oh, yeah, and what's that? It obviously has something to do with me, from the tone of your voice."

"Sure does. Rumor has it you're suffering from a terminal Don Juan complex."

Frankie chuckled and went on chuckling. He was highly amused.

Bill smiled, feeling comfortable, relaxed, and more at ease with himself than he had been for a long time. He knew that with Frank in Venice, for a few days he would be able to shake his depression, dispel the horrific images of war, and recharge his batteries completely.

Now Bill motioned to the waiter, ordered two more drinks, and said, "It's not such a bad reputation to have, when you think about it. After all no man can be a Don Juan unless women are interested in him."

"Only too true. As they say, it takes two to tango. By the way, I ran into Elsa in Beirut a few weeks ago."

"Elsa?" Bill frowned, looking puzzled.

"Don't tell me you've forgotten Elsa Mastrelli, our guardian angel from Baghdad."

"*That* Elsa! Oh, my God, how is she?"

"The same. Still covering wars for her Italian news magazine, still playing Florence Nightingale, ministering angel, and earth mother all rolled into one. At least, so I've been told."

"She was really great. Is she still as attractive?"

"Yes. Well, slight correction necessary here. Elsa has matured, looks more interesting, more experienced, even a bit war-weary, tired. But yes, she's still a knockout, a good-looking woman with a lot of savoir faire. In other words, she's grown up. We had a quick drink at the Commodore and reminisced about Baghdad."

"That was one hell of a time in our lives, Frankie!" Bill exclaimed animatedly. "My God, I'll never forget it . . . January of 1991. Only four years ago, but it seems so much longer, don't you think?"

"It sure does. We took some real chances, Billy, in those days."

"We were only twenty-nine. And very daring."

"Also very stupid, if you ask me." Frank threw Bill a pointed look. "No story's worth dying for."

"No, it isn't. But we didn't even think about dying, let's face it. And our Baghdad coverage made both our careers. Weren't we lucky that CNS was the only television network allowed to stay on in Baghdad? And that you and Elsa were the only print journalists given permission to stay on with us to cover the Gulf War?"

"All thanks to you and that enterprising producer of yours, Blain Lovett. What happened to him, is he still with CNS?"

"No, he went to NBC, then moved over to CBS. He's still there, doing very well, but no longer going out on foreign assignments. By choice, I guess."

"He was great, the way he networked. What a wheeler-dealer he was."

Bill grinned, remembering his former producer. "He had his act down pat, making his important contacts before the war started. Long before. And the Iraqis loved his schmoozing. He charmed a lot of them well before the conflict began and so they favored him. And we were home free when holy hell finally did break loose."

"I'll never forget the day he told you that our Iraqi minders were letting CNS bring in all that television equipment from Jordan," Frank said. "Including that satellite phone. I, for one, was flabbergasted."

"So was I, Frankie, and where would we have been without it? That phone was our only link to the outside world, and CNS was the only network getting coverage out for the world to hear and see."

"It did wonders for CNS, pushed them to the top of the pile in live news coverage in particular. And actually, Billy, we were fortunate to come out of that debacle alive, all things considered, and all those direct hits the hotel took. And there was Elsa, what a terrific little trooper she was . . . "

Frank paused as he realized that he had lost Bill's attention. "What's wrong?" he asked.

"Nothing."

"Something's wrong. You're not listening to me. And you have the strangest expression on your face."

Bill turned to Frank. "I don't want you to look now, but it's that woman over there. At the other side of the bar. Did you see her come in?"

"How could I fail to miss her? She's the only other person here except us. So, what about her?"

"I almost knocked her over earlier today. Collided with her this afternoon as I barreled around the corner, on my way back to the hotel. I chased her hat."

"*Chased her hat?*"

"Oh never mind, and don't look at me like that."

"Like what?"

"As if I'm nutty."

"Well, you are a bit crazy, Billy, and so am I, thank God. Life's too damned hard not to be slightly crazy from time to time. How else are we going to deal with all the stress and tension? Anyway, what about this woman?"

"I was very taken with her this afternoon. I wanted to get to know her better."

"I can't say I blame you. She's interesting-looking. Is she Italian?"

"I don't think so, even though she looks as if she might be. I'm pretty sure she's an American, certainly she sounds it. Anyway, her hat flew off as we collided, so I ran after it. I also ran after her as she thanked me and walked off. I wanted to invite her to have a drink with me. It's funny, Frankie, but I didn't want her to go."

"Why didn't you ask her to have a drink?"

"I tried to, but she was hurrying, almost running. I was right behind her, and so naturally I saw her with the man she was meeting. Just my luck that she's involved with someone. For all I know he might even have been her husband. I watched them embrace. Still, I must admit I've thought about her for the past few hours, off and on."

"There's only one thing to do."

"What's that?"

"Go over and invite her to have a drink with us," Frank suggested. "You'll get the lay of the land pretty quickly."

"I guess you're right." As he spoke, Bill pushed himself to his feet and strode across the bar, walking in a direct line toward the young woman.

She looked up from a notebook she was holding and smiled when she saw him. "Hi!" she said, sounding friendly.

"Since you wouldn't let me buy you a new hat, could I at least buy you a drink?" Bill began. "My friend and I would love you to join us for . . . drinks *and* dinner."

"That's really nice of you both, but I can't. I'm waiting for a friend. I have a previous engagement," she explained.

Bill looked crestfallen. "Just my luck, er, er, our luck. Well . . ." His voice trailed off and he half turned to go, and then he swung around to face her again. "You're an American, aren't you?"

"Yes, I am. From New York."

"So am I."

"I know."

"My name's Bill—"

"Fitzgerald," she supplied, eyeing him, looking suddenly amused. "I know who you are; in fact, I watch your newscasts all the time, Mr. Fitzgerald."

"Call me Bill."

"All right."

"And you are?"

"Vanessa Stewart." She thrust out her hand.

Leaning forward, Bill took hold of it, and shook it. He discovered he did not want to let it go. "I have a great idea," he said and finally released her hand.

"You do?" She raised a dark brow and her large silver-gray eyes were quizzical as they focused on him intently.

Bracing his hands against the back of the chair and leaning forward, drawing closer to her, Bill said, "We must be the only three Americans in Venice at the moment, so we *must* spend tomorrow together."

"*Tomorrow?*" Her brows drew together. "Why tomorrow?"

"It's Thanksgiving."

"Oh, my God, I'd forgotten."

"Well, it is. Thursday, November the twenty-third. And it would be a crime if the only three Yanks in Venice didn't celebrate this most American of all holidays together. Join me and my friend, Francis Peterson of *Time*. Come on, what do you say?"

"Very well, I'll join you, but only on one condition."

"What's the condition? Shoot."

"That we have a proper Thanksgiving dinner with turkey and all the traditional trimmings."

Bill's face lit up in the most engaging way, and he grinned boyishly. "You've got a deal!" he declared.

She smiled up at him. "Then I'll be happy to come, thank you very much. Shall we meet here in the bar?"

"Good idea. Champagne first, and then on to our turkey dinner with all the trimmings. What time?"

"Seven. Is that all right?"

"Perfect." From the corner of his eye Bill saw the Italian, Giovanni, entering the bar. He inclined his head and politely took his leave. Moving away from her table swiftly, he retraced his steps across the room.

Frank had been watching Bill alertly, and now he said, "What happened?"

"She can't join us tonight. For obvious reasons. The Italian is on the scene again."

"Is that him over there now? The guy she met this afternoon?"

"Yes. Giovanni. However, she has agreed to have dinner with us tomorrow night."

Frank looked impressed. "That *is* an accomplishment, old buddy. How did you do it?"

"I reminded her that it's Thanksgiving, pointed out that we were more than likely the only three Americans in Venice, and added that it would be a crime if we didn't celebrate the holiday together."

"And she agreed?"

"On one condition."

"And what's that?"

"A turkey dinner. She wants a traditional Thanksgiving meal with all the usual trimmings."

"You didn't promise it, did you?"

"Sure I did. Why are you looking skeptical, Francis?"

"Where the hell do you think you're going to find a turkey? In Venice, of all places, for God's sake! This is pasta land, Billy."

"I know, and don't worry. Just trust me."

"But Bill, a *turkey*—"

"Did I ever let you down in Baghdad? Who's the one who always managed to find the most delectable stuff in that war-torn city . . . from Johnnie Walker to cans of corned beef."

"Well, you were pretty good," Frank admitted, grinning.

"I know what I'm doing," Bill remarked. "I booked us a table at Harry's Bar tonight. And we'll go there again tomorrow. Everyone from Arrigo Cipriani, the owner, and the maître d' to the youngest busboy knows me well. Please believe me, Harry's Bar will make us a real American Thanksgiving dinner. They'll get a turkey, no matter what. After all, the mainland's not far away."

"I know better than to argue with *you*, Billy. And what's the lady's name?"

"Vanessa Stewart. She's from New York. She knew who I was."

Frank threw him an amused look. "Good God, don't sound so surprised, Bill. The whole of America knows who you are. Your face is in their living rooms every day of the week."

4

"Do you think she's stood us up?" Frank said the following evening. He and Bill were sitting in the bar of the Gritti Palace, waiting for Vanessa Stewart to arrive. He glanced at his watch. "It's twenty past seven."

"Stood *us* up! *Never*," Bill answered in a jocular tone, with a quick laugh. "Two dashing war correspondents like us. Good Lord, Frankie, don't you know by now that we're irresistible?"

When Frank merely threw him a sharp look and made an exasperated noise, Bill added in a more sober tone, "But seriously, I don't think she's the type to do that."

"What makes you so sure?"

"I just am, trust me on this," Bill replied firmly. "I thought she seemed like a serious person yesterday, and although we spoke only briefly, I detected something in her, an air of breeding. I know she would have phoned us here by now if she weren't coming, to make some sort of polite excuse. I sensed that she was not flaky, not the flighty kind at all."

"If you say so. And I guess it's a woman's prerogative to be late," Frank responded. Then he and Bill exchanged swift looks and promptly sprang to their feet as Vanessa Stewart appeared in the doorway of the bar. She hurried in, gliding forward at a rapid pace.

The young woman, who was of medium height and slender, wore a burgundy-colored outfit made of crushed velvet and carried a matching wool coat. The narrow velvet pants were paired with a loose, tunic top, which, with its square neckline and long sleeves cut wide at the cuffs, had a medieval look about it. Strands of amethyst-and-ruby-colored glass beads were twisted into a choker around her neck, and small gold medallions gleamed at her ears.

Both men wore admiring expressions as she drew to a standstill in front of them, a look of concern on her face.

"Sorry I'm so late," she said in an apologetic voice, shaking her head. "So rude of me, but it was unavoidable. I was delayed at a meeting this afternoon. When I got back to the hotel it was late and I had to change. I didn't want to lose any more time by calling you in the bar. I thought it best just to dress and hurry down."

"Are you staying here?" Frank said.

"Yes, I am."

"It's not a problem," Bill exclaimed, wanting to put her at ease. Smiling warmly, he went on, "Vanessa, I'd like to introduce you to my friend Francis Peterson of *Time* magazine. And Frankie, this is Vanessa Stewart."

"It's very nice to meet you," Vanessa said, shaking Frank's outstretched hand.

"And I you," the journalist answered, offering her a welcoming smile, thinking how personable she was and how attractive, in an offbeat way. Bill had described her to him as being gamine, and it was true, she did have a roguish, saucy kind of charm. With her huge gray eyes in that small, piquant face and her short, curly, dark hair she looked very young and vulnerable. She reminded him of someone, someone he couldn't quite place.

Vanessa put her coat on a chair and sat down.

Bill said, "Would you like a glass of champagne or do you prefer something else?"

"Oh, champagne's lovely, thank you." She settled back in the chair and crossed her long legs.

Champagne was poured, and after they had all clinked glasses Bill said, with unconcealed curiosity, "You mentioned you were delayed in a meeting. So are you here on business?"

"Yes, I am." Vanessa cleared her throat, and went on, "I'm a designer. Of glass. I get most of it blown here. On Murano, to be exact. So I'm coming and going all the time."

"Are you a New Yorker?" Frank asked.

"Yes. I was born there."

"Do you live in Manhattan?"

She nodded. "In the East Fifties."

"Good old New York," Frank murmured. "There's nowhere else like it in the whole world."

Bill said, "What kind of glass do you design?"

"Vases, fancy bottles, big plaques and plates, decorative objects mostly, things to put on display. But I also make jewelry, like these beads." She touched the choker on her neck and explained, "But mostly I create objects for the home. Last year Neiman Marcus launched a line of mine, which I designed exclusively for them, and it's been a big success. That's why I'm here right now, to supervise the new collection."

"Oh, so it's currently being made, is it?" Bill said.

"Yes, at one of the oldest glass foundries on Murano. There's nothing like Venetian glass, in my opinion anyway. I think it's the best in the world."

"Where did you study in the States?" Frank probed.

"The Rhode Island School of Design, but also here in Venice. I did a graduate course for a year."

"So you lived in Venice!" Bill exclaimed. "How I envy you. I love this city."

"So do I." Vanessa's face took on a glow; she smiled at him. "La Serenissima ... the Serene Republic, and it's so aptly named, isn't it? I always feel truly content here, peaceful, yet very alive. Venice is a state of being, I think."

Bill looked at her closely. He knew exactly what she meant about Venice. Struck by her openness, he nodded, returned her smile, and found himself staring into her luminous gray eyes. He averted his face, picked up his drink, and took a quick swallow. He felt suddenly self-conscious of his awareness of her, of his sexual attraction to her.

Frank, conscious of Bill's sudden discomfort, said, "And tell me, Vanessa, where do you normally spend Thanksgiving?"

"With my mother, if we happen to be in the same place. And sometimes with my father, if Mom's away. It depends on the circumstances."

"You make it sound as if your mother travels a lot," Frank remarked, raising a brow questioningly.

"She does."

"For pleasure or business?" he asked, still probing.

"Her work."

"And what does your mother do?"

"She's an actress."

"In the theater?"

Bill sipped his champagne, leaning back in the chair, listening, thinking that Frankie was asking too many questions. But at the same time he wanted to hear her answers. She intrigued him in a way no woman had for the longest time.

"Oh, yes, my mother works in the theater, and in films," Vanessa said.

"Would we know her?" Bill leaned forward, focused his attention on her.

Vanessa laughed. "I think so. My mother is Valentina Maddox."

"Is she really!" Bill cried. "Well, now that I know who she is I must admit you have the look of her, a very strong resemblance, in fact."

Frank said, "And Audrey Hepburn many years ago, when she was in *Sabrina*. That's who you reminded *me* of when you first walked in. Hasn't anybody ever told you that you look like her?"

Vanessa was still laughing. She nodded.

Frank now asked, "Aren't your parents divorced?"

"Yes. But they're still friends, and they see each other from time to time. They both live in New York. Well, Dad does. My mother's really a gypsy, flitting around the world, going wherever her work takes her."

"Do you have any brothers or sisters?" Bill inquired.

"No." Vanessa sat up straighter and looked from Bill to Frank, then began to laugh again. "What a lot of questions you both ask!"

"We're journalists. It's our job to ask questions," Frank replied.

They walked to the Calle Vallaresso, just off San Marco, where Harry's Bar was located.

It was a cold night. Frost hung in the air and ringed the moon, a clear silver sphere in an ink-dark sky. Cloudless and clear, it was littered with a thousand tiny pinpoints of brilliant light.

The streets were relatively deserted. Only a few people were about. As the three of them walked along, they could hear the clatter of their own shoes on the cobblestones.

"Hollywood couldn't have done it better," Bill remarked at one moment, glancing at the sky. "Hung that moon up there like that. What a fantastic film set Venice is, actually."

Vanessa exclaimed, "That's what my mother used to say when she came to visit me! She has always thought Venice to be the most theatrical of places in the whole world."

"She's right," Bill said, taking hold of Vanessa's arm, guiding her as they went down the narrower streets in the direction of the famous restaurant. He loved the closeness of her, the scent of her perfume. It was light, floral. Enticing. Just as she herself was enticing. He was very drawn to her, just as he had been yesterday, but tonight the feeling was more powerful.

They walked on in silence for a few seconds until Bill said, "I suppose you know all about Harry's Bar."

"Not really," she responded. "I went there with my parents, but only once. Didn't Ernest Hemingway make it his hangout?"

"He did, yes, along with a lot of other writers and journalists and celebrities. It was founded in the nineteen thirties, when an American, Harry Pickering, the now famous Harry, borrowed money from a hotel barman. The bartender was Giuseppe Cipriani, and when Harry paid him back he gave him additional money to open a bar. And *voila*! The restaurant was born."

"I love stories like that," Vanessa said, and then shivered slightly, drew further into her coat.

"Are you cold?" Bill asked solicitously.

"No, no, I'm fine."

Frank, who had been silent during the walk to the restaurant, announced, "There's Harry's Bar, straight ahead. We'll be inside in a minute."

They were given a royal welcome when they walked into Harry's Bar. Once they had shed their coats, they were escorted to one of the best tables at the back of the room. "Welcome, Signore Fitzgerald," Arrigo Cipriani said. "And 'appy Thanksgiving."

"Thanks, Arrigo. Now, how about some Bellinis to celebrate the holiday?"

"Good idea," Frank said.

"That'd be lovely," Vanessa agreed, and once they were alone she turned to Bill, and said, "I've forgotten what a Bellini is. I mean, I know it's champagne but what's in it besides that?"

"Fresh peach juice."

"Now I remember! They're fabulous."

A great deal of camaraderie had developed between them in the short time they had known each other. Vanessa had taken their probing questions at face value, had not been offended, and they in turn had been struck by her attitude, realizing what a good sport she was. And so the gaiety and banter continued at Harry's, only to be interrupted when a waiter arrived at their table, presenting the menus with a flourish.

"I ordered a special main course for us all last night," Bill explained.

"Si, Signore Fitzgerald, I know. But you didn't order a first course."

"True, I didn't. What do you suggest?"

"What about *risi e bisi*, I know you like it." Looking at Vanessa and then at Frank, the waiter continued, "It's a wonderful risotto. Mmm." He kissed his fingertips. "Rice with peas, ham, and Parmesan cheese. Delicious."

"Sounds good enough to eat," Frank joked.

Bill grinned at Vanessa. "It is good. I think I'll have it. How about you?"

"All right. Thank you."

"We'll all have it," Frank added. "And let's take a look at the wine list, please, Antonio."

"Si, Signore Peterson." The waiter nodded and departed.

Vanessa pushed back her chair and said, "Excuse me for a moment," and left the table, heading for the ladies' room.

Bill leaned over and said to Frank, "So, what do you think of her?"

"She's lovely, and you were right, she's not a bit flaky. In fact, I think she's a very nice young woman, one who's rather serious by nature."

Bill said, "I like her."

"It's more than *like*, Bill, that's too soft a word."

"What do you mean?"

"You're bowled over by her, and you're going to get involved with her. She with you."

"I'm not so sure."

"About yourself? Or her?"

"Both of us."

Frank smiled broadly, and a knowing glint entered his black Irish eyes. "Oh Bill, my boy, take my word for it, you are heading for the big one here. She's irresistible to you, has all the things you love in a woman. As for her, she can't take her eyes off you. She's intrigued, flattered by your interest in her, and she hangs onto every word you say."

"I think you exaggerate."

"Trust me, I don't. I've got eyes in my head, and I've been watching you both for almost two hours now. You're both trying to hide it, but you're falling for each other."

"I wonder who that Italian is? Giovanni?" Bill muttered.

"We can't very well ask her. Anyway, she's not wearing any rings, at least not a wedding ring, only that crested signet on her little finger."

"But that doesn't mean anything these days. And she does spend a lot of time here, she said so."

"That doesn't mean anything either, Billy. I'm telling you, that young woman —" Frank stopped as Vanessa glided up to the table.

The two men rose, and Bill helped Vanessa into her chair.

Once she was seated, she smiled across at him, and said, "You reminded the waiter you'd ordered a main course last night. Not a turkey?"

"Of course it's a turkey. I ordered a traditional Thanksgiving dinner for us, and fortunately they were able to oblige. After all, that was your condition, Vanessa."

She stared at him for a long moment, and shook her head slowly. Her eyes twinkled mischievously when she finally murmured, "But I was only teasing. I never thought for one moment that you'd find a turkey in Venice . . . "

Bill stared at her.

Vanessa's touch was featherlight as she rested her hand on his arm. "You see, I *wanted* to spend Thanksgiving with you . . . with or without a turkey."

5

What Francis Peterson had predicted finally came to be.

Bill and Vanessa fell in love.

As Bill said much later, they probably did so on Thanksgiving night at Harry's Bar, although it took them several days to acknowledge their feelings.

During the Thanksgiving weekend they got to know each other better. In fact, they were a threesome, since they spent Friday and Saturday with Frank.

For these two days Vanessa became their guide, showing them places in Venice that not even Bill, the Venice aficionado, knew about. These were small, unique art galleries, museums and churches off the beaten track, bars and cafés known only to the Venetians themselves, shops where the best bargains were to be had.

At Bill's insistence, she took them out to Murano, where she did much of her work. They went to the island by *vaporetto*, a water taxi that took only seven minutes to get there.

Bill and Frank both wanted to see her designs, and so they visited the ancient glass foundry where her glass pieces were handblown. Both men were impressed by her stunning designs, her talent and creativity, and they realized she was a true artist.

That evening, at her request, they escorted her to a cocktail party given by an old friend of hers from her student days, who owned a palazzo on the Grand Canal situated diagonally across from the Gritti Palace. They needed a gondola to get there.

The two newsmen found the slightly ramshackle palace an amazing place, and were fascinated by its many treasures. Carlo Metzanno, their host, was an interior designer, and he had given the massive, centuries-old palace a great deal of style and elegance. As he showed them around, he explained the provenance of many of the art objects, paintings, and antiques. Prominently displayed were several extraordinary pieces by Vanessa. These were fluid, sinuous, and impressive.

The three of them stayed at the cocktail party for an hour, mixing with a colorful group of people including a couple of local artists, a famous French movie star, a playwright from London, and an American architect.

When they left the palazzo, the same gondola that they had hired for the evening took them to the Giudecca, the narrow sliver of an island across the Canale della Giudecca. Vanessa had invited them to dinner, and she had booked a table at Harry's Dolci, the charming and intimate "little sister" of Harry's Bar. After their meal they strolled over to the Hotel Cipriani for espressos and stregas before going back to Venice in the gondola. "We've become the three musketeers," Frank said as they took their seats, settling back to enjoy the ride to the Gritti Palace. "We're now old pals." Bill and Vanessa laughed, and Bill said, "I think that's swell."

Bill had planned what he termed "an adventure" for Saturday night. Once again, a gondola was hired for the evening, and this carried them down the narrow winding backwaters of Venice until they arrived at an old house that looked like a hole in the wall. It turned out to be a marvelous family restaurant, one Bill knew well, which was a popular eating place favored by Venetians in the know.

It was a gay evening filled with bonhommie. They laughed and joked, exchanging a lot of amusing banter. A considerable amount of genuine affection flowed between them. The two men had grown quite close to Vanessa, and she to them.

"Here's a toast, then," Frank said as the dinner drew to a close. "To dear friends—old and *new*." He clinked his glass of red wine to Bill's glass and then Vanessa's. Smiling at her genially, he added, "You're a good sport, kid, the way you've put up with us. Especially *me*, with all my questions. I've enjoyed being with you for the last couple of days. You've been like . . . a breath of fresh air."

Vanessa colored slightly, the flush rising from her neck to touch her face. Frank had teased her a lot, and now she was touched by his compliments, his unexpected courtliness.

"What a nice thing to say, Frank, thanks, and I've enjoyed *your* company."

"I'm going to miss you both," Frank went on, looking from Vanessa to Bill. "Most especially you, William Patrick. Battle-fields are not the same without you."

"I know," Bill replied, his eyes focused on his best friend. "I'll miss you, too, but who knows, we may well be covering the same story in the next few months."

"Could be," Frank said. "I hope so."

As they left the restaurant a short while later, Vanessa shivered and moved nearer to Bill, who put his arm around her protectively and drew her close against him.

Venice in winter, and especially in the evening, was mysterious, even frightening. The gondola glided down many dark waterways, heading for the Gritti Palace. Mist rose up from the murky canals, and there was no noise except for the slap of the oars as they hit the water. Everything was shadowy, eerie in the dim light.

On either side of the narrow waterways, buildings loomed up like strange inchoate monsters under the threatening sky. At times the mist was more like fog, thick and almost impenetrable. The dampness clung to them, seemed to penetrate their clothes.

The three friends stayed huddled in the gondola, shivering, fighting the cold, talking quietly until they reached the hotel.

"I'm glad we're back," Vanessa said with another shiver as Bill helped her to alight at the small dock in front of the Gritti Palace. "There are times when Venice at night frightens me, fills me with foreboding—" She cut herself off, feeling suddenly foolish. After all, she had two men to protect her, not to mention the muscular gondolier who looked like a prizefighter.

Since they each had their rooms on different floors, they said good night in the lobby.

Frank, who was leaving the following morning for Milan and then a direct flight to New York, kissed Vanessa on both cheeks. He gave Bill one of their customary bear hugs.

"See you, William," he said nonchalantly, walking to the elevator. Suddenly, he paused, turned around, and looked at them both for a split second, the expression on his face unexpectedly serious.

"Take care of each other," he said and disappeared behind the sliding doors of the elevator.

Bill and Vanessa remained standing in the lobby, staring at each other.

Vanessa's eyes were full of questions as she murmured, "What an odd thing for him to say—" She stopped, her gaze still riveted on Bill.

"Not really," Bill answered quickly. Then, after the merest hesitation, he went on, "You see, he knows how I feel about you."

"How is that?"

"I'm very . . . *drawn* to you, Vanessa."

She was staring up at him; she nodded. "I guess he knows I feel the same way."

"You do?"

"Oh, yes, Bill."

Bill inclined his head slightly. "So, Frankie *was* right. He sensed it from the beginning. He was quite positive he knew exactly how we *both* were feeling."

"He's very astute." She spoke in the softest of voices.

"He is. Do you want a nightcap? Or something hot, maybe? Hot lemon tea?"

"Not here, though," Vanessa said.

"Your room or mine?"

"Oh yours, please," Vanessa answered with a small, shy smile. "You have a suite, mine is nothing so grand."

Putting an arm around her shoulder, Bill led her to the other elevator at the far end of the lobby. The minute the door closed, he did what he had been wanting to do for the past three days. He took her in his arms and kissed her.

Vanessa kissed him back, and with such intensity he was momentarily startled. When the elevator came to a halt, they quickly pulled apart. As they stepped out, he noticed her flushed face. She was usually so pale.

Drawing a finger down one side of her cheek, he leaned into her and whispered, "You're burning up. Hot to the touch."

She looked at him swiftly but said nothing.

With their arms wrapped around each other, they walked along the corridor to his suite. After letting them in, Bill closed the door with his foot. Shooting the bolt with one hand, he pulled her into his arms with the other. Once more they clung together, kissing with growing fervor.

Suddenly Bill held her away from him and said, "Let's take off our coats." So saying, he helped her out of hers, struggled to shrug off his trench coat, and threw both on a nearby chair.

Silently Bill took hold of her hand tightly, led her into the adjoining bedroom and over to the bed. Vanessa seated herself on the edge of it, all the time watching him as he bent down and took off her shoes, first one and then the other.

After kissing each foot, he slid his hand under her wide, flared skirt, stroking her leg, moving up until his fingers caressed her inner thigh.

"Bill?"

"Yes?"

"Let's get undressed."

A half smile touched his mouth. With swiftness he rose, took her hands in his and pulled her to her feet, so that they were facing each other. Vanessa moved closer, placed her arms around his neck, kissed him on the mouth passionately. As she did so, he reached behind her and unzipped her wool skirt.

The skirt fell to the floor, lay in a swirl of purple at her feet. She stepped away from it, then swung back to him, her eyes focused on him with intensity.

Bill looked at her closely. What he saw surprised and pleased him. Her face was flushed, full of desire, and her silvery eyes brimmed with longing. For him.

Roughly Bill pulled her to him, bent his face to hers, and kissed her deeply. He slid his tongue into her mouth, let it graze hers, and she did the same, exciting him more than ever with her fervor and unabashed desire. He felt the blood rush to his face; he was aroused as he had not been aroused for years. He wanted her so much, had wanted her for days, and now he felt as though he would explode. He had an enormous erection. He pressed himself against her; she bent to his will, letting her whole body flow against his.

Leaning away from her slightly, he looked down at her breast, touched it gently. How taut it was under the thin silk blouse. Fumbling, he undid the first few buttons, put his hand inside her blouse. He kissed her breast, then sucked on the hardening nipple.

"Please, let's lie down, Bill."

Clinging to each other they staggered to the bed. She began to take off her blouse, but he stopped her.

"Let me do it," he said in a low voice. "I want to undress you. Please, darling."

She nodded. Her eyes never left his face as he opened her blouse. After slipping it over her shoulders, he began to kiss her neck, her arms, and brought his mouth back to her breast. As his tongue tantalized the nipple, he undid her bra. At last both of her small, rounded breasts were free and he buried his head between them.

Bill could feel Vanessa's strong hands in his hair, smoothing and stroking, massaging his neck and shoulders. He heard her soft moans as he moved from one breast to the other, tenderly kissing and touching them, inflaming himself as well as her.

After a moment he sat up, looked down at her stretched out on the bed. How exciting she was to him, so vulnerable in her delicate beauty. She wore a lacy, black garter belt and sheer, black stockings. Carefully he undid the suspenders and rolled down each stocking, took off one, then the other. His eyes ravished her body, so trim and lean, yet shapely. Unfastening the garter belt, he slipped it off.

She stared up at him, her eyes wide and unblinking. "I want you," she said in a husky voice.

He nodded, stood up, threw off his clothes haphazardly, lay down next to her. Taking her in his arms, he kissed her eyes, her lips, her ears. "I want to kiss every part of you," he whispered against her hair.

"I'd like that," she murmured.

He slid down the bed, brought his mouth to the core of her. She responded wildly, crying his name. Her body suddenly convulsed in a spasm, and she grasped his shoulders hard, gasping as she did so.

Before he could stop himself, Bill was astride her, lying on top of her. Both his hands reached up into her dark curls, and he covered her mouth with his, touching his tongue to hers. He needed to take her to him. Now. Without further delay. Bracing his hands on either side of her he raised himself up, stared down into her eyes.

"Yes," she cried. "Oh, yes, Bill."

His hands left her hair, moved on to fondle those taut breasts with their erect nipples. He pushed his hands under her back, then her buttocks, lifting her closer to him, fitting her body to his. He was harder than ever and slid inside her easily.

And she welcomed him with her warm and pliant body, cleaving to him, thrusting up to him. She became welded to him. She moved her legs, threw them around his back, as high as they would go, so that he could shaft deeper and deeper into the warm, soft core of her. And they found their own rhythm, moving faster and faster until they were frenzied.

Bill thought his heart was going to burst. He sank deeper and deeper into her until he was entirely enveloped by her. "Vanessa," he gasped. "Vanessa."

"Yes, Bill!" she cried. "Don't stop."

He brought his mouth to hers again, and holding her tightly in his arms, they came to a climax together, sharing their ecstasy. And their joy in each other was unparalleled.

6

"That was all too quick," Bill said, encircling her with his arms, pulling her closer to him. "I'm afraid I was overanxious."

"No, you were wonderful."

"I've wanted us to be together like this since the other afternoon, when I almost knocked you over."

"So have I."

"Really and truly, Vanessa?"

"Yes, honestly."

He felt her smile against his chest. Before he could stop himself, Bill asked, "Who's Giovanni?"

She swiveled her eyes to look up at him. "How do you know his name?"

"I heard you greet him the other afternoon, just after I'd chased your hat."

"I see. He's an old friend . . . we met when I was doing my graduate course here. We became close, he helped me in lots of ways."

"Are you lovers?"

"No." Vanessa hesitated, then added, "Giovanni lives with someone, has for several years . . . another man."

"Oh." Bill cleared his throat, and after a moment he said, "We asked you lots of questions, Frankie and I, but we didn't ask your age, being the gentlemen that we are. But how old are you, actually?"

"Twenty-seven. Soon to be twenty-eight. And you're about thirty-five, aren't you?"

He laughed. "Thanks a lot! And no, I'm thirty-three," he replied and kissed the top of her head. "You said you were staying another four days. That means you're leaving on Wednesday. Correct?"

"Yes, I have to work at the glass foundry on Monday and Tuesday."

"Can I see you in the evenings? Can we be together until you leave?"

"Of course, I want that too, Bill."

"Listen, I'm coming to New York in December. For the Christmas holidays, in fact. Are you going to be around?"

"Yes." There was a small pause before she continued, "Bill, there's something I must tell you."

He heard an edge in her voice all of a sudden and he frowned. "Go ahead."

Vanessa took a deep breath and plunged. "I'm married."

For a moment Bill did not respond, and then he moved up on the pillows.

Vanessa struggled free of his embrace, turned to face him.

They stared at each other intently.

Vanessa saw surprise mingled with hurt on his face.

"Don't be angry with me. Don't look at me like that," she cried.

"How do you expect me to look, for God's sake? I'm disappointed, Vanessa. You lied to me."

"No I didn't, we never mentioned my marital status."

"You lied by omission."

"What about your private life, Bill? Is there a woman in *your* life? You don't need a piece of paper to make a commitment to someone. Making it legal doesn't necessarily make the bonds any stronger, the attachment greater. Do you live with a woman?"

"No."

She sighed.

He said, "Do you live with him?"

"Sort of . . ."

"What does that mean?"

"He's away a lot. And I go to my studio in the Hamptons a great deal of the time. I have a barn and a cottage in Southampton. So we're not together often."

"And when you are? Is it a proper marriage?"

She shrugged.

"Do you sleep with him?" he pressed.

Vanessa did not respond.

"Your silence is golden . . . it means that you do."

"It's not a good marriage—"

His hard laugh stopped her short. "Ah, the misunderstood married woman!" he exclaimed.

"No, it's not like that!" She leapt off the bed, ran into the bathroom, and came back a moment later wrapped in a terry cloth robe. Seating herself on the edge of the bed, she took hold of his hand.

Bill looked at her, his face taut. He was trying to come to grips with his emotions. After making such passionate love he had been euphoric, a feeling he had long forgotten existed. And he had felt at ease with this young woman who had come so unexpectedly into his life. He knew he wanted to get to know her better, to spend time with her. Her announcement that she was not free had been a bombshell.

Vanessa exclaimed, "Please, Bill, don't be angry. Let me explain."

"I'm not angry, and go ahead, be my guest. *Explain*," he said and there was a sarcastic note in his voice.

Ignoring this, Vanessa said, "Peter's a lawyer, a show-business lawyer and very successful. He's away a lot, mostly in Hollywood. It wasn't like that at first, but his business has grown. And I'm traveling, too. I suppose, in a way, we've grown apart a bit. But he's a good man, and he's been very supportive of me, as I have of him. So we sort of . . . muddle through. It's not a great marriage, but it's not a bad one either."

"Have you never thought of leaving him?"

She shook her head. "He's a good man, as I just said. I wouldn't want to hurt him."

"What about you, Vanessa? Aren't you entitled to have a happy relationship with a man?"

"I don't think it's possible to build one's happiness on someone else's unhappiness."

"I know what you mean."

"In any case, Peter would fall apart if I left him. I just couldn't have his pain on my conscience."

"Do you have children?"

"No, sadly we don't."

"How long have you been married?"

"Four years."

"Do you still love him?"

"I care about him—" She came to a halt, looked thoughtful, finally confided, "Peter's been in my life for such a long time. We're good friends, and we have a lot in common. He's always encouraged me in my work, my career, never stood in my way. He's a nice person. I like him. I respect him, and I love him. But—"

"You're not in love with him, is that what you're trying to say?"

"Yes." Vanessa bit her lip and shook her head. "I mean, how could I be here with you like this if I were?"

Bill laid his head back against the pillows and closed his eyes. A small sigh escaped, and without opening his eyes, he said softly, "I just wish you'd told me you were married, that's all."

"I wanted to," Vanessa said. "I intended to, and then we started to have such a good time together. I liked you so much. I wanted to be with you, and I just thought you'd lose interest if you knew I had a husband."

He said slowly, "You should have been straightforward with me."

"Have *you* been with me?"

He sat up swiftly and stared at her. "Yes, I have. There isn't a woman in my life. You know I'm widowed. My God, the whole world knows I'm widowed. And I haven't had a really good relationship since Sylvie died. Oh, yes, there've been a few women, but I've never fallen in love, or had a meaningful relationship since my wife died six years ago. To tell you the truth, I thought that you and I might have something going for us, that this was the beginning of something special. I want a good relationship, Vanessa, I want to have another chance at happiness." He shrugged. "I guess I was wrong to think it might be with you."

Vanessa said nothing, looked down at her hands twisting nervously in her lap.

The awkward silence grew.

At last she said, "How do you *really* feel about me, Bill? Be scrupulously honest."

He gave her a hard penetrating stare. "We've just made passionate love, and you ask me that?" He gave a short laugh, pursed his lips. "Obviously I'm overwhelmingly attracted to you, turned on by you. I enjoyed making love with you. Let's face it, we've just had wonderful sex. I like being with you. I admire your talent. As I told you in the lobby a short while ago, I'm very taken with you, Vanessa."

"And I am with you, Bill. So much so I haven't really been able to think straight for the last couple of days. All I know is that I just want to be with you. Whenever we can. You're a foreign correspondent, you're obviously going to go back to Bosnia or somewhere else, and I have my own career . . ." She shook her head, and tears brimmed in her eyes. "I thought we would see each other whenever we could, be together as often as possible and . . . see what happens."

"Let things work themselves out in their own time, is that what you mean?"

"Yes. Whenever my mother was facing difficulties, she would always say to me, 'Vanny, life takes care of itself and a lot of other things as well. And usually it's for the best.' That's still her philosophy, I think."

Bill looked at her thoughtfully. "So, what you're saying is that you want to have an affair with me? A secret affair. Because you don't want your husband to be hurt. Am I correct?"

"It sounds terrible when you put it that way."

"But it *is* the truth. And as a newsman, I *am* a seeker of truth."

Vanessa shook her head, biting her lip again. Slowly, tears trickled down her cheeks.

"Oh, for God's sake, don't start crying!" he said, and reached for her, pulled her into his arms. He flicked her tears away with his fingertips, then tilted her face to his. Softly, he kissed her on the mouth.

When he stopped, she said, "Please tell me you're not angry with me, Bill."

"I'm not angry. Only selfish. I always want things my way, like most men. And listen, you haven't committed a crime. Anyway, why should you stick your neck out for me?" He laughed. "I'm always in harm's way . . . a bad risk."

"Don't say that!" she cried, her eyes flaring.

Tightening his grip on her, he brought his face closer to hers and whispered, "I *want* to be your lover. Now why don't you take off that robe so that I can start practicing."

7

It was an extraordinary day, clear, light-filled. A shimmering day. The sky dazzled. It was a perfect blue, unmarred by cloud, and the sun was brilliant above the rippling waters of the lagoon. The air was cool, but not as cold as it had been over the past few days, and the mist had dissipated.

On this bright Sunday afternoon, Bill and Vanessa walked through the streets and squares for several hours, holding hands, hardly speaking but comfortable in their mutual silence. Both were swept up in the beauty of Venice. They walked on past the Accademia, down the Calle Gambara into the Calle Contarini Corfù, until they came at last to the Fondamenta Priuli-Nani.

"Of course I remember this area now," Vanessa said, turning to Bill, smiling up at him as they headed down the street. "That's the old boatyard of San Trovaso, where gondolas are repaired," she continued, gesturing to the decrepit-looking buildings ahead of them. "I came here once with my father. He wanted to see the Church of San Trovaso. It's very old, if I remember correctly."

"Yes, it is," Bill replied. "It was built in the tenth century, and that's where I'm taking you now, actually. To the church. I want to show you one of my very favorite paintings. It's by Tintoretto.

And incidentally, gondolas are also *made* at the San Trovaso boatyard, it's one of the last of the building yards left in Venice."

"They've all more or less disappeared. So many of the old crafts have become defunct," she murmured, sounding regretful. "But, thank goodness, glassblowing hasn't!" she finished with a light laugh, grinning at him.

They continued on past the boatyard, and walked up over the Ponte delle Meravegie, the bridge of marvels. Within seconds they were approaching the Church of San Trovaso, its cream-colored stone walls and slender bell tower rising up above the trees, a sentinel silhouetted against the cerulean sky.

After they had entered the church, Vanessa and Bill stood quietly for a moment, adjusting their eyes to the dim light and the overwhelming silence. They both genuflected, and Bill threw Vanessa a swift glance but made no comment, realizing that she also must be a Catholic. They slowly moved forward, walking down the nave toward the altar.

Immediately, Bill brought Vanessa's attention to the two paintings hanging on either side of the choir. "Both are by Tintoretto," he explained. "The last two pictures he ever painted. In 1594. Come on, let me show you the one I love the most." A moment later they were in front of *The Adoration of the Magi*, Tintoretto's great masterpiece.

"I've always liked this particular Tintoretto myself," Vanessa volunteered. "It's absolute perfection. The colors, the images, the incredible brushwork."

"Wasn't he marvelous," Bill said, "A towering genius." He fell silent, simply stood staring at the picture, rooted to the spot, unable to tear his eyes away.

At this moment it struck Vanessa that Bill was mesmerized by the painting. Several times she threw him a surreptitious look, but she made no comment, not wanting to break the spell for him; she understood how moved he was by this great work of art.

Finally dragging his eyes away from the painting, he said, "When I look at this Tintoretto, and the other treasures in Venice, and consider man's incredible talent, his ability to create incomparable beauty, I can't help wondering how man can also be the perpetrator of an evil so stupendous it boggles the mind. It's hard to reconcile the two."

"But the two have always coexisted," Vanessa answered, putting her hand on his arm. "Venice *is* the total personification of visual beauty. It's there for us to *see*, to take pleasure from, wherever we look. The art, the architecture, the many different treasures that have been accumulated here over the centuries, the very design and layout of Venice itself—" She paused for a split second before she added softly, "You have just come out of Bosnia, where you witnessed inhumanity and savagery, cruelty beyond belief. And those images must still be in your mind, Bill. How can you not make comparisons?"

"You're right, yes, I know that," he said, and turning away from the painting at last, he took hold of her arm and led her down the nave, back to the front door of the ancient church. "I suppose the beauty of paintings and music help to make the hard realities of life . . . bearable."

"I think so."

Once they were outside in the sunlight, Bill blinked and shook off the images of the Balkans war that had momentarily overtaken him. He exclaimed, "It's such a long time since I've taken a gondola up the Grand Canal. Shall we do it, Vanessa? It's still the most spectacular trip, isn't it?"

"Absolutely. And I'd love it. It's ages since I've done it myself, and I guess the Grand Canal personifies Venice, doesn't it? Besides, I find gondolas a very relaxing way to travel."

Bill felt a sudden rush of happiness surging up in him. He knew it was because of Vanessa, her presence by his side. He put his arm around her, hugged her to him. "I'm glad we met, I'm glad we're here today in Venice. I'm glad we made love last night. I'm glad we have a few more days together." He stopped, tilted her face to his and looked at her, a faint smile briefly touching his mouth. "Whatever your circumstances are, Vanessa, you're the best thing that's happened to me in a long time." He kissed the tip of her nose. "Clandestine though it must be, I want our affair to continue." His eyes searched hers questioningly.

She nodded. "So do I. Whenever we can, wherever we can," she answered, and reached up, threw her arms around his neck, pulled his face to hers, and put her mouth on his. "There," she added, "sealed with a kiss."

He laughed, and so did she, and with their arms wrapped around each other they walked back the way they had come. Retracing their steps past the old boatyard, they went down the narrow streets until they came again to the Campo dell' Accademia, where Bill hired a gondola to take them back to the Gritti.

Immediately they were seated, Bill put his arm around Vanessa again and pulled her closer to him, realizing as he did that in only a few days this woman had come to mean so much to him. It didn't seem possible that he could care so deeply for someone other than Helena or his mother, but he did now. And it was all very sudden at that.

For her part, Vanessa was thinking similar things, and wondering how her life would ever be the same again. It wouldn't, she was positive. Not ever again. Because of Bill.

The two of them sat with their backs to the gondolier, who was in the prow. They were facing St. Mark's Basin, the vast expanse of water that rolled up to the quay.

Directly in front of them were the island of San Giorgio, the Church of the Salute, and the Dogana, the beautiful domed customs building. These buildings, known as the three pearls to the entrance of Venice, were turning golden in the late afternoon sunlight.

"The light of Turner," Bill said, leaning forward intently, looking at the sky. "Vanessa, do you see the changing light? It's gone a peculiar yellow, the yellow Turner captured so perfectly on canvas. I've always loved the paintings he did of Venice."

"So have I. And this view is the very best," she replied. "The entire city floating on water, the water changing with the light. The whole scene is . . . dreamlike . . ." Vanessa paused, thinking how truly lovely it was. Magical, almost otherworldly. It moved her; she felt the unexpected prick of tears in her throat, touched as she was by the beauty of this city.

Sky and shifting water merged, golden, then iridescent in the lowering light of the afternoon. All the colors of Venice were reflected now in the Grand Canal as they floated along it, heading for the hotel.

Fading sunlight caught the cupolas of the basilica, streaking them to silver, touching the pale colors of the palazzos, giving the pink, terra-cotta, ocher, and powdery yellow a dusky, golden cast. All these colors of La Serenissima blended in a delicate mix, with just the hint of green here and there. And everywhere the sense of blue . . . blues bleeding into watery grays.

The gondola slid slowly up the Grand Canal, past the ancient palazzos jammed close together, almost higgledy-piggedly, tall and narrow. The houses were built on stilts, just as Venice itself was built on pilings pounded into the sand, silt, and rock centuries ago.

Sinking, she thought, they say it's sinking. And it was, very slowly, even though some of the rot had been stopped.

Vanessa stared at the palazzos, all of them full of priceless treasures, works of art by the great masters, paintings, sculptures, silver and gold objects, tapestries, furniture. How terrible if it all sinks, she thought with a shudder. What a tragedy that would be.

Bill increased the pressure of his arms around her, and she leaned back against him. She was falling in love with him. She shouldn't, but she was, and she didn't know how to stop herself.

*   *   *

They sat in the bar of the Gritti Palace and had hot chocolate, tiny tea sandwiches, and small, delicious cakes. It was growing dark outside, the bright sunlight of earlier had dulled to leaden gray, and a wind had blown up, but it was warm inside, comfortable in the bar. They were enjoying being together, getting to know each other better.

At one moment Vanessa murmured, "You haven't really said where you're going from here, Bill. Is it Bosnia again?"

He was silent for a moment and then he nodded, his face suddenly grim. "But only to do a wrap-up. I won't be there longer than three or four days, thank God."

"The war must have been awfully hard to cover . . . I saw such horrors whenever I turned on the television. I can't imagine what it was like to actually be there."

"It was hell."

"It affected you . . . I know from the way you spoke with Frank."

"Yes, the war did affect me, change me. I've been a witness to genocide . . . the first war and genocide since the last war and genocide in Europe. That was in the thirties when the Nazis started persecuting the Jews, exterminating them, along with the gypsies and anyone else they thought needed killing off. I never imagined it could happen again, or if it did, that the world would permit it." He shook his head and shrugged. "But the world *has* permitted it, and the civilized world, at that. Excuse me, Vanessa, I shouldn't use that term. Nobody's civilized as far as I'm concerned. All any of us have is a thin veneer; scratch that in the right place and a monster will appear." He gave her a hard look, and went on, "As a newsman I have to be dispassionate, objective and balanced. Like a bystander, *watching,* in a sense."

Vanessa nodded. "Yes, I understand, but that must be very hard for you."

"It is now. At one time I could move around at will, from battlefield to battlefield, without being upset or disturbed. Bosnia has altered all that. The savagery, the butchering of innocent, unarmed civilians. My God, it was horrific at times . . . what we all witnessed. There are no words strong enough or *bad* enough to describe it."

Vanessa was silent.

After a moment she reached out and took hold of his hand, held it tightly in hers, knowing better than to say a word.

Bill was quiet for some time. He finally said, "I'm going to be doing a special on terrorism. I have two months to put it together. We'll start filming in January through February, so that we can air it in March."

"That's why you're not going to be based in Sarajevo?"

"Correct. I'll be traveling through the Middle East."

"Will . . ." She tightened her grip on his hand and leaned into him. "Will we be able to meet?"

"I hope so, darling. I'm counting on it."

"Shall we make Venice our place of rendezvous?"

He squeezed her hand. "I think that's a brilliant idea."

"When are you coming to New York in December?"

"About the fifteenth. I have two weeks' vacation due." He searched her face. "That won't present a problem will it, meeting in New York?"

"No, of course not. And I've a favor to ask," she said, smiling.

"Then ask it."

"Can I meet your daughter?"

"Do you want to *really*?"

"Yes, Bill, I do."

"Then you've got a date. I'll take you all to lunch. Helena, my mother, and you. It'll be great, having my three best girls out on the town with me."

8

New York, December 1995

Vanessa Stewart had always prided herself on her honesty. It was not only an honesty with those people who occupied her life, but with herself. For as long as she could remember, she had despised prevaricators and even those who merely half-fudged the truth.

But now on this icy December day she had to admit to herself that she had not been honest for a long time. At least, not as far as her private life was concerned.

There was no longer any question in her mind that she had lied to herself about the state of her marriage. And lied to Peter, too, by not forcing him to admit that their marriage was floundering, not working on so many different levels.

I've lied by omission, she thought, remembering the line Bill had used in Venice some ten days ago now. By not being open with Peter, I've only compounded our basic problem. I'm as much at fault as he is. And there was a problem. More than one, in fact.

Face the truth, Vanessa suddenly admonished herself. Be a big girl, accept things the way they are now. They're not the same as they once were; they haven't been for a long time.

A distracted look settled on her face as she focused on her marriage, the drawings spread out in front of her now forgotten.

She and Peter no longer communicated very well, hardly at all, really. The shared confidences of their courtship and the early days of their marriage had long since been abandoned. Their sex life was practically nonexistent. And whenever they did make love these days it was usually because they had quarreled. Peter had always believed that this was the best way of making up. Certainly the easiest for him, she now thought.

But quite aside from this, they spent a great deal of their time apart. They were always in different places, or so it seemed to her.

And their interests were very different. They had grown apart . . . as they had grown in different ways.

It's no marriage at all, Vanessa thought. It's just a sham, truly it is. We stay together out of . . . *what*? Suddenly she did not know why they stayed together. Unless it was out of habit. Or loyalty. Or lack of a better place to go. Or someone else to go to. Or laziness. Which one of these reasons it was, she had no idea. Perhaps it was all of them in combination.

Placing the pencil on top of her drawing board, Vanessa leaned back in the tall chair where she sat and stared out of the huge window in front of her. Her mind was racing.

Her design studio was in a building downtown in Soho, on the corner of Mercer and Grand. It was a fifth-floor loft looking south, and she had fallen in love with it at first sight because of its spaciousness and extraordinary natural light.

The view from her window was familiar to her, but it never failed to please her. She had not grown tired of looking out at her own special corner of Manhattan. The splendid nineteenth century buildings were lined up before her eyes, while behind them the pristine twin towers of the World Trade Center, all black glass and steel, pierced the afternoon sky.

Two centuries juxtaposed, she thought, as she did every so often. The past. The present. The future.

The future. Those words danced in her head.

What was *her* future?

Was it to continue to live this lie with Peter? This lie that was their marriage . . . no, the remnants of their marriage.

Or was she going to leave him?

Is that what the future held? A life without Peter Smart, the only man she had ever known, except for Bill Fitzgerald? Well, that wasn't quite the truth either, if she were scrupulously honest. There had been one other man in her life. Steven Ellis. Her college beau. Her first lover, her only lover until she had met Peter. And then married him.

And now Bill Fitzgerald was her lover. Her clandestine lover. Was it because of Bill that she was suddenly looking truth in the face? Had her relationship with him forced her to be honest for the first time in several years? More than likely. Yes, it's because of Bill and the way you feel about him, a small voice in her head whispered.

A deep sigh escaped her. She did not know what to do. Should she make Peter see their marriage for what it was, a sham? If she did, what would happen? And what did *she* want to happen? Peter might say they should start all over again, try to make a go of it. And where would she be then? Was that what she wanted? A future with Peter Smart?

What she had said about him to Bill was true. Peter was a good man, a decent human being. And he did love her in his own way. Furthermore, he looked after her well, and he had been extremely supportive about her work, had encouraged her career. Peter was a caring man in a variety of ways, and reliable, dependable, loyal.

And she was absolutely convinced he would be hurt and unhappy if she left him. He depended on *her* in so many ways.

Why would she leave Peter anyway?

Because of Bill?

Yes.

But Bill hasn't asked you to leave Peter. He hasn't made any kind of commitment to you, that insidious voice whispered. In fact, he rapidly agreed to an affair, a secret affair. He accepted the idea of being your clandestine lover. Actually, he suggested it, the voice added.

But Bill or no Bill, her life with Peter had grown . . . empty? *Yes.* Stale? *Yes.* Lonely? In many ways, *yes.* They didn't share anything anymore, at least that was the way she saw it, the way she felt. There was so much lacking in their relationship. For her, anyway. Maybe Peter felt differently. Maybe he expected less of marriage than she did.

And what did she want in a marriage?

Emotion. Love. Warmth. Companionship. True feelings shared. Sexual love. Understanding. Was that too much to ask of a man? Surely not. Certainly it was not too much for her to give.

Peter had not offered her many of these things lately, quite the contrary. And wasn't that one of the reasons she had ended up in bed with Bill in Venice? Yes, the little voice answered. But it had also happened because she was overwhelmingly attracted to Bill. Falling in love with him? Yes, it was happening. Hadn't she known that days ago in Venice?

Falling in love, Vanessa thought. More like falling into madness.

It was dusk when Vanessa left her studio and got into the waiting radio cab that she had ordered earlier. As the driver headed uptown, her thoughts again turned to the problems in her life. Wrestling with them was not proving to be very fruitful; certainly she wasn't coming up with any answers for herself. The only thing she knew for sure was that her Venetian interlude with Bill, the feelings they had shared, had only served to point up the unsatisfactory relationship she had with Peter.

Comparisons, she thought, I hate comparisons. They're odious. But, of course, how could she not compare the emotional closeness she and Bill had enjoyed with the aridness of her life with Peter?

It suddenly struck her that Peter was denying her his love, himself, just as he had denied her a child. Instantly, she crushed that thought, not wanting to confront it, or deal with it now.

On the spur of the moment, she leaned forward and said to the driver, "I need to make a stop on the way uptown. I'd like to go to Lord & Taylor, please."

"Okay, miss," the driver said, and turned left off Madison when they reached East Thirty-ninth Street. He headed west to Fifth Avenue, where the famous old store was located.

The driver parked the cab on the side street, but Vanessa walked around to Fifth Avenue and stood looking at the Christmas windows. They were always the best, she knew that from her childhood. The windows were full of wondrous mechanical toys, breathtaking scenes from famous fairy tales and the classics, magical to every child.

Pressing her nose against the window, as she had done when she was a child, she smiled inwardly, watching an exquisitely made toy ballerina, dressed in a pink tutu, pirouetting to the strains of "The Sugar Plum Fairy." The music was being piped out into the street, and it brought back such a rush of forgotten memories that Vanessa's throat tightened unexpectedly.

Her mother and father had always taken her to see *The Nutcracker* if they were in New York over Christmas, just as they had brought her here to see the store's windows before going inside to meet Santa Claus and confide her Christmas wish.

Sometimes they had not been in Manhattan at Christmas, but in California or Paris or London, depending on her mother's current movie or play. Or what her father, Terence Stewart, was directing at the time. She was an only child, and they had always taken her with them on location or wherever they went. She had never suffered because of their theatrical careers; she had had a lovely, and very loving, childhood and had remained extremely close to her parents.

Eventually Vanessa turned away from the window, suddenly overcome by feelings of immense sadness and loneliness. An aching emptiness filled her, as it so often did. It was a feeling that threatened at times to overcome her. Somehow, she always managed to throw it off. She knew what it was—the longing for a child. But Peter did not want the responsibility of a child, and so she had buried the longing deep inside herself, sublimated the desire for a baby in her work. But, occasionally that terrible yearning gripped her, as it was doing now. She tried to still it, wishing it away.

Pushing through the swinging doors, Vanessa went into the store, her mind focusing on Helena, Bill's little girl. She was looking for something truly special. Helena was six, and there were so many things to buy for a child that age. Taking the escalator, she rode up to the children's department, spent ten minutes looking around and left empty-handed. Nothing had caught her eye.

As she hurried across the main floor, Vanessa stopped to buy tights and winter boot socks, then picked up eye makeup she needed before returning to the cab.

When she arrived at their apartment on East Fifty-seventh Street, Vanessa was surprised to find her husband at home. He usually never got in from his law office before seven in the evening at the earliest.

She shrugged out of her topcoat in the foyer and was hanging it up in the closet when he came out of their bedroom.

He was holding a couple of silk ties in his hand, and his face lit up at the sight of her. Smiling hugely, Peter said, "Hi, sweetie."

"You're home early," she answered, walking forward.

He nodded, kissed her on the cheek as she drew to a standstill. "I wanted to get my packing done before dinner."

"Packing?" A frown marred the smoothness of her wide brow. "Where are you going?"

"To London. Tomorrow morning. I have to see Alex Lawson. As you know, he's filming there at the moment. Anyway, his contract for his next two movies is finally ready, and I've got to go over it with him, walk him through it. It's a bit more complicated than usual."

"Oh, I see."

"Don't look so glum, Vanessa. I'll be back in ten days, certainly in time for Christmas."

"Does it take ten days to walk an actor through a contract? Or is he particularly dumb?"

"Vanessa! How can you talk like that about Hollywood's biggest heartthrob," he said and laughed a deep-throated laugh, amused by her comment. "You, of all people! Coming from a show business family as you do."

When she made no response and moved away, Peter took hold of her arm and gently turned her to face him. "I thought we'd go somewhere special for Christmas. Mexico . . . Bali . . . Thailand. Anywhere you want."

"But my mother will be in New York for Christmas . . ." Her voice trailed off. Suddenly she felt depressed.

"All right, then we'll stay here; it was just an idea. But no problem, no problem at all, sweetie." He went back into the bedroom.

Vanessa followed him, placed her Lord & Taylor shopping bag on the bed, and sat down next to it.

Peter spent a moment or two sorting ties, then he turned around and gave her a puzzled look when he saw the expression on her face. "What's the matter?" he asked, walking over to the bed, looming up in front of her.

She met his steady gaze with one equally as steady, but the expression on her face was thoughtful. Her husband was thirty-eight years old. Slim, attractive, a man in his prime. He had a genial personality, natural charm, and was popular both with his friends and clients. A brilliant lawyer, he had become highly successful in the past few years, and the success sat well on him. Peter Smart had everything going for him. And yet his personal life was abysmal. She ought to know; she shared it with him. It was empty, arid, pointless. As was hers. Didn't he notice this? Or didn't he care? Then it suddenly hit her like a ton of bricks: Was there another woman in his life? Is that why he had nothing to give *her* anymore?

"You're looking odd," Peter remarked in a quiet voice.

She cleared her throat. "I'm sorry you're going away; I'd hoped we could spend a quiet weekend together. I want to talk to you, Peter."

He frowned. "What about?"

"*Us.*"

"You sound serious."

"I feel serious. Look, you and I . . . things are just not right between us these days."

He gaped at her. "I don't know what you mean, Vanessa."

"What's our life about?" She gave him a penetrating stare. "We seem to be . . . drifting apart."

"Don't be so silly!" he exclaimed with one of his light, genial laughs. "Our life is very much on track. You're a doer and an achiever, and you have a career you love. You're doing extremely well, and you've accomplished so much with the design studio. I'm going great guns at the law firm. Things couldn't be better on that score. So why do you ask what our life is all about? I don't understand what you mean."

All of a sudden she knew that he didn't, that he was genuinely puzzled. She exclaimed, "But we're never together. We're always in different places, and when we are in the same city, you constantly work late. And when we're at home you haven't got a lot to say to me anymore, Peter; and there's another thing, we don't seem to be as close physically as we were." It was on the tip of her tongue to ask him if he was having an affair, and then she changed her mind. He might well ask her the same question, and then what would she say?

Peter was shaking his head, looking miserable, the laughter of earlier wiped out of his eyes. He threw the ties onto a chair and sat down on the bed next to her, took hold of her hand. "But, Vanessa, I love you, you know that. Nothing's changed. Well, I guess it has. I'm successful, very successful, and in a way I never dreamed I could be. This is the big one for me, the big chance, and I don't want to screw it up. I can't, because what I do now, how I handle everything now, is for our future. Yours and mine. Our old age, you might say."

"Old age!" she exploded. "But I don't care about that! I want to live now, while I'm still young."

"We are living, and living very well. And doing well. That's what counts, sweetie." He gazed into her eyes, and said more softly, "I guess I've been neglecting you lately. I'm sorry." He put his arms around her, tried to kiss her, but Vanessa drew away from him.

"You always think you can solve our problems, our disagreements, by making love to me," she said.

"But you know we always *do* solve what ails us when we're in bed together. We work it out that way."

"Just for once it would be nice to make love with you because we *want* to make love, not to get us over one of our quarrels."

"Then let's do it right now."

"I don't want to, Peter. I'm not in the mood. Sorry, but this little girl doesn't want to play tonight."

He recoiled slightly, startled by her sarcastic tone, and said slowly, "Is this about the baby? Is this what all this talk of drifting apart is about? Is that it, Vanessa?"

"No, it's not."

"I know I've been tough on you about having a baby—" he began and stopped abruptly.

"Yes, you have. You made it perfectly clear that you didn't want children."

"I don't. Well, what I mean is, I don't right now. But listen, sweetie, maybe later on, a few years down the line; maybe we can have a child then."

She shook her head and before she could stop herself she said, "Perhaps we ought to separate, Peter. Get a divorce."

His expression changed immediately and he sat up straighter on the bed. "Absolutely not! I don't want a divorce and neither do you. This is silly talk. You're just tired after all the work you did in Venice, and the schedule you've set for yourself with the new collection."

Vanessa was regarding him intently, and she realized that he was afraid of losing her. She could see the fear in his eyes.

When she remained totally silent, Peter went on swiftly, "I promise you things are going to be different, Vanessa. To be honest, I thought you were happy, excited about your design career. I hadn't realized . . . realized that things weren't right between *us*. You do believe me, don't you?"

"Yes," she murmured wearily. "I believe you, Peter." She got up off the bed, and walked toward the bedroom door. Dismay lodged in her chest. "There's not much for dinner. Shall I make pasta and a salad?"

"Certainly not. I'm going to take you out, sweetie. Shall we go next door to Mr. Chow's?"

Vanessa shook her head. "I don't feel like Chinese food."

"Then we'll go to Neary's pub. Jimmy always gives us such a great welcome, and I know you love it there."

9

Vanessa surveyed the living room of the cottage through newly objective and critical eyes. There were no two ways about it, the room looked shabby and decidedly neglected.

She did not care about the shabbiness; the faded wallpaper, the well-washed chintz and worn antique rug were all part of its intrinsic charm. It was the feeling of neglect that bothered her. She knew that the entire cottage was scrupulously clean, since it was maintained by a local woman. But the living room, in particular, had a lackluster air to it.

Bill would be arriving in a few hours to spend the day and part of the next with her, and she wanted the cottage to look nice. Since he spent so much of his time roughing it in battle zones and second-rate hotels, she felt the need to make it comfortable, warm and welcoming for him.

When her parents had divorced several years ago, they had not known what to do with Bedelia cottage. Neither of them had wanted it and yet they had been reluctant to sell it, oddly enough because of sentimental reasons. They both had a soft spot for it.

And so they had ended up giving it to their daughter. Vanessa had been thrilled.

It was located at the far end of Southampton and stood on three acres of land that ran all the way up to the sand dunes and the Atlantic Ocean.

The cottage was not in the chic part of town, nor was it very special, just a simple, stone-and-clapboard house, about forty years old. It had four bedrooms, a large kitchen, a living room, and a library. There was a long, covered veranda at the back of the cottage which fronted onto the sea.

Once the house was hers, she had turned the old red barn into a design studio and office and converted the stone stables into a small foundry with a kiln. It was here in the studio and foundry that she spent most of her time designing and executing the handblown glass prototypes she took to Venice to be copied and produced in Murano.

Being as preoccupied as she was with work, Vanessa did not give the cottage much attention. Piles of old newspapers and magazines, which she had saved for some reason, were stacked here and there; current books, which she hoped one day to read, were piled on a chest and the floor; and, several large vases of dried flowers, which had looked so spectacular in the summer, had lost their color and were falling apart.

Glancing at her watch, she saw that it was just eight o'clock. Bill was arriving at one. Mavis Glover, who had looked after the cottage for years, usually came at nine.

Suddenly deciding not to wait for her to appear, Vanessa made a beeline for the piles of books, carried them to the library next door and found a place for them all on the bookshelves. For the next hour she worked hard in the living room, discarding newspapers, magazines, and the bedraggled dried flowers.

Finally, standing in the middle of the room and glancing around appraisingly, Vanessa decided she had made a vast improvement. Because the room was no longer cluttered, the furniture was suddenly shown off to advantage. The French country antique pieces stood out. Their dark wood tones were mellow against the white walls and the blue chintz patterned with pink and red tulips, which hung at the windows and covered the sofas and chairs.

Not bad, not bad at all, Vanessa thought, and hurried out to the large family-style kitchen. Last night, when she had arrived, she had put the flowers she had brought from the city into vases; now she carried one of these back to the sitting room. The second one she took upstairs to her bedroom.

This had once been her parents' private sanctuary, and to Vanessa it was the nicest room in the cottage. Certainly it was the largest. It had many windows overlooking the sand dunes and the ocean beyond, and a big stone fireplace was set in one of the end walls.

Entirely decorated in yellow and blue, the room had a cheerful, sunny feeling even on the dullest of days. It was comfortable to the point of luxury.

Hurrying forward, Vanessa put the vase of yellow roses on the coffee table in front of the fire, and then went into the bathroom to take a shower. Once she was made up and dressed she would start on lunch while Mavis cleaned the rest of the cottage.

As she stood under the shower, letting the hot water sluice down over her, Vanessa luxuriated for a moment or two in thoughts of Bill. He had arrived in New York last Friday, December the fifteenth, as he had said he would. That was five days ago now. They had managed to snatch several quick drinks together on Sunday and Monday. He was busy with CNS most of the time; but when he was not, she did not want to intrude on hours he had set aside for his daughter.

"I'll drive out to the Hamptons on Wednesday morning," he had told her over their last drink at the Carlyle. "I can stay over until Thursday, if that's all right with you. How does it sound?"

It had sounded wonderful to her, and her beaming face had been her answer to him.

She could hardly wait to see him, have his arms around her, his mouth on hers. At the mere thought of making love with him, her body started to tingle. She snapped her eyes open and turned off the shower.

No time for fantasizing, she chastised herself, reaching for a towel. Anyway, within the space of a few hours she would have the real thing. They would be together.

Once she was dry, Vanessa dressed quickly, choosing a heavy red sweater to go with her well-washed blue jeans. Since it was a cold day, she put on thick white wool socks and brown penny loafers. Her only jewelry was a pair of gold earrings.

Once she had applied a little makeup and sprayed on perfume, she ran downstairs to prepare lunch for Bill.

He was late.

Vanessa sat in the small library, leafing through *Time* and *Newsweek,* wondering where he was, hoping he was not trapped in traffic.

Foolish idea that is, she thought. It was a Wednesday morning in the middle of December, and the traffic had to be light from Manhattan. It was only in the summer that it became a nightmare. She was quite certain Bill would find it straight sailing today; she had given him explicit driving instructions, and, anyway, the cottage was easy to find, just off the main road.

By one forty-five, when he had still not arrived, her anxiety was growing more acute by the minute. She was just deciding whether or not to call the network when she heard a car drawing up outside and she rushed to the front door.

When she saw Bill alighting, then taking his bag out of the trunk, she felt weak with relief. A moment later he was walking into the house, his face wreathed in smiles.

He took hold of her at once, pulled her into his arms. She clung to him tightly.

"Sorry, darling," he said against her hair. "I was delayed at the network and then it was tough getting out of New York this morning. A lot of traffic. Christmas shoppers, I guess."

"It's all right . . . I thought something had happened to you."

"Nothing's going to happen to me," he said, tilting her face to his in that special way he had.

"Let's go into the living room. It's warmer," Vanessa murmured, taking his arm. "I've got white wine on ice, or would you prefer scotch?"

"White wine's fine, thanks."

They stood together in front of the roaring fire, sipping their wine and staring at each other over the rims of their glasses.

"I've missed you, Vanessa."

"I've missed you too."

"You know something . . . I think about you all the time."

"So do I—I think of you, I mean."

"It's funny," he said softly, looking at her closely. "I feel as if you've been in my life always, as if I've known you always."

"Yes. It's the same for me, Bill."

He shook his head, smiled faintly. "I didn't dare touch you when we were in the bar of the Carlyle . . . you're very inflammatory to me."

She stared at him, saying nothing.

He stared back.

Putting his glass on the mantelpiece, he then did the same with hers, moved closer to her, and brought her into the circle of his arms. He kissed her hard, pressing her even closer to him, wanting her to know how much she excited him.

Vanessa tightened her embrace, responding to him with ardor, and this further inflamed him. Bill said in a low, hoarse voice, "I want you so much, want to be close to you."

Pulling away from him, she nodded, took hold of his hand, and led him upstairs to her bedroom.

There was tremendous tension between them. They undressed with great speed, sharing an urgent need to be intimate and closely joined. As they fell on the bed, his hands were all over her body. Loving hands that touched, stroked, explored, and brought her to a fever pitch of excitement.

They could not get enough of each other. He continued to kiss her, and she returned his kisses with the same intense passion she had felt in Venice. And Bill luxuriated in the nearness of her, in the knowledge that she longed for him, needed him so desperately. He felt the same need for her. It was a deep, insatiable need.

Stretching his body alongside hers, he took her suddenly, moving into her so swiftly he heard her gasp with surprise and pleasure. As she clasped him tightly in her arms, her legs wrapped around him, they shared a mounting joy.

Vanessa lay quietly in his arms.

The wintry afternoon sunshine cast its pale light across the yellow walls, turning them to bosky gold.

The only sound was the light rise and fall of Bill's breath as he drowsed and, far beyond the windows, the faint, distant roar of the Atlantic Ocean.

She found the stillness soothing.

Their lovemaking had been passionate, almost frantic, and even more feverish than in Venice. Their need for each other had been so overwhelming, it had stunned them both; afterward they had stared at each other in astonishment. Now this tranquillity was like a balm.

Stretching her body slightly, trying not to disturb him, Vanessa took pleasure from her sense of satisfaction and fulfillment. How different she was with Bill; she even surprised herself. Each time they made love, they seemed to soar higher and higher, reach a greater pitch of ecstasy. It always left her reeling.

In some ways, Vanessa no longer recognized herself. She

knew she had undergone a vast change since meeting Bill Fitzgerald. He brought out something erotic and sensual in her, made her feel whole, very feminine, very much a woman.

Pushing herself up onto one elbow, Vanessa looked down at him. The tense, worried expression he invariably wore had disappeared. In repose, his face was smooth, free of pain and concern. He looked so young, very vulnerable. And he touched her deeply.

Vanessa was aware that they had an intimacy of heart and mind as well as body, and it pleased her. They genuinely understood each other, and this compatibility gave them a special kind of closeness that few people shared.

She knew she was in love with him. She knew she wanted to be with him. For always. But was that possible? How could it be? She was not free. She had a husband who loved her, who was terrified of losing her. And for her part, she owed him loyalty and consideration.

Troubling thoughts of Peter insinuated themselves into her mind. She pushed them to one side. Too soon to think of the future . . . Later. She would think about it later.

In the meantime, she was absolutely certain of one thing. With Bill Fitzgerald she was her true self, without pretense or artifice. She was the real Vanessa Stewart.

She brought a tray of food and a bottle of white wine upstairs to the bedroom, where they had a picnic in front of the fire. And after they had devoured smoked salmon sandwiches, Brie cheese and apples, and downed a glass of wine each, they dressed and went out.

The thin sun still shone in the pale azure sky and the Atlantic had the gleam of silver on it. It was a blustery day with a high wind whipping the waves to turbulence.

Bundled up in overcoats and scarves, their arms wrapped around each other, they walked along the dunes, oblivious to the world, to everything except themselves and their intense feelings for each other.

At one moment Bill stopped and spun her to face him, looked down into her expressive gray eyes. "I'm so happy!" he exclaimed. "Happier than I've been for years."

"What did you say?" she shouted back, also competing with the roar of the ocean.

". . . happier than I've been for years," he repeated, grinning at her, catching her around her waist, pulling her to him. "I love you," he said, his mouth on her ear. "I love you, Vanessa Stewart."

"And I love you, Bill Fitzgerald."

"I didn't hear you," he teased.

"I LOVE YOU, BILL FITZGERALD!" she screamed at the top of her lungs.

His joyous laughter filled the air.

She joined in his laughter, hugging him to her.

And then, holding hands, they ran along the sand dunes, buffeted forward by the wind, euphoric in their love, happy to be alive, to be together.

Later that evening they sat in front of the fire in her bedroom, listening to Mozart's violin concertos.

Vanessa, suddenly looking across at Bill, saw how preoccupied he was as he stared into the flames, noted how tensely set his shoulders were.

"Are you all right?" she asked in a soft voice. When he did not respond, she pressed, "Bill, is something wrong?"

He lifted his head, looking directly at her. But still he said nothing. Disturbed by the sadness on his face, she went on, "Darling, what is it? You look so . . . unhappy . . . even troubled."

He took a moment, averting his eyes, focusing again on the fire. Finally he said, "This is not a game for me."

Frowning, she gaped at him. "It isn't a game for me either."

Bill said, "This afternoon I told you I loved you. It's the truth."

There was such a questioning look on his face she couldn't help but exclaim, "And I love you. I *meant* what I said, Bill. I don't lie. Do you doubt me?"

He was silent.

"How could you possibly doubt me?" she cried, her voice rising. "It's not possible to simulate the kind of emotions you and I have been sharing since we met."

"I know that, and don't misunderstand my silence," he was quick to answer. "I know you have deep feelings for me." Leaning forward, he took hold of her hand, gripped it in his. "I just want you to know that I'm serious about you—" He paused, pinned his eyes on her. "I'm playing for keeps."

Vanessa nodded.

"Just so long as you know," he said.

"Yes, I do, Bill."

"I'll never let you go, Vanessa."

"You might change your mind," she began, but halted when she saw the stern expression on his face.

"I won't."

Vanessa sat back on the sofa, gazed abstractedly at the painting above the fireplace.

He asked in a low voice, "What are you going to do?"

"I'll tell Peter I want a divorce."

"Are you sure?"

"Yes, I'm sure."

"So am I. I've never been more sure of anything in my life." Moving closer to her on the sofa, he put his arms around her and held her against him. And he knew he had the world in his arms. She was the only woman for him, the only woman he wanted.

10

New York, December 1995

Bill had asked Vanessa to meet him at Tavern On The Green at twelve-thirty on Saturday, and as she walked into the famous restaurant in Central Park she realized what a good choice it had been.

Always festive at any time of year, it was spectacular during the Christmas season. Beautifully decorated Christmas trees were strategically placed, strings of tiny fairy lights were hung in festoons throughout while branches of holly berries in vases and pink and red poinsettias in wooden tubs added an extra fillip to the seasonal setting.

The magnificent Venetian glass chandeliers, which were permanent fixtures in the main dining room, seemed more appropriate than ever at this time of year.

Bill spotted her immediately. Rising, he left the table and hurried forward to meet her.

As he came toward her, she thought how handsome he looked, and he was extremely well-dressed today. He wore a navy blue blazer, blue shirt, navy tie, and gray pants. He was bandbox perfect, right down to his well-polished brown loafers.

Grabbing her hands, he leaned into her, murmured, "You look great, darling," and gave her a perfunctory kiss on the cheek. "Come and meet the other two women I love," he added as he led her to the table, the proud smile still in place.

Vanessa saw at once how attractive and elegant his mother was, and she seemed much younger than sixty-two. Dressed in a dark red wool suit that set off her beautifully coiffed auburn hair, she looked more like Bill's older sister than his mother.

Sitting next to his mother was undoubtedly the most exquisite child Vanessa had ever seen. She had delicate, perfectly sculpted features, wide-set cornflower blue eyes that mirrored Bill's, and glossy dark blonde hair that fell in waves and curls to her shoulders.

"I've never seen a child who looks like that," Vanessa exclaimed softly, turning to Bill. "Helena's . . . why she's positively breathtaking."

He squeezed her arm. "Thank you, and yes, she is lovely looking, even though I say so myself."

They came to a standstill at the table, and Bill said, "Mom, I'd like to introduce Vanessa Stewart. And Vanessa, this is my mother, Drucilla."

"I'm so glad to meet you, Mrs. Fitzgerald," Vanessa said, taking his mother's outstretched hand.

"Hello, Miss Stewart." Drucilla smiled at her warmly.

"Oh, Mrs. Fitzgerald, please call me Vanessa."

"Only if you call me Dru, everyone does."

"All right, I will. Thank you." Vanessa looked down at the little girl dressed in a blue wool dress, who was observing her with enormous curiosity. "And you must be Helena," she said, offering the six-year-old her hand.

"Yes, I am," Helena said solemnly, taking her hand.

"This is Vanessa," Bill said.

"I'm delighted to meet you, Helena," Vanessa murmured, and seated herself in the chair Bill had pulled out for her.

"Now, what shall we have to drink?" Bill asked, looking at all of them. "How about champagne?"

"That would be nice," Vanessa said.

"Yes, it would, Bill," his mother agreed.

"Is this a celebration?" Helena asked, gazing up at Bill, her head on one side.

"Why do you ask that, Pumpkin?"

"Gran says champagne is only for celebrations."

"Then it's a celebration," Bill responded, his love for his child spilling out of his eyes.

"And what's this celebration?" Helena probed.

Bill thought for a moment, looked at his mother, and answered, "Being here together, the four of us. Yes, that's what we're celebrating, and Christmas, too, of course."

"But I'm not allowed champagne," Helena remarked, staring at him, then swiveling her eyes to Dru. "Am I, Gran?"

"Certainly not," her grandmother responded firmly. "Not until you're grown up."

Bill said, "But you are allowed a Shirley Temple, and that's what I'm going to order for you right now." As he was speaking, Bill signaled to a hovering waiter, who promptly came over to the table and took the order.

Vanessa said to Dru, "It was a great idea of Bill's to suggest coming here for lunch; it's such a festive place."

Dru nodded. "You're right, it's fabulous. Bill tells me you met in Venice. When he was there with Frank Peterson."

"Yes . . ." Vanessa hesitated and then, noticing Bill's beaming face, she went on more confidently, "We spent Thanksgiving together."

"The only three Americans in Venice on that particular day," Bill interjected. "So we had no alternative but to celebrate together. And a good time was had by all."

"I'd like to go to Venice," Helena announced, looking from her father to her grandmother. "Can I?"

"One day, sweetheart," Bill said. "We'll take you when you're a bit older."

"Do you work with my daddy?" Helena asked, zeroing in on Vanessa.

"No, I don't," Vanessa answered. "I'm not in television, Helena. I'm a glass designer."

The child's smooth brow furrowed. "What's that?"

"I design objects, lovely things for the home, which are made in glass. In Venice."

"Oh."

Vanessa had been carrying a small shopping bag when she arrived, and this she had placed with her handbag on the floor. Now she reached for it, took out a gift tied with a large pink bow, and announced, "This is for you, Helena."

The child took it, held it in her hands, staring at the prettily wrapped present. "What is it?"

"Something I made for you."

"Can I open it now, Daddy?"

"Yes, but what do you say first?"

"Thank you, Vanessa." Helena untied the ribbon, took off the paper, and then lifted the lid off the box.

"It's quite fragile," Vanessa warned. "Lift it out of the tissue paper gently."

Helena did as she was bidden, held the glass object in her hands carefully, her eyes wide. It was a twisted, tubular prism that narrowed to a point. Its facets caught and held the light, reflecting the colors of the rainbow. "Oh, it's beautiful," the child gasped in delight.

"It's an icicle. An icicle of many colors, and I made it specially for you, Helena."

"Thank you," Helena repeated, continuing to hold the icicle, moving it so that the glass caught the light.

"It is very beautiful," Dru murmured, turning to Vanessa. "You're a very talented artist."

"Thank you."

Bill said, "May I look at it, Helena?"

"Yes, Dad. Be careful. Vanessa says it's fragile."

"I will," he murmured, his eyes smiling at Vanessa as he took the icicle. "This is quite wonderful," he said, and then nodded when the waiter brought the champagne in a bucket of ice. "You can open it now, please," he said.

After the glass icicle was returned to its box and put on the floor next to Helena's chair, and the wine had been poured, Bill lifted his flute. "Happy Christmas, everyone."

"Happy Christmas," they all responded.

Helena took a sip of her Shirley Temple and put it down on the table. Turning, she stared hard at Vanessa, and, with undisguised inquisitiveness, she asked, "Are you Daddy's girlfriend?"

Taken aback by the child's candor, Vanessa was speechless for a moment.

Bill answered for her. "Yes, she is, Helena." He smiled at his little daughter, then looked over her head at his mother, raising a brow eloquently.

Drucilla Fitzgerald nodded her approval. And she did approve of this pretty young woman whom she had known for only twenty minutes. There was something about Vanessa that was special; she could tell that, being the good judge of character that she was. Vanessa was to be encouraged, Dru decided. Anyone who could bring this look of happiness to her son's face had her vote of confidence. He had been so lonely after Sylvie's death. And morose for years. She had not seen him so buoyant, spirited, and full of good cheer for the longest time. Suddenly, she felt as if a weight had been lifted off her shoulders.

"Let's order lunch," Bill said. "Do you know what you want, Pumpkin?"

"Yes, Daddy. I'd like to have eggs with the muffin, like we did last time."

"Eggs Benedict," Dru clarified. "I'd love it too, but I don't think I'd better. Not with my cholesterol. I suppose I'll have to settle for crab cakes."

Bill looked at Vanessa. "Do you know what you want?"

"I'll have the same as your mother, Bill, thank you."

"And I'll keep Helena company, go for the Eggs Benedict," he said.

Helena touched Vanessa's arm. "Are you going to marry Daddy?"

Vanessa was further startled by the child's outspoken question, and by her precocity. She glanced swiftly at Bill.

Dru sat back in her chair, observing the three of them.

Bill grinned at Helena and said, "You ask too many questions, Pumpkin, just like Uncle Frank does sometimes. And we don't know yet whether we're going to get married or not . . . we need to spend more time together, get to know each other better."

Helena nodded.

Bill went on, "But you and Gran will be the first to know if we do. I promise you."

Later, as Bill helped Vanessa into a cab, he whispered, "Not a bad idea my kid had, eh?"

"Not a bad idea at all," Vanessa replied.

"Take this, darling," he said, pressing something into her hand.

"What is it?" she asked, looking down at it, realizing that it was a key. "What's this for?"

"The suite I booked at the Plaza. For us. Suite 902. Can we meet for a drink later tonight? Say around nine?"

"But of course," she said and slipped the key into her bag.

11

Venice, January 1996

It had been raining all afternoon, hard, driving rain that was still coming down in an endless stream. The sky was the color of anthracite, pitted here and there with threatening black clouds, and below her the Grand Canal was swollen, looked as if it might overflow at any moment.

Vanessa turned away from the window and moved into the room, shivering slightly. Although Bill had turned up the heat earlier, when she had first arrived from the airport there had been a chill in the air. It was a dampness that seemed to permeate her bones. She tightened the belt on the bathrobe she was wearing and shrugged further into it as she huddled in a chair near the radiator.

Vanessa was glad to be back in Venice with Bill. It was the first time they had seen each other since Christmas. He had left New York at the end of December, to travel through the Middle East and Europe. Tel Aviv, Jerusalem, Amman, Beirut, Ankara, and Athens were some of the cities on his list. He was busy preparing his special on international terrorism for CNS; time was of the essence since it had been scheduled to air early in March.

Bill had arrived at the Gritti Palace a day earlier than Vanessa, flying in from Athens the night before just as she was leaving New York. They would have five days together in their favorite city. She had work to do out at the glass foundry on Murano. Bill was going to polish his script for the show, and they would be together in the afternoons and evenings.

A smile touched her mouth as she thought of Bill and her love for him. He meant more to her than she had ever imagined possible. He was the man of her life. For the rest of her life. They were meant to be together, and there was nothing that could keep them apart. She knew that now.

A small sigh escaped as she thought of the past few weeks. Apart from seeing Bill, meeting his mother and Helena, December had been a ghastly month for her. Peter had stayed in London longer than he had intended, and after his return to Manhattan he had left almost immediately for Los Angeles. He had been away so much she had barely had a chance to discuss their private life, and Christmas had been miserable for the most part.

Finally, early in January, she had cornered him one evening when he returned from the office earlier than usual. Endeavoring to be as gentle as possible, while displaying no weakness whatsoever, Vanessa had told him she wanted a divorce.

Peter had reacted badly, overreacted really, and had been adamant that they remain married. Even though he had agreed, in the end, that their relationship was no longer what it had once been, he nonetheless refused even to consider divorcing. Very simply, he balked at the idea and wouldn't listen to her. At least not that particular evening.

Vanessa had come to realize that there was only one thing to do, and that was to get on with her life, lead it as she saw fit, and be independent. Ten days before leaving on this trip to

Venice, she had taken her courage in both hands and left Peter, moving all of her clothes and possessions into the loft in Soho.

The loft had once been an apartment before she had turned it into a studio-office, and it had a good-sized working kitchen, a full bathroom, plus a guest toilet. Once she had purchased a sofa bed and installed it in the back storage room, turning this into a bedroom, the loft had become a comfortable place to live. Most important, it had made Peter realize just how determined she was to end their marriage. Her departure had a tremendous impact on him; he at last understood how serious she was about a divorce.

As her mother had said to her, "Actions make more of a statement than words ever could, Vanny, and it's best to end this now, while you're both still young enough to start all over again, find new partners." Both of her parents had been very supportive of her decision to leave Peter. However, she had not told them about Bill, deeming it wiser to keep her own counsel at this moment.

Vanessa heard Bill's key in the lock and glanced at the door as he came in. Getting up, she went to him, her face full of smiles.

He had gone downstairs a few minutes earlier to pick up a fax which had arrived from New York. Now he waved it and said, "Neil Gooden and Jack Clayton *love* the footage so far. Neil says he can't wait to see the rest of it." Bill handed her the fax. "Here, read it yourself, darling."

She scanned the two pages, digested everything, and handed it back to him. "Congratulations, Bill. From what Neil says, you've worked miracles and in less than three weeks. Aren't you thrilled he thinks it's going to be a smash?"

"From his mouth to God's ears," Bill said with a huge grin, and putting his arm around her shoulders he walked her over to the sofa.

"I do think it's coming together, though. I just need to cover two more cities and then it's a wrap, as far as the field reporting is concerned. When you go back to New York, I'll head for Paris, work there a couple of days with my crew and the producer. Then we'll all go on to Northern Ireland, make Belfast our last stop. Incidentally, I've finally come up with a good title."

"What is it?"

"I'm thinking of calling the special *Terrorism: The Face of Evil*. What's your feeling about it?"

"I think it sounds good. And it says exactly what you mean."

He nodded. "Yes, I guess it does. What I've managed to do is cover terrorism around the world. I've been filming interviews with experts, and some terrorists who are in jail in Israel. I'm backing up the new stuff with footage of past acts of terrorism, from the 1972 killing of the Olympic athletes and Lord Mountbatten's murder by the IRA to the Lockerbie crash, the World Trade Center bombing, and the Oklahoma City explosion. I've endeavored to make it very personal, very intimate. I want it to hit home, touch the average American. I'll be using some interviews I did with survivors of terrorism, and relatives of victims of terrorists. I'm quite gratified by the way it's come together." Bill got up, walked across to the mini bar, and took a bottle of mineral water from it. "Do you want anything, Vanessa?"

She shook her head.

Bill strode back to the sofa, sat down next to her. After taking a sip of water, he placed the bottle on the coffee table and placed his arm around her. "Moving into the loft was a very good idea, Vanessa. It's shown Peter how serious you are about a divorce."

"Yes, it has. He phoned me yesterday, just as I was leaving for Kennedy. And while he didn't actually *agree* to a divorce, he did sound more amenable, if a little crushed. I have the feeling he's beginning to accept the idea."

"That's a relief." Bill looked at her intently. "Did you tell him about me? About us?"

"No, I didn't, Bill. I didn't think it was necessary. And anyway, it would be like a red flag to a bull. Very inflammatory."

"I don't care if he knows, you know. I'm a big boy. I can look after myself."

"Yes, but why rub salt in the wound? Anyway, Peter really has come to accept how bad our relationship has been for the last few years . . . I prefer to leave it at that."

"Whatever you say, sweetheart, you're the boss."

She gave him the benefit of a loving smile.

He leaned closer, kissed her on the mouth. "The concierge just told me Venice will be flooded by seven o'clock. No Harry's Bar tonight, I'm afraid. We'll have to eat here."

"That's fine, Bill. The restaurant downstairs is good."

"Oh, but I thought we would have room service, eat here in the suite."

"Yes, if you want, I think it's more comfortable anyway, and I don't have to get dressed."

He nodded and reached for her. "My thought precisely."

"You once suggested that we make Venice our point of rendezvous," Bill said to her much later that evening, after they had made love, eaten dinner, and made love again. "And I think that's a great idea. It's going to be very convenient for me."

They were in bed and Vanessa lay within the circle of his arms. She swiveled her eyes to meet his. "What do you mean?"

"When I've finished the special on terrorism, I'm being assigned to the Middle East. I'll be based either in Israel or Lebanon, that's up to me. But whichever it is, I can fly straight up to Venice. It's an easy trip. I'll try to be here whenever you're working at the foundry in Murano, if only for a couple of days, or a long weekend."

Her face lit up. "Oh, Bill, that'll be wonderful, being able to see you every month. Well, more or less. Why the Middle East, though?"

"I didn't want to go back to Bosnia, as you know, even though there's trouble there again. There always will be, too, if you ask me. And the peace accords are very fragile, not likely to last, especially if the UN troops leave. Still, I wanted out, and Jack Clayton was aware of that ages ago. So he asked me if I'd like to go back to the Middle East to cover the whole area. I know it well, and Frankie's in Lebanon. So it'll be like old home week." He grinned at her. "As I'm telling you this, I'm beginning to realize that I will base myself in Beirut, set up camp with Frankie at the Commodore Hotel."

"When will that be, darling?"

"In March sometime. I'll be cutting and editing at CNS in New York in the middle of February, preparing the special. And then I'll go."

"I thought everything was quiet in the Middle East right now."

"As quiet as that area will ever be. There are always rumblings of some kind, somewhere, be it Iran, Libya, Saudi Arabia, Syria, Israel, or Iraq. You name it. Flare-ups happen all the time," Bill explained.

"If your assignment starts in March, when do you think we can meet here again?"

Bill held her closer, smiling at her, his blue eyes crinkling at the corners. "In March, of course. The end of March."

12

Venice, March 1996

"Are you sure there are no messages for me?" Vanessa said, her eyes focused intently on the concierge standing behind the desk at the Gritti Palace.

"No, Signora Stewart, no messages." His faint smile seemed almost apologetic as he added, "No, nothing at all. No faxes, nothing, signora."

"Thank you." Vanessa turned away from the desk and walked rapidly toward the elevator.

Once she was back in her room, she sat down at the writing table in front of the window and gazed absently out at the Grand Canal.

It was a cool, breezy Saturday in late March, but the sun had come out and given a certain radiance to the afternoon. Yet she was hardly aware of the weather; her thoughts were focused on Bill. She opened her appointment book and stared at the date. It was March the thirtieth, and she had been in Venice for four days, working at the foundry on Murano. Bill was supposed to have arrived on Thursday afternoon, the twenty-eighth, to join her for a long weekend.

But he was forty-eight hours late, and she did not understand why. After all, it was not as if he were in a war zone and in any danger. Beirut was quiet at the moment; he had told her that himself. She dismissed the idea that something might have happened to him.

It struck her then that he could have gone somewhere else in the Middle East to cover a story. He had talked about Egypt and the Sudan to her when he had been in New York in February. They had been able to meet only once at that time because he had been busy editing his special on terrorism, and then he had had to leave for Beirut.

Yes, that was most likely the reason he was late. Right now he was probably on a plane, flying to Venice from some distant spot. This thought cheered her, but an instant later she was worrying again. If he had been delayed because he was caught up on a story, why hadn't he phoned her?

Frowning to herself, Vanessa reached for her address book and quickly found the number of the Commodore Hotel in Beirut. Glancing at the hotel's chart for direct dialing to foreign cities, she picked up the phone and punched in the numbers for Beirut and the hotel.

It was only a second or two before she heard the hotel operator saying, "Hotel Commodore."

"Mr. Bill Fitzgerald, please."

"Just a moment, please."

She heard the ringing tone. It seemed to her to be interminable. He did not pick up. He was not in his room.

"There's no answer," the operator said. "Do you wish to leave a message?"

"Yes. Please say Vanessa Stewart called. He can reach me at the Gritti Palace in Venice." She then gave the operator the number and hung up, sat staring at the phone.

After a few moments, she rose and walked over to the coffee table. Picking up the remote control, she turned up the volume on the television set. The CNS weatherman was giving the weekend forecast for the States. She sat down on the bed and watched CNS for the next couple of hours.

World news. American news. Business news. Sports news. But no news of Bill Fitzgerald, chief foreign correspondent for CNS.

Later in the evening, for the umpteenth time that day, Vanessa checked her answering machines at the Manhattan loft and the cottage in Southampton. There was no message from Bill.

At one point she ordered sandwiches, fruit, and a pot of hot tea. She had not eaten anything since breakfast, and suddenly she was feeling hungry. After her light supper she watched CNS until the early hours, although she did so with only half an eye. It was mostly repeats of everything she had seen earlier, and her mind was elsewhere anyway.

On Sunday morning, after she had drunk a quick cup of coffee, Vanessa dialed the Commodore Hotel in Beirut and asked for Bill Fitzgerald.

Once again, there was no answer in his room.

This time, Vanessa asked to be put through to Frank Peterson. She clutched the phone tightly, listening to the ring, hoping that at least Frank would pick up. He did not.

After a split second the hotel operator was back on the line. "I'm sorry, both of them seem to be out, miss. Would you like to leave a message?"

"Yes, for Mr. Fitzgerald. Please ask him to call Vanessa Stewart at the Gritti Palace in Venice."

Vanessa spent a miserable Sunday, waiting for the phone to ring and watching CNS and CNN on television, alternating between the two cable networks. At one point she checked her answering machines in the States, but there were no messages. Not a whisper from anyone. She even phoned the international news desk at CNS headquarters in New York. But they wouldn't give her any information about Bill's whereabouts.

By late afternoon she had given up hope of Bill arriving. In any case, she was due to leave for New York on Monday morning, and so she got out her suitcase and began to pack. She did so in a flurry of emotions—frustration, anger, disappointment, worry, and dismay.

That night, when she went to bed, Vanessa was unable to sleep. She turned restlessly for hours, praying for morning to come.

Eventually she must have dozed off because she awakened with a start as dawn was breaking. As she lay there in the dim, gray light Vanessa finally acknowledged what she had been denying all weekend: The real reason Bill had not shown up was because he was no longer interested in her. Their affair was over for him. Finished. Dead.

No, she thought, he cared too much. I'm wrong.

And yet deep down she knew she was right. There was no other possible reason for his absence.

She closed her eyes, remembering all the things he had said to her . . . that he loved her . . . that he was playing for keeps . . . that he was serious about her . . . that this wasn't a game for him. He'd even encouraged her to divorce Peter. Why did he do that, if he hadn't meant what he said?

Well, of course he meant those things when he said them, that niggling voice at the back of her head muttered. He was glib, slick, smooth. A wordsmith. Clever with all those wonderful words that tripped off his tongue so lightly. Wasn't that all part of his talent? Hadn't he told her that his grandmother had always said, when he was growing up, that he'd kissed the Blarney Stone?

There was another thing, too. He was back in the close company of Frank Peterson, his best friend, his alter ego. Frank was a man Bill had characterized as a womanizer with a terminal Don Juan complex. Those had been his exact words. Maybe they were off somewhere together for the weekend. Bill was very close to Frank, and impressed by him. And perhaps some of Frank's habits were contagious.

Suddenly she felt like a fool. She had been sitting here waiting for Bill for four days and there hadn't been the slightest word from him. As chief foreign correspondent for CNS he had access to phones wherever he was. He could have called her from anywhere.

But he had not, and that was a fact she could not ignore.

Dismay lodged in the pit of her stomach and she found herself trembling. Tears sprang into her eyes and she sat up, brushing them aside as she turned on the light, looked at her travel clock. It was five o'clock. She sat on the side of the bed for a moment, endeavoring to pull herself together. As painful as it was, she had to admit that she had been dumped. Why, she would never know. She began to cry again, and she discovered that she could not stop.

13

"Over the years, I've discovered that the more you love a person, the more they're bound to disappoint you in the end," her mother had once said to her, adding: "And, in my opinion, men understand this better than we do. That's why they rather cleverly spread their bets. Always remember that, Vanny. Don't give all for love. And don't be duped."

But she had given all for love. And she had been duped. And she had remembered her mother's wise words far too late for them to matter.

Was it true? Did men spread their bets when it came to women? Was that what Bill had done?

Certainly she had loved him a lot, put all of her trust in him. And in the end he *had* bitterly disappointed her. But no, wait, it was so much more than disappointment, wasn't it? He had humiliated her, made her feel foolish, even ridiculous, and he had hurt her so badly she thought she would never recover from that hurt. It cut deep . . . deep into her very soul.

She had been so open with him, so honest, baring her soul, her innermost secret self. She had given him everything she had to give, far more than she had given any other man, even her husband.

Seemingly, her gifts of love and adoration had meant nothing to him. He had discarded her as easily as he had picked her up in the bar of the Hotel Gritti Palace.

Unexpectedly, and quite suddenly, she remembered something he had said to her about Frank, something about Frank hedging his bets as far as women were concerned. Perhaps all men did that.

Vanessa let out a long sigh and walked on across the sand dunes, her heart heavy, her mind still fogged by the pain of Bill's defection.

It was a fine, clear day in the middle of April—cold, with a pale sun in a pale sky. The Atlantic Ocean was calmer than it had been for days despite the wind that was blowing up.

She lifted her eyes and stared up into the sky when she heard the *cawk-cawk* of seagulls. She watched them as they wheeled and turned against the clouds.

The wind buffeted her, driving her toward the beach. She hunched down farther into her heavy duffle coat and stuck her gloved hands into her pockets. She felt dispirited to the point of depression.

She was well aware that her depressed emotional state was because of Bill Fitzgerald and what he had done to her. She found it hard to believe that he had disappeared from her life in the way that he had, but it was true. At times she even tried to tell herself she didn't care. But of course she did.

Their love affair had been so intense, so sexual, so passionate in every way and so ... *fierce.* He had swept her off her feet and into his bed and then out of his life when he had grown tired of her. Just like that. *Puff!* She was gone. Had their affair been too hot? Had it burned out too fast for him? She was not sure. How could she be sure ... of anything ... ever again?

Vanessa felt the splatter of raindrops on her face and immediately looked up. Thunderheads were darkening that etiolated sky, turning it to leaden gray, and there was the sudden bright flourish of lightning, then the crack of thunder.

Turning swiftly, she walked back to the cottage at the edge of the dunes. She made it just in time. It was a cloudburst. The heavens opened and the rain poured down.

She locked the door behind her, took off her duffle, and went into the library. Here she turned on lamps, struck a match, and brought the flame to the paper and logs Mavis had stacked in the grate.

Since she had returned, Mavis Glover had taken to coming almost every day, fussing over her, bringing her fruit and vegetables and other groceries. Once Mavis had even offered to pick up newspapers and magazines, but Vanessa had told her not to bother. She was not interested in the outside world; she had cut herself off from it.

She had returned from Venice and moved out to Southampton permanently. She had turned herself into a virtual hermit. She had unplugged her telephone and pulled the plugs on the radio and the television. In fact, she vowed she would never look at television again as long as she lived.

She was out of contact with everyone. Out of action. The only person she saw or spoke to was Mavis.

Licking my wounds, she thought now as she sank onto the sofa in front of the fire. Licking my wounds like a sick animal.

The truth was, she did not want to see anyone, not even her mother. The world was well lost for her.

Peter had sent the divorce papers; they had arrived yesterday by special delivery. She had laughed loudly and hollowly when she had seen them. As if they mattered now. She had pushed for the divorce when Bill was a part of her life, and now seemingly he had discarded her.

The anger flared again in her and with it came the hot, endless tears. Pushing her face down into the cushions, she cried until she thought there were no tears left in her.

*   *   *

She sat up with a start. The fire had almost gone out. Glancing at the mantelpiece, she focused on the clock. It was just five. Time to go to work.

Pushing herself up off the sofa, Vanessa looked out of the window and saw that the rain had ceased. The late afternoon sky, washed clean of the dark clouds, was clear again.

After putting on her duffle coat, she walked slowly across the lawn to the red barn, then stopped for a brief moment as she passed the small copse of trees to the left of the house. Years ago her mother had planted hundreds of daffodils, and she had added to them since she had owned the cottage.

Many of them were pushing their golden heads upward, fluttering in the breeze, pale yellow beacons in the soft light. How fresh and springlike they looked. So pretty under the trees. Her eyes filled. She brushed her damp cheeks with her fingertips and walked on.

Once she was inside her studio, Vanessa focused on her work. Going to the drawing board, she switched on the light above it and was soon sketching rapidly, drawing spheres and globes, until she found her way through the many shapes springing into her mind. She settled, at last, on kidney and oval shapes.

Her work had become her salvation. She found it hard to sleep at night, and so she had reversed her routine. From five o'clock until eleven she created her designs in the barn. She had a drink and ate dinner at midnight, and then read half the night, until fatigue finally overcame her.

And once the designs on paper were finished, she worked in the foundry, hand-blowing the glass pieces. As she did she would ask herself how she would ever be able to go to Venice again. She would have to because of her work. But she knew she must find another hotel. She would never again set foot in the Gritti Palace.

14

Beirut, April 1996

"You were *there*, Joe! What really happened?" Frank Peterson exclaimed, his voice rising slightly. His face was pale, and he looked strained and anxious.

Leaning over the table, he pinned his eyes on Joe Alonzo. "What the hell happened to Bill?" he demanded again.

Joe shook his head. He looked as if he were about to burst into tears. "I'm telling you, Frank, it was over before I could blink. We were in West Beirut, not too far from here, near the mosque. We all got out of the car, Mike, Bill, and me. Bill started to walk toward the mosque; Mike and I went to the trunk, to take out our equipment. Suddenly this big Mercedes slid to a stop. Three young men jumped out, grabbed Bill, and hustled him into the car. Then the Mercedes sped off."

"And you didn't follow it!" Frank said in a hard, tight voice, staring at the CNS soundman. "Jesus, Joe!"

"I know, I know, Frank, I can guess what you're thinking. But the point is, Mike and I were stunned for a second. We couldn't believe it."

"And so you didn't react."

"We did, but not fast enough! Within a few seconds we ran to our car, raced after the Mercedes, but we couldn't find it.

645

The damned thing had just disappeared. Literally, into thin air."

"These local terrorists know all the side streets and back alleys," Frank said, and eyed Joe thoughtfully. "And if you and Mike hadn't been taking your equipment out of the trunk, you would've probably been grabbed as well," he asserted in a quieter tone.

"Damn right we would!" Mike Williams said, coming to a halt at the table where Frank and Joe were sitting in the bar of the Marriott in the Hamra district of Beirut.

Frank jumped up at the sight of Mike, grabbed his hand and shook it. "Join us, Mike, I've just been talking to Joe about Bill's kidnapping."

"It's a hell of a thing . . . we're at our wits' end . . ." Mike sat down heavily. He looked tired and worried. "When did you get back to Beirut, Frank?"

"Last night. From Egypt. I was covering a story there when the new trouble between the Israelis and Hezbollah erupted. The civil war is over, everything's on the mend, and then they start skirmishing again. But did they ever *really* stop?"

"I doubt it," Mike replied. "Still, it's the first time the Israelis have attacked Beirut directly in fourteen years. And with laser-homing Hellfire missiles, no less, shot from four helicopter gunships off the coast. My jaw practically dropped when it happened two days ago."

"Yeah, but the Israelis were actually responding to Hezbollah's bombing of Israel," Joe pointed out quickly.

Frank nodded. "And after Israel's attack on Beirut, Hezbollah retaliated yesterday by sending another forty rockets into Israel. The war of attrition continues."

"Nothing changes much," Mike murmured and motioned to a waiter, ordered scotch on the rocks.

Frank said, "I couldn't believe it when I saw the story on CNS about Bill's kidnapping. My God, I'd just left him when he was taken. I flew out of Beirut on March twenty-seventh and he was grabbed the next day. And for most of the time I was away I thought he was having a good time in Venice."

"He never made it to Venice," Mike responded. "I'm sure you realize the network sat on the story for a few days, hoping he would be released quickly. When he wasn't, they got it on the air at once."

"Who's behind it? Have you heard anything?" Frank probed.

"No, we haven't," Joe answered.

"I was just on the phone to Jack Clayton," Mike explained. "The network still doesn't have any information. Nobody's claiming this, the way the bastards usually do. It's a bit of a mystery. Total silence from all terrorist groups, according to New York."

"It's got to be Hezbollah," Frank said in a knowing tone. He turned from Mike to Joe, raising a brow. "Who else but them?"

"You're right," Joe agreed. "That's what Mike and I think, too. At least, we believe that the Islamic Jihad is behind it. You know better than anybody, Frank, that the terrorist arm of Hezbollah is full of wackos. They're the ones who took Terry Anderson and William Buckley, and they're not known for fast releases."

"Terry Anderson was a hostage for seven years," Frank muttered.

"Don't remind me," Mike said dourly. "By the way, we've been in touch with Bill's mother."

"I spoke with her myself from Egypt," Frank answered. "As soon as I knew what had happened. It's remarkable the way she's holding up."

Joe volunteered, "We try to call her every few days. Unfortunately, there's not much we can tell her."

"Hearing from you helps her a great deal, I'm sure of that." Frank lifted his glass, downed the last of his scotch. Leaning back in his chair, he thought for a moment about Vanessa. He had tried to reach her for days, but there was no answer at her left or the cottage in the Hamptons. "What's the network doing about trying to find Bill?" he asked.

"There's not a lot they can do," Mike said. "Bill's picture has been circulated throughout Beirut, the whole of Lebanon, in fact. And a great deal of pressure has been put on the Lebanese and Syrian governments, and right from the beginning. Even though the story wasn't released immediately, the CNS top brass were on top of the situation at once, the same day Bill was snatched.

"And pressure was put on the White House as well. Let's face it, Frank, there's nothing anyone can do until an organization claims the kidnapping as theirs. Only then can the U.S. Government and the network start pushing for Bill's release."

"I always kidded him, said he was bulletproof," Frank began and stopped when Allan Brent, the Middle East correspondent for CNN, stopped at their table.

"We've just had a news flash," he said. "Hezbollah is claiming they have Bill Fitzgerald."

"Oh, Jesus!" Frank cried.

"How long ago was the flash?" Joe asked.

Allan Brent glanced at his watch. "It's now seven, about six-thirty, thereabouts."

Mark Lawrence, who was covering Bill's kidnapping for CNS, appeared in the doorway of the bar. When he spotted the CNS crew with Frank and Allan Brent, he hurried over. He said to Mike, "I guess you've heard that the Islamic Jihad has Bill."

"Yes," Mike said. "Allan just told us."

"I hope to God Bill's all right," Frank cried. "I *pray* to God he's all right. That group is fanatical, unstable, and unpredictable."

*   *   *

It was always dark in the cramped, airless room.

They had nailed old wood boards over the windows and only thin slivers of light crept in through the cracks.

Bill Fitzgerald turned awkwardly on the narrow cot; his movements were restricted by handcuffs and leg chains. Managing at last to get onto his back, he lay staring up at the ceiling, trying to assess what day it was.

All along he had attempted to keep track of time; he figured he had been a hostage for almost two weeks. When he asked his various guards, they wouldn't tell him. All they ever said was, "Shut up, American pig!"

He felt dirty, and wished they would allow him to have another shower. He had only been permitted two since his capture. His clothes had become so filthy he had begged them to give him something clean, which one of his guards had done yesterday. *Finally.* Cotton undershorts, a T-shirt, and a pair of cotton pants had been thrown at him, and he had been unchained in order to change into them. The clothes were cheap, but it was a relief to have them.

He had no idea where he was, whether he was still somewhere in Beirut or in the Bekaa Valley, that hotbed of Hezbollah activities where the Iran-backed militia was in control. So many hostages had been held there.

Bill didn't even know why he had been taken, except that he was an American and a journalist. But he *was* certain of one thing—the identity of his kidnappers. They were young men of the Islamic Jihad, the terrorist arm of Hezbollah, and dangerous. Some of them were slightly crazed, on the edge, capable of anything.

They kept him chained up, shouted abuse at him, beat him every day, and gave him little food or water. And what food they did provide was stale, almost inedible. Yet despite their continuing mistreatment of him, he was not going to let them break his spirit.

Bill kept his mind fully occupied as best he could.

He thought mostly of his child, his mother, and of Vanessa, the woman he loved. He worried about them, worried about how they were reacting to his kidnapping, how they were handling it. He had faith in them, knew they would be strong; even his child would be strong.

As he lay staring at the dirty ceiling, he envisioned Vanessa's face in his mind's eye, projected her image onto the ceiling.

How lovely she was, so special, and so very dear to him. And how lucky he was to have found her. He knew they would have a wonderful life together. The first thing he was going to do when he was free was make a child with her. She wanted one so badly; she had confided that to him the last time they had been together.

He had worried about her for the first few days he was in captivity, knowing she was alone in Venice, waiting for him. And with no idea why he had not shown up.

Bill heard the key turning in the lock. He focused his eyes on the door and steeled himself for his daily beating. In the dim light he saw one of his captors entering the cell.

"Put on blindfold," the young man said, walking across the room, showing the grimy rag to Bill.

"Why?" Bill asked, endeavoring to sit up.

"No speak, American pig! American spy!" the young man shouted and tied the blindfold around Bill's eyes roughly, pulled him to his feet, and led him across the cell.

"Where are you taking me?" Bill demanded.

"No speak!" the terrorist yelled, pushing Bill out of the room.

15

Vanessa sat up with a jerk, feeling disoriented, blinking as she looked around the library. Dimly, in the distance, the thudding noise that had awakened her continued.

She pushed herself to her feet, hurried across the room and out into the hall. Instantly the thudding sounded louder, and she realized that someone was hammering on the front door of the cottage.

She ran across the hall, shouting, "I'm coming," and flung open the door. Much to her surprise and consternation she found herself staring into the face of Bill's mother.

"Dru!" she exclaimed, completely taken aback. "Hello! Have you been knocking long?"

When his mother did not answer, but simply stared at her blankly, Vanessa went on, "Why have you come to see me? What are you doing here?" Her brows knitted together in a frown when suddenly she became aware of Dru Fitzgerald's troubled face and bloodshot eyes. She also noticed that she looked painfully thin. "Dru, what's the matter?" she asked, urgency echoing in her voice.

Dru leaned against the door jamb, unexpectedly breathing hard, as if she was experiencing some sort of difficulty. She managed to say, "May I come inside, Vanessa?"

"How rude of me to keep you standing here. Of course, please come in. Can I get you anything?"

"A glass of water, please. I must take a pill."

Vanessa took hold of Drucilla's arm and escorted her into the cottage. After leading her to the sitting room, and settling her in a chair, she went to the kitchen for the water.

A moment later Vanessa returned. She handed the glass to Dru, waited for her to take the pill, then said, "I can tell you're distressed about something. What's the matter?"

Drucilla Fitzgerald, staring intently at her, realized with a small jolt that Vanessa did not know what had happened to Bill. How that was possible she wasn't sure, but, nonetheless, she was quite certain it was true. Dru wondered how to tell her. Tears flooded her eyes, and she clasped her hands together to stop them from trembling.

Vanessa was about to ask her again what was causing her upset when Dru cleared her throat, reached out and took hold of Vanessa's hand.

Dru said slowly, almost in a whisper, "I've been trying to reach you on the phone for days." No longer able to control herself, she began to weep. She groped in her wool jacket for her handkerchief.

"I've had my phone turned off," Vanessa explained, and as she said these words she had a terrible sense of foreboding. "It's Bill! Something's happened to Bill, hasn't it?"

Dru continued to cry, her sobs almost uncontrollable, her pain even more apparent now.

Vanessa went and sat next to her on the sofa, put her arm around Dru's shoulders. "I'm totally in the dark, Dru. I've had not only the phone turned off but the television as well. I've cut myself off from the world for the past two weeks."

Dru turned to look at her, the tears streaming down her pale face. Her mouth began to tremble. "He's dead," she said in a voice that was barely audible. "My son is dead. My only child has been taken from me in the most cruel way. Oh Vanessa . . . Vanessa . . . Why did they kill him? They shot him. He's never coming back. He's gone. Oh, whatever shall we do without him?" She continued to weep, gasping, holding her arms around her body. Her sorrow was unendurable.

Vanessa was gaping at Dru. She had gone cold all over, and she was stunned, reeling from shock, unable to respond for a moment. Her eyes welled, and she began to shake. At last, she said, "I don't understand . . . *who* killed Bill?" Choking on these words, she was unable to continue, just held onto Dru tightly. The two women clung together, sobbing.

Eventually, through her tears, Dru said, "It was Hezbollah. The Islamic Jihad. They kidnapped Bill, Vanessa. I realize now that you didn't know, otherwise you would have come to Helena and me, to be with us."

"When?" Vanessa gasped. "When was he taken?" Her voice shook and fresh tears flowed; she knew the answer even before Dru spoke.

"March the twenty-eighth," Dru answered. "It was a Thursday. They took him that morning in Beirut. He was out with the crew, Joe and Mike—"

"Oh, my God! My God!" Vanessa cried out, pressing both of her hands to her face, trying to stem the tears. They slid through her fingers, fell down onto her cotton shirt, leaving damp splotches. "I was waiting for him in Venice, and he didn't come! I thought he'd lost interest in me, that it was over between us. But he couldn't come, could he? Oh, Dru, Dru . . ."

"No, he couldn't. He loved you, Vanessa, he wanted to marry you. He told me that. He also told me that you were married, that you were getting a divorce."

Vanessa swallowed hard. "Bill was mine and I was his and that was the way it was. How could I have forgotten that?"

Drucilla sighed and looked into Vanessa's face sadly. "When we're in love, things are always very extreme, intense . . . "

"I love him with all my heart. I shouldn't ever have doubted him in Venice. I should have known something terrible had happened, something beyond his control."

Dru was silent for a second, and then she said softly, "You were feeling hurt."

Vanessa suddenly lost control again and started to weep bitterly. "When was he shot?" she asked through her tears.

"We're not sure." Dru found it hard to continue. She brought her hand to her trembling mouth, and took a few moments to regain her composure.

Slowly, she went on, "Andrew Bryce, the president of CNS, and Jack Clayton, Bill's news editor, came to see me yesterday." Pausing, she took a deep breath before saying, "To tell me themselves that the Islamic Jihad had just announced they had executed Bill. They left his body at the French Embassy in Beirut, who have given it to the American Hospital to send home."

"But why did they kill him?" Vanessa cried. "*Why*, Dru?"

"Andrew and Jack don't know. No one knows. The Islamic Jihad haven't said anything. They've given no explanation."

The two women who loved Bill Fitzgerald sat together on the sofa, not speaking, lost in their own troubled thoughts, silently sharing their heartbreak and sorrow.

After a while, Vanessa spoke. Looking at Dru, she said, "Where is Helena?"

Dru covered her mouth with her hand once more, the tears starting afresh. After a moment she said, "I brought her with me. I hadn't the heart to leave her. She's walking the dunes with Alice, the nanny. The child's heartbroken, she worshiped him so."

Vanessa nodded. Rising, she walked across the room to the window, stood looking out at the dunes, her mind full of Bill and the love they had shared. She thought of his child. And she came to a sudden decision.

Turning to look at Bill's mother, Vanessa said, "I think you and Helena should stay here with me for a few days, Dru. Bill would want us to be together."

Much later that night, when she was alone in her bedroom, Vanessa wept for Bill once more. She wept for the loss of the man she loved, the life they would never share, and the children they would never have.

It was a long night of tears and anguish. There was a moment when guilt reared up, but she crushed it before it took hold. It was a ridiculous waste of time to feel guilty because she had doubted him briefly. He would be the first to say that, just as his mother had.

As dawn broke over the dunes, Vanessa came to understand that her grief would last for a long time, and that she must let it run its course. Bill Fitzgerald had been the love of her life, and she had lost him in the blink of an eye. Lost him because of some insanity on the other side of the world. It was wrong, all wrong. He had been far too young a man to die.

It should not have happened, but it had, and she was alone. Just as his child and his mother were alone, bereft and lost without him. They were her main concern now. She would do what Bill would want her to do . . . console and comfort them.

They needed her. And she needed them.

16

"I'm glad Alice listened to you, Dru, and took her vacation," Vanessa said, stirring the chicken soup she was making, peering into the pot on the stove. "It would have been foolish of her to cancel it, when she had it all planned. But you know, she never did say where she was going."

Dru did not respond.

Vanessa said, "Where has she gone, actually?"

Still Dru did not answer and Vanessa swung around, exclaimed, "My God, what's wrong," threw down the wooden spoon, and rushed across the kitchen.

Drucilla was leaning back in the chair, her face drained of all color, starkly white against her red hair. She was clutching herself and wincing.

Vanessa bent over her. "Dru, what is it?"

"Pain. In my chest. My left arm hurts. I think I'm having a heart attack."

"Don't move! I'll get the car. Southampton Hospital's not far away. On Meeting House Lane. I'll have us there in a few minutes. Just don't move, Dru. Okay?"

Dru nodded.

Vanessa ran to the garage, backed the car out, parked it near the cottage, and leapt across the lawn to her studio. She had left Helena drawing there earlier. Pulling open the door, she called, "Helena, come on, we have to go!"

"Where?"

"To the hospital. Your grandmother's not well."

"I'm coming," the child shouted fiercely, jumped off the stool, and flew across the floor. "Is it her heart?"

"She thinks so, yes," Vanessa said, took hold of Helena's hand, and ran with her to the cottage. "Get in the car, honey, and I'll be out in a minute with Gran." As she spoke, Vanessa helped Helena into the backseat and fastened the safety belt.

Inside the house, Vanessa grabbed her handbag from the hall closet, and dashed back to the kitchen; Dru was slumped in the chair with her arms still wrapped around herself.

Bending toward her, Vanessa asked, "Dru, do you feel any worse?"

"No. Just the same."

"Can you make it to the car?"

"Yes, Vanessa. If you help me," Dru murmured in a weak voice.

Together the two women walked slowly across the kitchen and outside to the car. "Try not to worry. You're going to be all right," Vanessa said as she fastened the seat belt around Dru, praying that she would be.

And she kept on praying all the way to the hospital.

"Mrs Fitzgerald *has* had a heart attack, fortunately not too severe," Dr. Paula Matthews said, drawing Vanessa to one side of the waiting room. "She's going to be all right, but she will have to watch herself, take care of herself."

"Yes, I understand, Dr. Matthews, I'll see that she does. In the meantime, how long does she have to be in the hospital?"

"A few days. Five at the most. She's in our cardiac care unit, more for observation and a rest than anything else." The doctor smiled at Vanessa, then glanced at Helena, who was sitting on a chair near the window. "I've never seen such a beautiful child," she said. "You're very lucky."

"Yes," Vanessa murmured, not knowing what else to say.

"Anyway, I know Mrs. Fitzgerald's anxious to see you both, so let me take you to her room."

A moment or two later Vanessa and Helena were sitting by the bed where Drucilla lay looking pale and weak. "I'm so sorry, Vanessa, to put you to all this trouble," Dru said in a low voice. "What a nuisance I am."

"Don't be so silly," Vanessa exclaimed. "You're not any trouble to me at all. And Helena and I are going to come and see you every day."

Helena said, "And Vanessa says we'll bring you things. Like books and magazines." She smiled at her grandmother. "And flowers, Gran."

"Thank you, darling," Dru murmured.

"Please don't worry about Helena," Vanessa went on, taking hold of Drucilla's hand, squeezing it. "She's no trouble, we'll be fine together."

"But your work . . ." Dru began, looking worried.

"I can do my work and take care of Helena," Vanessa reassured her. "Just think about yourself and getting better."

"I don't know how to thank you."

"Thanks are not necessary, Dru, you know that. And I'm here for you, whenever you need me."

"Bill told me you were a loving woman, and he was right," Dru said. She averted her face for a moment, blinking back tears. Then, turning to look at them both again, she forced a smile. "A hospital's no place for you two. Go and have lunch, and I'll see you tomorrow."

"'Half a pound of tuppeny rice, half a pound of treacle. Mix it up and make it nice. Pop goes the weasel!'" Vanessa sang, leading the child around the room in a circle, holding both her hands.

Helena laughed, much to Vanessa's relief. She had been in floods of tears all morning, suddenly reacting to her grandmother's departure for the hospital the day before. Drucilla's heart attack, coming so quickly after Bill's death, had been too much for the little girl to handle.

Vanessa understood Helena's concern for her grandmother, but she had not been able to stem her tears, or comfort her. At least not until now. The little game they were playing seemed to have helped. It had brought a sparkle to the child's eyes.

"What a funny song," Helena said. "What's a weasel?"

"A little furry animal with a bushy tail that lives in the woods."

"How do you know this song?"

"When *I* was six, I was living in London for a while with my parents. I had a nanny who was English. She taught me the song."

"Can you teach me?"

"Of course. Sing along with me, Helena. Here we go. 'Half a pound of tuppeny rice, half a pound of treacle. Mix it up and make it nice. Pop goes the weasel.'"

Helena sang with her, and they went round and round in circles, holding hands. After half a dozen times Helena knew the words, had committed them to memory.

She laughed merrily and clapped her hands. "I'll sing it for Gran when we go to the hospital this afternoon."

"What a good idea, Pumpkin."

The smile slid off Helena's face and she recoiled, gaping at Vanessa.

"What is it? What's wrong?"

"Don't call me Pumpkin. Only Daddy calls me that. It's his name," she cried fiercely, and burst into tears.

Vanessa went to her, put her arms around her, held her close. "I'm sorry, Helena, I didn't know. Don't cry, honey. Please."

But Helena could not stop sobbing, and she clutched Vanessa as if never to let her go.

Vanessa smoothed her hand down the child's back, endeavoring to comfort her, to soothe her, making hushing noises.

After a while the sobs lessened, and Helena grew calmer. Vanessa led her across the studio to the sofa, lifted her up onto it, and sat down next to her. Taking a tissue from the box on the coffee table, she wiped Helena's eyes, then drew her into the circle of her arms. "In a little while we'll go into town and have a hamburger for lunch. How does that sound?"

"Can I have french fries?"

"Of course."

"And an ice cream?"

Vanessa smiled at her. "Yes, if you want."

Helena nodded; then she bit her lip, suddenly looking tearful again.

"What's wrong, honey?"

"Is Gran . . ." Her bottom lip trembled and tears shimmered on her long lashes. "Is Gran going to die?"

"No, of course not! Don't be silly!"

"People die of heart attacks, Vanessa. Jennifer's grandmother did."

"Who's Jennifer?"

"My friend."

"Well, *your* gran isn't going to die, I promise you that."

"But she's in the hospital."

"I know, and she's getting better. I explained to you yesterday, the reason Gran is in the hospital until Friday is because she needs a rest. That's all. Her heart attack wasn't a bad one, honey. Trust me, she'll be all right."

"They're mending her heart at the hospital."

"Yes," Vanessa murmured, giving the child a reassuring smile.

"Gran's heart is broken. It broke the other day. When the men came."

"Men?" Vanessa repeated, momentarily puzzled.

"Daddy's men. From the network."

"Oh, yes, of course."

"They told her my daddy is dead and it broke her heart."

"Yes, darling . . . "

Helena gave Vanessa a piercing look. "Is Daddy in Heaven?"

Vanessa swallowed. "Yes," was all she could manage.

The child continued to look at her closely. "With my mommy?"

"That's right. They're together now," Vanessa said, striving hard for control.

"When is he coming back, Vanessa?"

"Well . . . well . . . you see . . . he won't be able to come back, Helena. He's going to stay with your mother . . . he's going to look after her." Vanessa averted her face, brushed away the tears.

Helena seemed confused. She frowned hard. "I want him to look after me."

"I know, I know, but he can't, honey, not right now. Gran's going to look after you."

"But what if she dies too?"

"She won't."

"How do you know?"

"I just do, Helena."

"Why did the men kill my daddy?"

"Because they're bad men, darling."

Helena stared at Vanessa and started to weep again. "I want my daddy to come back. Make him come back, Vanessa."

"Hush, hush, honey, don't cry like this," Vanessa murmured, endeavoring to soothe her. "I'm here. I'll look after you."

Helena pulled away, looked up into Vanessa's face. "Can we live with you?"

For a moment Vanessa was taken aback, and then she replied, "We'll have to talk to Gran about that."

Helena nodded.

"By the way, where has Alice gone on vacation?" Vanessa continued, wanting to change the subject, distract Helena.

"To Minnesota. To see her mom and her brothers and sisters. Alice has a great-grandmother and she comes from Sweden."

"Tell me some more about Alice."

"Well, she takes me to school and picks me up from school, and she takes me to Central Park and she plays with me."

Vanessa leaned back against the sofa, relieved that the six-year-old was now chattering normally, that she had managed to divert her.

17

On Friday morning Drucilla Fitzgerald was released from Southampton Hospital.

Vanessa and Helena were there to pick her up and take her back to Bedelia Cottage on the dunes. After the three of them had lunch together, Vanessa sent Helena to draw and paint in the studio. She needed to be alone with Dru for a short while in order to talk to her.

"Helena's a lovely little girl, she's a real credit to you," Vanessa said as she and Drucilla relaxed over a cup of herb tea in the sitting room. "We've become very good friends."

Dru smiled and nodded. "I know. She told me, and she sang 'Pop Goes the weasel' for me. She enjoyed herself with you, Vanessa, and I'm so glad she wasn't a problem."

"No, not at all, Dru," Vanessa began, and paused, then said, "But I think . . ." She shook her head. "I was going to say I think there's a problem, but I don't mean that at all."

Dru was frowning, looking perplexed. "What are you getting at, Vanessa dear?"

"I remember that when I was little I worried about a lot of things. All children worry; Helena worries."

"About my health, is that what you mean?"

"Yes. Children can easily feel insecure, and threatened,

when a parent is sick or in the hospital. And I believe Helena feels very vulnerable."

"Yes, I'm sure she does, but she'll be all right, now that I'm out of the hospital. However, it'll take her a long time to . . . get over her father's death." Drucilla choked up. It was a moment before she finished softly, "It'll take us all a long time."

"Yes, it will . . ." Vanessa's voice trailed off as she stood, walked to the window, and gazed out at the sea. It was a deep blue on this mild afternoon in early May, streaked with sunlight and no longer bleak and uninviting. In her mind's eye she saw Bill's face; he was never out of her thoughts. She focused on his little daughter, and she knew exactly what she must say to Drucilla.

Turning swiftly, Vanessa came back to the sofa and sat down next to Bill's mother. She gave her a thoughtful look, and said, "Before your heart attack, you told me you had no relatives, and I was wondering if you had ever appointed a legal guardian for Helena?"

Drucilla did not seem at all startled by this question, and she answered evenly, "No, I never have. We never have. It didn't seem necessary. But I know what you're getting at, Vanessa. You're wondering what would become of Helena if I were to die. Isn't that so?"

"Yes, it is. You're a young woman, Dru, and this heart attack has been a . . . well, a sort of warning, I think. I know you'll look after yourself from now on, and you're not likely to die until she's grown. But—"

"You're only voicing what I was thinking as I lay in that hospital bed this week," Dru cut in. "I've worried a lot about Helena, worried about her future. I'm sixty- two, as you know, and I aim to live for a long time. Still, you never know what might happen. Life is full of surprises and shocks . . . "

"Would you consider me? Could I become Helena's legal guardian, Dru?"

"Oh, Vanessa, that's lovely of you to volunteer, but would you want that kind of responsibility? I mean, what if I did die while she's still little? Would you want to care for a child . . . you're young, only twenty-seven, and one day you're bound to meet someone else. To be the guardian of another man's child could be a burden . . . a stumbling block to a relationship."

"I don't see it that way, Dru, I really don't. If I were Helena's legal guardian I would fulfill my obligations to her, no matter what the circumstances of my life. I realize you don't know me very well, but I am sincere and very trustworthy."

"Oh, darling, I know that. Bill loved you so very much, and certainly I trust *his* judgment. Besides, I'm a good judge of character myself, and the day I met you, at Christmas at Tavern On The Green, I knew the sort of person you are. I felt then that a weight had been lifted from my shoulders because I could see how changed Bill was because of you. He was so happy. And I suddenly feel as if a weight has been lifted from me again." Dru took hold of Vanessa's hand and held it tightly; suddenly her eyes welled. She said, "I can think of no one I would like more to be Helena's legal guardian. I know that with you she would always be safe."

Vanessa's eyes were also moist. "Thank you, Dru. As soon as you're up to going to New York, I'd like to make an appointment with my lawyer. Or yours, whichever you prefer. We will set all this in motion. Is that all right with you?"

Dru nodded. "I hope to live to a ripe old age, but it's good to know you're there in the background."

"I'd like us to be together, Dru; I'd like to get to know Helena better, and you too. I was wondering, would you consider spending the summers here with me?"

If Drucilla was startled she did not show it. Without hesitation, she said, "I'd like that, Vanessa, I really would. And I know Helena will be happy. She loves it here."

"Then it's settled." Vanessa leaned closer, kissing Dru on the cheek. "There's something else I have to tell you."

"Yes, what is that?"

"Frank called very early this morning. He's come to New York . . . with Bill's things . . . from his hotel room in Beirut. He wants to come and see us tomorrow. Is that all right?"

Drucilla found it hard to speak. She simply nodded her head and held Vanessa's hand all that much tighter.

"He was my best friend, I loved him," Frank said quietly, looking at Bill's mother. "Everybody loved Bill. He was such a special man."

"He's dead and our lives will never be the same," Dru murmured, her face ringed with sorrow. "But we must go on, and bravely so. That's what he would want."

"Only that," Frank agreed. "He was the bravest man I ever knew. He saved my life. Did you know that, Dru?"

"No, I didn't," she replied. "He never told me that, Frank."

"He wouldn't, he was very modest in his own way—"

"Uncle Frankie!" Helena cried as she appeared in the doorway with Vanessa and rushed forward into his arms.

Frank held her tightly. She was part of Bill, and she looked so much like him, he thought. His throat tightened and for a moment he couldn't speak, so choked up was he.

Frank looked over Helena's head, his eyes meeting Vanessa's, and he nodded slightly. Then, releasing his godchild, he went to greet Vanessa, embracing her. "I'm so sorry, so very sorry," he said.

"So am I," she whispered. "I loved him, Frank."

"I know. He loved you . . . I have something for you." Drawing away from her, Frank reached inside his jacket, took out an envelope. "I found this in Bill's room at the Commodore in Beirut." He handed her the envelope.

She stared down at it. *Vanessa* Bill had written across the front. She bit her inner lip, pushing back the tears when she saw his handwriting. She stared at it for a long moment, afraid to open it.

Dru, watching her carefully, said softly, "Perhaps you'd like to be alone when you read it, Vanessa. We'll leave you."

"No," Vanessa said. "It's all right . . . I'll go . . . outside." She left them in the sitting room and went across the back lawn and down to the dunes, clutching the letter tightly in her hand.

There was a sheltered spot where she often read, and she sat down there for a while, staring out at the sea, thinking of Bill, her heart aching.

Finally she opened the envelope and took out the letter.

Beirut
Monday, March 25th, 1996

My very dearest Vanessa:

I know I'll be seeing you in a few days, holding you in my arms, but I have such a need to talk to you, to reach out to you tonight, I decided to write to you. Of course you'll be reading this letter when I'm there with you in Venice, since I'll be bringing it with me.

The next few lines blurred as her eyes filled with tears, but after a few moments she managed to recover, and went on reading.

I don't think I've ever really told you how much I love you, Vanessa—with all my heart and soul and mind. You're rarely out of my thoughts and all I want is to make you happy. You've brought me back to life, given new meaning to my life. And now I want to share that life with you. You will, won't you, darling? You will be my wife and as soon as that's possible?

In my heart I can hear you say yes, yes, yes in that excited way you have. And I promise you I'll love and cherish you always. You know what, let's make a baby in Venice. I know how much you want a child. And I want it to be mine. I want to know that part of me is growing inside you. So let's do it this weekend, let's make a baby.

I've never told you this before, but in the last six years my life has been hellish. Three people I loved very much died on me. First Sylvie, then my father, and finally my grandmother. Their deaths broke my heart.

But over the past few months I've come to understand that the heart broken is the strongest heart.

Bill.

Vanessa sat there for a long time, holding the letter. And then she folded it carefully, put it back in the envelope, and rising, she walked slowly across the dunes and into the cottage.